A descendant of Huguenots and Essex smugglers, Jan Middleton has a degree in English Literature from London University and has taught to A level in state and independent schools, always endeavouring to open her students' eyes to the cultural, social and historical contexts of novels, plays and poetry. She has a passion for writing, history and music and enjoys discovering stories from the past through meticulous research. Jan lives in a 17th century thatched cottage in an ancient Devon village with her family and Black Labrador.

For Jon, Tamsin and Imogen.

Jan Middleton

BRIGHT SHADOW

AUSTIN MACAULEY PUBLISHERS™

LONDON ∗ CAMBRIDGE ∗ NEW YORK ∗ SHARJAH

A CIP catalogue record for this title is available from the British Library.

ISBN 9781398436763 (Paperback)
ISBN 9781398436770 (Hardback)
ISBN 9781398436794 (ePub e-book)

www.austinmacauley.com

First Published 2022
Austin Macauley Publishers Ltd®
1 Canada Square
Canary Wharf
London
E14 5AA

Thank you to my friends who love historical fiction and were game enough to balance a huge A4 ringbinder on their laps in order to read and critique *Bright Shadow*. You said you would prefer a proper book – so here it is!

This is the true story of Princess Katherine Plantagenet, fourth surviving daughter of Edward IV and Elizabeth Wydville. I stumbled across her in a little history book produced by Exeter University containing a factual essay by Margaret Westcott, entitled "Katherine Courtenay, Countess of Devon 1479 - 1527". A Plantagenet princess who had lived in my home county of Devon! I was intrigued, and began to research her life, discovering an extraordinary and compelling story.

As the self-proclaimed "daughter, sister and aunt of kings", Katherine clearly defined herself by her royal connections. Sadly, this would eventually destroy her own family: the nephew who once called her "his favourite aunt" would one day execute her son. Her own natural death in 1527 probably saved her from the appalling fate of her first cousin Margaret Pole, who was butchered on the scaffold in 1541 – simply for being a Plantagenet.

I have tried to stick closely to historical fact, using reputable sources to present the events in Katherine's life and only allowed myself a little dramatic licence in the creation of her autumnal romance with the fictitious Benedict Haute. Whilst writing, I became aware that Katherine was very much "the camera" through which significant people and episodes in history could be viewed.

Even the earliest commentators on Katherine note how she endured extraordinarily traumatic reversals of fortune; her life swung through periods of wealth and adversity with no certainty of positive outcome. She is a shadowy figure in history. No portrait or tomb effigy exists, just a couple of representations in stained glass windows but I hope my imagined narrative serves to illuminate her story, and that she can burn as brightly in your imagination as in mine.

Jan Middleton
Devon
January 2022

Names: *The repetition of Christian names during this era poses a difficulty – far too many Edwards, Richards, Elizabeths and Katherines! Some authors opt for making changes but I am going to presume that a comprehensive list, a family tree, clarity when they are introduced into the narrative and, on the reader's part, a genuine interest in "who's who" will suffice. Where possible I have used different spellings or diminutives, or given characters their full title. For example, I have left Catherine of Aragon as "Catalina" throughout.*

List of main characters listed chronologically as they enter the story

Those in italics are fictitious.

1479 – 1485 The Girl
Plantagenet Family (House of York)

Katherine's family:

her father: King Edward IV
her mother: Queen Elizabeth Wydville
her sisters: Elizabeth (Bessy)
                 Mary (dies young)
                 Cecily
                 Anne
                 Bridget (becomes a nun)
her brothers: *The Princes in the Tower*
                 Edward V
                 Richard (Dickon) Duke of York

her uncle: Richard, Duke of Gloucester, later Richard III
               Anne Neville (his wife, formerly married to Edouard, Lancastrian, Prince of Wales, son of Queen Marguerite of Anjou and King Henry VI)
               John of Pontefract (his bastard son)
               Edward (Ned) his legitimate son, also a Prince of Wales

her grandmother: Cecily Neville (mother to Edward IV and Richard III)

Francis Lovell: friend to Richard III
Harry, Duke of Buckingham (descended from Edward III)
Kate Wydville, his wife (younger sister to Queen Elizabeth)

her first cousins: Princess Margaret of Clarence, niece of Edward IV
               later known as Meg Pole. Known to history as the Countess of Salisbury.
               Prince Edward/Ned of Clarence (nephew of Edward IV)

her maternal uncles: Sir Anthony Wydville and Lionel Wydville
her adult half-brothers: Thomas Grey and Richard Grey

Sir John Nesfield: soldier and warder of Westminster Sanctuary

Joanna: nursemaid and, later, Katherine's children's nursemaid

Elyn: nursemaid

Thomas, Lord Hastings: friend to Edward IV and Privy Councillor

Thomas Bourchier: Archbishop of Canterbury

her first cousins: Jack de la Pole, Duke of Suffolk and Edmund de la Pole (later Duke of Suffolk)

Jane Shore: Mistress to Edward IV, Thomas Hastings and Thomas Grey

Lord Stanley: Councillor to Edward IV

Archbishop Rotherham of York

1485 – 1509: The Wife

The Tudors

King Henry VII
Queen Elizabeth of York (Bessy)
Lady Margaret Beaufort (Lady Stanley, My Lady the King's Mother)
Prince Arthur of Wales
Prince Harry of York
Princess Margaret (marries James IV of Scotland)
Princess Mary (marries King Louis of France and Charles Brandon)
      {Prince Edmund
      Princess Elizabeth
      Princess Katherine} died young

Perkin Warbeck (who may have been Katherine's brother Richard, Duke of York, King Richard IV)
Lady Kateryn Huntley (a Scots noblewoman, wife to Perkin Warbeck)

Princess Catalina of Aragon, later Queen Catherine

Lord Edward Courtenay, Earl of Devon
Lady Elizabeth Courtenay, his wife
Lord William Courtenay, their only child, husband to Katherine
      Katherine and William's children:
           Lord Edward Courtenay dies aged 6
           Lord Henry (Hal) Courtenay (marries Gertrude Blount)
           Lady Margaret (Meggie) Courtenay
           (marries Lord Henry Herbert of Raglan, *"Somer"*)

Captain Christopher Darch, Warder at the Tower of London
Avis Darch, his wife

Patch, a Fool

Sir James Tyrrell, a supporter of Richard III
Thomas More, a young lawyer

Philip le Bel, Hapsburg Archduke of Burgundy, married to Juana, Catalina's sister

Thomas Kyme, third husband of Princess Cecily of York

Rob Anning, a steward on the Courtenay estates in Devon
Christian Anning, his wife
Damaris Anning, his daughter
Adam Anning, his son

Philippa, daughter to Joanna, Katherine's maid and confidante
(NB Katherine definitely had a beloved maid called Philippa, whose wedding
dress she paid for!)

1503 -1509 *The Traitor's Faithful Spouse*

Isabel Darch, granddaughter of Christopher and Avis Darch, marries Adam
Anning

Charles Brandon, a friend of Henry VIII, later Duke of Suffolk and husband of Princess Mary

Gertrude Blount, wife to Hal Courtenay
Lady Elizabeth Boleyn
Mary Boleyn (later Lady Mary Carey)
Anne Boleyn

1511 – 1527 *The Countess Katherine*
Bessie Blount, mistress to King Henry VIII
Cardinal Wolsey
Sir Benedict (Benet) Haute, an imagined, distant cousin of Katherine's on her mother's side. Katherine really did have a great aunt Joan Wydville, who had married into the Haute family.

Places
Thames-side royal palaces:
Eltham
Westminster
Greenwich
Sheen
Richmond
Windsor
The Tower of London (also a prison)

Kenilworth Castle, Warwickshire

Castle of Guises, Calais

Courtenay homes:
Warwick Lane, City of London
Colcombe Castle, Colyton, East Devon
Columbjohn, near Exeter (now part of the National Trust Killerton estate)
Tiverton Castle
West Horsley, Surrey (now a centre for the performing arts)

Cheneygate, Westminster Abbey Sanctuary

Yorkist strongholds:
City of York
Middleham Castle, Yorkshire
Sheriff Hutton
Pontefract

York Place (Wolsey's London home)

The Red Rose (Hal Courtenay's London home)
Brecknock Castle, Brecon, Powys – home of the Duke of Buckingham
Raglan Castle, Monmouthshire – home of the Herbert family

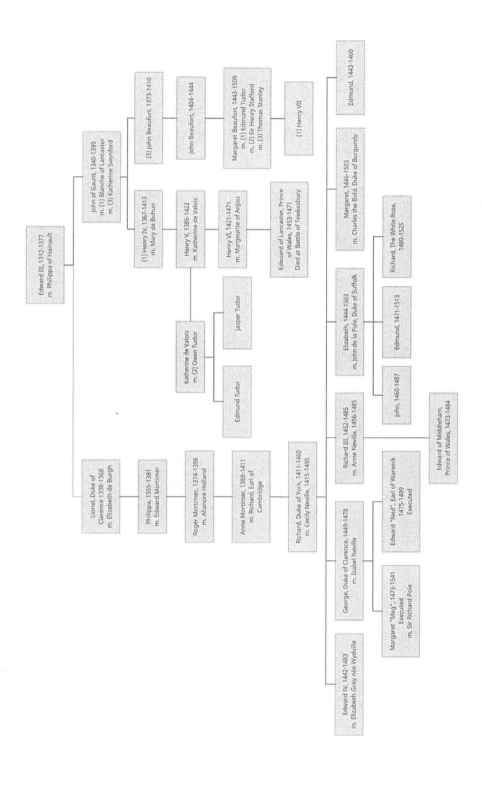

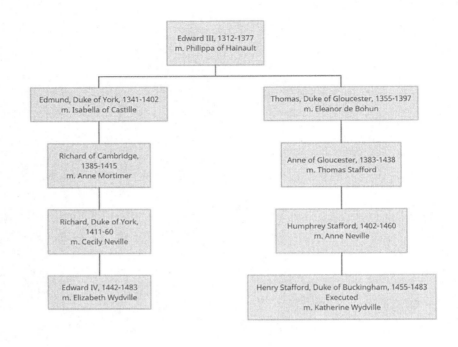

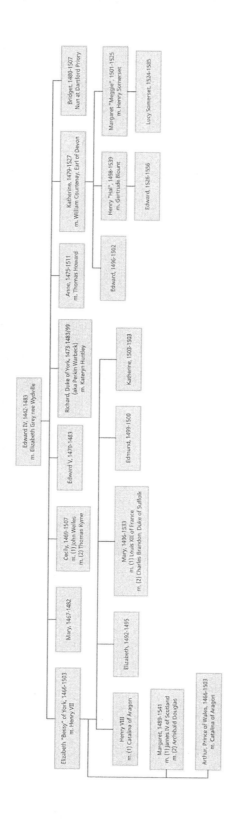

Prologue
Tiverton Castle, Devon: Friday Afternoon 15th November 1527

It was a beautiful day to die. Overnight, the autumn storm had swept through the Exe Valley, relentlessly stripping leaves from the trees and whipping them into great bundles – tumbling them into the fast-flowing river and swirling them downstream towards Exeter, the estuary and the sea. Daylight brought a welcome calm. A robin proclaimed his territory with insistent piping and by late morning the sun in Scorpio was sending intense autumnal rays to ignite the very last, lingering brown leaves on the oaks to a translucent orange, and make the usually grey castle walls glow with unseasonable warmth.

It filtered through a casement window and fell upon the open page of an illuminated Book of Hours, making the gold, blues and reds glow like jewels upon the creamy parchment. In her chamber, the excellent Princess Katherine, Countess of Devon, born Plantagenet, a Courtenay by marriage – daughter, sister and aunt of kings, was content. Her brown eyes were closed and her hands were still. Her fair hair, only slightly laced with a few silver strands at the temples, lay neatly brushed beneath her cap of finest holland. The final prayers had been said by her chaplain and she waited quietly and willingly for God to take her to His presence.

Her breathing was shallow now but her thoughts were clear. She knew that soon she would lie forever in the chapel on the south side of the handsome church of St Peter, only a stone's throw from her window. This was her own choice but something of a sadness too, for in her heart she wished that the dust of her body might mingle with that of her parents at Windsor, or her beloved sister Bessy in the abbey at Westminster.

Yet she knew that others of her family also lay alone across England: her husband William these past sixteen years in splendour at Blackfriars where the brothers said a daily obit for his soul; her sisters: wayward Cecily at rest in the church of the old Plantagenet palace at King's Langley and gentle Anne, sleeping for eternity amongst the Howards in quiet Thetford, and devout Bridget in the nuns' simple graveyard at Dartford Priory. She, Katherine, was the last of the royal sisters. Even young Arthur was alone in his royal tomb at Worcester.

Her brothers lay somewhere in unmarked graves. So many years of never mentioning them. Never daring to speak their names. Treason to suggest that bright-eyed Dickon might still live. Treason to wonder if anyone other than Richard had killed them. *But before sunset my immortal soul will have left this earth and if I speed through purgatory I may meet them all again – those beloved faces lost to me for so many years.*

Her eyes flew open with a sudden thought. Her serious daughter-in-law Gertrude Blount and maid Philippa were by her side. She registered the shock in Gertrude's eyes – saw the pupils dilate with sudden fear but Philippa's warm, capable hand lifted her own from the cool linen sheet.

"What troubles you, Your Grace?" Her broad face swam into view. Katherine locked eyes with the kindly woman who had been her devoted servant for so many years. She struggled to speak; her throat was parched and at first her lips refused to open but the need to know was powerful.

"Will I see my Uncle Gloucester? And Henry Tudor?"

There was a gasp from Gertrude and a dry cough from the chaplain who sat at the foot of the bed.

"Ah, Your Grace – there be naught to fear. All will be well." Philippa's voice was firm and reassuring. "Father James, come to her again. Comfort her."

She heard the shuffling step of the old priest as he approached. He pressed the smooth rosary beads into her hand once more and she fumbled to wind her fingers around them.

"God is merciful, Your Grace," he whispered.

She clutched at his sleeve. "To those who would murder the innocent?"

He leaned over her and spoke softly, for her ears alone. "No, Your Grace. Of that I am certain. God sees all. God knows all. But *you* are shriven and sure to find a place soon in His heaven. Go in peace, good soul."

She sighed. "Open the window," she whispered, "I would feel the air."

"Open the casement, Philippa," she heard her daughter-in-law order, and the broad elm floorboards creaked a little under the maid's heavy tread…

She heard the rasp of the casement and then felt a rush of air upon her cheeks. In the distance the River Exe rushed onwards, white froth scudding on the surface. The chamber was refreshed by a welcome coolness but the resilient noonday sun shone in too.

"The sun, in splendour," breathed Katherine. She closed her eyes, expecting to return to tranquillity but, instead, three suns and three crowns burned upon her retina. *Ah, well. It is to be expected. After all, I was born a York princess.*" And she turned her face towards the symbol of her house.

The Girl
1479 – 1483

1

August 1479
"In those days you would have seen a royal court worthy of any leading kingdom, full of riches ... and most delightful children. There were five girls ... fourth Katherine ..."
(The Crowland Chronicle)

Katherine:
My Yorkist royal family lived in luxury in a court designed to dazzle any visiting foreigner. We glided effortlessly up and down the Thames on ornate barges between the royal palaces – Westminster, Windsor, Sheen, Eltham and Greenwich – eating the finest food; listening to the most talented musicians; laughing at the players; praying in the most exquisite chapels. In winter we had blazing fires, furred gowns and all the old festivities of Christmas and Twelfth Night. In summer we made leisurely royal progresses through towns and villages of England where the people shouted with joy to see their king and queen with their beautiful children. Everything was protocol and ritual, pageants and songs, ceremony and etiquette. Cupboards and tables were bedecked with gold and silver and altars adorned with jewels. My father the King had reconstructed England after decades of civil war and the confidence of his court shone like a lantern over all England. All thought they we were safe forever in that radiance.

God's favour also shone upon us. After all, had not my father King Edward returned from exile and regained control of his kingdom? Had not the Lancastrian cause finally been defeated in the water meadows of Tewkesbury? Now, not one but two young princes stood as heirs to continue the Yorkist dynasty into the next century. Handsome little boys, with open, honest faces and noses sprinkled with freckles, beloved by their older sisters, Bessy, Mary, and Cecily. The years of bloodshed were over. Warwick the kingmaker was dead in the mists at Barnet and Henry the saintly but mad king dead in the Tower. Edouard of Lancaster, his dubious heir, slain too at Tewkesbury and his poor, exploited young widow, Anne Neville, rescued and now safely married to Gloucester, the king's loyal younger brother. Marguerite of Anjou, the captured old queen, was ransomed by her cousin the French king and sent packing across the Channel. And only a year ago George, the Duke of Clarence, my father's treacherous, turncoat middle brother had been put to death privately in the Tower. Wickedness and intrigue were at an end. England breathed freely again. It now belonged to House of York and there were surely none who wished otherwise.

On a showery mid-August afternoon the Queen laboured to give birth to her eleventh child at Eltham. The wooden shutters were closed and she could hear the Kentish summer rain pattering against them. In the hearth a fire had been lit, which made the chamber insufferably warm. Between the fierce contractions she sighed. At forty-two, many women were past child-bearing but her own fertility, coupled with the insatiable attentions of her younger husband, seemed to know no limits. The tightening band of pain came again and Elizabeth shifted on the pallet bed, trying to close off her mind to everything except the need to bring this next Plantagenet child into the world. There was no time to move to the birthing stool. She felt the sudden, familiar circle of burning, the exquisite torture of birth, followed by the slither of fluid as the child was expelled from her body. Within seconds she heard the indignant mewling of a newborn and exclamations of satisfaction from the midwife. Tears slid down her cheeks – relief for her own survival thus far, and for the living baby.

"A son?" she asked, through lips dry and bitten from trying not to scream. A queen does not cry out; she just clutches the bed-ropes harder.

"Another beautiful daughter, Your Grace. Another princess." The midwife smiled encouragingly. After all, the queen had already borne five boys, even if two were the sons of her first husband and one had died. Ha! Judging by the king's interest in her there might yet be more! She stifled a chuckle behind her hand.

A cool hand gently soothed Elizabeth's brow. Her eldest daughter, called Elizabeth too, but known to all as Bessy – a gentle name, sounding like a whisper of silk, judged old enough at thirteen to witness the birth of this sibling because soon she might be leaving home to marry into the French royal family and bear children herself. She had been white-faced, seeing her mother's pain but her training as a princess won through and she had stationed herself stoically at Elizabeth's head, ready with the moist linen cloth and the wooden biting block.

"Lady Mother, a princess is always welcome. His Grace the King, my father, will be pleased."

Oh yes! He'll be pleased because another girl can be married abroad into some European royal family. She knew her own daughters could never marry for love, as she herself had done twice – once aged sixteen in another lifetime and again fifteen years ago. A droll half-smile touched her lips as she remembered her younger self – the Lancastrian widow who they said had bewitched a Yorkist king with her silver, slender beauty and refusal to settle for anything less than being his lawful wife. It was certainly true that she had refused to be just another mistress, yet Edward's capitulation to her terms had come as an extraordinary surprise. No reigning king had ever married for love, and to a commoner. But Edward had said, quite cheerfully, that she had the beauty and bearing of royalty if not quite the full pedigree. And had not Jacquetta, her own mother, been born into the noble family of Luxembourg and once married to John of Bedford, an English prince? Yes, but she had thrown it all away for the sake of love when she took her second husband, the squire John Wydville. It was hard to believe Jacquetta was dead these seven years. Together they had worked a certain May magic over the ardent Edward of York; Jacquetta had been determined to snare him for her eldest daughter. A clandestine wedding and three days of secret passion ensured that Edward was hers. Days long gone. Since then she had had to learn to share him with countless other women but gradually she had realised that his unfaithfulness did not mean any alteration in her status as queen, or an end to their own relationship. This child was evidence of that.

Elizabeth sighed and gave herself up to the ministrations of her women, who removed the holy girdle and gently sponged her clean. She felt the warm water trickle over her thighs. The soiled and blood-stained sheets of the pallet bed were removed and Elizabeth was helped into clean linen then settled in the bed of state. Her hair, left loose for the birth so as not to impede the passage of the babe, was gently re-braided whilst the baby girl was washed, anointed with honey and rosewater, swaddled and given to the wetnurse to be suckled. Elizabeth always recovered fairly easily from childbirth; surely it was no sin to be proud that her body swiftly regained its lithe shape, even after so many pregnancies? Even now, she surreptitiously ran her hands over her belly beneath the sheets and knew it would not be long before she was back in her close fitting gowns.

A polite knock sounded at the door. Outside, the king's physician had been waiting patiently for news. Bessy opened it and Elizabeth heard an exchange of low voices and then the sound of brisk, firm footsteps fading into the distance. This was soon replaced by a scuffling and chattering.

"Lady Mother, I have sent word to my father." Bessy was clearly enjoying her important role but then the serious formality in her voice gave way to girlish enthusiasm. "My sisters are here and would see you, Mama!" Smiling, she ushered them in: twelve-year-old serious Mary, ten-year-old bouncing Cecily and seven-year-old quiet Anne. In a moment, decorum was forgotten as they rushed to the bed. Mary seized her mother's hand and kissed it tenderly; Cecily hung back for a moment, then burst into tears and not to be outdone, took and kissed the other hand. Anne's gaze slid across the room to where the new baby snuffled at the nurse's breast.

"Girls, let your lady mother breathe!" Laughing, one of the ladies-in-waiting bustled round them, wiped the tears from Cecily's face and gently released Elizabeth from their frantic grip.

"Here, Your Grace, some birthing ale to sustain you."

Elizabeth took the cup and sipped. A warm glow spread through her. Again she felt that feeling of relief and triumph that she had survived and read the same in the eyes of her ladies and daughters. No woman would ever wish another ill in childbed. A welcome calm now descended upon the room. The tension of the last few hours dissipated and for a while they all relaxed in the luxury of feminine companionship. Sweet herbs were strewn to freshen the chamber – lemon balm, lavender, chamomile and mint. The baby was inspected by her older sisters and pronounced acceptable. They sat by the nurse, watching the infant suckle.

"When will my father come?" asked Bessy.

As if on cue, the door was flung open and Edward Plantagenet stood there, a broad grin across his florid face. He was so tall he had to duck to avoid the lintel. He had never stood upon ceremony at the birth of his children but had always come to see Elizabeth as soon as possible, despite the shocked tuttings of the midwives and the flutterings of the ladies-in-waiting. Now he crossed the room in two strides and stood proudly at the foot of the bed. Bessy, Mary, Cecily and Anne wriggled beneath his arms into his embrace. In private family life Edward was happy to dispense with formality.

"I am glad you are safely delivered, wife. Praise be to God."

"Amen. I have borne you another daughter, Edward." Elizabeth had never apologised for her girls. She had proved herself capable of producing boys in her first marriage, and had waited patiently for the next two, who had duly appeared. Her mind flickered back nine years to the birth of Edward, Prince of Wales. In the face of Warwick's rebellion, her husband had fled into the Low Countries. Alone, in sanctuary at Westminster, with only her mother to assist her, she had finally given birth to his heir in the Jerusalem Chamber but it had been another five months before he had returned in triumph to rescue them. But then she had known that he would. From her bed she stole a covert glance at this man who raised her from commoner to queen but whose faithfulness was as variable as a weathervane. Even amongst the women serving in her rooms today she knew there must be several he had bedded. She noted how his eyes followed them. She also noted his expanding waistline and high colour.

Ruefully, he controlled his gaze, re-directing it fondly over the four girls wrapped around his waist and legs. "Well, there is plenty of room for one more! Where is the little maid?"

Joanna the nursemaid rose and presented the baby whose face was just visible above the tight linen bands that bound her tiny limbs straight. But she was wide awake and regarded her father intently. Edward was enchanted, as he had been with every one of his children, male or female, legitimate or bastard. Master Arthur, baseborn son of his first delightful mistress Elizabeth Lucey and Mistress Grace, whose mother he could not quite remember, had been accorded places in the royal nursery. He would provide for them all. This one was particularly attractive – not red and squashed like some newborns but with skin that looked like soft, rosy satin.

"What would you name her, husband?" Elizabeth knew that if she deferred to him he was quite likely to let her choose. She had managed him skilfully since the day they had met, beneath the oak trees in Grafton Forest. Sure enough, he immediately smiled at her. Like many big, genial men who genuinely liked women, he always preferred compromise to conflict. He liked to be generous where he could.

"You may have the choosing, my dear. A reward for your hard travail."

"Katherine," said Elizabeth. The name was one of her personal favourites. She pronounced it the new English way, softening the "th", rather than the hard French *Katrine*. "Katherine, after my sister." She saw a narrowing of his eyes.

His younger cousin Buckingham had once railed against his arranged marriage as a child to her Wydville sister. Handsome, blond, arrogant Harry Stafford, Duke of Buckingham, descended from Edward III and fiercely proud of his Plantagenet blood, had thought it demeaning to be tied to an upstart Wydville. Yet *that* Katherine had been the sweetest of children, a beautiful girl and now a faithful wife and mother in distant Wales. For some reason Edward disliked Harry and excluded him from his Council. She thought quickly. "And after St Katherine, of course." No-one could object to a child named after such a holy saint.

Assuaged, Edward agreed. "The bravest of women; may she be likewise. There was another Plantagenet Princess Katherine too, a hundred years ago, who married into Spain."

"My brothers will like her," remarked Bessy. "She is already very pretty, is she not?"

"Well, I think she rivals even Cecily, who was said to be *very handsome* when she was born." Edward twinkled at his third daughter.

His heart filled with pride and satisfaction as he contemplated how he could use these five princesses to forge alliances across Europe or help to maintain peace in England. As his own sisters, Margaret, Anne and Elizabeth had played their part in strengthening the Yorkist cause, so would these lovely girls. He envisaged a glittering future where his daughters might wear the crowns of France, Burgundy, Scotland, Castile, Aragon, Portugal – even further afield – and yet relations between these countries were proving so unstable. The terms for Bessy's marriage to the French dauphin seemed to drag on endlessly; Edward had begun to wonder if Louis was quite so committed to the idea of the alliance.

Bessy tugged at his sleeve. "Father?"

Edward came back to reality. The newborn was being offered up for his blessing. He touched her soft head with his huge hand and planted a gentle kiss on her forehead. She smelled like newly-baked bread. Her sisters followed in turn, and the baby Katherine gazed back solemnly.

"She will be christened tomorrow, Edward?" None of Elizabeth's children had been frail at birth but she still feared for their tiny immortal souls.

"Of course, my dear. Here in the chapel at Eltham if you wish."

"May we be her godmothers, Father? Mary and me? We are old enough." Bessy's face was bright with sisterly love and tenderness.

"Should we allow this? Are they important enough?" Edward appealed in mock horror to his wife's ladies-in-waiting, who duly laughed at his joke.

"Please, Father! You promised!" urged Mary. "We know all our prayers and can teach her."

"As long as *you* promise not to step on the chrisom and fall over," replied Edward gravely.

"I carried the chrisom for my brother the Prince of Wales when I was only four," declared Bessy, and added mischievously. "You may not remember, Papa. You were not there."

Edward met his wife's eyes, each remembering the reunion after the long months of separation and hardship.

"You speak truly, Bessy. But we had better balance you both with very elderly godfathers. And now I think it best we leave your mother and new sister to sleep awhile before the bell summons us to Evensong."

Outside, the clouds cleared completely by late afternoon and soon the pepperpot turrets of Eltham were touched by evening sunlight. Swans glided across the great lake, their black webbed feet paddling strongly under the surface, the white feathers of their wings stirring slightly. Tomorrow, in the warmth, the water lilies would unfurl again. A messenger, in the blue and murrey livery of the house of York, galloped out of the courtyard and across the moat, and took the road to Westminster to tell the world of the birth of Princess Katherine. In his newly constructed Great Hall, King Edward IV sat at supper upon the dais, dressed in his finest purple robes, and reflected upon his good fortune. He called for more food and, when he thought his two eldest daughters were not looking, caressed the enticing breasts of Elizabeth Shore, called Jane, the merriest of his many mistresses. In her bed, his wife Elizabeth Wydville lay listening to the sounds of music drifting up and the frequent shouts of raucous laughter. She hated this period of confinement when the court forgot about her but knew that it meant six weeks of peace and quiet before being required to resume her wifely duties.

2

"Edward IV spent the ensuing Christmas at his palace at Westminster, often clad in very expensive clothes ..." (The Crowland Chronicle)

Katherine: I was a very small girl but knew that I was a princess. I understood that my father was a king and the most important, powerful and handsome man in the land, and my mother, the queen, the most beautiful. I had learned that my Plantagenet family was not always of one accord and that in the past bad things had happened. One part of my family was called York and the other Lancaster. My grandfather of York died fighting for the throne and so my father took his place. I had so many uncles, aunts and cousins that it was impossible to count or name them.

Twelfth Night 1483

Richard, Duke of Gloucester, sat with his brother's family in the Great Hall at Westminster. After a season of leading Edward's invasion army against the Scots he was bone weary. The summer campaign had been drawn out but successful: Edinburgh and Berwick had fallen to him; the Scots king, James, usefully imprisoned by his own nobles in Edinburgh Castle and Scotland now stumbling along under Edward's creature the Duke of Albany. Who knew what the next year would bring? He would much rather have stayed upon his own estates in the north this Christmas but Edward had insisted he travel south, to be paraded, lauded and rewarded as the King's victorious lieutenant-general.

It was the last night of feasting; the huge Yule log still burned bright, crackling in the hearth, and garlands of holly and ivy festooned the stone walls. On the high table, intricate subleties of marchpane had been admired – amazing

31

sugary constructions of the King's favourite residences, and now, amid much laughter, pieces were being broken off to eat.

He motioned to a servant to bring him a piece of sugar Fotheringhay, the whole gatehouse, and placed it carefully in front of him, where he would remember it later. Suitably wrapped, it might stand the journey home to Middleham in the new year. His children would like to see it. The rich smell of hundreds of honeyed wax candles filled the air, along with the cinnamon of the spiced wine in the hanap in front of him. Richard sipped moderately, never a man to want to become inebriated – always watchful and alert. He fiddled with the ring on his left heart finger and surveyed the hall.

As the lutes and hautbois played and the tabours beat time, he counted five pretty nieces – nearly all blue-eyed and blonde – just the odd surprising variation such as little Katherine whose eyes were as brown as his own, and Cecily, who was dark haired. The legacy of their darker Plantagenet grandfather. He had not seen them since last Easter and noted, with an ache in his heart, how strong and healthy they were. All were gorgeously clothed: lovely in expensive Venetian golden silk shot through with peacock blue – the older ones shimmered as they danced and the two little ones sat with their nursemaids like obedient poppets at the foot of their mother's chair of estate, watching in wide-eyed wonder. He wanted to love them, wanted to care for them as deeply as he cared for his own young son up in Yorkshire but it was the sight of their mother that prevented it. He watched her now, smiling as she danced before them with her debonair brother Anthony, Lord Rivers, who had come with the Prince of Wales from Ludlow. In her mid-forties, she was nearly twenty years older than his own wife, Anne, yet she moved like a girl. Like a Circe.

Richard distrusted her and hated the way her Wydville relations had inveigled themselves into every position and family of worth in England over the last fifteen years. He had been a boy of ten when Edward had married her, in awe of her beauty and elegance but at a loss to understand what had made Edward throw aside the prospects of a marriage with Bona of Savoy and choose the impoverished widow of a Lancastrian knight. Richard loved his brother but over the years had despaired of the way he allowed Elizabeth to influence his decisions. She might well have given him two heirs but had also brought Edward a tribe of stepsons and brothers-in-law – the Rivers did indeed run high in England. What business did a queen's family have to interfere with the running of the realm? She looked up as she turned in the dance, caught his eye and inclined her head graciously. *Haughtily, more like. Arrogant. Beautiful. Deadly. Surely responsible for the death of my brother George, Duke of Clarence.*

He thought back to those dramatic days three years ago when George had stupidly plotted rebellion and how quick Elizabeth Wydville and her family had been to persuade her husband that he must be removed. She had seized her opportunity to wreak her revenge for the part George had played in the executions of her father and brother after the Battle of Edgecote. She had hardly spoken to Richard when he arrived in London this Christmas; instead, she had shown by her expression how she resented all the praise being heaped upon him for the Scottish victories.

He inclined his own head to her, graciously, coldly, then turned to take in Edward, presiding over this final evening of celebration from his canopied throne, wearing his crown as custom decreed at Christmastide. Another flowing, sleeveless gown – this one of crimson, edged with ermine. Just how many outfits did Edward think it necessary to wear over the course of a few days? And how many women was it necessary to ogle? How much food did he think one man should put away? Lucky that Edward had such height, or he would struggle with his girth these days. He was a great king, there was no doubt and Richard had been happy to be his loyal lieutenant on the battlefield against Lancaster but it had become obvious that Edward's fighting days were over; he seemed to be drifting into a life of indolence and debauchery. Richard sighed – his brother wrote frequently, urging him to come back and visit more often, to get to know the young princes his nephews but that was rather hard to do when Edward also ordered him to the Scottish borders. Since George's death, Richard had preferred to spend any spells of freedom on his lands in the north – the distant windswept castles of Middleham and Sheriff Hutton where, in the cooler, fresher, heather-scented air he could attempt to think more objectively about his feelings.

His innermost sentiments, about George, were horribly confused. For so long Edward had never wanted to believe that George was ready to turn traitor and lay siege to the throne he had fought so hard to achieve, and maintain. But, reflected Richard, Warwick the Kingmaker, infuriated by Edward's unsuitable marriage, had been ready to "unmake" him and replace him with a younger, more compliant version. How tangled and treacherous those years had been! Plot after plot – like being trapped on some interminable wheel of fortune. Edward imprisoned – Warwick on the verge of victory – Edward's escape (with *his* help, and Hastings') – Warwick and George escaping to France – Warwick's

33

abandonment of George and a new plan to put the Lancastrian pretender Edouard on the throne. And so Richard and Edward had cut their losses and sought refuge in the Low Countries. Edward had had no money, so (and Richard smiled to remember it!) had offered the Dutch ship's master his robe lined with marten fur. Ah, well, Warwick had not achieved the support he thought would come; no-one knew who to trust anymore and he seemed to have forgotten that the English detested the French! They were weary of fighting and changing kings. And so he and Edward had returned, landing at Ravenspur, rallying vast numbers to their side; edging down England (reunited with a most contrite George, even …) and so finally to Barnet, in a surreal mist, and Warwick, that *proud setter-up and puller down of kings* dead on the forest floor. Yet it had taken Tewkesbury to finally rid the realm of the poison of the Lancastrians.

There was a moment at Tewkesbury which Richard preferred to blot from his memory – when Edouard of Lancaster, so-called son of Henry VI, had been captured and brought before Edward in his tent, defiance and arrogance glittering in his eyes. They had given out that he had *died on the field,* which was true in a way, although Richard could not recall quite how far they had allowed him to run across the meadow before they brought him down. The red mists descended and the pretender died in a melee of stab wounds. Had he been responsible? Or George? Or Hastings? Or even young Thomas Grey?

Richard looked down at his slender hands encircling the hanap. How can it be, he thought, that a man's hands can wield the sword in battle, the dagger in the dark and still be the instruments that caress a woman's body, or a child's hair, or when placed together can be the channel to prayer? There was another memory he rarely allowed to surface: an octagonal chapel in the Tower, on a May evening – the final elimination of the last one who stood in the way of the House of York. Poor King Henry – his prayers the only things his bewildered wits could master. That night Richard had learned just how far his brother Edward was prepared to go to secure his destiny. The sickening thud as wood landed upon skull and the metallic smell of the blood that trickled over the flagstones.

A trumpet fanfare. Edward's sons, the two young princes, entered and ran eagerly down the steps together. Both had recently come from Ludlow. The Prince of Wales was clad in white cloth of gold and the little Duke of York in pale green satin. Richard knew that the boys were not often together with their sisters but the past two weeks of celebration had rekindled their familiarity. Now they sauntered to join the other children. The elder had his arm flung carelessly over the younger one's shoulder. About three years between them, much like me and George, thought Richard. He could not forget the way George had loved him and looked after him when as children they had been sent into safety in Burgundy with just the clothes on their backs.

Ah, foolish George! Forgiven for his part in Warwick's uprising, but utterly incapable of settling to a role as the King's brother, as he, Richard, had done. The shock on George's face on the day four-year-old Bessy had been named the heir apparent; when he realised *he* was no longer Edward's heir. Of course, it was ridiculous that he should have thought Edward would not have children.

But then that was George – given to fantasies and stupid ideas. Jealous and petulant when crossed and capable of foolish, impulsive acts of revenge. The last straw had been his part in spreading malicious rumours about Edward's legitimacy. And then, after Isabel's death, his hare-brained scheme to marry into the Burgundian royal family … Richard struggled to come to any sensible assessment about his wayward brother. *Why did I not plead for him?*

And yet, wryly, Richard recognised his own shortcomings too. He knew full well how his prolonged absences from court gave the Wydville family more space for influence over his nephews. *Do they even recognise me,* he wondered. *Thank God Edward is hale and hearty, even if he is looking a bit portly these days. I will come down more often. I will visit the boys at Ludlow, and show them that their father's youngest brother can be as much of an uncle as those upstart Wydvilles. More. I am their royal uncle. Their only royal uncle. I will bring Anne and my own Edward south this spring, and build bridges.*

The music ended and his eldest niece, Bessy, returned breathless and glowing to her place next to her uncle. Strands of strawberry-blonde hair escaped her jewelled net. Richard rose and offered her his hand to steady her as she stepped onto the dais. He remembered her as a sweet-tempered child and noted that she had grown into a bonny young woman of nearly sixteen. In her features and figure he saw her mother reflected but in her colouring, charm and geniality she was her father. She was very much aware of her status as the eldest princess, and the need to converse pleasantly with important guests but there was something sincere and wholesome about her. Now she turned to thank him with a face full of honesty and interest. Although she barely knew him her courtesy was exemplary.

"His Grace, my father, is so pleased you came, Uncle. I wish you were with us more often, sir. How fares my Aunt of Gloucester and my sweet young cousin? Could they not have come with you this year?"

"They have not been in good health and preferred not to travel at this time of year." He felt he could hardly tell her how Anne hated Elizabeth Wydville with a passion and refused to leave Yorkshire.

"Of course. I understand. But I am sorry for it. My brothers would have played with your boy." She gestured down the hall, where the boys sat together, beyond the dancing, entertained by tumblers. Their shouts of delighted laughter rang out as the acrobats leapt and twisted through the air. He thought of his own boy, hundreds of miles away, probably in bed. These Plantagenet children were all on show, evidence of Edward and Eizabeth's fertility and charmed existence. Even the youngest one, Bridget, had been brought to be displayed at this lavish festivity.

The dark eyed child, Katherine, had escaped from her nurse's care and made her way confidently towards her beloved eldest sister. At three-and-a half she was like a miniature version, dressed in the same blue-green cloth of gold with a cap of pearls over her dark blonde hair.

"Bessy?" She was scrambling up but lost her footing and fell heavily, losing one of her soft kid slippers. The next dance had begun and no-one noticed her. Undeterred, she sat solemnly for a moment and rubbed her knee. Richard found himself smiling, marvelling that the little maid had not burst into tears.

"Oh, goodness, Katherine!" Bessy swept her up. "Where have you come from?"

"No shoe," said Katherine mournfully, sticking out a bare little foot.

"Allow me." Richard was glad to have been pulled out of his reverie by Bessy's conversation. Sometimes, the past years weighed heavily upon him; it was good to be reminded that life was now more certain, despite the Wydville faction. He did not want to be a soldier tonight. Retrieving the slipper from the sweet rushes he knelt to restore it, fitting it swiftly and expertly. Hands that could kill could be used for the homeliest tasks. He met Bessy's smile over the child's head.

"There, you did not think I could do that, did you?"

She dimpled. "You are kind, my lord Uncle. Katherine, say thank you."

Richard met the steady, brown-eyed gaze of the small girl. He knew he was being assessed. The intelligence of her appraisal surprised him; she was using her instincts to work out his worth.

"Who are you?" she demanded imperiously.

"Katherine! Oh, Uncle, please forgive her; she is very young."

"I am your Uncle Richard, child. And once I had a little girl like you at home. Well, I still have her but she is not so little these days. And she is Katherine too. She is twelve now."

He was aware of Bessy's gasp of surprise. "You must know I have other children, Bessy, as does your father. I have a son, John, too." A moment of regret in his heart, for the bastard John of Gloucester was a well-grown, feisty, merry boy, full of energy and a stark contrast to his pale half-brother, Edward of Middleham. Both boys were precious to him, but ...

"I am sorry, sir. I did not know." If she was embarrassed, she hid it well. She knew that men took mistresses but wondered how her mother, or her Aunt Anne Neville felt about it. Or how she, Bessy, would feel. "It is good to have brothers and sisters," she ventured, "howsoever we gain them." She was genuinely fond of her own half-sister Grace, who served in Elizabeth's rooms, and of Arthur, a friendly and undemanding young man. They were the two she knew about. Suddenly her voice caught in her throat and tears brimmed in her eyes.

Richard took her hand in concern. "I know, my dear. Your sister, Mary."

Bessy clutched Katherine tightly and nodded. "We were so close in age, sir. I miss her. It was so sudden." A May morning, just seven months ago, and Mary dead in her bed. "God's will be done, sir." Since Mary had left them Bessy and Cecily had closed ranks; the three years between them becoming less important as they grew up, although Bessy took her role of eldest sibling seriously. Cecily could be impulsive and needed careful handling.

Another fanfare of trumpets as Edward rose. He was looking down the line of dancers, as if seeking out someone in particular. Richard followed his gaze and saw his favourite mistress, Shore's wife, her hand on the arm of their mutual friend Lord Hastings. Bessy lowered her eyes. Elizabeth Wydville made a speedy assessment of the situation and swept her heavy court dress into a low curtsey to her husband and sailed away in the opposite direction, attended by her brothers Anthony and Lionel. *Ah well,* Richard considered; *maybe the womanising is no bad thing really, if it keeps the Wydville witch at arms' length.* Edward set his crown firmly on his head and with a lascivious smile set off to claim his lover from his best friend. Richard sipped his wine.

Bessy hid her face in Katherine's pearled bonnet. She hated it when her father showed his affections for the Shore woman so publicly. She felt her sister's little body grow heavy and realised that she was dozing. She stole a glance at her Uncle Richard but he seemed lost in thought again, as she had seen him for so much of this evening. Bessy hugged Katherine closer, breathing in the sweet rosewater scent of her hair. Katherine was no longer the baby of the family; that place was now filled by little Bridget, named after a Swedish saint because one day she would be given to God, not a foreign prince. *One day, we shall never see each other again: I will be in France, and Katherine will be in Spain. I have lost one sister this year ... oh, God, why do you ask this of me? My mother sees all her sisters – they come to court – they are part of her life. I must go away to a land I do not know, to people I have never seen, to a man who may never love me. And yet ... it means I will be a queen one day.* She rested her chin upon Katherine's head and contemplated the lot of princesses.

Puffed from exertion, Edward finished his dance and passed Jane Shore on to young Thomas Grey who clearly could not believe his luck. He staggered back to his chair of state, collapsed back on to the cushions and summoned his brother to sit with him. They presented an extraordinary contrast: Edward built like an over-sized Greek god; Richard like a slight centaur. Edward's square, red face framed by chestnut gold waves; Richard's pale skin stretched over high, taut cheekbones. Edward resplendent in an astonishing ostentatious, trailing, furred gown lined with crimson damask; Richard neatly turned out in a close fitting doublet of expensive, pure, deep black relieved only by a narrow collar of gold and rubies.

Edward applauded the music, called for his choristers to give them songs, drank long and hard, wiped his mouth fastidiously then turned to Richard. For all his corpulence his eyes gleamed with the intelligence Richard knew so well.

"You recall the Tudor boy in Brittany? I have recently come to some sort of agreement with his mother. I think now I would rather have him home; restore him to some sort of status and wealth – make him grateful. What do you think?"

"Have him where he can be watched more easily, you mean," commented Richard dryly.

"Something like that. Marry him, even, to one of the girls. Anne perhaps, or Cecily now the Scots alliance is off. Katherine is too young, more's the pity. Ha! If Louis goes back on his promise I would even give him Bessy!"

"Ah, get him out of Europe and turn him back into an English lord?"

"Secure his loyalty to me, not to Brittany, or France or even Burgundy. Out there he's unpredictable. His mother wants him home." Edward had often preferred to win over his enemies, wrong-footing them with apparent affability.

"And you don't fear him? There are some would call him the heir to Lancaster."

"Why would I fear him? Who is left who would want to follow Lancaster again? I have two fine, healthy sons. By the time I'm in my grave they will be men. He's tainted with bastardy. No, no-one's interested in him in England, except his mother. And one of my daughters would keep him sweet-tempered. Though Cecily might run rings around him!" He drained his hanap and called for more.

Richard mused into his own cup, swirling the wine as if he might see into the future. The firm singing of the choir resounded up to the hammerbeam roof, the trebles of the boys blending with the deeper voices of the men.

"Make we joy now in this feast
In quo Christus natus est
A patri unigenitus
Through a maiden come to us
Sing we of him and say
Welcome; Veni Redemptor ventilium."

"And what does Her Grace the Queen think to your plan?"

"She is aware of it. She sees the sense of it. She has no particular love for Lady Margaret Beaufort, and I don't doubt but that the feeling is reciprocated, but a match would be useful."

"Thus it has ever been," sighed Richard. "We all must marry for pragmatic reasons – land, money, titles … oh, except you, Ned. I do recall *you* married for love!"

Edward eyed him keenly. "You do not love Anne? Little Anne, rescued from Lancaster; rescued from the kitchens by her hero, Dickon!"

"I have every respect for Anne," said Richard stiffly.

"But you would not have taken her without her lands," observed Edward dryly, "or the fortune she brought you. And come to think of it, *she* would not have had *you,* had you not been the only one able to protect her interests. Christ, will I ever forget you and George like two rutting stags fighting over Isabel and Anne's inheritance!"

Richard inclined his head in acquiescence. "We tried your patience sorely, brother."

"I marvelled at the legal arguments you both produced."

"Without land we are nothing. George knew that as well as I."

A silence fell between them, filled again by the music of the choir, now wistful and lilting in a minor key. The achingly beautiful voices of the boys soared to the high notes. All through the hall people paused to listen. In the moment the romance of the words seemed to mean more than their religious significance.

"Of a rose singen we
Misterium mirabile
The rose, of flowers she is flower
She ne will fade for no shower
To sinful men she sent succour
Mira plentitudine. "

The last notes hovered on the air, as the haunting *tierce de Picardie* resolved itself. There was huge applause and the yule log erupted into a spray of sparks as someone threw a handful of bones from his trencher and the fat spat in the flames.

Edward reached over and clasped his brother's hand warmly. "Aye, I married for love. Elizabeth brought me nothing but her beauty. But she is not your enemy, Dickon." He gave a sudden, characteristic shout of laughter. "She just doesn't like you much! Never has done, I'm afraid. Probably jealous. She's the same with Hastings. Just doesn't like those who try to make me see things differently. Like any wife."

"She sometimes seems to question my loyalty," conceded Richard. "I am sorry, Edward, but I think I can never be close to her."

"And you have no need to be, Dickon. All I ask is that you respect her as queen and the mother of my children. As you have ever done. Now, why not

40

bring Anne and the boy down for Easter? For the Garter service at Windsor? They would like that, eh? A bit of warmth and colour after a cold Yorkshire winter?"

Edward called for Richard's cup, and his own, to be refilled. The choir from the Chapel Royal started on their next song.

"Blow thou Northern wind
Send thou me my sweetling
Lovelier on earth
Blow, thou Northern wind."

Richard knew that the only time Anne would come south would be if Queen Elizabeth were dead or locked up. Both highly unlikely.

On her seat on Bessy's lap, dark eyed Princess Katherine stirred. She watched her father and the man who had told her he was her uncle, and wondered if now they had finished talking together they might swing her up towards the lovely carved angels on the roof and the gilded statues of the kings. She ran to them, and they did.

A few days later, just as Richard was preparing to return to his own city residence, Crosby Hall, he found young Katherine again, sitting alone on a staircase just outside the royal apartments. She smiled when she saw him, certain now who this uncle was – not as handsome and tall as her Wydville half-brothers and uncles, for sure, but clearly dear to her father, the king. Something in Katherine's pensive expression made him pause. He bent down and lifted her chin.

"What is wrong, child? Why are you here on your own? Where is your nurse? Your sisters?"

"Mama is angry," confided Katherine, "she is shouting." And added, "Bessy's not going to be a queen."

Richard thought quickly, interpreting a three-year-old's grasp of European politics. Since childhood, Bessy had been addressed as Madame la Dauphine of France, in anticipation of her eventual marriage. It could mean only one thing – the French marriage was off. Edward would be apoplectic with rage. Richard called for an attendant for the child then made his way up the stairs to his brother's private bedchamber. The guard at the door bowed and let him in. Edward was by the window, gazing out over the Thames. The January waters were grey and choppy. He was dressed only in his shirt and hose and Richard realised how the loose over-gowns had disguised his belly at the Christmas feasts.

"Ah, Dickon. You have heard." His voice was tight with fury.

"Louis?"

"And Maximilian of Burgundy. They have signed a treaty at Arras. The news came late last night after you left me. And now Louis' son will marry the Burgundian heiress, not my Bessy. And Burgundy will give France two of her best provinces. Ah, Christ, Dickon, what a mess!" He turned to face his brother and Richard saw a vein pulsing in his forehead. Suddenly, with a savage gesture, Edward swept the table clear. Documents, ink pots and sand flew through the air. He sank on to a chair, clenching his fists. "All my life – all the years I have been king – always I have worked towards trying to make this country a better place for us all – security, peace. *Peace*, Dickon! Yes, I have made war; I have fought battles – God knows I send *you* to fight my battles because I can't do it all alone – but in the interests of keeping this country *safe*! A secure and strong kingdom for my son Edward when he grows up."

"I know this, my brother," murmured Richard. The ink had spattered his travelling cloak but did not show against the black.

"And these marriages – Cecily to Scotland, Bessy to France – now come to nothing! Where do I go from here, Dickon? What's it all been for? Who will be my allies? Who can I trust?" He raised a face ravaged by lack of sleep and excess of drink. "Stay, Dickon. Do not go back yet. Stay and help me make some sense of it. Ah God, Elizabeth will tear me to shreds for this."

"Ned – I hear you, but after Parliament has met tomorrow I must go home for a while. What's done is done. Louis and Maximilian will not be changing their minds. We need time to think – to consult with your other advisors."

"I trust none as I trust you, Dickon. Not Hastings, bless him, nor Elizabeth's brothers ..."

Richard felt a fleeting moment of triumph. "Then give me time, Ned. I swear I will be back by Easter. I will stay if you command me, but I have not seen Anne, or my son, for weeks now. I have duties and appointments that need my attention." He allowed himself to grin. "Christ, Ned, you have appointed me to so many new lordships, stewardships and offices that if I *don't* go you'll have chaos at home as well as abroad! " The joke was well -timed. Edward's face began to relax. "We have the whole summer ahead of us to sort this out. Seek out new alliances. God's blood, Ned, there are other countries beyond France and Burgundy."

"I will help too, Papa." A small voice, but cheerful and confident. Katherine had performed her usual trick of evading servants and had followed her uncle, slipping into the chamber. Unless the king was actually with his Council the guards had long learned to admit his children, even if the queen despaired of her husband's indulgent behaviour. Edward found himself being surveyed by two pairs of penetrative brown eyes – eyes he recognised as having belonged to *his* father. Richard felt a small hand slide into his. "We will make Bessy a queen one day, won't we, Uncle?"

Richard squeezed her fingers gently. "Assuredly, Princess."

Edward held out his arms to his child and she climbed onto his lap, reaching up to stroke his face. He slumped in the chair and closed his eyes. Then she held out her right hand, as she had seen her mother do to lords and ambassadors. She tried to remember what her mother said on such occasions. "You have our leave to go, Uncle."

A sudden memory came to Richard of himself as a small boy facing the Lancastrian soldiers in the market place at Ludlow and how his mother, Cecily Neville, grandmother to this girl, had shown no fear but held out her hand to the terrifying Duke of Somerset, simply expecting his homage to her status and femininity. He hid a smile, bowed and kissed Katherine's hand.

"Look after His Grace, your father, Katherine. Until April."

She nodded, watched his courtly exit then turned her attention to her father again. He seemed exhausted and she thought he might like to sleep. On the bed was one of his grand furred robes. She eased herself off his lap, crossed the room and pulled the robe off the bed. It was heavy but she managed to drape most of it over his lap and tuck it round him. She found a tasselled cushion and eased it behind his head. Satisfied, she left him and went in search of her sister Bessy, to tell her not that they would find her another prince to marry.

3

Katherine: *My father was simply a shadow, tall and wide, who fell upon my life so briefly and was gone. The sun of York, blazing in glory, was ignominiously extinguished by the waters of the Thames. I was very little – just three and a half years old but my sisters told me I was a bright child who watched and listened intently. I relied upon the tales they told me to piece together any understanding of that time (I never entirely trusted Anne's version as she was only eight herself, but Bessy and Cecily were young women …*

"The king … took to his bed during Easter; and in his palace of Westminster surrendered his spirit to his Maker." (The Crowland Chronicle)

9ᵗʰ April 1483: Westminster Palace

The sorrow in the king's chamber was palpable. The air was malodorous with male sweat, urine and vomit. On the bed, the vast bulk of Edward IV, just nineteen days away from his forty-first birthday, lay silent and inert after five days of agony. His features seemed to have collapsed into a morass of pasty flesh. Harsh bristles stood out on his chin, giving him an appearance not dissimilar to a fat pig.

Queen Elizabeth Wydville was assailed by a grief so physically intense she wondered if her next breath would actually come. She fell forward onto the body of her dead husband, for a moment utterly defeated by the calamity of the event. Edward was still warm – the fever had been so intense. She clung to him as someone drowning might hold on to the most rotten log. This body, with which she had coupled thousands of times; the arms that had held her; the golden hairs on his chest in which she had entwined her fingers; the mouth that had pressed upon hers... but already the priest and barber-surgeon were gently lifting her that they might close his glassy eyes.

"Your Grace, he is gone." Her champion. Her saviour. Decadent and debauched but still her husband. Possibly. Certainly. Still the king. Gone.

Harsh sobs burst from Lord Hastings, Edward's best friend, chamberlain and partner in whoring and gambling. Old Archbishop Bourchier eyed her with wary compassion. Her brothers Lionel, the Bishop of Salisbury and Sir Edward, the sea captain, stood in the corner, whispering urgently with her adult son Thomas Grey, Lord Dorset. Thomas Stanley, Margaret Beaufort's husband, stood dry-eyed, gauging the moment, occasionally transferring his weight from heels to toes and back again.

She stared at the men, Edward's council, who packed the chamber. It was incomprehensible – only ten days ago Edward had been hale and hearty, enjoying the prospect of a fishing trip on the Thames but the east wind had lashed the rain, causing the expedition to be abandoned. Water had swamped the boat and they had all been soaked, returning laughing to the palace. Edward had taken to his bed, declaring it was the only place to warm up. Only five days ago they had all been certain that his chill would pass but today, in the early hours, they had called her, saying the king had but hours to live.

Then time had seemed to stand still. She had held his hand, watching his chest rise and fall – each time more laboured. He had known what was happening – had implored them all to forget their differences and unite for the sake of his son, a twelve-year-old boy soon to be burdened with kingship. With tears coursing down his face he had insisted Elizabeth's son Thomas Grey should place his hand in that of Lord Hastings. Had insisted upon a codicil to his will stating that his brother, Richard of Gloucester should be the Protector of the realm till young Edward should come of age. Had urged her Wydville brothers to forget their rivalries with the Duke of Gloucester and work for the common good. Had ensured that all of this was documented and witnessed. Then, and only then, Bishop Morton heard his confession in private.

One of his physicians touched her elbow and bowed. "Your Grace, you should retire for a short while. There are … things … which must be done … for His Grace the king."

"No, no…not yet. His children are outside. They must say goodbye."

"Maybe in a little while, Your Grace, when we have…"

"Now!"

At her command the door was opened and her five daughters and one son entered. Bessy held the hand of young Richard; Cecily had two-year-old Bridget on her hip; Anne held hands with little Katherine. They all stared at the vast bulk of their father on the bed, naked above the tangled sheets. There was a dreadful silence.

Elizabeth felt a rising hysteria. Somewhere in her consciousness she recalled a folklore story that once, hundreds of years ago, a tidal wave and terrible flood had swamped the lands of Kent, Sussex and Hampshire. A surge of water had submerged villages many miles inland, overwhelming and drowning their inhabitants. She felt like she was there now – about to be swept away by something utterly beyond her control. She was shaking like a mad thing. Her children did not know which was the worst sight – their dead father or distraught mother. No-one moved in the chamber.

Then Lord Stanley cleared his throat. "The king is dead. Long live the king. Long live King Edward V!"

Prince Richard was saucer-eyed. He realised the enormity of the event. "Can a boy be king, Lady Mother? Can he? How will we tell my brother Edward? Will we send a messenger? Can I go? Who will tell him? He will be sad. I am sad, Mother, I am –" He burst into tears. Blindly, Elizabeth reached for him, drawing him into her embrace where he cried noisily and snottily on to her kirtle. Bessy and Cecily exchanged glances and closed in around their mother. Anne ran out, sobbing. Katherine's steady gaze took in the scene; it seared itself into her brain: the pewter bowl containing red-flecked sputum and one of her father's huge hands that dangled over the side of the bed. She watched as the doctor lifted those hands and crossed them over the king's broad chest. Katherine felt upset – she had promised Uncle Richard that she would look after her father, the king but he was dead. She knew what dead meant. Dead meant being completely still. Then they put you in the ground. Or in a church, under the floor. Dead meant your soul went somewhere else. She would need to pray hard that her father's soul went to Heaven. She ought to get started on that straight away. Maybe Uncle Richard would be back soon and help to sort things out. He had promised. Bessy could have been Queen of France but not of England because even though she was the oldest she was a girl. Her brother Edward in Ludlow would be king.

Thomas Grey knelt by Elizabeth, whispering urgently. "Your Grace, my mother, my Wydville uncles agree – we need to talk."

Her eyes swivelled to hold his. This boy of hers, Dorset, son of her first love. True to her. True to her family. *Her* family. There was no-one else to protect her now – she was no foreign princess who might call upon her powerful relatives to safeguard her interests. Neither France nor Burgundy nor Spain nor Scotland would care what happened to her. But she had her brothers, and her grown sons. And a network of supporters – families related to her across the southern counties of England.

"Mother, we will come to your chamber within the hour. Just us." She nodded brusquely. She understood. A new focus was gripping her: the importance of planning the next few days and weeks, of ensuring that the boy in Ludlow was brought quickly and safely to London and surrounded by those who loved him. The king is dead; long live the king. Edward IV was useless to her now; her future was invested in her son Edward V. She allowed herself to be led from the room to her own apartments where she took food and drink for the first time in hours. She sent words of comfort to the children, trusting in their servants to see to their needs. Her ladies-in-waiting approached her cautiously, offering her a laver of warm rosewater and clean linen. She rinsed her face and held her arms above her head, allowing them to unlace and remove the gown and shift she had worn for two days and nights. Sighing with relief, she accepted the fresh clothing just as quick knocks sounded at the door.

Edward and Lionel Wydville, and Thomas and Richard Grey entered quietly. The women were dismissed. A heavy silence hung in the room. Lionel padded to the door again and checked that no-one was listening. Elizabeth looked from one to another, slowly, searchingly, her nerves as taut as an archer's bow string. Thomas Grey broke the tension, reaching for the wine on the table and stuffing slices of manchet bread into his mouth.

"God, I haven't eaten for hours."

"All is being taken care of, my sister. The king will be buried in his new chapel at Windsor," said Lionel gently. "Edward and I will be present."

Elizabeth nodded. "I know it was his wish."

"But his other wishes -" began her son Richard Grey.

"Are not so easy to follow," finished her son Thomas, still chewing.

Her younger brothers and oldest Grey sons were close in age, mid-twenties to early thirties. Tall, long-limbed, fair and blue-eyed – unmistakably from the same family. They had become accustomed to wealth, status and power in the last few years. They were unwilling to relinquish it to Richard of Gloucester.

"The most important thing," said Lionel earnestly, "is to write to Anthony and make sure he brings our nephew Edward to London as quickly as is decently possible, that we may get him crowned before Gloucester gets here."

Elizabeth clasped her hands. "But the king's instructions. Gloucester as Protector?"

Richard Grey chuckled derisively. "Our Edward is nearly thirteen. Mother. He is no babe like the third Henry. He knows who loves him. He adores *you* and he worships my Uncle Anthony. He won't want Gloucester. If we can just get him crowned he won't need a Protector. Why would he need anyone but us? We can send Gloucester back to his beloved Yorkshire, his thin wife and sickly son."

Thomas nodded eagerly. "We're quite important enough to make laws and govern by ourselves, without Gloucester poking his nose in."

"But Hastings will tell him of Edward's final wishes."

Thomas snorted. "His final ravings, more like, while he was deep in fever and pain. The Council would prefer to pass over such wishes. We don't want Gloucester in that role. No Regent ever laid down his power, save reluctantly. There are enough of us."

"You are sure?" She scanned their faces for uncertainty but saw only confidence.

Edward Wydville covered her hands with his own. It felt good to have a man she trusted hold her so. "Sister, we are in a strong position and can make it even stronger. To be sure, Gloucester will come south for his brother's funeral but Richard here will go to Ludlow with all haste and confer with Anthony, and Thomas here will go to the Tower as Constable and guard the Treasury. I will be in the Channel with the fleet. Gloucester is over two hundred miles away. Your son Edward is safe with Anthony. It is a shorter ride from Ludlow than from Yorkshire."

"And more pleasant," said Lionel cheerfully, "the daffodils and primroses will be out. Spring comes later in Yorkshire. Your son Edward will soon be with you. Anthony and Richard will bring him into London. Why, you will hear the cheering from Westminster! Our young king. The future is ours, Lisbet, you may be sure of it."

The use of her old childhood name brought tears to her eyes. "Very well. Bring me my writing tablet. It will be so good to see Anthony again. If anyone can reason with Gloucester it is he."

The lights burned long that night in Westminster. In one room, the embalmers worked quickly and expertly on the old king's body that he might be displayed for all to see in the Abbey before being chested and removed to Windsor. In another, a goose quill scratched and flew across parchment; sealed with the ring of Lord Hastings. At dawn the first messenger left, not on the road west to Oxford, Worcester and the Welsh Marches but north to Middleham. In her bed Katherine Plantagenet woke several times, prayed for her father's soul, as Elyn her nurse had instructed her, and wondered what would happen tomorrow.

4

Katherine: *Sometimes, in a quiet moment, my children asked me whether I could remember my royal brothers. Most children follow a beloved brother or sister's coffin to the grave side. It is nothing unusual in any family. But my brothers simply disappeared. Edward I hardly knew at all but I remember he had our mother's silvery-blond hair and once popped a comfit into my mouth. Richard is clearer in my memory for he spent more time with us. He was always running and hated to sit still ...*

"To King Edward IV succeeded, but for a lamentably short time, his son Edward V." The Great Chronicle

Ludlow, April 16th 1483

Anthony Wydville, Lord Rivers, courtier, scholar, champion of the jousts, governor and favourite uncle of the two young York princes, walked in the outer bailey at Ludlow to clear his head. On this fresh, mid-April morning scudding white clouds sailed onwards, west towards Wales and underfoot the spring grass was beginning to grow. His leather boots darkened where the moisture had flicked upwards with his strides. The bulk of the castle rose up behind him, its crenellated towers standing sentinel over the borderlands: Beacon Tower, overlooking the town; Mortimer's Tower facing Wales along with the four towers built by the Normans all those years ago. Fifty years ago, the Yorkists had taken control of this lovely edifice on its rocky promontory above the fast flowing Teme; Edward IV had spent his boyhood here and chosen it for the court of his young sons – a place where young Edward could learn about ruling through the Council in the Marches of Wales. And how well he had been progessing! Knowing how much Ludlow meant to his family, the prince was buckling down magnificently. Until a few days ago. It was never easy to tell a boy his father was dead but young Edward had reacted courageously, fighting back tears and simply saying, "My mother will need me, Uncle." Anthony knew he was praying now at the altar of the circular Romanesque chapel in the inner bailey.

Elizabeth's letter had shaken him at first, speaking so urgently of the need to bring Edward back to London as soon as possible, under armed guard. For the life of him, Anthony could not quite think why such speed was necessary or indeed, why they would have need of more than a modest retinue. In any case, the boy needed a few more days yet to get used to his new situation. The Council had sent word that May 4th was the date for the coronation so Anthony judged they could delay their departure until after the St George's Day service. By then Richard Grey would be here too. The roads were fairly dry; it would not take more than a few days. The news from London was good – his kinsmen seemed to have everything under control. I wish I might be with Elizabeth now, he thought, for she has always been a one for drama, even when we were children; invariably he had always had to be the calm one. He would remain so now, and try to ease, not rush, young Edward into his destiny.

Anthony breathed deeply of the clean Shropshire air. He was a well travelled man – Santiago, Rome, Venice – yet the sweet springs here at Ludlow captured his heart. For ten years he had lived here happily and usefully, dispensing justice throughout the principality of Wales. He relished the autonomy he had been given and the trust his brother-in-law had placed in him. He thought of the Duke of Gloucester, up in Yorkshire. The King in the North. This tragic news would hit him hard; Richard had shown immense loyalty over the years. Anthony knew that he hated the Wydvilles but also knew him to be a man of high principles. He hoped they might both guide young Edward towards becoming one of the best kings England had ever known. The boy is so promising, he thought; intelligent, even clever; as pious as he grandmother Cecily Neville would wish and with a tender heart. He has his father's charm and a strong sense of family; he loves his mother and siblings dearly, even if most of his life has been spent here with me in Ludlow. I have nurtured him for duty and government and he's nearly ready – just two or three more years and it will all come good. It's sooner than any of us would have wished, but God's will be done.

A few sudden heavy drops of rain ushered in an April shower. Anthony turned back to the castle to seek the warm apartments of the Great Chamber where Sir Thomas Vaughan and Sir Richard Haute, chamberlain and controller of young Edward's household would be waiting. Together they would spend the day helping the boy to compose his first letters as king. They could start by informing the corporation of King's Lynn. Why not? They had to start somewhere. And he would write to Gloucester too.

York, April 23rd 1483

The news from London, brought by Hastings' messengers who galloped day and night had indeed hit Richard hard. It changed everything. As Anthony Wydville had sought the clear air at Ludlow so did Richard stand in the herb garden of St Mary's Friary, searching his soul for answers. It was cold in Yorkshire. The wind blew from the north, gusting around his head. He pulled his cloak tighter, his fingers numb now. He had been out here for an hour or more, pacing up and down the pathways, thinking, while the final preparations to ride south were being made. Now his men were shouting that the horses were saddled, the baggage wagons packed and their journey could begin in earnest. From all over the north men were gathering to ride with him.

Two facts would not leave Richard's mind. A country with a boy king sits on shifting sands. It was impossible for a twelve-year-old to rule a kingdom facing political crisis: war with France and Burgundy; money down the drain on marriages that now would never materialise. Secondly, the Wydville greed for power knew no limits. Ignoble upstarts, clinging to the skirts of Elizabeth. The House of York could so easily be swept away by the queen's family. She hated him; he had always known it. She would never stand to see her boy under his influence – not willingly. *Ah, Edward, why did you have to die before you had time to shape your boy in your own image? He is only half-made, and that half is Wydville, not York.* And the Council, dominated by Wydvilles while men like Harry Buckingham were left out in the cold. What would their future be under such a Council? Already Dorset was boasting of being the boy's *uterine uncle.* What place would there be for him, Edward's paternal uncle?

Richard was playing for time. Yesterday, the nobility and gentry of York, summoned by him, had prayed for the late king's soul in Requiem Masses in the Minster, and had all sworn an oath of fealty to young Edward. But then Hastings' next letter had come, warning him of the Wydvilles' intention to crown the boy on May 4th. And then Buckingham's enigmatic message, not in a letter but delivered in person by his agent Persivell: *"My Master is ready to help you in any way that is wanted, with a thousand good fellows if need be."* Buckingham, the Wydville-hater, doubly descended like me, he thought, from our grandsire Edward III. What does he see in this moment? A chance to take a step nearer the seat of power? Edward had kept him at arm's length, denying him a place upon the Council. He would see the new regime as an opportunity to be counted – have his Plantagenet blood recognised. And why not ... the old nobility of England must surely want to contribute in these new times. Richard sent a message arranging to meet him on the ride south. Buckingham would ride east from his estates in Brecon.

The main thing is to stop the boy reaching London without me. If they crown him they will say a Protector is no longer needed – the Council will assume those powers. He had written to the Council from Middleham, stressing his loyalty, citing his rights under Edward's will. Thank God Hastings had apprised him of that. From Elizabeth herself he had heard precisely nothing.

He swung himself up into the saddle, glad to be on his powerful stallion White Surrey. Cheers rang out from his followers. All would become more clear as he rode south, he was sure of that. They clattered through Micklebar Gate, iron horseshoes striking sparks, and he glanced up at the place where once the heads of his father and brother Edmund had been displayed on spikes by that Lancastrian bitch Marguerite of Anjou. Richard felt a sudden surge of certainty – their deaths, and Edward's early demise would *not* be in vain. The House of York *would* triumph, and not in the form of a Wydville boy.

A courier came galloping up alongside him. "Your Grace! News from Lord Rivers!"

Richard held up his hand to halt the retinue and seized the parchment with its dangling seal. He tore it open and scanned its contents swiftly. Anthony Woodville was bringing the boy to London and suggested a rendezvous at Northampton. Richard frowned. Was this a genuine, cordial attempt on Rivers' behalf to offer some sort of co-operation with him, as Protector, or some Wydville plot to stall him whilst the boy was sent on to London with others? And why still no word from Elizabeth? He threw the document at his secretary and spurred White Surrey forward. It was thirty miles to Pontefract.

5

Katherine: *They say that memories are built upon a sound, a smell, a glimpse, a feeling – some little thing that connects with the mind, in the same way that a key will turn in a lock. I know that when I see a full moon I am always crossing the courtyard at Westminster and then a door closes behind me, making me a prisoner ...*

*"**The king's mother, hearing of the arrest of her brother and sons, fled with her possessions from the royal palace of Westminster to the abbey to take shelter in the security of that privileged place ...**" Crowland Chronicle*

Westminster, May Day 1483

It had been a strange three weeks. The outside world slewed into mid, then late April. Green buds began to swell on the apple and cherry trees in the orchards beyond the city walls. Soon they would burst into frothy pink and white blossom. Each morning Katherine was woken by cries of gulls come upstream on the Thames; their strident squawking entering her dreams and causing her to surface to another day. Interestingly, her Lady Mother had not sent her back to the nursery at Eltham but kept her close at hand with her older sisters. Bridget, though, had developed a hacking cough and was confined to the apartments at the Royal Wardrobe, watched over by her nursemaid, Joanna.

Inside the palace everyone seemed to be waiting for something. Her father's funeral came and went, unattended by any women, who mourned in privacy, but her uncles Edward and Lionel reported back to them how nineteen peers of the realm, ten bishops and hundreds of Edward's staff had filled the graceful Chapel of St George. Katherine leaned against her mother's knee as her uncles described the burial. They told how the men of his household had thrown their staves of

54

office into the grave and the heralds their coats-of-arms. Katherine did not like to think about that; she preferred the part where Sir William Parr had ridden her father's coal black charger, caparisoned in his gorgeous trappings of golden leopards, up the nave, battle axe in hand and offered Edward's knightly achievements at the choir door. In her imagination she heard the stallion's hooves striking upon the stone. Did Sable snort and whinny, she wondered, knowing how close his master was?

"There was such a crush as you have never seen," said Lionel, "but all was done properly."

Elizabeth Wydville's lovely face was a mask. She betrayed no emotion as her brothers spoke of how Edward's own coat of gilt mail, with his arms embroidered in pearls, gold and rubies upon crimson velvet, was hung near the tomb. Bess and Cecily wept to hear about the banner of taffety, with the royal arms, suspended above.

"Why could I not have been there?" demanded the young Duke of York. He had been petulant for days, having wanted to go to Ludlow to fetch his brother but Elizabeth would not hear of it.

"Because you are a child!" Elizabeth's patience with him finally snapped and her voice was sharp and tense. His bravado crumbled and he sobbed again.

During those days, Katherine was not sure what to do with herself. Elyn, her nurse, dressed her each morning, washed her face and combed her hair but barely spoke. There were no lessons. Bess, Cecily and Anne simply waved her away, too sad to entertain her, and her brother had no use for girls, he said. In the mornings she sat silently in a window embrasure, with her simple embroidery, keeping out of everyone's way. She spent her afternoons in the Westminster gardens by the river with Elyn, picking the pale pink lady's smock, purple fritillary, early forget-me-nots, dog violets and swaying Lenten lilies that grew wild in the beds the gardeners had not yet tended. She brought them back to the chamber she shared with Anne, where they wilted quickly. She found a sheltered willow arbour, and curled up there, watching the boys and men planting and weeding. Nobody seemed to care where she went during these hours. On chillier days she wandered alone through the palace, through state and private rooms; she climbed stairs to the towers and looked out over the vista of the city, seeing the soaring spire of the East Minster, St Paul's. At meal times she decided to behave as well as she knew how – eating and drinking quietly, ensuring her elbows were off the table. Each evening she presented herself for her Lady

Mother's blessing but Elizabeth hardly seemed to notice her; her eyes were constantly straying to the door, to the window. Time stood still except for the bells announcing the other liturgical hours. Katherine joined her family in the chapel, knelt dutifully like a little stone effigy and fixed her eyes on the jewelled crucifix, as the priest intoned sonorously in Latin and swung the golden censer. Clouds of incense flew around her head and filled her nostrils and throat with its cloying power. Fervently, she recited her psalter, to prove to whoever would listen that she knew it. There was a new bidding prayer: the household were enjoined to pray for *Our dread king Edward V, the Lady Queen Elizabeth and all the royal offspring.* Katherine had difficulty imagining the affable brother she had seen at Christmas as a *"dread king".*

On the evening of May 1st she was mentally and physically exhausted, glad to go to bed even though the chamber was still light. She fell asleep quickly and hardly stirred when Anne and Elyn crept in a little later. In the early hours, however, she was woken by a commotion: horses' hooves clattering across the courtyard below her window, urgent shouts and yells. Katherine lay for several minutes, her heart racing. Both courtyards were usually silent at nights, the guards on duty while the palace slept. On the truckle bed, Elyn started up in alarm. The cresset burning by the bedside flickered in a sudden draught. Anne was awake and out of bed, opening the shutters to see what was happening below.

"Elyn! Rouse the girls!" Her sisters Bessy and Cecily were in the room, long hair loose and flying. "Help us dress them and bring them to my Lady Mother! Hurry!"

Katherine felt herself lifted from her bed by Bessy and set upon her feet. Bessy grabbed the light wool tawny gown hanging on the pole and pulled it down over Katherine's head. She flung open chests and found cloaks, shoving two under her arm and throwing a third over Katherine's little shoulders.

Elyn, in her shift, was rendered speechless but obeyed, helping Cecily to dress Anne who gasped indignantly. "I don't want to get dressed! It's not morning! What is happening? What are you doing? Cecily, *stop it!"*

Cecily slapped her. "Don't ask questions. There's no time." Shocked, Anne stood still.

More people were crowding into the room now, men and women from the Queen's household whom Katherine recognised but could not name. They came with more candles, and their grotesque shadows were thrown up like giant insects against the walls as, frantically, they grabbed whatever could be moved: stools, coffers, even the tapestries off the walls. Katherine opened her mouth to speak but shut it as Bessy pushed her feet into her leather shoes. She met Anne's frightened eyes.

"Anne! Where are your boots? Your strong ones?"

"I don't know, I –"

"Here," Elyn had found them and Anne, too, was finally shod.

"Elyn, my Lady Mother says you may choose whether you come with us," said Bessy.

"Your Grace, where are you going? Where are you taking them?"

"To Sanctuary," said Bessy shortly. "Now."

Elyn gave a sob of fear but nodded. "Do I have time to dress, Your Grace?"

"Just your kirtle, Elyn, and boots and cloak, like the rest of us. Then follow us. Come on, Cecily and Anne. "

The two elder girls hurried the younger ones through unlit stone passages, down dark stairwells and out into Palace Yard, the main courtyard, lit by flaming brands. Everywhere was chaos: scores of men carrying burdens of household goods upon their backs, disappearing out of the gates towards the Abbey precincts. Katherine gazed in astonishment at servants with fardels of clothes, bedding, plate, criss-crossing the courtyard. In the midst of it all was her mother, issuing imperatives in a shrill voice Katherine had never heard before. She had an outraged Prince Richard firmly by the hand; he too had been dragged from his bed and stood with tousled hair, in yesterday's shirt and wrinkled hose halfway down his legs. The points of his doublet dangled free. He was bawling fit to bust. Elizabeth suddenly saw her two oldest daughters.

"Bessy and Cecily, for God's sake take Dickon and do not let go of him for a single second until you are safely through the doors. Anne, I need you to be as grown up as you can be and hold Katherine's hand. Is Bridget brought here yet?"

"Word has been sent, Mother. Joanna will meet us there."

"Thank God. I am so sorry, Bessy; I never meant for this to happen again but it is our only refuge. And this time will we take what we can."

A lathered horse galloped into the courtyard; a man flung himself out of the stirrups. It was her adult son, Tom Dorset, his usually handsome, arrogant face etched with anxiety.

"It's no good; I could raise no army in the city, Lady Mother. I had to leave the Tower. I will come with you. And my Uncle Lionel will join us. There is nowhere safe for us." He looked like a frightened boy rather than a man.

"What news of my brother Edward?"

"At sea, Mother, in the Channel."

Trepidation flashed across Elizabeth's face. "Then we must go now, as swiftly as we can. I do not know who is for us anymore and Gloucester will be here soon,"

Katherine felt Anne take her hand and they followed the strange train of people and belongings, out of the palace gates and across the short distance to the Abbey. The sky was clear and the stars were out, lending a surreal, magical atmosphere. Katherine wondered if they were actually going into the Abbey but they passed the Great West Door and instead made for Cheneygates, the Abbot's lodgings. Joanna the nurse was waiting there in the moonlight, with Bridget in her arms. The child was still coughing miserably, her rasping breaths cutting through the night air. A large wagon had trundled behind them, loaded with the biggest pieces of furniture. It ground to a halt, the wheels screeching as the brake was applied.

"Your Grace! We can never get these in! The door is too narrow!"

Katherine thought her mother looked rather like a mad witch. Her hair was escaping from her coif and her face was contorting into mixed expressions of fear and fury. Wildly, she swept her gaze along the walls of the building.

"There! Where it is weakest! Knock it down!"

The men looked at her in disbelief. "Your Grace, this be Sanctuary. We cannot -"

Elizabeth screamed at them, "Smash it down, I say! Everything must go in!"

In the doorway the worried looking Abbot of Westminster wrung his hands. "Your Grace, my Lord Duke of York, Princesses, oh, and my Lord of Dorset ... I bid you welcome. May you find safety here, under my protection. I swear I will do all I -"

Already they were pushing past him, into the gloomy interior where just a few candles burned. The door slammed shut behind them. Katherine stood with her family amidst the flotsam and jetsam of their lives: chests, packs and random pieces of furniture; feather mattresses upended against the walls and clothing spilling out of over-stuffed coffers. Her half-brother Thomas looked frozen with disbelief. Bessy and Cecily still had hold of a sniffing, hiccuping Richard but now released him. The small boy sank down on to the floor. Outside they could hear the sound of dull thuds as part of the wall was being broken down. Abbot John Eastley swallowed hard and tried to look as though the arrival of the Queen and her children, and the wanton destruction of his courtyard wall, were everyday events. He fell back upon his innate hospitality – the time-honoured role of an abbot faced with unexpected guests.

"Well! Some refreshment, Your Grace? Yes, a glass of wine and some cakes. Come through into my privy chamber."

It was utterly bizarre to be eating honey cakes and buttermilk at five o'clock in the morning but Katherine found she was suddenly ravenous and helped herself eagerly from the platter a silent young monk held out to her. Joanna took some buttermilk for Bridget and sat on one of the coffers, helping the little girl to sip. The adults were conversing urgently, working out practicalities.

"I can put my three best rooms at your disposal, Your Grace," said the Abbot. "The Jerusalem Chamber, the dining hall and this chamber. You will remember there is a small courtyard where the children may play."

"You remember, Bessy?" The Queen's voice caught in her throat. "You were but four. You played there with Mary."

Bessy nodded, unable to look at her mother. Suddenly it was Cecily who was weeping.

"Oh, my Lady Mother, who will come to us here? Who will save us? My father is no more!"

Her last few anguished words unleashed something awful In Elizabeth. Before their eyes she hurled the cup of wine aside, sank down upon the rushes and cast herself forward. A dreadful moan of abject despair escaped from her prostrate form. Only the Abbot had the courage to kneel beside her, his black Benedictine habit bunched up, showing beneath thin, bare calves threaded by purplish veins and long feet with thick, yellow toenails.

"Be of good courage, Your Grace. All will be well yet." But Katherine heard a note she recognised in his voice. The same well-meaning tone used to her and Bridget to reassure when it meant nothing of the sort. It was impossible that her mother the Queen should be lying on the floor. It scared her.

"Mama. Get up. Please get up." She knelt beside the Abbot and tried to lift her mother's head. All that happened was that Elizabeth's headdress finally came apart and skeins of her knee-length hair unravelled over the rushes. Her sisters were beside her, also trying to raise their mother. Elizabeth's breath came in a great gulp and rivers of tears were flowing down her face. Her words came out in a torrent of wretchedness.

"Cecily is right! We were here once and we are here again – and this time my husband cannot save us! He will never come! Oh, God, he is dead! He always came! He always came back! He will come no more! Who will stand for us? Gloucester has taken my brother Anthony and my son Richard, and my kinsman – and he has my son Edward in his keeping. Sweet Mother of Christ, what will he do? "She raised grief-stricken eyes to the Abbot and Tom. "What will *we* do?"

With sunrise there came a hammering on the door. Archbishop Rotherham of York burst in, delivering the Great Seal of England into Elizabeth's hands. He knelt before her, tears in his eyes, declaring his loyalty. Elizabeth held the heavy metal seal like a talisman; the bright rays of the sun filtered through the high, arched windows of the Jerusalem Chamber and the bronze flashed as she stood by the empty fireplace, slowly turning the disc over and over, and staring at the images of her husband on horseback, sword aloft, and sitting on his throne before Westminster.

"As long as you have this, Your Grace, nothing can change in England," declared Rotherham stoutly, but Katherine saw how his mouth worked to keep his emotions under control.

"This is … brave of you," whispered Elizabeth, "They will surely strip you of your office when they know."

But within a couple of days she managed to recover some of her equanimity. Their beds were set up in the Jerusalem Chamber and the dining hall reserved for the servants' beds and daytime activities. A cell was found for Thomas Grey in the monks' dormitory. Elizabeth kept the Abbot's privy chamber as her own space. Food was sent from the monks' kitchen and arrived cold and unappetising. Strangely enough, anyone could enter sanctuary so they lived in constant fear of who might bang next upon the door. Her mother's brother, Lionel, joined them a few days later, slipping secretly into the lodgings. His white prelate's robes billowed as he sank into the proffered chair. He was unwashed, unshaven and haggard.

"The news changes hourly, Your Grace. Our brother Anthony and Sir Richard Grey have been taken north to Sheriff Hutton and Middleham. Gloucester entered the city yesterday with the young king. The citizens –" he paused, searching Dorset and Bessy's faces for clues as to how much he should disclose to his sister.

"Yes? You might as well tell all, sir," said Bessy, "for concealment of news will not help us."

"The citizens are told that we Wydvilles meant to take over London; Gloucester has produced wagonloads of weaponry said to be ours."

Tom Dorset groaned.

"My son, the king?"

"Taken to the Bishop's palace."

"And Gloucester?"

"Rides high with the Council, for he has made all swear loyalty to the king."

"There, Lady Mother!" exclaimed Bessy, "that is not so bad, surely? My uncle of Gloucester does surely mean to honour my father's wishes!"

"They will not administer your husband's will whilst you all remain in sanctuary," continued Lionel, "which means -"

"That we are destitute," finished Elizabeth. "Unless you have brought money with you, brother? Or you, Tom, did you bring gold from the treasury?" Her tone seemed mocking.

Lionel shook his head, "I have nothing, except the clothes I stand in."

"There was no time, Lady Mother." Tom paused, then blundered on. "And in any case there was hardly anything left. Your husband's jewels had to be pawned to pay for the funeral expenses."

Cecily looked alarmed. "How on earth will we eat, Lady Mother?"

Elizabeth gave a short laugh, "Through the generosity of my Lord Abbot. Until his purse runs out."

"But last time, did they not bring us food?" began Bessy. "You told me, Mama, there was a butcher, and nuns brought bread and eggs, and the people left gifts, too, every day."

"Then, the Londoners loved your father," replied Elizabeth. "Like me, they simply had to wait for him to come and rescue us all."

Cecily looked horror-struck. "How long must we stay here, Lady Mother?"

"Until I can trust Gloucester, which may be never."

Katherine was only managing to follow tiny threads of the conversation but Cecily's question made some sense. She crept to her mother's side and laid a tiny hand on her knee. "So will we live her for ever, Lady Mother?"

"Most likely," said Elizabeth. She rose and went into the Abbot's privy chamber, slamming the door behind her.

* * *

61

On May 10th Richard was in control when the Council met in the Star Chamber at Westminster – a new Council, devoid of Wydvilles now: his close friend Francis Lovell; Buckingham, who had proved staunch and supportive at Stoney Stratford; loyal supporters of Edward IV like Hastings and Bishop Stillington; his nephew John de la Pole, son of his sister the Duchess of Suffolk; carefully chosen new faces like the young king's former tutor John Alcock and John Russell the Bishop of Lincoln. Some old wily faces remained – Lord Stanley, with his inscrutable expression. The window was open and a welcome breeze from the Thames refreshed the stuffiness of the room where they had been in session for three hours. A sudden waft lifted some of the papers on the table. Carefully, Richard anchored them with the corner of the sand box then looked at the expectant faces. They had just formally accepted him as Protector.

"Your Grace's loyalty to the late king is beyond reproach," said Hastings, whose eyes still brimmed whenever he mentioned his friend. "I declare, Dickon, my Lord, that nothing more has happened than we've successfully transferred the rule of the kingdom from two of the queen's relatives to two of the king's!"

Thumps of approval on the table.

"Then I take it we are agreed, "said Richard briskly, "that I may have the tutelage and oversight of the king's person?"

Murmurs of assent. Lord Stanley stood up and bowed first to Richard and then to Harry Buckingham. "May I congratulate your lordships on the way you brought young Edward to London without any bloodshed. No more than a cut finger!"

There were low chuckles from most of the men present.

Buckingham waxed lyrical. "It was the devil's own job, was it not, Dickon, to part the prince from the queen's proud kinsmen! The lad did not seem to recognise their faults – and tried to tell us how he wanted his mother's family and none other. Sweet Mother of Christ, the boy does not seem to understand that he's a Plantagenet! He'll need some education on that!"

"Aye!" put in Francis Lovell.

He's spent too long with Rivers at Ludlow – what did they teach him there? He should have been sent up to Middleham to you, Dickon! It's a crime that he does not know his father's family."

Richard seized the moment. "True enough, and you all know we shall have no security unless Lord Rivers, Sir Richard Grey and the other two are dealt with."

"Dealt with?" Bishop Moreton looked at him quizzically. "How do you mean, Your Grace? You have them prisoner, I believe, but after the coronation it might be politic to release them. What further harm can the Wydvilles do once His Grace is crowned, with you as Protector?"

"They have committed treason, "snapped Richard. "God's nails but they would have had me killed. Why else did they head the boy off to Stoney Stratford while Rivers detained me at Northampton?" He was desperate to get them all onside but clearly it would not be easy.

Buckingham poked a finger in the air at Bishop Moreton. "I tell you, my lord, that if we had not smelt a rat, and very quickly too, you would be subject now to Rivers sitting here, with his brothers and his Grey nephews, and my Lord of Gloucester, and me, dead in a ditch at Northampton!"

"But treason, Your Grace? We would need hard proof of Rivers' ... I am not sure that we have sufficient evidence to ..." began Bishop Stillington and looked appealingly at his fellow councillors.

"Treason is indeed a strong word, sir, "said John Alcock, in a considered tone, "and can lead in only one direction. Like Bishop Stillington I believe we must consider the situation much more carefully before we could possibly endorse your view of Lord Rivers."

He gazed somewhere beyond Richard's head, fixing his eyes on the tapestry on the wall behind and then upon the star-spangled ceiling. His thoughts were of the letter he had received telling of a weeping young king, when all his familiar household servants had been summarily dismissed.

Archbishop Rotherham had kept his eyes firmly on the floor for most of the meeting. Yesterday, he had been sent to wrest the Great Seal back from Elizabeth – a scene he would rather forget, for the Queen had wept and wept, calling him a traitor. Princess Bessy had been stony-faced, the little prince had called him rude names, and this morning Richard had demoted him from his position as Chancellor *You were somewhat foolish, Archbishop.* Yet so far he was not dismissed from the Council. He cleared his throat. "Sir, I would urge you to have some concern for the dignity and safety of the Queen."

Richard leaned forward, rested his elbows on the table, linked his fingers and rested his chin on them, regarding Rotherham silently for a moment. No-one else spoke. Finally, Richard sighed. "I have every concern for the Dowager Queen and her children. But I can hardly be held responsible if she refuses to come out of sanctuary. Why does she choose to remain in a place reserved for criminals? She places her own dignity and safety in jeopardy."

"Sir, with the greatest respect, Her Grace is frightened," ventured Rotherham.

"Frightened? When we have just agreed to mint coins in the name of her son?" Richard's voice was icy with frustration. "All that is required of the Queen Dowager is that she accepts me as Protector, as was her husband's desire, and accepts that her family shall have no further influence over our young king."

Buckingham roared his approval.

At the far end of the table, the kindly old Archbishop of Canterbury, Cardinal Bourchier spoke up. "I think that when we tell her that the king's coronation is now re-scheduled for June 22nd she will feel more reassured."

"Then by all means send word to her," said Richard. "And while you are about it, tell her that her brother Captain Edward Wydville is denounced and must disband his fleet in the Channel. If he refuses I shall arrest him." He looked around the table. "I do take it that we are all now agreed that the Wydville faction shall never more be allowed to think they can rule our kingdom?"

Again, murmurs of agreement.

"Well, then, gentlemen. We shall meet again soon." Richard was already on his feet, gathering papers.

"Your Grace," interposed Bourchier, "how is our sovereign lord, the young king? I would like to be able to take good news to his mother. She has not seen him since Christmas. You will recall that he is my young kinsman too."

Richard paused in the doorway. "He is well, sir. Some slight toothache, but otherwise well."

"What we need to do," said Buckingham, "is move him now to a more appropriate lodging. What do you all say if the King takes up residence in the Tower? It is a more fitting place than in your palace, eh, Lord Russell?"

"Indeed, sir. His Grace the King would feel more at home in the royal apartments he knows, I am sure."

Richard nodded assent. "Will you see to that then, Harry?"

Buckingham's blue eyes flashed with enthusiasm and self-importance. For so long the late King Edward had excluded him from any position of authority, despite his noble birth. With Dickon it was already different; Dickon respected his status and seemed to value his friendship. His star was rising.

6

Katherine: *My world had been blown apart, forever. All I knew was that my father was shockingly dead and that together with my mother and my sisters I was in a place called Sanctuary. They told me that in Sanctuary God would keep me safe but I sensed it was a lie.*

"On Friday 13th June Lord Hastings came to the council at the Tower, where, on the orders of the Protector, he was beheaded." The Crowland Chronicle

June 13th 1483

When it was fine, Katherine and her sisters spent their time in the tiny courtyard at Cheneygates. Above, a square of sky was visible, like a piece of blue patchwork, and an occasional high cloud drifted by. It was like being cut adrift together in a small boat. Bessy and Cecily were reading aloud, a leather bound volume of *The Canterbury Tales* propped up in front of them on an old lectern begged from the monks. Anne lay on her stomach on a pile of cushions, listening. Katherine could not follow the story so sat propped up, next to Anne, eyes closed, feeling the warmth of her sister's body and of the sunshine upon her eyelids. If she blotted out this place then, in her imagination, she could run again down familiar wide, green garden paths at Eltham and smell the fragrance of roses. She fingered the pink gown smoothed over her knees, embroidered with white roses. Her nails picked constantly at the thick silk knots and chains. They grew dirtier by the week; as the silk unravelled the roses were lost.

The young Duke of York sat in the shade, playing chess with one of the novice monks drafted in by the Abbot to keep the boy amused. They were managing to provide him with some rudimentary lessons but as the days wore on he was dreadfully bored, hemmed in by the lack of space and lonely for the company he was used to of boys his own age There was no riding here, or practising at the quintain; no-one to play sword-fighting with; no-one to teach him how to hunt with his peregrine falcon. His half-brother Tom Dorset was no fun either. But Brother Jerome was quite good at chess.Every morning Elyn and Joanna slipped out to buy bread. Elizabeth sent them with silver plate to sell in order to have a supply of cash. They returned with as much news as they could glean from their families in the city, the guards they knew at the palace and servants in other noble families. They smuggled letters in to Elizabeth from supporters – messengers loitered outside the Abbot's House, waiting for either girl to appear. Neither Elyn nor Joanna asked questions about whose seals were on the folded-up messages they pushed into their sleeves or beneath their shifts. They simply delivered them to Elizabeth who mouthed her thanks silently, took them and disappeared into the Abbot's privy chamber. There was also one who came with her golden curls concealed under a hooded gown, to see Thomas Grey – and spend an illicit hour with him in the monk's cell. When Elizabeth had first recognised her she had screamed at Tom for being an utter fool, but the whore had proved useful, carrying messages from an unexpected source...

In this way she had kept track of some of the events in the outside world: she knew now that the Council was split – some beginning to doubt Gloucester's true intentions. She knew that he was buying favour – that Harry Buckingham had received spectacular grants of land and power in Wales. She knew how others were living off the promise of future favours. She knew that her brother Edward had escaped Gloucester's pursuit in the Channel and had sought refuge in Brittany with Lady Margaret Beaufort's son, Henry Tudor. She knew too, that there was growing disquiet in the city about why Gloucester still detained Anthony, Richard Grey, Lord Haute and Thomas Vaughan in prison, and questions about why the royal family remained in sanctuary. She knew that her son the young king was now in the Tower, attended by Dr Argentan who wrote of Edward's aching jaw and melancholy mood.

Most interesting recently had been an unforeseen letter from Lord Hastings. Despite her personal detestation of the man, Elizabeth was pragmatic enough to recognise that his loyalties lay with his late master and friend – reading his words she realised that this devotion centred firmly on Edward's heir.

"Your Grace, I grow uneasy. I do worry about my Lord of Gloucester's desire to lengthen the Protectorate beyond the coronation. Neither am I sure about why

66

he extends such generosity to my Lord of Buckingham. My Lord Stanley has urged caution. My Lord Rotherham and Moreton share my unease...."

Sitting in the cool of the Abbot's dining hall, with Hastings' letter in her lap, Elizabeth could hear Bessy and Cecily's light voices outside as they alternated between the rhyming couplets of *The Knight's Tale.* The older girls were coping well with this enforced confinement. Bessy had initiated a routine of reading, prayers, singing, board games and needlework. After her initial outburst Cecily had simply lain on her bed in the corner of the Jerusalem Chamber, refusing to communicate with anyone but Elizabeth had overheard the stoical Bessy speaking of the selfishness of such behaviour. Gradually, Cecily had mastered her distress and begun to help Elyn and Joanna with the personal care of the younger children. Now Katherine had declared that she wanted only Cecily to comb her hair and wash her face.

A door banged at the rear of the house – the little door through which Elyn and Joanna came and went without too much notice, and through which other visitors were occasionally admitted. Light footsteps came pattering down the passage and Elyn appeared in the doorway, red-faced and sweating, her coif awry, the pupils of her eyes dilated with horror.

"Oh, dear God! I have run all the way! Oh, Sweet Jesu, my side!"

"Elyn? What is it? Where have you been? Where is the bread?"

"Your Grace! They have killed my Lord Hastings!"

Elizabeth rose in disbelief. She clutched the letter to her breast. "What on earth do you mean, Elyn? What are you saying?"

"Lord Hastings, madame! They have cut his head off! In the Tower! This morning! The whole city is on fire with it! I am come from my father's house!"

Suddenly, Lionel was in the Hall, too, grim-faced. "It's true, Elizabeth. I have just had word from one of my men. The Council met this morning at the Tower, and Gloucester accused Hastings of treason – said he was plotting with you, and our family. Before the poor man could defend himself Lord Howard and men in armour burst in and dragged him out. They laid him on a log and took his head off."

"And what else?" whispered Elizabeth, white with shock.

"Rotherham and Morton in prison, taken to Wales, and Lord Stanley taken under armed guard to his own house in the city."

"God help us." Elizabeth held out the letter to her brother. "Take this, Lionel – it's from Hastings – and burn it. Now! Do you hear what I say?"

"Lady Mother, how did you come by such a letter?" Bessy stood in the doorway, framed by all her sisters. "Elyn, did you bring it?"

"No, no, My Lady. Not that one. It was brought by –" Elyn stopped, and her face turned from red to puce.

"Bessy, it was brought by Mistress Shore."

Bessy turned incredulous eyes upon her mother. "You are in communication with *that woman?"*

"*That woman* has secretly visited your brother Tom, here, and yes, she has brought us news. Bessy you must know that we have family, and kinsmen, and their retainers out there who would help us against Gloucester."

"And the Shore woman has been acting as your go-between? Carrying letters from Hastings? How, in God's name did she get in?"

"In disguise. As a nun." Elizabeth was acutely aware of how incongruous, even ludicrous this sounded.

Bessy gave a shout of appalled laughter. "And now you are found out? Oh God, Lady Mother! Why must you plot? Why must you endanger us all even more? Why can you not make peace with my Uncle of Gloucester and release us all from this captivity? What harm would he wish us? My brother's crowning is all arranged!"

Katherine stood in the shelter of Cecily's arms and watched the furious interchange between her mother and her eldest sister. They looked like two cats about to fly at one another.

"You allowed that *whore* in here? Where my sisters and brother slept? You would speak with her?

"Bessy, you forget yourself," said Elizabeth. "Mistress Shore brought us news because she loved your father."

"Because she shared three men's beds!" Bessy's voice rose in fury.

"Bessy, calm yourself," said Lionel. "There is more you should know before you choose to rail against us all. Gloucester has written to the civic council in York, asking for an armed force to aid and assist him against our family. He says we are trying to destroy him."

"And are we? Are we, Lady Mother?"

"Bessy! You must understand – I do not know what to think, or who to trust."

"No, Lady Mother, you just refuse to trust my Uncle of Gloucester because you have ever hated him! I do not know why – my father would never tell me, but he *did* tell me, as he lay dying, that he thought *his* brother the best person to

68

have charge of Edward, not *your* brothers. *You* would not even speak to my uncle of Gloucester at Christmas. Have you ever spoken to him? Have you ever tried, just for one moment, to look for what my father saw in him?" Bessy was wild-eyed with passion. Lionel looked as if he had no idea how to deal with shrieking women. Cecily laid a restraining hand upon her sister's arm.

"Bessy, listen to me and listen well. In my heart I think that Gloucester may intend some harm towards your brother the king. There, I have said it."

Horror washed across Bessy's face. "What are you suggesting?"

"You know what I am suggesting. Do not make me say in front of your little sisters and brother." She turned to her brother. "Lionel, Tom cannot be found here now."

"He is gone, already. I do not believe Gloucester or Buckingham will harm women but I must go too. They will not respect sanctuary now."

Elizabeth embraced him. "Then go, as quickly as you can. Lie low, and do whatever you need to do to keep yourself safe. Where will Tom go, do you think?"

"He spoke of France. If he can find a ship sailing tonight, he will go to Edward, who is with the Tudor. Be of good heart, sister. We will meet again soon."

Bessy watched silently as her uncle kissed her mother goodbye. She felt Cecily's hand creep into hers. The sisters formed a sort of chain, linked by hands. Young Richard appeared from outside, cross and bothered.

"What was all the noise about? You all disturbed my game of chess with Brother Jerome. With all your shouting we could not hear ourselves think," he added disapprovingly. "I wish there was somewhere else to go, to get away from you all. I wish I was with my brother."

* * *

June 14th 1483

Richard, Duke of Gloucester and Lord Protector of England, lay in bed at Crosby Place. He had not slept – or, if he had, he could not remember it. He had watched the midsummer twilight turn to a few hours of darkness then watched again as dawn hardened on the walls. Beside him his wife Anne Neville still slumbered, even though the bright sunshine was filtering through the shutters and dust motes danced in the air. She had arrived from Middleham yesterday, to find her London home in a state of consternation following the events of the morning. Now her narrow shoulders rose and fell, her breathing faintly rasping. Occasionally she coughed and Richard winced to hear the dry-sounding lungs. He studied her face: the pale complexion, arched brows, snub nose and determined little chin. Beneath the blue-veined lids were her serious hazel eyes and tendrils of nut-brown hair escaped from her nightcap. She was no beauty but pretty, in a slender, almost childlike way. At twenty-six she looked more like sixteen. Yet there was a core of steel in Anne's personality, a single-mindedness inherited from her father the Kingmaker. As she dreamed, Richard saw his son, Edward of Middleham, in the high set cheekbones and the involuntary movements of her lips. Edward was the bond that held them together – both fiercely attached to the little boy who, like his mother, seemed to catch every cough and cold under the sun.

Yesterday's events at the Tower preyed heavily upon his mind. That Hastings should have so betrayed him, turning his coat back towards the Wydvilles! There had been no alternative but to act when the facts had been laid bare. Letters, between the Wydville witch and Hastings – carried to and fro by the whore who had warmed Edward's bed, and Hastings' and Thomas Grey's. Why had Hastings decided to seek out the Wydvilles? *Had he truly meant to betray me? Fool, fool of man – he left me with no alternative but to act decisively, as my father Duke Richard of York would have done; as my brother Edward would have done. As I did at Stoney Stratford when I seized the young king from Anthony, Lord Rivers. As I will do again if I have to. I cannot flinch from my duty. I have to do whatever it takes to ensure the boy is my king. If I have to destroy others then I can do it. I never wanted this ... I was content with my life in the north. I never asked for this ... but it has come to me. And I must make it work.*

Beside him, Anne stirred, opening her eyes and turning towards him. She propped herself up on one elbow, coughing a little as she adjusted her position. Richard passed her the glass of honeyed small ale left by their bedside at night. She sipped gratefully then regarded him anxiously. "My Lord? Are you well? Have you slept at all? " His anger last night had frightened her. She had never seen fury like it. She knew him to be high-minded, intelligent and utterly pragmatic. She did not fool herself that he had married her for love; he had chosen her for the vast Warwick estates he so craved, which had made him a virtual king in the north. But then what man would not have done so? That was the way of the world. She had often seen impatience in him yet she had never seen deliberate injustice, or cruelty. He respected her; he was fond of her; they had known each other since childhood and their shared memories anchored them. He knew how to rule well in the north, mastering his rivals in a brave and God-fearing way that brought security. She believed that loyalty and honesty were the cornerstones of his character. Yet she acknowledged that aspects of his character remained ever elusive, even from those who thought they knew him well. Yesterday, ire had come upon him like quicksilver, because one he had trusted had betrayed him. Anne shuddered. It beggared belief. Hastings, who had been the one to send word of Edward's death when Elizabeth had stayed silent; Hastings, who had warned of the Wydville intrigues. A hundred times in the past twenty hours she had pictured his handsome head being pushed down upon the log in the shadow of the White Tower; imagined the flash of savage steel in the noonday sun and seen the red blood flow on to the green grass. A man executed without any form of trial. She had no idea how she had managed to fall sleep. Maybe from sheer disbelief and exhaustion.

"What will happen to his family, Richard? Will you punish them, too? The eldest boy is but sixteen." Her voice was uncertain but courageous. Richard moved her plait of walnut-brown that had fallen over his arm.

"I will not attaint him. His wife can retain his land and goods." His voice was tight.

"She will bless you for it," she responded with relief. "It is the right thing to do. Neither she nor the children are to blame." She had feared he might be ruthless as his brother Edward had been at her brother-in-law Clarence's execution. Buoyed a little by his response she ventured further. "And my sister Isabel's son? You must remember Dorset had his wardship but what will happen to him, now Dorset is fled?"

"What do you think best?"

She was pleased that he seemed willing to consult her. "That he should come to us, at Sheriff Hutton or Middleham, and be with his sister and your children?" She spoke carefully, making it seem a request rather than a statement, including the two York bastards, John and Katherine. Some appeal to Richard's sense of family might secure safety for her dead sister's child. "He is no threat, my lord; I hear he is behind in his lessons and lonely for company."

"Then arrange it."

She breathed more easily now. From outside the door they could hear sounds that told them the household was stirring. Footsteps of maidservants on the stairs;

clunking of wooden buckets; quiet calls. Like an ordinary day. As if the world was not turning upon its head.

"And what will you do today?" she dared to ask him.

He found he could not tell her what was in his mind. What he had been turning over in the recesses of his brain for the last six hours. That having possession of one of the York princes was not enough. "Think," he replied shortly.

"Does the council meet again today? After ..."

"In divers places. With divers people." He could never trust the council again. He needed to split them and learn who was with him. He leaned over to kiss her cheek, then called for his page to help him rise and dress. Anne watched from the bed as he leaned over the laver and rinsed his face in hot water, then sat to be shaved. The boy helped him to pull his nightgown over his head and offered fresh linen. The flesh of his torso was white compared with his face, neck and forearms. Richard's back was twisted – a feature she had hardly noticed in his younger years but which was becoming more pronounced with time. She feared it pained him but he never spoke of it. The subtle padding in his outer clothing hid it well. Now his page helped him into a indigo- coloured overgown and held out a shallow tray of jewels. Richard selected three rings of gold and rubies, and slid them on to the thumb, fourth and fifth fingers of his right hand. The page settled a collar of gold, pearls and dark jasper over his shoulders. He glanced back at her.

"And what will *you* do today, my dear?"

"Write to our Edward. And now send for Isabel's Edward. So many Edwards – and Richards! Maybe we should have chosen differently for our son. Do you remember, my love, how we considered Edmund, or Thomas, or even Humphrey, that your mother might not be confused?"

He knew she was trying to tease a smile out of him, to send him on his way with a lighter heart but it would not come. "They are the names of princes, not of kings," he said. Anne looked at him in astonishment. She waited until the page had left the room then slipped off the bed and came to his side.

"What are you saying, Richard?" she asked softly, "that you envisage our son as king one day?"

He could not tell if she was appalled or excited. "Stranger things have happened," he said quietly. "You came south when you knew Elizabeth was in sanctuary."

She threw him a calculated smile. "My father always intended me to be a queen."

June 16th 1483

Prince Richard of York deigned to allow his little sister Katherine to play with him. He had thought about teaching her to play chess but on Bessy's advice settled instead for instructing her about the names of the pieces in the chess set. Bessy and his mother were barely speaking. It was a dull morning; prayers with the monks were over, breakfast had been bread (again!) and Brother Jerome had duties to attend to. In the courtyard the square of sky was grey, a summer shower expected any minute. Male company was in very short supply – Richard was uncertain as to whether the monks with their tonsured heads, thick black robes, cowled hoods and silent footsteps qualified as real men. As far as he was concerned real men were like his Uncle Anthony or grown up brothers – wielding swords and riding in jousts, laughing and dancing – not scratching away on vellum in chilly cloisters or on their knees in the herb garden. Of course, a man had to spend *some* time on his knees praying to God but then he would get up again and ride out to gallop across the downs and through forests, following the sound of the hunting horn.

"The king," said Katherine, as he produced the ivory figure from behind his back. She picked it up and, giggling, made it walk along the floor.

"What do you think our brother is doing this morning?" Richard found himself thinking this every single day since they had heard that Edward had been moved to the Tower. Richard liked the Tower, with its view of the river and all the boats. At the Tower there were archery butts, and stables, a menagerie of wild creatures and all sorts of interesting places to explore.

"Walking? Like this?" suggested Katherine. "In the garden."

She had not been at the Tower for several months but could just about recall the areas she and Elyn had roamed in – certainly enough space to run about and play.

Richard joined in her game. He picked up two more chess pieces. "And a bishop comes to visit him, with a knight," he agreed.

"Good day, my lords," said Katherine solemnly, bowing her king.

"Good day, Your Grace," said Richard, dipping his pieces so that their heads touched the rushes. " What is Your Grace's will?"

Katherine thought hard. She pondered upon what she might want, were she to be stuck on her own in the Tower. She looked up at Richard's impish face, with its mop of curly bronze hair, very much in need of Cecily or Elyn's attentions with a comb. "I'd like to see my brother, please," she said firmly.

Thudding again on the main door. It echoed through the dining hall where they sat and brought Elizabeth out of the privy chamber. Various members of the Council had visited over the past two weeks, begging her to change her mind and quit sanctuary. Some had spoken gently; others unpleasantly. She had listened politely then asked them to leave. In the past three days, since Hastings' execution, she had lived on a knife edge – daily expecting some force to try and expel her.

"My Lord the Archbishop of Canterbury," announced the awestruck monk who had opened the door. Before her stood Cardinal Thomas Bourchier, the man who had crowned her nearly twenty years ago. His red robes and hat seemed to fill the room like embers from a fire. But the old man was not alone; following him into the hall came several other members of the Council whom Elizabeth knew well: John Howard, the Earl of Surrey and John Russell, the Bishop of Lincoln. Alarmingly, in their wake came four armed guards in the livery of the Duke of Gloucester, the white boar emblazoned on their chests. Bessy and Cecily had been at their needlework in a corner but stood up in apprehension.

"Madame," said Bourchier. He was eighty years old and not to be hurried in his speech. He bowed. Katherine looked at his hands, clasped in front of his red gown, fascinated by their mottled flesh. She gazed at his face where the old skin hung like a cockerel's wattles beneath his chin. Faint specks of spittle hung on his nether lip like a spider's web. She had never seen anyone so old. The other men, the ones in livery, smelled unpleasant – stale sweat and sour breath. A gut-wrenching fear suddenly gripped her belly. With all the animal instincts of a small child she was afraid. "Madame," he said again, as if cranking himself into verbal action. "I am come to ask you to surrender your son the Duke of York into the care of the Protector, the Duke of Gloucester."

"No," said Elizabeth.

"Because," he continued as if he had not heard her, which was probably true, "because it is not seemly that the young duke should not attend his brother's coronation. Indeed he may be returned to your care *after* the coronation."

Elizabeth searched his face. "Do you speak in good faith?"

His old eyes watered. "Aye, Madame. I swore loyalty to the heirs of your sovereign lord King Edward IV on his deathbed. My Lord Protector is anxious that our young king should have company and support at this time."

The Bishop of Lincoln nodded. "It is hard to understand, Madame, why you feel he should remain here. After all, a child of his age has no need of sanctuary for he has not sinned. Sanctuary is for grown criminals." Katherine thought he sounded rather like a snake. She would not have been surprised to see a forked tongue flick out.

"Indeed it would be better if *all* the children left this place," said John Howard. "God's teeth, Your Grace, why would you want to keep them here? You have made your point and failed. Hastings has lost his head for it and others held prisoner. Give it up; come out and support your son as he is crowned. Or if you persist with this charade then at least allow the lad to have his brother for company."

Bessy looked carefully at her mother. In the last couple of days she had felt immensely frustrated with Elizabeth. If it was true that she had plotted, then the intrigue was exposed and the perpetrators punished. She did not believe that the uncle she had spoken to so comfortably at Christmas could mean harm to women and children. It had been two months since her father had died but Bessy felt she had lived two years since then, forced into some nightmare existence. She yearned for her old life, and wanted it for Cecily, Anne and Katherine too. She wanted young Richard to stand proudly by his brother and swear allegiance, as her Uncle Dickon had once done as a child of nine at *his* brother's crowning. *Loyaulte Me Lie. Uncle Dickon's motto.*

"Lady Mother, you should consider this. Our Richard is driving us mad here. You know it; he is miserable without his playmates and his horse, and his hawk, and his puppy. It's bad enough for us girls"

"Mama! Please let me go! I can tell Edward all our news and play with him at chess, and practise our archery as we did at Ludlow! And help him learn what to do at the coronation!" Richard's bright hazel eyes were shining with a ten-year-old's enthusiasm.

Cardinal Bourchier stood silently, head bowed. He was loath to mention that scores of armed men waited outside the Abbot's house. The Dukes of Gloucester and Buckingham had given him half an hour before they threatened to breach sanctuary.

Richard tugged at his mother's hand. "If my brother needs me, I should go."

Elizabeth dropped her other hand on his hair, teasing out the many knots with her fingers. She knelt to his level and kissed him. "Then take him, sir, for I know that if I do not give him up others will take him from me."

Two of the guards stepped forward and each took one of Richard's arms, lifting him off his feet so he dangled like a puppet between them.

"No!" said Bessy sharply. "There is absolutely no need for this! You will treat the Duke of York with the dignity he deserves!" She moved forward and pulled at the guard's arm. He shook her off. The mood in the Dining Hall changed. The two bishops were bundling the aged cardinal away down the passage to the main door and Richard was being swept away too. The door opened and a shaft of daylight filled the entrance. The Queen and her daughters, suddenly panic-stricken, crowded behind the men but stopped in the doorway. Outside they could see serried ranks of soldiers with halberds that glittered with raindrops. They heard the ominous crunch of a hundred pairs of leather boots shifting on the cobbles. Elizabeth took in the scene with horror but she dared not take one step over the threshold. Bessy looked dumb-founded.

Elizabeth felt a movement against her legs; Katherine had wriggled between their skirts and was darting across the concourse towards the soldiers. Her high little voice rang out indignantly. "These men are hurting my brother. Tell them to put him down!"

John Howard raised his hand and the boy was released. He came to stand next to his little sister, brushing himself down indignantly. Katherine looked pleased. She patted his arm.

"*Now* you can go to our uncle, and *he* will look after you."

Howard motioned with his hand again and the boy was lifted up and on to the pommel of his saddle. His arm tightened around the child's middle as his stallion shifted on the cobbles. Young Richard twisted to look at him.

"Are we going to see my uncle?"

"Aye; he waits for you in the palace."

"Then let us not tarry, sir." He waved down at Katherine, then to his mother and sisters in the doorway. "Goodbye! And please come to my brother's crowning next week!"

"Tell Richard of Gloucester I have always known him – and what he intends towards my family." Elizabeth Wydville shouted clearly from the doorway.

"Aye, Madame," retorted Howard. He nudged his chestnut forward until he was only feet from the entrance to the Abbot's house. "You have said it yourself

76

– *your* family. Not this boy's family. He is a Plantagenet, like my Lord of Gloucester, like our young king, like all your daughters. You cleave to your Wydville supporters at your peril."

With a flourish of reins he turned his horse. The soldiers presented arms, wheeled around and fell into two columns through which Howard proceeded, followed by Lincoln and Bourchier. Slowly, they all moved away from Cheneygates, heading back to the palace, where Richard of Gloucester waited in the Star Chamber. Katherine stood, waving, A light summer drizzle was falling, dampening her hair. Bessy and Cecily dashed from the safety of the doorway to retrieve their little sister, pulling her back into the gloom of sanctuary, past their weeping mother slumped against the door and back down the passageway into the Abbot's dining hall. The room seemed to reverberate still with the drama of what had just happened.

Katherine extended her fist and showed her sisters the little chessman gripped in her palm.

"What shall I do with him?"

Cecily hugged her. "Put him carefully in Richard's box – until we see him again. He . . . he would not like to lose one of his pieces."

"Why does our Lady Mother cry?" asked Katherine curiously.

Bessy swallowed hard. "She is sad to see Richard go."

"But our uncle will take good care of him. And our brother the king will be so pleased to see him. They will have dinner together today."

Elizabeth remained sitting in the open doorway for over an hour. Eventually the sound of hooves and marching boots was heard again, making their way down the streets that led eastwards by the river to the Tower. She sat there until the last vestige of sound had faded away, to be replaced by the bells of the abbey ringing for matins and the start up of the monks' even chanting.

7

Katherine: *You must understand that the inter-marriages amongst the old families at court created a veritable spider's web of relationships. Plantagenets, Nevilles, Staffords, Beauchamps, Bourchiers – all united and divided in dizzying spirals of love and hatred. Harry, the Duke of Buckingham, was cousin to everyone: to my Uncle Richard, to Lady Margaret Beaufort, to Anne Neville ... his grandfather had died in battle for the Lancastrian cause; he had been the ward of my father, who had carefully ignored him, and upon my father's death he saw his chance to become the devoted friend of my Uncle Richard.*

Harry Buckingham lay sprawled across a chair in Richard's hall at Crosby. His long legs, elegantly hosed in fine, cream linen, stretched out in front of him. He allowed his arms to hang loosely, and flexed his fingers individually as he waited. The young Duke of York had been safely delivered to the Tower that afternoon and the reaction of both boys had been touching. Edward had embraced his younger brother with tears in his eyes and given stiff, formal thanks to both men. The trouble was he showed no signs of warming to his Uncle of Gloucester – was stony-eyed and tight lipped in his presence, and for all that he was not yet thirteen had a unbending haughtiness about him. A Wydville haughtiness. When addressed by Gloucester he answered with cool politeness but nothing more. The tailor from the Wardrobe arrived to take measurements for their coronation robes, which seemed to lift his spirits and excite the younger lad, so Gloucester and he had withdrawn and returned to Crosby Place. They found Bishop Stillington there, hovering in the Great Hall, seemingly anxious to speak to Gloucester alone. Gloucester had taken him into his privy chamber. Buckingham waited with good grace.

A good half an hour passed. Buckingham could hear voices behind the door; he grew bored and somewhat peeved that Gloucester did not invite him to share whatever Stillington had to come to discuss. Eventually the door opened and

Gloucester appeared – his face a strange parchment shade, his lips like two lines of ink. Without speech he motioned that Buckingham should enter.

It was a pleasant room, lit by tall lancet windows that faced the river. The morning's rain had stopped and now bright sunlight poured in. Bishop Stillington sat hunched in a chair by the fireplace.

"You had best hear this, Harry," said Richard.

Bishop Stillington looked up. "You wish me to repeat it all, my lord?"

Richard eyed him levelly, twisting the ring on his smallest finger round and round. "The world will need to hear it, so begin with my Lord of Buckingham, who is of my family, and whom I trust." He moved to stand by the window and leaned both hands against the wall, as if for support, stretching the muscles of his back.

Stillington cleared his throat fussily. "I have searched my conscience and can no longer withhold what I know."

Buckingham looked puzzled. "You have a confession to make?"

"Of sorts."

"Then best seek out one of your fellow bishops, sir, rather than us!" quipped Buckingham but pulled up short at Stillington's anguished expression, aware that his joke had fallen flat. Richard was still turned to the wall, his face hidden.

"It concerns the late king, and his marriage." But it appeared the bishop could say no more. His hands trembled and his eyes brimmed.

Suddenly, Richard turned. "Oh, get to the point, Stillington! Tell Harry what you have just told me – that there is no way we can put young Edward on his father's throne!"

Buckingham looked baffled, but a momentary gleam of interest caused his pupils to dilate. "Say on, sir."

Stillington drew a deep, steadying breath. "Before Edward of York met Dame Elizabeth Grey he was enamoured of many other women. With the ardour of his youth he could not resist – "

"– a pretty face! Ha! Like you, Dickon before you married Anne! And you have young John and Katherine to show for it! They should have married you as a child, Dickon, like me."

"My bastards are acknowledged and cared for, as befits their status," replied Richard coolly, "but I do not seek their advancement beyond what is right and proper in the eyes of God and the law."

"His Grace King Edward loved a certain lady, who would not be his mistress. The Lady Eleanor Butler."

"Shrewsbury's daughter," interjected Richard." Of noble birth, Harry. Her mother was a Beauchamp. She was sister to Norfolk's duchess and niece to the Kingmaker. No strumpet."

The bishop's voice now came in staccato sentences. "The lady was a widow. A little older than Edward. I married them. A simple ceremony. No witnesses. When he tired of her the lady was urged to keep it secret. She took refuge with the Carmelites nuns in Norwich."

Buckingham let out a slow whistle of incredulity. "You believe this? You believe that your brother knowingly committed bigamy when he married Elizabeth? Come on, was he that foolish? Have we been living these twenty odd years with a lie?"

"This is what the bishop tells me, in good faith. Why should he lie, Harry?" replied Richard quietly.

Buckingham gave a snort of cynicism and looked directly at Stillington. "Because Edward once put you into prison, sir, for speaking out of turn, and you desire some revenge?"

"If you think that, my lord, I am sorry. I do not look for revenge or reward. I am over sixty years old; I have served my king and my God well enough, I think, and would be glad enough of a peaceful old age, but in the light of current affairs I cannot keep this to myself any longer. If you think I woke this morning and invented this, you know me not." There was a stricken dignity to his mein.

Buckingham now looked thoughtful. "And Edward was then stupid enough to take Dame Grey to wife? Another woman who would not leap to his bed without a ring on her finger!"

Richard sighed. "He was my brother and I loved him like none other. But you know he was ever a dolt where women were concerned, Harry. His Achilles' heel. There is likely a score of Plantagenet bastards in the homes of merchants all over London, and likely in the homes of lords too." He stopped, then added, "And in the Tower, and at Cheneygates."

The full import of Stillington's words registered now with Buckingham. "So his children with Elizabeth are bastards? The boys? The princesses? That is what we are now saying, is it not? By Jesu, this changes our world. When did she die, this Eleanor?"

Stillington swallowed, his Adam's apple moving like a bird's egg up and down inside his throat. "Fifteen years ago."

Buckingham did rapid calculations. "So, after Bessy, and Cecily but before the boys were born."

"Aye, but Edward did nothing further to sanctify his marriage to Elizabeth," said Richard quickly. "He did not put it right. Even though he knew. This means the boys, and all the girls, are as much bastard as my own John and Katherine. And God's blood, Harry the more I think upon it, the more I even wonder at his second marriage. Who was *there?* Jacquetta of Bedford, now dead and some other misguided priest. I take it, that was not *you,* that time, Stillington?" His words came at the bishop liked barbs. He began to pace up and down. "My father, and my brother Edmund did not die at Wakefield that bastards might sit upon this throne! My father was descended through the third Edward, from his mother *and* his father – the legal, rightful, truthful heir! It was what he held to all his life; what was taught to me by my mother. Ah God, what was she taught to Edward too, yet he chose to ignore it."

"They say the Wydvilles bewitched your brother," said Buckingham quietly. The dangerous word hovered in the afternoon sunlight.

"The Wydvilles! The downfall of this kingdom, Harry! And when that boy looks at me with his Wydville eyes, and smirks with his Wydville lips, and turns away with his Wydville scorn, I see no Plantagenet there, Harry! Do you?"

"The Council must now hear this, " said Buckingham briskly. "I am afraid you must tell your tale again, Bishop, But no doubt it will be easier the third time."

8

Katherine: *On a few occasions, as I was growing up, I met my grandmother Lady Cecily. She was so old her skin was like parchment but I remember that they told me she had once been called the Rose of Raby because she was so beautiful. She dressed like a nun and prayed all the time. Our family was so large I was surprised she even knew who I was but she gave me a beautiful Book of Hours that had been hers as a girl, and she told me to be proud of my Plantagenet name and Yorkist blood ...*

June 21st 1483

Baynard's Castle, the Yorkist stronghold and home of Cecily Neville, rose up vertically from the Thames like some river-god's residence. Its symmetrical turrets, sharp gables and three storeys of windows gave it an air of strength and power. Cecily rarely visited London these days; she had retreated to the castle at Berkhampstead to avoid Elizabeth Wydville and to follow a life of religious devotion, but Richard's letter had brought her quickly to the capital.

In the private chamber where she had once slept with her husband, Cecily considered her youngest son kneeling before her. So like his father in looks, temperament, demeanour – and ambition. Her blue-veined fingers rested lightly on his head and gently ruffled the hair as black as a raven's wing. Of all her sons Richard was the one she acknowledged to be the most intelligent; the one with the strongest sense of duty and piety. Edmund had died twenty-three years ago at seventeen – taken prisoner then cruelly hacked to death on the bridge at Wakefield by the Lancastrian Clifford; Cecily had known that if he was old enough to fight then he was old enough to die too, but at the time it had brought her much sorrow. Golden Edward had taken his place with so much promise and courage but then married so foolishly, compromising the Plantagenet dignity she held so high – and George, her darling, rash and mischievous, rapacious and disloyal, yet always her beloved boy. How she had pleaded with Edward to forgive him, spare him … yet the only concession won had been a private execution. Now Richard had come to her with Bishop Stillington's tale of Edward's own stupidity. It did not surprise her. After sixty- seven years nothing ever surprised her.

"You know what I have ever thought of the Wydvilles, Dickon."

"Aye, Lady Mother." For the last ten years, since Edward had ordered George's execution, Cecily had played little part at Court, appearing only for ceremonial events. Elizabeth's influence upon Edward had hurt her sorely.

"This gives you a chance to put it *all* right."

Richard contemplated the carpet beneath his feet. His mother had always lived in luxury.

"To take the crown away from young Edward is the right thing to do? You believe so?"

"I believe what I have ever believed – since the first days of marriage to your father. That the York claim is legitimate and God-given. We have to hold fast to what is right and true if our argument is to hold water. You offer this kingdom something without stain. Your son is as much my grandson as the boys in the Tower, but more so because he was born within a marriage that will never be questioned. "She paused. "And he has no witch for a mother."

"So you would have me proclaim these boys, and their sisters, as bastards, and step forward myself." His words were a statement, rather than a question.

Cecily's hands moved to the bejewelled crucifix hanging against her breast. He looked up and in the beautiful, austere face, swathed in its wimple and barb, saw compassion and wisdom, and cynicism – and his own naked ambition.

"Stillington's story may be a fiction," she said slowly, "as much a fiction as the ridiculous notion that Edward was not your father's son – that I lay with some archer in Rouen! Oh, do not look shame-faced, Dickon; I am not stupid – I know you might use even that story to your own advantage, except that you also know I would never speak to you again. But it is the Plantagenets born to rule, my son, not the Wydvilles. And it's too late now to appease them. You need to cut them out, like the disease they are." There was a silence between them. "But no harm to the girls, Dickon." She surveyed him as if he were a terrain she wished to cross. "There must be truth between us, as there was between your father and me."

"And George's son? Your grandson Edward of Warwick?" Richard looked deeply into his mother's eyes.

Cecily sighed. "By rights, yes. But he is strangely simple, Dickon. Like a child of three or four, even though he is eight. His tutors report that he can learn no letters."

"Anne is bringing him into our household now that Thomas Grey is fled."

"Good. He may blossom a little under her care. God knows the poor boy has known no loving parents and can hardly remember his own sister. Elizabeth should have taken him in when George died, but she would not. Part of her revenge. I begged Edward to receive the children into the royal nursery but she would have nothing to do with them. And, anyway, he is removed from the succession under George's attainder."

"Which could be reversed if Parliament so wished it," reflected Richard.

"True, my son, but who in their right minds would choose another child when a grown man stands ready?"

"Oh, Mother, if I am to move forward now, I need to know I have your blessing. I cannot bring myself to open my heart to Anne yet, though I believe she would support me."

"Don't underestimate her, Richard. She holds Elizabeth Wydwille responsible for her father's death. The prospect of revenge may be sweet to her. I am sure she would rather her son be the next Prince of Wales than any Wydville cub."

"She would not sanction me harming those cubs, though."

Cecily shrugged. "You may not need to do so. As I said, who would support a mere boy when a capable, true born Yorkist man offers himself? Have you confided in Harry Buckingham?"

"He was there when Stillington came. It was politic to share it with him for if I keep him at arm's length I can never be sure of his loyalty. He thrives on feeling he is important; on land and money, and titles and influence -"

"Oh, Richard! As do all you men!"

"But he is rightly proud of his own line and would take his place by my side, I think. Edward ignored him, because the Wydvilles told him to. He will see a better future with me. I have already raised him as high as I dare."

"Does he look for more?" asked Cecily.

"He will always *look* for more."

"Then be wary of him, Dickon, for the best of men will turn."

Richard gave a hollow laugh. "You think I have not learned that? Mother, remember where you sent me to learn – to Warwick, who turned upon my brother!"

"I have lived to see all, Dickon, is what I would say to you. Cousins and brothers who kill each other; mothers and daughters at odds –"

"Mother and sons?" asked Richard quietly.

Cecily seized his hands and held them between her own. "The past is the past. Edward chose that woman and not a hound from hell could have dragged him from her bed. God seems determined to give me a long life and I have no son now but you, Dickon. Tell me, do you believe you can be a good king?"

He stared down for long seconds, breathing out with emotion. "I do believe so, Lady Mother. I believe I could be the king my father wished to be when mad Harry near destroyed this realm." He reached out to touch Cecily's crucifix. "I swear to you, Mother, that my governance would be to bring peace."

"Then above all else you must stress your concerns for proper justice; the people must believe that you will listen to their grievances that you act for the common weal of all. That is the king England needs. Do not alienate people, Richard, or you will fail."

"You should have been a man, Mother," remarked Richard ruefully, "England would have done well under your rule!"

"Hush; do not speak against God's ordinance," said Cecily primly, but then her old eyes blazed into mischief, "but yes, I have often thought so." She still held his hands between her own. "Your men may meet here, Richard, for discussion. Your father would be proud."

Outside the tall walls of Cecily's home, London pulsated in the tight, midsummer days. Rumour snaked up and down the narrow streets where the upper storeys of the wooden houses conspired together. In the deep storerooms of the merchants' homes, men whispered together behind great rolls of fabric, carpet and tapestries; on the dockside men sat in the shade of the barrels of wine, pitch and sacks of grain, exchanging the latest news. Outside the East Minster of St Paul's, Master Ralph Shaa, brother to the Mayor of London, preached his sermon "Bastard slips shall not take deep root" and men learned of the illegitimacy of King Edward's children. Listening to him were the Duke of Gloucester, the Duke of Buckingham and other great magnates. Men saw the sorrow on their faces.

"So, tell me, Lady Mother," said Bessy, her voice laced with disbelief and sarcasm, "did you know you were never married?" In the past few days their relationship had changed radically. The loss of Lionel and Tom Grey, the departure of little Richard, and now the unbelievable information that her marriage had been a sham, had sent Elizabeth spiralling into abject despair. She was beyond weeping now and just sat in a state of numbness, her hair uncombed, her linen unchanged, new lines appearing daily on her brow, and by her mouth and eyes. Her age, held at bay for so many years by charms, potions and self-belief, now showed itself quite plainly; her body seemed to sag and her feet shuffled through the rushes. For hours she had neither slept, nor eaten but just stared mutely into her hands.

Her daughters were at their wits' end to know what to do with her. Bridget tried to climb up on to her lap but Elizabeth seemed oblivious to her. Eventually the two youngest girls settled for propping themselves up against her knees. Anne was too big for that and simply brought a joint stool and sat as close as she could. The two older girls conferred for a while in the courtyard then returned. Finally, Bessy threw all parental respect aside and resorted to seizing her mother's shoulders and shaking her forcefully. "Enough! Enough, Mama!"

Elizabeth wanted to sink forever into some abyss of darkness but the sheer strength of Bessy's physicality assaulted her senses and the arrow-directness of Bessy's question reached her.

"We *were* married. In the chapel at Grafton," she said dully. "I would not lie with him until then."

"Like another lady, then!" shot Cecily. Her young heart was full of disbelief and a sense of terrible betrayal – a feeling so intense it actually hurt in her chest. The two eldest girls had slowly absorbed the full meaning of the news Elyn had heard in the streets, and which Lord John Howard had confirmed in a short visit.

"But our lives have been a lie!" exclaimed Bessy. "Or what they say is a lie! Which is it, Mama?"

Elizabeth twisted the heavy Welsh gold wedding band on her left hand, then pulled it over her knuckle and laid it in her lap. She looked at it for a while then picked it up between finger and thumb and offered it to her eldest daughters. "I believed this to symbolise my marriage to the king of England," she said simply.

"It is my only evidence. But others say not. And I cannot gainsay them. You will learn, both of you, that women have no choice. No defence when things go wrong. No saviour except a man who wants what is between her legs or in her womb."

At least she was talking to them again. "So you *did* know?" Bessy was insistent.

"No, I did not. But I am not surprised. I knew he had had women before me. All knew it. I knew he had children too." She made a strange sound – half a sob and half a laugh.

"That was the argument he gave to his mother, who thought I was not fit to be his queen. He told her that he was fertile and so was I. That we had both had sons. That it was better than marrying some foreign princess who might turn out to be barren. That shut her up." She bit her lip. "But the woman they speak of was an earl's daughter and your father could not have persuaded her into bed with a whispered promise."

"Did you know her, Mother?" a small voice from Anne.

"No, she was gone from court before I arrived. I remember seeing her in Marguerite of Anjou's rooms when I was a young girl first sent from Grafton. She was the same age as me, a pretty girl, married young, then widowed. Your father liked … a woman with some experience …"

Anne looked puzzled. Cecily shuddered but Bessy pressed further. "But if it is true, then why did this lady not fight for her place as queen? Why did she not tell her father, or tell Warwick?"

"You judge all women by your own courage, Bessy. There are those who are afraid. And who knows? Edward had stopped loving her. Mayhap she loved God more."

Cecily placed her hands on the stone embrasure of the window and gazed up through the cloudy glass at the blue sky beyond. "I thought this was the worst; I truly did, but then I thought that you might come to some accord with my Uncle Gloucester and somehow we would all go in peace to my brother's coronation. But it's not to be, is it?"

Elizabeth's chin trembled, "No. It's not to be. Your brother will not be king now. And you are no longer princesses. I do not know what is to be, or even what tomorrow will bring."

"Does it bring letters, still?" asked Bessy acerbically. "I only ask, Mother, because it would be useful to know if you plan on further plotting. Cecily and I would like time to compose our faces into the right expression."

"I can do faces," announced Katherine. "This is Elyn, when she is cross …
this is Anne, when she's dreaming … this is you, Bessy, when you are angry with
my Lady Mother … oh, and this is the old man who took Richard away!" She
was contorting her face into a variety of extraordinary expressions, ending with
a passable impersonation of Archbishop Bourchier.

"You had best practise a new one," said Bessy tartly, "the face of a plain Kate,
rather than a Princess Katherine, for that, apparently is who you are now."

Katherine looked puzzled. "Why? Who says so?" She scrambled up and
stamped her foot. "I shall fight them!"

"Jesu, you were named well, Katherine, the bravest of us all!" Bessy felt
herself close to hysteria but caught her breath and held it down.

"Mother, what will he do?" asked Cecily, "and what will he do with our
brothers?"

"I hope he sends them back to us," said Katherine.

Elizabeth pushed tendrils of greying hair out of her eyes and tucked them
behind her ears. It was her first gesture of any purpose in days. "My guess is that
he will send them north – while he works out what to do with them."

Bessy offered a faint smile, of sorts. "Well, they are boys, when all is said
and done, and maybe they will enjoy the adventure. The Council would never
allow harm to come to them, surely? There will be a future for them, eventually.
Look how well my Uncle Richard treats his own bastards -"

Elizabeth's brows furrowed." How do you know of them, Bessy?"

"He told me himself, at Christmastide."

"His girl is called Katherine, like me," piped up Katherine. "I think he loves
her."

"He will never love *my* children," said Elizabeth. "He sees you all as
Wydvilles, not Plantagenets."

"Well, can you blame him, Mother?" fired Bessy. Your actions have not
helped us – any of us!" She found that a feeling of bitter division was beginning
to wind itself around her very soul. She had always identified herself as her
father's daughter, a proud Plantagenet princess who would one day take her place
as a queen of a powerful European country and in so doing help forge friendship
and alliances for her father's England – *her* England. Although the prospect of
leaving her family saddened her, she had imagined herself as the mother of the
future king of France, putting Plantagenet blood back where it belonged on the
throne of France. She had imagined visiting her homeland and seeing her father's

pride. When Louis had pulled out of the marriage negotiations just before her father's death, Bessy had pinned her hopes on her Uncle Richard helping to broker another prestigious match. With whom, Bessy had no idea, but she was still sure of her status as England's most marriageable princess. As far as she could see, her mother's panicked flight into sanctuary, open hostility to Richard of Gloucester, and recent plotting served only to jeopardise her chances, and those of her sisters. And now all was destroyed, for what foreign prince who would marry a bastard daughter of Edward IV?

"What can *we* hope for?" asked Cecily. Her dark blue eyes stood out vividly in her pale face. Her fine black brows furrowed with worry. In her fifteen years Cecily had known nothing but luxury and finery, cosseting and adulation. Like Bessy, she had been brought up to know that one day she would leave to represent her family – probably into Scotland. Her father had teased her about how she would need a royal wardrobe of furs against the northern cold yet, like Bessy's betrothal, it had all come to nothing. The two girls spent hours talking about what the future might hold for them now. How could their little brother secure good husbands for them? Their hope lay with Richard, as Protector.

Elizabeth looked world-weary. "We must stay here, and wait."

Katherine: *"Memories of that time come in fragments, like pieces of a dark glass vessel shattered when it falls on the stone flags at a Christmas feast ..."*

The summer evening was warm and still. The bells for Vespers and then Compline called the monks to prayer. Their chanting of the psalms drifted once more through the abbey precincts as Elizabeth and her small household knelt before the portable altar she had brought into sanctuary. It was the same one that had been in her rooms in all her confinements. Katherine loved the gilded figures carved all around the edge: the Blessed Virgin, Christ on the Cross and the apostles. One of the priests had shown her Saint Katherine, martyred upon her wheel and Saint Christopher, carrying the Christ Child on his back. These were her favourites, and when the candles were lit she always looked to see them, glowing and beautiful.

Compline was the final office of the day – a time for contemplation and preparation for the night ahead. In the peace of their devotions her mother and sister Bessy seemed calmer. The Abbot had sent yet another priest to lead their prayers, his pleasant voice delivering the familiar Latin words like a steady cascade. Katherine felt herself nodding. Sometimes it was hard to stay awake. Her body jolted suddenly but no-one seemed to have noticed. She peeped out from beneath her lashes to see her mother and sisters all with their eyes firmly shut. She wished she was back at the palace at Westminster, or the nursery at Eltham, where no-one had shouted or argued, and evening had been a time of games and music until bedtime. There, the door curtain of her chamber had been drawn at 8pm and she had slept soundly till morning. Here, there was no special bedroom for her and despite the difference in their ages the four oldest princesses were forced to spend much of their time together. Only little Bridget was put to bed early, in a corner of her mother's room.

It was the moment of the final benediction. The priest was intoning:

"Thou has put gladness in my heart,
More than in the time that their corn and their wine increased.
I will both lay me down in peace, and sleep:
For thou, oh Lord, only makest me dwell in safety."

But before they could all depart in peace for the night, they were disturbed by the sound of urgent voices in the passageway. Katherine saw Bessy's eyes fly open from prayer and flash swiftly to Cecily, who shook her head. The priest cast a look of surprise but continued. Katherine waited for the knock she knew would come – a series of thumps which made the heavy oak door quiver.

"Your Grace! It is Nicholas Haute!"

Elizabeth hauled herself to her feet but looked like someone roused from a deep sleep, uncertain and disoriented. Katherine could see her mouthing the name as if trying to recall to whom it might refer. The priest laid down his prayer-book and looked questioningly at her. Her heavy-lidded eyes, already dilated as the light of the summer evening faded, seemed enormous.

"Lady Mother, it must be news about our Uncle Anthony, and our brother Richard Grey," said Bessy quickly. Elizabeth nodded mutely and Bessy moved to open the door.

A young man stood there, grey with exhaustion, his recognisable green Wydville livery covered in dust from the road. He sank down into an obeisance and stayed there, as if the weight of his head was too much for him to bear.

"Tell us," commanded Bessy. "Tell us all."

"At Pontefract, yesterday, at sunrise -" his voice cracked with emotion. "My Lord Anthony, and my Lord Richard, and poor Sir Thomas Vaughan – on the battlements." From somewhere he summoned courage and looked up. He was no more than sixteen or seventeen, smooth-faced and tow-haired, his blue eyes full of misery. "They were executed, Your Grace."

The priest moved quickly to catch Elizabeth. She neither screamed nor cried out but simply sank against him, breath escaping from her lips in a hiss of lamentation. He was forced to take her whole weight as she collapsed forwards, her full breasts against his chest. The look of alarm on his face, at finding himself holding the Queen in so intimate a way, would have been comical in any other situation. Katherine backed into Cecily's arms as Bessy knelt beside the weeping boy.

"You have to tell us all you know," she said more gently. "You are an Haute cousin?"

"Aye, from Ightam, my lady, in Kent. Her Grace's aunt, sister to her father, is my great aunt. They sent me because I said I could ride the fastest." The story came tumbling from him now : how at grey Pontefract, three men were led out on to the battlements of the castle and beheaded then their naked bodies thrown into a common grave at a nearby monastery, the deep sandy soil shovelled over them in minutes. How his uncle, Richard Haute, controller of the young king's household, had been pardoned but was in disgrace.

He raised tear-stained eyes to Bessy and Cecily. "There was no permission from the Council. The King simply ordered it."

Cecily had instinctively covered Katherine's ears with her palms but now released her and seized Nicholas Haute, shaking his shoulder." What do you mean, cousin, *the King?"*

The boy's expression slowly changed from one of anguish to incredulity. "You have not heard?"

Cecily snorted. "We hear only what others choose to tell us." She turned balefully to the priest who, with distaste, had managed to prop Elizabeth against the wall. "What do *you* know, Father?"

"London is rife with rumour," began the priest uncomfortably. "There is much confusion, my lady."

Nicholas Haute took a deep breath. "It is said that the Council have begged the Duke of Gloucester to take the throne. My Lord of Buckingham told them that kingship is no child's office. Men say that Gloucester refused at first but then accepted. The coronation will be on July 6th."

Katherine watched as, very slowly, Bessy sat on the floor in front of her mother. Elizabeth had still made no sound but sat motionless, her head between her knees. Bessy stretched out her hand and lifted her mother's chin. When she spoke her voice was calm.

"See, Lady Mother, where you have brought us. You and your Wydville family. Cecily, Anne, Katherine, Bridget and me – we are Plantagenets, not Wydvilles. Edward and Richard were Plantagenet princes but *you* did everything to make sure they were surrounded only by Wydvilles – a *wall* of Wydvilles! I do not care if I never hear that name again!"

Elizabeth stared at her daughter, dumbly. Bessy gave a deep, exasperated sigh. "We cannot go *on* like this, Mother. You have no-one else left to turn to now. Face the truth." She twisted round to the priest and the boy. "So what do *men say* of my brothers, in the Tower?"

Both looked acutely uncomfortable. Nicholas Haute because he had been brought up to be chivalrous and protect the weaker sex from harm and distress; he had delivered his message and could not bear to be the harbinger of any more misery. Bessy's bitter words about the Wydvilles unsettled him. His own family supported their more illustrious cousins. All his life he had dreamed of meeting the glamorous queen, her sons and daughters - and claiming them as kin, but now he wanted nothing more than to be gone. He shook his head, pretending he knew nothing. The priest avoided Bessy's direct gaze. He had never set eyes on the woman and girls before tonight; he had thought it interesting to come and see the infamous Wydville queen and her pretty daughters. He knew what stories were now circulating – that the princes had not been seen for days now – but decided it was not his place to tell.

Bessy gave them both a look of contempt. "Go," she snapped.

Shame-faced, Nicholas Haute backed through the doorway, sketched a quick bow and was gone. The priest gathered together his things and also bowed. "I trust Her Grace will feel better in the morning," he said awkwardly.

Cecily's upper lip curled in a savage, sarcastic smile. "Her husband is dead; her marriage is dead; her brother is dead; her grown son is dead; her princely sons are lost – but yes, I am sure she will feel better in the morning."

Katherine and Anne watched as their two older sisters lifted their mother, put her arms over their shoulders and half carried, half-dragged her to her bed.

Katherine: *"At night, in sanctuary, I drifted into terrible sleeps where men fought each other with daggers and princes ran shrieking from shadows ..."*

9

"The attendants who had previously ministered to the young king's needs were all kept from him. He and his brother were transferred to the inner chambers of the Tower proper." Dominic Mancini

The Tower of London June 27th 1483

Richard crossed the drawbridge and rode under the gatehouse archway into the Tower's inner ward. In front of him rose the high walls of the White Tower, the formidable donjon built by French William four hundred years ago. Richard steeled himself; he knew he had to make this visit alone, in person, to speak with the young boy whose throne he had chosen to take.

The princes had been moved into the White Tower, their apartments comprising two chambers, one for sleeping and one for daytime. Richard dismounted, threw his reins to his servant and ascended the wooden stairs built on to the side of the tower. The interior was cool and dim after the warmth outside. He was met by Dr Argentan, young Edward's physician, the last of the servants from his former household, who bowed, formally and warily, then ushered Richard up another two levels and into the day chamber where a window opened on to the Constable's garden but not visible from any public view.

"The boy has been told I am here?"

Argentan inclined his head again. "His Grace is dressing; he will be here directly."

Richard swallowed hard. "The correct form of address for my nephew is now my lord Edward, not His Grace." He looked around: the room was untidy and a thin layer of dust coated virtually everything. A half-finished Latin translation lay upon the table next to a quill, ink pot and sandbox; a chessboard balanced on another small table, the pieces neatly in place ready for a new game; a bow and a leather quiver full of arrows were propped up in a corner. All evidence of a scholarly boy's daily life.

"Is my lord Richard still abed too?"

Dr Argentan smiled slightly. "No, sir, he is up betimes every day and likes to help with the Constable's dogs. He'll be there for a while yet; he likes to brush them and feed them. His Grace – my lord Edward, is suffering a little with toothache and I give him a sleeping draught to help him at night. That is why he rises later. And he spends much time in prayer, too."

The door from the adjoining chamber opened quietly and Richard was face to face with his eldest nephew. *The boy is tall for his age; he has grown an inch or so even since Christmas,* thought Richard. But apart from his height he was pure Wydville: he had Elizabeth's silvery blond hair, her high cheekbones and deep-set eyes. He stared at his uncle. They had not seen each other since the day they had entered the capital back in early May. Edward's eyes held the glittering insolence of youth – the look of a boy who despises the adult with whom he is forced to speak. All his life he had been a king in training, used to deference. It did not occur to him to offer any greeting. His lower jaw was swollen slightly and he was pale.

Richard motioned to Dr Argentan to leave them. He hesitated but Edward gave him a quick nod and he slipped out of the room. Uncle and nephew stood alone; the six feet between them a continent.

"Edward," began Richard, but the boy cut him short.

"They tell me you have murdered my dearest brother Richard Grey, my dearest Uncle Anthony and my dear friend Thomas Vaughan," said Edward flatly. A pall of melancholy seemed to hang over him.

Richard was silent for a moment. He knew now he could never win this boy over. He could never, in a million years, hope to make him see things in a different way. Why would he, raised and nurtured by Wydvilles?

"It is the death prescribed to traitors," he replied.

"And what do you intend to 'prescribe' to Dickon and me, *Uncle*?" The final word dripped with hatred and sarcasm. "Must we, too prepare to be sacrificed?"

Richard was taken aback by the boy's directness. He had braced himself for an awkward conversation but not this blatant hatred. "You cannot be king, Edward. Your parents' marriage was not valid." He tried to speak evenly. "Parliament and the Council have accepted this and asked me to take the burden of kingship upon myself. Your future is in your own hands. I can send you and

Dickon to my estates in Yorkshire while the furore calms down; you can grow up there, as I did, in safety, and in due time return to my court as my young, beloved relations, sons of my brother." Edward stared at him. "You will have a life of dignity, and every opportunity to marry well, and serve me."

"Serve *you?* Who do you take me for? I am my father's heir. It is you who should serve me."

The lad has courage, thought Richard, *you have to grant him that.* "Edward, this is not what I looked for when your father died in April. I was ready to stand as Protector, as your father wished, until you came of age. But two things have changed that – no, hear me out, boy. Firstly, most of the noble families of this land will not accept your mother's family as the power behind the throne. Secondly, your father's penchant for marrying women he wanted to bed has made the Church see you, and all your siblings as illegitimate – and as such you may not inherit. Do not blame me, boy, for the situation your parents have wrought."

Edward turned a look of cold fury upon him, and winced as a flash of pain coursed through his jaw. "You are lucky, Uncle Gloucester, that I am only twelve. If I were four years older you would have to face me on a battlefield for I swear I would fight for my crown, even as my father fought for his." His voice rose." I do not believe what you say about my parents' marriage. I do not believe it! When I am grown I will return and take my crown back! You are a usurper! You seek to depose me, and take what is mine for yourself! You are evil! You are -" his words collapsed into a tide of passionate sobbing and he flailed his fists upon the table.

Richard regarded him with an odd mixture of compassion and distaste. He searched for some vestige of his brother in the boy but could see only Elizabeth. Hear only Elizabeth. Where was the Neville, the Plantagenet, the Yorkist? He felt a strange cold feeling settling in his blood – this boy's threat to rise up, as a grown man, was not to be taken lightly. *Cut them out, his mother had said, like the canker they are.*

"I came here this morning, Edward, to try and explain things and answer your questions." He sighed deeply. "God knows, I do not want you to become some embittered cur, dying on a battlefield like Marguerite of Anjou's son, or to have to flee this land and live in exile, like Margaret Beaufort's Tudor boy. See sense! You have a brother, and five sisters, and I am prepared to provide for you all, see you all educated and raised as befits your status as royal bastards. But you *cannot* be king now, and you *will* never be king in the future." He found that he had approached the boy – was standing over him. Edward rose rapidly, the chair clattering to the floor behind him. To Richard's astonishment he felt a sudden thump in the chest as Edward pushed him backwards – he lost his footing and fell heavily, landing on the base of his spine.

Edward's face was contorted with hatred but he was also shocked at what he had done. Dr Argentan must have been listening outside for he flung open the door, rushed in and helped Richard to his feet, casting a look of horror at the boy. The impact had been hard, and Richard felt pain radiating all the way up his back. He leaned heavily on Argentan for a moment, trying not to groan.

"I can see there is no point me even trying to talk to you," he said between gritted teeth, as he tried to straighten up. "I will think upon what to do with you and your brother." He pushed Argentan aside and quit the room without a backward glance. On the way down the staircase he almost collided with a young boy running up – ten-year-old Richard, his namesake. The child's face flushed with recognition and excitement.

"Oh! My Uncle of Gloucester! Bessy said you would come to see us! Good morning, sir!" He cocked his head with concern. "Are you hurt, sir? Can I help you?"

Richard had searched fruitlessly for traces of his brother in young Edward, but in this boy he saw it all: the dark blond hair flecked with russet; the open, honest expression and the full lips that might one day be sensual. If *this* boy had been the elder things might be different. The child's face was smeared with dirt and his shirt none too clean. He looked more like one of the stable boys than a lord. With a pang, Richard realised that there were no women here to tend to the child. He was proferring his hand but Richard found he could not take it. To feel the warmth of that young flesh would be too much.

"My young lord!" Dr Argentan was shouting urgently down the stairs. "Come up now!"

Young Dickon was nonplussed; he looked up the stairs and then back at his uncle. He dropped his hand. "Will you come again, sir? I could show you Sir Robert's spaniels, or we could look at the lions in the menagerie. They are very fierce but I like to watch them. Edward and I have heard them roaring..." Richard elbowed his way past him and ran down the staircase, bile rising in his throat. The child's chatter faded. In the courtyard he paused, breathing hard, then yelled for his horse. It took a minute or so for his servant to reappear, leading a reluctant

White Surrey, who had clearly been enjoying some refreshment, for a few wisps of hay hung from his creamy muzzle. Richard swung himself up into the saddle, gathered the reins then looked up at the window. He saw the two boys framed there: Edward white-faced and Dickon bewildered, until Dr Argentan pulled them back, and quietly closed the casement.

July 6th 1483 Westminster

"On 6 July, Richard Duke of Gloucester received the gift of royal unction and the crown ... At the same time and in the same place his wife Anne received her crown as queen." Dominic Mancini

It was early on a Sunday morning. Katherine had been woken early by the sound of the Abbey's sanctuary bells clanging joyously, along with the compelling clamour of peals from steeples and towers all over the city. The air was thick with celebration. The very walls of Cheneygates seemed to reverberate with a sense of anticipation. Katherine kicked off the bedcovers and stretched then peeped across to where her older sisters lay. Bessy was wide awake too, lying on her back with her hands tucked behind her head, listening intently. Cecily stirred in her sleep and opened her eyes slowly but then, in an instant, was fully alert.

"It's today, isn't it?"

Bessy nodded silently, then looked across at Katherine. "Kate, wake Anne, then Cecily and I will help you both to wash and dress. Elyn and Joanna aren't here this morning."

An hour later and the sisters were in the little courtyard. It was a blessedly fresh, breezy summer morning, the square above their heads a perfect azure. The bells' noise was incessant. Their ears had become accustomed though. Elizabeth refused to join them, keeping to her room, but even with all the windows closed the sound of the city's rejoicing permeated through every crack and cranny.

"They will be walking barefoot now, to the Confessor's shrine, from White Hall," said Bessy, gazing upwards at the heavens.

"Barefoot?" asked Katherine in astonishment." Won't they have dirty feet?"

Bessy smiled. "They will walk upon a gorgeous cloth. As our parents did."

"Mama had her own coronation," said Cecily quietly, "but the Abbot says *they* will be crowned together."

"It happens," replied Bessy, "when a married couple become king and queen at the same time."

"The bells are so loud! Do you suppose Edward and Dickon will hear them, in the Tower?" said Anne. "Or is it too far? It's strange to think they are only two miles away from us." She turned her face up wistfully to the sky, their only physical link with the outside world.

"I should think all London can hear them," said Bessy dryly. "That's the whole point."

The girls had brought their usual throws and cushions and spread them out over the sparse square of grass. So early in the morning most of the courtyard was still in shade but later it would blaze with heat before the afternoon shadows fell again.

As the morning wore on the bells fell silent, then they heard music wafting on the air – anthems they recognised, then great cries of excitement and acclaim. Fanfares from trumpets and low rattles of kettle drums.

"I wish we had wings," said Cecily wistfully, "and could fly over the roof to see what is happening. What do you think they are wearing? Something very purple and gorgeous no doubt." She looked down ruefully at her stained cherry-red gown that only three months ago had been her heart's delight but now suffered from lack of brushing and proper care. It was as much as their servants could manage to procure clean linen for them on a weekly basis; it had proved too expensive to send it out for laundering and the monks in the abbey laundry did not like to handle female shifts so Joanna had to creep in while they were at services. Even in the confined rooms of the abbey sanctuary Katherine, Anne and Bridget were growing like young weeds and yesterday Elyn had snipped the toes off the ends of their soft leather shoes to procure longer wear. They would last them over the summer, she said, for they were not walking anywhere.

Bessy strained her ears to catch the new sounds. "Well, it's over and done with now, and they will return to Westminster Hall, for the banquet,"

"Who do you suppose carried her train?" mused Cecily.

Bessy laughed. "You'll never believe it, but they say it is Margaret Beaufort, Lord Stanley's wife. She likes to keep her eye on the future."

Cecily cast a sideways glance at her sister. "As we must do?"

The two younger girls had been awake so early they were now drowsing in the sunshine.

"This is the strangest morning, I give you that," sighed Bessy. "If I am honest, I do not know what to think. Our father trusted Richard absolutely, Cecily – I cannot stop thinking about that. And it may be that his right to the throne is valid – I can't stop thinking about that either."

"But I do not want to be illegitimate, Bessy. It feels so wrong."

"Look on the bright side. No-one is going to send us to France, or Scotland, or anywhere else anymore. I expect our uncle will find some eminent English noblemen for us. There will always be someone glad to marry the daughter of a king. He has married his own Katherine to Lord Herbert. And quite frankly, Cecily, at the moment I feel I would marry anyone to get out of here!"

Cecily stifled a giggle. "You don't mean that. You *don't!* You *wanted* to be queen of France!"

"I *did*," agreed Bessy, "but I never really wanted to leave England, and you, or Anne and Katherine."

Cecily smiled but then a shadow passed over her pretty features. "Our brothers?"

Bessy at once became serious too. "Ah, Sweet Jesu. If only I knew. They might as well be two hundred miles away."

"Do you think what Mama says is right? That he would harm them?"

Bessy lay back on the cushions, trailing her fingers through the few hardy daisies. The summer was proving to be a warm one and for nights now she had lain awake in the sticky, sultry darkness, struggling to make sense of her confused thoughts and feelings, relieved when an early dawn brought light again, and some coolness. She knew that men would stop at nothing to take a crown. She understood that men would kill to keep a crown. This was normal; this was her world. Sweet boys grew to be ambitious men. Kill or be killed. Maybe somewhere, in another time, another place, things were different...

"I think," she said slowly, still teasing out her line of thought even as she spoke, "that he would not *wish* to harm them. But he will if they stand in his way."

Cecily scanned her sister's face with her intelligent dark blue eyes. "Are they in his way? He is crowned today."

Bessy rolled over on to her stomach. She laid her cheek against the grass and parted the blades with her fingers. So close to the earth, she could see individual particles of soil between them.

"Do we truly know our brother Edward, Cecily? I mean *know* him, like I know you, and you know me? Do you love him, as I love you, and you love me?

100

As we love Anne and Katherine?" She smiled fondly at her young siblings, curled up like little puppies. She reached out for Cecily's hands and entwined her fingers into her sister's. "We have been taught to love him, as we were taught to love our father – as we will have to love our husbands. But I am not sure that is the same sort of love I feel for you or my sisters."

Cecily gasped with shock. "Shhh! Don't say such things!" but she gripped Bessy's fingers with her own.

"But it's true," insisted Bessy. "We may not question men. Do you think the world will always be like this, Cecily? Ha! What a question! I could not say this to anyone but you. Don't look so horrified!"

"I am not horrified, but it is surely wrong to speak so."

"I cannot help the thoughts in my head."

There was a soft rustling sound and the sisters looked up to see their mother in the archway. Her face was blotched from lack of sleep and anxiety, her gown creased. Without speaking she crossed to them and eased herself down on to the cushions. Absent-mindedly she stroked the heads of Katherine and Anne, who surfaced from their doze.

Bessy made an effort to ensure that her tone was mild, not accusatory. "Lady Mother, it is over. My Uncle of Gloucester now sits upon the throne. We need to look to the future – all our futures."

"I will not leave sanctuary," said Elizabeth. "And neither will you girls, without my permission. He has my boys. He will not have you too."

Cecily and Bessy exchanged covert flickers of lashes.

"Mama, we cannot live here forever," said Cecily gently.

"No. We still have supporters who may bring Richard down."

"Mama!"

"I could get all of you away, in disguise, beyond the English Channel, to somewhere you would be safe -"

Bessy found it impossible to remain composed. "You would risk our lives? The little ones too?" She had a sudden urge to place herself between her mother and the younger girls, as if to ward off their mother's intentions.

Elizabeth spread her hands helplessly. "If anything happens to your brothers we must be sure that your father's line survives."

Bessy stood up. In frustrated fury she hurled a silken cushion across the courtyard. The two younger girls were round-eyed in astonishment. Katherine

101

scrambled to her feet and retrieved it, clutching it against her stomach. *Bessy is the same height as Mama, now.*

"When will you stop *plotting?* Why, our uncle will come to think that Cecily and I threaten him as much as you do! Mama, we just want to *survive* this! We just want to live in freedom!"

Elizabeth regarded her eldest daughter with puzzlement. The dutiful child had changed into a headstrong young woman she barely recognised. The two boy princes had left her sphere of influence early – she had accepted that. Edward had gone to Ludlow with Anthony at a young age and returned to London only infrequently; Dickon had spent months away too. Quite rightly they had been raised in a world of men, given their own households when infants and reared to be independent – but the girls – she had only ever been half a day's travel from them; she had set out and supervised their daily routines and visited frequently. They had grown up revering her, compliant, respectful and obedient. Now she was baffled by Bessy's resentment. All she wanted was to protect their interests – to keep alive some flickering flame of hope. As usual, feeling insecure drove Elizabeth to be lofty and distant.

"I suggest you think upon the Fifth Commandment, daughter," she said coldly." I expect your obedience, not your defiance. I expect Father Piers will find time to hear your confession."

Bessy blushed scarlet and her sisters lowered their eyes. Elizabeth swept back to her room.

That evening the servants reported what they had seen of this new king: Elyn had managed to catch a glimpse of him returning to the palace after the coronation. "A doublet of blue cloth of gold, wrought with nets and pineapples, Your Grace! And a long gown of purple velvet, with ermine and thousands of lamb-fleece hangings! Then purple cloth of gold, and crimson and white damask!"

"How very colourful. They could not miss him, then," replied Elizabeth, curtly.

10

September 1483

The weather broke within the week. The sky turned a sullen grey, the temperature dropped and soon heavy raindrops were coursing down the lancet windows of the Jerusalem Chamber. In the city outside the street channels soon filled and overflowed. The stink of the summer was gone but the filth was carried down every thoroughfare until it emptied into the Thames. Joanna and Elyn returned from their daily food forage soaked to the skin. Although Elizabeth had brought many treasures and jewels into sanctuary her reserves were steadily dwindling; over the past three months she had sent plate to the Wydville supporters and knew that more would be required if her latest plans could be pulled off.

The spat between mother and daughter had calmed to a simmering resentment on Bessy's side, and a clear expectation of better behaviour on Elizabeth's. She had the upper hand, for there was absolutely no possibility of Bessy either managing or choosing to leave. A long waiting game lay ahead. Cool, wet August gave way to a chilly September and even more rain.

They heard that Richard had left the city to go on a royal progress to show himself as king in midland and northern towns. There was no news at all from the Tower – no messages or letters. Nothing. The weeks were long and dismal. Elizabeth's secret plans for spiriting her daughters abroad had come to nothing. This became apparent one morning when a dark haired, broad-shouldered man entered the Abbot's dining room unannounced just as the family were finishing an unappetising meal of bread and cheese. Elizabeth was economising and whilst there might be meat tomorrow today was more meagre fayre. Katherine hated the bread; it was hard to chew, stuck against her teeth and cloyed on her tongue. She wished the Abbot would send bread from his own table – that was white, and fine.

The man sketched a bow. "Dame Grey." Katherine saw her mother start at this shockingly plain term of address. It was made even more ordinary by broad vowels of the man's Yorkshire accent. "I am sent to inform you that the Council of His Grace the King has ordered that guards be posted around these lodgings." There was no malice in his tone, just a statement of fact.

Katherine studied him. He did not look like a bad man. He had kind brown eyes, with creases around the edges, and his mouth was fixed in a kind of rueful expression that looked as if it wanted to be a smile. However, Elizabeth had composed her features into what Cecily called "Mama's blank face."

"Of course. And you are?" she asked disinterestedly.

"Sir John Nesfield, Dame Grey. I am to command the guards."

"Then you had best do so." Disdainfully, she turned her head away from him, effectively dismissing him, as she had done to servants thousands of times in her years as queen. Ignoring him completely, she walked past him back into her private room.

Bessy rose, and wiped crumbs away from her mouth. "You must excuse my mother, sir. She finds it hard not to be the queen anymore. I thank you for your courtesy in coming to tell us about the guards."

"I take it that these *guards* are not to keep *us* safe from intruders?" asked Cecily archly

Nesfield's mouth did break into a smile. "No, my lady. It's more a case of keeping a close eye on v*isitors.* And those who leave. The comings out and goings in, so to speak."

Bessy smiled back. "At least you have the decency to be honest with us. Thank you."

"There is nothing you ladies need fear. My guards will not enter your rooms, unless I order it."

Unafraid, Katherine tugged at his hand. "I used to be a princess," she told him gravely.

He knelt on one knee and kissed her hand. "I know it, my lady. I served your father, King Edward."

"Tell us," said Bessy simply. She gestured for him to sit at their bench. He moved his sword out of the way and joined them, sitting down heavily.

"I was with King Edward in exile in Burgundy and returned with him when he took his throne back from the Lancastrians. I was in his retinue when he came here to sanctuary to find the Queen and new born son. I remember *you* then my

104

lady, just about the height of this little maid." He ruffled the top of Katherine's head. "And I was with him at Tewkesbury too."

"You were very loyal, sir," said Bessy quietly. "And yet you now serve our uncle?"

"I am loyal to the best interests of the House of York, my lady."

Bessy liked his directness. "Can you tell us anything about my brothers?"

At once, a troubled shadow crossed his face. "Not really, my lady. There is no news as such."

"But something has happened. I can tell by your expression."

He sighed heavily. "A few weeks ago there was an attempt to free your brothers. Fires all over the city – meant as distractions whilst men tried to storm the Tower."

The bewilderment on Bessy and Cecily's faces told him that they knew nothing of this. He felt sorry for these two lovely girls, trapped here by their scheming mother.

"Who?" breathed Bessy. "Another of my mother's …" her voice trailed away with emotion.

Nesfield hesitated, then judged that telling of the failure of conspiracies was more likely to dampen than inflame enthusiasm.

"Wydvilles. Lady Stanley probably. Like as not my Lord of Dorset. It came to nothing for as ever we were well warned. Tell your mother it's really not worth it, my lady."

Bessy stared at the floor and saw how the rushes were yellowing. The Abbot's housekeeping was not as thorough as in the royal palaces. She raised her head and looked directly at Nesfield. "And my brothers?"

He cleared his throat noisily. "Well, they are now confined within their rooms – understandably – but I am sure they are well cared for, my lady."

"Who looks after them?" asked Katherine curiously.

"I confess I do not know, my lady. But the constable of the Tower, Sir Robert Brackenbury, is a good man. He will be keeping them safe."

"But then why do we have no letters, or news?" Cecily found that tears were pricking at the corners of her eyes.

"I cannot say, my lady." He looked distressed. "If you wish to write I will see to it that your letters are taken to Sir Robert. But do not seal them. I will have to read them first."

Bessy sighed. "We came here nearly five months ago with our mother, sir. She brought us here to be safe because she could not judge men's intentions. We do not know what sort of king our uncle will be, and it is hard to gauge what he now intends towards us all. This is what makes our mother so fearful. But truly, we are weary of this."

He took her hand gently and kissed it, as he had kissed Katherine's. "It will come to an end, lady, but not just yet. Try to keep your mother from too much intrigue!"

11

Early September 1483 Brecknock Castle, the Welsh Borders

In green and peaceful Brecknockshire, in his castle high above the fast-flowing river, Harry Buckingham waited for news. Daily, the confluence of the Honddu and the Usk swelled with the autumnal rains, their waters beginning to trickle then flow on to the natural floodplains where the cattle and sheep anxiously started seeking higher ground. He had left Richard's progress in early August, stealing away in the middle of the night to ride hard westwards to his land in the Welsh Marches. He knew what the rumourmongers were saying – that he was not satisfied with the rewards Richard had heaped upon him after the coronation – that as a direct descendant of the third Edward he was greedy for more. To some extent they were right, but there was something else they did not know.

Buckingham was seated at his desk in the chamber above the Great Hall, where estate business was conducted. From the tall, narrow windows he could see the stout walls intended to protect the town from Welsh attack, and the square tower of the little grey cathedral. Somewhere in the castle his two eldest children, five-year-old son Edward and four-year-old daughter Elizabeth were playing hoodman blind – he could hear their distant squeals of laughter. Two-year-old Henry was no doubt trying to join in. In their private solar his wife lay upon her bed, resting in the final month of her latest pregnancy. Kate was Elizabeth Wydville's sister, which made his offspring first cousins to the royal children. Buckingham liked his children. He enjoyed playing with them, romping on the floor as their tiger or lion, whilst they rode on his back, clutching at his doublet and shrieking. He loved to make them laugh. Which is why when Richard breathed of his intentions towards the boys in the Tower he had sickened in his heart. It was a step too far. He wanted no part of it. The more he thought about it, the more he found he was moving away from wanting to support Richard. He had sensed it before and now felt vindicated. Now he had spoken with Morton, and daily they expected news from Tudor's supporters he felt calmer.

His wife had been surprised to see him return home so soon and astonished that he had travelled with just a few trusted servants, not the grand retinue who usually accompanied him behind the streaming Stafford standard with its golden knots. The hot summer had been a long one and she fretted about her sister mewed up in the Westminster sanctuary – and wanted to know if he brought any news of her and her family. Kate was twenty years younger than her royal sister; Elizabeth had been gone to court and then to her first husband John Grey's home at Groby while Kate was still a small child, but she had come home to Grafton after John Grey's death – the sad, but glamorous big sister whom Kate had adored. She could faintly remember the golden giant that was Edward Plantagenet coming to woo Elizabeth and when the baby Princess Bessy had been born Kate was in her element as a young aunt.

"Your sister and her daughters are well, but Richard has set a guard on them after her last crazed scheme to send the girls away."

"And my royal nephews?" Kate's usually pretty face had looked puffy and worried. She was struggling with this pregnancy, often feeling sick even in these later months, and finding it hard to do much more than sit about. Coming to London for Richard's coronation had been impossible for her, even though her husband had carried the King's train. Buckingham felt a sudden, unexpected wave of tenderness towards her. Their first few years together had not always been easy; at times he had felt that her status as a mere gentleman's daughter did not match his noble blood, even if her sister was Edward's queen. They had been married as children – Elizabeth's way of ensuring that the Wydvilles were linked to the old nobility. But they had grown closer; Kate had her sister's beauty without the attendant coolness and arrogance. His childish resentment had faded, to be replaced by genuine affection for the girl who put him first, who loved him dutifully as her husband and father of her children, and seemed to care little for politics. She loved her sister but accepted that her loyalties lay with her husband.

Buckingham felt a sudden desire to unburden himself of his innermost thoughts. In bed that first night home, close to Kate's warm body in the darkness, with his arms wrapped around the swollen belly that would soon be his next child, he told her his fears. He felt her muscles tense against him and a movement of her right arm told him that she was crossing herself.

"Infanticide? Holy Mother of God, that is a mortal sin, Harry!"

He felt the near-term babe kick under his hand. Kate shifted her position to ease her discomfort. Outside the rain was beginning again, the autumn winds whistling around the castle towers but the thick hangings of their bed created a private world.

"Is this why you have come home?" she breathed against his ear.

"He says he must do it. That it is the only way for future peace. He says his mother approves. There was an attempt to free them, just before we left London, and I think that decided him."

"If they were grown men, Harry ... but *boys!* Why, in all the years when the Lancasters and Yorkists fought each other, no-one ever harmed innocent children! Not Warwick, or Marguerite of Anjou, or Richard's father. None of them would stoop so low."

"But if it is the price to be paid for peace, for all of us?"

"Harry, I am but a woman; I know little of warfare but I think that to kill children is a heinous crime. Where will it end?"

"I saw them, in the Tower. I visited two or three times. After all, they are my nephews too, because of you. Edward did not like me because I had been with Richard when we took him at Stoney Stratford but he unbent a little when I took him books. He likes poetry, you see. And the young one – is so merry ... he likes spaniels, as I did at his age. "

"Oh, Harry!"

"I cannot be part of it. Every part of me abhors the very thought. And Kate, I find myself wondering if now I must stand against him. God knows, it is not yet two months since I helped to crown him, and he had given me such honours, but ..."

"But you cannot put your own soul in peril, Harry. I *know* you."

He kissed her forehead. "You know me better than I know myself."

"But what to do now? He will surely want you back by his side. "

"I can never go there again. I must declare for young Edward. It is the only way. And there is more, Kate."

Reaching in the darkness he found the tinder and candle and lit it. Their enclosed world was softly illuminated. Pulling the hangings aside he slipped out of bed and went to where his travelling bags had been stacked against the wall. Fumbling inside one he eventually produced a stained roll of parchment, covered in neat handwriting. He jumped back into bed and drew the covers up. Kate propped herself up on her pillows.

"This is from Lady Stanley. Margaret Beaufort. Read it."

In the dim candlelight Kate read carefully, saying the words aloud, under her breath, as she had been taught to do as a girl in the schoolroom at Grafton Regis. She had received a good education and was thankful for it. Her intelligence was another thing that had drawn she and Harry closer – unlike many men he liked having a wife with whom he could discuss affairs of importance. The letter stunned her.

"She asks you to join with her son in bringing down the king. She asks you to write to him. Will you do this?"

"If Richard has the boys killed people will say I had a hand in it. I am seen as his foremost supporter. My God, they may even say *I* did it, or advised him!"

She laid her head upon his shoulder. "No, Harry. Surely not."

"As God is my witness, Kate, I thought he would put them with the Clarence children. But I was wrong. So I must find a different way now. Pledge myself to restore young Edward before it is too late. Tomorrow I will speak with Morton."

Kate could see the irony. "He was sent here to be under your guard!"

"Which buys me time."

Bishop Morton was surprised, to say the least, to find himself before Harry Buckingham and being offered a glass of his best wine and a seat by the fire. The last time they had met, on that fateful morning of Hastings' execution, Morton had seen only scorn and distaste on Buckingham's face as Gloucester's soldiers had dragged him away. He had to admit that imprisonment in Brecknock Castle had been no great hardship – he was well fed and slept upon a comfortable mattress, not in any dungeon but in a small room above the gatehouse, with a good view of the town, where the Stafford guards could keep a close eye on him. His only complaint was that the room was not warm enough; the damp brought rheumatic pains to his sixty-four-year-old bones. Now he regarded the twenty-eight-year-old duke with interest and judged it best to say very little until he could read him more easily.

Buckingham swilled his wine nervously. "I will come straight to the point, Morton. I have left the King's progress."

"Indeed, sir. And how does that affect me, prisoner as I am in your fine home?" asked the bishop mildly. He saw a vein pulsing at the side of Buckingham's head.

"Because I feel we may now … work together. In a common purpose."

Morton would not make it easy for him, he knew. But they lived in times so turbulent, so dangerous, that the alliance of old enemies in new friendships was nothing unusual. For the last fifty years the lines of treaties between the noble families of England had been constantly redrawn, affinities swerving like weathercocks in a storm. Morton was using silence cleverly. Buckingham tried to match him but failed. The wily old fox had so many more years of experience at his back.

"The King – Richard – confides in me – has confided in me."

For all his familiarity with the world of subterfuge, Bishop Morton had no idea what Buckingham was about to say next. When he heard the words falling quietly from Buckingham's lips he recoiled in genuine horror.

"Have the boys done away with? He actually said that?"

"He trusts me. I think he felt he had to tell someone. I think he wanted my approbation as well as his mother's."

"By leaving him so suddenly he will know that you do not support him. He is astute, Buckingham."

"I left word that Kate had summoned me – that she was like to be ill in childbed."

"A man leaves his king for his wife?" Morton looked disbelieving. "Well, boy, you *have* burned your bridges."

"Aye, I know that well enough. And I know he will have my head off, upon a log, like poor Hastings, if I ever meet him anywhere except upon a battlefield, so you had best tell me what you know of those who would see him brought down."

That Buckingham had made a momentous decision was crystal clear. Morton felt a gleam of satisfaction that the conspiracy against Richard could be glossed with such a name as Harry Stafford, Duke of Buckingham. Candidly, he told him of the network in the south – the true Yorkist men from Edward IV's household who despised how Richard had pushed his sons aside for the sake of his own ambition; of the scions of the Wydville family who waited – in Salisbury, in Guildford, in Kent, in the Channel, in Brittany, ready to rise. But there was an area he still had to probe.

"Tell me, do you make this choice because you cannot stomach seeing children's bloodshed, or because you see some glimmer of hope for your own ambitions? You have reminded us countless times, sir, of your illustrious ancestors. There are those who will say you want the crown for yourself. Will you set this aside to back Henry Tudor?"

"You may as well ask why Henry Tudor would invade, just to remove Richard and place young Edward back on the throne," retorted Buckingham.

"That's easy enough to explain; he wants to come home. His existence as a refugee in Brittany is not easy – he relies too much upon the goodwill of the Duke there. Richard has made it clear that there is no place for him in England and that he will not reinstate his title as Duke of Richmond. The late King Edward was just about to do that, and was even talking of a marriage to one of the princesses. Lady Stanley was hoping Richard would do likewise but he'll have none of it. So she has washed her hands of Richard now and is willing to join with the Wydvilles to bring about her son's return. I think he will be content to be a royal brother-in-law."

Harry contemplated the flames dancing in the hearth. Those that leapt high were bright but those that licked the logs at a lower level endured longer. "If, under Edward V, I can retain all that I have been given: Constable of England, the lordship of the Marches and the control of the royal lands, then I am content too." And at that moment he believed it. "I can never condone the slaughter of innocents. I will not become a Herod."

"Then we have many letters to write tonight," said Morton. "I take it you have men trusted to lay down their life for you?"

So now they waited. Letters had been despatched in secret to Brittany, London and other places. The uprising would happen. Henry Tudor would set sail. Edward V would be freed. Richard Plantagenet would be defeated in battle, or incarcerated in the Tower himself to await his fate. And history would remember him, Harry Stafford, as the man brave enough to repent of ever lending his support to the usurper. Under young Edward's rule he would rise and rise – the beloved uncle Buckingham. And if the boy died young, well … As for Henry Tudor, if the duchy of Richmond and his mother's love proved not quite enough he would be dealt with too. *I am descended from the best king England has ever known.* Buckingham strolled over to the window and looked out over his lands. If the other rebels could raise armies all over England … why, he could easily do the same in Wales.

12

Early September 1483 Westminster Sanctuary

Nesfield may well have said to try and keep the sun from rising, or the moon from waxing and waning, thought Bessy a week later, because intrigue was what fed Elizabeth's soul. She had spent several days complaining loudly of pains in her head and stomach, declaring that her usual remedy of a mint infusion was doing no good. She vomited up her food, seemed to be burning up with fever and pleaded with Bessy to speak with Nesfield about allowing a doctor to attend her. Nesfield visited and looked worried when he saw Elizabeth's white face and how she lay inert upon her bed. Cecily mopped her brow and held a small basin. Little Bridget's bed had been moved into the hall, next to Katherine's, for fear of infection.

"Who would she wish to see?"

"Anyone," said Bessy, "who could make her feel better."

A faint voice came from the bed. "Could it be Lady Margaret's doctor, Bessy? The Welshman who is so good with women's ailments."

"Would you allow it, sir? I have my sisters' health to think of, too. If we should all fall ill ..."

Elizabeth retched loudly again; a trickle of green bile spread across the sheet and Nesfield found himself agreeing that Elyn should be sent to Coldharbour, Lady Margaret's residence, to request a visit from her valued servant.

Dr Lewis Caerleon came in the afternoon. He consulted briefly with Elizabeth then came out to speak with Nesfield. "I have given Dame Grey medicine to soothe her head, and she will sleep a while, but I crave your permission to return this evening to check on her progress. I fear her humours are much disturbed. The next few hours are vital."

Nesfield hesitated but registered the genuine concern in Bessy and Cecily's expressions. Although a seasoned soldier and sailor, at heart he was a kind, chivalric man and women's distress always moved him. When the new King Richard had ordered him to command the guards outside the Westminster sanctuary he had found himself agreeing readily. He could not see how a visit to an obviously sick woman, from the doctor of the lady who had attended Queen Anne at her recent coronation, and whose husband was loyal to York, could pose any threat to King Richard's security. "An hour's visit," he said. "No more."

Dr Caerleon returned at dusk. He slipped in via the postern door and presented himself to Bessy and Cecily who were seated by the empty fireplace in the dining hall, wrapped in woollen cloaks against the evening chill. He was old, at least sixty, tall and stooped, with rather wild curly grey hair flattened under a leather skull cap and wore the dusty dark robes of his profession. His fingers were long and tapering and he spoke in the sing-song accent of his homeland.

"I am permitted to see Her Grace for a while."

Bessy registered the deferential address but did not react. "We will come with you, sir. My mother has been sleeping."

They entered Elizabeth's room and to Bessy and Cecily's surprise their mother was out of bed and seated in her chair, dressed in a clean gown. A steady fire burned in the hearth.

"Come in, Dr Caerleon. You have messages for me from Lady Stanley?"

Bessy started in astonishment, then it was as if the shutters over a window had suddenly been opened. Her mother was no more ill than the man in the moon.

"Cecily, stay outside the door and make sure no one comes near. If you see Nesfield or one of the guards approaching come quickly to warn us." Elizabeth's voice was so firm that Cecily was taken aback and obeyed without question, closing the door carefully behind her.

"You must tell me quickly. The Princess Elizabeth must hear this."

Caerleon opened his leather bag and took out a small roll of parchment sealed with a red wax disc imprinted with the unmistakable badge of the Beaufort family – the portcullis. Silently, he handed it to Elizabeth who broke the seal and scanned the contents. Their tall shadows danced on the walls. Minutes passed. Elizabeth finally looked up. Huge tears ran down her cheeks and splashed on the letter, causing the ink to blur. But no sound escaped from her lips. She crumpled the letter and returned it to Caerleon, who placed it carefully in the fire where the flames suddenly flared and consumed it, then settled back to gentle flickering.

"So they are both said to be dead?" Her voice was the quietest of whispers.

Bessy felt her legs turn to water and pressed herself back against the door for support.

"And she believes this to be true?"

Caerleon nodded.

"And she offers me a way forward, even though my princes are no more."

Bessy closed her eyes. In front of her swam two young faces, one with a slightly arrogant smile, framed by straight, silver-gilt hair and the other with a freckled nose, topped by an unruly tangle of russet-blond curls. Two boys, on their ponies, setting out for Ludlow, waving at their sisters on the steps of Windsor castle. Two boys watching the tumblers at Christmas; two boys playing chess; two boys shooting at the butts in the Tower garden; two boys, asleep in their shared chamber … She was aware that she had slid down the door and was now on the floor. From far away, through a roar of blood in her ears she could still hear her mother's voice, low and savage.

"Tell your mistress that I am in agreement. But I will not write it. You must commit my words to memory. Tell her that her son can have my daughter. If that is the price for defeating Richard so be it."

"The risings are planned for next month, Your Grace. Your Wydville relations have it in hand and Buckingham will be the figurehead. Tudor will cross from Brittany."

"And I will be avenged."

"I will visit again in a few days. Nesfield has no suspicions."

"I can keep vomiting awhile. God knows I have reason now."

He was gone as unobtrusively as he had come, skirting past Bessy on the floor and Cecily in the passage outside. Cecily slipped into the room and looked round-eyed at her sister prostrate on the rushes and her mother with her head in her hands.

"Mama? What is it?"

But Elizabeth's composure cracked. She was sobbing as she had done when she had been told about the falseness of her marriage, and when she had heard of Anthony and John Grey's deaths. And yet, this wailing was different too – it contained a misery and depth of tragedy Cecily had never heard before in her life. Bessy also seemed possessed by some extraordinary emotion Cecily had never previously witnessed. She sat up, dry-eyed, but with her fists clenching handfuls of the rushes, her chest heaving and her mouth working over two words. "No. Never. No. Never." Cecily wanted to flee into the passage, and yell for Elyn or Joanna but some animal instinct told her to shut the door instead, so that the distress, whatever it was, should be theirs alone. She threw herself down on her knees next to her sister, pulled her round and cupped her face in her hands so that she could make eye contact

"Bessy! Stop it! You have to tell me!"

Elizabeth's keening continued, like that of a wounded animal.

"We have to make Mama stop!" Cecily hissed. "The guards will hear! The little ones will hear and be afraid again!"

Bessy gulped long and hard and was clearly making an effort to regulate her breathing. Cecily scrambled to her feet and turned her attentions to her mother. This needed more than a disrespectful shake. She steeled herself, swung her right arm back and delivered a stinging slap to Elizabeth's cheek. Her hand burned with the impact. All three of them were shocked into absolute silence and then stared, wild eyed at each other. Bessy was the first to speak. She pointed at her mother.

"She has sold me in marriage to Margaret Beaufort's son."

Cecily was uncomprehending. "He is of the House of Lancaster. Mama would never do that."

"Oh yes, she would. Wouldn't you, Lady Mother?"

"But what has happened that is so dreadful – why is she so very distressed?"

A hot spot of raised scarlet pulsed now on Elizabeth's cheek, where Cecily had struck her. She raised her hand and fingered it, wonderingly, then rubbed away the remaining wetness from her face. Staring into the fire she spoke. "He has murdered my princes, and I will see him, and his family, dead."

It took Cecily a few seconds to process her mother's words. Aghast, she whirled back to Bessy for some sort of confirmation. Bessy nodded, slowly, tragically. Then her defences crumbled and she crawled across the rushes to lay her head in her mother's lap. Cecily could not speak because a huge lump had lodged itself in her throat and an horrendous weight pressed upon her chest. She too sank down and cast herself against her mother's knees. She had no idea how long they stayed like that. Hours maybe. The fire had turned to charred embers and the candles burnt to stubs by the time anyone moved.

Katherine woke in the small hours to find Bessy and Cecily's beds empty. Next to her Bridget slept soundly and in the corner Anne was also breathing steadily but occasionally muttering in her dreams. The Abbot's house seemed filled with a palpable sorrow. Katherine heard the latch of her mother's door clicking and then her sisters appeared like ghosts, holding hands and seeming to have to support each other to make the few steps across the room. In the shadows Katherine thought they looked like old women and was too afraid to call out. She watched as they knelt before Mama's little altar and saw how they bowed their heads, as if their necks were like fragile stalks too weak to hold up blooming flowers.

"Into your hands, Lord, we commend the spirits of your servants Edward and Richard," Bessy was whispering. "Look after them, Lord, for they are innocent of any wrongdoing."

Katherine understood in that moment that her brothers were dead. Dead like her father. Dead like her Uncle Anthony. Dead like her siblings Mary, and Margaret and George, whom she had never met. Fearful of disturbing her sisters, she lay back, her heart pounding, her young mind whirring with questions she knew she could never ask: How? Had they died of a summer fever in the Tower? Had the plague come and covered them in spots? How come they had died together? Where would they be buried? At Windsor with Papa? In the Abbey with her brother George?

The next morning, when her mother told the rest of their little household that the royal boys were murdered, and by the order of their uncle, Katherine screamed and screamed.

117

13

"Then he came to York, where his little son and heir ... was knighted and made Prince of Wales." John Rous

"At York he was joyfully received of the citizens ... the queen followed also with a crown upon her head, who led by the hand her son Edward ... as in show of rejoicing they extolled King Richard above the skies ..." Polydore Vergil

Sunday 8th September 1483: Feast of the Nativity of the Virgin Mary

The towns of central and northern England had put on a brave show to welcome their new king, whatever they privately felt about him; whatever the rumours circling his progress like carrion crows. In the still, hot days of July, he and Anne left stinking London far behind and rode up through the cool Thames Valley to Reading, then on past golden, ripening wheatfields to Oxford, then by the side of the fast-flowing River Severn to Gloucester, Tewkesbury and Worcester. Then they headed northwards, to Anne's Neville heartlands of Warwick and Coventry, Leicester and Nottingham and so finally, by late August, into Richard's strongholds of Pontefract, Middleham and York.

As they travelled, the landscapes gradually transformed, from fertile plains to windswept moorland. Accents changed too; the broad, flat comfortable Midlands dialect gave way to the clipped, harsher northern language, almost incomprehensible to the southerners in Richard's party, who had never before ventured far outside London. It mattered little to Richard that the wind blew harder and the rain fell more heavily as the summer drew to its close; once at Nottingham he felt he was coming home and by the time he entered York he had left the world of Westminster far behind. It was as if a burden had shifted from his shoulders.

York did him proud. Riding through Micklebar Gate, with Anne waving confidently at his side on her chestnut mare, he heard the crowds cheer wildly at the sight of their northern lord and lady turned king and queen. He hardly had time to think of those dear heads once displayed so grotesquely on the spikes above him. Instead, he was swept into the city itself, dazzled by displays of colourful tapestries and fabrics hung like tournament banners from every window. The next three weeks were a whirlwind of activity; the city council had prepared pageants portraying his descent from Edward III, and speeches galore. The rotund mayor, sweating in his ceremonial scarlet, knelt to present the keys of the city, and offered bags full of gold, but Richard refused them politely, as he had done in all the other towns, saying he would rather have their loyalty. Every night he and Anne fell into bed exhausted but laughing. Reunited with her little son Anne was in her element; she coughed less and smiled more, saying she felt much more suited to the bracing air of the north, and could they not make their home here for much of the year?

When Richard saw his eight-year-old son standing on the steps at Middleham Castle he thought his heart might break. They said the boy had been waiting for hours, running up on to the battlements time after time to look for the first signs of the outriders and straining his ears for the sound of the heralds' trumpets. He was so much like Anne, with her soft brown hair and snub nose. Richard took his slight frame into his arms, and felt the slender arms wrap around his neck. *My son. My own Edward. You will be king after me now.* He released him and allowed Anne her turn to hold the child close to her heart. Edward of Middleham led his parents to his chamber, eager to show them the hound puppy they had given him when they had left four months ago.

Anne turned a joyous face to her husband. "Are they not *both* grown? I swear I do not know whose legs are the longest!" She joined her son on the floor, to play with the little harrier who yapped and growled and stood on his head with excitement.

Richard felt a sickness in the pit of his stomach. Only six weeks ago he had seen those same long, spindly legs of early adolescence on two other boys. Young Dickon was a well grown lad, promising the height of his father and Edward, at twelve, was just entering his growth spurt. There really wasn't much between them. Where had Tyrrell put their bodies? Did they lie together in a tangle of limbs, in some shallow grave in the Tower precincts, or had he smuggled them out for more decent burial, maybe at Windsor? One night, at Worcester, he had shared with Buckingham what must happen to the boys – had explained to him that it was for the good of the state, a terrible price to be paid for future peace in the land. With the boys gone, England could settle to its Yorkist destiny. In ten years they would be footnotes to history, forgotten like countless other royal bastards. But Buckingham's reaction had said it all. For all his arrogance and ambition he recoiled as if stung, his eyes widening for a spilt second. His words had been carefully chosen – *You must do as you think best, cousin* – had stayed to share a glass of wine but in the morning his bed and his horse's stable were both empty. *My Lord of Buckingham has been summoned hastily to Brecknock, Your Grace, where his wife is near her time.* He had sent letters after Harry, urging him, then commanding him to return but heard nothing.

Today his own Edward was to be invested as the new Prince of Wales in the Archbishop's palace. Up here in the north few spoke of the other young princes – they had never been seen and so commanded little sympathy. The north had easily consigned them to bastardy and oblivion, much like Edouard of Lancaster. Richard shivered, despite his furred gown, at the realisation that his own son was the third boy in twelve years to be named Edward and Prince of Wales. But this time it would be different. *Do not think about other boys. Think only of this boy.*

It would be a grand ceremony. James Tyrell had arrived in York with all the necessary raiments from the royal Wardrobe – he had ridden hard from London and met briefly with Richard. *Is it done, Tyrrell? It is done, Your Grace.* And that was all. Life goes on. He found he could not tell Anne, or even his close friend Francis Lovell, who had been his faithful follower since childhood. Richard found that the best way of dealing with it was to blank it out in his mind, the same way in which he had once coped with the knowledge of how his father and brother Edmund had died. How he had dealt with his brother Clarence's end. Put it out of mind and concentrate on what needs doing next.

That evening, in the Archbishop's palace chapel just by the mighty Minster, Richard formally invested his son as his heir. In one way it seemed ridiculous, girding an eight-year-old child with a sword, but Edward held himself upright, his brown eyes huge with awe. Richard placed the wreath of estate upon his head; it slipped rather lopsidely and the boy giggled nervously. Anne leaned over and straightened it lovingly, her fingers lingering against his cheek. The golden ring was placed upon his finger and the golden staff of office put into his right hand.

Edward turned, as instructed, to face the audience of archbishops, bishops and prelates, and all the retinue from London. Behind him on the high altar the silver and gilt figures of the twelve apostles glittered in the candlelight. He could hear his father's voice, firm and confident, ringing around the spacious chapel:

"'We therefore, following the footsteps of our ancestors and with the assent and advice of the said prelates, dukes and barons of our realm of England, we have determined to honour our dearest first born son Edward, whose outstanding qualities, with which he is singularly endowed for his age, give great and, by the favour of God, undoubted hope of future uprightness, as prince and earl, with grants, prerogatives and insignia and we have made and created, and do create, him Prince of Wales and Earl of Chester... And we invest him as the custom is by the girding on of the sword, the handing over and setting of the garland on his head, and of the gold ring on his finger, and of the gold staff in his hand, to have and hold to him and his heirs, kings of England, for ever.'"

After the Mass, the trumpets sounded. The Bishop of Durham bowed and Edward proceeded down the central aisle, flanked by his mother and father. Close behind came a group of excited young men, knighted to mark the occasion, amongst them Richard's illegitimate son, John of Pontefract. They spilled outside into the chill of the late evening where the citizens of York waited with anticipation. Richard looked upwards and saw a flock of long-tailed swallows circling – summer was well and truly over and the last visitors leaving. Already a few of the leaves on the ancient oaks in the Archbishop's garden were turning amber. Edward stood up tall and gripped his golden staff, then waved with his free left hand. A roar of approval went up:

"A York! Long live King Richard! Long live Queen Anne! Long live Prince Edward!"

Two hundred miles away, a four-year-old girl lay in her bed in the Abbot's dining hall at Cheneygate and watched the shadows gathering on the wall. Her hands and feet were cold and her cheeks still damp with tears. She did not want to sleep because of the fear that she might die. The fear that some faceless giant might creep along in the night, snatch the pillow from under her sleeping head and use it to stifle her. Or the giant might bring daggers and stab at her. Or he might carry a huge stone and crush her. For these were the ways in which Katherine Plantagenet imagined a child could be murdered.

"Realising that he was hemmed in and could find no safe way out he changed his attire and forsook his men ...." Crowland Chronicle

18th October 1483 Herefordshire

It was under fifty miles from Brecon to Hereford through the Wye Valley but it might as well have been five hundred. For two weeks the rain was incessant, falling from the sky as if God fully intended another Noah's flood. The water poured not only from the heavens but down the hillsides and off the fields, finding every possible route of descent, swamping the bridleways until they were indistinguishable from the ditches. The streams raged like rivers in full spate and the rivers became passionate tides charging towards their destinies. The ground was so saturated it gave way underfoot and the men who had followed Buckingham began to desert in droves. They did not need much of an excuse, for although initially attracted by the tale of a Welsh-born hero, who would reinstate the boy king Edward, they had been reluctant to join a rebellion and any short-lived enthusiasm quickly waned in the face of cold, wet and mud. For days now they had straggled behind, numbers dwindling every time the sergeant attempted a head count. They wanted their own dry homes and beds. Apart from a handful of loyal followers, Harry Buckingham found himself alone, for Morton had gone to Ely to raise his own followers.

Now he sat on his horse, drenched through. The Stafford banner held by his page was a sorry sight of soaked silk, occasionally flapping dismally in the wind. In front of him a tributary of the Wye had overflowed its banks and halted their progress, for the field had been transformed into a quagmire. Even his saddle was sodden and the reins slid through his fingers like slime-covered serpents. The men who had ridden on ahead reported that the River Severn foamed with fury. They had never seen anything like it: cottages swept away – corpses and carcasses floating downstream. The centuries-old crossing place had entirely disappeared, the contours of the land no longer familiar. There was simply no way of reaching Thornbury, the designated mustering place. He felt tears pricking in his eyes and a sense of utter desolation as the reality of his situation hit home. His world had fallen apart. Why would men not flock to join him and follow him, as they did Richard? He remembered how the ordinary men of Yorkshire had clamoured to be at their lord's side, and thousands had marched down the Great North Road and camped outside the city walls in the week before the coronation. *Which I organised,* he thought bitterly. *I was the one who handed him the crown.*

Those who remained with him had taken shelter under trees almost leafless after the storms; they afforded little protection and the group shifted about in uncomfortable silence.

"My lord! What next?" One of them was brave enough to shout. They had stayed with him thus far but now it was clear that their "rising" had no future

Buckingham did not even bother to turn in his saddle but lifted his hand in a gesture of defeat and dismissal. His horse lowered its neck and shivered. He heard the sound of heavy squelching as the other horses turned heavily in the mud, then began to move back across the field. He could not hold these last few men against their will and clearly they needed no second telling. Within minutes they had gone. The only sound was the dull roar of the water. High above, a buzzard circled slowly on the air currents in the gunmetal sky.

He searched his mind for possibilities. Returning to Brecon was out of the question, for Richard's men would already be there. He had no idea where his nearest allies might be – no idea if the other men mentioned by Morton had risen successfully or not. Kate and his two boys waited at Lord Ferrers' manor at Weobly; it was only six weeks since the birth of baby Anne but bravely she had followed him with the boys, leaving the girls in the care of their nurses. *Holy Mother of God, what have I done? Let my little girls be safe at Brecon.*

There was nothing for it but to lie low for a while until he could be certain of what had happened elsewhere. Kate and the lads would be safe enough – Ferrers had not particularly wanted to offer them hospitality but he would not turn a woman and her children out – and with any luck she would follow his instructions to give Edward over into the care of his great uncle William Knyvet. He had to put his trust in others. He thought rapidly – where could he go? Where would be safe? Somewhere remote … Somewhere Richard would never look … No castle, or manor …Why Wem! Wem, two days ride away, north of Shrewsbury but the home of old Ralph Bannister whose family had served his for three generations. And if things were really bad, from Wem he could head up into North Wales and the ports. *But not like this, not looking like Henry Stafford, second Duke of Buckingham. I am a fugitive now. Best look like one.*

He swung down from his saddle and dragged the waterlogged caparisons from his horse's back. He tore off his own surcoat and trod it into the mire. Underneath he wore a plain leather doublet and dark hose. He stripped the tassels from the horse's bridle and threw them away. Luckily the creature was so tired, hungry and coated with mud up to his hocks he did not look like the mount of a lord. For good measure Buckingham drew his dagger and hacked a little at his mane and tail and looked with grim satisfaction at the effect. There was no need to do much to his own appearance – he was already blathered in dirt, his boots filthy and his face besmirched. He mounted again and leaned forward to pat the horse's neck.

"Come on, Bruin my friend, you can get me to Wem. There will be a dry stable there, and some apples, no doubt."

Totally alone, probably for the first time in his life, Harry Buckingham wiped his reins as dry as he could and kicked his weary mount northwards to Shropshire.

14

"With what kind of death these children were executed is not certainly known ... so great grief struck generally to the hearts of all men ... they wept everywhere." Polydore Vergil

Late October 1483

Bessy found that grief for her brothers came in waves. The best way of coping, she discovered, was to keep busy – at least as busy as it was possible to be, sequestered in sanctuary, so she set herself tasks each day: *read this book; finish this embroidery; start a new one; practise my lute; translate this passage from Latin into French; think of stories to tell the little ones. Above all, do not think about how they might have died.*

Elizabeth alternated between bouts of inconsolable weeping and expressions of dire revenge. During the latter she prowled about their three rooms like a lioness, calling upon God, the Virgin Mary and all the saints to see that Richard Plantagenet roasted in hell. The kindly abbot offered to pray with her; Cecily said it was to prevent their mother wearing out his flagstones. Cecily's sorrow was a dry-eyed affair, punctuated by little sudden sobs and scurrying into corners. Anne curled up like a sorrowful puppy, trying to make sense of what the grown-ups had done and Katherine seemed little concerned in the daytime but screamed at night, woken by nightmares that left them all emotionally exhausted. In the end Bessy and Cecily took it turns to lie with her, arms around her, ready for the first twitchings and moanings that presaged the visitation of her terrors. Waking her proved the best thing; she would cling to them, sobbing in distress, babbling incoherently of giants and pillows and knives and stones. Even little Bridget, whom they thought too young to understand, sensed something was wrong and withdrew into silences.

Bessy had her own nightmares and was sure that Cecily did too. Yet one morning she surfaced early from a light sleep, struck with a sudden thought. *Why, if my brothers are truly gone, that makes me my father's heir! As I was before they were born! Sweet Virgin, if my Uncle Richard lies about my parents' marriage then that makes* **me** *the rightful queen of this realm!* She sat up, her heart pounding. She shook Cecily awake.

"Cecily! You are my heir!"

"What?" Cecily's eyes were heavy with fatigue. It was hard enough to sink into any sort of restful sleep and she did not appreciate being woken. "What, Bessy? It's the middle of the night!"

"No. It's early. And I have just realised something. I should be Queen of England. Not queen as Mama is – was – because she was married to the king, but *properly Q*ueen!"

In the darkness of a cool October dawn they could barely see each other but Cecily could make out Bessy's slim outline sitting bolt upright in bed. Cecily snuggled down under her covers. Their exchange was conducted in hissed whispers.

"How can you be the queen when our uncle has been crowned king?" She felt it was a perfectly reasonable question. "What are you going to do, Bessy? Join Mama in her plotting? Send messages to all her Wydville clan begging them to declare for you? Challenge Uncle Richard in combat?" Cecily's scorn was often her mode of defence when feeling defeated.

"No, of course not – I am just saying. And it means *you're* the heir, Cecily!"

There was a thump of pillows and a creaking of the bed ropes as Cecily tossed back towards her sister. "I'll tell you what it means, Bessy; it means danger for both of us. While the boys were alive we were nobodies – just girls – but now people *will* think of us, and remember us, and say they act in our name – and we can't stop them. Mother will have you married off to Henry Tudor before you know it; she might even *send* you to him, and most likely you'll drown on the way to Brittany, and then she'll send *me!* And if you do live then God knows who she'll find for me. And what will our Uncle Richard do, when he returns to London and thinks about us? Why, he'll probably put *us* in the Tower and have *us* killed too!" She turned over pointedly to face the wall.

Later that day Bessy took her courage in both hands and knocked on her mother's door. They had not spoken much since the terrible news and Elizabeth had not mentioned Henry Tudor again. Elizabeth was seated, several letters in her lap. Bessy sighed; clearly, there was no end to her collusions. She curtsied, a rare throwback to the days of formality of court. If Elizabeth was surprised at her daughter's restored civility she did not show it, but motioned that she should be seated too. The Abbot's Privy Chamber was a spacious, with a broad stone fireplace. Some of his finest tapestries hung on the walls, depicting famous biblical scenes. There was plenty of room for the bed, chests and the furniture Elizabeth had brought from the palace. *If you half close your eyes*, thought Bessy, *you could almost imagine we are back at Westminster, or Windsor, or Eltham, or Sheen.* She sat down gracefully, playing a game with herself that she was in her father's presence chamber; she spread the skirts of her gown and tucked her feet in tidily. She closed her eyes. *Now my mother will tell me what foreign guests we shall entertain at supper this evening; the King of France's envoy will be here and I must dance and sparkle!*

But with a jolt she was back to reality. She opened her eyes to see Elizabeth gathering up her papers and placing them carefully in the fire. For a week now they had had the luxury of fires in all three of their rooms, carefully tended so that they did not go out – a blessing in the chilly, wet weather and incredibly useful for disposing of secret missives.

"Out of interest, Lady Mother, just how *do* your letters get past Sir John's guards? One would think we were under siege, yet still you receive messages."

Elizabeth smiled a tight smile. "Elyn has been making eyes at one of the guards. He's from Kent, where our Haute relatives live. His mother was a maid at Ightam and he knows not his father. Elyn has told him he is probably our distant cousin. He is completely smitten. And he has a brother who serves in Lady Stanley's household as a groom."

Despite herself, Bessy laughed. "Oh, Mama! How do you do it?"

"But the news is not good, Bessy. The risings against your uncle have failed. I believe my brothers Lionel and Edward, and son Thomas Grey are safe in Brittany by now but Harry Buckingham has been found and arrested. God know where my sister Kate is. I fear that Richard may now come and break sanctuary." She lifted her hands in a gesture of helpless supplication. "I have done everything a mother could do to keep our hopes alive but it has come to naught."

Bessy swallowed hard. "Mama, this morning I suddenly understood more. I am Papa's heir now, am I not? I had not thought of it before. I suppose girls don't. If I marry Henry Tudor it could put an end to all of this, couldn't it? All these decades of killing and hating."

The papers in the hearth suddenly ignited in a brief, energetic blaze. Elizabeth's face was riddled with anxiety; the high forehead was still smooth but around her eyes and mouth deep lines had been etched in the past six months.

"That, my daughter, was Margaret Beaufort's idea. But her son will not come now. He was so close, so ready to invade – but he received word that things had gone wrong and he returned to France." She took Bessy's hands in hers. "And now Richard will punish all those who have not managed to escape to be with him."

"Including you?"

"Oh, Bessy, he knows I am at the heart of it. I do not expect his mercy. And Anne Neville hates me."

Bessy blanched. "But he would not hurt us? Women and girls?"

Elizabeth looked even more pensive. "Men have always had ways of destroying women they fear. They may not kill us but they lock us away. A nunnery. An island."

"An *island?"*

"Your cousin the Lancastrian King Henry had a sister-in-law whom they accused of sorcery and witchcraft and banished her to the Isle of Man, and then the Isle of Anglesey. Eleanor, she was called; my mother Jacquetta knew her well."

Bessy looked aghast. "And you think my Uncle Richard will do the same to you? To us? Put us on an island and let the world forget about us?"

"I just don't know, Bessy. Maybe he will be satisfied that all the men involved are dead or fled."

"Mama, do you believe now that our boys are dead?" Bessy asked the question bravely and directly.

Elizabeth grimaced. "What did your tutors teach you about the past?"

"How do you mean?"

"Your Plantagenet ancestors. The second Edward. The second Richard. The sixth Henry. Men will stop at nothing when they reach for the crown. Absolutely nothing. Your own father included."

"But that was war. He killed his enemies in battle."

"The sixth Henry did not die in battle. Your father's brother, George, did not die in battle. They died in the Tower. Your beloved father, Bessy, showed his

128

brother Richard how to take a crown. And that is why I do now believe my royal boys are dead."

"Then maybe we must blame my father as much as my uncle for what has happened," said Bessy quietly. "Mama, do you think the world would be a different place if a woman could be queen? A real queen, who rules?"

"I hear tell of the Queen of Castile, Isabella. She has proved what a woman can do but she has a strong husband at her side, and he is a king too. I cannot foresee a world where a woman could ever be queen alone. Do you remember there was once a queen called Matilda? They say God and his saints slept while she and her cousin Stephen brought this country to its knees. No, England would never stand for it."

"Mama, I am glad that we are talking again. I think what matters now is that we survive."

"Bessy, I do believe that Henry Tudor will try again, one day. His claim is slight, but his power may be strong. Our power may now be weak, but your claim is strong. Think on it, my daughter. Think on it."

15

December 1483, Westminster

Harry Buckingham had died in the market place in Salisbury. His rank had been respected, consequently it was the axe that separated his head from his neck, and his right hand from his arm, rather than being strung up on the gallows, but he was dead, nevertheless. He'd been difficult to track down, thought Richard, until he'd made the foolish mistake of seeking shelter with an old servant. The money on his head had proved far more attractive to Ralph Bannister than the idea of looking after him. Richard winced slightly as he recalled Lovell's tale of how they had found him in Bannister's little orchard, gathering a few late apples. Harry Stafford. Once his loyal friend, once the man who had agreed that England needed a better option than a boy on the throne. A man he had showered with rewards – land, titles, money, restoration of his Bohun inheritance – what more had he wanted? *Did he think I would not last? Did he go over to Tudor because he saw me as a doomed ship? He knew those boys had to die. He knew it! He would have done the same himself, in my shoes. Lovell knows; Lovell understands. I did not order it out of hatred, or because I wished harm to my brother's sons – but because I had to. God knows, Edward had to have George killed in order to keep England safe. We both had our cousin Henry killed, to keep England safe. I ordered that two boys should die, to keep England safe. It is a price worth paying.*

Richard woke with a start. He had slumped forward on the table. His hat had fallen off and his hair was in his eyes. He felt a weariness every day now – a sense that things would not come right, however hard he tried. *Focus upon doing the right things,* his mother had said, *proper justice.* Well, he had dealt with the risings against him and administered fair justice: those found guilty of treason against their anointed king were dead; those who had been misled were pardoned and sent home; he had been lenient with Margaret Beaufort, putting her husband in charge of keeping her in order – *fair justice; deprive her of her title; give her estates to her husband and make that husband keep her in check in the future.* He'd been fair to Hastings' widow too, back in the summer – no attainder and a burial in Windsor. Buckingham's wife need not fear him, either, even if she was a Wydville. He would be fair to Elizabeth Wydville too, if she would see sense and come out of sanctuary.

There was a rustle of silk behind him and two cool palms covered his eyes. He leaned back into Anne's gentle hands and she moved her fingers lightly over the tense muscles of his temples, then his jaw and down his neck. He exhaled slowly.

"You are tired, my lord." Her voice was compassionate and loving. Anne had always loved him, from when she was a small girl at Middleham when she was one of the richest and most important heiresses in the kingdom, a pawn in her father's plans to control England. Warwick had married Isabel, her sister, to George, thinking to make him king when Edward would not come to heel, and when that failed Anne had been sacrificed to Warwick's next political move – to have her as the Lancastrian Edouard's wife, Princess of Wales and the next queen of England. Richard knew that Anne loved him loyally, intensely – saw him as the saviour who had rescued her from the horrors of the Lancastrian royal family; rescued her from the grasping George who would have put her in a nunnery to seize her part of her mother's Beauchamp/Despenser fortune. And that much was true. But had she realised that his love for her was built upon her wealth too? She had brought him Middleham, and the fidelity of the north. Richard made himself love her in return; over the years his regard for her had definitely evolved into something like love – he was glad to be in her company, in her bed, in her arms and had never been unfaithful to their marriage. But he could not allow her into the secrets of his heart. She would never know his frustration at having only one living legitimate child; never know that sometimes he looked at her physical frailty and wondered if God would bring him the chance of a second wife one day. She would never, ever know about the two boys who had been smothered in their beds, the life snuffed out of them like unwanted puppies.

Now he forced himself to smile. He pulled her round and down onto his lap, where she loved to sit. She weighed nothing; it was as if a bag of feathers had been placed on his knees. The heaviest part of her was the nut-brown hair coiled up under her coif. She laid her face against his cheek and he could feel the heat radiating off her; a spasm of coughs suddenly erupted from her and for a moment

131

she shook uncontrollably. They did not speak of it; it was just Anne's cough. She had always coughed, especially when away from Yorkshire. The air, here by the river, and the smells of the city, did not suit her.

Outside, a few flakes of snow were trying to form. Occasional flurries skittered past the windows. There had been hard frosts earlier in the month and the city merchants spoke of a winter when the Thames itself might ice over. In the north, Richard and Anne had seen many winters when the snow lay feet deep but here in the south it was not so common. Richard was glad of the warmth here in his rooms, for many chambers in the palace had only wooden shutters through which the cold crept insidiously. He was glad too of the furred gowns that kept the cold at bay. Anne's throat and wrists were bound in ermine, and over her silken gown she wore a surcoat of thick, sapphire – blue wool.

He held her until her breathing regulated; the density of the cloth did not prevent him from feeling the bird-like structure of her bones. She pulled back from him until she could look into his eyes. "For a few days I thought … I had hoped ..." her voice trailed away. There had never been another pregnancy after Edward, no miscarriage or stillbirth – just nothing. It was another area of silence between them. They prayed. What else was there to do? It was God's will. And sometimes kings did not have a vast family of sons. But mostly they did. After all, that was the role of a queen. The sadness in her soulful brown eyes was telling. As much as he could not share his private thoughts with her, so she kept her own secrets hidden away. How could a man ever understand a woman's agony of seeing the blood return every month, like a red tide of betrayal? She yearned for, prayed for, pleaded with God, even bargained with God for another child but He did not hear her. There was still time – she was not yet twenty eight – but she felt as if the sands of her life were sliding inexorably through some pitiless opening, narrow but always unsealed. Never once had Richard rebuked her for this barrenness or turned hard eyes upon her but sometimes his stoic silence was worse to bear than another man's disappointment.

Anne ran her fingers over his face, feeling the lines etched around his eyes, across his forehead and by his mouth; they were deeper than last year. She knew what caused them.

"Is there still no word, Richard, about where they might be? Could Buckingham's men have taken them into Wales? Could Margaret Beaufort have hidden them somewhere on her Midlands estates before you had her arrested?" The mystery occupied her mind and actually kept her from brooding too much upon her own troubles. "It may even be that some Wydville supporter has them. Should you go to Elizabeth and confront her yourself? It's too bad, Richard, when you meant to move them up to Yorkshire and bring them up honourably. But what I don't understand is how *anyone* actually got them out of the Tower – I mean, you would think *someone* would have seen *something.* Could the guards have been in the pay of Buckingham, or the Tudor? Have you thought about that?"

He could hardly bear her innocent questions. Fortunately, she did not seem to pause long enough to expect answers and moved on. "Just how long does Elizabeth think she can stay in sanctuary? You would think this winter weather would freeze her out! Those poor girls, they must be so cold and fed up. When she gives up this stupid game we must have the girls at court, Richard, and show everyone that we mean only good towards them. I could find them husbands – I would like to do that, to help them in some small way. I know what it feels like to be frightened and powerless."

There was a knock on the door and Lord Francis Lovell entered. She had known her husband's best friend since childhood too and although he bowed low, and courteously, she knew him well enough to dispense with any needless ceremony in such a private setting. Jumping off Richard's lap she swiftly crossed to embrace him. Like Richard, he was slightly built, but finely toned with muscles like whipcord and a light step.

"Francis! It is good to see you! How is Agnes?" Her father Warwick had married Francis into her family, to her first cousin.

"She is well enough, Your Grace."

"Anne. My name is Anne, Francis. You know you can use it as you always did. Is she coming to court for the New Year? I dearly love to have family around me, since Isabel." Isabel, her sister, who lay behind the high altar in Tewkesbury Abbey. Poor Isabel. Better at producing Yorkist heirs but dead at twenty five.

Richard rose too, and flung an arm around Lovell's shoulders. "I can see you have something more important to tell us than mere family news; it's written all over your face."

"It's news from Brittany, Dickon. You are not going to like this. The Tudor has sworn an oath in the cathedral at Rennes that he will marry Princess Bessy. Lady Bessy, I mean."

Richard could immediately picture the scene in his mind's eye: the vaulted ceiling and the altar aglow with gold and silver; the pale winter sunlight filtering in through the high arched windows as Henry Tudor knelt on the cold stone slabs.

"Ah, so he's made it public, then? A clever move. Who was with him?"

"Morton, Dorset – all the Wydville exiles, Dickon. They pledged their allegiance to him, and he promised to marry Bessy."

"A *fait accompli*, then," retorted Richard with a derisive laugh, "unless we come up with a more tempting solution. Any ideas, Anne?"

She forced a smile. "He has no money, my lord, He is descended from bastards. He can be no threat to you. Why would anyone in their right mind choose to follow him now?"

Richard looked thoughtful. "Every man has his price, eh, Francis? Shall we offer pardons and a second chance to them? What would it take to bring them back?"

Anne suddenly seized his arm. "Richard, if we can get Elizabeth out of sanctuary, and bring the girls to court, as I suggested, then you will have Bessy where Tudor cannot lay hands on her. She is a sweet, biddable girl, they say, so surely she will obey her anointed king? Her father's brother?"

Ah, thought Richard, but I am also her brothers' murderer.

"We can find her a more suitable husband than Henry Tudor," continued Anne, "and the second girl too, who is of marriageable age." A fleeting stricken look passed across her face. "But Richard, they must be *honourable* men; I would not have them suffer as I did when I was made to wed the Lancaster prince." She spoke so rarely of that awful time in her youth that both Richard and Lovell were slightly taken aback. Richard pressed his lips to her hand.

Lovell looked away, fumbling inside his doublet to bring out a travel-stained document. "This is from the Duke of Brittany, or at least from his advisors. They want our help against the French king who encroaches on their borders. If we give them money, and arms, they are willing to make sure we can lay our hands on Tudor."

"Well then, Francis, there is your mission! Off with you to the court of your namesake, Duke Francis, and see what you can do. You have always wanted to play the diplomat. Now's your chance." Richard felt a new surge of hope; if anyone could pull it off it was this thoughtful friend whose loyalty he knew was beyond doubt.

Lovell bowed deeply, touched by the faith his king placed in him. However, he hesitated too, for there was more he had yet to say. He would rather Anne were not present but there was no help for it. He bit his bottom lip and looked up at Richard.

"There is just one more thing, Dickon … my lord.... Your Grace." He found himself lurching into formality.

Richard eyed him quizzically.

"The people cannot understand why you do not say where the York boys are. The rumours are not good..."

"I do not know where they are." *That much is true.*

Anne turned serious eyes upon Lovell. "It *is* terrible not to know, but someone took them from the Tower. They could be anywhere – even with their aunt. A boat down the Thames – a journey across the sea to Burgundy. Why, it's what *I* would have done. Goodness knows, it's what Richard's own mother did all those years ago when his father died at Wakefield. The more I think of it the more certain I am."

Lovell looked uncomfortable. "That's not what most seem to think, Anne. There are dark rumours."

"What on earth do you mean?"

Richard felt as if he was pushing some heavy weight to the far recesses of his mind. "He means, my love, that the people think I have harmed them. It's all right, Francis, I am neither deaf nor blind to what is said."

Anne sat down, her pupils dilated with shock. Inside her furred wristbands her hands were shaking uncontrollably.

"And have you?" It was a simple, direct question. There was a long silence. Lovell stared miserably at his feet and Richard pushed his hair back off his pale face in a quick, angry gesture of distress.

"What do you think?"

"I think …" she said slowly, "I think I cannot think that." She rose awkwardly and curtsied deeply to her husband, her fingers touching the chair arm for support. "I will see you at dinner." How she crossed to the door she did not know. The silk train of her gown soughed quietly then she was gone.

"Ah, God, Francis."

"Dickon, you did what you had to. I would have done the same, were I in your shoes. Anne is tender-hearted but she is no fool. She's Warwick's daughter, after all, and if *that* doesn't teach you about hard decisions, I don't know what does."

"It will be another thing we will never speak of."

"Probably best that way."

"And your advice for dealing with what is whispered up and down the streets of London? And throughout the south of my kingdom?"

"In the same way. Best not to speak of it. As long as it is thought they may still live, our enemies will be less likely to rally for Tudor, or use young Warwick as a figurehead."

Richard looked appalled. "George and Isabel's boy? God's truth, Francis, the lad is backward. Anne keeps him now at Middleham with our Edward. It would be terrible if the malcontents tried to use him. I *have* to keep him safe."

"Then, as I said, say nothing. Let the Londoners have their rumours for now and put your faith in the north. You can be a great king, Dickon, and when you call Parliament in January you can begin to show just how great. Once the people see you doing good all else will be forgotten."

The two men came together in an embrace that held every emotion of their childhood and youth together. Both wept a little. They held each other's shoulders, for a moment like lovers. Then Lovell knelt and kissed Richard's ring.

16

Over the last four months life in sanctuary had settled into a quiet existence. Richard's first Parliament had convened in late January, confirming his position as king. There was no going back. Since Christmas the time had crawled. The news from France was scarce. Each week Elizabeth looked for letters from her brothers or son Thomas Grey but now virtually nothing permeated through Richard's network of spies and guards. As for Henry Tudor, apart from his bombastic declaration that he would marry Bessy, little had been heard of him either. His mother was silenced for the time being and his supporters lay low in the Breton heaths and villages. Richard was replacing the rebels with men he could trust – rewarding his men from the north with land and offices. Elizabeth had entertained some hope that her favourite sister Katherine, Buckingham's widow, might be allowed to join her in sanctuary but Richard had poured scorn on the idea and instead placed Lady Buckingham and her children under the close supervision of the St Clare Sisters at a convent near the Tower. As he put it, with exasperation, "Why should I allow another tribe of Wydvilles into sanctuary when I am trying to get the ones in there *out?*" So hardly anyone ever visited now, even to try and persuade Elizabeth to leave. It was, she thought, as if Richard was leaving her to fester away what remained of her life. The cold, dark days of January and February had slowed time down. Without exercise and with limited occupations, her daughters had grown pale and listless like young plants starved of sunlight.

"Just how many cousins do we have, Bessy?" To pass the time Cecily had set herself the task of drawing up a family tree. Her penmanship was skilful, as was her ability to draw representations of people. Now the evenings were stretching out a little there was more light for reading and writing. The large oak table in the Jerusalem Chamber was strewn with parchment and inks that Cecily had charmed from the stores of Brother Jerome, one of the Abbey scribes. She had a pumice stone to smooth the surface and a knife to sharpen her quills. One advantage of being in sanctuary was that there were no tutors to say a girl should not be engaged in such an activity. Cecily was absorbed by her work and questioned her mother constantly about the illustrations she should put by names, to the point that Elizabeth remarked that if she was a boy she could be sent to join the College of Heralds.

Bessy peered over her sister's shoulder. Cecily had drawn long lines with offshoots and little shield shapes. Sometimes she had added a tiny male or female figure.

"Good heavens, Cecily, we don't know all our cousins! What family does?"

Cecily leaned back, easing her cramped shoulders. She smiled ruefully, "You're right; I'll just stick to the main ones, the ones on Papa's side that matter. Look, this is our father's sister who married the Earl of Suffolk – the de la Pole family. How many children do they have?"

Bessy made a face of comical dismay. "I don't *know!* There is John, the eldest, and Geoffrey the next one, and more boys, and a little one, Richard, and some girls – you must remember Elizabeth, Anne and Catherine who came sometimes to court at Christmas?"

"Hmm ... and their badge?" She called across to her mother, "What is the de la Pole badge, Mama? What should I draw?"

"Leopards' faces," replied Elizabeth, galled by Cecily presumption that Wydville cousins now counted for nothing yet amused by her second's daughter's tenacity. It was an early evening of rare harmony and togetherness. Bessy was easier to manage these days, often lost in her thoughts, and less inclined to berate her mother. There was, however, an unspoken issue: would they now be facing another season as guests of the Abbot?

Little Katherine was engaged in producing a neat alphabet on a scrap of parchment. Her tongue protruded with the concentration required not to smudge the precious ink. In the last few months they had all realised her precociousness – at four-and-a-half she could already form her name in square, even letters and was quick to recognise words in her sisters' prayer books. Bessy delighted in teaching her; she had sent Elyn out to track down the lutemaker who had supplied the royal family in the past, and begged him for a small instrument that Katherine might begin to learn the fingering. Anne was not really interested, and Bridget too young, but in Katherine Bessy had an eager pupil. The little girl could hold a tune too; her voice was mellow and she copied rhythms well. In a way, living so closely with her older sisters provided Katherine with extraordinary opportunities to listen and converse. If they had been in their normal environment at Eltham or Sheen, she would have been separated from them, with just her nurses and younger sisters.

Now Katherine looked on critically as Cecily drew. "That is a cat," she announced. "It looks like Tibby." Tibby was the Abbey's plump tabby cat – a good mouser, who sometimes deigned to sit on Katherine's lap to be stroked when not too busy.

Bessy burst out laughing. "It *does,* Cecily! It looks nothing like a leopard."

"Well, I have never seen a leopard, except on coats of arms," she replied with dignity.

"Mama, what do we know of our de la Pole cousins?"

Elizabeth laid her embroidery on her lap. "Richard has the eldest boy in Yorkshire now, at Sheriff Hutton. He was here, though, when they came to take your brother. I saw him. They have all declared allegiance." She added waspishly, "Your Aunt Anne of Suffolk would rather look after the interests of her own boys than think of what has befallen her brothers' sons – the rightful heirs."

"Well, would you not have done the same, in her position?" asked Bessy quietly. "We all guard our own, Lady Mother."

Cecily looked up from her writing and laid the quill thoughtfully against her cheek. "Mama, how will Henry Tudor marry Bessy, if he is stuck in France and Bessy is stuck here in sanctuary?"

Katherine's dark eyes were saucers in the fading light. "Is Bessy going to marry someone? Stop poking me with your foot, Anne!"

Bessy gave a small, tight smile, and patted her knee invitingly. Katherine abandoned her writing and climbed on to her sister's lap, her favourite place in the whole world. No-one felt as soft as Bessy, not even Mama; no-one felt as safe as Bessy. She fingered the golden chain around Bessy's neck, staring intently at the square pendant with its plum-coloured garnets and creamy pearls. "Will you leave us when you marry?"

Bessy felt three pairs of eyes upon her: Anne ventured a grey-blue gaze veiled by half-closed lashes; Cecily's dark blue eyes holding a huge question; Katherine's trusting brown irises only inches away. Elizabeth did not look at her daughter but stared into the middle distance, focusing on the tapestries.

"I have decided that I will do whatever God tells me to do to keep you all safe. I don't know what that means yet, but if I can help you all through marriage, even to Henry Tudor, then that is what I have resolved to do. But you are right, Cecily, I cannot do it from within these walls."

"Then we shall have to go," said Katherine solemnly. "You'll have to let us out, Mama."

"So we can start living," said Cecily, pointedly.

Katherine: And believe it or not, a few days later something quite extraordinary happened. My Uncle Richard swore an oath in front of the lords, mayor and aldermen of London that if my mother would leave sanctuary he would ensure our safety. If we agreed to be "guided, ruled and demeaned by him" he would protect us, for the love and loyalty he had borne towards his dear brother, the late King Edward IV and would, in time, find us husbands who were "gentleman born". Our options were limited: remaining in sanctuary, taking the veil or seizing the chance of offered freedom. My mother gambled that Richard was not in a position to risk the consequences of harming us. Neither Elizabeth nor Cecily were keen to be nuns.

So we emerged, like seven white ghosts, shaking the dust and damp from our skirts, raising our pale faces to the thin April sunshine, blinking like new-borns. Wonderingly, we retraced our footsteps back to the royal apartments at Westminster, where once we had lived. Elizabeth, Cecily and Anne were summoned by Queen Anne Neville and they were gone in a heartbeat, away to the north, to the court of the new king at Sheriff Hutton where they would join our orphaned Warwick cousins, Margaret and Edward Plantagenet, who also lived with our uncle.

What to do with the rest of us? Well, in a sense our captivity continued but in a fairly benign manner. My lady mother, Elyn, Joanna, myself and my silent little sister Bridget were loaded into a cushioned cart and trundled away with Sir John Nesfield to his new home at Heytesbury in Wiltshire. My mother grudgingly admitted that Sir John was a good man, even if King Richard had set him to watch our every move. I remember holding back the thick curtains to peep as we passed through villages, hearing the peal of church bells and feeling the living warmth of the little spaniel given to me as a new pet.

A memory surfaces of a grey stone manor house, where Spring sunlight floods through the small panes of mullioned windows on to honey-coloured wooden floors. Dank river smells are banished and instead there is a bubbling stream and sweet scents of beeswax and blossom, clean linen and baking bread. I wake naturally to birdsong, not the cold lapping of water or the harsh clang of the Abbey bell. The ancient landscape rolls away endlessly; sheep graze in the wide pastures and larks soar in the blue heaven. Sir John still watches us, but at a distance, benevolently, and pleasure replaces pity in his kind brown eyes, for what is there to watch? Two little girls, who run to see the lambs, the piglets and the calves, racing each other round the orchard, jumping over the pale Lenten lilies on pretend ponies, and a widow who simply sits quietly with her sewing and two attendants in the shade of the apple trees. Sir John does not know that she is thinking of two boys who should be riding too, on real royal ponies with tossing cream manes and swishing tails, wearing gold caparisons embroidered with suns of York. She never mentions them, though, so Bridget and I are silent too. At five years old I knew I once had two brothers but I did not know where they could have gone. And I never dared ask.

17

Elizabeth and her youngest daughters had only been at Heytesbury for a few weeks when a messenger galloped into the courtyard one morning, flung his reins at a servant and raced indoors to see Sir John.

Elizabeth was in the still room, last summer's dried lavender spread out in front of her, its heady, soporific fragrance rising from the table. The door was ajar and the first warm sunshine of the year formed a little pool on the flagstones. Elizabeth felt a huge relief in this new-found freedom, for although she was technically under house arrest Sir John administered it with a light touch. He had no wife, so had willingly agreed to her request to take charge of the still room with all its herbs.

Being Queen of England seemed another world now. There had been no point in not accepting Richard's terms; if her royal boys were dead then she had to live for her royal girls. She had to believe that the day would come when her fortunes would rise again. Meantime she would live the life of the lady of the manor in a quiet corner of Wiltshire. Years ago, as a girl on the Wydville manor at Grafton, she had learned all the lore about medicinal herbs in readiness for her life as John Grey's wife and a lifetime as mistress of Groby Manor. Well, she had ended up as Queen of England – a far cry from running a country estate, but now there was something soothing and in recalling and using her old skills. The days passed easily enough; there were even some nights now when she slept through. Yet still, when morning came and she surfaced to consciousness, her first thoughts were of her two royal sons and she tortured herself with images of how they might have met their end. To come into the still room, and move slowly amongst the bunches of dried plants hanging from the wooden pegs, inhaling their aromatic scents, was balm to her soul.

The door creaked as it opened fully and Sir John stood there with a grave face.

"Well, there is sad news indeed from Yorkshire, Dame Grey."

142

Her heart missed a beat. *Please God, not Bessy, or Cecily, or Anne!* But Sir John was talking of somebody else – some boy – *"The Prince of Wales". Who does he mean? My Edward has been dead these nine months by all acounts.*

"It's said the King and Queen are inconsolable," Sir John was saying sadly, "their only boy, gone so suddenly."

In a flash she understood. So the revenge she had wished upon her sons' murderer was coming good!

"They were at Nottingham when the news came from Middleham. They have gone mad with grief."

Elizabeth looked at him curiously. "What do you expect me to say? That I am sorry? I say he has got the first of what he deserves, and that there will be more to come! He took my sons and now God has taken his." She ran her hands through the lavender and a puff of its sweetness spiralled upwards. "I thank you for telling me, Sir John, but I will not be praying, merely rejoicing." His eyebrows shot up at the candour of her tone. "And that's not treason, by the way. It's called motherlove."

He could think of nothing to say to her, so bowed formally and left her. Elizabeth's mind raced through new possibilities. Without an immediate male heir what would Richard do? *Now he knows what it's like to lose nearly everything. People's thoughts will shift again ... Bessy will be thought of again...*

The summer of 1484 passed largely without incident. The only change was the departure of Sir John Nesfield, for Richard had ordered him back into the fleet. The poor man was captured by the French off Scarborough and held to ransom. Fortunately Richard paid swiftly and Sir John returned to Heytesbury with enough tales of seafaring and deck-fights to keep Katherine and Bridget totally entranced. He told them he was now appointed Esquire of the Body to the king in recognition of his good service and might expect a summons to join His Grace at any time.

Letters came fairly regularly from Bessy and Cecily, their happiness pouring off the page. Anne Neville had welcomed them warmly. Richard treated them with every courtesy. Their wardrobes were replenished. They hunted and hawked, danced and sang and received gratifying attention. The new queen was making sure that young Anne's education resumed; each morning she learned alongside her Warwick cousins. Bessy wrote of how well she liked young Margaret Plantagenet – *a sensible girl, Mama, and very fond of her little brother.* But with the death of Richard's heir the situation would have imploded up there. *It is rumoured that he will choose Edward of Warwick as his heir, but I do not see how that could be, Mama, for the child struggles to understand the simplest of lessons.* Then there was Bessy's most recent letter: *I have met my cousin of Suffolk, Mama, John de la Pole. He is handsome and kindly! Some say my uncle the king will choose him to be his heir. He is appointed leader of the Council of the North and now the king's lieutenant in Ireland. Be happy for us, Mama. We are living again.*

Katherine:

And in the following winter, my big sisters visited unexpectedly from the north, braving the frosty roads to be with us after Twelfth Night. I was shy at first, especially of Bessy who seemed a stranger – a grown woman, like my mother. She was tall, stately and fair and dressed in beautiful velvets and furs, given to her by our Uncle Richard the king, looking like a queen from a tapestry. When my Lady Mother exclaimed at the richness of her apparel she smiled nonchalantly and said that the King liked to see her dressed in the same manner as his wife.

It was a joyous reunion. Bessy and Elizabeth smiled at Sir John and, with blushes, asked for time to talk of women's matters. He bowed politely and left them to their fireside whispers. Cecily and Anne, together with Elyn and Joanna, scooped up Bridget and Katherine and took them outside to throw snowballs until Elizabeth opened the casement window and said they should come in before they froze. Then Cecily and Anne played chess in a corner; Bridget slept and Katherine leaned against her mother's knee and feigned sleepiness as the flames danced and flickered out of the logs and her cold toes thawed. Almost lost amid the crackles, she heard two soft voices in muted discussion. She stole a glance up and was surprised to see her mother's and sister's blue eyes dark and sparkling with excitement.

"She coughs blood," whispered Bessy.

"There is a chance for you," breathed Elizabeth, "in good time."

"There is no word from Brittany, Lady Mother. Nothing. Yet Richard would make me queen, I am sure of it." Bessy's voice was a caress upon the air. "He has ever loved me, since I was a little girl."

"Could you do it? Marry the man who had your brothers killed?"

"I told you, Mama, I will marry anyone who can make life better for all of us. Never again will I live in hiding. If I marry Richard and have children then my Yorkist grandfather's blood will rule England. I have thought long and hard. I think he must have ordered my brothers' deaths but in a way I can understand why. Oh, not accept it, Mama, never that, but I see why. Neither of your sons can ever be king now but if I can be a queen I can honour their memories in my heart." There was a brittle edge to Bessy's tone, "All that matters is that we all go forward now. In whatever way we can."

"You will be someone's queen," replied my mother, "I will make sure of it."

How many queens can there be, Katherine wondered.

In late March 1485, news came from London that Queen Anne had died. Warily, Sir John conveyed the information to Elizabeth, who composed her lips and said, "How sad. I shall pray for her soul." A week later another horse and rider galloped into the courtyard scattering the ducks. Another message from the capital: Uncle Richard had indeed found a *"gentleman born"* for Cecily. He was Ralph Scrope, a younger son of old Lord Scrope of Upsall and brother to the new lord who supported the king. Apparently the wedding had already taken place and Cecily sent to the Scrope family home in North Yorkshire. Katherine could see that her mother was furious with this *fait accompli* – she tore the letter into shreds, threw them to the ground and walked away, leaving them to be caught up in the easterly gusts and ferried back to London.

"He's done it so that no-one else shall have her!" Cecily, who might once have been Queen of Scotland, would have to settle for a minor English lord. Katherine wondered why Cecily should be married before Bessy; such niceties had always been very important between them, as between her and Bridget.

However, much can be learned in the kitchen, she discovered, in the summer when you are six-years-old and wish the escape from your nursemaid for an hour or so. You can hide under the great table, safe behind the willow baskets full of vegetables. It was best to be there just before noon, when the servants congregated to eat after a morning's hard work. They were hungry and thirsty, and lingered over their ale and food, inclined to gossip. Here she learned far more than she should, and understood far more than anyone imagined.

Fat Cook was carving slices from a giant ham. "'He's not likely to marry my lady Bessy now," she said confidently, and quite loudly in her strong Wiltshire voice, "not now people say as how Queen Anne were poisoned, God rest her soul.

However much he wants her, or she wants him, it's just disrespectful. And she's his niece, which can never be right."

"They do say Henry Tudor might still have her, though," mused Ralph, Sir John's steward. "If he comes, of course." Katherine knew him to be a fair-minded man because his bow to her was just slightly deeper than to Bridget. "He took that vow to marry her, and says as how he will honour it. Mind, they do say as how he would have had my lady Cecily if my lady Bessy were taken from under his nose. That's why *she's* been married off to one of the King's supporters, faster than fire. The others are too young to matter, bless them."

"He's ready – and he'll land in Wales, or Cornwall mebbe, or Devonshire, or Dorset even. Makes no difference to me what beach he chooses! I just want some peace at last." This third voice was that of Walter, the horseman, who taught Katherine to ride.

Beneath the table she inhaled the earthy scent of carrots and stroked their green fronds. She wondered whether Cecily had liked being married "faster than fire" to a man she did not know.

"Aye! Who cares who sits on the throne as long as there's no more battles," declared the cook, slapping ham onto trenchers," I lost my man years ago at Towton even though he fought wi' King Edward. Who wants those times again? Rivers running red with blood! Widows and orphans!"

"We shall have to have one last battle," said Ralph, reasonably, "to decide it once and for all. Happen King Richard will win and marry some foreign princess – there's talk of Portugal or Spain, and have a new family, and we'll all be to rights again. He'll find someone for Lady Bessy – maybe there's a nice Portuguese prince for her."

"Or the Tudor will win, and marry my lady Bessy, and that'll be an end to it too, thank God."

"Shame about them boys." Fat Cook's voice was tinged with regret "Shame she weren't rightly married to the old king. We would never have had all this trouble." She snorted with laughter. "And then I'd be cooking for a queen and two princesses, not a whore and her little bastards!"

She paused for a moment and Katherine heard a slurp of ale. "Mind you, if the King is thinking of sending her to Portugal, or if Tudor has her, as you say, Ralph, it must mean she is a princess again, surely?"

"Blessed if I can say," replied Ralph.

Katherine wondered what a whore could be. And what a bastard was. She made a mental note to ask Elyn about these interesting words. She wondered whether she would ever be a princess again. And where Cecily might be with her new husband. And whether she would ever see Bessy again.

And then, in the muggy heat of a dying July, Sir John was finally summoned to join Richard's army at Warwick, for news had come that the Tudor had set sail at last, bolstered by French money. It seemed that custody of Elizabeth Wydville and her little girls was overlooked for a few days. She seized the moment. One evening Katherine and Bridget waited dutifully in the little chapel, for their mother to join the household at compline, but instead a rather flustered Thomas came running from the stable.

"Dame Grey's palfrey is gone!"

Ralph Stephen rose from his knees in consternation. He had been left in charge until Sir John's replacement arrived. "What do you mean, gone?"

Walter made a helpless gesture with open palms. "The black mare is gone, and also the old bay."

Katherine stifled a giggle. Her mother was an accomplished rider, and Elyn was well-used to horses too. Now she understood what they had been whispering about for the last two days. From beneath her lashes she stole a look at the nursemaid Joanna who simply kept her eyes closed, her head bowed and her palms together in respectful prayer. Katherine did likewise. Ralph strode down the little aisle towards them, grabbed Joanna by the shoulder and yanked her up. "*Where* is Dame Grey, and the girl Elyn?"

Joanna maintained a brave and convincing innocence. "I know not, sir. I saw them last this morning and Her Gra – Dame Grey bade me spend the day with the children. I took them for a walk, and they played by the stream. I am sorry, sir, if I did wrong. I made sure they were clean and tidy for prayers."

The steward gave a shout of frustration. Pushing Joanna aside, he leaned over and seized Katherine, pulling her off the bench and into the aisle. Bridget burst into tears but Katherine rubbed the top of her arm and met the steward's tight-lipped fury with candour.

"Do *you* know where your Lady Mother has gone?"

"No," said Katherine truthfully, but added helpfully, "but she rides fast and will be miles away by now." She noted the changing complexion of the steward's face, from its usual sallowness through a sudden florid flush that threatened towards purple. "I hope you won't get into trouble, Ralph," she said primly, "for losing my Lady Mother."

18

Katherine

Eventually, the shadowy myth that was Tudor came out of Brittany like an avenging, snorting dragon. Learning of my sister Cecily's marriage to one of Richard's household knights, and hearing whispered rumours that Richard might actually marry my sister Bessy, he was finally galvanised into action. He landed at Mill Bay, near Pembroke, with his rag, tag and bobtail of a French army, and prostrated himself upon the sand, declaring that God should judge him by his actions. He rode through the Tudor heartlands of West Wales, gathering Welsh soldiers, and passed through the gateway to England, Shrewsbury. Finally, he collided with my uncle's army in Leicestershire, at a place they called Redemore Field, not far from Stoke Golding. In two hours of a summer's morning the fate of my country, and my family, changed forever.

"Let me say the truth to his credit: that he (King Richard) **bore himself like a gallant knight ... honourably defended himself to his last breath ..."** John Rous

"And as for me, let me assure you this day I will triumph by victory or suffer death for immortal fame." King Richard III, before the Battle of Bosworth Field (Chronicle of England, Rawlinson)

2Ist August 1485

Richard Plantagenet, King of England agreed with William Stephens, the steward of Heytesbury: there had to be one last decisive battle before England could finally face a future of peace. He was resigned to it, as if he had always known that like his father and brother he would have to fight for his right to the crown. Simply removing his nephews was not enough. It was as if he had lived with the spectre of the pretender Henry Tudor wavering just beyond his sightlines for years. Yet he also knew that this was not exactly true. The idea of Tudor as a real, flesh and blood enemy was really only of two years' standing. So much had happened in two years. Two years since he had shared with Buckingham what must happen to the royal boys; nearly two years since he had stood next to Anne and his own Edward on that lovely evening in York, when the warm northern voices had roared their approval. Just one heady evening when he had allowed himself to think that it might all be his, and his son's.

When he thought of Edward and Anne he felt numb, then some dreadful wave of emotion threatened to unman him. He prayed for their souls, telling himself that they were surely with God now for all eternity yet could not rid his mind of the horror of their passing. Edward, burned up by fever and Anne wasted away to nothing – a paper-thin creature whom they would not let him visit in her final days for fear that he might catch her disease. *And they say I poisoned her!* His dreams were unbearable; his son and wife appeared, reaching out imploring hands, mouthing silent reproaches, then turning from him and fading into gaping black holes. For a few mad days he had wondered if Bessy's kind spirit might fill the void but his advisors were horrified beyond words. *Marry your niece, Your Grace? It is forbidden! It is evil! Incestuous!* But he had known that she would have said yes. Her motives were less easy to fathom – the strangest mixture of revenge for her brothers and pity for him that he should ever have been driven to such a decision. He knew that Bessy knew. Which meant that Cecily knew too. But both young women had seemed driven by some extraordinary force which overrode their hatred and sorrow – a simple desire to live. With Bessy, some kind of goodness might have eventually risen above the evil. But it was not to be and if he died tomorrow Tudor would make Bessy his queen because she was his passport to acceptance.

A summer evening breeze stirred the bright blue, red and gold of the colours of England raised above Richard's campaign tent. They had marched from Leicester, through the villages of Sutton Cheney and Market Bosworth, finally making camp here at Ambion Hill near the marshy plainland between Dadlington and Stoke Golding. Loyal men, led by those who had kept faith: his nephew John of Lincoln; Lord Howard of Norfolk; Shrewsbury, Kent and Westmoreland; Francis Lovell – lords and knights prepared to die for him. Others he was less sure of – Northumberland, for instance, had brought his army but was keeping his distance.

The camp was alive with the sounds of nearly fifteen thousand men readying themselves for battle at dawn: cannons dragged creaking through the moist soil; men cursing the weight of the stone missiles that would pulverise the Tudor dragon's flesh; the *swish swish of* sharpening of swords, halberds and pikes; the clink of oiled chain mail as squires burnished their master's armour one last time. Darkness fell and the warhorses chomped, snorted and shifted uneasily in the ranks, pawing the ground with their huge hooves, sensing some strange, palpable emotion midway between terror and excitement.

It was utterly impossible to sleep. Richard had tried, stretching out on his camp bed, in his shirt, telling himself sternly that a tired commander was of no use to his army. Always, he had been able to sleep before a battle – a few snatched hours to refresh mind and muscles but tonight his brain refused to co-operate. It was the same with food; they had brought him food and wine but although he chewed the meat he could not swallow and ended up spitting it out. The wine alone stayed down.

In the small hours he stood in the doorway of the tent gazing at the inky skies, at the moon and stars playing hide and seek behind the swirling clouds. Away to the northwest, faint glows and pinpricks of light signalled where Henry Tudor was camped with the old Lancastrian Lord de Vere of Oxford and his mongrel army of French mercenaries and Welsh misfits. Richard wondered just how many English lords and knights had chosen to stay on their estates and have nothing to do with this final settlement of scores between York and Lancaster. And what about the Stanleys? Where, in God's name, had the artful husband of Margaret Beaufort, and his equally wily brother, placed themselves? There was no sign of them and their six thousand men in the main camp. However, Richard had Lord Stanley's heir, twenty-three-year-old George, Lord Strange, captive in the camp – hostage for his father's loyalty. *Christ,* thought Richard, *the man is recently married to a Wydville bitch. How can I trust these people?*

There was a tramp of boots nearby and a swinging lantern. Two figures loomed out of the darkness, a man and a youth, and Richard recognised the familiar form of Francis Lovell. Lovell, whose love and loyalty were almost painful to bear. Lovell, who had indeed gone to Brittany, played the diplomat (or spy, depending how you saw it) and almost been successful in persuading the ageing Duke to hand Tudor over, but the Dragon had slipped away into France

151

where he had begun to call himself King of England and assemble his army. Richard peered into the light of the lantern and suddenly saw his own features reflected.

"Your Grace," Lovell bowed. "I have brought your son to you, as you wished."

"Well, my John, my Captain of Calais!"

The slender boy at Lovell's side sank to his knees in front of Richard. The soft, weak light gleamed for an instant upon a neat head of raven-black hair and then a face of porcelain fairness, with high cheekbones and peat-brown eyes. A proper Yorkist boy, not some blond Wydville hybrid. A healthy boy who never coughed, or complained of stomach gripes, or toothache – a boy who had spent his childhood simply growing towards manhood, steadily and thoughtfully. He was so nearly there, but not quite. Richard gazed upon his illegitimate son, John of Pontefract, and could have wept for the irony of life. The boy's mother was now but a hazy memory; Richard had not seen or heard of her in sixteen years but her name was Katherine, and she had been as soft as lambswool in his own teenage arms in Pontefract Castle all those years ago. For that reason he had always harboured a sentimental liking for the name and bestowed it upon the other accidental product of his passionate youth, his bastard daughter. And suddenly he thought of his brother's child, another little Katherine Plantagenet, who had held his gaze so steadily with same brown eyes that Christmas two and a half years ago. *Where was she now? Ah, Heytesbury, Bessy had said. And where was Bessy? Safe in Yorkshire – hidden from Tudor.*

Richard motioned the two men dearest to his heart inside the tent. The interior was lit by a couple of candles and shadows danced on the curved sides. Thick druggets covered the ground. His body armour for tomorrow hung on a pole and on a table sat the helm he would wear, a golden circlet sitting firmly on its rim. John stared at it in astonishment and dismay.

"You surely do not intend to fight marked out as king, Father?"

Richard placed an arm around his shoulders. The lad was seventeen and exactly the same height. "I have nothing to hide. Those who fight for me must know me and see me leading them."

"But *they* will know you, too!"

"Aye, and be afraid, when they see that England already has a rightful king."

"But most kings go into battle with decoys, Father. "

"Not this king."

John turned appealing, mournful eyes upon Lovell. "Tell my father not to, my lord. He will listen to you."

Lovell smiled. "Your father is right. It is all, or nothing tomorrow. But fear not, John, it will be *all,* for God will be with us, as he has been at all the battles we have ever fought in."

"Then let me fight, too, I am old enough. You were my age when you led the vanguard at Barnet. You told me!"

Richard hugged him fiercely and kissed his cheek. "I had more training than you. I knew what I was doing. If there was one thing that Warwick did well it was in teaching us to be fighters, eh Lovell?"

"I have skills, Father!" declared the lad indignantly, "I have trained long and hard, too."

Richard sighed. "John, you know I would love nothing better than to have my son at my side but your sight is not keen, and beneath a helm you would be almost blind. Besides which, I know you fell from your horse less than a week ago and your left leg stills pains you. I will not risk it."

"Is that why you sent for me? To tell me I cannot fight for you?" The young man was almost in tears.

Richard fought back his own emotions. "I wanted to see you before the battle. You have always brought me luck, John! Do you remember when you were a small boy at Middleham and they brought me three new destriers to choose from, and you picked out White Surrey because –"

"Because he took the apple from my hand without biting me – and I said you needed a well-mannered horse, as well as a brave one."

"And you were right. White Surrey has carried me well these past six years. He will do the same tomorrow. I want you to leave now and return to Sheriff Hutton, where your cousin, Lady Bessy, waits. Look after her, John, until good news comes. Take my blessing and be my talisman."

His final words were unwavering and clearly dismissive. Lord Lovell moved to the doorway and held back the heavy drape, ready for John to pass through but the boy knelt again, openly weeping.

"I wish I had been born your true son, Father."

For years Richard had quelled such an idea but the truth was hard to resist at such a moment. "Ah, God, John, so do I."

"Will you take this, Father, and wear it close to your heart tomorrow? For luck?" John fumbled in his sleeve and withdrew what looked like a small piece of greenery. Then Richard saw the unmistakable yolk-yellow flowerheads of gorse, the *planta genista* of his family. Wordlessly, he reached out and took it between finger and thumb, carefully avoiding the sharp thorns.

When his son had gone he laid the sprig next to the helm with its golden crown. For luck.

19

"The day is ours, the bloody dog is dead." (Earl of Richmond, afterwards King Henry VII. *"Richard III"* by William Shakespeare

"And moreover, the king informeth you that Richard Duke of Gloucester, lately called King Richard, was slain at a place called Sandeford and there was laid openly that every man might see and look upon him." Circular letter of King Henry VII after the Battle of Bosworth Field, preserved in the archives of the city of York.

Katherine

As I grew up, the stories of that morning at Redemore Field became part of my consciousness. There were so many different versions, depending upon who told the tale. By all accounts it was a most savage battle. Whatever men said of Richard Plantagenet – murderer of princes, wife-poisoner – none could deny his bravery as he threw his destiny into the hands of God. They say he galloped towards Henry Tudor, knocked down Sir John Cheney, the tallest soldier living; killed the Tudor's standard bearer and came within feet of the Pretender himself. Oh, how different my life, my sisters' lives, might have been if, at that moment, luck had been on his side.

Up on the hillside was the Stanley army. I do not believe the Stanley brothers ever had the slightest intention of declaring for the Yorkist king. Old grudges run deep, and William Stanley hated the way the families of the Northwest had gradually come to see Richard Plantagenet as their lord. What's more, the men who surrounded my uncle on that field of battle were those who had benefited so much from his kingship – who had received offices previously held by the Stanleys. Little wonder then, that when Stanley finally moved his men down that fateful slope it was to end that situation and restore his family to power. My uncle the king lost his helm and was hacked to death by their halberds. Again and again blows were rained down upon his bare head before he was dragged from his horse and disappeared under their swords, axes, daggers and bills.

And so my family's hold upon the throne of England came to an end. I often wonder what King Richard's final thoughts must have been. Did he even have time to think, in that melee of flashing steel and spraying blood? Did he think of my brothers, or his own brothers, or his dead wife, or his son, or his own father, or my sister Bessy? Or were his thoughts only of the need to extinguish the fire of the Red Dragon who threatened to consume his kingdom? I remember a man with the darkest of hair which fell like a blackbird's two wings either side of his pensive, sensitive face. I remember my father's joy in his company. I remember that he had a daughter with my name. I remember him lacing my shoe. I remember them telling me that he had murdered my brothers.

It was all over within two hours. Before mid-morning England had a new king. Henry Tudor watched impassively as the Stanley men stripped Richard Plantagenet of his armour. As they hauled off the linen undershirt and padded gambeson, a handful of little trinkets and pieces of cloth fell in the mud: a silken white rose; a small silver badge of a white boar; a tiny golden crucifix on a thin chain, and a sprig of gorse, still fresh and bright. A soldier cried out with glee and scooped up the metal talismens but trod the fabric rose and piece of gorse into the soil. They dragged off the linen braies and then slung the naked body over the back of a mule. Tudor made no comment as the creature moved slowly off the field and Welsh and Breton men at arms came forward to stab at the bobbing, bony, bare buttocks. He heard the sickening crack as Richard's pelvis broke under a sudden, savage onslaught from a heavy pikestaff.

"We have found the crown!" A shout of triumph from somewhere and Thomas Stanley was brandishing something slender and gold, then holding it aloft before he placed it upon Tudor's head. It was slightly dented. The soldiers cheered wildly, "God Save King Henry!"

"Where shall we take the body, Your Grace?" asked William Stanley.

Henry Tudor pursed his thin lips and looked as though he had never been less interested in anything in his life. He surveyed the flat marshlands and distant horizon. He raised his right hand to settle the circlet more snugly on his head. It rested on his temples.

"Il y a une église près d'ici?" he asked finally. French came more easily to him than English. He thought and dreamed in French.

"There is a Franciscan abbey in Leicester, Sire."

"Bien. Les frères peuvront trouver une tombe par là pour lui."

The Tudor had hardly broken sweat. His war horse had not even one speck of mud on his caparison. He gave orders that they should all repair to Leicester so that the citizens should see with their own eyes the dead, defeated king and the new, victorious one. Within an hour or so the thousand or so Yorkist corpses on the battlefield had been stripped of their valuables by oafish Breton mercenaries and the living prisoners rounded up and roped together. Some groaned with pain; others offered silent, unyielding hostility. The air was rank with the metallic stench of blood and large flies were already settling on the raw wounds of the fallen horses and men. As Henry Tudor gathered up his reins he saw where Richard's standard lay trampled in the wet ground, the golden leopards of England flattened and the fleur de lyses imprinted with great hoof marks. He motioned that it should be picked up. Like the crown, it was his now.

He entered Leicester in the afternoon. When the citizens saw the battered corpse of the king, and ranks of blank-eyed prisoners, they knew which way the wind was blowing and welcomed the five thousand Welsh and Breton soldiers without question. That night, and the next, the taverns and the brothels were filled with their strange accents, incomprehensible to the Midlanders who simply took their coin and hoped to be rid of them as soon as possible. After all, what did it matter who was king?

As it passed over Bow Bridge the exhausted mule had stumbled and almost fallen against the stone walls. Richard's head, with its felon's rope around the neck, had swung like a cow's full udder against the parapet. Then he had been pulled off the animal and left for several hours lying in the market place under a proclamation that Henry Tudor was now king, seventh of that name, and that his reign was dated from the day before the battle, so that all who had fought against him were traitors. Scores of drunk, raucous townsmen emulated the soldiers in spitting and urinating over the pale flesh. At dawn, the Abbot sent two brothers to recover the poor corpse; they pulled their cowls close to hide their horror at the state of it. There were no further instructions so they took it to the Abbey's infirmary where it was sponged of its clotted blood and mire, and wrapped in a monk's shroud before being laid in a hastily dug grave in the choir of their church. The Abbot, who was a Yorkshireman, defiantly set candles and ordered a

Requiem Mass. In the morning Henry Tudor set out for London. On September 3rd he made a triumphal entrance into the capital and gave thanks to God for his glorious victory at St Paul's Cathedral.

20

Katherine

When Henry Tudor seized the throne he had already decided to create a new dynasty. The name Plantagenet became a filthy word, a token to be cast away on the midden. We were afraid to even utter it. He kept his promise to marry my sister, Bessy; she and my mother chose cynical realism. Margaret Beaufort too. She saw it as the only way of securing her son's tenuous hold on the throne. The fact was that Bessy was the true queen regnant, her father, brothers and uncles all being dead – and the whole of England knew it, but Henry Tudor stamped all over this truth with his warhorses and obliterated it with his battle standards.

The narrow-eyed man controlled us all for the next twenty four years, breathing his vile dragon breath across my life. And always at his side, always watching me, my sisters and my mother was **his** *mother. At Sheriff Hutton, with all King Richard's followers defeated or, like Francis Lovell, fled into obscurity, Bessy found herself in new company: Margaret Beaufort arrived to keep her son's future wife under her thumb, and whilst he made himself at home in our capital she brought Bessy south.*

When Elizabeth had arrived at the palace of Sheen, the lovely royal residence granted to her by her husband in years gone by, it was entirely empty of Richard's followers and still staffed by servants who had once been hers. She settled herself back into her old rooms to wait. It was a gamble, but whether Richard Plantagenet or Henry Tudor was to prove the victor, she judged that her days as an exile were over.

News of the battle and its aftermath came swiftly. Elizabeth could not contain her excitement and looked daily for the summons nine miles upstream to Westminster. In Wiltshire, her youngest daughters were told that their Uncle

Richard was dead and that their sister Bessy would now marry the new king and become their queen. It seemed the wheel of fortune had finally turned again. Elizabeth sent messages to Heytesbury that the little girls must be drilled in manners and etiquette – the importance of keeping their eyes downcast until spoken to. She fussed at the memory of the state of their few gowns and sent urgent messages to Lady Margaret Beaufort that she and all her daughters would need clothing from the Royal Wardrobe. News came that Bessy and Lady Margaret were travelling south, and with them were the Warwick children, Ned and Meg, and Cecily, apparently liberated from the Scrope castle at Upsall.

"Imagine!" Katherine said to Bridget, as they meandered in the orchard at Heytesbury, on a warm September afternoon, selecting windfalls to take to Fat Cook. "He has never been to London before! He has never even seen Westminster!"

She did not always expect a response, for much of the time Bridget seemed to inhabit her own private world. She understood everything around her but rarely spoke to anyone except Katherine. She liked order, and hated loud noises; she often seemed unwilling to look at people directly but preferred to gaze into the distance, a faraway look in her eyes.

Now she picked up a large apple up from the lush grass and inspected it a close quarters. "He won't be much of a king, then, will he? Our father knew everything, and everyone – and everywhere."

Katherine pretended not to be amazed that her little sister had said so much. She merely nodded. They had few memories of their father and were somewhat confused as to whether *Our Father, who Art in Heaven* might be him, although the Heytesbury priest had looked pained when Katherine asked him.

They collected more apples, making a lovely pile in the basket. Katherine pondered on Bridget's truth.

"Well, our sister will have to teach him then. *She* knows how to be a queen. *She* knows Westminster – every nook and cranny, I should think. She can tell him where the offices are, and the Wardrobe, and the jewels."

"He won't like that," observed Bridget sagely. "Men don't like being told things by women." She did not speak again that day.

They never got to taste the apples they had picked, for the next day a horse-drawn litter bearing Yorkist arms arrived to take them back to London. They passed again through the hamlets, villages and small towns that had last seen them eighteen months before. Now aged six, Katherine took more notice. Joanna pointed out the mysterious henge on the Great Plain, its inscrutable stones standing sentinel and casting long shadows in the evening sunlight. They trundled on, leaving Wiltshire behind, through the woods and villages of Hampshire and into Surrey, staying at manors and monasteries where all the talk was of the new King Henry Tudor. Men and women stood in the fields as they passed by, curious to see the daughters of the old King Edward; they leaned upon their hoes, or called their oxen to a halt, shaded their eyes with their hands and watched. Katherine and Bridget waved enthusiastically. Occasionally some woman would approach, bow low and present a basket of fruit from her orchard. Once, a baker stopped them and pressed good manchet loaves into their hands.

They passed through the little town of Basingstoke on market day, following all the carts laden with cloth. Word spread quickly about important travellers in the wagon painted with the sun of York and as they halted outside the church of St Michael to water the two horses a little group of nervous civic dignitaries was already waiting. The two male attendants sent by their mother to keep them safe on the road drew up alongside; one lifted the leather flap and peered in. "The townsfolk wish to welcome you."

Joanna pulled a face. The journey was tedious, the roads bumpy and her head ached. Bridget was having a silent day; the travelling upset her.

Katherine smiled at him. "I will greet them, sir. Help me down."

Steps were brought and Katherine was handed out of the wagon. If the good folk of Basingstoke were surprised at the sight of a six-year-old girl they hid it well. Katherine beamed upon them.

"I am Katherine Plantagenet of York, daughter to King Edward and sister to Princess Elizabeth!" Her young, high voice rang out like a silvery bell. "I thank you for welcoming me and my sister Bridget to your town of ..." her voice faltered for a few seconds but the man at arms saved the day and coughed behind his sleeve. "... your lovely town of Basingstoke!" declared Katherine triumphantly. She was sure neither Bessy nor Cecily could have done it any better. "And how delightful to meet you all," she added for good measure, remembering the phrase her mother had often used. "We are going home to London," Katherine told them, now well into her stride, "because my sister Elizabeth is going to marry the new king. The fighting is over and I am sure we will all be safe now. And I think I am a princess again."

Basingstoke had not seen a princess before but its residents were clearly delighted with their good fortune. She was small, it was true, and not dressed like a princess, but she was graceful, pretty and charming. They were enchanted. In the south, support for old King Edward and his poor young sons was strong; some men from the town had ridden out in the rebellion a year ago. King Richard was dead now and their own Princess Bessy would be their queen.

"God save the Princess Katherine!" yelled an enthusiastic voice at the back, taken up by all the group. Shouts of approval and appreciation hovered in the warm September air.

Finally they came into the valley of the Thames, and along the ancient, straight road to Egham and Staines, where a smart barge awaited them. It was not flying the royal standard, and the oarsmen wore no definable livery, but was nevertheless a fine vessel. On a fresh morning in mid-September they were rowed on the final leg of their journey, downstream towards the city. Katherine and Bridget refused to sit undercover; the stiff breeze brought roses to their cheeks and droplets of water from the fast-sculling oars flew through the air to land on hands, lips and eyelids. Katherine screamed with laughter, and even Bridget smiled, and the indulgent oarsmen rowed even more enthusiastically, responding to their passengers' joy. The barge left a rippling wake that spread to the banks. After a time the river widened considerably; the oarsmen could feel the ebbing tide and their facial muscles relaxed.

They began to see wharves, interesting boats, and great cranes reaching up into the sky. Katherine could never remember feeling so excited. They passed by Westminster Palace and saw the dark bulk of the Abbey behind it. Joanna told her there was nothing to fear anymore. No-one would ever force them back behind the walls of sanctuary. Then the great river bent to the right. On the north bank stood the lovely homes of England's richest noblemen, with gardens and orchards stretching down to the riverbank and private jetties.

At last they passed the Blackfriars Monastery and the oarsmen began to steer the barge towards the bank. They had reached their destination: Coldharbour, the new home of the new king's mother, Lady Margaret Beaufort. It had been home to many over the years, including royalty, and lately the Royal College of Heralds, but Henry Tudor cancelled their grant to make sure his mother had a London home to suit her new status. Another small barge was moored at the jetty, flying a small but unmistakable Wydville pennant.

Katherine was handed out by a burly oarsman to a servant in Stanley livery who set her down gently on the landing stage. Her legs felt suddenly wobbly after several hours spent on the river. She realised she was ravenous, too. Then she looked up the path that led through the gardens up to the great house itself and saw four familiar forms walking quickly towards her. Within seconds she was in her sisters' arms – a tangle of sleeves, and tears of relief and joy. Bridget had disembarked too and was flying to her mother's embrace, and the six of them were laughing and crying all at once.

"I am just arrived, too," said Elizabeth.

Bessy took her youngest sisters each by the hand. "We have such things to show you!"

"And such people," said Cecily.

"Where have you been all this time, Cecily? Where is your husband?" asked Katherine, then wished she had never said anything, for Cecily's bright eyes brimmed with sudden tears. She caught an anxious glance between her mother and eldest sister.

"You are to go straight to the Great Hall, to Lady Margaret," said Bessy, and added wryly, "Cecily, Anne and I have learned to do exactly what she says, and when she says it. And Mama, she has a new title. We no longer address her as Lady Stanley, but as My Lady, the King's Mother. You had best practise it on the way." Elizabeth's finely plucked brows rose a little higher.

They walked up along the gravel paths through the alleys of late roses towards the stately mansion, its red brick chimneys and turrets standing out against the blue sky. Katherine heard the bells of city churches beginning to strike the hour of None.

Cecily was agitated. "Oh dear, you were late. We shall have to wait now, while Lady Margaret attends her devotions."

Fortunately, the waiting offered scope for Elizabeth and her youngest to tidy themselves, then they were conducted into the Great Hall where Margaret Beaufort, Lady Stanley, awaited them, seated on a carved stool on the dais. She rose as they entered, a small, bird-like woman dressed in black, like a nun. She was younger than Elizabeth but looked older, as if time and anxiety had shrunk her. Little more than a child when she gave birth to her son, her life had been devoted to the Lancastrian cause whilst paying lip service to the Yorkists. She had inveigled her way into Edward IV's favour, even carrying Bridget to the font for her christening. Now she stood in triumph over them all. Anne, Katherine and Bridget had no memory of her but to Bessy and Cecily she had been a familiar figure at court.

Well, thought Elizabeth, *indeed the tide of fate ebbs and flows for us all. Once, this creature carried my train at my coronation; now she sits in judgement over our futures.*

There was a moment of fine interest as Elizabeth Wydville and Margaret Beaufort gauged who would incline her head first. For a horrible moment Bessy thought both would stay bolt upright. It seemed each was affixed to some sort of invisible ramrod. Elizabeth Wydville held out till the very last second; after all, she was an anointed queen and Margaret Beaufort simply the daughter of a duke who had died in ignominy. But then a thought flashed through her brain – this was the woman whose idea it had been to marry Bessy to her son, and in doing so save them all from obscurity. There would be a life for all of them at court and who knows what road it might lead them back towards...

"Lady Margaret." Elizabeth bobbed the tiniest of acknowledgements. Perhaps it was only her nose that dipped forwards, but it was enough.

"Lady Elizabeth."

So not Your Grace, but then not Dame Grey either.

They stepped forward and exchanged a cool kiss of welcome. Margaret Beaufort did not relinquish her place on the dais; the extra inches brought her level with Elizabeth's height,

"I have had the pleasure of your elder daughters' company these last few weeks. My son, the King, has now commanded all your daughters into my keeping and guiding, as well as their Clarence cousins."

Katherine was listening hard to this conversation. *Commanded into Lady Margaret's keeping and guiding?* She tried very hard to keep her eyes on the floor, as her mother had instructed, but two years of fearfulness got the better of her.

"Mama, I don't want to – *ow!*" Cecily had trodden hard upon her foot, crushing her toes.

"I trust your son is well?"

"My son, the King, is in excellent health."

"And he resides at –?"

"Baynard's Castle." The way in which she said the name implied that all Yorkist homes were now Tudor residences.

"And he will visit my daughter Bessy soon?"

"You may depend upon it. In the meantime we shall be a bustling household, Lady Elizabeth. They shall have tutors, and plenty to occupy themselves." She turned a gimlet eye upon her charges. "You will have comforts and respect as befits your station but I keep a pious house."

Katherine opened her mouth then shut it again. Her left foot would be bruised tomorrow.

21

"**O, now let Richmond and Elizabeth,**
The true successors of each royal household,
By God's fair ordinance conjoin together." (William Shakespeare, "Richard III*")*

Katherine: *Whatever my sister Bessy truly felt about her new situation she kept it hidden. Providing for the future of her remaining family seemed to be her lodestar.*

Henry Tudor arranged to visit privately, meeting Bessy in the presence of their two mothers. It seemed to the eighteen-year-old that she was playing a role in some existence outside her own body, watching herself performing the essential daily functions of waking, washing, dressing, praying, eating and sleeping. Sometimes she observed herself talking with Lady Margaret, and heard a quiet voice agreeing that she looked forward to meeting her saviour, the man from Brittany. Then she witnessed snatched, secret conversations with her mother, and heard the same composed voice agreeing that all her endeavour should be for the moment when the crown would be placed on her head.

After the maids had taken away the cooling bath water, Elizabeth and Cecily helped her to dress, while Anne, Katherine and Bridget sprawled on her bed eagerly picking through a box of jewellery like a trio of bright-eyed magpies. Bessy smiled faintly as they held up various chains and rings, draping and adorning themselves as only small girls can. The box had been found at the bottom of an old chest in the room allocated to her. She returned to watching her reflection in the polished metal mirror that occasionally flashed with sunlight as the ivory comb moved through her thick, strawberry-blonde hair. Elizabeth said she should leave it loose, as a mark of her purity; if the Tudor had any doubts they must be swept away in this first encounter. *What had he heard about*

Richard? Would he believe the stories that she might have become his queen? Would he think she had encouraged such an idea? She held out her arms as Cecily laced her sleeves and then dipped her head to receive Katherine's offering of a collar worked with tiny enamelled daisies.

"It's pretty, Katherine. Thank you."

"I found it at the bottom of the box."

Elizabeth peered at the intricate design. "Ah, daisies – marguerites. This house once belonged to the Lancastrian queen, Marguerite of Anjou. She must have left the casket behind here when she fled north. Yes, wear it, Bessy. It may please him to see some symbol of his own house."

"How adept we are," said Cecily dryly, "at changing our allegiances. Mama, you were once the wife of a Lancastrian knight and ended up a Yorkist queen. Bessy was born a York princess and will become a Lancastrian queen. We ought to laugh, really."

"A *Tudor* queen," said Elizabeth.

"What happened to your husband, Cecily?" Still no-one had provided Katherine with a satisfactory answer to such a burning question. For a moment she thought Cecily was about to slap her – but Bessy's hand came up swiftly to catch Cecily's swinging arm.

"Did you like him?" persisted Katherine.

"I did not know him long enough to tell. I met him once. On the day they made me marry him. I cannot even remember what he looked like."

"Where is he now? "

"How should I know?"

Elizabeth put a warning hand on Katherine's shoulder. "No more questions. It upsets Cecily." All knew that her young husband had found himself on the losing side at Bosworth. Cecily was bewildered yet furious. Her wedding ring was stripped from her finger and she was no longer my Lady Scrope. Like any princess, a pawn to be used in the game of political expediency. Elizabeth Wydville had assessed her daughter's figure with anxious eyes but Cecily had remained as slender as a willow wand and Ralph Scrope was never mentioned again.

Lady Margaret arrived, puffed up with excitement and self-importance, and conducted Bessy and her mother to the solar, the room behind the Great Hall where generations of women, merchants' wives and daughters, as well as princesses and queens, had passed hours in sitting, conversing and sewing. It was strange to find a man in such a feminine room. Bessy registered his tall height and spare build. He was nothing like her father, nothing like her uncle. He was neither dark nor fair but a nondescript, lightish brown; his thin hair fell either side of a sallow face, and a pair of narrow, pale blue-grey eyes regarded her shrewdly. She spread her skirts in a deep curtsey and felt his dry hands cover hers, then the brush of dry lips on her forehead. She was aware of the wide, elm floorboards and saw how dust had settled on them. No-one had thought to sweep the solar for this momentous meeting of York and Lancaster.

He did not raise her, but dropped her hands, leaving her on her knees. He was speaking, but not to her – to his mother. His accent was strange – English, but with a pronounced rough Breton edge, the French of soldiers and artisans. Bessy had always known that this day would come, when she would stand before her future bridegroom for appraisal, and she was not afraid, but in her thoughts the meeting would be in some palace, with an audience of delighted diplomats, and with her hand tucked safely into the great padded sleeve of her father. There should have been fine wine, and sweetmeats, with feasting and dancing to follow, before a long ceremony in some exquisite cathedral. Her parents had always said some of her family would travel with her to her new country, to see her happily and safely settled. But her father lay rotting in Windsor; her uncle lay rotting in Leicester. Her brothers lay … somewhere. Elizabeth Wydville was in the room, but seated quietly somewhere behind her.

"My son, the King, is pleased to note that she is comely in appearance, and that it looks as if she will find child-bearing no particular problem."

Elizabeth rose and also curtsied before this son-in-law to be. "I have borne ten children, sir, and my own mother fourteen. Bessy will be no different. She understands her duty."

My duty to my father. To my dead brothers and my living sisters. To my York heritage. Not to you.

The King spoke again and Bessy strained to follow his curious voice. What was he saying? That he was most eager to honour his vow to marry her but that affairs of state must come first; there was much to do to settle the country after the upheaval of the summer months. The people were exhausted, traumatised. There must be a coronation as soon as possible; Parliament must meet and his household set in order before he could think of welcoming a wife to Westminster. And of course, there was dispensation to secure from His Holiness, for were they not cousins in the fourth degree? In the meantime he would visit her often – they would dine together here at Coldharbour and she might come with his dear Lady Mother to Woking, where he would be staying in the forthcoming weeks. He would be delighted to send her material and furs against the refurbishment of her winter wardrobe. She should say what colours she preferred. And in due course, if Parliament agreed, her family might use their titles again: *the Dowager Queen; the Princess Elizabeth; the Princess Cecily ... and whatever the younger ones were called.*

Bessy still kept her eyes firmly fixed upon the floorboards through all this. He was making things crystal clear: there would be no immediate joint coronation but the trade-off was that she and her sisters would be restored to legitimacy. *Well, of course, Henry Tudor, for how else can you bring yourself to marry me?*

And now he *was* raising her to her feet, and kissing both her cheeks. Kisses of cordiality and respect. Lady Margaret was pink with pleasure. The tips of his fingers brushed against the enamelled collar and his left eyebrow arched quizzically. He took Elizabeth's hand and held it against his lips for a fleeting second. Then he was gone with his mother, treading lightly down the spiral staircase to the Great Hall, out into the courtyard, through the archway, down the path through the rose garden to the jetty where the royal barge waited to row him back a few hundred yards upstream to Baynard's Castle. Bessy realised she had not actually spoken a single word to him. Could she ever learn to love him as a man?

Katherine: *A month later he had himself crowned in our Abbey in a lavish ceremony. They say his mother wept with happiness. But not all the extravagance, pomp and proclamations in the world could make people really believe in him as king, much less his claim to have been placed on our throne by "divine aid". He was no obvious heir; just someone in the right place, at the right time. It was insulting to my sister that he did not require her presence at his coronation. Rather, he deliberately excluded her and so avoided any suggestion of a joint monarchy. He would not have it said that he ruled in her right. My sister Bessy made no comment. She had a stillness, a madonna-like beauty that captivated men and women alike. We worshipped her. She was our princess of York, to be translated into our queen by tragedy, circumstance and pragmatism. However, Henry Tudor made sure that he emerged alone from the great west door of the Abbey to walk across to the feast in Westminster Hall.*

The Act that had made me and my sisters bastards was repealed and it was ordered that all copies should be burned. Much to my mother's relief, the stories of my father's dalliance with Eleanor Butler began to sink into obscurity. There was no-one left in England with any will or reason to revive such rumours. Those who had supported my Uncle Richard had either disappeared like Francis Lovell or were imprisoned, like his bastard son, John. Some made the decision to stay, declare their new loyalty and survive. Such a one was my cousin John de la Pole. If there were mutterings across Europe we did not hear them.

My mother revelled in the restoration of her dignity, pre-eminence and name. And absolutely no-one spoke of my dead brothers. It was as if they had never existed. Sometimes I wondered if it had all been a dream: had we really lived all those months in the rooms in sanctuary? It was as if I must date my real life from when the Dragon triumphed on that marshy plain in Leicestershire.

However, it was another three months before he remembered his vow in Rennes and married my sister. He had to be reminded by the Lords Spiritual and Temporal that such a union would end the mortal hatred that had divided England for decades. At the time I had no idea of my sister's courage, or the depth of her goodness; these were qualities I came to recognise as I grew up. All I knew was that she consented to the marriage. Fortunately, he allowed her a day of magnificence and a gown of silk damask and crimson satin over a kirtle of white cloth of gold, and dressed himself in gold too. He weighed my sister's heart finger down with a band of heavy gold. Then he left her and went on a tour of his new kingdom, smiling with satisfaction when he saw the towns displaying his new symbol, the red rose merged with the white. Even York, the beating heart of my family, prostrated itself beneath a new, enormous Tudor rose. I wondered whether my sister had to point him in the direction of the Great North Road

22

Katherine: *We posed a problem, us Plantagenet girls. He feared what we symbolised. Yorkist supporters might claim us in marriage; at any moment our mother might agree to unions that could make us figureheads and undermine the Tudors. Her own marriage had suddenly been declared valid again, which meant we were definitely princesses once more but our futures were unclear. Would Henry Tudor offer us to foreign royalty or would he chose to bury our identity in marriages with loyal Lancastrians? Cecily was sure that he had spent weeks searching all the rooms in the Tower to make sure that our brothers really were no more. But he never found their poor bodies. He could never prove that my uncle had killed them. He could not even prove that they were dead. Two years had changed everything in England.*

Westminster, Spring 1486

The first time he saw Katherine was when the Plantagenet girls formed a little line, in order of height and age, before his throne and court. He was two months married to Bessy, returned from his progress, and she was already pregnant, sitting on a velvet-covered stool at his feet, her lovely face inscrutable beneath her gable headdress. The announcement had just been made to the court; it was as if Henry needed the world to know that his new dynasty was already secure – that God was showing his favour yet again. Elizabeth was not present; Cecily said Henry Tudor distrusted her and would rather she kept to her own rooms. His own mother had the room next to his private chamber.

My Lady the King's Mother now stood at Bessy's shoulder. Katherine felt a wave of terror; in her black gown, mantle and white wimple this tiny woman looked like a raptor. Her fingers were claws; her eyes swivelled. At any moment she might soar and then swoop.

As the eldest, at sixteen, Cecily was desperate to appear confident. She lifted her chin defiantly, only too well aware that her recent, colourful matrimonial history was the hushed gossip of the court. Second in line stood Katherine's cousin, Margaret of Clarence, called Meg, summoning all the dignity and courage of her twelve years to stand straight and tall but giving herself away by the flaring of her long Plantagenet nostrils as she breathed composure into her fear. Anne, at eleven, stared at her shoes. Bridget, the baby aged five, was blank-faced and detached. As for six-year-old Katherine – she swallowed and swallowed with rising panic, then suddenly darted out of place in the line to clutch her sister Bessy and hold tight to the furred cuff of her sleeve.

Henry Tudor stood up, dressed in the same expensive black as his mother. Katherine thought that if she did not know he was the king then for all the world she would mistake him for one of the clerks that haunted the palace of Westminster with their inky hands and stooped shoulders. How in God's name could he have wielded a sword on the field at Bosworth, she wondered. He stepped down to where she stood, still grasping Elizabeth's gown and quietly, deftly, prised her fingers open, then closed his own over them and she felt him tug her up to her feet. She dared to look at his face, though she knew one should not stare directly at a king. His eyes were disconcerting. One seemed to return her gaze whilst the other wandered over the room. She hid her other hand behind her back.

"Which sister is this?" he enquired.

"Katherine, Your Grace," replied Bessy, "who is small, but knows her own mind." A sharp intake of breath, a ripple of courtiers' laughter round the chamber and Katherine did not know whether to feel mortified or proud. Her heart pounded.

"She will do well to be obedient, not independent," retorted My Lady the King's Mother.

"This girl's place is to listen to her elders, obey without question and accept the King's will in all that she does." Her face seemed to have contorted itself into something resembling an old lemon, and her tone was as sour. "And all these girls should do likewise."

"Indeed," said Bessy smoothly. She had reached out and Katherine felt her fingers link into her concealed ones.

"And when we find them husbands they will be thankful."

"Indeed," said Bessy serenely. Katherine felt her hand being squeezed reassuringly.

"We shall find husbands for them all," announced Henry Tudor. It was hard to tell whether this was delivered as a promise or a threat.

"As princesses, my lord, they are especial treasures." Bessy spoke with the courage that comes from being pregnant with the next heir for England, Margaret Beaufort's eyes goggled in her head at the very idea that this line of young girls could be considered princesses. Clearly she thought that only her beloved son's future daughters could ever have a right to that title. She had never been called such. She was just the great-great granddaughter of a king, with her own great-grandfather base-born. A Lady, yet never royal except in her own mind. It seemed she might pop with outrage but suddenly Henry Tudor took her hand too, and then, to Katherine's horror, transferred hers into his mother's. Bessy slid her fingers away and Margaret Beaufort grasped Katherine so tightly her little silver ring dug painfully into her palm.

"We will keep them close, my Lady Mother, and in due time, you will have the choosing of their husbands."

Mollified, she beamed upon her son, looked daggers at her daughter-in-law but mercifully loosened her hold on Katherine. None could argue with what Bessy had said, for Henry had surely married her as a princess of York – had selected her to appeal to and appease the people of England who longed for peace. And if Elizabeth was a princess why then, so were her sisters. They might have princes and kings to husband. Or not.

"And pray, which is the one said to have been already married?" Henry Tudor scanned the line. Cecily flamed scarlet to the very roots of her dark hair at being spoken of so rudely and publicly.

"Your old marriage will be annulled," announced Henry. Cecily looked astounded. "And let us hope that you will be as happy with a new husband as my dearest wife."

Bessy rose now; Katherine thought she would go to Cecily but instead she ran a hand down the front of her gown, lightly skimming but drawing all attention to the precious womb where the future Tudor heir lay. She then laid that hand upon Henry Tudor's arm and spoke clearly. "Cecily understands her duty. She will go to the husband you choose for her as willingly as I did to mine." Her words were like sweet music somehow laid over a minor key. Katherine saw Henry's lips purse but he laid his own hand on top of Elizabeth's. Cecily took courage, and set her jaw even more firmly. Katherine quaked at the defiance in her eyes but, surprisingly, a hint of approval hovered at the edges of Lady Margaret's lips.

"The girl is my godchild, and my brother, Lord Welles, has need of another wife. She can become a good Lancastrian and serve us well. But not just yet."

Not just yet? Enigmatic words. There was a flicker from Henry's eyes to his mother's and then the briefest of an appraising, sweeping glance at Cecily. Bessy had to come safely through childbirth first, of course, or Cecily might well have found herself as Henry's second wife, rather than Lord Welles'.

Katherine: *He always had a plan. Always. I grew up in his court and knew that nothing ever happened without his knowledge and sanction.*

That September, a month after her seventh birthday, Katherine became an aunt for the first time. Bessy was taken to the ancient priory of St Swithun at Winchester, that her child might be born in a place of legendary English kings. She laboured through a stormy night, shocked by the extent of the pain, but biting down upon the piece of wood they placed in her mouth and writhing through the contractions that threatened to tear her apart. She could not imagine how she would ever face such pain again. At the worst moments Elizabeth Wydville held eye contact with her daughter, willing courage and survival into her distended frame. Even Margaret Beaufort stopped talking about God for five minutes and allowed Bessy to crush her hand.

The baby was small but adorable. His father sent word that he was to be called Arthur. Bessy shrugged; his name did not matter – what was important was the triumph that here was one York boy who would never disappear into the Tower. He might bear the name of Tudor, but her father's blood, and that of all his Plantagenet forebears, ran through his veins and could be seen in his blue eyes and little thatch of golden hair. She listened as the bells of Winchester began to ring at dawn and imagined the bonfires that would be lit across the country. Four days later Cecily carried him proudly to his christening, through the cathedral hung with cloth of gold to the raised font near the altar, at the shrine of St Swithun. Two hundred torches lit his way and a taper was placed within his tiny fingers. Katherine was deemed too young to play any formal part but marvelled at the colours, and the music, and the fine things to eat.

After the birth Bessy felt strangely light-headed and feverish; she saw the looks of concern on the faces of her mother and sisters as they sponged her with cool water. Many a woman lost her life in the days after delivery. There were hours when Bessy lost all sense of time and place, and simply swam in a strange sea of heat. Faces loomed before her, laughing: her father, her two uncles, George and Richard, as she had known them as a child; her brother Richard Grey and her royal brothers. She glimpsed her grandmother, Jacquetta and Queen Anne Neville, holding her little son Edward by the hand. All stretched out their arms to her, inviting her to join them. Muzzy with fatigue, she pushed them all away and tried to crawl back to consciousness. She must not die! She must live! For her family's sake she must live!

Henry sat with her when the baby was brought back from his baptism and placed in her arms. "You must honour the tradition and be the first to call him by his name," he instructed quietly. Through a hot haze, Bessy felt the slight weight of the child but she could not hold him steady. Henry Tudor beckoned to Katherine who stood at the foot of the bed. "Climb up, and help hold your nephew." Uncertain, Katherine looked to her mother. Elizabeth nodded quickly and the little girl scrambled up onto the gorgeously hung bed of estate, wriggling next to her sister so the baby could be propped against her. With a superhuman effort, Bessy spoke: "I call my son Arthur, and ask for God's blessings upon him." Then she slid into a void.

Later, when all the ceremony of gift-giving was finally over, and the King had returned to his own rooms, Bessy found her sore body and mind returning to some blessed coolness. She opened her eyes and looked around the chamber: Cecily was still next to her with a basin and cloth; Arthur's wet nurse was suckling him quietly in a corner. Katherine sat next to her and played with her little nephew's tiny pink toes which wriggled with ecstasy. Her mother and Lady Margaret were inspecting the impressive pile of glittering, bejewelled silver and gold plates and cups. Bessy looked briefly at the gifts but longingly at her child.

"May I not feed him?" she pleaded.

Elizabeth came to the side of the bed and stroked her daughter's hand gently. These days she was strangely subdued. The position of status and influence she had anticipated as mother of the queen had simply not happened. Her son-in-law made it abundantly clear that if she was to stay at court she must keep a low profile. He was polite to her but distant. At least he had allowed her to be present for the birth of her first grandchild. Her reward for behaving herself was to be the baby's godmother. "It is not the business of queens, my daughter," she said and added quietly, "you need more children. To be safe."

Margaret Beaufort, turning a lidded, golden cup in her hand, nodded emphatically. "We must have you back in my son's bed to make another child." Clearly, her version of being safe meant something different.

Katherine tore her gaze away from her new-born nephew; her beloved sister looked wan and she noted the look of despair that she sometimes wore herself when asked to do the seemingly impossible.

"How long must I stay here?" asked Bessy

Elizabeth looked at her critically. "A month should see you churched, I should think. I usually recovered very quickly. I was concerned at first but you have not torn, or lost much blood, and the fever has not taken hold."

"How lucky you are, my dear," said Lady Margaret. "I am sure you may look forward to another babe within the year."

Katherine did not miss the flash of outrage in her sister's eyes. "He must crown me first," said Bessy, flatly. "He must keep his side of the bargain." Not since the time of William of Normandy had an uncrowned queen given birth to an heir.

They returned to London in late October. The baby prince was left at Farnham, with his own little household. Bessy had wept but Elizabeth gently reminded her that that was how it had been for her, too. The heir to the throne did not belong to his mother. She had done her duty in producing him but now she must leave him to the care of others. One day he would move further away, to Ludlow, to learn how to be a king. With her subsequent sons, Elizabeth assured her, it would be easier. Bessy reached for Katherine, and hugged her closely as the royal litter made its slow way back to the capital.

Within days they attended Cecily's second wedding. John Welles was nearly forty, with greying hair and a slight paunch, and Katherine giggled wildly as the bride was dressed in her new tawny velvet gown. "This will make you half-aunt to the King!" The permutations of relationships never ceased to amaze her. Cecily, however, accepted her latest husband with good grace and Lady Margaret seemed to admire her for it. The groom might not have been the foreign prince Cecily had once hoped for but at least he was kind. At the wedding he covered her trembling hand with his own and smiled upon her with warmth. She met his eyes and then spoke her responses firmly and he kissed her gently. Katherine was learning fast that happiness is elusive – a state to be snatched at and enjoyed when offered. There was no doubt that now Henry Tudor and Margaret Beaufort had their male heir, and Bessy looked likely to provide others, they had simply found a solution that prevented Cecily from marrying a greater man who might unsettle the Tudor hopes. At least Lord Welles looked as though he might cherish her.

23

"This year was Stoke Field where by the king's power was slain the Earl of Lincoln"
The Great Chronicle of London

Katherine: *But Henry's place upon my father's throne; my brother's throne; my uncle's throne was far from secure. Yes, Prince Arthur grew daily but soon I heard talk of a boy in Ireland who claimed to be my cousin, Edward of Warwick, Meg's brother.*

It was Christmas and the court was at Greenwich. Gifts had been exchanged and on New Year's Day Bessy and Henry donned their crowns for chapel and the feast that followed. On the surface all was harmonious but the rumours swirling round London had put Henry into a dark mood. The festivities prevented him from being closeted with his advisors. Now they sat together on the top table in the Great Hall awaiting the entrance of the golden wassail cups but Henry was making no pretence at good humour.

Bessy found it a challenge to make complete sense of her new status. Queen, yet uncrowned. It was hard to read Henry. That he valued her as the mother of his son was beyond dispute for he treated her with respect and kindness in public and in private. Yet he was in no hurry to crown her, and was not willing to allow her much financial independence. Bessy had learned that her settlement as his wife was less than either her mother's or even Marguerite of Anjou's. He was obviously eager for another child but in the last three months had not forced himself upon her. He seemed to be waiting for some signal from her – a rare consideration from a husband, according to her ladies. He was a bundle of contradictions. Bessy felt he liked her as an individual but regarded her family with great wariness. She wished she could speak to him more candidly for she felt the same: as a man he did not displease her at all, but she could never forget that his victory on the battlefield marked the end of her family's power. And now there was this trouble in Ireland. One of Henry's men had just been whispering in his ear – no doubt updating him with the latest news from Dublin.

Bessy did her best to smile upon the Steward and Treasurer who bowed low before her, but the knuckles gripping the arms of her chair were white.

Goblets of steaming Wassail wine were presented to the couple. At any other time Bessy would have loved the sweet, thick taste of spiced fruit and honey but now it was all she could do not to heave.

"Whoever this boy is, he is a danger to us," said Henry quietly. "Apparently, he now refers to *me* as "The Welsh milksop who's stolen his throne." "

"But the boy is *not* my cousin of Warwick! How can it be? How can anyone believe such nonsense? And even if he came to England do they not think I not would recognise my own cousin?" Bessy felt sick with exasperation. "And in any case, we know where Ned is." Her eyes clouded. Despite her pleas, her husband had removed the sweet, biddable boy from Coldharbour and placed him in the Tower. It was a barrier between them. That Henry distrusted her family was all too apparent. She knew that the root of the trouble lay not with gentle young Ned but with her grown-up cousins, sons of her Aunt Elizabeth who had married the Duke of Suffolk. John, William, Edmund and Richard de la Pole were proud of their Plantagenet blood even if they had sworn allegiance to Henry Tudor. She knew that her husband was having great difficulty in separating Elizabeth Plantagenet, the Yorkist princess, from Bessy, his wife. She feared it would be a canker in their marriage.

"What are you going to do?"

"Wait," said Henry shortly. "Wait until I know for certain which of your relations is behind this conspiracy." He took a sip of the mulled wine and looked sideways at Bessy. "I rather suspect your Plantagenet aunt in Burgundy."

Bessy returned his look with a cool stare of her own. "I do not know that aunt. I have never met her. Though I believe she hates me for my marriage to you, sir."

"Does you honoured mother correspond with her?"

Bessy took a deep breath and mustered her courage. "I do not know, sir. Perhaps you had better ask her." She was saved from further conversation with her husband as the choristers burst into cheerful song. Bessy felt a sort of misery creeping over her. Even though baby Arthur grew chubby and stronger in his cradle at Farnham she knew that would not necessarily preclude her mother from her habitual scheming. Henry had not invited her to share the Christmas season with them; Elizabeth was alone at Eltham. It was all too easy to imagine the thoughts running through her mother's mind: not every baby lives; some women die in childbirth – in which case the insurance of a male heir of undisputed, legitimate Plantagenet blood could still be a prize worth pursuing. But *Ned? My mother knows as well as I do where Ned is. There must be someone else behind it all, someone using this boy as a smokescreen for his own purposes.* John de la Pole, Earl of Lincoln, would be likely to raise Elizabeth Wydville high again whereas Henry Tudor clearly regarded her as an unfortunate nuisance. But where was the sense in that? *Unless ... unless somewhere in her heart my mother believes one of her sons yet lives. If she thinks there is some remote chance that the boy in Ireland, whoever he claims to be, might be her son. And if he is? If by some miracle one of my royal brothers still lives, then what is the future for my own child Arthur? Are we all destined for another lifetime of killing?*

Further down the hall Katherine sat at the same table as Anne, Bridget, Meg and some of her Wydville cousins. They had all been given comfits – sugared fruit and marchpane animals; she toyed with the sugared plum on her plate, picking it up and running her tongue over the sweet exterior, delaying the pleasure of sinking her teeth into the flesh. The choir sang lustily, bestowing musical blessings *"Love and joy come to you,"* but Katherine was suddenly aware that Meg was hunched over, hiding her face, and that tears were trickling through her fingers. On her wrist was a silver bangle and dangling from it a little silver barrel – a poignant reminder of her dead, disgraced father. Katherine put down her comfit and stole an arm around her cousin's shoulders. She leaned in, close to Meg's ear and breathed the only words of comfort she could think of.

"Meggie? Meggie, my brothers were taken too."

Kings take boys. It is what they do. You can't stop them. Kings take whoever they like, whenever they like.

The way Ned had been taken was imprinted on Katherine's memory forever. They had been all together at Coldharbour, in the weeks before Henry Tudor's coronation, hard at their lessons as decreed by My Lady the King's Mother. Katherine had sailed through her translation and was happily embarking upon a second when the door had opened and four of the King's soldiers stood there. They hustled Ned away from his Latin lesson, down the stairs to the waiting barge. Poor boy, not inclined to learning and happiest on the floor playing with his hound puppy. Poor boy, unable to help his birth and place in his family – the last Plantagenet boy.

Meg had screamed and tried to place herself between her brother and the yeoman of Henry's new guard. The new Tudor rose masqueraded on their broad chests. The tutor stood by, helplessly wringing his old hands with distress. Ned's ink-splattered manuscript fluttered to the floor like an injured wing. His puppy and Katherine's spaniel yapped furiously.

"You cannot take him! He has done nothing! He is faithful to the King!" Meg flung herself at the nearest guard who simply used one hand to push her off and hold her at arm's length.

"Save my brother!" she screamed. "Somebody please save my brother!"

So Katherine ran. She dodged the second man, slipped under the armpit of the third and was running, running like the wind, her thin velvet slippers pounding along the passage to her sister's private apartments. She arrived, sobbing for breath, and demanded entry. Bemused, the man-at-arms swung open the door and she stumbled in but to her horror the chamber was deserted. No music. No laughter. Nobody. Bessy had been taken up to Westminster with her mother and Lady Margaret to visit the Royal Wardrobe and select furs for the coming winter. Katherine's knees turned to jelly and she sank down upon the polished floorboards, her feet stinging with pain. In the distance, the dogs still barked and Meg still shrieked like a banshee as they dragged her brother away. Katherine crawled to the window, hauled herself up to peep over the edge and saw, like a scene from a mummer's play, how Ned was being carried down the garden path by the burliest of the guards towards the landing stage where a small, dark barge waited. His legs thrashed helplessly and his mouth was wide open in a silent scream. Bessy had returned to Coldharbour in the evening, shocked at Meg's distraught state. For days she would not speak but sat in the window looking down river towards the Tower. Bessy realised why Henry Tudor had sent her upstream to Westminster that morning.

For Katherine it was a defining moment in her young life – a realisation that her sister being queen did not necessarily mean safety. She was fearful and resentful, uncertain who she could trust and at the age of seven already haunted by images that came in the night to disturb her sleep: her father huge and dead; her uncle Richard with his head split in two; her princely brothers fighting for breath (for by then she had heard the stories of how they had been smothered); her half-brother Richard Grey laying down his head upon the block at Pontefract.

There was no-one she could turn to for her mother seemed to be staying away from court forever; it was hard to be alone with Bessy, and Cecily was miles away.

The winter of 1487 slowly edged its way towards spring, and the stories circulating round London were as feverish as they had been almost four years ago. Another Plantagenet boy was in the Tower, but was he alive or dead? Come to think of it, who had ever seen him? He had escaped! No, he had been murdered, like his cousins the princes, No, he was in Ireland! To quell such talk, Henry Tudor decided to prove to London that Edward of Warwick was very much alive, but very much loyal to the new royal family and not in the least bit interested in his Yorkist heritage.

Katherine saw her cousin again one cold February morning when Henry ordered them all to walk from Westminster through the streets of London to a service at St Paul's Cathedral. The idea was that the people of London should see for themselves that Edward, son of the Duke of Clarence, was with his family and certainly not in Ireland. Ice lay on the puddles and frost on the roofs of the houses. Katherine's breath hung in the air and a weary winter sun was mostly blocked out by the tall gables. In her furred cloak, Katherine was round eyed with disbelief, for she saw Henry offering his arm to her mother, and close behind them My Lady the King's Mother smiling and chatting to her sister Bessy and her cousin Meg. Meg was white with anxiety, casting desperate glances everywhere, searching for her brother. Cecily and her husband John Welles were also in the procession. Just behind them was a solitary figure – young Ned, thinner and taller, but dressed well in warm furs and velvet. Katherine saw her de la Pole cousins too, tall and handsome young men. Together with Anne and Bridget, she brought up the rear of the party, accompanied by her half brother Thomas Grey and Wydville uncles Richard and Edward, men now riding high in the favour of the Tudor king.

It was a long walk across the city to the cathedral. Despite the cold, the Londoners had come out in their hundreds to see the royal family go by. Mostly they seemed just curious to see this strange parade of Plantagenets and Tudors. To all intents and purposes they looked like a big, happy family, the Queen's relatives happily reconciled to the new order. They were not to know it was nothing more than an elaborate puppet show. Henry waved genially, and Elizabeth Wydville inclined her still lovely head. Lady Margaret distributed alms, assisted by Bessy and a tight-lipped Meg. Ned of Warwick walked eagerly, glad to be out in the fresh air, waving enthusiastically.

"*Should* he wave? Should *we*, Anne? " asked Katherine anxiously.

"I think so, I think it would help. I think the King would like it."

"Bridget, we must wave. Look, see what Anne does and we will copy her."

So the three younger York princesses lifted their hands in their furred gloves and joined in the charade. It helped to keep them warm as they headed towards the great spire that soared over all London.

Katherine had never been to St Paul's before. They passed into the interior where the February light flooded through the exquisite rose window. They processed to the shrine of St Erkenwald where they all knelt devoutly. Her heart thudded in her chest in case she should do anything wrong. She caught Ned's eye and saw the sadness there, although he managed a tiny smile for his favourite little cousin. His lips seemed to be moving – praying? No, she realised he was mouthing "Kaspar", the name of his puppy. Katherine nodded quickly, allowing her right hand to indicate height, then brought her left hand up to meet it; to anyone watching it looked more like a grand gesture of prayer.

The King, his mother and the Queen bowed their heads and prayed devoutly. Meg of Clarence was not allowed to stand near her brother or exchange any words but her gaze reached out and locked into his innocent, awed expression. She forced a smile. Katherine felt a tear slide down her cheek and put our her tongue to catch it lest anyone should see. A motley crew of Wydville, Plantagenet and de la Pole blood gazed fixedly at the shrine as the mass got underway. Behind them a thousand Londoners shuffled. And a lonely, abandoned eleven year old boy yearned for the comfort of his sister and his puppy. After the service they returned in procession to Sheen, where Meg and Ned were allowed a precious couple of hours together – not alone, in full view of the court, and Meg was ordered to smile and be joyful. Darkness came early in February, though, and by evening Ned was being rowed back up the river to his rooms in the Tower.

But as the primroses showed their hopeful little faces in the green banks, and the first haze of bluebells shimmered in the woods beyond Eltham, the boy in Ireland still claimed to be him. In Burgundy, Edward IV's sister Margaret supported his story and sent two thousand German troops to his aid. John de la Pole, Earl of Lincoln and formerly heir to Richard III, who had knelt next to Katherine in St Paul's, fled the court to support him too. Some fools crowned him king in Dublin, and then Lincoln returned with an army of eight thousand to challenge Henry Tudor. The boy rode a white pony at the head of the troops. England trembled with fear and excitement: could the Tudor's rule be so short-lived?

They met at East Stoke, near Newark. Henry donned the same armour he had worn to fight at Bosworth and rode the same war horse. He watched with satisfaction as his commanders out-thought de la Pole's Irish and German mercenaries and within three hours the field was strewn with dead Yorkists who rolled down the gently sloping valley into the River Trent, leaving a trail of blood. Henry was furious, though, when they told him that Lincoln had died fighting, for now he would never get to the bottom of the conspiracy. The whole sorry episode had shown him that despite Bessy as his wife and despite his new heir there were still those who could not accept his rule. The boy was found wandering among the dead on his white pony. It turned out that he was just a joiner's son from Oxford, with the outlandish name of Lambert Simnel, who had been groomed for the part of impersonating Ned of Warwick. Henry could not fathom it. Had Lincoln hoped to be a second Kingmaker, with a false, puppet king – or might he have removed the boy at a later date and claimed his own inheritance. It was said that Francis Lovell, King Richard's loyal friend, had fought too but escaped.

Not only was it the end of Lincoln, it was also the end of Elizabeth Wydville's time at court. She had supported Lincoln, said Henry. She had sent letters and money to support the Yorkist cause and to betray her own grandson, Prince Arthur. Perhaps she would now prefer to live at Bermondsey Abbey and meditate upon her crime, suggested Henry. And perhaps it was also time to send Princess Bridget to her destiny as a bride of Christ.

Bessy gathered her three youngest sisters round her late at night. They had already retired to bed but faithful Elyn and Joanna had roused them, put fingers to their lips and then ushered them quickly through shadowy passages to the Queen's apartments. Bessy was alone and in her night-gown, her fair hair loose about her shoulders – something they rarely saw these days, now she was a married woman. Katherine saw that her sister's eyes were glittering with unshed tears. A high red spot burned in either cheek.

"Has somebody else died?" asked Katherine abruptly. "Is it Cecily? Or Ned?"

"No, no ... nobody has died. But we shall not be seeing much of Mama from now on. She is going to live away from court, with the monks at Bermondsey."

Katherine regarded her sister suspiciously. "Mama does not like monks. Not to live with, anyway. She said she had enough of them when we were in sanctuary."

"Why, Bessy?" Unobtrusively, Anne was slipping into Cecily's vacant shoes, filling her place as Bessy's confidante, despite the nine years between them. She was quiet, thoughtful and mature beyond her years. Positioned between the characterful vivacity of Cecily and Katherine it was all too easy to overlook Anne but her watchfulness and common sense were proving helpful.

"My husband says he cannot afford for her to live at court. He says the expense is too great."

"Is it because he thinks she still plots?"

"Probably."

"What does Mama plot?" asked Katherine.

"And darling Bridget, will be leaving us too."

Katherine felt a stab of fear. She did not understand why Bridget spoke so little but knew that she was often called upon to act as her mouthpiece. The youngest princess was still oddly dreamy and preferred her own company. "Will Bridget go with our lady Mother?"

"No. It is time for her to go to the life our parents always intended for her."

Bridget cocked her head with interest. "I am to serve God," she said solemnly.

Bessy pulled her youngest sister close in a fierce hug. "It is what Papa and Mama always planned for you. We all know that. I had hoped to keep you longer but -" her throat tightened. Henry Tudor had been impassive on the subject: Princess Bridget had been promised to God since birth and could now begin her religious life. The Dominican nunnery at Dartford was large and wealthy – a suitable place for a young lady of high birth and pious intention. Two younger sisters were enough to have to provide for in a worldly sense – finding suitable husbands and providing financial settlements would be hard enough. Expense enough.

Bessy swallowed hard. "I think it will suit you, but if you hate it, my darling – if you truly hate it, you must tell us. No-one will make you take the veil against your will. At first you will be a boarder, with other girls, and in time you can take your vows, if that is what you want. You can write to us all, and I am sure there will be visits. There is a great library there, Bridget, and many kind, clever women who will teach you and look after you well."

Katherine's hand stole over Bridget's. "Will he send me there too?"

"He's not *sending* anyone! It has never been a secret that Bridget will be a great religious lady."

"Nobody told *me* that," said Katherine indignantly

"Well, maybe you were not listening. Why, she will probably be Prioress one day, and live in fine state!" There was edge of desperation, though, to Bessy's voice that Katherine did not miss.

Anne was doing her best to support Bessy. "It will be nice and quiet there, Bridget. There's sure to be lovely food."

With a great effort Bridget looked directly at her sisters. "I can say prayers for all of *you,*" she said thoughtfully. "I can be the one who speaks to God when you all don't have much time, and I can be the one who helps to keep you all safe." It was the most anyone had ever heard her say.

In the morning, when Elyn came in to open the shutters and assist the Queen to rise to hear Mass, she found the four sisters fast asleep together in Bessy's bed. Bessy lay in the middle, her arms around Anne and Katherine, whilst Bridget lay curled at their feet. Elyn started; they looked for all the world like stone effigies in a country church.

Katherine: *How could a six-year-old child know whether she wanted to be a nun or not? My grandmother Cecily Neville had suggested it at Bridget's birth, and named her for one of her favourite Swedish saints, and my parents had liked the idea, but I am sure it was never meant for her to go into the nunnery at so tender an age. I loved Bridget so much – she had been the constant companion of my childhood, my playmate, bedmate and shadow. But she had been deeply traumatised by our time in sanctuary and the loss of our brothers. I think my mother and my eldest sisters somehow knew that she would not be able to live in the world like the rest of us – that to ask her to become somebody's wife and a mother would be utterly beyond her resilience. Yet when I lost her to her religious life it still felt like another body-blow from Fortune. My mother was not banished to Bermondsey permanently but Henry Tudor was simply not prepared to finance a queen dowager.*

After the battle at East Stoke, the boy called Lambert Simnel was brought to Westminster and stood, bare-headed, in St Stephen's Hall. He was little more than a child with a tear-stained face and legs like twigs. Katherine and Anne stared, for they saw in his face and tearful expression a shadow they half-recognised. A fair-haired boy with blue eyes; a straight nose and a high forehead, he bore a startling resemblance to her own brother Edward, lost in the Tower four years ago. And yet … and yet Edward would be older...This was why they had had to say he was Meg's brother, Ned. To make it fit.

"This is *not* my cousin," declared Bessy clearly. Her voice rang up to the hammer beams. The huge hall was thronged with Henry's officials. "He is some poor boy, exploited by others." She turned to her husband and suddenly dropped to her knees, pleading, as was her right as the queen. "Be merciful, Your Grace. I know you would not wish to kill small boys."

Her words hung on the warm air like heavy, dark damsons on a fruit tree. Somewhere, on the edge of memory Katherine saw a dark blue doublet. For all her position as a re-instated princess, for all the love of two sisters whom she saw daily she still felt a deep, abiding fear and a crushing sense of uncertainty.

24

"This year Queen Elizabeth was crowned at Westminster with great solemnity upon Saint Katherine's day." The Great Chronicle of London

Katherine: *And then, a full year after Arthur's birth, with Lambert Simnel spared and happily turning a spit in the royal kitchens, and Ned of Warwick gazing unhappily from his window in the Tower, Henry Tudor finally kept his promise to have Bessy crowned at Westminster Abbey. We travelled up the Thames in a flotilla of barges from Greenwich. I remember the thudding beat of the drum as the oarsmen pulled, but it was an easy trip as the tide flowed with us, willing Bessy towards the crown so rightfully hers. It was a happy day, for my sister Cecily was with us again. The water danced and glittered in the late autumn sunlight, seagulls joined us and cawed before soaring back towards the estuary and I was dazzled by my elegant sister in her white gown of cloth of gold and mantle of the same, edged with ermine. A diadem of precious gems blazed above her long, fair hair. The east wind caused us all to shiver but Bessy set her face upriver as if she were the figurehead rather than the gilded dragon. At the bow a huge royal ensign unfurled as the wind picked up and the leopards and lions of England danced to celebrate my sister's reward for her fertility.*

November 1487

"He has to crown you. The people will stand for little else. With a Yorkist queen he might be safe." Her mother's words came on the wind to Bessy as they swept past Bermondsey Abbey in the fast water. The sisters saw a group of tiny figures on the lawns, most in dark habits but one, unmistakeably in bright blue, waving and waving.

"Bessy! Cecily! Anne! See, our Lady Mother!" Katherine shrieked with delight and waved madly. Henry Tudor would not allow Elizabeth to share this day but nevertheless she had found a way of letting her daughters know she bore witness to Bessy's triumph.

They drew up at the Westminster water stairs and Katherine heard the joyous clang and clamour of the abbey bells and the excited shouts of the people reverberating through the air. It was but a few minutes' walk across the palace precincts she knew from her childhood, to the abbey. Cecily had the honour to bear Bessy's train but Anne and Katherine pressed close.

They processed along the beautiful blue and golden carpet laid upon the paving stones. Scores of people thronged to catch a glimpse of their queen – this daughter of Edward IV. Their faces loomed close, their fingers stretched out. Katherine could smell their sweat and their stale breath and shuddered but Bessy smiled serenely and surged forward proudly towards the arched entrance. "This is where our father walked to claim *his* crown." She spoke low so only her sisters could hear.

There was sudden scuffle as a boy reached forward in her wake. Katherine's brain registered his eager face, like bright coin – she saw the knife in his hand but more the smile upon his lips. He looked about her own age. He fell upon the carpet and she remembered her mother's laughing words of reminiscence about her own crowing – about how the people of London thought it their right to take home a souvenir of this momentous occasion – a tiny piece of the blue carpet, as soon as the king or queen passed by. Then, pandemonium as the guards lunged forwards and seized him. Swords flashed, pikes plunged and blood flowed. Crimson flecks flew into the air and stains spread along the azure wool.

"No!" screamed Katherine. "He means no harm!" Henry Tudor's men had never been to a coronation before. They were Bretons. They spoke no English. They knew nothing of English customs.

But they were hustled from the sunlight into the dim interior of the abbey and the great door thudded behind them like a thousand heartbeats in one. They stood, petrified. On the other side of the door they heard sounds of metal hissing through air, and terrible shrieks of agony and groaning. Then a strange, eerie silence. Then trumpets burst forth in a riotous fanfare of welcome. Trembling, Cecily wiped scarlet blood into her scarlet gown. Anne and Katherine did the same, feeling a stickiness under their fingers. Bessy was untouched – still shining in her white, gold and ermine. Their pupils adjusted from the sunlight to the candles. Katherine's eyes slid down to the carpet which continued to snake its way up the endless nave to the altar where her sister would be anointed and crowned. "Te Deum" crashed through the air and Elizabeth of York processed slowly to her destiny, with Cecily still clutching her train and Anne and Katherine behind, trailing tiny ruby droplets of English blood.

Katherine's cousin, Meg, was ear-marked for Richard Pole, whose mother was half-sister to My Lady the King's Mother. They were at their embroidery in their chamber one morning a few weeks later when the door opened and Bessy entered, attended only by Grace Plantagenet, bastard daughter of Edward IV, who divided her time waiting upon Bessy, and Elizabeth at Bermondsey. Grace had been part of their lives since childhood, trusted with their secrets.

Bessy took a deep breath. "A marriage has been arranged for you, cousin. To Sir Richard Pole."

Meg raised her head like an interested bird. "Plantagenet to Pole," she remarked. "Reduced to a single syllable. Ah, well."

A skein of rich crimson silk dangled from Meg's needle like blood. She stabbed it suddenly into the tapestry and screamed. She dealt the box of threads a savage kick and wooden spools clattered to the floor, the colours colliding like shards from a smashed stained glass window. With her right arm she swept the tapestry hoop to one side and then, to her cousins' horror, began to hit herself on both sides of her head.

"Is it not enough that my brother is kept in the Tower?" she sobbed, beating her own temples. "Must I too be taken from you all and hidden away in some castle in the country?"

Grace, who served them, yet was one of them too, swept Margaret into her arms and held her tight whilst Katherine scrabbled on the floor after the spools.

"*You* may keep the name!" sobbed Margaret into Grace's shoulder. "For you it holds no fears, but for us …" Grace looked stricken.

Bessy had rushed to the door and slammed it shut. She sped back to Meg and took her from Grace, seizing her by the shoulders. "Be quiet and listen to me! Richard Pole is a good man, a decent man. Yes, yes, a Lancastrian, I know, but one who will keep you safe. That is all that matters now, to be kept safe. To live! I cannot keep your brother Ned safe; God knows what happened to my own brothers but I *can* keep you, my beloved girls, from harm. Some sort of contentment does come from marriage and children. Cecily is not "hidden away", is she? She comes to court. As long as I am queen you know you are all safe."

Her outburst was over but Margaret shuddered with emotion and raised a tear- stained face. "But what will happen to us when you are gone?"

Bessy was taken aback. "When I am gone, cousin? Whatever do you mean?"

"You have to have more children. Arthur is not enough, is he? And each time you risk your life! Each time we will live in dread that you will not return to us."

Whilst Bessy paled somewhat, Grace produced a handkerchief and gently wiped Meg's face. "Her Grace had little trouble with Prince Arthur, cousin. Why, look how many babes her own mother had, and her grandmother before her! Her Grace comes from a line of strong women! None die in childbirth!"

"It is God's will, Meg, what happened to us, but I can assure you that I intend to stay on this earth for many years to come and do my utmost to keep you all in favour with His Grace the King and My Lady the King's Mother."

25

"Where I have no worldly goods to do the Queen's Grace, my daughter, a pleasure with, neither to reward any of my children, according to my heart and mind, I beseech Almighty God to bless Her Grace with all her noble issue ... I give Her Grace my blessing, and all the aforesaid my children." (The will of Queen Elizabeth Wydville, dated 10th April 1492, Bermondsey Abbey)

Katherine: *The remaining years of my childhood seemed to pass without drama. To my relief, Bridget seemed content with her life at Dartford Priory; her letters were full of descriptions of the nuns she was growing to respect, and her love of the ordered life. In the nursery at Eltham Palace gentle Arthur had been joined by a bouncing, bossy little sister, Margaret, and an impatient, red-haired baby brother, Henry. I saw my mother occasionally. Her departure from court life inevitably distanced her from us all. By the time little Harry was born Bessy privately declared that there was really no point in Mama trying to plot with anyone anymore, for the Tudor dynasty was firmly in place. I saw that Henry Tudor treated his queen with great respect, and was glad for Bessy's sake. I was delighted with my new position of favourite aunt; the new royal children filled the void left by my brothers' sad deaths.*

Then, a couple of months before my thirteenth birthday, the unthinkable: my mother was dying. She lay upon her bed at Bermondsey, watching the dust motes dancing in the shafts of sunlight and pretending that she had no pain. The King gave permission for us to spend time with her in her final days. Anne and I were regarded as the chief ladies present but at seventeen and twelve we did not necessarily feel comfortable in this role. I envied Bridget, who had special permission to come from the priory at Dartford and simply knelt by our mother in her robes of a novice nun, and prayed. Cecily was far away in Lincolnshire with her newborn daughter; Meg was gone with her new husband to Farleigh

Hungerford Castle where she awaited the birth of her first child. She wrote that she prayed every night for her poor brother alone in the Tower. I was careful to put her letters in the fire but as our barge rowed past the Tower I looked up and willed Meg's love through its thick walls. Bessy sent word from Sheen that she would come to our mother if she could but she was also heavily pregnant, with her fourth child.

Bermondsey Abbey 8 June 1492

Elizabeth Wydville was sleeping. Her wimple had been removed that she might draw her breath more easily in these last hours. Katherine looked upon her mother's legendary face: the high forehead, the bow lips, the sculpted cheekbones, heavy lidded eyes and the wisps of silver hair escaping from her simple linen coif. She had seen the portrait that captured her as a young queen; very little had changed, save for a few lines around her eyes and mouth. Such beauty defied time. She saw each of her sisters somewhere in her features.

I love her, yet I am just one of twelve children who have demanded her attention. Katherine knew her mother had lived primarily for her boys – what mother would not? Yet for the most part those boys brought her such sorrow: Richard Grey, executed at Pontefract; Edward and Richard lost in the Tower. Thomas Grey had sent word that he would pay all funeral expenses, for Elizabeth had nothing and had requested absolute simplicity. Katherine looked around the room and saw just one plain wooden crucifix upon the wall, one simple table which bore her book of hours and one wooden clothing pole upon which hung an unadorned blue gown. Where were her jewels? Her money? Her pictures? Her furniture? Her tapestries and Turkey carpets? Her silver plate? The things Katherine remembered from sanctuary and her rooms at Westminster? The trappings of her regal status? Then she remembered why Elizabeth was here – forced into religious retreat by Henry Tudor. The very idea that Elizabeth Wydville would have chosen pious contemplation for her later years! A snort of irreverent laughter escaped her lips and devout Bridget gave her a reproving look. Katherine ignored her. She loved Bridget dearly but the nuns had made her insufferably pious.

Katherine sighed. The time had come for Elizabeth Wydville to make her way to God but there were so many questions left unanswered. *Oh, my mother, why did you think that your boy-king son could be guided by Wydvilles and none*

193

other? Who did you regard as your little sons' murderer – Richard? Henry Tudor? Yet you would have married Bessy to either! Is a crown worth so much? Did you plot with Margaret Beaufort? With John de la Pole? Are you guilty of bewitching my father? In the past two years Katherine had come to know so much more about her family history. She no longer listened under tables; instead, she asked questions of those who could remember and would tell her: Elizabeth, Grace, Cecily. Much of it mystified her: cousins against cousins; brothers against brothers; uncles against nephews – and at the heart of it all her mother trying to decide whether her living eldest daughter or missing youngest sons had most claim upon her ambition and loyalties. A web of such complexity it defied explanation. What would history make of them, she wondered?

Much to Katherine's gratification, her tutor had declared her intelligent enough to follow his teaching of some of the stories of past centuries and monarchs. She now knew of William who had come from France and conquered the Saxons, and of four hundred years of Plantagenet forebears who were crowned in the abbey at Westminster. She had made some sense of the broad sheet of vellum which showed how she was descended from the third Edward and wondered at the extraordinary claims of her brother-in-law, who might be the grandson of a French princess but was only the great-great grandson of John of Gaunt (through a dubious Beaufort line forbidden from the throne). She had seen her own illustrious and wholly legitimate line from Prince Edmund, made doubly certain through marriage to Plantagenet heiresses. She was in no doubt that Henry Tudor had no right to call himself king. "But," her tutor whispered, with one eye towards the door, "the English have never tolerated a queen in her own right since the catastrophe of the Empress Matilda." Katherine looked at him squarely and suggested that one day they might have to.

Now she was glad it was a summer morning, for the sun was high in the sky and there was a welcome warmth permeating even the stone walls of the abbey. The hours drifted by; afternoon merged into honeyed evening without any change in temperature. Katherine walked in the garden and picked a full blown white June rose which Bridget laid upon their mother's pillow.

"Here's a red one too, Bridget, for Mama was the daughter of a Lancastrian knight, and the wife of one too, when she was not much older than us."

They waited for three days, taking it in turns to sit in the monks' herb garden or in the cool of her room. The Prior looked in from time to time, bowing his tonsured head. When Elizabeth had first arrived she was viewed with suspicion and some distaste; her history as a king's lover and scheming dowager queen cut no ice with the monks but they had come to accept her, for her generosity and smile, and had treated her with respect.

Once, Elizabeth stirred and they offered her wine. She sipped slowly from the cup – plain wood again, not the jewelled hanap she used in the past.

"Are we waiting for anything?" Her words were faint but lucid.

"Maybe for Her Grace the Queen," replied Anne quietly

"She will not come. He will not allow it."

"She is confined, my Lady Mother," explained Katherine

"Oh yes," she responded, "I do know it." Each seemed to mean something different.

"A new prince or princess, "added Katherine encouragingly, for she knew her mother dearly loved news of her grandchildren.

"Bessy does her best to keep you all safe." She sighed." But I cannot wait for her. Your father calls to me. He needs me at Windsor." Suddenly her eyes were wide with recognition and joy; she struggled to push herself up from her pillows, reached her arms forward in loving certainty then fell back. The rose petals were crushed and scattered around her.

Katherine: They buried her at Windsor, next to my father. I wished we could have gone with her but custom forbade it. Yet our bastard sister, Grace Plantagenet bravely refused to leave her side, and because Bessy cried so hard Henry Tudor relented and allowed it. So Grace told us how our mother completed her final journey in the quiet of a late evening on Whit Sunday, as the sun's rays slanted along the surface of the river and faded into the reeds. The rowers' oars barely splashed as they cut through the silken water. Two swans glided with them for a while; a family of ducks paddled and quacked alongside. The funeral was short, and devoid of any splendour. There was no music, no ceremony other than a few prayers. Grace described how she stood by the altar (where they had levered up a huge slab) and watched as my mother's coffin was lowered into the brick-lined vault. Then she was gone forever.

A few days later we were at least permitted to attend a Requiem Mass for her soul. The chantry in St George's chapel was truly lovely, and a fitting place for a queen. Above our heads the beautiful new fan vaulting was like stone lace; the candles threw intricate shadows across the walls and the floor. Their scent of beeswax mingled with cloying incense. I had never seen my father's resting place before. Bridget and I clutched Anne's hands as we knelt and prayed. As we turned from the grave and made our way out into the court, I realised that we were orphans now.

That night, the three sisters slept in the castle before Bridget had to return to her contemplative life. They were bedfellows again as they had been in sanctuary. It was muggy and impossible to sleep so they talked and wept into the small hours, sharing memories of their childhood. Anne whispered of a father who would carry his little daughters high on his shoulders and of brothers with smiles as broad as sunbeams. They promised to love each other as long as they lived. Bridget was composed and reassured them that she had always dreamed of dedicating herself to God and had found a new, safe family and the comfort of prayer. In the morning Anne and Katherine held her tight, planted kisses on her lips then waved her off as she mounted a gentle palfrey and set off on the road that runs by the river to Staines, from where she would be taken back to Dartford. She would take her vows soon and they did not know when, or if, they would ever see her again.

A week later Anne and Katherine were rowed back to Sheen where they entered the dark rooms of Bessy's confinement and told her careful stories of their mother's last days. Margaret Beaufort was much in evidence, fussing as usual over the protocol and etiquette attached to an event as important as the birth of a Tudor.

For the first time Katherine was judged old enough to attend her sister during her confinement. She saw the walls covered with rich, patterned tapestries of silver and gold thread; the windows closed and covered with similar hangings – no images of animals or humans for fear that such things might harm the unborn child. In the hearth a fire was blazing, despite the July heat. The royal bed was ready, with its beautiful linen, and at its foot the pallet upon which Bessy would actually give birth. Jewelled crucifixes, candlesticks and images stood upon the newly erected altar, and gold and silver plate adorned the cupboard. Whilst her mother lay dying, Bessy had been sealed up in this world of crimson, silver, gilt and ermine, away from men.

Bessy was very near her time, her fingers and ankles unpleasantly swollen. She was relieved beyond measure to see her sisters and begged for details of Bermondsey and Windsor. When Margaret Beaufort was forced to leave the room for a few minutes, for the sake of her own comfort, Katherine searched her mind for snippets that would bring her sister solace. *Our mother spoke of you in her last moments; the scent of honeysuckle was in the air; she knew she was going to our father...* the last piece of information caused Elizabeth to gasp with joy. She remembered her father so clearly. She was sixteen again, the apple of his eye, a daughter to affiance into the best royal house of Europe. She spoke of how she remembered him returning in 1471 after the Battle of Tewkesbury, and sweeping his five year old princess into his arms. *"Even before he went to look at Prince Edward"*. Katherine felt envious. She remembered nothing, apart from a figure that towered above her.

"He meant *me* to be an Empress," says Anne wistfully. "Though when I think about it there is something quite funny about that idea." She smiled because she was shortest of the sisters. Bessy, ever kindly, propped her huge belly with cushions so she could lean over and cup her face.

"You would have made a splendid wife for Maximilian!" They were laughing now – a blessed relief after days of grief. "Katherine, don't pull a face. He loved you too. I remember how he said you should be promised to Juan, Prince of the Asturias when you were born, because you were so beautiful! I remember how he carried you in his arms at Eltham in the Great Hall, to show you off to the court and ordered the heralds to play a fanfare for the future Queen of Spain!"

The door opened again. Margaret Beaufort returned to hear the last few words of this exchange. Despite her gravid state, Bessy was as quick-witted as ever. "My Lady, do enlighten my sister – was there not a Katherine, daughter of your Lancaster ancestor John of Gaunt, who married into Spain?"

Henry Tudor's mother relaxed her expression. "Indeed so. And there is another Katherine in Spain now, though of course they call her Catalina, directly descended from that English princess. My son thinks she will make a good bride for Prince Arthur when the time comes". She bustled away to re-position the statue of Our Lady on the little altar.

Katherine smiled ruefully. "I might have liked to be a queen of Spain, Your Grace, but not if it meant leaving you."

Bessy looked deep into her eyes. "We will find you a good husband, sister," and added very quietly, "Someone who will keep you safe and be honoured to have a Plantagenet bride. You too, Anne, of course. Cecily is safe. Meg is safe. I can do the same for you both. It is easier for girls. Trust me. "

"Lancastrians?" Katherine had one eye on Lady Margaret who was now thankfully most occupied with inspecting the fresh linen just brought in by a maid.

Bessy leaned even further into her cushion to muffle her words. "Well, hardly Yorkists, my little sister. Where would we find one of those today? I was thinking of handsome, pleasant young men who would love you both for your sweet selves. "

"No more Scottish princes?" asked Anne warily. "The King once suggested sending us all north to marry assorted members of the Scottish royal family."

Bessy snorted with laughter. "And we were all highly relieved when the Scots king perished at the hands of rebels at Sauchieburn! No, I will look for good English nobleman who will agree to let you both come to court and stay with me forever," Tears suddenly flooded her eyes." I cannot lose my sisters. I cannot."

"My Lady," Katherine called to Margaret Beaufort, "Her Grace the Queen wishes for some air. May we not open the window?"

The King's mother looked anxious. "The air could be dangerous. But Her Grace may have a little more light if she wishes."

Katherine:

Fortunately we did not have to wait too long for this next royal baby. She was born on Saturday July 2nd and Henry Tudor must have felt a little guilty for he agreed that she might be named Elizabeth after her grandmother so recently deceased. She was like a fairy child, tiny and unmistakably Wydville with her silver blonde hair. She was baptised and taken from Sheen to the royal nursery at Eltham where her siblings were introduced to her. I loved the peace at Eltham – it is where I, too, was born and I felt comfortable there, reassured that some part of my early childhood had not been spent in the dank rooms of sanctuary. I knew then that this was the place I dreamed about: the plesaunce, where I learned to walk between the apple trees, the parkland where deer roamed and where the great oaks cast their shade over buttercup-filled meadows.

Edward IV had built the Great Hall in the years before Katherine's birth. To her, it symbolised her family who once lived in this place. At dinner she allowed her gaze to rise up to the soaring, vaulted hammer-beam roof and rest upon the intricate carvings of the falcons in a fetterlock badge. She pretended that it was

198

her own family who still sat upon the dais: if she half closed her eyes she could see shadows of her older brothers in their rightful places and the outline of a blond giant who laughed uproariously as his fool tumbled and turned. She saw her mother, graceful in her butterfly headdress, smiling upon her beautiful daughters and turning to catch the eye of two handsome young men – her Grey sons. Seated next to her, raising a silver goblet in a toast to her beauty, was her beloved brother, Anthony, cultured and debonair. There was music, and colour, and a whole future of stable Plantagenet rule in this England finally at peace with itself. Then the vision faded. Rubbing her eyes, Katherine looked again and saw Henry Tudor, My Lady the King's Mother and Bessy – all quietly eating. How the world had changed in ten years.

The latest little Tudor was installed with her retinue of nursemaids and rockers, although her sister Margaret did not stand on ceremony. She shook back her auburn curls, peered into the cradle and poked the tightly swaddled babe. "Is she real, Aunt Katherine?"

Prince Harry hardly had time to acknowledge his new sister. He paused briefly on his way to more interesting things and glanced at her. "Yah!" he declared, which could have meant anything, then turned away.

Six year old Arthur regarded her seriously. "She is a sweeting," he announced. "I do not mind another sister." He was already a kind boy, his mother's son. He was rarely seen in the nursery because as the heir he was being brought up in his father's world, groomed for future kingship.

King Henry came with Arthur, to look upon his expanding brood. Two princes. Two princesses. The Tudor dynasty firmly established. Bessy had kept her part of the bargain and played her part to perfection. Katherine could see the satisfaction in his narrow face. Yet he was not a natural father; he did not know what to say to Arthur, who gazed at him in awe, or how to manage boisterous Margaret who wanted him to admire her favourite poppet. Young Harry had not even noticed his father, so intent was he upon pestering his nursemaid to pick him up. Henry was relieved when Bessy entered the nursery and the two eldest children clustered round her, adoration in their eyes. Even Harry transferred his attention to his mother, struggling to get down and toddling to grab her hand. Bessy was determined that her children should know her and spent days here at Eltham, directing their household.

Harry hung off her like a burr but she knelt and put her free arm around Arthur's slim frame, holding him close. "How do your studies go, my son? Is Mr Rede pleased with you?"

He leaned into the mother he saw so rarely, eager for her warmth and approval. She smelled of flowers and fresh linen. "I have written a prayer in Latin, Lady Mother, for my new sister." She kissed his light brown hair, enjoying the luxury of having this little Prince of Wales still at home before he set out to establish his own court at Ludlow Castle.

"And you, Margaret? What have you been doing?"

Margaret sighed and scowled. "Making a gown for my poppet, Lady Mother, but the stitches are hard. Look, I pricked my finger!" Woefully, she held it up for inspection.

"Persevere, Margaret. It will come with practice."

"Ma! Ma! Ma!" shouted Harry.

"Katherine, take him, will you?"

Harry was firm and wriggly in her arms. He pressed his hot face into the cool of her neck. "Ka! Ka! Ka!" Already she was his favourite aunt because she was more of a big sister and would play with him but she had soon discovered that the only way to keep him sweet-tempered was to indulge him. It went against her better instincts but struck her as the safest option – he had been known to bite when thwarted. Katherine sensed that Bessy worried for this fiery little boy – feared that if left uncurbed he might grow into a child others would not like but Henry Tudor laughed and said Harry would make a fine archbishop one day. Privately, Katherine thought it was most unlikely.

Now, amidst the chatter, Katherine realised that the King was taking his leave of his family, saying he and Arthur must return to Westminster and then Arthur would travel on into Shropshire. Katherine shivered. Once her own brother Edward had lived in the same rooms at Ludlow, seen the same views over the River Teme, worshipped in the same round chapel in the courtyard, watched the same starry sky from the battlements and dreamed of a far-off day when as a grown man he would become a worthy king. Never to be …

"Arthur!" Bessy laid her hand upon her son's head that he might feel her blessing. "Take heed of Mr Rede, and be respectful of all those who care for you and guide you." Her voice faltered slightly but she recovered." I will visit you at Ludlow."

Katherine wished she could see into the future. She knew it was treason in her heart but she longed for the day when this gentle-hearted, half-Plantagenet boy would be king, instead of Henry Tudor, with his suspicious eyes.

26

Katherine: I was *fourteen. Old enough now to follow most of the rumours that lapped at the edges of my brother-in-law's court. He longed to feel safe upon the throne he had wrested from my family but I was learning that he could never drop his guard. Eight years had passed but there were still those who looked for a chance to restore the White Rose. Sometimes I thought of my cousin Ned growing to lonely adulthood in the Tower but never glimpsed for six years. I heard how Lambert Simnel had left the kitchens and was training as a falconer. Henry said there would always be pretenders to his throne so he tried to laugh off the whispers of another boy who surfaced in Europe. Merchant ships from the Low Countries, docking in London, in Southampton, in Harwich, were all on fire with the news.*

" **... the great malice that the Lady Margaret of Burgundy beareth continually against us, as she showed lately in sending hither another feigned lad called Perkin Warbeck ...which called himself the second son of King Edward IV"** Letter from King Henry VII, 20th July 1493, at Kenilworth (archives of the Earl of Shrewsbury)

1493

The court had been at Kenilworth for the summer and Katherine had loved the progress through England. Not since Heytesbury had she travelled any distance from the London palaces. She was enchanted by the old castle with its warm red sandstone, lavishly appointed chambers and the grand staircase that led to the Great Hall, from where she could look out over the shining Great Mere. In fresh Warwickshire they were far away from the smells and plagues of London in the summer heats. But rumour had pursued them all up through the counties of

Berkshire and Oxfordshire. Katherine knew that Kenilworth had been chosen, not for its romantic associations with Henry Tudor's ancestor John of Gaunt, but because it sat squarely in the middle of England, and from its doughty keep the Tudor army could sally forth to whatever coast the Pretender might choose for his invasion.

Katherine sat in an open window, looking out over the jousting yard where a group of young men were practising their skills at the quintain and allowed her thoughts to consider what she had lately overheard. In her ears were the thuds of lance upon shield, the scrunch of the horses' hooves in the sand and the crazy whirr of the spinning, man-shaped target. A cry of triumph went up as one of the young lords was successful.

She had learned a new name this week: Perkin Warbeck. A name that sounded faintly ridiculous as she tried it out aloud. It had coarse edges and lay thick upon her tongue like a piece of rough pastry. The name of a farm boy or a shoemaker's apprentice. Inside her head she spoke another name but ensured that her lips did not move. *Richard Plantagenet, Duke of York.* She tried the two names together, balancing them to see if there was any point at which one might complement the other. Was there any remote chance that these two names could be one and the same person?

Another shout of approbation as another young man hit the quintain. She thought about her aunt, far away in Burgundy, whom she knew hated Henry Tudor with a passion and longed for revenge for his crimes against the House of York. For two years she had been sheltering a boy growing to manhood – a boy with light russet curls and noble bearing – a boy who now declared himself to be the youngest prince lost in the Tower ten years ago but miraculously saved from death because of his youth and innocence.

In the last few days Katherine had found out that others believed in him, either through expedience or because he represented a myth they were so desperate to see become reality. Her knowledge had been gleaned in whispered conversations with Cecily, visiting from her home in Hertfordshire. Every day they sought some pretence to be alone together. Sisters who wanted to gossip.

"He was in Ireland! Then taken to France! The French king says he is truly our brother!" Yesterday in the rose garden, Cecily had been wild with excitement, her dark blue eyes sparkling with intensity. At twenty four she looked no older than eighteen. She was happy in her marriage to a man who valued her spirited personality and was proud of her beauty. John Welles supplied the fatherly nature she so missed, tempered with amused tolerance of her fiery passions and her sometimes wild imagination. One of the most unexpected outcomes of her new life was her relationship with Margaret Beaufort. Fond of her half-brother, the King's mother seemed to like Cecily because she had made him happy. "John says I remind her of herself when she was young". Bessy, Anne and Katherine had looked astonished.

When Cecily offered to take the children outside to play, she insisted that Katherine should join them. Katherine held three-year-old Harry by the hand while Margaret skipped ahead with her pet greyhound. The nursemaid trailed along behind, out of earshot, carrying little Elizabeth who was a few weeks past her first birthday but showing no signs of wanting to walk. Cecily had left her own little girls at her home to come and spend a few precious weeks with her sisters.

"Katherine, I can remember Dickon so clearly! I will never forget they day they took him."

In the open air words can just float away on the breeze. *As long as we are careful, thought Katherine, we can speak.* Above them the massive bulk of the castle walls absorbed secrets with the sunshine. She glanced covertly around the garden but they were alone, apart from the nursemaid. Harry clamoured for his freedom and then charged off in pursuit of his sister, running up and down the alleys heady with the perfume of late summer roses. Beds and beds of red roses.

"And what does our sister say?"

"What can she say? She dare not speak a word. And she thinks of what it will mean now to *her* son, to Arthur. We cannot expect her to choose between her own son and a brother she has not seen for ten years. But there are placards all over the city urging people to rise up!" Cecily's voice was hardly above a whisper but infused with zest. "My husband says there are rumours everywhere of a White Rose invasion!"

Katherine gazed across the sea of red roses and tried to imagine waves of white ones. Could it ever be? "But Cecily, what will it mean? For Bessy and the King? For all of us?"

Her sister plucked a red rose and tore the petals off, one by one, allowing them to drop back on to the soil. "My husband is a good man, a kind man. But you and I, Bessy and Anne – we come from different stock."

Ahead, Margaret was bellowing with outrage – Harry had caught up with her and pushed her over. She had landed amongst the roses and their thorns. Harry was standing with his hands on his hips, laughing triumphantly at his sister's discomfiture. Fortunately, the nursemaid set off to sort him out.

"But we can do nothing, Cecily. We are women. And as you say, Bessy has her own sons to think of. She has to be a Tudor now. Our brothers –" she had dared to say those words, "- are long gone. *He* is so powerful. What good can come of it?"

"If Arthur and Harry must step aside for a rightful king, so be it," Cecily's words were so low Katherine could barely hear them yet they cut deep into her ears. "And our aunt in Burgundy is a woman, yet she dares to declare for him."

"But if it means fighting again? Cousin against cousin? Englishmen dead in their thousands in battles up and down the land?"

Cecily just tossed her pretty head and went to help the nursemaid who was not able to hold little Elizabeth *and* prevent Harry from further mischief. To Katherine's astonishment Cecily slapped Harry's sturdy little legs. He tried to hit her back, red in the face with anger, but being accustomed to young children she held him easily at arm's length.

"Cecily, you can't –"

"Oh, I can – he may think he is important but he cannot be allowed to behave as he pleases. He knows he deserved it, too. What do you say, my young prince? Will you run and tell your mother that Aunt Cecily smacked you?" Her voice held a challenge that Harry could not meet. "Because, if you do, I shall tell her why. And your grandmother will smack you again. She does not like disobedient boys."

The nursemaid was wide-eyed. Margaret scrambled out of the rose bushes, nursing scratched arms and hands. Harry stamped his foot defiantly. "No like Aunt Sissly," he declared, pulling free and running to hide his head in Katherine's skirts. "Like Aunt Kaff'rin. My fav'rite aunt."

And so now Katherine watched the young men of the court honing their skills, wondering whether this new generation would be called upon to fight for real – whether they must gallop out of the tilting yard on to battlefields, whose side they would choose and how many more families must be wiped out in the name of her own. Suddenly, she was aware of her chest tightening and tears blurring her vision. A picture came into her mind of Bessy running across the precincts at Westminster – another queen fleeing into sanctuary with a brood of small children, two little princes and two princesses, whilst a king called Henry Tudor rode to meet a young man with a white rose in his helm somewhere on English farmland. Land that would surely shake to the sound of thundering hooves, air that would be thick with screams of the dying and running red with blood. An involuntary sob was torn out of her.

"Your Grace?" Through wet lashes Katherine looked down on the yard. A slim young man, somewhat older than herself, was sitting easily on a steaming but handsome bay horse. He had removed his helmet and his chestnut hair stuck up comically; he tucked the headgear under his arm and she saw how his forehead, cheeks and chin were marked by lines from its pressure but there was concern in his dark eyes. She had seen him before, at some of the feasts and ceremonies here at Kenilworth and at Westminster, but could not place him.

"Good day, Your Grace," he said, and she caught the respectful emphasis upon her title. Not all used it; to some she was simply the Lady Katherine.

Katherine nodded politely. She did not think she should respond *After all, I am a princess and he is but a knight.* He opened his mouth to speak again, looked hesitant, closed it, then said suddenly, "Forgive my presumption, Your Grace. I thought you looked sad."

He *was* being presumptuous. Katherine knew she should rise, turn on her heel and walk away from the window in frosty silence but his eyes were warm with sympathy and sincerity. The horse tossed his head, shook his mane and snorted softly.

"You see, Seaton thinks so too."

"Seaton?"

"He is named for his birthplace, Your Grace – Seaton is by the sea in Devon. There is a long shingly beach with red cliffs on one side and white on the other."

"I have never seen the sea," Katherine responded, despite herself.

"That is a pity, Your Grace. You would like it. I am sure. "

She wanted him to stay for a minute, so that the thoughts of battle and blood could be swept from her mind.

"What colour is the sea, sir?"

He considered for a moment. "It can be blue like the sky – or green, like the grass – or grey, like the clouds – or even silver, like a looking glass – or some days dark as lead. But I like it best when it is like an opal – when all the colours merge and glow."

Katherine was astonished. She had never really spoken alone with a young man before. She did not know what more to say but he continued in an easy tone. "My home is in Devon, we have many manors in the county. From our castle at

Colyford it's only a short ride to the coast, so I have seen the sea in all its moods and colours."

It was clear that he thought she knew who he was so it would be embarrassing now to ask his name. She wondered whether he knew about the rumours that had come from over the sea about Perkin Warbeck and for a moment wished she could ask him but that would be dangerous for them both. Caught between mortification and apprehension, she simply inclined her head in silent acknowledgement. He did not seem perturbed but bowed politely.

"Well, with your permission I must go now. Seaton!" And suddenly the horse was sinking his forelegs, inclining his own magnificent head in a deep bow. Katherine burst out laughing at the skill of the performance, then young Sir William Courtenay gathered his reins and the two of them wheeled away across the yard, throwing up a cloud of earth-dust. Katherine's heart was racing. Perkin Warbeck was a thousand miles away in the Low Countries. She wished she had had the courage to ask the young man his name.

27

Greenwich August 1494

It was late morning. The sun in Leo sent shafts through the narrow windows of the palace and warmed patches of the blues, greens and reds of the tapestries on the walls. There was no breath of wind and trees were still outside. Summer was clinging on, with the Kentish fields parched and tawny; the leaves with that dark green fullness that comes before they begin to turn. The streets of the capital were hot and stifling but at Greenwich there was usually a breeze from the estuary. Not today, though.

At fifteen, Katherine was now well-used to her role as lady-in-waiting to her sister. It was not an onerous duty. On the contrary, she enjoyed and cherished keeping Bessy company – making music with her; reading with her; helping with embroideries; dancing and being on hand when foreign dignitaries were at court. There were ladies of the bedchamber to attend to Bessy's personal needs but Katherine and her sisters had lived so closely together in the past, with few attendants, that helping Bessy to bathe, or dress, or arrange her hair seemed second nature. Often Bessy would dismiss her women to be alone with Anne or Katherine. It provided a welcome opportunity to talk without being overheard.

This morning Bessy had risen late. At twenty eight, and the mother of four children, she was just beginnng to put on weight. Her slender, girlish figure was giving way to a more matronly outline. As Katherine held out a clean linen shift Bessy looked down at her body ruefully. "I do not seem to have inherited Mama's ability to look years younger than her real age! How she managed to have a waist like a weasel after bearing twelve children I shall never know!"

"She was extraordinary," agreed Katherine.

Bessy appraised her sister critically. "I believe *you* and Cecily to be the ones who have her figure. Look at Cecily – two children now and you would think

208

she was still a maid. It's Anne and me who will have to put up with Papa's plumpness!"

"Anne is not plump!" protested Katherine, laughing, "she's just well-rounded."

"She had best stop eating so much then. She does not have my height."

"Have we changed much, since we were all children?" Katherine helped her sister step into one of her favourite gowns and laced the back. Bessy then sat in front of her looking glass and shook out her hair ready for combing. It was still her best feature – thick and wavy, rippling over her shoulders and down her back. It was a queeen's right to wear her hair loose when she wished but Bessy now hid it modestly beneath her favourite headdresses, just leaving a tantalising little glimpse of at the top.

"It was always said I was a fair mix of our parents, unmistakably Papa's with my red-gold hair, whereas *you* have Mama's blondeness. Yet *you* have the brown eyes that come from our grandfather of York, and Cecily has his dark hair. Anne is Papa to the life, blue eyes and his smile; dear Bridget – well, I doubt she cares much about her hair these days but the last time I saw it, like yours, it was blonde."

"It's funny to think she is only twelve miles away from us here. She will take her final vows next year."

"She is content, Katherine. And safe. Dartford offers her the tranquillity she craves. You must not think of her as lost to us. I send money for her regularly and I know that she prays for us daily."

"Was she … *normal,* as a very little girl? Before we went into sanctuary?"

"I am not sure. I was not with her much when she was very small; I was already at court and you and she were in the nursery. I did not know you very well – until we were all forced to live together all the time. I remember that she had been ill, with a cough and a fever, and for a while we were not sure if she still heard properly."

Katherine was intrigued. It was not often that Bessy seemed willing to talk about those far-off days. She ventured further. "I can remember many things very clearly."

"I think that is wishful thinking, Katherine. You were but four years old."

"The same age as you, then, the *first t*ime our Lady Mother went into sanctuary," Katherine responded, carefully and politely. She was standing just behind Bessy's shoulder, ready with the pins. The edge of her face, too, was caught in the bright silver oval. Bessy stared into it; Katherine held her gaze. She knew full well that four-year-old little girls can remember some things vividly. Not the exact sequence of events, or day to day details – but images that flash cruelly upon the imagination; smells that evoke feelings; snatches of words that whirl through the mind and the way the touch of something once felt under pudgy young fingers can open floodgates of fear and distress. Nightmares that invade sleep.

"Well, I am sure such memories are best forgotten. We are safe now." Katherine could tell that she was creating a forced brightness in her tone. "Goodness, you are a king's daughter, and a queen's sister, aunt to princes and a princess yourself again. Let that be enough." The four words were more of a plea than a statement.

The comb slid through her hair more easily now. Katherine caught up the wavy tresses and began braiding, then carefully looping and pinning. They were silent together – but each aware of a tension. When she finished, Katherine reached for the linen coif then the black and gold, stiff, elaborate gabled headdress which she placed upon Bessy's head, tucking away the last strands of flyaway hair. The embroidered golden lappets hung down either side of her face. Her gown was dark red with patterned collar and cuffs. She suddenly seemed remote and queen-like.

"Will you tell me more of your memories?" Katherine dared to asked

Somewhere between them, dangling unseen, were three names. Three dead names. Not inscribed on any tomb. One was always avoided and two were engraven in their hearts where none could see. *What would my brothers look like today? Edward would be twenty four and Dickon twenty one. And my royal uncle – the same age as my father when he died. Did I dream those days of my childhood?*

Bessy rose, and smoothed her gown. She ran her fingers over the enamelled roses of her necklace then put out her hand to touch Katherine's cheek. Leaning towards her, she planted a gentle kiss on her forehead and Katherine breathed in her perfume of crushed flowers.

"Memories can bring little peace to our hearts. It is far better to look to your future, Katherine, as I have done," she advised. "Indeed, there is no other way for us." The precious time alone together was over; already the other noble ladies-in-waiting were bustling in with Bessy's shoes, a stole for her shoulders and a list of the foreign ambassadors she was to meet that day.

The future, for Anne, at least, was mapped out. John Howard, the Earl of Surrey, who had fought for Richard III at Bosworth, and then sat contritely in the Tower for three years as his punishment, even refusing to escape when he had the chance, was also looking to his future. Upon his release he reminded Henry Tudor of the decade-old betrothal between his son Thomas, and the Princess Anne of York. Bessy had kept very quiet about it. She did not forget how Surrey had taken her brother Dickon from sanctuary that day, but she saw how he began to rise in her husband's favour. Henry did not hold grudges against those who set out to prove their loyalty to the new regime. Thomas was young, and his star was rising. Bessy judged him to be a safe choice for Anne.

Katherine: *I grew up in a dangerous year. In October, my rumbustious little nephew was pronounced to be the new Duke of York. Part of me wanted to believe that the King was making some attempt to honour my family name, but I struggled to believe such kind intentions. Cecily said she was convinced it was all to demonstrate that our brother Dickon was truly dead, and that The Feigned Lad in Europe could not possibly be he. I am afraid that Prince Harry received far more attention than was good for him. In his tiny suit of armour he strutted through Westminster Abbey like a proud little partridge.*

The celebrations to acclaim the new Duke of York went on for weeks. London glowed in the autumn sunshine – a spectacle of gold and blue, from the jousting arena hung with cloth of Arras to the embroidered cushions on the seats where Katherine and Anne sat with five-year-old Princess Margaret anchored between them. It was the perfect St Martin's summer – unbelievable days of warmth even though leaves were falling from the trees. Katherine enjoyed watching the jousting. She marvelled at the speed at which the young men of the court galloped down the lists towards one another, their horses' hooves flinging up the sawdust and dirt; she closed her eyes at the moment of contact, flinching at every *"thwack!"* of lance upon shield and only opened them to the cheers of approval from the spectators. Little Margaret presented the prizes but loved all the contestants so much she wanted to reward every knight. Solemnly, she stepped forward with the bags of gold and silver and stood before the great horses whose necks glistened with sweat and foam. Katherine scanned the victors, wondering if the young man who had spoken so kindly last summer at Kenilworth might be among them.

The King liked the idea of Anne being married to one of his loyal followers. The Howard family liked the idea of their heir marrying a princess but diplomatically never said so. Anne looked at Thomas Howard and with Bessy's encouragement pronounced him to be acceptable. Thomas Howard looked at Anne and saw a succession of sons with royal blood. After the marriage, arranged for early February, she would retire from Bessy's service and begin a new life on her husband's estates. For now, Katherine clung eagerly to the last few months of her sister's quiet, sincere company. Cecily's marriage had proved an unexpected success; John Welles allowed her to come to court for all sorts of festivities – Katherine hoped that Anne's husband would be equally loving and tolerant. Time would tell.

Within weeks Nature had righted herself and the first frosts came that lasted over the Christmas season and into January. Light snow fell, transforming the dirty streets and lying like white velvet on the rooftops. Anne went to Greenwich to prepare for her marriage but Henry, Bessy and the court moved to the royal apartments at the Tower. Katherine was filled with acute anxiety. The lodgings were comfortable and totally separate from the main body of the Tower, but she could only think that this was the place where her brothers had last been seen alive and where her young cousin was still incarcerated. She lay awake at night, listening to sounds so different from all the other riverside palaces. She was alert to every step, every creak, every mutter. In the icy air all sounds were intensified: boots marched on stone; metal keys clanked; animals in the menagerie roared and the cold Thames lapped rhythmically at the water gates. Somewhere in this vast, ancient place her cousin Ned lay awake and alone, now a young man of twenty bereft of family and friends. Katherine wept into her pillow, thinking about him. What must it be like to be imprisoned here? Was he thinking, even now, of his lost royal cousins, and his own father, brought here to drown in a butt of malmsey wine? They would not tell her where he was held and she found herself surreptitiously sneaking glances at all the windows whenever she crossed the courtyards or took the air upon the walkways.

It seemed that the court lived in a perpetual state of high alert. Katherine noticed how the number of night-time guards had doubled, and that the identity of anyone entering the Tower precincts was checked and re-checked. Faithful Elyn, who now served as one of Bessy's body servants, complained loudly when she returned from visiting her family.

"Jesu, they *know* who I am! Do they think I am hiding Perkin Warbeck under my cloak?"

The days spent at the Tower were short on daylight but long in hours. Bessy and her ladies-in-waiting whiled away grey mornings and dark afternoons playing cards and devising ideas for the entertainments at Anne's wedding which was now only days away, and Bessy's birthday which followed it. Katherine looked forward to leaving the brooding fortress and travelling downstream, back to the light and space of Greenwich.

Then, suddenly, the court was ignited by the startling news that Sir William Stanley, brother-in-law to Lady Margaret Beaufort, had been arrested for treason. Bessy and a handful of her women were seated by the fire on a raw morning in early February when the King himself was announced. All the women rose and sank into deep curtsies. He bowed formally to his wife before kissing the cheek she offered and then motioning that she should be seated again. Her women tried to lose themselves against the walls.

"Well, it seems the conspiracy around the Feigned Lad has crept to our very hearth. Lord Clifford has told me the whole sorry story. " Stanley was the Lord Chamberlain and the overseer of all that happened in the royal apartments. Henry Tudor was white with anger, shocked by the betrayal so close to home. Katherine felt her hands trembling as she tried to gather up the deck of cards. "But he will not stab me in the back," barked the King, "because I shall strike his head from his body." A ripple of consternation ran round the room.

"What does your mother say?" Bessy folded her hands in her lap and looked up at her husband.

"That the man is a viper. She agrees that he must die."

"And my Lord Thomas Stanley?"

"My mother's husband is as appalled as she is."

Katherine turned her face away, towards the fire. The soft skin of her cheek skin began to prickle with its heat. All knew that the King's spies had been everywhere in the last few months, combing through households, alert for any whisper of support for the Feigned Lad in Europe.

"And what do you think has been found at his home in north Wales?"

"I cannot imagine, sir."

"Enough money to pay for an army, and clear evidence of his Yorkist sympathies."

Katherine was sure his eyes were boring into her. She tried to lower her head even further into the furred neckline of her gown. How on earth could Bessy like this man? She had never heard a word of criticism pass her sister's lips concerning her husband and now she simply waited; there was no trace of curiosity on Bessy's face or in her demeanour. *What evidence,* wondered Katherine, with her eyes fixed firmly on the floor.

"Yes, a Yorkist livery collar, with all its symbols of treachery!"

White roses, thought Katherine, *and sunbursts, and fetterlocks, and ostrich feathers – all proudly blazoned in my father's day to proclaim our family.* She closed her eyes and they danced before her, in church windows, on shields, on tapestries, on jewellery, on the collars her father's followers men wore around their broad shoulders.

"I have told you what I think of the Stanleys, husband. They turn their coats to suit their own interest."

For a moment Bessy's ladies held their breath in horror. That the Queen should dare to speak so openly! Katherine was aware of her breakfast churning in her stomach. Henry gave a guffaw of cynical laughter. "Indeed – I should have heeded your wise words, my dear. There will always be those who betray me, even if I have given them everything. But to find a traitor in my own family – my mother's brother-in law, whom I have raised high!" The women in the room seemed like frozen statues – who knew whether some relation had also betrayed the King?

Astonishingly, Henry sighed and sat down heavily in the chair opposite his wife. He did not speak but his anger seemed to subside. Bessy signalled to her ladies to leave and they scuttled out in relief. Katherine rose hastily to follow but Henry's hand reached out and grasped her wrist.

"I have news for the Lady Katherine. She may stay."

He released her quickly but her wrist burned. She remained standing, head bowed. He rarely addressed her directly. She ate in his company, danced before him, followed in his wake in processions and played with his children but had never held a sustained conversation with him. He had not invited intimacy from his wife's family. Katherine's heart thudded in her chest.

"It has occurred to me that your sister may be advantageously married into the Courtenay family."

He was not consulting her, but beginning a discussion with his wife – gauging her reaction. Katherine bit her bottom lip and pressed her fingernails into her palms.

"The Courtenays are an old and noble family," said Henry, "loyal to me, and to my Lancaster ancestors. These things matter."

He wishes to bury my York identity in some jumped-up English family, as he has done with Cecily, Meg and Anne. He will marry me to some man who was with him in Brittany, as a reward for his loyalty. William Stanley's support of the Feigned Lad has spooked him.

"They would be acquiring a rare and precious pearl," said Bessy. "A princess. Your sister-in-law."

"In the past many English princesses have married into the leading families of England," said Henry.

"Yes," considered Bessy, "the Nevilles, and the Mowbrays, and the Mortimers." It was what she left unsaid that had the most impact. Those families had been all but wiped out. "I would not call the Courtenays a leading family, but I can see why they would want such a strategic alliance. They would feel they could claim kinship with you."

Henry looked at her sharply. "They have not asked for it. It is my idea. I thought to offer your sister as a reward for their allegiance."

At least he is honest. But must he speak of me as if I am some commodity, to be bartered or bought, even when I am actually standing next to him?

It was as if Henry had read her thoughts. He directed his insightful gaze at Katherine. "I am sure your sister recognises the importance of marrying where her sovereign thinks best. Lady Katherine?"

Katherine mustered every ounce of her courage to look at her brother-in-law. At thirty eight deep grooves marked his mouth and his eyes were heavily lidded. The streaks of iron grey at his temples aged him. *How must he feel, when he wakes each morning, and knows there is a boy out there who wants his throne? Ah, but once he was that boy himself, a Lancastrian nobody in Brittany who coveted my Uncle Richard's place. He knows what it is to be a pretender, and he knows that with enough support, and luck, pretenders can find their way to their heart's desire...*

"I am mindful that I must marry where Your Grace pleases," she whispered.

"When are you sixteen?"

"In August, Your Grace?"

215

"And you have your courses?"

Katherine felt a hot blush rise up her chest and knew that her face was turning crimson with embarrassment. She appealed to her sister in dumb anguish. That he should ask such a question, so openly – as if she were some heifer or filly! He laughed, apparently amused by her discomfiture.

"Your modesty does you credit, my dear, but it is something the Courtenays will want to know."

"And will they want her pregnant, before they agree to her union with their family?" There was a biting edge to Bessy's question. Katherine was aghast. She had heard of such goings-on but never in royal families. A sardonic smirk had crept into the corner of Henry Tudor's mouth and a sudden, awful realisation swept across Katherine's comprehension: *he had not agreed to marry Bessy until ...they had all said Prince Arthur had been born a few weeks early, but what if ...*

"My dear, you are alarming your sister! I am merely ascertaining that we may offer her to the Courtenays in good faith. Are you content with this match, Lady Katherine?"

Katherine could not bring herself to point out that no specific man had been mentioned. She was to marry " a Courtenay" – it might mean anything: a middle-aged widower with children already, like Cecily's husband, or some child who she would have to play with for six years while she waited for him to grow up, or (heaven forbid!) some old man in his dotage, with unspeakable infirmities. Fortunately Bessy came to her rescue.

"Who exactly do you have in mind?"

"Sir Edward Courtenay has one son, as yet unmarried. You must remember him, Bessy. The lad came up from Devon and was one of those knighted at your coronation."

Bessy was frowning, sifting faces and names. Scores of new young men circled around the fringes of the Court, hoping to be noticed, willing to carry out the King's business. "Ah, William Courtenay. The one who likes jousting. The one who has taught his horse to do tricks."

Katherine caught her breath in an involuntary gasp of amazement. There could not be such luck in the whole wide world! She sensed a relief as powerful as her own in Bessy's demeanour. She was also alert to the waves of sisterly communication, unspoken but palpable in the short space between them. It was as if Bessy was urging *Take this opportunity! It is your best hope!*

Katherine sank into a well-executed curtsy before Henry Tudor. Her knees no longer wobbled and her breathing was even. "I am content, Your Grace, and I thank you for your interest in my future." Best that he should think her compliant. Katherine could now see and understand exactly the game Bessy had been playing these past ten years. A smile threatened the corner of her lips as she thanked God for her good fortune but she fought it and managed to present an entirely serious face to her brother-in-law. Bessy had also made an obeisance before her husband.

"I do ask, sir, whether Katherine may remain with me at court after her marriage."

Henry Tudor gave circumspect attention to the top of his wife's gabled headdress and the net holding Katherine's blonde hair in place. Whilst the political world swirled around him at least he felt in control of the women in his family and could afford to be magnanimous. This one remaining sister could cause no trouble once allied to the Courtenays. Indeed, allowing her to remain at court could be a useful tool in ensuring Bessy's continuing loyalty.

Tiverton Castle, Devon Summer 1495

William Courtenay was twenty years old. His favourite things in life were his courser, Seaton, his new suit of jousting armour and his new position as Captain in the King's army. His father, Sir Edward, never stopped telling him how lucky he was to have been born at a time when the family had been restored to their earldom and their estates – nearly one hundred manors across the south of England, with sixty in Devon alone. After supper, and several glasses of good Bordeaux wine, Sir Edward could talk for hours about the Courtenay history: how their crusading ancestor Reginald de Courtenay had argued with the French king come to England with Queen Eleanor of Aquitaine and married the Lady Hawise of Okehampton. William had seen Okehampton Castle, perched high above the little town on the edge of a bleak moor and much preferred Tiverton and Colcombe, where the landscape was more forgiving, the winds less bracing and the journey time up to London along the Great West Road a few days shorter.

Sir Edward was also very clear about *what* had brought them all to this happy state of affairs: loyalty to the Lancastrian cause over decades. Courtenay blood had been shed at Towton and Tewkesbury and then endured years of exile in Brittany with Henry Tudor, the rightful heir. Sir Edward had endless stories about his experiences carrying letters between Margaret Beaufort, Elizabeth Wydville and the Duke of Richmond – how he had dodged Yorkist spies at Plymouth, sailed to Roscoff and galloped across the Breton moorlands to deliver messages to Henry Tudor in Vannes. Then, twelve years ago, they had set sail again and on Redemore Plain, he had raised his standard for the Welsh Dragon and hurtled down the hillside to engage in armed combat with King Richard's army. It did not take many cups of wine before he was proudly displaying the scars he had received that day – scars that had earned him the grateful thanks of the new king.

William leaned his head against Seaton's powerful neck and ran his hand down the horse's foreleg, checking for any inflammation. It was warm and comforting in the stables, with wholesome aromas of clean straw, polished leather and horse-flesh. The Earl of Devon's heir could not imagine a better place to spend a July afternoon. Most of the horses were out in the fields but Seaton had banged his leg a few days ago and deserved a bit of pampering. William trusted his groom but liked to double-check everything himself. Seaton whickered softly, his large nostrils dilating with pleasure as William stroked his side. His huge muscles rippled; he shifted position slightly on his immense haunches and swished his silky black tail.

"Will we like her?" murmured William into the horse's satiny bay coat. "Will we manage a wife?"

The news that he was to marry the Princess Katherine of York had come as a shock. William had accepted that marriage to an heiress of his father's choice was an inevitable fact of life, but had imagined she would be from solid Devon stock – a Courtenay cousin from Powderham, or a Champernowne or one of the Edgecumbe girls, or even a Pomeroy. The idea of becoming the Queen's brother-in-law, and by default a close relation of the King, was astounding. His mother was excited beyond measure at the prestige the family would gain from such a union, though also worried beyond measure as to how a Plantagenet princess, used to the luxuries of royal palaces, would cope with the draughty castles of her new family. Sir Edward soothed her, assuring her that Tiverton could rise to the occasion with a few new tapestries, and reminded her that Courtenays had married English princesses before, though he could not quite recall who.

"In any case," William told Seaton," we are to live in London, where my wife will attend the Queen. You and I will still come and go, though."

William thought back to the betrothal, a ceremony held at Windsor before the royal family had begun their summer progress through the Midlands and

North West. He could still feel the cool, slim hand that had been placed in his, and remembered with joy the shy smile Katherine had offered him. She was nearly sixteen, as slender as an ash sapling and her blonde head reached his shoulder. Her eyes were like the deep pools of the river Exe, dark and expressive. In a moment of hilarity he realised that he liked them because they resembled Seaton's – the same trust and spirit. In the few snatched moments of private conversation he tried to tell her how he felt.

"I am so honoured, Your Grace. I never expected -"

"Nor I, sir. I am so lucky."

How a princess, destined to be Queen of Spain in her cradle (so his mother had enlightened him, in hushed, awed tones) could possibly consider herself to be fortunate as the future wife of Courtenay from Devon entirely mystified him.

Seaton nosed at his fist, eager for the handful of oats he had brought. William opened his palm and allowed him his treat: he felt the tickle of the thick velvety lips and smiled at the steady, satisfied chomping. What could he take to Katherine, as a gift? What on earth would please a girl who probably had everything? He thought it unlikely that Sir Edward had any spare money for jewels. Seaton's head suddenly came up, his ears pricked with interest. Out in the fields he could hear one of the mares neighing to attract the attention of her wayward foal. The yearlings were galloping up and down joyously, their hooves thunderous upon the baked red earth. In that moment William Courtenay knew exactly what he would take as his wedding gift to his wife, come the autumn.

28

Eltham Palace, Kent Summer 1495

Katherine was indeed content. The wheel of fortune seemed determined to gather her and swing her upwards. For the first time in her life she found herself contemplating a future. Bessy's advice, offered out of pragmatism and sisterly concern, she now saw as wise beyond measure. William Courtenay attracted her; she liked his firm, well-shaped hands and his strong, lithe build. She liked his thick, unruly brown hair, which glinted with reddish highlights as it caught the sun, and his generous mouth that showed good white teeth when he smiled. She liked the way he spoke humorously yet respectfully to his mother, who tried to look as though an alliance with England's royal family was an everyday occurrence in her family. He had kissed her lips gently after the betrothal ceremony, and held her hand as naturally as a brother, but unlike a brother had slipped his arm around her waist and whispered that he thought her beautiful.

The wedding was arranged for late September, when Bessy and Henry returned from their summer progress. This year, Katherine did not travel with them but remained at Eltham with the children, under the jurisdiction of Margaret Beaufort. Bessy fretted about her little daughter, her namesake Elizabeth, who was slow to walk and talk – like Bridget she often seemed far away, in a world of her own. The contrast was even more striking because Harry and Margaret were such loud, boisterous children, forever pounding at top speed through their nursery palace – disputing over everything and appealing to "Aunt Kaff'ryn" to arbitrate in their differences.

"Only boys can be kings!" declared Harry scornfully, as they played with their mother's long-suffering Fool, Patch, in the Great Hall. It was a wet morning and Patch was giving them pick-a-back rides, jumping over the benches. Katherine sat with little Elizabeth on her knee; the child was like a pale goosedown feather, ethereal in her blondeness. Harry had just declared Patch to be a royal destrier, the mount of their father, and ordered Margaret to wait until he changed back into a lady's palfrey. Furious, Margaret shouted that she was older than him, and a better rider, and that she could ride a king's horse any day.

"Well, you can't, because you are a girl, and girls can't be kings, so you can't."

Affronted, Margaret kicked the nearest bench and howled at the pain in her toes. Patch raised his eyebrows comically – Harry was stuck to his back like a limpet, both hands gripping round his neck.

Katherine was fond of this wilful little boy but sometimes he just needed taking down a peg or two. "Harry, that's not strictly true. In England there is no law against queens; it's just that for hundreds of years kings have had sons."

Patch whinnied quietly and pawed his foot. Harry looked down imperiously upon his two sisters. "Well, you *won't* ever get to be a king, or a queen, either of you, because there is Arthur, and me," A sudden thought struck him. "Aunt Kaff'ryn – if my father dies, and Arthur dies, I will be king, won't I?" Patch whistled loudly – it was treason to talk of the King's death. Katherine kept her composure; children should be answered honestly.

"You know that will not happen, Harry, for Arthur will have his own sons by then."

"But if he doesn't?" persisted the four-year-old prince.

Patch the Fool suddenly reared up and tipped the Duke of York backwards on to a pile of cushions. "Us destriers, my young lord, we know when our knights lose concentration, whether they be kings, princes, dukes or earls – and we throw 'em off!" He galloped round the Hall, shying at imaginary obstacles. Harry lay amongst the cushions and roared. Margaret applauded. Harry scrambled to his feet and hit her. Three-year -old Elizabeth burst into tears.

Katherine composed her features into a disapproving scowl. "Harry. If you behave badly I will write to Her Grace the Queen your mother, and tell her." She knew this would have some effect for Harry adored his mother. His face crumpled immediately. His bravado deflated.

"Don't tell, Aunt Kaff'ryn. Harry will be good." He came to her side, sniffing. Margaret glared at him, and aimed a kick at his shin, which missed. Katherine sighed and hoisted the sobbing Elizabeth on to her hip. Fortunately. Lady Darcy, lady mistress of the children's nursery, appeared from the doorway behind the dais. Katherine thought she had been alerted by the rumpus and had come to rescue her, but was surprised to see her comfortable, middle-aged features etched with anxiety.

"Your Grace! Let me take the children! We are to remove to Westminster within the hour!"

Patch regarded her quizzically. "Why the haste, Mistress?"

"News from the coast," she said shortly, taking Harry and Margaret by the hand.

Katherine's heart missed a beat. "An invasion?" she breathed.

"Aye, but a failed one. "Lady Darcy lowered her voice. "My Lady the King's Mother says the Feigned Lad was sighted off Deal, and sent his men ashore but they were dealt with by the King's men, and he sailed away. They say he will go to Ireland or Scotland. Lady Margaret thinks the royal children should be at Westminster, where we may all be better guarded."

He is like a phantom, flitting around the coast of this island in the sea mists.

Patch was by her side. "Let me take the little princess. Hush, sweeting, old Patch will carry you to your nursemaid. We'll be off on the river soon." He took the tiny child tenderly.

"Who is this Feigned Lad?" asked Margaret, her sharp seven-year-old ears had heard the name before. "What is he to do with us? Aunt Kaff'ryn?"

"Truly, I do not know." She was glad to be able to tell the truth. "Come. Let us do as Lady Darcy bids us, for we must catch the tide."

Westminster September 1495 aged 16

Cecily and Anne pinned her into her wedding gown. It was made of costly white damask, with crimson velvet sleeves and an ermine collar.

"I'm sure I have never seen anything so grand, little sister," observed Cecily dryly. "Does our dear brother-in-law think so highly of the Courtenays that he seeks to impress them? You and I, Anne, did not have anything this magnificent. Are you in his special favour? Do you smile winningly at him over supper?"

"Hardly," said Katherine. "This is re-fashioned from Lady Anne Percy's gown when Harry was made Duke of York last year. Even this gold circlet was worn by her. Bessy remembered, and sent to the Wardrobe."

Anne giggled. "My husband says the King is miserly and trusts no-one to count his money but himself!"

Cecily sniffed. "He certainly keeps Bessy very short. He has it down to a fine art – when Bessy is in debt, which she is most of the time, she has to borrow from him, then pay him back."

Katherine held up her arms as Cecily attached the costly sleeves. She frowned, "Then how has Bessy helped us – you and me, Anne? For William tells me she brokered our marriages herself. The King refused to pay any dowries. Did you know that?"

"I guessed it. I think we have our Grandmama Cecily Neville to thank – for when she died last May Bessy inherited her Mortimer and Clare property."

The three sisters were alone in the hour before Katherine's wedding. They were in the bedchamber that had been Cecily's as a girl, overlooking the fast flowing Thames. Memories of their childhood were strong today as the last of them prepared for a new life.

"It *is* better like this," said Anne. "Sometimes, when I think back to what might have been, I know we are fortunate in many ways. *They* are gone, but *we* have each other."

Cecily glanced at the door. On the other side, they could hear the quiet hub-bub of excited conversation from the ladies-in-waiting who would help conduct Katherine to St Stephen's Chapel.

"Maybe one is not gone," she whispered. "Or at least, not *gone* entirely, just gone somewhere else."

Katherine swung round and her gorgeous sleeves knocked the pot of pins out of Anne's hands. They cascaded to the floor.

"He is in Scotland, at the court of King James," said Cecily swiftly, "and they say that he will marry a Scottish heiress, and the Scots king will give him an army to take his rightful throne."

"Shut *up,* Cecily!" hissed Katherine. "Someone will hear!"

"But he could be our -"

"Shut *up!*" Katherine's hand shot out of the hanging sleeve and delivered a smart smack to the corner of Cecily's mouth. The gilt trimming caught her lip and made it bleed. Cecily dabbed the scarlet drips defiantly.

"He *will* come, and when we see him we will know if he is -"

There was urgent knocking and laughter at the door. Anne shot a frightened look at Cecily and moved to open it. Bessy's favourite unmarried ladies in waiting spilled into the chamber like a flight of butterflies, all gauzy veils and slender arms, surrounding Katherine with exclamations of delight; Cecily was able to slip away to bathe her mouth.

Behind the ladies, her brother Sir Thomas Grey, Marquess of Dorset, was waiting to conduct her to her marriage. Katherine smiled nervously; Bessy told stories of the older half-brother, the womaniser who had been with them in sanctuary, then fled to Brittany. She knew that Henry Tudor did not trust him – Thomas had been used as security against the French loan that allowed him to invade England and was now obliged to give written assurance that he would not commit treason against the Tudors. It was hard to believe he was a brother – old enough to be her father and a stranger with whom she had exchanged no more than pleasantries. Once slim and handsome but now inclined to fleshiness and thinning hair as grey as his name. Married to an heiress and with countless children yet still known as a lecher. But now he offered her his arm, with a droll smile.

"Who would have thought it, my little sister? Our mother would have been proud on this day. Your royal father, too."

For a fleeting moment Katherine heard Elizabeth Wydville's voice, confident and edged with arrogance; clear-toned and regal.

"I think my parents would have preferred to see me wed into Spain, or France, sir."

"Take it from me, my dear, parents are happy to see their children married into security, and the Courtenays are certainly that these days."

She took his arm and he tucked her hand comfortably into the crook of his elbow. It was not far to walk across the palace precinct to the beautiful royal chapel. Katherine had expected to be married in a far more modest setting and suspected Bessy's influence upon the King. She ascended the stone stairway to the upper level, for the royal chapel was built above the one used by the household.

Trumpets blared a short fanfare as she arrived. Katherine was startled but Thomas Grey chuckled. "Our sister the Queen will have her way today. She is determined to see you married properly!"

The chapel was flooded with that unique, golden light of late September. Katherine walked slowly down the central aisle, past the colourful wall paintings towards the great stained glass window at the far end. The choir stalls were filled with the bright faces of boys from the Chapel Royal. Lord William Courtenay was waiting for her, his honest hazel eyes alight with pleasure. Thomas Grey transferred Katherine's hand into his, and the ceremony began.

After the Nuptial Mass, Katherine and William exited into a warm afternoon. The chapel had no bell tower but a celebratory peal burst forth from nearby Westminster Abbey.

"Bells, too!" Katherine heard Cecily just behind her. "We didn't have that, either, did we, Anne?"

William grinned at her, the breeze lifting his wavy chestnut hair from his forehead. "I bet they didn't have a wedding feast in Westminster Hall, either!"

On that day, Katherine felt herself the most fortunate of girls. Blessed with a husband who clearly adored her; honoured by a loving sister, and with her velvet-slippered feet set upon a path of unexpected good fortune. The ghosts of her childhood hovered somewhere but when Lord William Courtenay pulled her into his arms that night she banished them from her consciousness.

The Wife
1496 -1509
1

"Katherine the youngest daughter was married to Lord William Courtenay, the son of the Earl of Devonshire, which long time tossed in either fortune, sometime in wealth, after in adversity ..." Edward Hall, Chronicler

Katherine: *And so began the happiest period of my life. Despite being two people thrown together in marriage by a most unlikely set of circumstances: a King's desire to curry favour; an Earl's ambition and a sister's desperate yearning for my safety, we were also our own selves. In each other we discovered those rare ingredients – compatability, friendship and mutual respect. We both knew that others were using us for their own ends but we did not care. My only sadness was the death of my sister's child, the little Princess Elizabeth, just days after my wedding. A fever, a cough, a runny nose and a rash – and she was gone from us, slipping away in the night as if stolen by faeries. I thought Bessy would go mad with grief. Children died every day, but not **her** children. Henry Tudor wept too, but whether from a father's sorrow or because he had lost a valuable asset I could not tell. They laid her to rest in the Abbey, on the right hand side of the altar and I prayed that my sweet little niece would inherit eternal life in Heaven. At least she had a grave and in due time a tomb of grey marble and a copper-gilt effigy. My royal brothers had no such memorial.*

There was soon another child to fill Bessy's arms, the merriest of all my nieces and nephews, named Mary for the Queen of Heaven. And within a year I had my own child too, a healthy little boy whom my husband cheerfully agreed should be called Edward, after my father and lost brother. My esteemed father-in-law always thought it was in honour of his good self and we chose not to disabuse him. Childbirth came easily to me, as it had to my mother. William and

I joked privately that we would one day have enough descendants to rival any English dynasty.

Rumour and gossip still swirled around the Feigned Lad. My sister Cecily was right when she said that the Scottish king would uphold his cause. We heard that he had been married to the Scots king's cousin, Lady Kateryn Huntley, and that they had their own child. As I rocked my newborn son in his cradle the Feigned Lad and Scots James marched south, only to turn back through lack of money. Then came three years I shall never forget – events seared upon my soul as surely as those times in sanctuary ...

London Summer 1497

"Edward Plantagenet, Earl of Warwick, of whom you have heard before, being kept in the Tower, almost from his tender age, out of all company of men and sight of beasts ... so much that he could not discern a goose from a capon." Edward Hall, Chronicler

Henry Tudor needed more money. Specifically, to finance his campaign against the perfidious James IV of Scotland and the wretched Feigned Lad. In the far south of his realm, the good folk of Cornwall did not see why they should have to pay taxes to fund an army marching northwards. Across the peninsula, from the Lizard to Bodmin, tempers frayed and finally exploded. Why should they pay, when good King Edward Plantagenet had given them their Stannary Charter over a hundred years ago by which they were exempted from such high contributions? With outrage in their hearts they marched across the moorland, led by An Gof the Blacksmith, across the Tamar, through green and rolling Devon; on into the flatlands of Somerset; onwards across the ancient plain of Salisbury; onwards into Surrey – hoping that the stout-hearted men of Kent, who had rebelled against arrogant kings and their tax collectors in days gone by, would flock to their West Country brothers' banner. They wished, they said, to enjoin the King to rid himself of his evil advisors

The King's army was in the north, led by Anne's father-in-law the Earl of Surrey. Henry Tudor winced when he realised thousands of disgruntled Cornish, Somerset and Wiltshire men were waiting at the edge of his capital. Hastily he set to mustering all the men he could. Luckily for him, the oldest inhabitants of London remembered their grandfathers' stories of how the Kentish rebels had once stormed through the city, killing and looting. How they had razed the Savoy palace to the ground, broken into the Tower and dragged an archbishop to his death, and rudely kissed the king's mother for good measure. In panic, they nailed wooden boards across their shops; cried "Every man to harness!" and rushed to defend the gates and walls of their city.

As Henry Tudor settled his bejewelled salet upon his head and prepared for battle, Lady Margaret Beaufort, Bessy, Katherine and the youngest children fled from vulnerable Eltham to the security of the Tower.

At dawn, on the morning of June 16th, after a sleepless night, Katherine crept out of Bessy's rooms in this, her least favourite royal residence. She smiled winningly at the young man-at-arms, who took her for a servant in Elyn's cloak, and let her pass, and soon she was standing upon the ramparts, looking eastwards to the Black Heath. There was an early morning heat haze rising off the marshlands and a low, deep murmur in the far distance.

As far as she knew, William was still in Exeter with his father, having been involved in defending the city from the Cornish rebels.

Right Well-beloved Wife

The Cornishmen marched through. We reached a compromise without bloodshed or siege. I truly believe they wish only to speak with the King and make him realise the unfairness of his levies, and rid himself of evil advisors, but if they should come unto the walls of London I beg you to take our son from Eltham and go with your sister into safety.

William

Safety. Katherine shuddered. Who, of her family, had ever been safe in this place? She knew Bessy felt the same. This fortress was no refuge for children of the House of York. Somewhere nearby, her cousin Ned still languished, aged twenty one but now never seen or visited. Meg's devotion to the brother she had not laid eyes on in five years was pitiful. Her letters were never answered and her pleas for news fell on stony ground. When she came to court to wait upon Bessy she told them how her husband advised against even mentioning her brother's name, let alone asking permission to visit him.

"God's teeth! My Lady, you should not be here! You must return to the White Tower, where we can best protect you." A ruddy-faced captain, with weary eyes and a stained leather jerkin, had recognised her, and was trying to steer her away from her vantage point.

"How many are there?" She strained her eyes to the horizon where the rising sun was beginning to burn away the mist; dancing glitters indicated where Henry Tudor's men had gathered in their armour, ready to fight. The Cornishmen's idea that they would talk to the king had long since evaporated. They even had a leader now – a nobleman named Aubney.

"They say about fifteen thousand, my Lady, but they have no horses, and no artillery."

Katherine sighed. "Why must men fight and die?"

The captain regarded her sympathetically. "Because we have causes we believe in, I suppose, my Lady. We fight when we think we are right and those we fight against are wrong – whether it's true or not." He had a stout honesty she liked.

Katherine leaned her elbows on the parapet. "And you think these Cornish men are wrong – to refuse to pay the taxes? Would you want to pay them, if you were Cornish?"

He looked at her warily. "I am true to my King. Now please, come with me back into the Keep." He was a decent man, and worried about the level of defence he could muster to keep these royal ladies safe.

"I will come," responded Katherine, "on one condition. What is your name?"

"Darch, my Lady."

"Your Christian name?"

"Christopher, my Lady." He looked distinctly uncomfortable. Overhead a lone seagull circled, screeching.

"Do you know where the Earl of Warwick is kept?" If Katherine had run him through with a poignard he could not have looked any more shocked. She caught the flicker of assent in his expression; he fought to hide it but she knew.

"Would you take me to him, Christopher? For no more than half an hour? Now, while everyone is so caught up in other events? He is my cousin. I have not seen him for ten years." The words came tumbling out. "We loved him as a boy. His sister grieves so much. If I could but see him, and tell her …" Suddenly she realised the absolute folly of what she had just requested. Why, this man had just said he was true to the King – he would be more likely to march her back into the White Tower under armed guard and have her accused of treason.

Yet some instinct urged her on. "I am no threat, Captain, to you, or him, or anyone. His sister can no longer come to him because she lives elsewhere."

Christopher Darch stared at her. There was a century of silence between them whilst the seagull landed on the top of the wall and squawked at them. Katherine could smell the sour tang of the river and hear the water lapping at the gateway beneath. She tugged at a ring she wore on the forefinger of her right hand. "You can have this. It is a garnet, with pearls. You can give it to your wife, or sell it and buy something for your children."

It was six o'clock in the morning. The night guards would soon be handing over to the day time men at arms. Many had gone with the King to the Black Heath. Even though the Queen, the children and her close relations were here to be kept safe, the Tower could not boast much of a defence. The permanent prisoners were not well-guarded. Captain Christopher Darch knew what he should do: he should return this young lady to the royal rooms in the White Tower and lock her in. Instead, he found himself executing the swiftest of nods.

"Come now. Say nothing. Follow me."

He bundled her along the ramparts and down a steep stone flight of steps, then through an archway and along a cobbled path. The inner ward of the Tower was like a little village street with doorways and alleyways. Surprisingly they passed no-one although Katherine could hear distant voices and clanging, as of pots and pans. They were approaching the point where the inner ward connected with the outer, and where a sturdy, grey stone tower stood sentinel. He led her under its tall archway then pushed her flat against the wall by the door, and pulled up the set of keys which dangled from his thick leather belt. The largest he inserted into the lock and turned. It grated slightly and Katherine hardly dared to breathe. Then he had whisked her inside and was locking the door behind himelf. They were in a small guardroom with steps leading upwards. He indicated with his thumb.

"Up there. Ten minutes."

Katherine climbed the tight, narrow steps, steadying herself against the cold stone wall. A studded oak door. An iron latch. She lifted it slowly and the door swung open. The room was squarish with two lancet windows. The floor was covered in straw and a pallet bed lay against the wall. On the bed a human form lay hunched under a coverlet. There was nothing else in the room; no books, no sign of games, music or other pastime. The straw was fairly clean but there was a musty smell, as if of mice or old food. In the early morning sunlight cobwebs were easily distinguished, festooned across the walls and ceiling. A large spider scuttled for the open door. Katherine's heart hammered in her breast. The latch had creaked and the form on the bed turned over. A thin, boyish face, with several days' worth of fair stubble. Dirty blond hair. Meg's grey-blue eyes. The long Plantagenet nose that defined so many of her family.

"Ned?" She did not dare speak above a whisper.

He watched her, as a maltreated animal might regard its next keeper. *There are ten minutes in the world in which to bring him some vestige of comfort.* The only thing to do was talk to him.

"Ned. You will not recognise me. It has been so long but I am little Katherine, your cousin. We were once together as children. I want you to know that we do not forget you. Not me, or Bessy, or Cecily, or Anne ... or Meg. " His eyes filled with disbelief, then wonderment, then with tears. A fat globule spilled out and ran down his pale cheek. "Meg is at Ludlow. She has a good husband. She has children. She ... she comes to court. She prays for you, every day. She says she thinks of you when the sun rises and when it sets." He did not move but just lay on his side. He looked towards the windows where the light filtered in. "Every day, Ned, when the sun rises. Now. Your sister Meg is thinking of you now. " *How many minutes left?*

"Bessy has tried, Ned, but the King won't listen. Not yet. Maybe one day. When it's safe."

Outside there was a cheerful, masculine whistling and then a burst of tuneful baritone that faded as its owner walked away into the inner ward. What on earth could she say to this young man whose life was being drained away in this chamber? What sort of mind could order such an existence for a fellow human being? Ned had grown to manhood in a space no bigger than Seaton's stable. The cruelty of it all suddenly threatened to overwhelm her but somehow she mastered her emotions. She wanted to approach him but he emitted an acrid smell of sweat and under the bed was an open pot in which a fat turd swam in dark yellow urine. A film of shame crossed his face.

"Oh no, Ned. Nothing is your fault." Despite her good intentions she was near to sobbing. *How many more minutes?* "It may end. There is a boy in Europe, who might be – Oh, Sweet Jesu, have *hope,* Ned. Do not give up *hope.* "

He was mouthing something. *What is he saying? Can he speak?*

"Kaspar? Yes, I remember Kaspar! He went with Meg to her new home."

When his voice finally came, it was rasping and quavering. Not a man's voice but with slips in pitch as though it was still a boy's treble cracking into uncertain maturity. "Tell Meg. I miss her. I love her." He pushed himself up on his elbows but then seemed defeated by the effort and collapsed down again, face in the filthy pillow, his long arms dangling almost to the floor. It seemed he would not look at her again. Katherine took a deep breath and crossed the short distance across the chamber. She leaned down and kissed the back of his head; under her lips his hair was soft and thick, though dense with greasy dust. Then she ignored the foul stench from beneath and simply took his nearby hand and folded it against her heart.

"Do whatever you can to survive, Ned. It's what we all have done, to get this far. Better days will come for you, as they have for me. Farewell, my precious cousin. May God keep you."

Captain Darch let her out of the Garden Tower as easily as he had admitted her. He locked the door behind him. An armed guard of ten men came marching across the grass. Katherine kept her eyes downcast.

"Please keep inside, my lady. Do not venture out again. It is too dangerous," said Captain Darch in a firm voice. He was conducting her up the wooden staircase to the White Keep's only entrance. As she passed back from the fresh air back into the dim interior he pressed something into her hand and muttered close to her ear.

"I do not want your ring, my Lady. God sees what is right and what is wrong."

"Keep it, sir," she whispered, and pressed it back into his palm. "A token of my esteem. You have done me and my family a great service today."

He saluted the solitary man-at-arms on duty and was gone.

Katherine smiled apologetically at the guard. "I just needed some air. The captain brought me back." She sped up the staircases, up three flights, back to the rooms where she could hear the familiar sounds of the children stirring. Six-year-old Harry appeared, half-dressed and trailing a wooden sword.

"There's going to be a battle today, Aunt Kaff'ryn," he announced gleefully. "My Papa will kill the bad men."

"More than likely," said Katherine. She took his hand and led him into Bessy's chamber. Her sister was dressing, pale with anxiety. Only a handful of women had come with them, to attend upon her and the children.

"Katherine? Where have you been?"

It was better that Bessy should never know. Time and time again she had pleaded with her husband over Ned but he was imperturbable. The last half an hour had been like some surreal dream. Best that she remembered it as such.

"I could not sleep; I went outside for some air – but the guards returned me. We have to stay here now."

"Until my Papa the King has killed the bad men!" shouted Harry. Bessy knelt down until she was at her son's level and took him by his shoulders.

"We must pray that your father the King is successful today, but we must also pray for all those souls who will lose their lives. War is never a good thing, Harry, especially between men of the same realm. You would do well to heed that."

Harry was caught between his natural obstinacy and his genuine love for his mother.

"But can I fight the bad men, Mama, if they come here?"

"They will not come here, Harry."

He looked disappointed. "Well, it's a good job my brother Arthur is in Ludlow, because he is no good at fighting. When I am older I shall ride out with my father. I shall fight the French! Or the Scots! Or the Spanish!"

"I am sure you will, but in the meantime you will come to Mass. Run and ask Elyn to tie your points."

Outside there was the sudden, insistent clanging of the Tower's tocsin bell – the signal for all men-at-arms to take to their stations. In the city all the churches began to echo the warning until within minutes it seemed the whole capital was reverberating with consternation. Katherine grabbed her sister's hand. "It is starting. Where is Lady Margaret?"

"She went to be with the children as soon as she had said her prayers. *Our* sweet children she calls them. She declares she will protect them with her life if needs be."

"Well, if I was a Cornishman I'd think twice about attacking a castle with Lady Margaret inside it."

Notwithstanding her anxiety about their situation, Bessy snorted with laughter. "Come, we had best all be together. Jesu, Katherine! What is that smell? The cloak you are wearing! Harry's dog must have pissed over it in the night. Take it off and leave it here."

It was all over by mid-afternoon. Henry Tudor rode back in triumph through the city to the East Minster of St Paul's. Just as at Bosworth and Stoke, he had merely sat on his horse and observed. The Cornish leaders had all been captured,

233

their followers dead or fled. What resistance can a farmer or fisherman with nothing more than a wooden stave offer to a king's cavalry, infantry and archers, even if the best is in the north? Two thousand men fell – trampled, hacked, pierced, stabbed or spitted. As evening fell, Lady Margaret, Katherine and Bessy stood in silence in the shadow of the White Tower. The infamous An Gof was brought in chains to the Tower. Henry Tudor's soldiers handed their prisoner over to Captain Christopher Darch, who gravely took custody. He would be executed within days. No mercy would be shown to the commoner; he would be hanged, his entrails torn out before his eyes, then deftly chopped into four whilst still alive. His body parts would be sent to all quarters of the kingdom to deter other would-be rebels. Lady Margaret's eyes gleamed with satisfaction. "So perish all those who would defy my son, the King!" she shouted down, from the steps.

Michael An Gof was a giant of a man, broad-chested and with legs like tree trunks. He dwarfed the two soldiers who flanked him. His dark, curly hair was matted with blood. His Celtic blue eyes were glazed with exhaustion but he raised them to stare at My Lady the King's Mother.

"Tudors!" he spat the word with derision. "You'll not last long!" His accent was thick, each vowel drawn out to its limit. As they dragged him away his scornful laughter still rebounded off the walls.

Lady Margaret was holding Harry by the hand. She had said he should see the men his father had defeated. The huge man had unnerved him somewhat but now he jigged up and down with excitement. Bessy turned on her heel and went back into the White Tower, giving terse orders that their bags should be packed immediately. There was enough light still for them to be rowed back up to Westminster. Katherine was relieved beyond measure to leave the Tower with its constant atmosphere of foreboding. As they passed under the Garden Tower she stole a glance upwards and thought she saw a shadow at the window. The children were helped into the barge: eight-year-old Margaret ashen-faced, but trying to appear grown-up; Harry now bawling with exhaustion; Mary quiet in her nurse's arms and Katherine's own little son, Edward, wrapped up against the night air. Captain Darch placed him into her arms.

"A fine boy, my Lady. I pray he thrives. I have one much the same age." The barge rocked as the oarsmen took up their positions. The lanterns were lit, casting strange shadows across the river and up the side of the Tower walls. They were just waiting for Bessy and Lady Margaret. Katherine swallowed hard.

"I thank you, sir. For your kindness. I will not forget it."

Bessy and her mother-in-law came pattering down the darkening, glistening jetty. Captain Darch stood smartly and handed each into the barge. Furs were wrapped around them all and the oarsmen pushed off into the rising tide. It was only a few days to midsummer and the moon was high too; the light was ethereal. Katherine watched as the Tower faded from sight, its distinctive skyline disappearing with the curve of the river. She thought of Ned, facing another lonely night amongst the thousands he had already endured and the thousands that might lie before him. Silent tears slid down her cheeks on to her sleeping son's head. Lady Margaret snored softly, lulled by the rhythmic plash of the oars. Bessy sat stony-faced, young Margaret's head lying in her lap. Eventually there were cries of welcome as the barge approached the Westminster Pier. More lanterns flashed as the barge glided in and thudded quietly against the moorings. Servants were there, to take the children, exclaiming about their bravery and talking of hot food and warm beds. As usual Lady Margaret took precedence and Bessy said nothing, allowing her little moment of triumph before she followed her up the jetty. Despite the late hour the King was waiting in his privy chamber to greet his mother and wife – to tell them of his victory.

Katherine disembarked wearily, taking the hand offered to her in the darkness. As she found her balance on the jetty the hand became an arm which crept around her waist. Dazed with fatigue she tried to push it away, taken aback at such impudence, but then her legs were lifted up too and she found herself staring into a face she loved more than life itself.

"William! Sweet Jesu, William!"

"Katherine! Right well-beloved!"

All protocol was forgotten. And he was kissing her, carrying her in strong arms all the way up the pier towards the lights of the Palace. The tension within her broke, and she sobbed against his doublet.

Their private room looked out on to the courtyard. Katherine had not been here for weeks, and William for four months. Puffing with exertion, he deposited her on the bed, then pulled off her shoes and his boots. It was nearly two o'clock in the morning. Expertly, he unlaced her gown and her sleeves, helped her to remove her kirtle and gently eased the little gabled headdress from her brow. He pulled the pins from her braids and her thick blonde hair sprang loose. Then he flung off his own gown, unlaced his doublet from his hose and shucked himself out of both. They were each left in their shifts. Someone had lit beeswax candles and put a jug of small ale on the table. He poured them both a cup and joined her on the bed.

"You did not fight today?" She was raking his body with her eyes for signs of injury.

"No. Father and I arrived from Exeter two days ago and they had already shut the city gates. We had to stay without. It was chaos. You?"

"We left Eltham when we heard the rebels were in Kent. We were in the Tower for nearly ten days."

"Our son?"

"He is well. He has more teeth and is pulling himself up on every joint stool he can find. Or every dog."

He leaned back against the carved bedhead and she snuggled into his side, laying her right cheek upon his breast, her left hand upon his heart, her left leg raised and over his. It was how they liked to lie. They were too tired for anything more.

"I cannot believe you are here. It has been four months." She stretched up and kissed his chin. "How is Seaton?"

"Happily installed in the royal stables and eager to see his favourite mistress." His hand stroked her back and the top of her legs.

They drowsed for several minutes. "William, I have to tell you something. This morning I saw my cousin, the Earl of Warwick." Instantly he was awake again, with a soldier's alertness.

"What? You glimpsed him somewhere? Were they moving him?"

"No. I made a captain take me to him."

"Jesu Christ, Katherine! You did *what?*"

"*Shhh!* No-one saw me. It was just for a few minutes. I have told no-one else."

They were both sitting up now. William wore an expression somewhere between horror and comical dismay. Katherine clasped her knees and looked beseechingly at her young husband. "William, my dearest lord. I *had* to. For Meg. I didn't plan it. It just happened. I never thought he would agree but he did."

"And?"

"It was awful. The room is so small, and dismal. Ned has nothing. Meg's fears are right, I think. He has no company, or anything to pass his time. He hardly spoke. Oh, what threat is he, William? A poor, simple, innocent young man? I fear he could not tell a goose from a capon."

"Shh! Keep your voice down, my wife. You know full well why he is a prisoner. Because of who he is. Katherine, you must not tell the Queen, or any of your sisters. You must not even write to Meg. It's too dangerous."

"But Meg is desperate to know how he does!"

"You will see her at Christmas, when they bring Prince Arthur."

"Christmas! That is six months away."

"And your secret will keep."

He lay down again and held her close, pulling the sheet and woollen coverlet round them both. Sometimes Katherine's ancestry and family caused him concern. *My own child is now someone whom others might seize upon in the name of the house of York. How ironic is that, when the King regards us as old Lancastrians and eager supporters of the Tudors? How, in God's name, do I keep my own children safe from their mother's legacy of Plantagenet blood?* Katherine had relaxed in his arms and was now breathing regularly, the troubles of the last few days smoothed from her face by sleep. *I shall have to live a very long life, making sure that neither Edward nor any child to come ever looks back into their royal bloodline.* In marrying him to Katherine, he realised, his father had done far more than ally the Courtenays to the Tudors. Unwittingly, he had created a hornets' nest.

2

8th September 1497

Henry Tudor sat in his private chamber at Westminster, staring at the document offering the latest intelligence about the Feigned Lad. That the creature was an impostor he was in no doubt, at least when he talked with his closest advisors. Alone, he was less certain. Sixteen years upon the throne and still no sense of permanence or security. He drummed his fingers on the table top. His mind ran in circles. What must it be like to be a king beloved of the people? He had no idea. The only person in his life who offered him love was his mother – and her love had ever been a kind of fierce, possessive adulation; he could do no wrong in her eyes. Love was not something offered by Bessy. Respect, yes. Deference, yes. Wifely dutifulness, yes – he had four healthy children to prove that. But her cursed family! When he tried to prise out of Bessy her thoughts about the Feigned Lad she simply turned away in silence and he had no idea what that silence meant. A yearning that the boy might indeed prove to be her brother? Or a fear that her own sons would be set aside, or even worse? Would she be ready to give up her queenship to a young man whose title her husband had usurped?

He was not afraid of combat. *God knows, I am a king who took my crown on a battlefield, and who has defended it since!* Yet he was now a good deal older; his joints ached some days and a whole day in the saddle was not necessarily his choice of pastime. Mostly, being king of England perplexed him. You would have thought, he reasoned, that bringing an end to the pernicious fighting that had soaked the very earth country in blood for forty years would have brought him some estimation, some vestige of thanks and appreciation. Instead, he found himself surrounded by conspiracy – no wonder then, that he chose his advisors for their loyalty rather than their pedigree. Those who best content me, thought Henry, are those who demonstrate their support.

The paper lying in front of him informed him of the Feigned Lad's proclamation, stating that the Tudor, who called himself king, relied upon and rewarded low-born men to do his will. Henry's fist came down upon it in a thump of rage and frustration. Next to it was a slim leather-bound volume of accounts, also detailing the network of intelligence-gatherers he was forced to deploy to keep abreast of whisperings and unrest, from Cornwall to Northumberland.

Wax dripped down the thick candles in their pewter holders. The shutters were firmly fastened against the ill humours of the night. On the other side of the locked and guarded door was his presence chamber, with his throne and cloth of estate, where only this afternoon he had received emissaries from the Spanish monarchs Ferdinand and Isabella. To Henry's mind, if he could marry Prince Arthur to a daughter of two of the most powerful rulers in Europe, the English would simply have to acknowledge him as an astute king. But the Spanish ambassador murmured of how worried their majesties were about the possibility that others might yet dispute the Tudor right to the throne. Henry groaned, and laid his head upon his accounts book. His eyes grew heavy and his mouth fell open. A thin line of saliva dripped on to the red, tooled leather.

A knock sounded on the other door to his room, the one that connected his apartments to those occupied by his mother. Margaret Beaufort came in, her dark over-gown trailing through the fresh rushes. She stood for a moment, observing her son, before coughing. Henry snorted out of his sleep, eyes flying open. She moved forward to stand next to him, laying her hand upon his shoulder.

"There is news, from Cornwall. He has landed." She gripped his arm tightly. "They have declared him Richard IV."

"Which he is not."

"Which he is not," she affirmed. "What will you do?"

Henry dabbed at the wet spot on his book. "Send word to Courtenay that he must hold Exeter against him."

"You need to call him by his ridiculous name, now. This "Feigned Lad" nonsense only makes him sound mysterious. We have a name for him – use it."

"It's a nickname. No-one knows his real name."

"It's a foolish, common name and if we use it enough people will realise he is not who he claims to be. Perkin Warbeck is not a man to challenge for the throne of England. He is at best the offspring of some Flemish watergate keeper; a servant; a pot-boy." There had been many times in her life when Margaret Beaufort had wished herself born a boy. Then she could have borne the Lancaster

239

standard herself. A proud, moral and pious servant of God, she knew she could have pulled down the decadent Edward Plantagenet. Instead, they had married her as a child to Edmund Tudor and she had suffered agonies as this son had been torn out of her thirteen-year-old body. But she had accepted her destiny and decided that her revenge upon the world would be to see her flesh and blood take root as the rightful dynasty. She was not about to let some boy from Tournai uproot the family she had planted and nurtured.

She moved a chair so that she could sit directly opposite Henry, and leaned forward with urgency. "When you capture him, you must execute him. No putting him in the kitchens as you did Lambert Simnel. He is a thousand times more dangerous."

Henry rubbed his furred collar between his thumb and middle finger. "*If* we capture him. He seems to have a remarkable instinct for evasion."

She snapped her fingers in front of his face. "I said *when* you capture him. His luck has run out – I know it. Bring him in chains and hang him."

Henry looked slighly pained. "I cannot necessarily do that, Lady Mother, for if he is Perkin Warbeck he is no Englishman therefore cannot be accused of treason."

Lady Margaret was on the edge of exasperation. "You are the king! You can do what you like with him. Once you have him."

"The said Perkin and his accomplices assaulted the City of Exeter at two gates, that is to say the North Gate and the East gate, where by the power of the Earl of Devonshire and the citizens he was put off ... albeit that they fired the gates ... the Earl of Devonshire was hurt in the arm with an arrow ..." The Great Chronicle of London

Exeter, Devon Sunday 17th September 1497

The walled city of Exeter held its breath. Outside, camped in the fields, sprawled the army gathered by Perkin Warbeck on his march up from Cornwall. The rebels had appeared so suddenly, marching upon the North Gate, drums pounding and with voices raised in crazy, blood-curdling aggression. The bells of the city's many churches had clanged the alarm at four in the morning, shaking its inhabitants awake, urgently calling men from their everyday occupations:

240

weavers, fullers, tanners, blacksmiths, butchers and bakers rushed out of their homes and shops to sharpen every type of weapon they could find. At each corner of the town the gates were firmly barred. From the crenellated walkway of the watchtower on the North Gate a small group of men assessed the challenge they faced.

Sir Edward Courtenay peered into the dawn light. "Ha! He's come well-prepared. Look, they have siege ladders."

Through the mists of a September morning his son William tried to focus on the rolling countryside to the north. The Exe glinted where it met the Creedy at Cowley Bridge. Grazing land abutted the city's ancient walls, with their Roman foundations and stout Saxon stone work. Beyond that was the rising ground of the royal hunting grounds of Duryard. He could make out dark, miniature figures swarming like ants over the green grass; many were busy alongside long, thin structures – unmistakably ladder-like,

"What else will they have?"

Sir Edward shrugged. "Whatever they've managed to lay their hands on between Bodmin and here."

"Thank God we managed to get in last night. Who else is with us?"

"Some good local men: Thomas Fulford, John Croker and Edmund Carew. Piers Edgecumbe got wind of it all a few days ago and galloped like the wind up from Cornwall. They're not all traitors to the King down there."

The mists were lifting even as they spoke, revealing the shocking extent of the rebel army – line after line, stretching back towards the confluence of the two rivers.

"There's a good few thousand, Father. How many can we count on?"

Sir Edward turned to the grave-faced man standing alongside him. "Master Atwill? You are the mayor of this fine city. What is your best estimate?"

"We are eight thousand souls, sir. But that includes women, children, the elderly, the monks and friars."

"Well," said Sir Edward briskly, "every lad over ten should be able to follow orders, and if the holy brothers wish to see another day they would be wise to set their consciences aside for a while. I will not ask them to fight, but they can bring up the arms and supplies to those who do. I suggest we all go down now. We can expect some sort of attack this forenoon."

They walked back to the city carfax and turned left into the High Street which was by now a hive of activity. The men of Exeter were galvanised into action, dragging timber to shore up the gates and racing from their houses with an extraordinary assortment of weapons. Doors banged; women were boarding up street level windows with grim determination. In front of the Guildhall a scarlet-faced fellow, clad in homespun russet, paused momentarily in front of the Mayor and the two well-dressed gentlemen.

"We can fight, sir! Look, here's the bow my grandfather carried at Agincourt! It's been under my father's bed for decades but is well-oiled and will serve!"

William smiled at his eagerness. "I trust you have the arrows to go with it?"

The man grinned back over his shoulder as he ran on, "Quivers full of 'em, my lord! I knew they'd come in handy one day!"

At the Blackfriars' house, where they had taken up lodging, William and his father ate a hasty breakfast of bread, bacon and ale. Then they dressed in their thick pourpoints and selected their armour. William stood still whilst his squire attached the steel plackert which would protect his chest and stomach. His father gave him a level look. "Not too much, William. It's not a jousting tournament. You'll need to be fleet enough to run and use your sword."

"Well, it will certainly be different to last time, Father. He seems determined to make a fight of it, rather than just pass through."

"It's the city he wants, lad. He will have been advised that if he can take and hold Exeter he will have something to make others think. So far all he has done is flit about Europe, and Scotland, and Ireland. He'll be wanting to take root somewhere and Exeter is as good as any."

William dismissed the squire and waited until the elderly friar, in his black Dominican robes, had cleared the table and flapped off to the kitchen in his thick leather sandals.

"Father, who do *you* think he is? " He kept his voice low.

Sir Edward grimaced as he adjusted his swordbelt to sit more comfortably round his broad waist.

"You mean, is he your long-lost royal brother-in-law?"

William gestured helplessly. "But what if he is?"

"He stands no chance, William, whoever he is. He's declared his hand now but it won't last long. Oh yes, there are those who cling to the old York romance, and those who are disaffected enough to throw in their lot with him, but in the long run? The King will hunt him down as surely as he pursues the stags in the forest. It won't have a happy ending. Look, William, ever since our family married into the Beauforts we've pledged allegiance to the Lancaster cause and now the Tudors. I'm not about to stop now. If this pretender is indeed Katherine's poor brother then I am sorry for him, and for her, and the Queen, but it still means I will capture him if I can."

"Do you *like* the King, Father?"

"Jesu, William! *Liking* the man has nothing to do with it! He has raised us, restored our title and wealth, allied us through marriage. In the next generation the Courtenays will be first cousins to the Tudors. *That* is why we are here at his bidding to defend Exeter. Put your sallet on."

As they made their way back to the city's North Gate William found himself thinking about Katherine. In the dark privacy of their curtained bed she had confided her sister Cecily's story that their mother had believed her second royal boy might have somehow escaped from the Tower and been spirited away into the Low Countries. He knew that Katherine felt torn in two by her loyalties. She loved her thoughtful nephew, Arthur; spent hours with Harry and the two girls Margaret and Mary. She had no desire for their young lives to be torn apart as hers had been as a child. And yet, as she so often whispered, *what if?* If the Feigned Lad really was King Richard IV, surely he would look favourably on the sisters he had once adored, and take them to his heart. William was not quite sure, though, what fate might befall Henry Tudor, should King Richard IV be restored. And what would the Courtenays and Howards have to do? Turn their coats for the sake of the princesses they had married?

An hour later William had an excellent view of the young man, practically his own age, who yelled up at Sir Edward Courtenay to surrender the city. He was tall, sitting easily upon a grey stallion with a plumey mane and tail; he rose in his stirrups, balancing perfectly as the horse sashayed a little. He was bare-headed but wore a thin gold circlet low on his brow, embellished by what William realised were small white roses. His cloak was deep blue, embroidered with golden suns. He looked every inch a young king come to claim his own. William saw the Adam's apple in his father's leathery throat working up and down.

"There will be no surrender, Perkin Warbeck! I hold this city for the King!"

"So be it, sir. Then I fear we must fight for it." He inclined his head courteously. His voice was cultured, with no trace of guttural Flemish. His whole demeanour was that of a young noble.

The next five hours were a blur of desperate defensive fighting. The Feigned Lad mounted a most extraordinary attack upon the North Gate whose thick oak panels groaned and splintered as rock after rock was flung at them. The rebels seemed to have constructed some rudimentary form of trebuchet hurling huge stones which smacked and thudded with incredible force. Weakened, the gates yielded slightly and sharp steel pried through as the men on the outside attempted to split the wood further. However, it was difficult for the rebels to break through by the north way, for they were fighting uphill; the Exeter men held firm, routing their assailants successfully. From the ramparts of the city walls they rained arrows down upon the rebels and buckets full of scalding water and hot pitch. Then word came that a similar assault was happening at the East Gate. William had never seen anything like it, never heard anything like it.

Sir Edward, despite his fifty years and broadening girth, was everywhere, yelling commands, encouraging men, constantly assessing the situation. That he was in charge, and confidently so – was an eye-opener for William who had never quite known how far to believe his father's stories of Bosworth Field. And when the first rebel fighters surged over the siege ladders into the streets of Exeter, William also witnessed how his father could fight.

They came like rats – a pack of wild eyed, wiry Cornishmen more used to slithering through the passages of their tin mines but now screaming as if pursued by devils. They leapt triumphantly on to the narrow walkways of the wall, brandishing their daggers. At the East Gate the hand to hand fighting was bloody. William had long since ripped off his steel helmet, preferring the freedom of movement above any idea of protection. It seemed to him that his whole world had closed down to the frantic melee in the narrow, streets. He found himself pushed back some distance from the gate, not far from the Rougemont Castle. Again and again he faced some new opponent – a madman wielding a timber axe, whose arm he sliced through in one swing of his sword; another who came at him with a halberd, forcing him to execute some sort of backwards dance over fallen masonry – his luck held and the man tripped up, his weapon clattering down into the gutter where an Exeter apprentice seized it gleefully and aimed a wild chop at its original owner. Crimson blood flowed, trickling through the cobbles. Wide-eyed with shock at what he had just done the apprentice then screeched with blood-lust, pulled out the halberd and headed back into the fray.

William stood, blowing hard, his heart pounding, his whole body shaking; the next second he was fighting again, this time a textbook duel against another swordsman with murder in his eyes. This was no miner or fisherman, but a rebel of higher birth, boasting a fine pair of leather boots and a gleaming long sword that he wielded with dangerous dexterity. Their blades clashed and sparked;

William tried to find his balance on the uneven ground, his brain on fire with everything he had ever been taught: advance, slash, parry, thrust … his opponent's weapon hissed somewhere above his head – William ducked and bobbed up again. His foe had over-reached slightly and rocked on the balls of his feet, trying to regain a firm footing. William saw his chance and thrust hard. His blade sank, met resistance then suddenly sank into the softness of flesh – a look of astonishment then agony flashed across the other man's face as he sank to his knees then rolled away. For all his army training and jousting skills, William had never actually killed another fellow human before. He tasted bitter bile in his mouth and then was vomiting on to the street. His breakfast and the man's blood mixed together in the runnels at the side of the thoroughfare.

"My Lord Courtenay!" A well-built man in his mid-thirties was at his side. William recognised Edmund Carew, an affable neighbour from Mohun's Ottery, with whom he had often jousted and traded the odd horse or two.

"Sir Edmund!" They grinned at each other. Edmund's thick dark hair was standing on end and the sword he carried as bloody as William's. Together they fought their way back in to the main body of the fracas at the far end of the High Street.

"Look! Your honoured father needs us!" He pointed up at the top of the East Gate where Sir Edward was back in control. The siege ladders had been pushed away and for the moment there were no more Cornish. William sniffed – there was an acrid smell wafting over the walls and tell-tale smoke rising.

"William! Edmund!" His father was yelling from the top of the gatehouse. "He's trying to burn his way in! We need to meet fire with fire!"

William understood instantly. The Feigned Lad thought to burn down the gates but if there was fire *inside* too, the rebels would have no hope of making their way through yards of conflagration. He shouted instructions to the Exeter townsmen – to bring whatever combustible materials they could find and within minutes men, women and children were arriving with firewood from their own homes, wooden barrels from the brewery, boxes from the tannery, piles of dry wool from Rack Street. Monks staggered from the cathedral with spare wooden scaffolding. John Atwood, the Mayor, was calm and authoritative, sending for brands from houses where fires burned daily in the hearths. Soon the East Gate entrance was piled high with all manner of burnable material, ready to be ignited.

"What more?" William looked at Carew. "How else can we repel them?"

Edmund Carew thought quickly. The fire would be an excellent defence but there was no harm in another layer.

"Ditches, in front of both gates, and earthworks from which we can defend. If they do get through the gates the smoke will obscure the ditches and with any luck they'll just tumble in!" He was pleased with his plan, and gave orders immediately. The Exeter citizens' ingenuity knew no bounds – spades were brought from every vegetable garden, every stable, every graveyard and before long tradesmen, merchants and monks were digging with the enthusiasm of small boys. By the hour the ditches grew wider and deeper and the spoil used to bank up a defensive mound.

The Mayor looked on in admiration and satisfaction. "That will sort them!"

By late afternoon it was clear that the Feigned Lad's efforts were bearing little fruit. The fires had worked well, the rebel army taken aback by such tactics. The streets were safe, with scores of Cornish either dead, or captured and herded into the cellar under the Guildhall.

William, Edmund Carew, John Croker and Piers Edgecumbe all joined Sir Edward on the city wall walkways as the Exeter churches began to call the hour of Vespers. The four younger men were exhilarated with the successes of the day but Sir Edward looked less optimistic. "They have fallen back to lick their wounds but they will try again tomorrow."

"How many do you think they have lost, sir?" Edgecumbe's tone was respectful.

"I'd estimate three or four hundred, and Atwil says we've taken a hundred or so as prisoners."

"And few losses on our side," said Croker.

"Aye, the men of Exeter can be proud of themselves. But it's not over. He wants this city and he's not giving up yet."

Edmund Carew's dark brows knitted in thought. "We could have guns mounted by the morning, Sir. The city has portpieces but not much in the way of balls to fire from them. No stocks, I mean. And not many men who know what to do with them. "

William's face brightened. "They'll fire anything – glass, old iron. Anything that we can ram down them."

Sir Edward was not convinced. "I dislike bombards, William. As dangerous to those who use them as the enemy they are trying to hit! And as Edmund rightly points out, we lack skilled crews."

"But we can have a go! We understand the theory of it and Edmund can tell us all what to do. Carew?"

"How far away do you think the King's army is, sir?" John Croker was a Tavistock man, firmly ensconced on his Devon estates; his rich burr no different to that of his tenants.

"Messengers went twenty four hours ago, when we first sighted the Pretender's army. They went down by ropes over the western side of the walls and should be well on the Great West Road by now. The King is at Woodstock. A few days away."

"Well it's clear that Warbeck has no artillery, and if he thinks we have plenty he'll not linger here to see his men blown to pieces. I think we should do it. Get the guns into position tonight, fire on him in the morning and see what transpires. William's right; I can show some sensible men what to do."

Exeter remained on edge. Darkness fell and uneasy clouds scudded across an inky sky. There was no moon. In the rebel camp a few fires burned, glowing pinpoints that the anxious monks could see from the tower of their great cathedral. In the tall, gabled houses of the Fore Street and the hovels nearer the river men and women lay awake for a second night. If any had entertained any secret sympathies for the cause of the young man who besieged their city they abandoned them now, telling each other they were loyal to King Henry and sweet Queen Bess. In the house of the Blackfriars Sir Edward snored, worn out by the day, dreaming of portpiece guns that spewed live fish over the walls of the city. He shifted in his sleep, with some odd awareness that maybe the fish were better off in the Exe. William lay sprawled under a coarse linen sheet and a quilted cover. The good friars had provided hot water in a large barrel for bathing and it had felt good to sluice the day's filth and blood from his body. He hoped that the man he had left dead in the street by the castle would receive a decent burial; the monks had trundled the corpses away for interment in consecrated ground. Whether you fought and died for a crowned king or a man who said he was king, you deserved to lie in peace, reasoned William. He said a prayer for the soul of the unknown Cornish gentleman, for he had left this life suddenly and unshriven. There would be a family asking questions, seeking answers. A wife maybe. Perhaps a child or two. William felt distinctly uncomfortable at taking life. *But it was him, or me. If I had not killed him it would be Katherine receiving news and weeping and my children growing up fatherless.* For he had two sons now. Six months ago Katherine had given him little Henry, a name chosen judiciously to mark the Courtenays' loyalty to their king. Katherine disliked the name, he knew, and the baby was soon "Hal" to their entire household. He thought of them all where he had last seen them six weeks ago: young Edward and Hal with their cousins at Eltham and Katherine either with them, or attending Bessy at nearby Sheen, or Greenwich. He hoped Henry Tudor had the sense to send word from Woodstock and ensure they would stay far away from any conflict.

Katherine had not yet travelled to Devon to see the rich green and red landscape that would one day be hers by right, when his father died. She had never yet clapped eyes on his childhood home at Tiverton, or the other Courtenay estates at Colcombe, or Okehampton. In good time, he thought, as he drifted into exhausted sleep … his father had fought like a man half his age today.

Exeter's carpenters and their apprentices did not sleep. By the hour of Prime, the guns were in place on the city walls, raised up on hastily constructed platforms. Buckets of musket balls, broken glass, shards and lumps of iron from the smithies sat alongside. Each gun was attended by an apprehensive yet willing crew, under Edmund Carew's command. Strong-armed laundresses, their kirtles hooked up to their knees, brought up more buckets of water and piles of soaked linen to cool the barrels of the guns. Metal containers of hot coals were ready to serve the wire primer.

William wondered where on earth Edmund had found supplies of gunpowder – the unstable saltpetre, sulphur and charcoal mix. He eyed it warily as the men used copper scoops to ladle it down the barrels. When the first guns fired the entire walls seemed to shake down to their Roman foundations. The guns were only portpieces, such as might be used at sea, but the thunderous explosion they produced was impressive. They recoiled like dragons reversing, spewing smoke and soot in all directions. The men who had operated them were stunned, then cheered wildly as they peered over the walls to see the results. Over the next hour the guns were fired, reloaded and fired again in the direction of the Feigned Lad's camp. He tried again with his siege ladders and for a short space of time there was fierce fighting again on the walkways and in the nearby streets but the suddenly the rebels seemed to lose heart.

"They realise they are beaten!" crowed Edmund Carew. His face was black with soot, his two brown eyes standing out like walnuts in white circles.

"Lord Edward is hit!"

William was in the middle of supervising the ramming of a gun when he heard the shouting to his left. Rather, he heard his father's roar of fury; a stray rebel arrow had flown up and over the wall and more by luck than judgement had embedded itself in the top half of Sir Edward's arm. By the time William reached him he was propped up against the wall, eyes closed, white-faced with pain, enduring the attentions of Exeter's barber surgeon. Blood ran off his elbow. The barber surgeon was swiftly applying a tourniquet made from strips of linen, twisted into a short piece of wood.

"How bad is it?" William had seen festering wounds before and feared for his father's survival.

The barber surgeon did not look up from his work. "He's lucky. The head is not deeply embedded. I should be able to get it out with an arrow spoon. If I can get the wound cleaned quickly I think he will keep the arm. We must take him back to the Blackfriars' House. There is a friar there well skilled in herbs and healing."

"William?" Sir Edward's voice was faint but clear. "I leave you in command. He's all but given up. Allow him to proceed from the city. He won't get far."

William blinked hard. He watched as his father was lowered down from the wall, tended carefully by men from the Courtenay estate and taken to safety. Edmund Carew joined him and flung an arm affectionately round his shoulder. The streets were now thronging with Exeter's citizens, their faces bright with expectation. At their head came John Athill, their Mayor,

"It is over, Lord William! The lookouts have seen men running away. The guns have won the day! Thank you, my lords, for saving our city."

"Look, William, he's down below. He wants to parley."

William removed his sallet and raked his fingers through his hair. Sweat ran freely from his forehead, down his nose and cheeks, dripping off the end of his chin. "Where is our standard?"

To great cheers, the Courtenay arms were raised high above the fire-damaged East Gate. The golden flag fluttered in the breeze, its azure lions and three red roundels dancing in their quarters. William looked down on to the fields, and the little church of St Sidwell's. Beyond lay the road that led back to his home at Tiverton. The Feigned Lad's army was much reduced in size and scattered about. But riding towards him was the young man himself, flanked by two outriders. They came right up under the city walls. The Feigned Lad looked up, his face handsome and composed in the morning sunshine.

"I am Richard Plantagenet, fourth of his name! With whom do I speak?"

"I am Lord William Courtenay, heir to the earldom of Devon."

Interest and curiosity flashed across the Feigned Lad's features. "Husband to the Princess Katherine?" The silence on both sides of the city walls prickled with intensity.

"The same."

"A shame we had to fight, and lose good men, Lord William."

"There have been none slain on this side." William spoke the truth. The defenders of Exeter were weary and some hurt, but no deaths had been reported.

The Feigned Lad leaned forward and patted his grey stallion's neck. "I congratulate you on the defence of your city. I ask as a favour that you allow us to depart without further molestation." His English was fluent, but the "r"s more rolling, the vowels just slightly flattened and the tiniest hint of husky intonation. *Like an Englishman who spent many years travelling in the Holy Roman Empire.*

He does not have a quarter of the men who stood with him yesterday. And they will probably desert him before tomorrow. William raised a hand in acquiescence. The Feigned Lad saluted him, as one soldier to another and began to turn his horse. Then he stopped, and called over his shoulder, "And give my love and respects to your wife!" He kicked hard and the grey stallion galloped away. William stood long on the gate tower with Edmund and John Athill, until the Cornish rebels were specks in the distance.

"Impudent young dog!" exclaimed Edmund Carew. "To insult your wife, William!"

.

Katherine: *He did not get far. By the time he reached Taunton the Cornishmen deserted him as rats do a sinking ship. They knew that the King's forces were not far away and most valued their lives above loyalty. Three days after Exeter, he had fled down to Hampshire where he sought safety in the famed sanctuary of Beaulieu Abbey but the King's men found him and dragged him back to Taunton. Here my brother-in-law came face to face with the Feigned Lad who had tried his patience for so many years. He dragged him back to Exeter, from where my husband wrote to me.*

Right Well-Beloved Wife

My father is recovering from his wound and will go from here home to my mother at Tiverton. The King has been within Exeter these last three weeks. He is most eager to show his gratitude to those who protected his fair city from the Pretender, whom he forced to march behind him, to show all that his cause is

250

now entirely lost. The King lodges at the Treasurer's house by the cathedral and yesterday the captured prisoners were shown to him, with halters round their necks. He has shown great clemency in pardoning most, though the ringleaders were hanged upon the Southern Hay. Those who gave succour to the rebels as they came up from Cornwall will be fined. The King has given his cap and sword to John Athill, the Mayor, as a mark of his regard and says both must be carried before the mayor in all future processions. Master Athill is most pleased.

I must tell you of something strange. The Feigned Lad's wife has been brought up from Cornwall where he had left her for safekeeping with the monks at St Michael's Mount. The King seems most taken with her (and indeed she is remarkably beautiful) and has promised her a place at your sister the Queen's side. The young lady wept openly, for it is said her firstborn is dead. The King is minded to bring Perkin Warbeck back to London and show the people he is an impostor, and no threat. I will travel with them. My love to you and our sweet boys.

Given under my signet at Exeter.
William

3

"From thence to Sheen, whereto Her Grace was brought the wife of Perkyn ... which said wife was a Scottish woman and a daughter of the Earl of Huntley" The Great Chronicle of London

Westminster late October 1497

"He expects me to take her as one of my ladies-in-waiting!" Bessy looked up in astonishment from her own letter, written in Henry Tudor's unmistakable hand.

"I know. William told me as much." Katherine bent her head over the shirt she was embroidering for her husband. "She is very beautiful, apparently."

They were seated together in a deep embrasure overlooking the gardens. Bessy stared at Henry's signature. "And he says she must be furnished from the Royal Wardrobe as soon as she arrives."

"What are we to call her? My Lady the Feigned Lass?" Katherine snipped off the end of a piece of black silken thread, and held up the shirt to the light to assess her stitching.

Her sister looked troubled. She laid down the letter quietly and folded her hands in her lap. At the far end of the room her musicians played gently, a soothing background against which her ladies had been chatting and sewing for an hour or so. Patch the Fool was endeavouring to entertain them, too, producing eggs from his ear. Bessy forced a smile at his antics. There was enough noise to mask her words.

"Well, she can hardly be addressed as the Duchess of York, and Mistress Warbeck sounds somewhat out of kilter, so I suppose we go back to her name before marriage. Lady Kateryn Huntley. Oh, dear God, Katherine, she might be our sis -"

"Shh! Don't say it. Cecily is already too indiscreet – I think she has sent messages of friendship."

Bessy's hands fluttered up in dismay but she hid them again in her lap. Katherine rose and called brightly, "Her Grace is going into the garden for a little while. The rain has stopped. No, no, we do not need company – just our cloaks."

Outside, the gravel walks were shiny from the recent shower. The air was sharp and fresh after the stuffiness of Bessy's rooms. There was always something comforting about the familiarity of Westminster; they knew every path and turn from their childhoods. A man-at-arms from her household accompanied them but Bessy waved him away with a charming smile and he retreated to a seat, glad to rest his legs. Bessy had little notion of privacy for her life as queen was, by its very nature, very public. Her women bathed and dressed her, and kept her company, and attended her at every moment. Whether with the children at Eltham or at one of her own homes, like Sheen, protocol demanded that her person should be guarded and attended. She thanked God that her sisters were in England and not queens of distant lands, for it was only with them she could ever be herself.

They wrapped their cloaks more firmly against the bracing easterly gusts and walked down the broadest path towards the river. If anyone should look from the windows they were in full view – just the Queen and her beloved sister enjoying a breath of fresh air. "Laugh, Bessy, as if I am telling you a good joke."

"He is doing it to test me, to see if I will ask her questions about her husband. She will have attendants in his pay who will report back to him"

"Then never ask her."

Bessy raised pitiful eyes towards the sombre skies. "I *remember* him. Cecily remembers him. We watched him ride away with Lord Howard. "

At the end of the terraced gardens the autumnal Thames flowed blank-faced towards its estuary, its currents swirling and eddying in shades of pewter-grey, oyster-brown and verdigris. The tide was just beginning to ebb and the banks were emerging, slick and slimy with mud and weeds. Katherine felt a memory similarly exposed.

"Mama cried for days."

"She did."

"Cecily thinks something happened afterwards, something Mama did not know about for a long time. She is convinced that Dickon was smuggled out of the Tower. She's convinced that the Feigned Lad is he."

Silently, Bessy watched the river. A few craft were out on the water, merchants' boats whose billowing sails would propel them towards Europe. What would they bring back? Silks from Venice? Spices from the East? Wood from the Baltic? Had a boat once sailed past here sixteen years ago – a plain, insignificant boat, with a precious, princely cargo? Had a brave little boy huddled in the cabin, trying not to cry as he skimmed past his home and his family to an unknown, dangerous future? Had there really been someone loyal enough to York to spirit its last heir away, without even his mother knowing the truth?

"Cecily has had a terrible time, losing her two girls to fever. And now her husband ails too. She clings to ideas that comfort her. It's understandable."

"And what do *you* think, Bessy?" Katherine's words were a quicksilver shoal, slipping immediately below the surface.

"Truthfully? I have no idea. And he is a man now. Would we know him? Will we be able to tell? And if we recognise him, what can I do? What is the right thing to do? I have my own sons now!"

"Bessy, your man has left his bench. He's worried that we are so close to the water. Laugh again. Imagine I have just said something hilarious. That's good. William writes that the King is bringing him to London any day now, and we *will* see him."

"Oh, Sweet Jesu. It would be a miracle. And yet – it could destroy us. We have had enough destruction, you and I, and Cecily and Anne, and Bridget, to last a lifetime. "

"We have all survived, thanks to you. We are all content, thanks to you. And if he is who we hope he is, then all that matters is that he lives – not that he is king."

"He is no child, no Lambert Simnel, to think that working in the kitchens is a lucky escape. And he has lived with our Aunt Margaret in Burgundy, and with kings, and emperors. If he is truly who he says he is he will not give up. He will think back to how our grandfather and father fought again and again to win what they believed was theirs by right. But what will he do to my boys? Arthur is the same age as Dickon was when -"

"Turn around, Bessy. Put on your smile again. Your man is waiting to escort us back, and for all we know he is Henry's man too."

The thirteen years between them had shrunk away as if to nothing in the last two. Katherine becoming a mother intensified their bond, and her blend of spirit, common sense and compassion was of huge comfort to Bessy. Little Edward

Courtenay and the Princess Mary shared the same nursery and were firm friends – plump, rosy toddlers with their maternal grandfather's good-temper, and indolence. Bessy kept Katherine close by, but both paid almost weekly visits to Eltham where Bessy sat for hours teaching Harry and Margaret their letters. Harry, at six, was proving quite precocious and could already produce a fair, if over-large, imitation of his mother's handwriting. Beautifully written letters came from Arthur in Ludlow, respectful and loving, requesting his mother's blessing and praying for *the accomplishment of your noble desires,* a phrase that made Bessy smile at its serious tone. All were musically gifted, could sing sweetly and were learning to play a variety of instruments. Bessy indulged them with the finest of tutors. The miniature lute that Bessy had once procured for Katherine in sanctuary was stowed away safely; one day Katherine hoped for her own daughter.

The blessings of children brought heartache too, though, as her sisters had learned: the loss of Cecily's two little daughters, and Anne's stillborn baby, as well as Bessy's little Elizabeth. God gave life, but He took it too, and however much it was His will the reality was so hard. As they made their way back to the palace Katherine thought of the Lady Kateryn Huntley, who they would soon meet, and how she must be grieving for her newly-dead child. What was worse, to have your husband arrested by the King and likely to hang, or hold your dead babe in your arms? Without a husband there could be no more children. Without a child your very heart was pierced.

William's letter did not lie, thought Katherine, she *is* remarkably attractive but she has the air of a wary young filly, who does not know when her master will next bridle her, or saddle her, or even feed her. In the public setting of the Great Hall at Sheen, she curtsied deeply and elegantly to Bessy but Katherine did not miss the trembling hands or the way she had set her jaw in such a way as to counteract any emotion. Katherine recognised and understood such things. She wished she could reach out to this girl and simply say "Welcome, sister," but that could never be.

Bessy sat under her cloth of estate, with Margaret Beaufort at her side. Her face gave nothing away. This was just another pretty girl to be admitted to her household, in recognition of her birth and position as the Scots king's cousin. The rest of her ladies tried valiantly to contain their own intense desire to know more, even when Lady Kateryn sat amongst them and took up an embroidery frame, or a hand of cards, or when she lifted her kirtle in the dance and they glimpsed the slender ankles clad in the finest of kersey hose, lined with cypress lawn, such as only the queen and her sister usually wore.

It was as if she, Bessy and Katherine had made a secret pact: *We will say nothing about the man we want most in the world to discuss.* She appeared every morning in Bessy's rooms. Quietly and efficiently she responded to every direction and passed pleasantries when addressed but she never once initiated conversation. She gave no indication that she was a grieving mother, or a wife whose husband was even now being brought to the capital as a prisoner, to be placed in the Tower.

On the day that Perkin Warbeck rode into London, under armed guard, the citizens were agog with curiosity. It was reported that he waved cheerfully as his fine grey stallion clattered over the drawbridge into the Tower, for all the world looking like a prince embarking upon a sojourn at one of his palaces. A few days later Henry Tudor entered Bessy's rooms flourishing a piece of parchment.

"He has confessed!" he announced exultantly.

Margaret Beaufort flushed with relief and pleasure. She crossed herself feverishly then embraced her son. "This is the end of it then, all these years of foolishness. You can have done with him, and the people will thank you for it. I would advise you to hang him high, Henry, and send the quarters of his treacherous body north, south, east, and especially west, to show what happens to impostors."

A jitter of apprehension rippled round the room and there was a stifled sob from the corner where Lady Kateryn sat but Bessy affected not to hear either. She did not miss a stitch in the fine embroidery upon her lap. She pushed the needle through again and drew the silken thread through steadily.

"Are you not interested in the nature of his confession?" demanded Henry. Bessy wished he would not choose such public moments for his announcements but maybe that was part of his game too – thinking that at some point she would crack and show concern for the Feigned Lad. But he seemed unaware of how her life had been spent mastering and hiding her true feelings. Having Katherine close by helped; their anxieties had been played out in private – now they could both sit calmly, with the turbulence of their thoughts known only to one another. She could only hope that Lady Kateryn might instinctively grasp at the same demeanour. How had a confession been obtained?

"I am sure it will do us all good to hear it," said Lady Margaret, casting suspicious eagle-eyed glances around the room.

Henry unrolled the document and spread it in front of Bessy. It was very long, and sprang back into its cylindrical shape. Irritated, he secured it at the top with her embroidery box and rolled it out again. It spiralled down; the neat, secretary handwriting continued in an unbroken block, filling all the parchment. He watched her for a reaction.

"It looks very detailed. What does it say?" She guessed that he had probably devised it himself. She was not wrong.

"It says that he is not who he claimed to be. It says he is a boy of no education from Tournai in Flanders. He admits that his father is merely a poor burgess, Johann de Werbecque, and his mother a Katherine Faro. So poor that they farmed him out to any relative who would take him in. Just an ignorant boy who joined a group of travelling merchants and went with them to Ireland where he dressed up in their silks and attracted the attention of English Yorkists who seized upon him and persuaded him to play the part of your dead brother the Duke of York. Just as Lambert Simnel was persuaded to be your cousin of Warwick."

"Then all is well, Henry. Then he is no threat to you, or to our son Prince Arthur. What will you do now?"

"I have decided that he can come here, where I can have him watched every day. He will be under guard of course but as you say, he can no longer pose any threat. I will have his confession printed for all to read."

Margaret Beaufort's expression hardened even more than usual. "This is a mistake! He should be executed. Why, other Yorkist -" she stopped herself abruptly, suddenly aware that she was not alone with her son in his privy chamber but in his wife's rooms. She could not be seen or heard to criticise him. Katherine, sitting close enough to Bessy to have an uninterrupted view of the document hid a smile behind her hand. The King's version of the Feigned Lad's past seemed to be an extraordinary concoction of over-detail and fantasy. Surely the bit about being dressed up in silks smacked of the legend of Tristan? Now what was happening? The King had crossed to where Lady Kateryn was quietly weeping in the corner.

"You see, my dear, he cannot hurt you further. You were as much deceived as any. You are not to blame. The marriage will be annulled and you will be free of him. Free to resume your life. I shall send word to your cousin the king in Scotland." Kateryn sobbed afresh which appeared to satisfy Henry. "Poor soul, you have been much abused."

When he left, his mother glided after him. Several of Bessy's ladies crowded around Lady Kateryn, offering their sympathy and consolation. Katherine could hear snatches of their conversation:

"… will soon forget …"

"… and the King will ensure that your new husband is …"

"… much better to put this behind you …"

"… and how dreadful that you were so deceived …"

"… the Queen is so kind; she will not allow …"

Then Lady Kateryn's own lilting, Scottish voice, rising above them all in an hysterical scream," I cannae bear it!" She pushed them all aside and prostrated herself before Bessy.

"Please, Your Grace. I beg you. Give me leave to retire."

Bessy nodded gravely. "You will be welcome again when you have composed yourself, Lady Huntley. Do not run; you may fall and injure yourself. Please join us again for prayers this evening." When the distraught Kateryn had been helped back to her own room, Bessy's ladies broke up into small groups, talking in hushed whispers. Katherine signalled to her musicians to play and they embarked upon a soothing set of tunes. Bessy lay back in her chair, eyes closed, allowing the gentle music to wash over her.

4

Courtenay House, Warwick Lane, City of London
November 1497

Katherine entered the gateway of her new London home and looked around in admiration and satisfaction. The square court was spacious, paved with stone and flanked by three storeys of offices and sleeping accommodation. Directly ahead was the Great Hall and leading from it the butteries and kitchen. Above, she knew there would be a quiet solar for private family time. The half-timbered galleries spoke of recent work, the oak still pale and smooth. Over the rooftops the bells of the East Minster at St Paul's sounded the Sext, the hour for midday prayer.

"I hope you like it," said William. "Of course, when my parents come to London we must share it, but otherwise it is ours. Plenty of room for our whole household, anyway. It's a busy part of the city but that's all to the good, I think, and not far for us to ride to attend the King and Queen."

"I cannot believe it. I cannot remember anywhere I could truly call my own home." She had never before been mistress of any house; since the age of four she had only ever lived in grace and favour rooms in the Tudor royal palaces.

"Well, you have others too; you just haven't seen them yet! The Courtenays have manors all over Devon, not to mention a castle or too. My father thought the family needed a London base now that you and I seem destined to spend so much of our lives here, though he and my mother are content enough in Devon."

She turned to her young husband and standing on tip-toe kissed his cheek. Newly-shaven that morning, he smelled fresh and clean – of expensive castile soap and lavender-strewn linen. "Lord William Courtenay, I brought you nothing, yet you give me everything."

His arm stole around her waist. "Katherine, right welbeloved. You have given me two fine boys and your heart. I can think of few married couples at court as content as we are."

For a moment Katherine allowed herself the luxury of leaning against him. All her life the world, her religion and experience had taught her that women were inferior to men: expendable, few deemed worthy of education, incapable of independent action or thought, bound to serve and obey their husbands in word and deed. Upon marriage even the most wealthy heiress saw her title, lands and possessions pass into her husband's legal keeping. With William, though, it was different. Yes, he expected her to defer to him in public; yes, he ordered all the important things in their lives – and yet here was a man whom she knew truly loved her. Even in the company of others, he asked for her opinion on all things; his white-faced anxiety and loving messages when she had entered her two confinements had assured her of his sincerity. He had confessed himself a little astonished to discover that his wife was fluent in three languages, and possessed reading and writing skills far in excess of his own, but laughed it off with cheerful good humour, *what can you expect when you marry a princess?* At least, he joked, with a twinkle in his eye, his wife had no training in jousting … as far as he knew. It was true, she had brought very little to their marriage – no vast estates or associated incomes. His parents had married him to her in firm expectation of how a link with the Tudors would benefit the Courtenays for generations to come. Who knew what rewards might lie ahead for loyal followers of King Henry? Now he returned her kiss, knowing that he adored her as a man might adore the Queen of Heaven herself. He hoped that such a thought was not blasphemous.

The children were already settled in the new nursery rooms. They would stay for the winter months but return to their royal cousins at leafy Eltham, or Hatfield or one of the other summer palaces in the warmer, sickness-ridden months of the year. Bessy had promised that both boys, and any future children, would be educated as befitted their status.

As they rode back to Westminster, through the lanes and fields that linked the two cities, Katherine drew her horse alongside her husband's. Seaton whickered to the pretty bay mare, William's wedding gift. With her four white socks and white, rose-shaped splash on her forehead, she was unmistakably his daughter.

"Ha! You recognise her, old boy! And I'll wager you remember her mother, a most beautiful black mare by the name of Velvet!"

Katherine glanced round. They were trotting along the Strand, the riverside road lined with the grand houses of the bishops and nobles. One of their household guards rode ahead, bearing the Courtenay standard now impaled with symbols of her own royal descent and two rode at a respectful distance, out of earshot. Now that they had left the densely populated city streets it was safer to talk. Katherine enjoyed riding out; she sat astride her mare confidently, at one with the creature's gait. As they passed by the entrances to various mansions servants in livery acknowledged the Courtenay colours and bowed.

"What will we do, if Bessy and Cecily recognise him?"

"Katherine, I have told you. If you value your life, and my life, and our children's lives you will do nothing. The King will never allow your sisters, or you, to speak to him. "

"Do you think it is a test? Bringing him into court, to see how my sisters react?"

"Undoubtedly."

"The King says he is uneducated. That must be a lie, for you said he spoke perfect English at Exeter. Kateryn Huntley says he plays the organ beautifully and wrote her the most wonderful love letters before they married."

"I thought you were never allowed to be alone with her, to talk?"

"We're not, but our servant Elyn, who was with us in sanctuary all those years ago, is still given to making friends with the right people and sometimes cannot help telling us the gossip."

"Please tell your sisters to take great care. There is nothing that the King does not know about. It's over, anyway. It doesn't matter who he is any more, for since his capture and his confession all support has just melted away." He reached over and laid a hand on Katherine's reins, pulling her mare back into a walk. "I can imagine how Her Grace the Queen must feel – no, that's wrong, actually I cannot even begin to imagine, but I just don't think anything can be worth it any more. And if Perkin Warbeck, or whatever his name is, has any sense or feeling he will try to avoid bringing more misfortune upon others."

Katherine: *And then came the day when I saw him. I had imagined it would be in some public place – at dinner in the Great Hall, or at chapel but instead it was whilst we were out hunting in the fields and woods beyond Sheen. He had been at court for days, they said, in the King's rooms, always with a guard or two in his wake but remarkably cheerful. The weather suddenly entered a settled spell, the days short and cold but thankfully still, sunny and dry. We had been cooped up in my sister's rooms, whilst rain and wind had beaten at the shutters, heartily sick of sewing, reading and other sedentary activities. Every topic of polite* *conversation had been exhausted; everything we wanted to discuss seemed too dangerous. So when the invitation came to join the King in his pursuit of the hart my sister needed no second bidding.*

The hunting grounds at Sheen stretched for thousands of acres – flat land, with woods, thickets and open ground ideal for galloping on a bright, frosty December morning. It was one of the last opportunities to hunt the stags before the closed season of mid-winter. The royal party clattered out of the courtyard at Sheen as soon as the sun was up, the gentlemen equipped with their long bows and huntsmen with sharp knives to finish off any kill cleanly. Somewhere in the King's retinue, jostling amongst scores of courtiers, Bessy and Katherine knew the Feigned Lad rode too. The winter sunlight caught upon polished stirrups, buckles and badges; the cold air was alive with anticipation; the horses and greyhounds sensed each other's zest for their instinctive desire to race and run.

When the first hart was scented, the huntsmen's horns blasted their nasal signal and the hounds streamed forward, eyes bright with excitement. Katherine found herself galloping alongside several lords – she recognised her de la Pole cousins, Edmund and his younger brother Richard, who both waved and threw her admiring smiles. Momentarily, William drew up alongside, curbing Seaton's massive stride for a few seconds to match those of the bay mare. He shouted to her above the thud of the pounding hooves, "Stay with the crowd, Katherine! Don't get lost! And watch for rabbit holes!" then was gone in a glorious stampede of horseflesh as the young lords showed off their stallions' pace.

Katherine's mare was unsettled by the scent of the male horses who had surrounded her; her smooth stride faltered and she cavorted to the left, throwing up her head. Katherine sat down in the saddle, fighting to shorten her reins and bring the creature back under full control. Ahead she could see the ground becoming uneven as they galloped towards the coney warrens. All the other riders had veered around to the right to avoid their horses coming to grief – in a panic-stricken split-second Katherine registered that although the mare was slowing it would not be in time. Sure enough she stumbled, and Katherine was pitched forwards. She was halfway up the mare's neck, sliding off, and braced herself for the inevitable impact. It came. She hit the ground hard but the morning sun had thawed the frost leaving the turf springy and muddy. She lay on her back, utterly winded, and saw the mare come to a surprised halt a few hundred yards ahead. Above her the expanse of sky was that pale blue of an early winter's morning and crows were circling, cawing as they flew from the leafless treetops. Then a figure blotted out the light. Hands were taking hers and someone was speaking.

"My lady, stay still for a while. Are you hurt? Your legs? Arms?" She could not place his accent.

She closed her eyes and considered her limbs, one by one. "No, no I don't think so."

"There is no blood. You will have bruises, but I think you will live." The last phrase was delivered with a mischievous chuckle.

Katherine opened her eyes again and struggled to sit up. At her side was a young nobleman in his mid-twenties, dressed in elegant dark green. His grey stallion was taking the opportunity to crop the grass nearby. He was good-looking, with a square jaw, hazel eyes and curling hair the colour of an autumn leaf. Two more horsemen were now approaching; one flung himself from his saddle and was running towards her.

"My Lady Courtenay! Cousin Katherine! What happened?" It was her cousin Edmund de la Pole, son of her aunt Elizabeth of Suffolk, brother of the dead Lincoln who had led the rebellion against the King shortly after Bosworth. This cousin had sworn loyalty to the new Tudor regime but nevertheless Henry Tudor had demoted him from Duke to Earl – a reminder to keep him in his place. Katherine looked from one man to the other. Edmund was slightly older but there were similarities in their facial features and colouring. There were many de la Pole brothers, Katherine knew, but she struggled to name the younger man who now set off to bring back her mare.

Edmund helped her to her feet and brushed the worst of the mud off her gown. "I must thank your brother" she began.

Her cousin took her hands again. "Not *my* brother," he said in a low voice.

The young man was back, leading the bay mare. He held her bridle while her cousin laced his fingers together and boosted Katherine back into the saddle. "Do you feel you can carry on?" She nodded. As she gathered up her reins the other young man moved from one side to the other, ensuring that her feet were settled firmly in her stirrups. Then he looked up, smiling directly at her.

"I am glad you turned out a fearless rider."

The Earl of Suffolk flashed him a look of warning. "No, Dickon."

"Dickon?" The name was a dry rustle in the back of her throat.

263

He shrugged. "Or Peter, or Piers, or Perkin. Or Richard. Whatever you like really. Did you turn out a good chess player too?"

"That's enough!" said Suffolk. "I'll look after her. Ride on, before they miss you."

The young man swept her a cheeky bow and vaulted on to his horse, pulling up its head from the grass. He patted its neck affectionately, in the same easy way that William communicated with Seaton. "I call him Soleil, even though he's grey, because he is so ... splendid. What do you call your mare?"

"Rose," she whispered, "but I do not say what colour," then watched him gallop away towards the wooded area where the distant tooting of the horn proclaimed a kill. She turned beseeching eyes upon her Suffolk. "You think he is ...?"

"I don't think anything, cousin. I find it's best not to. Come on, we'll catch up in time for dinner."

Tables had been laid in the open air, laden with pasties, cold meats, cheese and bread. Braziers had been lit and servants were busy heating pokers ready to thrust into the huge jugs of spiced wine, to mull it. Tendrils of smoke curled into the air. Scores of men and women of the royal household dismounted and claimed seats on little stools and chairs near to the fires; the air was dense with animated chatter: accounts of the morning's chase and kills. Eyes sparkled and laughter rang out. A temporary pavilion had been erected for the King and Queen under an ancient oak, to allow them to dine in comfort; the tree stretched gnarled branches to the sky like old fingers. Tapestries had been hung and a cloth of estate suspended from the branches. Katherine looked for William but could not spot him. Her cousin Suffolk delivered her safely to the entrance and helped her to dismount. She winced at the bruise she knew would soon grace her back.

Inside, Henry and Bessy were sitting side by side, flanked by the nobles of the court. Bessy's ladies-in-waiting who had not wished to hunt had joined them now, conveyed in litters. Pausing for a moment, Katherine's eyes roved over those outside, searching for the young man in dark green. She spotted him at some distance from the main party, sitting nonchalantly on a fallen trunk in front of the tethered horses. Suffolk conducted her through the throng to Bessy's side.

"Your Graces," he bowed low, "I came across my cousin Katherine, whose mare had been indulging in a few sideways antics. Thankfully she is unhurt but deserves a comfortable seat and some refreshment." Katherine saw a cloud of irritation pass over the King's face. He preferred not to be reminded of the network of family relationships between his wife and her many cousins. Suffolk judged the moment and made his excuses, offering a perfectly executed final bow, and a swift kiss on Katherine's hand. Thankfully, Katherine slid into the cushioned chair next to Bessy, who looked askance at the mud on her clothes.

"Jesu, Katherine, what happened?"

She shrugged. "As our cousin Suffolk said, my mare misbehaved and I fell off."

"Why was Suffolk not riding ahead with the other gentlemen?"

"I have no idea."

A servant set a cup of steaming mulled wine before her and she sipped gratefully, enjoying the delicious spiced warmth that stole through her body. A rich venison pasty soon restored her too. A furred cloak was brought and she pulled it around her shoulders. The brazier and the number of bodies in the makeshift tent soon created a soporific warmth.

"I do so love these last, unexpected days of pleasure outside," Bessy's words were wistful, "before we all retreat indoors for weeks."

"It is Christmastide soon, and Cecily will be here, and Meg and Prince Arthur from Ludlow. And you love being at Sheen."

"True. Oh, look, Katherine, here comes William. He shot the first hart, you know."

William was negotiating his way through the packed pavilion to reach her. Henry Tudor rose to his feet. "My Lord Courtenay! Congratulations! A fair shot indeed! All that practice on the walls of Exeter has honed your skills!" His courtiers roared their approval and banged the trestle tables, causing the platters to bounce. Henry Tudor clearly enjoyed their reaction; it was not often that he could quip and make men laugh. "And we hanged the Cornish rebels as our huntsman will the hart – is that not right, Courtenay?" William flushed. More applause and Thomas Howard, the Earl of Surrey, Anne's husband, jumped up on to the table, waving his cup wildly.

"So perish all Your Grace's enemies!" Deliberately he tipped his cup up and a stream of dark red wine gushed out, ran over the white cloth and pooled on the ground. Howard stamped his foot and flourished the vessel high above his head. *He curries Tudor favour like a fawning spaniel,* thought Katherine, *and he must, for surely his grandfather and father fought for York at Bosworth.* She tried to imagine Anne, miles away on the Norfolk estates in East Anglia, still grieving for her stillborn child. Quiet Anne, who never complained of her lot, and hoped

265

to be a duchess one day, but whose husband regarded her only as a laurel for his support for the Tudors, and kept her far from court. She could sense William's obvious distaste for Howard's crass behaviour.

Henry Tudor's shrewd, slate-like eyes had narrowed and he was looking through the open front of the little pavilion to where the young man still sat astride his log. He could have been some piece of statuary, for he did not move a muscle – just sat, with his grey stallion tethered behind him. All eyes followed the King's. A hush of expectation fell.

"Well, there is the young rebel himself. Call him hither," said Henry Tudor.

Thomas Howard leapt off the table, bounded out of the tent and caught the young man by the collar of his fashionable cloak, pulling him into the King's presence. Katherine felt Bessy stiffen. Surreptiously, she draped her own mantle over her sister's hand then felt for Bessy's fingers under the fur. The young man never looked at them. Never once did he allow his eyes to flicker in their direction. Instead, when Howard released him, he simply adjusted his collar and bowed before Henry. But he did not speak.

"Well, Perkin Warbeck. We were just speaking of Exeter," said the King. "You remember Exeter? Of course you do, it was but twelve weeks ago. And you remember my Lord Courtenay?"

The young man dipped his head in polite acknowledgement. "A fine opponent. Brave and honourable."

"He beat you soundly, did he not? And you were forced to flee? Oh, and then you were caught, and *then* you remembered that you were not who you said you were." Henry Tudor's lip was curling in a sardonic smile.

"And how *are* your family?" enquired Thomas Howard solicitously. "All those relations in Tournai!" The tent was filled with shouts of raucous laughter. The young man did not lose his composure but grinned good-naturedly. He offered his hand to William.

"My thanks for your mercy, sir."

Again, Henry's adherents hooted with laughter. *The whole thing is like an interlude,* thought Katherine – *an entertainment carefully devised to make us all smile.* All around her men were splitting their sides. Under the furred cloak she felt Bessy's nails digging into her palm. Thomas Howard was whispering in Henry Tudor's ear.

"Courtenay!" the King held up a hand to quell the noise. "What do you say to a horse race against young Warbeck? Flanders flesh against good English stock? Your great bay against his grey?"

"We should lay wagers!" shouted the excited Howard.

Henry turned towards Bessy. "The Queen dearly loves to gamble. She must, of course, place the first bet. What shall it be? Lord Courtenay or Master Warbeck?"

He is hateful, thought Katherine, *utterly hateful. He thinks to test her loyalty in such sly ways.* She pressed Bessy's hand as hard as she dared but her sister was in full control of herself and managed to sound as if she were merely indulging her husband in his games.

"Regretfully, I cannot stake money on Master Warbeck. A golden sovereign, though, upon my Lord Courtenay's horse."

The young man looked at her for the first time and gave her a dazzling smile. "I understand completely, Your Grace."

The young men poured out of the pavilion with much commotion and hilarity, half-carrying William and the Feigned Lad between them. Their horses were led forward; neither stallion was enamoured of being dragged away from his bag of oats and saddled again. They snorted, rolled their eyes and shifted their hind-quarters uneasily.

"Where shall we race to, Your Grace?" asked William. Seaton was foaming slightly at the mouth, champing down upon his bit.

The King gazed across the flat landscape of the hunting grounds to a stand of oaks in the distance. "From here, to the trees, and back," he decreed. Thomas Howard beckoned one of the huntsmen forward; his horn would serve as the signal to start.

Katherine sighed. There was no danger to either rider or horse; it was just another impromptu jape – and yet there seemed to be an undercurrent. What would happen if the Feigned Lad managed to best the king's brother-in- law? It was almost as if Henry had thrown down some ridiculous challenge to rile the young man into doing something foolish.

The horn rang out and both horses leapt forward, racing away across the short tussocks. Soon they were just specks in the distance and the household fell quiet, watching them round the oak trees and begin the sprint back. As they drew nearer Katherine could see each man low over his horse's neck; William had loosed the reins to give Seaton his head and the stallion was flat out, snaking along the grass like a mad thing. Soleil's gait was more flowing, speaking of his Moorish bloodline. They came back into earshot, hooves resounding on the hard winter ground then lost in the delighted roars and yells of Henry Tudor's courtiers. William veered across the impromptu finishing line a length ahead of the Feigned Lad. Both men pulled up, their horses heaving and sweating. Winded, William lay backwards, his head nearly touching Seaton's tail; the Feigned Lad slipped from his saddle and handed his reins to a groom.

"It seems I must congratulate you for a second time, my Lord Courtenay."

"This year the King kept his Christmas at Sheen, where upon St Thomas's Day a great fire within the King's lodgings ... so continued into the night ... by violence whereof much and great part of the old building was burnt and much harm done as in hangings ... rich beds ... howbeit, no Christian creature perished which was the King's singular comfort, considering the great and notable court that was there holding ..." The Great Chronicle of London

When they returned to the palace at Sheen it was to find that the Christmas visitors had arrived. During the darkening afternoon Prince Arthur had ridden in from Ludlow in the company of his Governor, Sir Richard Pole and Meg. Not long after, Cecily's party also clattered over the little wooden drawbridge.

"If we had Anne, and Bridget, it would be perfect," said Katherine. She hugged her sister fiercely, noting the shadows beneath her lovely eyes and the new, fine lines by her mouth. The loss of her girls and her husband's ill-health were taking their toll. She was still dressed in dark blue mourning for her little daughters.

"Anne will surely come at Easter, and Bridget will be thinking of us all even now, and praying for us!" Bessy accepted her sisters' and cousin's curtsies then gathered both women in her arms. She dismissed her waiting women and the four Plantagenet princesses sat by the firelight as evening fell. There was no feasting tonight, just a quiet supper served in Bessy's rooms.

"Well?" Cecily did not need to say more.

"We *have* seen him. But it is impossible to speak with him alone." Bessy kept her voice low. "And truly, it's impossible to say. I look for the little boy I once knew sixteen years ago but whether I can see him in the face of a grown man ... I just don't know."

"*I* will know!" said Cecily, "I was the one who combed his hair and washed his face. *I* will know in an instant!"

"Cecily, you won't. You will see what you want to see. And, forgive me for saying this, but I think your grief for Lisbet and Annie will make you want it even more. Is it true that you correspond with Lady Kateryn Huntley? That you call her "sister" in your letters?"

Cecily's eyes widened. "How do you know that?"

"Do you not think that my husband has eyes everywhere? Your household is no exception. Have a care. Henry is indulgent towards Kateryn but only so long as she dances to his tune. He likes to see her as the poor innocent victim, duped by the Scots king and the Feigned Lad. She is being very careful to appear so. Your letters could be her downfall."

Meg put an arm around Cecily's slender shoulders. "I write to my brother but he never replies. I don't know if he ever receives my letters, or if he can even read. I think Bessy's right. I think the King does have spies in all our homes."

"Jesu!" spat Cecily. "How can you bear to be married to him, Bessy?"

Katherine moved to the door and opened it carefully. The corridor outside was empty. Bessy's ladies had melted away, glad of an hour to themselves. A yeoman of the guard was on duty but at the far end. If they had been at Westminster such privacy would have been impossible but here at tiny Sheen she had an opportunity. The three faces by the fire looked at her expectantly, framed by their gable hoods and lappets. No longer the faces of girls but of mature women, used to wealth but marked by intense worry and grief. She shut the door quietly and leaned against it.

"I have things to tell you all. Meg, I have seen Ned, and spoken with him. When we were at the Tower in the summer. No, shh! Don't cry!" She rushed to her cousin and sank on her knees beside her. "He is well and sends his love and he knows you think of him every day of your life." She judged her words to be a fair rendering of the awful truth. "Better days will come, Meg. They will. And today I spoke with the Feigned Lad."

The three women were clearly thunderstuck. Bessy's mouth opened as though she would speak but she was lost for words. Cecily clutched at the rosary hanging from her waist.

"Sweet Mother of God, tell us quickly! What did he say?"

"Not much. That he hoped I still played chess, and that his horse is called Soleil. But I am sure our cousin Suffolk believes in him. He called him Dickon. And he let William win today, deliberately."

Cecily fumbled in her bodice and produced a letter. "His wife believes in him. Kateryn lived with him for nearly two years and has never once doubted him. She says he has told her of all his childhood memories."

"Our aunt in Burgundy could have furnished him with those *memories,*" replied Bessy bleakly. "And his education. And he has been touted round Europe in the company of princes. He has learned how to carry himself in their company. Oh Cecily, there are explanations for everything! And throw that on the fire, now! Jesu, you are as bad as Mama ever was! What's wrong with you? Have you no memories of her foolish plotting and scheming? Do *you* want to end up banished to Bermondsey with the monks?"

Meg took her hand and stroked it very gently. "I understand, Bessy, that it's better if he is *not* Dickon. Better for all of us really. It means that your Arthur goes forward into the future as our king, and he will be *such* a good king! He works so hard at his lessons and strives to learn all he can from my husband about ruling the Marches. England can look forward to years of peace and prosperity."

"But what if *he* is? Would you deny him his rightful place, Meg? And the release of *your* brother?" Cecily was practically hissing.

Meg jumped to her feet and pulled Cecily from her seat, holding her by both shoulders as if to shake her. "And what would *that* mean for Bessy and Arthur, Harry, Margaret and Mary? Would you have another generation of children ripped from their birthright as we were?"

"He would not blame them," said Cecily sullenly.

"As the King has not blamed Ned, by keeping him in the Tower all these years? Or us, married to bury our Plantagenet names in the furthest corners of England? See sense, Cecily! Arthur and Harry are just boys, as Edward and Dickon were boys – and a man's ambition to be king can sweep aside all sentiment, all compassion."

Cecily pushed her away and flounced to the window where she stood trembling, looking into the darkness of the December evening. Sconces burned bright at the end of the drawbridge and along the approach to the palace. Quietly, Bessy rose and joined her sister, slipping an arm around her narrow waist.

"Cecily, please. It breaks my heart when we disagree. What would you have me do? "

Katherine watched her two beloved elder sisters. Angrily, Cecily shook off Bessy's touch and leaned her forehead upon the hard stone of the window's mullions. Her mouth twitched with emotion. "You have become his creature, Bessy. A Tudor creature!"

"That is unfair, Cecily. I had no choice. You, above all, know the truth of that. I married him to keep us all safe! Meg, forgive me, we are all proud of the name our fathers gave us but all Henry sees is conspiracy after conspiracy to topple him from the throne. And there's something else. We are trying to persuade the Spanish to honour the agreement to marry Arthur to Catalina, the youngest Spanish princess. Think what that would mean for England! An alliance with the most powerful nation in Christendom! But the Spanish ambassador keeps mentioning how concerned Ferdinand and Isabella are about the legality of the succession. They will not send Catalina if there is any breath of further conspiracy."

"So what should we hope for?" asked Katherine.

"That the Feigned Lad, whoever he is, sees that *we* have survived, and values his own survival. If I could talk to him, I would tell him to live a quiet life: find a tranquil, green corner of England where the rivers run clean and the larks soar high in the sky, and raise a new family who know nothing of the name we all bear."

"He was lucky to escape Exeter with his life," said Katherine. "William expected him to be hanged when the King brought him from Beaulieu. Cecily, please listen to Bessy. If he is who we hope he could be then let us pray for his survival." She felt for her own coral rosary hanging from her waist and her fingers closed around the familiar, cool beads.

Cecily looked from her sisters to her cousin, scanning their faces. "I am weary. It was a cold journey from King's Langley and John is ailing." Bessy nodded a reluctant acknowledgement and Cecily left the room.

Meg's mouth pursed in thought. "She hankers after a purpose; a cause. Losing the girls has left such a void and she knows she is not likely to have more babes, with her husband so ill. Don't judge her too harshly."

"I don't," said Bessy heavily. "But she is like a moth to flame. She has all Mama's passion and I fear where it will lead her."

"Too close to the sun," said Katherine.

"We are all tired," said Bessy, "and you have travelled far, Meg, over the last few days. Things will be better in the morning. Cecily is always more sensible after a good night's sleep."

The Courtenays had lodgings at the front of the palace, on the upper floor with views across the river to the abbey at Syon. Katherine opened the shutters and the crisp air gusted into the room. William was lying on his back, snoring softly after many cups of wine. Night air was said to be dangerous but she loved the way it cooled her hot forehead and sent shivers into her lungs. In the moonlight, the water meadows glittered. The sky was darkly beautiful, studded with diamond stars. *Winter plays host to such beauty.* The stars, she knew, influenced many things: the weather, the crops, her own personality and the workings of the inner parts of her body. Bessy said that Henry Tudor was obsessed with the foretellings of the stars; he was forever urging his Italian astrologer to draw up new charts listing the good fortune that lay ahead for the new dynasty. Which stars had informed Henry about Perkin Warbeck, she wondered, squinting to bring the faraway spangles of light into better focus.

As her eyes adjusted to the darkness she saw the outlines of the clipped hedges on the edge of the garden, and the walls behind. A frost was forming on the tops, bouncing light back to the moon. A faint pink was tingeing the white – like some strange reflective glow. Puzzled, she leaned out as far as she dared, straining to see and listen. A sudden flow of fear coursed through her, from head to foot.

Almost instantaneously, screams rang out from somewhere further along the front of the building and from the inner courtyard the chapel bell began ringing the unmistakable tocsin alarm.

"William!" She was by her husband's side, shaking him awake. "William, for Jesu's sake! Fire!" *Thank God my children are in Warwick Lane. Oh, God, Bessy! Cecily! Meg! The princes and princesses!* William was groaning out of a heavy sleep.

"Jesu! My head!"

"Never mind your head! There's a fire somewhere! We have to get out!" She was moving towards the door but he snapped into consciousness with a soldier's instinct.

"No! Don't open it! It may save us!" He was off the bed and dragging the sheets from the layers of mattress. "Quick, Katherine, is there any water in the laver?"

She seized the large shallow bowl the servant had left for her to wash in. William was ripping strips of linen and then soaking them in the few precious inches of water.

"Wrap these around your head. Make sure your mouth is covered."

Wordlessly, she obeyed him. They looked like two corpses prepared for the grave.

"William, look at the door." Her voice was muffled behind the fabric. Tendrils of smoke were visible at the bottom of the thick oak.

"It's the window, then. Take off your gown; you'll never squeeze through otherwise."

She looked at him in horror. "Are you mad? We will break every bone in our bodies! "

But he had thrown the mattresses off the bed and was frantically releasing the bedropes.They spooled upon the floor. He knotted ends, working with absolute determination, pulling and testing as he went, then tied one end around the thick, carved bed post. He poked his head out the window and shouted down below where people who had escaped from the ground floor were gathering in anxious throngs.

"Right, Katherine. Do not think twice. The rope will hold you, I swear. Lean back and imagine you are walking down the wall like a pathway. Hold the rope out before you. I will not let you fall. Think of our children. GO!" He pushed her towards the window. She had divested herself of everything but her shift. "God's truth, but you are beautiful, wife."

Her eyes held his for a second. "I promised to obey you, husband, but I did not imagine it would be like this."

He lifted her into the window. She looked over her shoulder and down below saw people holding tapestries, sheets – anything to break the fall of those crazy enough to leap. William was putting the rope into her hands and in a dream she watched herself edging backwards out of the narrow window. It was a tight fit; she felt the stone scraping against the skin of her hips and shoulders. Tentatively, she began to lower herself, the will to survive overwhelming her fear.

"Look up! Look at me all the time, Katherine!" William was framed in the window. Through her thin soled shoes she could feel the hard, rough surface of the wall and the palms of her hands burned as the bed ropes passed through. Her ears were filled with rushing blood and beyond that the sound of crackling, and popping as precious glass window panes gave way.

From below came urgent shouts. "There's no more rope, my lady! Let go! We will catch you!" Panicked, she looked up again at William.

His eyes were steady. "Do it, Katherine! It's just a few feet!"

The fall seemed miles. She closed her eyes and waited for the sickening pain of broken bones, or oblivion. Instead, all the breath in her body was forced out in one great "Oouf!" as she hit something thick and forgiving.

"We have you, my lady! You are quite safe!"

She tumbled out of a tapestry, held by at least six or eight men, and rolled across the freezing grass, then scrambled to her knees, pulling the soaked linen strips from her face. Strands of loose hair stuck to her cheeks and lips. Someone dropped a cloak over her shoulders. She flung her head up, to watch William's descent, but to her horror he was no longer at the window.

"My husband! William! William!" She was screaming his name like a banshee.

Then a familiar form was at her side. Bessy. "He is too big to get through the window. But the fire is mostly on the other side, in the wardrobe rooms. He can make it."

The burning palace was ejecting its inhabitants in scores. Most fled towards the river banks to escape the intensity of the heat but others simply stood open-mouthed in the gardens, watching the spectacle of flames leaping out of the roofline into the night sky. Orange, yellow, red – with flashes of blue and green, dancing and spiralling. There was no saving the building.

When William came staggering towards her, his hair singed and his shirt and hose black with smoke and soot, Katherine burst into hysterical tears. He looked like some hellish figure from the wall-paintings in the chapel – a creature from the fires of purgatory. She threw herself into his arms and he dripped black water over them both. "Some resourceful fellow had the same idea as me, but had a whole jugful of water! We doused ourselves and ran for it!"

"Is everyone out?" A calm, authoritative voice rang out. Henry Tudor. "Well, my Lady Courtenay, you took a dramatic route of escape and no mistake." His tone was one of mixed admiration and amusement.

The whole royal family were gathering around Katherine and William, exclaiming at their state, although everyone was clad in some faintly comical assortment of garments – half-dressed, or half-undressed; the children in their night-shifts; Bessy, Cecily and Meg with their hair streaming down their backs.

274

The King had lost his doublet and his shirt hung out over his hose like a man caught in some whore's bedroom.

"Papa! Papa! Did you have to run, like us?" Prince Harry was jigging up and down in excitement, wide-eyed at the sight of the burning palace.

"Indeed I did, Harry. Fire waits for no man, not even kings. The floor of the gallery collapsed behind me. But the worst is over. They will contain it now." He gestured to where lines of men were organising themselves to pass buckets from the river and the wells. "The fire will burn itself out overnight."

His mother, Lady Margaret, was gliding across the garden towards them, pristine in her nun-like habit and severe wimple. "God be praised, we are all safe. But they say the wardrobe apartments are utterly destroyed. Razed to the ground. We shall have to send to Westminster immediately for replacement clothes for you all."

"Is anyone killed?" It was Cecily's voice.

Katherine caught the look that flashed between the King and his mother.

"Apparently not." Lady Margaret sounded almost disappointed.

Katherine could taste the acrid smoke at the back of her throat. She felt William's breath close to her ear and his whisper. "I need to check on something. Stay with your sister." He slipped away into the blackness.

Prince Arthur was gazing up at the roof of the palace and flinched as a reverberating thud heralded the collapse of yet another set of wooden beams and a few more flames spurted skywards. "It's awful, Mama. Sheen was one of your favourites. "

Bessy's face was masked in the shadows but her voice was firm. "If no-one has lost their life, then that is enough for me. God has smiled upon us. We can rebuild."

By morning the extent of the damage was obvious. Pillars of stone stood up like jagged black teeth where once the Great Hall and adjacent galleries had stood. Half-burned staircases led to nowhere now, and what few roof beams remained were charred like brittle bones. The court was to de-camp to Byfleet Manor, the nearest royal residence, for Christmas itself and the men were already saddling their horses; mercifully, their stabling was at some distance from the main palace. The women and children were to make most of the journey by barge.

In a gown borrowed from Cecily, Katherine stood on the landing jetty and looked back at the ruins of the palace. A thin, watery December sun was trying, but failing, to bestow a little warmth. She shivered. Bessy was busy settling the children and their attendants into the first craft, putting Meg in charge. Cecily came down the pathway with a few of her servants; they carried her husband, John Welles, in a chair. He coughed and coughed, and gave a wan, apologetic smile. Lady Margaret came fussing around her half-brother, ensuring his place in her own barge.

Cecily waited by Katherine's side for the Courtenay barge. "What did William find out?"

Katherine kept her voice low. "That he *was* lodged in the Wardobe. But somehow he got out before the fire took hold. He is safe."

"I'll bet our royal brother-in-law is not best pleased. There is talk that the fire was no accident – that it was set deliberately at the foot of the stairs of the Wardrobe -"

"Shh! Look, here comes his wife."

Lady Kateryn had been accorded a place in Bessy's barge, as one of her ladies-of-honour. She was dressed in her habitual black, her auburn hair vivid against the plain hood. As she passed Cecily and Katherine she lifted her eyes and they read an expression of grateful thanks. Cecily reached out a hand but Katherine caught it in her own. Kateryn was assisted into the Queen's barge and took her place in the midst of Bessy's other women. She sat silently, staring at her lap. The first three barges pushed off into the main current of the river. It was only a few miles upstream to Chertsey, where horse-drawn litters would meet them.

The Courtenay craft drew up alongside, its pennant flapping in the wind. Katherine and Cecily stepped aboard and settled themselves in the curtained cabin.

"I have missed this," said Cecily, leaning back into the cushioned seats. "You have no idea how bad the roads are north of London. It takes days to travel anywhere. I used to love being on the river when I was a child! Edward and Dickon loved it too -"

"Cecily, please -"

"Cecily, please, what? May I not talk about my brothers?"

"It is best not to."

"Don't be silly," she snapped. "There is no-one to eavesdrop here. Or do you think Henry Tudor has spies even on your boat?" She pulled back the curtain to prove her point. There was no-one near the cabin. The helmsman stood at the far end, in the stern, and the men rowing could hear nothing above the creaking of the oars, the beat of the drum and their own exertions.

"So what does William think?" demanded Cecily. "Did someone help Dickon escape?"

"We don't know for sure that he *is* Dickon," remonstrated Katherine.

"But you said yourself that you believe he is!"

"No, I didn't. I said our cousin of Suffolk thinks so. The things he said to me … anyone could have told him."

"When I see him, I will know."

"So you said, but I don't think it will be that easy. And I beg you, think of the consequences."

"Katherine, you were a very small child. You do not know what it was like to see our family ruined. If our brother Edward had lived we would have been queens in Europe! Look at us, married off to Lancastrian cronies -"

"Oh, Cecily. John is a *good* man. And William is the best husband I could have ever hoped for. We are blessed -"

"Blessed? *Blessed?* With a man twice my age, who is dying before my eyes, and two dead daughters? And what will Henry Tudor do with me when John dies? Marry me to some other of his followers? I tell you, Katherine, if I see that the Feigned Lad is truly my brother I will proclaim it from the mountain tops and see what Henry Tudor does then!"

Katherine sighed. It was very hard to argue with an older sister. She understood Cecily's fragility but knew it left her vulnerable to what Bessy had termed their mother's impulsive "passion". Cecily was unpredictable, and without the steadying hand of her husband likely to immerse herself in something at least foolish – at worst what might be called treasonable. Living away from court she simply did not appreciate the King's paranoia about enemies and pretenders.

"He will probably put you in the Tower, Cecily. Alongside our poor cousin Ned."

"Don't be ridiculous. No-one puts women in the Tower, not even a Tudor."

The barge pulled rhythmically through the water, gathering speed. The cadence of the movement was soothing. Wrapped in warm furs, and exhausted by Cecily, Katherine felt her eyelids grow heavy; the past twenty four hours had been so tense and then dangerous. She allowed herself to drift away.

Katherine: *Cecily never did get her chance to see the Feigned Lad, for when we arrived at Byfleet her husband was so ill Lady Margaret sent him to her physician at her manor at Woking, and Cecily had to follow. I have to admit that Bessy and I were relieved. The young man trailed in the royal family's wake as we moved from palace to palace in the winter months, and then with us again in the summer progress of 1498. Always, he was lodged in the Wardrobe rooms, which of course had to be locked at night to guard our precious possessions. I never spoke with him again, but he always smiled at me and bowed low when I passed. Once, he winked at me. He was never allowed to be alone with Lady Kateryn and was himself accompanied at all times by two of Henry Tudor's men. They posed as his companions, and clearly enjoyed his company, but never let him out of their sight. Meanwhile, all the talk was of the grand marriage planned for my young nephew Arthur – of the alliance to be made between the kingdoms of Spain and England – of the great future that lay ahead for us all. I continued to serve my sister, and my husband served the King. At our home in Warwick Lane our two little boys grew, safe in their nursery, and we spent as much time there as our duties allowed.*

5

"O my heart! And O, my heart,
It is so sore!
Since I must needs from my Love depart
And know no cause wherefore!" poem by King Henry VIII

June 1498 Westminster

There was a commotion in the line of women following the Queen back to her chamber after early morning Mass in St Stephen's chapel. Someone had fallen. Someone was sobbing. Bessy turned. "Good heavens, Katherine, what has happened? Run and see."

Katherine wriggled her way through a dozen or more of her sister's ladies to where she found Kateryn Huntley prostrate on the floor, crying as though her heart would break, a piece of paper clutched in her hand. Bessy's two yeomen of the guard, loyal and affable men, looked on, distinctly uncomfortable, as if they knew what had upset her. Katherine knelt beside her, and touched her arm.

"Lady Kateryn, let me help you. Please, come into the Queen's rooms. No, no-one else need come – she is too upset." There was no response, except the level of sobbing increased. "Pick her up," she ordered the guard, "and carry her."

The man nodded and scooped up the weeping young woman, bearing her gingerly through the doorway into Bessy's chamber where the Queen, white-faced, motioned for him to deposit her in her own great chair.

He lingered awkwardly. "It's her husband," he offered. "She's just found out." Katherine shoo-ed him away, and closed the door anxiously.

"Tell us," said Bessy simply. "Of all people, we are the ones you can tell."

Kateryn's dark brown eyes were enormous on her tear-stained face. Her whole body trembled. She fought to compose herself but was incapable of speech for at least a minute. Bessy drew up a stool and sat close, stroking her hand. Finally, her light Scots accent lurched with emotion.

"He is taken. Your husband will show no mercy this time." Neither Bessy nor Katherine spoke but waited as Kateryn appeared to breast huge waves of distress. "A window was left open, and he climbed out while his warders slept. He did not get far – to the monks at Sheen, but the Prior would not give him sanctuary. Your husband's men seized him and put him in the stocks before they marched him to the Tower."

Katherine felt a terrible shadow fall again upon her life. "The Tower? Where is he lodged?"

"Where he can see no sun, nor no moon, they say! And they have beaten him." She began to cry again, tears of bitter woe. Katherine realised that Bessy was crying too. Silent tears slid down her cheeks and she made no attempt to wipe them away.

"I can do nothing, Kateryn," whispered the Queen. "I have no power. I cannot be seen to plead for him. You must understand that. I had hoped he would settle for living here with us, for having some sort of life he could enjoy."

Kateryn shook her head. "No, he wanted what he said was his by right. We wanted each other back, too. He was a dear lord to me, Your Grace. A loving father to our child." She lifted her gaze to meet Bessy's. "I am afraid of your husband. He will have mine killed, and then I do not know what he will want from me."

"But he's done nothing!" exclaimed Katherine, "apart from escape, I mean. He has raised no army, nor spoken against the King. They cannot kill him for climbing out of a window!"

Bessy shook her head slowly. "Henry won't give him a second chance. And it's different now – the Spanish are pressing for evidence that Arthur's future will be safe from all Yorkists before they agree to marriage with Catalina. He will use this as an excuse. In fact, he probably arranged it.

"Your husband has chosen his own destiny," added Bessy. "Whoever he is, he has done all of his own free will." A ghost of a smile played on her lips. "I am so glad you loved him, Kateryn. He had that, at least."

There was a brusque knock at the door, which opened immediately. Henry Tudor and his mother entered. They had both been present at prayers and must have heard the disturbance. Lady Margaret sketched the shallowest of curtseys to her daughter-in-law. Henry stared at Bessy. *He looks old,* thought Katherine.

His hair is grey and thin; his skin is pale and his teeth are some of the worst I have ever seen. He looks the same age as his mother, at least. How can Bessy bear to lie with him? If there had been any shadows in the room she would have stepped back into them to escape his notice but Bessy liked the morning sunshine, and now it was pouring in with the promise of another bright midsummer's day. Such light was unforgiving and uncaring though; it landed upon the tearful face of Lady Kateryn, and accentuated Bessy's pinched lips and the beginnings of a double chin.

"Wife?" The one word was loaded with suspicion. He had forbidden her to be alone with Kateryn.

"It is nothing, sir. Lady Kateryn felt faint; she has not slept well, and the incense was most powerful in the chapel."

Lady Margaret cocked her head. "I did not notice, my dear."

Kateryn passed a weary hand over her brow. "I am susceptible to swooning, Your Grace. Since I was a bairn. The slightest thing."

Henry appeared to nod. "And of course you will have heard about Warbeck." The King and his mother looked pleasantly at all three women. Katherine fought to control her composure.

"Indeed, sir," said Bessy levelly.

"Well, he will trouble us no more," said Lady Margaret briskly. "And as my son has told you, you are entirely free from blame, Lady Huntley. Do not trouble yourself any further about such a traitor. As far as my son is concerned, it is as if your marriage has never been, is that not right, Henry?"

"Legally annulled," agreed the King. "Your cousin James Stuart is entirely in agreement."

"What will you do with him, Your Grace?" Kateryn's voice was small but clear. *She is brave*, thought Katherine, *I would never dare to ask him, if I were in her shoes.*

Henry Tudor coughed. A dry, irritable cough. It troubled him most mornings. He cleared his throat repeatedly to loosen the annoying phlegm that lingered there.

"Well, I shall leave that to our laws, my dear. I am sure there is a correct procedure to follow. In the meantime we must have you merry! A new gown or two – something more cheerful. See how delightful Lady Courtenay looks this morning!" Katherine started in alarm and clutched a handful of her creamy embroidered kirtle. "Yes indeed, my wife will ensure that her seamstress visits you today. What better way to cheer up a pretty young maiden?" He seemed immensely pleased with his idea. "And jewel or two. Come along, Lady Kateryn, you may accompany my lady mother and I back to my rooms and choose something."

He was offering her his arm and she could not refuse. Bessy swept him a deep curtsey as the three of them left the room. The guard closed the door softly. Bessy exhaled long and quietly. "He is in love with her."

"Does he want her as a mistress?" Katherine had no idea how she had even dared to say such words but to her surprise Bessy did not seem distressed – merely puzzled.

"No, I think not. He has never strayed. It is not in his nature. He is not a lustful man."

"But kings have mistresses. The Scots king is a complete womaniser, William says."

"Well, I am saved from such a fate, as his mother would never allow it," said Bessy dryly. "Prince Arthur and Prince Harry are her Tudor treasures, and she will brook no possibilities of bastards who might threaten them."

"How could a love child threaten your sons?"

"You forget your history lessons, Katherine. The Beauforts were the bastards of John of Gaunt. She knows well enough what havoc could be wreaked in another generation. No, he will treat her to new clothes, and jewels, and insist upon her company but he will never touch her. Not as long as I am alive."

6

Katherine: *While the Feigned Lad languished in the Tower, London was overrun by Spaniards. Every week there was a flurry of letter-writing, or letter-receiving between their Catholic majesties, Ferdinand and Isabella, in far off Spain, and Henry and Elizabeth Tudor. I was called upon often to sit with my sister as she composed her replies. We wrestled with our Latin, and concocted triumphant phrases. She carried one of Isabella's letters tucked into her jewelled belt and sent another to her son at Ludlow. She encouraged Arthur to write his own letters too, to Catalina, and we admired the copies sent to us by Meg. My nephew Prince Harry would not be outdone, I remember – he produced his own letters in Latin, pushing them under my nose for approbation. "They are wonderful, Harry," I told him, "but it is your brother the Prince of Wales who is going to marry the princess Catalina, not you. Why not write to Sir Thomas More instead? He is always pleased to exchange words with a fellow Latin scholar." Delighted to think of himself as a scholar, Harry would rush off back to his tutors, leaving Bessy and I to smile.*

News came that Cecily's husband John Welles had died, and with typical generosity Bessy summoned Cecily back to court ("Where we can keep an eye on her!"). My sister confided that she was pregnant again; it would be her sixth child with Henry Tudor. Little Edmund was born in February 1499; there was no doubt now about how God's favour shone upon the Tudors. Three lovely boys, who would in time play their parts in shaping England to be strong and powerful.

Sometimes, when the sun rose or set, turning the Thames pink and orange, setting fire to the clouds or rising or disappearing behind the flat horizon, I would think of those two young men in the Tower, hoping against hope that one day they might each be allowed some sort of freedom. Once, my own son found me crying as I looked out from the top windows of our house in the city, directing my thoughts across the spires and roofs.

"Why are you sad, Mama?" Edward Courtenay was nearly four and loved his mother. He leaned against her full skirts and put his thumb in his mouth. He did not see her every day, for she was often at somewhere called "court", which he imagined to be a very important place for she told him it was where his aunt the Queen lived, with her husband the King. He was familiar with most of his royal cousins and liked Mary best; she was pretty and friendly and the same age as himself. Cousin Harry he was wary of – he liked to win at everything, whether fairly or not. Margaret was the eldest and rather scornful of small boys. Edmund was just a baby. Cousin Arthur he could not recall; he lived in somewhere called Wales and was very grown up. Edward only had one other cousin, a boy called Thomas Howard who lived a long way away and whom he had never seen.

When Mama was at home at Warwick Lane, Edward was her shadow. And Hal was Edward's shadow. The two-year-old trailed behind him, chubby legs akimbo. Occasionally their wonderful father was home too and would carry one small boy on his back and tuck the other under his arm. Papa smelled of leather, and horses, and Mama often sent him to wash before she would allow him to sit with them in the solar. Then, smelling of good soap, he would sit by the fire with Hal asleep on his chest and Edward tucked between his legs while Mama played on her lute or read to them. Sometimes Mama and Papa were gone for weeks because the King and Queen commanded it and the boys had to make do with their nursemaids, or occasionally Grandfather and Grandmother Courtenay came from a place called Devon to stay at Warwick Lane. If they asked nicely Grandfather would show them his battle scars and tell stories of when he was a young knight, fighting for his king.

One day Mama had told him that *her* papa had been a king. Edward was astonished.

"Where is he?" Dead, Mama told him. She explained that she could not remember him.

Edward lay awake for several nights worrying that his papa might die too, and he would not be able to remember him. Then he found Mama crying by the window.

They were on the top floor of their tall house, standing in the gable that looked out over the city. Katherine picked her son up and pointed out the spires of the churches and the giant cranes by the river where the merchant ships drew up and unloaded their cargoes. He could see gardens and orchards and green fields too, stretching away in the distance.

"Look, Edward, can you see the great abbey at Westminster? That is where kings and queens are crowned. Your ancestors."

"Am I a prince then, Mama? Like Harry?"

"No, my sweeting. But you will be the Earl of Devon some day. That's better than being a prince. It's safer."

Edward liked to feel safe. He liked it when Joanna closed the shutters and drew the curtain round his bed. He liked it when his father's big hand enclosed his, as they walked together through the stables to where huge Seaton lived and watched him munching his hay bag. He liked it when he knelt for his mother's blessing and she placed her hands on his wavy chestnut hair.

"Is it dangerous to be a prince?" He was rather proud that he knew such a long word. Many things were dangerous because Joanna said so: the river; Papa's sword; the streets of the city outside – which is why the great outer doors were locked and barred every night. In Mama's arms he was level with her face and he put his cheek against hers. He felt her long eyelashes on his skin.

"It can be very dangerous to be a prince," she replied quietly, "which is why I am glad you are not one, even though you *are* the grandson of a king."

"What was my grandsire king called?"

She smiled, mischief lighting up her lovely dark eyes. "Edward, like you."

"Lots of Edwards in our family, Mama," he said with satisfaction.

She looked wistful. "And Richards."

Edward thought hard. "I don't know any Richards, Mama."

"Best that you do not, my son."

Supper that evening was a quiet family affair. Cecily was staying with the Courtenays. Since returning to court she often lodged with them, drawing comfort from the everyday bustle of their happy family life. Her own existence as a wife and mother had been so cruelly wiped away and some days she seemed detached, rudderless. She would appear to lose herself in some little trance, then shake herself back into reality and reach for a small nephew to hold close. Hal struggled out of her grasp as fast as possible but Edward allowed her to hold him for a few seconds, sensing her need, before he too politely wriggled free. She no longer spoke of the Feigned Lad.

Wiiliam sent word that he was still detained at Westminster so they sat in the solar, eating together, whilst sounds of the household at supper floated up the stairs. Later, when the boards had been cleared, there would be music and dancing. It was not a huge household, compared to many of noble families in London; Katherine knew nearly all of her servants by name and took an interest in their welfare. Many came from the Courtenay estates in Devon. William was a firm but fair lord; his servants were assured of good food and a comfortable life in return for their absolute loyalty.

The house in Warwick Lane had fireplaces and enormous chimneys. The solar was snug on a November night and was lit by sweet-smelling beeswax candles.

"We can go down if you wish," said Katherine. "In fact, they are probably hoping we will."

"I don't think I will ever dance again," replied Cecily. "You do know what's going on, don't you?"

"Yes, of course I know. But what can we do?"

"Have you heard from Meg?"

"What would be the point in her writing? She knows we will be thinking of her. And praying for him. She knows we share her sorrow."

For the fate of Ned Plantagenet, the young Earl of Warwick, was sealed. A plot had been discovered (*fabricated, said Bessy*) whereby he had planned to set fire to the Tower, escape to Flanders and wage war upon the Tudor king. (*Though how anyone imagines a poor lad like Ned would be capable of anything of the sort is just ludicrous, said Bessy*).

"Do you think what they say is true, that Ned talked to Dickon, and sent him letters?" asked Cecily.

"No. I don't believe a word of it," said Katherine quietly. "Who on earth would have put him in the room above poor Ned? Yet I wish it *were* true. I wish with all my heart that they might have found some comfort in each other in that horrible place."

"I struggle to think of it now as anything but a prison, and a place of death."

Footsteps pounded up the wooden flight from the Great Hall to the solar. Katherine flew to the door. "It's William. He's very late. He will be hungry." When William strode in it was clear that food was the last thing on his mind. Katherine had rarely seen her husband out of temper; usually, his innate good nature and positive outlook solved most problems but now he entered the peaceful little room as if demons from hell were at his heels. The heavy door slammed behind him and the candles guttered. He was panting from exertion and his jaw was set.

"You need to hear this from me. Do not scream, or faint on me."

Katherine felt her heart lurch. "You have been at Westminster for three days."

"Aye. They have both been tried and both sentenced to death. Your cousin Warwick will be beheaded, and your – and Warbeck will hang."

A deep groan came from Cecily and she hid her face in her hands. Katherine was silent. William threw himself into the chair by the fire and began to pull off his boots. He loosened the lacings on his doublet and ran his hands through his hair. His handsome face was furrowed with outrage. "The King wants them both dead and he has found a way to do it."

"Oh, William, hush!" Even in the inner sanctum of her own home Katherine feared the utterance of rash words.

"Does Bessy know?" asked Cecily in a dull voice.

"I can't imagine otherwise," said William grimly.

"We need to go down to the Hall," said Katherine in a decided tone. "We need to show that we are glad to hear that traitors to the King are condemned to die." Cecily looked at her with a mixture of horror and astonishment. "*This* family – my husband, my sons, will not be dragged down by Henry Tudor. Oh, husband, I am a danger to you! My very name and blood means he might look our way one day if we are not careful. Don't fool yourself, William; there will be someone in this household in his pay. Some boy who cleans our boots, or some girl who washes our shifts. We need to make sure that word goes back that we never questioned these deaths."

Ten minutes later Lord William Courtenay conducted his wife and sister-in-law into the Great Hall of Warwick Lane, the very picture of affability and relaxed good humour. The hired minstrels struck up the rhythms of a lively carol and Lady Courtenay led her sister on to the floor whilst her husband watched indulgently. A chain of people threaded their way through the dance, laughing and singing. At the back of the room, a young servingman, recently hired by the steward, noted Lady Courtenay's smiles, Lady Welles' composure and Lord Courtenay's applause. He shrugged. There was nothing here to report.

"And upon the Saturday next was drawn from the Tower unto Tyburn Perkyn Warbeck … at which place of execution was ordered a small

scaffold … and there upon the gallows hanged, and after … his head set upon London Bridge."

"And upon the Thursday following was the Earl of Warwick brought out of the Tower … and so led unto the scaffold and there beheaded." The Great Chronicle of London

Katherine: *Poor young men. To die so cruelly, and alone. My cousin Ned was marched to Tower Hill on a dark November morning, in a thunderstorm. He had not seen the world outside his prison for years. It was a day to stay home, in the warm and dry; my sisters and I simply knelt before Bessy's prie-dieu at Westminster, telling our rosaries while the rain lashed the windows. God knows what Meg did, in faraway Ludlow. It would have been quick, I know, for the axe slices through flesh like butter. Perhaps he did not really know what was happening. I like to think that when they told him to lay his head upon the wooden block he had no idea that eternity awaited him. Afterwards, they took his poor body for burial near the tomb of his grandfather the Kingmaker. Meg had that, at least, for comfort. For the Feigned Lad it was different. The Bishop of Tournai, who visited him in his cell, declared that he was unrecognisable. They dragged his tortured, broken body tied face down on a hurdle from the Tower to Tyburn, where the common people are hanged. They hoisted him on to the gallows, placed the noose around his neck, whipped away the ladder and left him to swing for hours. When I cried in horror, William folded me in his arms and told me it could have been much worse. For some reason Henry Tudor stopped short of having him cut down, disembowelled and quartered. God alone knows where they buried him. Christ have mercy upon his soul.*

7

A new century dawned and Henry Tudor entered his sixteenth year upon the throne. The Spanish ambassador, de Puebla, wrote happily to his king and queen in the Alhambra Palace in Granada that England was now a place of tranquillity and obedience, thoroughly purged and cleansed of doubtful royal blood. He assured them that all was now in order for the marriage of the Infanta Catalina to the true heir, Prince Arthur of Wales. Katherine was glad. Arthur was a sweet boy, well brought up by Meg and her husband in Ludlow. When he came to court Katherine saw little of his father in him, either in looks or character. He was not such a freckled redhead as Harry but more auburn, with pale skin. At fourteen he had reached the stage in boys where his hands and feet seemed ridiculously big for his slender frame. His legs were long and thin and his Adam's apple enormous in his throat. His voice had cracked early, much to Bessy's amusement, but was showing every chance of eventually settling to a pleasant baritone.

Lady Margaret tried to claim him during his Easter visit to Hatfield Palace but after dutiful appearances at her side at Mass he politely excused himself, seeking out instead precious hours to spend in his mother's company. Spring was so welcome after the sorrowful days of winter and Bessy was overjoyed to have her eldest boy by her side again. They rode and hunted together in the great park, where the first primroses raised tentative, pale yellow heads as mother and son galloped past, laughing together. They flew their falcons together in a sky as blue as a dunnock's egg, watching them hover on the currents and plummet after their prey. On wet days they played cards amidst much laughter and tried out Bessy's new set of clavichords. Arthur tolerated his siblings with his usual good humour. Music was a love they all shared and Katherine frequently came upon Bessy with her three boys and two girls – Edmund in her lap, Arthur at the keyboard, Harry singing with gusto, little Mary proficient upon her lute and Margaret beating time with a tabor. With Henry Tudor involved with his Council the family were free to relax.

The royal family kept well away from London that spring, for the plague was raging. William and Katherine closed up the house in Warwick Lane and sent their boys down to Devon to the clean air of the Exe Valley. The winter had been wet and mild, and the new season warm, which meant that the pestilence lingered. Finally, the King gave orders that his younger children should stay on at Hatfield for the whole summer when Arthur travelled back to Ludlow.

On a May morning they stood in front of the arched entrance, waiting to wave Arthur off on his journey back to Wales. Elyn, who had served Bessy now for over sixteen years, came out with plump little Edmund in her arms and four-year-old Mary. Margaret stood with her mother and aunt. The young prince travelled with an impressive retinue of heralds and men at arms, headed by Meg's husband, Sir Reginald Pole. The horses shifted restlessly, swishing their tails and champing on their bits. A trumpet sounded the signal for departure. All were eager to be off, for the weather was sunny and the roads would be dry. Arthur knelt for Bessy's blessing before mounting his horse. She laid her hands upon his head, then kissed him affectionately.

"Give my love to Lady Pole, Arthur, and follow her guidance in all things. She loves you as her own."

Arthur grinned. "I know that, Lady Mother. She fusses over me as if I were a day old chick!" He swung himself up into the saddle.

"Well, you will soon be a husband, my son."

Arthur blushed as he took up his reins. "Catalina writes that she is learning French, Mama."

"Thank goodness for that!" exclaimed Katherine, stroking the nose of his white stallion, "I doubt it's very easy to conduct a romance in Latin! Why does she have no English? All these years they have known she would come to us yet no-one has thought to teach her."

"I will teach her, Aunt," said Arthur shyly.

Bessy smiled up at him. "She will come soon, my son. Your father will send ambassadors later this year to confirm her departure."

Prince Harry came bounding across the courtyard, his peregrine on his arm. "Listen, Papa has sent me bells for her!" The hooded creature obligingly shifted on his leather glove, with a gentle jingling. Arthur looked down on his little brother and raised an eyebrow.

"Behave yourself, Harry, until I see you again. Honour our mother. Work hard at your lessons. And don't kick Margaret or Mary." His sisters smirked.

Harry frowned. He did not like being reproved by anyone. Secretly, he was glad Arthur was going back to Wales and that he would once again be the centre of attention amongst the royal children.

They all waved until Arthur's entourage became mere specks in the distance and then disappeared behind the great stand of oaks. The haze of dust kicked up by the horses settled. Harry immediately scampered off back to the mews. Katherine felt a sense of happiness she had not known in many months. All the trees in the park were now in their pale green May leaf, and the grass was growing. The fruit trees in the orchards at Hatfield wore their pink and white blossoms like froth. She thought of her own small boys, probably running rings around their indulgent grandparents at Colcombe Castle in east Devon, where they liked to spend the early summer months. So far she had still not travelled into the West Country herself; Bessy claimed her company and service, which she gave willingly. There would be time enough for Devon one day, she thought.

"The King orders us to Calais," said Bessy, turning back towards the palace. "He says there is no plague there."

"Calais?" Katherine was astonished but excited. She yearned to see the sea, never forgetting William's description of it on their first meeting. She quickened her pace to catch up with her sister. "When do we sail? How long will we stay?"

"In a few days, from Dover. Henry has kept it a secret for he plans to meet with the Archduke Philip. They will be discussing Mary's betrothal to his son. Everyone wants to form alliances now ... now that they are sure of the Tudors. Arthur will have the lovely Catalina. Mary will have Charles, Margaret will have the Scots king – and who knows what princesses await Harry and my little Edmund." Katherine could tell that her sister was caught between pride and desolation at losing her daughters. It was, of course, a parent's duty to achieve the best possible marriage alliances for their children but saying farewell, maybe forever, to a much loved daughter, must be heart-breaking. Had their own mother once felt the same, she wondered. Yet how must she have felt when it became clear that none of the planned marriages would ever happen. Katherine wished with all her heart that Elizabeth Wydville had lived long enough to see her married to William Courtenay.

"Let's stay outside, Bessy; it's a beautiful morning. We can walk in the garden before dinner." She led the way round along the front of the brick-built palace, whose many windows glittered in the morning sunshine, and through a side gate into the sheltered walled garden. Purple violets and pink gillyflowers in pots added an air of gaiety to the well-raked gravel walks. The dew had long since burned off the grass. A turfed seat of chamomile seemed to beckon invitingly.

"The Bishop of Ely has a fine home," said Katherine. "I am glad he offers it for your summer progress."

"I love it here," agreed Bessy, seating herself in the shade. "I'd rather stay here than go to Calais, if the truth be known."

"It will be a wonderful home for the children this summer; plenty of fresh air and pony-riding, and Harry can fly his hawk to his heart's content. Elyn will take good care of them while you are away."

"And your children?"

Katherine laughed. "Edward adores his grandfather, and Hal adores Edward, so I fear they do not miss me overmuch. Joanna is devoted to the pair of them."

"No sign yet of another little Courtenay?"

"Bessy!" Katherine blushed at her sister's candid question. "God has not yet seen fit to bless us again, but I pray for it." She smiled. "I should love a daughter."

A shadow crossed the Queen's face. "They are indeed a pleasure, but they will be gone so soon. You and I have been so lucky, Katherine, to stay in England and be together, and Cecily too, though she does not always see it that way."

"Will she marry again, do you think?"

"The King is considering it. He will not allow her to marry just anybody. She is still a Plantagenet. Lady Margaret may have some other relation needing a wife." The bitterness she sought to conceal slid out in her last few words.

Katherine chose her words carefully. "Do you not – *accord* with my Lady the King's Mother?"

"Well, I must. And she has the best interests of the children at heart. There are things which we both like – books, for instance. But it's a relief when she goes away to her own homes at Woking and Collyweston." She contemplated her hands lying in her lap, the fingers slightly plump these days, the flesh puffing a little around her jewelled rings. "Quite honestly, it's a relief when *both* of them are miles away. Maybe one day, when Arthur -" she stopped herself quickly, glancing around the arbour.

"It's just us," soothed Katherine. "Well, Calais will be an adventure!"

"I suppose so. There will be feasting, and jousts. William will like that, will he not? I am to take fifty ladies – including Kateryn Huntley."

"Poor soul, she has kept herself to herself these last few months. She still wears black, had you noticed?" Katherine smoothed the embroidered pansies on her own cream-coloured gown, then ran her fingers through the springy chamomile. It released its subtle appley scent and she breathed it in deeply. "Do you think of him?"

Bessy held up her hand to shield her eyes from the sun which was encroaching upon their shady seat, then laid her forehead upon her palm. "They are all in my thoughts and silent prayers, and will be till the day I die. Our brothers, our cousin. Poor York boys."

The sisters sat quietly for a few more minutes until the bell of St Etheldreda's next to the palace walls rang out the hour of Sext. Katherine rose. "Will you go to prayer now?"

"I think we should, little sister. If only to make sure that Harry has some moments of calm before dinner."

"This year the king and queen in the beginning of the month of May sailed over from Dover to Calais and there tarried certain days ..." The Great Chronicle of London

Calais May 1500

Katherine loved the sea crossing from Dover. The royal family was aboard the warship *Henri Grace A Dieu* and she stood on deck watching in wonderment as the tall white cliffs diminished, then faded into the horizon. They had left on a morning tide and now a stiff breeze filled the sails, propelling the flotilla southwards. Three more ships constituted the King's Navy, together with the galleyasses Sweepstake and Mary Fortune, and a motley collection of merchant boats hired for the occasion. The Channel swelled beneath the craft. Looking over the side, Katherine could see myriad shades of blue and green, and white-brown spindrift which was caught up by the wind and tossed into the air. The gulls who had followed them out of port, screaming and swooping, had all but disappeared and now her ears were filled with the flapping of the great linen sails, the deep creaking of the ship's timbers and the rhythmic slap of the waves against the hull. A tang of salty air assailed her nostrils and fine spray misted her lips and cheeks. Laughing, she leaned into William, whose protective arm steadied her as the deck occasionally lurched.

"It's wonderful! I shall give up being a lady-in-waiting and become a sailor!"

William guffawed, his hair blown into his eyes by the wind. "An easy crossing, on a fine day – you are a fairweather sailor indeed, my love! Wait till there's a gale and the ship is groaning on her side before you make such declarations!"

She turned around to face France, straining her eyes into the far distance, wondering if the slightly darker smudge at the end of her vision could possibly be land.

"How long will it take to reach Calais?"

"It's just over twenty miles. The captain says we shall be in harbour by evening."

Katherine looked up at the four tall masts. High above, the royal pennants danced against the sky. "It's a fine ship."

"Aye, His Grace the King has done well to improve matters at sea. He can't afford many ships so encourages the merchants to build ones big enough for him to employ. And they must use English ships for their cargoes – and he says a ship's an English ship if the crew is half English!"

"He always has a plan," observed Katherine dryly.

"Well, we shall make an impressive entrance in Calais, whether Archduke Philip is watching or not."

"You have heard that he intends to betroth little Mary to the Archduke's baby son?"

William whistled. "A grand match indeed. England's on the up."

Katherine gave him a sly smile. "*I* was going to be Queen of Spain at one point, you may recall," she said mischievously.

"I much prefer you being Lady Courtenay," responded William, kissing salt water off her nose. "And I warrant if little Mary was old enough to know what's going on she would settle for a handsome Englishman on a fine horse before some long-nosed, long-jawed Hapsburg."

"Hush! She will be an Empress one day, and her husband will rule from Spain to Austria."

"That'll put her sister Margaret's nose out of joint then," observed William sagely.

Katherine giggled. "It's true! Bessy tells me that when she and Cecily were girls they fell out all the time over who would get the best husband!"

William held her firmly round the waist as the ship dipped into the waves. "It depends what you call a good husband. Who do you think won?"

Katherine looked up into his honest hazel eyes and felt the warmth of his virile young body against hers. She thought of Bessy and the cold fish that was Henry Tudor; Cecily and the kind but elderly dead John Welles; Anne and her arrogant, ambitious Howard husband, and Bridget in her nunnery. "Me," she said softly.

Twenty four hours later she found herself in an astonishingly transformed church outside the city walls, watching as Henry and Bessy prepared to greet their honoured guest, the Emperor Maximilian's son, Archduke Philip of Burgundy. The interior was cool, and divided into sections with huge tapestry hangings. How clever, she thought, to create a palace in a church! The best gold and silver plate had been brought from the castle, and the finest drapery unloaded from one of Henry's vessels. The whole church was heady with the sweet perfume of lilies and irises. A temporary dais had been built, where Henry Tudor sat upon a great carved chair, his cloth of estate over his head. Bessy sat just to his side, a fraction below, under her own cloth. Katherine had never seen her sister look so composed and regal, whereas Henry's eyes darted nervously from side to side, assessing the likelihood of dazzling the Emperor's heir.

"Do you think him handsome?" breathed a soft voice at her elbow. Kateryn Huntley was standing just behind her, striking in her customary black velvet and satin. "They call him Philip le Bel. And they call his wife La Loca."

"The Mad? Is she?"

"So they say. She goes crazy if he so much as looks at another woman."

"And does he?"

"All the time."

"Perhaps she is more sad than mad."

The Archduke Philip was bowing to Henry Tudor, for in Calais they were on English territory. He was dressed in expensive gold damask, with a sumptuously furred collar and a golden collar encrusted with rubies and emeralds. He straightened up and Katherine saw the long nose mocked by her husband. She also saw the way his glance raked openly and lasciviously over the Queen's ladies.

"Not so much handsome as arrogant," she murmured, and heard Kateryn's chuckle.

There was feasting and entertainments; the best of Henry Tudor's musicians and choir from the Chapel Royal had also made the crossing. Archduke Philip sat with the English king and queen, apparently listening attentively but all the time his eyes registered every female in the building, from the serving maids to Katherine and Kateryn who found themselves seated together at the high table. After the formal music, dishes of strawberries and cream, cherries and spice cakes were brought in and the Burgundian nobles and English courtiers attempted cordial conversation.

"Where is his wife?" Katherine whispered behind her hand. The absence of the Archduchess Juana meant that there were no Burgundian ladies.

Kateryn grimaced. "He never takes her with him if he can help it. He's left her behind in Brussels. She would cramp his style, so to speak."

Katherine nibbled a saffron cake. "And how do *you* do these days, Lady Huntley?"

"Well enough, I thank you, Lady Courtenay. Your sister is kindness itself and I am well provided for. It is no hardship to serve her."

Katherine tried to imagine the hurt and loneliness of losing an only child, and then a husband, and of never being able to speak about either. "You are very brave," she whispered. "My sisters and I will always stand as your friends. Maybe, in time …"

"He will never let me go back to Scotland. He will keep me here. Lady Courtenay… please tell your sister that I wish her no harm, ever. I do everything I can to avoid the King's attention. I wish he would not send me presents of clothing. Please tell her I would never…" she blushed furiously, dropping her eyes and seizing more fruit to hide her confusion.

"Oh, goodness," said Katherine in dismay," the Archduke is approaching us."

Philip le Bel glided towards the two women he deemed to be the most attractive in the English queen's court. He liked the look of both of them: young and shapely. The one in black would not meet his eye but the fair one, dressed in a becoming pink brocade tilted her chin and regarded him coolly. Both were clearly married, judging by their hoods, but Philip never let that put him off; indeed, a married woman was often a safer option, as any unfortunate pregnancy could easily be explained away and not rouse his wife to passionate anger. He held out his hand, inviting the lady to dance. His green eyes offered other things.

Katherine looked along the table. Henry Tudor was nodding. William's eyebrows had disappeared into his hair line and he was gripping his cup fiercely.

Clearly, he also knew of the Archduke's dissolute reputation. The hand proferred was pale, slim, manicured; the long fingers weighed down with rings. Katherine thought of William's – brown, broad and capable, with the Courtenay seal his only adornment. But there was no avoiding dancing with the Archduke. He had singled her out and to refuse would be unthinkable. Amidst applause, he led her on to the floor and to the top of the line. Other Burgundian gentlemen were bowing to English ladies and the musicians began a stately pavane. Katherine held her head high and drifted through the slow, elegant movements. At least there was little prospect of him having to touch her, although he seemed to find any opportunity to brush against her and as the dance ended his lips lingered on the back of her hand. With shock, she felt the tip of his tongue lick her knuckles. She would have escaped gladly but the musicians had struck up a bright galliard. Philip still had a firm hold of her and was swinging her into a space. The steps were like quicksilver, and involved a certain degree of athleticism. Normally Katherine loved it, and when Wiliam could be prevailed upon to dance he would seize her round the waist with glee in the *volta,* holding her close and then turning her in the air. Her pride in her own skills meant that she was dancing well, leaping and hopping through the six beats. The moment of the *volta* came and the Archduke leaned in to clasp her; with horror she felt his hands stray – one at the back on her buttocks and the other low down below her waist, his long fingers probing through the fabric of her kirtle.

William was on his feet, his face white with fury. Henry Tudor held up a hand in warning. William cast a beseeching look at Bessy. As the music ended and the dancers performed their final leap, the Queen stood and applauded enthusiastically.

"Your Highness, what honour you do my sister!"

Philip stood stock still, with Katherine's hand still trapped in his. A sheen of sweat shone on his brow. He stepped back, and executed a perfect courtly bow, bending low over his extended right leg. He kissed her hand again but this time Katherine felt the sudden nip of his teeth.

"A beautiful princess, indeed," he said in English, his accent thick and nasal, and added in French, "but who is the boor to whom they have married her?"

Katherine thanked her stars for her education. She responded in French so rapid and low that only Philip could hear her. "No boor, sir, but a gentleman famed for his sword." Her dazzling smile masked the warning. William was already advancing, and Philip transferred her hand to her husband's arm. "The pleasure was all mine," he said.

"The cheek of him!" protested William. "Damned foreigner! Archduke or no archduke!"

Katherine giggled. It was a warm summer's night and they lay together in a chamber within Calais Castle, the shutters open and a French moon gleaming upon their naked bodies. William's outrage had been almost comical, and his consequent arousal the cause of much mirth as far as Katherine was concerned. Their lovemaking had been passionate, though, an affirmation of how much they meant to each other. Katherine heard what other women said, and what the Bible taught, about how a wife must submit to her husband whenever he wished but in five years of marriage William had never forced himself upon her and never looked at another woman, even through the months of her two pregnancies. With William she knew herself to be blessed. To love him, physically, was a joy. To love him, emotionally was a secret treasure. She ran her fingers again down the line of dark hair that ran from his waist to his groin. William pulled the sheets up over their shoulders and kissed the tip of her nose. "Behave yourself, wife," he said.

The sojourn in Calais lasted forty days. William took great pleasure in defeating every single Burgundian opponent in the jousts, thundering down the lists on Seaton like a man possessed. "A plaisancè!" was the cry of the day, indicating the supposed friendly nature of the tournament but those Flemish knights facing William Courtenay were not entirely sure that he had heard it.

Aside from the serious discussions about the betrothal of the Princess Mary and the infant Prince Charles there were plenty of other distractions: hunting in the woods beyond the city and excursions to see the cliffs and dunes. From the castle windows Katherine gazed out across the Narrow Sea, or La Manche, as the people of the town called it, trying to imagine what was going on back in England. Messages came regularly, though, and she was glad to have reassuring news of her sons in Devon.

"Your mother says they are lively little knaves," she said to William one morning, a few days before sailing home. "What do you suppose she means?"

"They have probably given her the slip and spent the day in the stables," replied William cheerfully, "it's where I spent most of my time at their age."

After Mass, breakfast in the Great Hall was a bustling, cheerful affair. Fresh baked bread, ale and fish were served. Boats had sailed across from Dover the previous day bearing letters now eagerly opened. The hall was filled with an air of pleasurable anticipation that within a day or so they would all be home again. The plague was truly over in London. All could look forward to the rest of this lovely summer in a safe, green England.

Suddenly, there was a commotion at the doorway and a travel-stained messenger in royal livery was making his way towards the high table where Henry and Bessy were seated. A strange silence descended upon the bright room. Servants stood still. From behind the screen came a shout of laughter in the buttery, quickly stilled. Henry Tudor stood up, his sallow complexion paling. Always his thoughts were of possible new trouble – news of an uprising. The messenger was kneeling, holding out a letter.

"Your Grace, I am so sorry … I have ridden hard from Hatfield, and took the first boat I could …"

Henry took it, broke the seal with a snap and read it. A muscle twitched in his left cheek.

"Husband, what is it? From Hatfield? Is one of the children ill?" Bessy was at his side, trying to peer over his shoulder. Then she gave a piercing gasp of distress. "No! Not Edmund!"

Katherine had a sudden vision of Elyn holding up the plump little boy five weeks ago, taking his chubby hand to wave as his big brother Arthur trotted down the avenue of oaks. He was a beautiful child, robust and healthy, curious and forward, already with a vocabulary of funny words and a disarming, freckled grin. He was just like Prince Harry at the same age, but with a sunnier disposition. A fifteen-month-old child adored by his mother, sisters, nursemaids and aunts. Bessy had been so lucky with her children – just the loss of little Elizabeth. No miscarriages, no still births. She felt a lump come into her throat and suddenly longed for sight of her own boys.

Wordlessly, Henry had handed Bessy the letter and strode from the hall. She stood, stricken, tears in her eyes. The messenger was still on his knees, head bowed. She swallowed hard. "We thank you for your pains. It must have been … a hard journey… to have come to us so quickly. Please, take your rest." She looked around in mute misery and Katherine rose, knocking over her stool. She flew to her sister.

"Your Grace, Bessy, come into your private room." Other ladies-in-waiting were gathering like flustered birds. Kateryn Huntley quietly positioned herself under Bessy's shoulder and together they supported the Queen out of the hall and into a sunny little room. Katherine allowed in one or two of Bessy's closest women. She still clutched the letter in her fist and began to sob.

"He was so little, so *little!*"

"He is with God," said Kateryn. "And the angels." She took the Queen in her arms and held her close – the first physical contact they had ever had. Bessy seemed comforted and would not let go of Kateryn's hand.

"You, above all, Lady Huntley, will understand," she wept. Her tears soaked the black silk of Kateryn's gown.

8

Katherine: *So we returned home across a mizzly, drizzly grey sea to a sad little funeral at the Abbey. Henry Tudor was shocked by the death of one of his princes. On a long, light midsummer night tiny Edmund was laid to rest in the Confessor's chapel. His little coffin, with its poignant effigy, was drawn by a chariot with six black horses – so big a chariot for so small a person. Even Lady Margaret wept to see it. Prince Arthur wrote his mother such a beautiful letter, urging her to think of her living children who loved and needed her, but admitting that his "sweet brother" would be forever in his heart. William and I brought our boys back from Devon and held them close. Soon afterwards I found I was pregnant and in the spring of 1501 gave birth to my longed-for daughter.*

Warwick Lane Summer 1501

Katherine was in the Great Hall at her home, checking the final preparations for the dinner the Courtenays were due to host that evening. She was glad to be back in society again after her confinement and churching. In another month or so Bessy would ask for her to return to court but in the meantime she was enjoying time spent with all her children and the bustling life of her London home. She took huge pleasure in being the mistress of such a beautiful house. *If only Mama could see what I have.* Summer sunlight filtered in through the high, expensive glass windows. The long oak table gleamed after its polish and the best of her silver and gilt plate glittered. A manservant was bringing in baskets of fresh flowers to be arranged in the huge empty hearth and on the high table. The sweet perfume of roses and lilies wafted and lingered in the still air. Up above, in the minstrels' gallery she could hear low chatter and the tuning of lutes.

"The musicians know where to find refreshment?"

The servant nodded. "All is in hand, my lady. I am sure your guests will be most impressed." He hesitated for a moment and then added quietly, "I have taken the liberty of ensuring that we have white roses."

Katherine looked at him sharply. He was not one of the Courtenay household but someone hired in as extra help. She found his familiarity rather unsettling.

"As a young lad I served in your uncle's household. I come from York, my lady, where we like our white roses."

"I am sure you do," she said evenly, "but a variety of blooms would be more in keeping with Lord Courtenay's wishes. Please see to it that some other colours are added."

"Red, my lady?"

"Not necessarily red. Just some other colours, to offset the white, you understand. Whatever is easiest to procure before this evening."

He bowed, and left the room. Katherine felt her heart thudding in her chest. Tonight her father-in-law the Earl of Devon was in town and they were holding a dinner. Her cousin, the Earl of Suffolk was one of their guests. William enjoyed his company at court and of late had been drawn into his circle of young nobles who loved jousting and hunting. Katherine felt a little uneasy about the growing friendship. She knew that Bessy was fond of their aunt, the Duchess of Suffolk, and privately welcomed her whenever she came to London, but it was not easy to forget that her eldest son had risen up against Henry Tudor. Cousin Edmund was at court, and gave every appearance of loyalty but Katherine had witnessed his subtle support of the Feigned Lad. She worried about how Henry Tudor might construe William's association with someone so near to her in Yorkist blood. Bessy had whispered that Edmund was furious that the King had not rewarded his loyalty by giving him his late father's title of duke, and resented the money he had to pay into the Tudor coffers. William, however, had laughed it off: *"He's a fine fellow, Katherine. A bit rash sometimes but we can keep him in check!"*

Later that evening she sat next to her cousin and his wife at dinner. She had not been in his close company since that winter's day when she had fallen from her horse. Edmund de la Pole turned a flushed face towards her. His chin was greasy with chicken fat and he was already tipsy.

"You keep a good table, Coz. I should dine here more often! We cousins should show our good friendship."

"Please, have a care in my house, sir."

"Sir? *Sir?* Hey, William, your wife, my little royal cousin calls me *sir!*" He lurched forward to take her hand, which she withdrew and he knocked over a cup of wine. The stain spread over the pristine white linen cloth. Katherine saw his wife looking embarrassed and unhappy.

"We are *family,* Princess Katherine!" he proclaimed in a stage whisper, "Plantagenets, you and me! Plantagenets, through and through!"

Katherine looked around frantically. Thank God – her father-in-law was immersed in conversation with someone else but William had seen what was happening, even if he had not heard her cousin's words. Edmund was pushing back his chair and rising to his feet rather unsteadily. "A toast! A toast to the beautiful Lady Courtenay, our Plantagenet princess!" His deep voice rang out down the hall. All noticed the slurring of his speech. Katherine felt herself colouring. She did not blush easily but guessed that her face was probably turning a shade of crimson. "A true rose of York!" her cousin was declaring, and had hold of her sleeve, trying to haul her to stand by his side.

"That's enough, Suffolk." William had come along the rear of the dais and was behind him, pushing him back into his seat. "You're in your cups, man!" he hissed, "and being indiscreet." He turned a broad smile upon all his guests and household. "A toast, indeed, to our sovereign lord King Henry!" Katherine was relieved to see several of her husband's friends on their feet, responding quickly.

"To the King!"

"The King!"

But somewhere in the room, she feared, there might be someone likely to report back to Henry Tudor what he had seen and heard in Warwick Lane.

Neither were matters helped when a month or so later William came home from court looking aghast. Katherine was sitting in the solar, her baby on her lap. Little Margaret, named for Meg in faraway Ludlow, rather than for Margaret Beaufort, was thriving and growing daily. Katherine, who had sent Joanna away for a couple of hours, released the baby from her swaddling board and allowed her tiny limbs to kick freely. She gurgled with delight, treating her mother to her new gummy smiles and trying to catch her own feet. Her boys played on the floor at her feet. William closed the door softly behind him and took in the scene of his little family. Edward noticed him first and scuttled across to be the one whom his father would hoist up into the place of honour on his shoulders. Hal pulled at his boots. William lifted each young son and buried his face in their wavy hair which smelled of the rosemary Joanna used in their bathwater. Katherine was aware of his presence but totally absorbed by the baby, tickling her toes. But when her husband did not speak, Katherine looked quizzically over her shoulder.

William set the boys down. "Run away and find Joanna,"he commanded.

"No, she will not be back yet. I said I would have them."

"Then run away and find someone else." William opened the door and gestured that the boys should go. "Edward, take your brother to the kitchens. Cook will find you a honeycake, I don't doubt."

Wide-eyed at such an unexpected parental laxity, Edward clasped his little brother by the hand and led him out. Their footsteps pattered down the staircase. Katherine wrapped the naked baby up and held her close. "What is it?"

"Suffolk has gone," he said flatly.

"Gone? Home to Wingfield? Why? Is my aunt unwell?"

"If only. He has fled the country with his brother Richard and gone to Burgundy, to the Emperor."

"Ah, Jesu!"

"The King is furious."

"He would be."

"Suffolk is an idiot. I tried to warn him after he was so foolish here. But he's calling himself *The White Rose* and trying to attract followers. No doubt some will declare for him."

"But ... not you, William?" Katherine suddenly realised that she did not know.

"Of course not me!" he said, indignantly.

"Thank God," she said fervently. The baby objected to being held so tightly and began to cry. "Do you think Maximilian will support him? Surely not, now that little Mary has been betrothed to his grandson?"

"Politics is a grim game," said William. "But I think Suffolk has misjudged it all. In Spain, and the Holy Roman Empire they are looking for alliances with the Tudors now, not a way of dislodging them. It's only the French who would like to see him brought down. Suffolk and his brother are the last male heirs of York. I hope to God nobody is interested in them. I hope it for the sake of my own boys." He took the protesting baby from her and rocked her in his arms. "We could do worse, Katherine, than go home to my Devon lands for a while."

She thought rapidly. "No. That might be seen as some sign that we have something to hide. Better to stay where we can be seen, every day. Where we can demonstrate our loyalty. I am due back in Bessy's service now Margaret is three months old. Why, the King has only just granted you an annuity for ... what was it? Your *daily diligent attendance!* And he's really busy, with all the rebuilding at Sheen, and Greenwich, and persuading the Spanish it's time to send their princess. He will be focused on that, I am sure. All will be well. Bessy will speak for us if needs be."

William kissed the downy top of his daughter's head and groaned. "Why did I ever get involved with Suffolk?"

"You were not … *involved.* You hunted with him, dined with him … that's all."

"Wrote to him."

"*Wrote* to him? What about?"

"Horses, and lances, and armour."

"Hardly the stuff of treason," said Katherine briskly. "It will blow over, I am sure."

9

"In this year came first certain tidings that the daughter of the King of Spain was landed at Plymouth ..." Great Chronicle of London

October 1502

"News from Plymouth, Bessy. The Spanish princess has finally landed!" Henry Tudor strode into his wife's rooms, flushed with excitement. Her ladies moved away respectfully to the far corners of the spacious chamber. "Jesu, we have waited long enough! When did they say she left her family? May, wasn't it?"

"Poor child," said Bessy, "it will all seem very strange to her. The weather, the landscape, the language. Remember, she was nearly shipwrecked the first time they tried to set sail. I am told that the Bay of Biscay is a dreadful sea to cross."

Henry looked at her curiously. "I would not feel sorry for her, wife. She is lucky to be marrying the most eligible prince in Christendom."

"She is a girl, who has left a beloved family to come to a country she does not know, to live with people she has only heard about."

"It's no more than Margaret and Mary will have to do, when the time comes," retorted Henry impatiently.

"It would not hurt to write to her, now, and let her know how welcome she is, and that we intend to love her as much as our own children," said Bessy quietly. "And maybe it is we who are lucky, to have Spain give such affirmance of our position in Europe."

There were times when his wife delivered such truths that Henry Tudor was momentarily startled. She always chose her moments carefully – never in the presence or hearing of his mother. He had never had any desire for a consort who was politically astute and never asked for her opinion or advice. For eighteen years he had tried to forget that this woman had been a Yorkist princess and educated as such. She never crossed him, never argued or harangued him, but just occasionally a subtly placed, insightful comment would wrongfoot him and remind him of what he preferred to forget.

For a moment. Bessy was not sure if she had gone too far, and wondered what his reaction would be. To her surprise he nodded slowly.

"You may be right, wife. I shall write today and reassure her. Better than that, I shall set out and meet her and see her for myself. How far do you think she will have travelled? The latest news is from Winchester. She must be somewhere along the Great West Road. Arthur must have set out too, by now."

Bessy allowed herself a smile when she thought of her firstborn. A year had done much to improve his looks; at fifteen it was possible to see the man he would become. There was a delicacy about him that sometimes worried her but he refused to be mollycoddled and Meg wrote that he loved the open air life at Ludlow, riding out eagerly with Sir Reginald Pole to inspect the estates and villages in the Marches. "He *is* excited. He will be glad to meet her after all these years. If he has had the same news I expect he and Sir Reginald will be well on their way to London by now."

"Then we shall meet up, and welcome the princess together." Bessy had not seen her husband so apparently eager about anything for months. His visits to her rooms, and her bed, were sporadic; he seemed to spend most of his time closeted with his advisors. What she felt for him could not be called love. She had never loved him. Their relationship was best described as a blend of acceptance, tolerance, duty and respect. At times part of her had hated him – for what he had done to her cousin Ned of Warwick, and the Feigned Lad, but another part of her recognised that he had had little choice.

"I hope she's as fair as they have promised," said Henry, helping himself from a dish of nuts. "Ambassadors have a habit of exaggerating their princesses' beauty. You don't think they have lied in any way, do you?" He was suddenly anxious; he trusted no-one. "Do you think her health is good? Do you think she will bear children easily?" Cracking a walnut, he grimaced as it proved to be rather rotten and flung it peevishly it into a corner.

"De Puebla has been honest with us, I am sure," soothed Bessy. "Remember, he says she is not dark, like many Spanish ladies but quite fair, with blue eyes and auburn hair. Why, she will look like a true sister to Margaret and Mary."

"I need to see her for myself before the marriage takes place. We can't have her just turning up, all veiled. She might be deformed, or pock-marked, or squint-eyed, or –"

"Henry! Don't be ridiculous! We have seen her portrait! She is none of these things. Go and greet her if you must, but for goodness sake do not alarm the child."

He pursed his thin lips. He did not like to be reproved. "I just want to see what I have bought at such cost."

Katherine: *Bessy's warning fell upon deaf ears. Henry Tudor intercepted the Spanish princess' retinue at the episcopal palace at Dogmersfield in Hampshire but his demand to be admitted to her presence was met with horror by the Spanish party, He found his way barred by an archbishop, bishop, counts and countless others. They had received strict instructions they stated, from the Infanta's parents, that she should have no meeting or any manner of communication until the start of the very day of the solemnisation of the marriage. Imagine my royal brother-in-law, in the middle of a field, being refused entry to an English house by a score of Spaniards! Imagine him striding into the poor girl's bedroom, in his sweaty riding clothes, demanding that she lift her veil and let him see her face! Later that same day he took Arthur back with him. Fortunately, my polite nephew managed to salvage the situation. In later years Catalina would tell me the story of how Arthur had spoken to her in Latin, apologising for his father's behaviour. Within days they were married in London. The city went wild with joy.*

Westminster, London November 1501

"I am exhausted!" declared Bessy, standing still while Katherine unpinned her hood. She kicked off her shoes and collapsed gratefully on to her bed. "Forgive me, sister, but I think I am feeling my age. If I do not rest my legs I shall never walk again!" They had returned from yet another day of celebration following the marriage of Arthur and Catalina – a river pageant, a service at St Paul's and dinner at the Bishop of London's palace.

"These festivities are wearing me out!"

Katherine smiled. "There's is plenty more to come! Jousting tomorrow, with half of London watching. William can't wait."

Bessy gave a mock groan. "I do not have the stamina of my energetic brother-in-law. But it *has* been the most extraordinary week. I cannot remember when we were last all so happy. It's the beginning of a whole new era, Katherine. The King is delighted with her, and Arthur, and the way they have conducted themselves. I do believe the whole of England feels a new sense of peace and prosperity." Taking the cup of wine offered by her sister, she patted the space beside her.

Katherine discarded her own shoes and lay back on the tasselled pillows, luxuriating in the comfort of the layers of mattresses. She closed her eyes. She felt Bessy nestle down beside her, and heard her sigh of relief. At moments like these rank and formality were easily forgotten. She giggled. "I suppose we must pray now that Catalina is blessed with a son before too long. It will happen soon enough, if your son's words are anything to go by!"

Bessy propped herself up on her elbow. "Really? What have you heard?"

Katherine opened one eye. "William attended the Prince of Wales, and says that before he left him Arthur declared he felt *lusty and amorous* and he asked for ale in the morning, because he said he had *been in Spain this night."*

Bessy was silent. She lay down again and turned her face away from Katherine. Her mood seemed to have suddenly changed.

"Bessy? Your Grace? I am sorry, I did not mean to offend you … It was just men's talk. William tends to tell me all sorts of things. I am sorry. It was crude. I should not have said it."

"No, it's all right, I am not offended. It's just ... I worry about Arthur. He is not as strong as people think. He would have known it was his duty to consummate his marriage but I hope he does not … over-indulge. "

Katherine sat up, her hood askew, her fair hair falling over her shoulders. "You think he is frail, Bessy?"

Bessy turned over and they lay face to face. "Not *frail,* exactly. It's hard to put my finger on it, but I think he still needs time to mature. He thinks himself such a man, but I still see the boy."

"He was probably just boasting. Boys do. They have probably done no more than fumble under the sheets together. Time will put all right."

Bessy sighed. "She seems a sweet girl. And he is a dear boy. They have their whole lives ahead of them. They appear to like each other. I don't know why I am worrying."

Katherine took her sister's hand and stroked it gently. "Because you love him. Because you want the best for him. And you are right, she *is* a sweet girl. She will be glad to call you mother, being so far away from her own."

"Mmm! Henry thinks she should stay here at court this winter, and that Arthur should return alone to Ludlow. He believes they should wait a while before they live together as man and wife."

"Well, there you are then. Plenty of time for him to grow in strength, and for you to get to know her properly."

"I pray I may be closer to her than I have been to my own mother-in -law," said Bessy feelingly.

"Did Lady Margaret weep throughout the *entire* marriage service?"

"She did. Quite a feat really. Two hours of tears. More than she managed at Henry's coronation. If she becomes a great-grandmother I think she will float away in a sea of her own making."

Katherine chuckled, glad to have Bessy restored to good humour. The anxiety created by their cousin's Suffolk's defection to Burgundy seemed to have died down. Very little had been heard of him in the past year. Henry Tudor had taken great satisfaction in having him publicly condemned for treason and excommunicated. And thankfully there had been no sign of the King treating William Courtenay with anything other than his usual gratitude for good service.

Two days later the King seemed vastly amused by the sight of William in the tournament to further celebrate the marriage. Despite it being an English November, the tiltyard at Westminster was transformed into a land of artificial trees and fruit. The new young Princess of Wales took her place with Bessy, Cecily and Katherine in a stand hung with cloth of gold. They were joined by the King, Prince Arthur and Prince Harry to watch the spectacle. When Lord William Courtenay made his appearance, apparently riding on a red dragon, with a great tree in his hand, the sun suddenly emerged from behind the clouds. The citizens of London, who packed the stands on the east side of the yard, yelled and stamped their approval.

Catalina spoke quickly in Spanish, and one of her ladies translated. "The princess asks if the gentleman's horse *minds* being a dragon?"

Katherine found herself looking into the blue eyes of Arthur's young wife. *How strange,* she thought, *in another world I might have been married to this girl's brother. I might have gone myself to a strange land and new family.* She remembered that Catalina's sister was the unfortunate Juana La Loca in

310

Burgundy and that her precious only brother was dead. Juana's son, and Catalina's nephew, now betrothed to the Princess Mary, stood to inherit half the world.

"The gentleman is my husband, Your Grace, and his horse is the biggest show off there ever was. I should think he's rather enjoying being a dragon!" A rapid translation, and Catalina was smiling.

Bessy leaned forward. "The child has very little English. I have to talk to her in French."

Seaton the Welsh dragon was galloping down the lists to meet his opponent, a black stallion disguised as a sea-monster. William's tree was lowered at just the right moment and the knight on the other side, sporting a trident, unseated with a minimum of fuss. Hundreds of Londoners cheered enthusiastically as the unfortunate fellow toppled into the sand. Katherine glanced across and saw the two princes on their feet, applauding their Uncle Courtenay. The King watched too, at first smiling but then his mouth hardened, as if he had remembered something. Katherine felt a shiver of apprehension. William was removing his helm and trotting towards the royal stand, a broad grin on his face, his tree-lance slightly the worse for wear. Seaton performed his famous party-piece, his forelegs splayed and his dragon headgear bobbing down. Catalina clapped with child-like delight. The King smiled again.

The evening served to keep Henry Tudor in a good mood. In the grandeur of Westminster Hall there was feasting and dancing. Katherine always loved this place; like the Hall at Eltham it spoke to her of her own family. The same carved angels looked down upon her; the same images of past kings bestowed their regal stares. She gave herself up to the pleasures of the evening. Whoever was in charge of the pageantry had devised a stupendous production: Katherine marvelled as a fully-rigged ship, a castle and a mountain were wheeled in. The ship was clearly meant to represent Catalina's journey from Spain, for a girl sat within dressed in the strange hooped skirts and mantilla Catalina wore. Another girl, in the same costume, sat on top of the castle, which was lit from within so its "windows" glowed. Inside, Katherine recognised eight of Bessy's prettiest maids of honour, their hair loose and garlanded with flowers. Two gentlemen stepped out of the ship and announced themselves as Desire and Hope, paying homage to the girl on top of the castle but she disdained them. Then eight more knights rushed out of the mountain, laid siege to the castle and carried off the maids of honour into a dance.

311

The next minute Prince Harry seized his sister Margaret by the hand and Katherine found herself joining in the laughter and applause as the two royal children showed off. Taught by the finest dancing masters, the Tudor siblings were fully capable of the most demanding dances. Twelve-year-old Margaret revelled in the chance to steal attention from her new sister-in-law, triumphantly treading, swaying and twirling with her brother. Breathless, they paused before Bessy to bow and accept the storm of applause, then Harry flung off his furred gown and capered in his shirt and doublet while Margaret's long auburn hair flew about her shoulders.

Afterwards, Catalina presented prizes to the victors of the jousts. Katherine watched with pride as William stepped forward to receive a ring set with diamonds and sapphires. The young Princess of Wales must have spoken to him for the translator came forward quickly, and Katherine smiled to see William replying and miming a quick imitation of Seaton's signature bow. Catalina's serious little face lit up and she flung a happy glance back to where Arthur sat upon the dais. When William finally made it to her side, Katherine squeezed his arm affectionately. "You seem to have a Spanish admirer."

William grinned. "She likes horses, apparently. They have dancing horses in Castile, and she was reminded of them. What do you think of my prize?" He opened his palm to reveal a thick gold ring, its gemstones twinkling in the candlelight.

"Goodness, Duke Philip himself would be envious," she said impishly.

"Do not mention that man's name."

The night was drawing to a close. William was called to join the nobles of Henry's court in playing the part of serving men, offering spiced wine and comfits to the royal family. Katherine held out her golden cup and then sipped the thick hippocras, tasting the delicious cinnamon, ginger and cloves. The warmth spread down her throat and through her body. The sugared almond comfits she twisted into her silk kerchief, to take home to her boys.

When Arthur and Catalina finally made a ceremonial exit to return to Baynard's Castle, Katherine and William stood side by side as the young couple passed by, a fanfare of trumpets proclaiming their joy. They followed them outside into the courtyard then down to the Westminster landing pier, where the flaming torches flared into the midnight sky and the citizens of London still waited to cheer again for their Prince and Princess of Wales. Their barge pulled out into the stream, accompanied by a smaller one bearing musicians.

"God bless them," said Katherine quietly. "Long life and happiness to them."

10

"And soon after was the Lord William of Devonshire ... taken and committed to safe keeping for favouring the party of the Earl of Suffolk"
Great Chronicle of London

February 1502

The wraith that was winter fell upon England. Ditches froze. Rivers slowed to a silent crawl. The roads and trackways resembled nothing so much as expanses of solid mud, glazed with waves of ice that sparkled when the weak sun broke through, but mostly just thawed only to freeze again. In the north, snow blanketed the ground for weeks whilst the south shivered miserably in east winds that infiltrated wooden shutters and keyholes. Crouched by fires that barely burned but smoked incessantly, the poor endured the bone-chilling cold, and the rich moaned about how even their furs failed to keep them warm.

In Ludlow, the Princess Catalina of Wales mourned for her lost, warm homeland of Granada. They had warned her of the English winters but never had she imagined cold so intense, or rain so wet, or skies so grey. Kindly Lady Pole spoke of a spring that would come one day, of swallows and snowdrops, but Catalina stared out of the poorly glazed castle windows at a ghost-world. Her young husband tried to cheer her, with endless games of chess and cards but so often he retired to his own bed, complaining apologetically of a weariness he could not seem to shake off. In Norfolk, Anne Howard, who had once been a Plantagenet princess, buried yet another stillborn child in the cold, flat earth and endured the accusing glances of her infuriated husband. In her chilly cell at Dartford Priory, the twenty-two-year old nun who had once been Princess Bridget, shivered as she tried to read and asked permission to sit in the warm refectory instead. In London, the widowed Lady Welles, who had once been the vivacious Princess Cecily inadvertently opened a small wooden chest and found inside forgotten little embroidered linen shifts that had once belonged to her two dead daughters, and wept tears that froze almost immediately upon her cheeks.

At Westminster, February skies loured over the palace. A few sparse snowflakes scudded across the Thames but failed to stick, either to the buildings or the ground. Each morning the daylight struggled and by early afternoon seemed to give up entirely. The cold was intense and Bessy the queen simply could not get warm, despite the sweet applewood logs piled on the fire. The winter roads meant that letters from Ludlow were rare and she fretted over Meg Pole's month-old news that Arthur had taken a January cold. Katherine had been unwell too, confined to her bed in Warwick Lane with a hacking cough, and Bessy missed her cheerful company. Henry Tudor she had not seen for several days. More than ever now he spent time closeted with his Council and despite herself Bessy was forced to enquire for news of him from his mother, whose answers were vague or evasive: he was busy with state papers; his time taken up with examining accounts; he was writing important letters.

January had seen the excitement of Princess Margaret's betrothal to the Scots king. Henry Tudor was delighted at the political promise of such an alliance. Bessy had misgivings – the idea of her young daughter departing for a new life in Scotland, to a husband sixteen years her senior filled her with anxieties, although Margaret herself was delighted by her new status as a queen, especially as she now had her very own apartments at Westminster. It would be another eighteen months before she would be required to travel north, by which time she would be nearly fourteen. The Scots ambassadors assured Bessy that their master was intelligent, well-educated and handsome. Other sources reported the existence of a string of mistresses and at least four illegitimate children. Bessy sighed; the same could have been said of her own father, she knew, and yet he had also been a loving husband and father. For Margaret, eighteen months was a lifetime away as yet.

"Mama? Have you seen our finished portraits?" Bouncing into the room, young Margaret, with her auburn hair and orange sarcanet sleeves, was a flash of colour on such a dreary afternoon. Bessy's elderly lady-in-waiting obligingly moved away from the fire as Margaret flung herself down next to her mother. "My father the King looks very regal; you look most serene – and I look … well, I am glad I decided to hold my marmoset. Do you think my husband the King of

Scots likes monkeys? Oh, but will it be too cold for Merry in Scotland?" Her face looked so suddenly stricken that Bessy reached out for her hand.

"I am sure we can make him a fur jacket!"

Margaret's expression relaxed, "Oh, yes! Something in crimson, with ermine, to match my dress!" She bounded away to the window, to see if the snow still fell, then turned back.

"Is it true, Mama, that Aunt Cecily was once going to marry my husband?"

Carefully, Bessy set down her embroidery, pinning the needle to the linen. "Many years ago, yes. When my own father was king."

"And will Aunt Cecily mind, do you think? That I am Queen of Scots instead?" Margaret was well aware of her aunt's unpredictable emotions.

"Sweetheart, if all women minded about who our fathers *first* intended us to marry, we should be in a sad state!"

"So who was it that *your* father intended *you* should marry?"

"Mmm, let me see … I believe it was the Dauphin of France."

Margaret's mouth opened in disbelief. "But you married my father instead." "Indeed."

"Why? Did somebody make you?"

A sound somewhere between a gasp and a cough. For a moment Bessy had forgotten the presence of Lady Wake, who had known her since childhood, whose brother had been one of King Richard's advisors and executed after Bosworth Field. "Your lady mother made a very wise decision, Your Grace, if I may say so." Her face creased into a wrinkled smile.

Margaret looked at her curiously. "Are you *very* old, Lady Wake?"

"Old enough to remember *three* queens of England, and your lady mother is the best there ever was, or ever will be." The elderly woman's voice quavered with a sudden surge of emotion. "I am privileged to serve you, Your Grace. God bless you for the sacrifices you have made, and the peace you have bought to this land."

A cold lump lodged itself somewhere in Bessy's throat and she felt tears threatening to prick in her eyes. She fought to control herself and then looked up brightly at her daughter.

"You see, Margaret, what it is it have such loyalty in your household! I pray that you may find the same devotion. I pray too, that your marriage into Scotland puts an end to war and suffering."

It was clear that Margaret had never really thought about that. She was too busy contemplating the number of new gowns and pieces of jewellery her father said she might have to complement her new position as a queen. Such generosity was not a common feature of her father's personality and she was determined to make the most of it. The best part of it all was that her brother Harry was consumed by jealousy at the moment. At the thought of his resentful scowl, a sudden giggle escaped from her lips.

"Mama, did you know that Harry wants a bride? He says it's not fair that Arthur and I should have all the luck. He keeps asking who are the richest and prettiest princesses in Europe. I told him father will probably marry him to some ancient old crone and send him off to live in Portugal, or Sweden – somewhere really far away!"

"You should try not to tease him, Margaret; you know how much he takes things to heart. It's hard being a younger brother. His time will come, but not yet."

"He's so impatient, Mama. By the way, he doesn't want to be an archbishop now; he wants to be a soldier. He says he will win back France. He says Arthur will be glad to have a brother who can do all his fighting for him, because he could never hold a lance. Honestly, some days he is quite unbearable. I am glad I don't have to spend too much time with him anymore."

Thinking of her second son, Bessy pictured his cheeky grin and air of self-importance. In one way it was endearing, and she knew full well that much of his swagger came from an inner lack of confidence. Henry Tudor had invested all his interest in Arthur, and Harry sensed it. The things that interested the ten-year-old boy – archery, tennis, riding, and learning knightly skills – were not at the forefront of his father's daily life these days. It was a shame, thought Bessy, that Henry did not make the effort to spend more time with his energetic young son. Harry was clever, and wanted his father's attention but it was only ever Bessy who had time to admire his Latin translations. When she visited his schoolroom he would eagerly bring her his books, and loved to read to her. At heart he was a good boy, she was sure, but over-indulged by his grandmother, often taken for granted by his father and living in the shadow of his older siblings. She hoped that a role as a trusted brother would be his destiny in adult life, and prayed that jealousy would not cause as terrible a rift as it had between her own father and his brother George. She made a mental note to write to Arthur about it.

". . . and my lady grandmother says that she always knew it, which I think is quite unfair because Aunt Katherine will be devastated."

Bessy realised that during her reverie Margaret must have said something of import, for Lady Wake was frowning, and struggling to her feet.

"I will fetch someone, Your Grace. This is dreadful news."

"Margaret, say that again. I did not hear you."

"I'm sorry, Mama, I thought you knew."

"Jesu! Knew what?"

Margaret's colour rose to clash with her bright sleeves. "Father declaring that my Uncle Courtenay has been in league with the Earl of Suffolk."

"*What?* Where on earth have you heard this from? Who is telling such lies?"

"My Lady the King's Mother told me…" Margaret's voice trailed away when she saw the shock on her mother's face. "I wanted to thank my father for my new gowns, and I went to his rooms but Grandmother said he was with the Council, and must not be disturbed, and when I asked why, she said that they had all just learned who has been planning treason with my Lord of Suffolk."

A kind of sick horror gripped Bessy. Henry would show no mercy, of that she was certain. His whole reign had been afflicted by disloyalty and threats of rebellion. Every summer, it seemed, when the court set out on its progresses to rural shires, there was somebody ready to take advantage of the King's absence to whip up unrest. If there was even so much as a rumour of men connected with her cousin Edmund de la Pole, Henry's spies would winkle them out, frame them and destroy them. But the idea that William Courtenay might be involved? Bessy had lived long enough to know that anything was possible. She had to speak to her husband.

Thank God everyone was at Westminster this week. Without a word, Bessy left a crestfallen Margaret and stepped out of her private rooms. It was just a few minutes' walk through the old palace whose every nook and cranny was known to her. She waved away old Lady Wake and the two younger ladies-in- waiting, moving swiftly through the many passages and doorways towards Henry's side of the building. She trod silently in her fur-lined boots but her skirts soughed and whispered behind her on the cold stone flags and wooden floorboards. Startled yeomen of the guard stood to attention and saluted her as she passed. Icy draughts sliced across from ill-fitting shutters and doors left open; she shivered and quickened her stride, finally arriving outside Henry's council chamber.

318

The two men-at-arms on duty shifted awkwardly. They were from Henry's own household and not personally known to her. Bessy gestured impatiently to the closed doors.

"You will admit me."

"Your Grace, His Grace has ordered that no-one should disturb –"

"You will *admit* me."

When the door swung open Bessy's nerve almost failed her. Never before had she dared to intrude upon Henry's business as king. A long table took up a fair portion of the room. Henry was seated at the head, and ranks of his council either side. A bright fire burned in the hearth. The air was stuffy with the odour of masculine sweat. The colourful tapestries on the walls contrasted sharply with the dark clothing or plain clerical dress of most of the men. Henry wore an overgown of dark green, trimmed with black fur. At first he was not aware of her presence, immersed as he was in reading a document but the scraping back of chairs and the rising of the other men that made him look up. Bessy saw disbelief, then irritation, then resignation pass across his pinched features.

"My dear? Is something amiss?"

"I would speak with you, Your Grace." She swept a deep curtsey and kept her tone formal.

"Can it not wait until later? As you can see, we are hard at work." Nearly twenty pairs of eyes turned upon her, their curiosity piqued. Among them she recognised the cool, ambitious gaze of Anne's husband, Thomas Howard, and the lizard-like appraisal of Lord Stanley, the King's stepfather.

Henry Dean, the wise and kindly Archbishop of Canterbury, who had officiated at Arthur and Catalina's marriage, bowed to her, then to the King. "Your Grace, I am sure Her Grace would not be disturbing you unless she had very good reason. We should all be happy to retire for a while while you speak, should we not, my lords?" Already he was herding his fellow councillors towards the door, like a benign but insistent old sheep dog. As he passed her she heard him murmur, "Indeed, Your Grace, some of us will be glad of some respite..."

When they were alone Henry leaned back and laced his fingers together. The cast in his eyes was quite pronounced; he seemed to fix her with his right, whilst the left veered around. It was not always noticeable except in times of stress or tension.

"What is so your *very good reason,* Bessy?"

Of course, he knew exactly why she had come.

"What are you proposing to do with Lord William Courtenay?"

A silence pulsated between them. Henry released his fingers and drummed the tips lightly upon the table. "Jesu, news travels fast."

"Blame your dearest mother. May I sit down?"

He shrugged and gestured at all the chairs. Bessy chose the one exactly opposite him, at the far end of the table. *In another world, if I had been born a boy, or if this country could stomach a woman as queen in her own right, this would be my council table, and this man would be a nobody, in exile in Brittany.*

"Your Grace ... husband ... Henry. Please do not do this. It will destroy my sister, Katherine."

"Maybe that is something Courtenay should have thought of before he consorted with Suffolk."

"*Consorted?* What proof do you have of"–

"I have proof enough! Your precious cousin was hosting dinners before he fled – inviting his *close companion* William Courtenay, and then dining himself at your sister's house in Warwick Lane."

"Henry, please. My cousin Suffolk and William are no more than jousting companions. They are just young men of the same age, thrown together within your court. Lord Courtenay values his place and his future here; he would not risk his wife and children by getting involved with some foolish conspiracy."

"You think not? His father, the Earl of Devon commands much of the south west coast where Suffolk could land. No doubt Lord Courtenay has mentioned this to him."

"But the Earl of Devon is one of your most loyal supporters! "

"Men change."

Bessy felt helpless. Once Henry had decided to believe something he stuck to it. His spies would have convinced him.

"Will you try him ... for treason?"

Outside the snow had finally gained some momentum and was beginning to stick to the lozenge-shaped window panes. In the gardens it would be settling on the bare branches and gravelled pathways; on the river the boatmen would be huddling under thick cloaks and praying that the Thames did not freeze over and lose them their trade. In the bowels of the Tower so-called traitors would be lying spreadeagled on the machine of torture, the rack, sobbing out times, and places, and names.

"A spell in the Tower for Lord William will make his father think again. You may do what you wish for his wife and children. From your own money," he added.

It was his one and only conciliation. She would be allowed to keep Katherine and her three children safe.

"You may not warn them. If I find out they have been given presage ... Bessy, I do not do this out of personal malice. I do it to keep a throne for Arthur to inherit when I am gone." He looked at her coldly. "It is not my fault if *your family* cause you distress. Why can they not accept that this all ended at Bosworth years ago? Do you *want* me to pass on a realm still ravaged by Yorkist claims?"

"No. Of course not." Her voice was a whisper. "All I have ever wanted is for killing and suffering to cease in this country. That is why I married you." If he heard her last six words he gave no sign. He picked up a document again and Bessy understood herself to be dismissed. She rose and bowed her head. It felt like the worst sort of defeat, as if she had been made to feel things were her fault.

Returning to her own side of the palace, she found her ladies-in-waiting hovering anxiously. She made it clear that breathing any word of what they had heard about Lord Courtney's impending arrest would endanger his family, and see them all in the Tower. Kateryn Huntley bit her lip and nodded. Old Lady Wake pressed her hand. "We have lived through worse, Your Grace."

Margaret was where she had left her half an hour ago. She had picked up her mother's embroidery and was attempting a few stitches, a forlorn expression on her young face. Bessy gathered her up and held her close, this child on the verge of womanhood who must go and learn how to be a queen. They were a similar height, and Margaret rested her head in the nook of her mother's shoulder.

"How will I leave you, Mama? How will it be if things do not go well? If I ever have to choose between Scotland and England?"

"You will learn how do try to do your best for those you love best," said Bessy, staring over her daughter's bright hair in its pearled snood, at the window that was now quite opaque with snowflakes.

Warwick Lane

"And among them Lord William Courtenay, a man of great nobility, estimation and virtue, which married Lady Katherine, daughter to King Edward ... taken of suspicion and jealousy because they were near of blood

to the conspirators, than for any proved offence or crime." Edward Hall,
Chronicler

They came for him before dawn. Katherine's cough had been so bad she had
slept separately for a few nights, lying awake propped up on several pillows,
staring at the patterns on the bed-hangings in the glimmering light of one fat
candle burning by the bedside. The fever had subsided but her chest still felt raw
if she breathed too deeply. Every now and then she reached for the cup containing
a tisane of liquorice and honey and sipped gratefully. She was just beginning to
drift off into a welcome doze when a loud banging reverberated somewhere in
the inner courtyard. Men's voices were shouting. Despite her home being in the
heart of the city, a stone's throw from St Paul's, disturbances at night were rare.
The city's curfew and the presence of the nightwatchmen kept most trouble at
bay. In addition, the Courtenays kept their own night guard at the gatehouse to
the main street.

Katherine closed her eyes again and tried to ignore the sounds. Let their
steward rise and deal with whoever was causing the commotion. But the little
maid Philippa, Joanna's daughter, who slept on the truckle bed was awake and
opening the door, peering out into the dark passage way. In the distance
Katherine could hear that baby Meggie had woken, her cries hushed by Joanna.
She sighed, and slipped out of bed, reaching for her furred night gown. The fire
in the hearth was burning low but thankfully managed to keep the chamber from
freezing on this winter night; a few new flames flickered feebly as the draught
from the open door rushed in.

"What is it, Philippa?"

"I don't rightly know, my lady. Some bodies down in the Great Hall. I can
hear my lord though, now. Shall I go and see?"

Katherine nodded and lit another candle, placing it carefully inside a horn
lantern. The ensuing glow lit up her young maid's pale face and white shift.
Katherine pulled a coverlet from the bed. "Here, put this around you." The girl
was gone for a few minutes. Katherine shivered and felt the painful ache in her
chest again. So many in the household had been afflicted by this awful illness,
one of the older servants coughing himself into his grave only two weeks since.
So far neither William nor the children had succumbed.

Philippa was back, her breath coming in gasps, not from illness but fear. "Oh, my lady! Come quick! Come now! They are taking my lord! Soldiers from the King!"

Katherine: *I remember it as if it were yesterday. The doors from our Great Hall to the inner courtyard were wide open to the night and a freezing wind blew in. Ten men, in Tudor livery, with pikestaffs – and my husband being man-handled by them out into the darkness. No chance for him to speak, or remonstrate or even bid me farewell. He must have seen me, though, on the staircase leading down from the solar for I heard him cry, "Katherine! Look to the children!" They took him barefoot in his night attire and pushed him into a waiting chariot that trundled off down Warwick Lane and was swallowed by the night. Our own two guards crept shame-faced before me: "We were powerless, my lady. Powerless."*

The whole household was in a state of shock. At first light, Katherine sent servants to trudge through the snow to Westminster and the Tower, to glean whatever news they could. They returned with frozen feet and sombre faces. Suffolk's youngest brother, William de la Pole, had also been arrested, along with a whole raft of names Katherine vaguely knew to be connected with her cousin's heartlands in East Anglia. She felt horribly alone. Her parents-in-law were nearly two hundred miles away in Tiverton. The roads down to Devon she knew would be virtually impassable at this time of year and in such weather but one of William's men offered to go anyway. "*I will take my chance, Your Grace. I know the monasteries where I may stop upon the Great West Road and can find new horses as I go.*" It was his earnest use of her old royal title that brought tears to Katherine's eyes. But it would be weeks, not days before she could hope for support from William's family. If support was what they would give. In the meantime she had to be practical.

She sat before her looking glass in her own bedroom, peering at her own face. She was twenty two, a young woman in the prime of her life. True, she was still weak and flushed from fever and a cough but the worst was over. She unbraided her thick, wheat-blonde plait and shook her hair free over her shoulders. It fell to her hips, a familiar and comforting cloak. She pulled it forward over her face and sat for a few moments in its quiet shelter, taking stock of her situation. The first thing must be to ascertain where in the Tower they had put her husband. She thought of her cousin Ned, of what she had seen that day in the Garden Tower, and shuddered. But William had family. Friends. He could be sent warm clothes, and wood for a fire, and food. He might even be allowed his own servants. Surely it could only be for a few days? Surely Henry Tudor did not seriously think that William was involved with Edmund de la Pole?

No word had yet come from Bessy. Katherine felt herself trembling; she could not expect her sister to intervene – it would not be fair. She could no more look to Bessy to save her husband than had Kateryn Huntley. The Queen's concern must be for her own sons.

"My lady?" It was Joanna. Loyal Joanna. Katherine's own nursemaid all those years ago, who had gone with the Yorkist princesses into sanctuary. She had married but her husband had died young, leaving her with a tiny daughter, and when Katherine heard of her circumstances she had welcomed her immediately into the Courtenay household as nursemaid to her own children. Joanna was possibly the closest thing Katherine had to a mother figure, for she had been there at every stage of her girlhood.

Gentle hands lifted her hair. "Shall I braid it for you, my lady?"

Dumbly, Katherine nodded, and felt the familiar tug and glide as the ivory comb began to tease out the tangles. Joanna did not speak but simply continued the soothing, rhythmic movements. Deftly, she plaited the tresses and pinned them ready for the linen coif and whichever headdress Katherine might choose.

"There, my lady, I have not lost my touch. It makes a change from trying to tidy the boys' mops! Hal cannot sit still and Edward's hair is so curly!"

Suddenly, the tears she had repressed for hours came spurting like wellsprings and she was in Joanna's arms, sobbing her heart out. Great rasping sobs of terrible fear.

"Oh, my lady – Katherine. Oh hush, my sweeting – it will come to good. It will." For several minutes, Joanna held her as she had held her as a child, waiting till the waves of hysteria began to subside. "Now, first things first. You need to eat something, and take a cup of small ale. My lord William will need you to be so strong, for his sake and the children's." She had brought a small tray in with her, and now sat beside Katherine, offering little pieces of manchet loaf and encouraging her to take small sips. Like an obedient child, she chewed and swallowed, chewed and swallowed. Gradually, the sick tension in her stomach abated.

A quiet knock sounded at the door, and Philippa's little face peered around the jamb. She resembled nothing so much as a disturbed dormouse, her eyes huge with worry.

"My lady, there is a messenger come from court. From Her Grace the Queen." She held out a letter, from which Bessy's seal dangled. Katherine felt a surge of hope and reached out for it hungrily, breaking the wax and scanning the few lines of neat writing. This was in Bessy's own hand – a message sent privately.

My Dearest Sister

Be of good faith. I do not believe the King intends harm to my brother-in-law. I have leave to help you within my own household. Let the children be sent to Havering with Joanna where I will ensure they are cared for as befits their station. Do you come to me, as soon as you may. Burn this.

Your loving Sister

Elizabeth

Havering, Katherine knew, was a village in the Essex countryside, and the manors there in Bessy's possession as queen consort. In effect, she was offering a safe haven for the Courtenay children, presumably from her own purse. Katherine was under no illusions. William's arrest for treason was likely to be followed by seizure of lands and confiscation of property, leaving their children's inheritance in dire doubt. She had no income herself other than the pension settled on her at her marriage, again from Bessy's personal slender means. And how would William's father react? Would he welcome her to his fireside, with his grandchildren, or would he choose to distance himself from a woman whose Yorkist cousins caused the King such trouble? Many a father had had to put his king before his son, if he hoped to survive himself. *Such is the game we all play.* This beautiful house in Warwick Lane could no longer be her home if she had no way of paying the bills. The servants would have to go; some might find employment in other noble households, others would have to return to Devon and hope that the Earl might take them in.

Thank God for Joanna, who declared that Dagenham Manor at Havering-atte-Bower was exactly the place where she wanted to spend the foreseeable future. *I have a cousin who lives in the village of Romford, my lady. It's a healthy spot. The children will love the woods and fields. Have no fear for us. You know I love them as my own.*

Within two days, with the weather much improved, they were gone. Edward mounted proudly on his pony; Hal and baby Meggie with Joanna and her daughter Philippa in the litter. It would be a journey of twelve miles along the good road from London to Colchester, with plenty of inns where they might stop for rest and food. Katherine simply could not bring herself to even begin to explain to Edward what prompted their departure. She could not burden a six-year-old with the knowledge that his father had been taken prisoner. He sensed something, though; knew his mother was hugging him too fiercely as she said goodbye.

"Are you all right, Mama?"

"I am fine, my son. Now do as Joanna bids you. Say your prayers morning and night and help Hal to say his."

"Why are we going to Havering?"

"Because your aunt the Queen is kind enough to say you may."

"Will my royal cousins, Prince Harry and Princess Mary be there?"

"They may visit during the summer."

"But *you* will visit too, Mama, won't you? And my lord father?" Edward's chin trembled slightly for although, like all high-born children he was used to spending time away from his parents, he had loved the last few happy months at Warwick Lane.

She knew she must say something that if repeated by her son would not cause trouble.

"If the King allows it."

Edward nodded in reluctant understanding, for he lived in a world ordered by authority. He had to obey Joanna, who obeyed his mother, who obeyed his father, who obeyed the King. A thought occurred to him as he settled himself into his little padded saddle.

"Can my uncle the King do whatever he likes?"

"Yes." Then a spark of resistance flashed within her as she thought of William in the grey fortress down river. "But he is answerable to God, like each and every one of us."

Outside her home curious bystanders milled about; word of Lord Courtenay's arrest had evidently spread swiftly but to her relief no-one called out anything that might upset her son. Instead, there was a respectful hush as the chariot trundled away, followed by Edward riding between two Courtenay men-at-arms. A watery sun peeped over the rooftops, bringing the city to a new day.

The snow of previous days had turned to dark slush, melting into the filthy channel that ran down the centre of the street. Just around the corner the great bells of St Paul's rang out the hour of Terce, the first of scores of city churches between Warwick Lane and the Tower. Katherine turned to pass through the gatehouse, quelling again the fear and panic that kept threatening to overwhelm her.

"À York!" A solitary, defiant voice in the thin February air.

"À Courtenay!" More voices joining in; a confident chorus.

"God bless Your Grace, and keep his lordship safe!"

London voices. Ordinary people who lived and worked in the streets, who would now return to their homes to continue with their day's work. Shopkeepers, tradesmen and their apprentices, good wives and servants. People for whom the Courtenay leftovers were always a source of extra food and who valued Courtenay patronage of their stalls and warehouses. Katherine did not dare look around to see who had called out but raised her hand in a fleeting, quiet gesture of acknowledgement.

Later that day she mounted Rose and rode to Westminster, holding her head high as she entered the main courtyard. Making her way to Bessy's apartments she could feel the looks of pity from the courtiers who passed her and heard their whispers. To her surprise, she was met by Kateryn Huntley, a small, dignified figure in black velvet.

"Come this way, Lady Courtenay. The Queen is in her presence chamber."

Bessy was sitting under her cloth of estate. Katherine looked askance, for in the circumstances she had expected a private, even furtive entrance to her sister's household.

She glanced around, recognising the familiar faces of Bessy's women, a few of her musicians and a couple of male servants, and saw nothing but expressions of sympathy. To her relief, Lady Margaret Beaufort was not present but the young Queen of Scots stood by her mother, doing her best to appear at ease.

"Sister." Bessy held out her hand formally, and Katherine knelt to kiss it, tears welling in her eyes. "We are glad to see you recovered from your illness, and glad to have you back in our service. You are most welcome."

"I am thankful to be here."

Bessy motioned to her musicians that they should play, and her ladies that they should return to their duties, and under the cover of calm melodies on the clavichord and lute, led Katherine to a deep window seat.

"Sister, they took him from his bed. He needs linen, and warm clothes, and food, and firewood. I cannot bear to think what the last two days have been like for him."

"Hush. Do not distress yourself. All those things shall be sent today. "

"But I cannot … I have no ..."

"Money. I know. But I have. And I will pay for everything. For you, the children and William. For as long as it takes."

"Bessy," she whispered, "I am sure he never conspired with our cousin against the King. He's no foolish romantic, to go following a white rose. He saw the last one trampled into the dust." She stole a covert glance across to where Kateryn Huntley sat at cards with young Margaret.

"That's what I told Henry, and I am fairly certain he means only to hold William as an example, not to bring him to trial."

"But for how *long?"*

"*That* is the part I cannot tell. You must give me a few days, possibly weeks, to see if I can find out more."

It seemed to Katherine that in all her life Bessy had stepped forward like a guardian angel to succour her sisters. Now she bowed and leaned her forehead against Bessy's hands, her heart too full for words.

11

Katherine: *So my dear lord languished in the Tower and the days turned into weeks, and winter edged into spring. I was not permitted to visit but we exchanged letters and I knew that he had received all Bessy's presents of clothes and food. They held him in the Beauchamp Tower, which he assured me was comfortable, and next door to the Lieutenant's lodgings. Being William, he put a cheerful face on the worst of happenings and wrote little notes to Edward and Hal, never mentioning his imprisonment but always full of jokes and fun. As the weeks passed it seemed that Henry Tudor was content to have proved a point, and was not baying for my husband's blood. We heard that Edmund de la Pole had shrugged off the suggestion that the Courtenay family had known of his plans to flee. This resulted in a message from Devon, inviting me to make my home there with my parents-in-law if I so wished. William wrote that he would be content if I did so, but then something happened to change all our lives ...*

"**Also in the month of April ... died the noble prince Arthur, eldest son of our sovereign lord at Ludlow.**" Great Chronicle of London

"**When His Grace understood that sorrowful heavy tidings he sent for the Queen, saying he and the Queen would take the painful sorrows together.**"

April 4ᵗʰ 1502 Greenwich

A spring evening in London. The day had been full of showers and blustery breezes but finally the waters of the Thames were less choppy, and in the west long ribbons of rose and coral streaked the sky. The newly-renovated palace of Greenwich also settled down into peace and quiet after a busy day, for the court was in residence and its chambers, courtyards, staircases, corridors, gardens and pleasure grounds had seen a flurry of activity. Its new brick frontage glowed in the sunset then, as night fell, gables and turrets were silhouetted against an indigo sky. The brewster locked the brewery door behind her and sighed, for her night would be short. The dairymaid double-checked that her butter was cool on the slate slabs before she too sought her bed. In her own apartment Margaret, Queen of Scots, lay awake and wondered what it would be like to share her bed with a grown man. Her little sister Mary slept with her thumb tucked comfortably in the corner of her mouth. Prince Harry turned over and banged his pillow furiously before slipping back into a good dream about hawking. Henry Tudor slept alone, the curtains of his bed firmly drawn. Bessy the queen slept alone too, a letter from Ludlow still held lightly in her hand.

After midnight, a solitary barge moored at the palace's landing stage and a cloaked figure made haste up the steps and across the silent lawns to knock urgently at the gatehouse door. He was admitted at once, and led through hushed passageways where night torches burned low in their sconces. In a small room two other men sat in chairs by a log fire, occasionally drowsing; occasionally making quiet conversation; occasionally reading. They could not remember the last time their night duty as Henry Tudor's waking privy counsellors had been disturbed. But they would never forget this time.

When the messenger from Ludlow held out his two letters, his hands shaking and his eyes ringed with misery, they knew exactly what news he brought. Breaking the seals of Sir Reginald Pole and his wife Lady Margaret Pole, each counsellor forced himself to read the content then each stared at the other in horror.

"God's teeth; this changes everything."

"How is he to be told?"

"How is *she to be told?*"

"He must be told first."

"By whom?"

"We must send for his confessor. The greyfriar."

More secret comings and goings in the night. Word sent to the next door monastery of the Franciscan Observants and a grey-cowled figure quitting the vigil of night-time prayer in the chapel to hasten to the door of the King's privy chamber.

Henry Tudor was half-awake when he heard urgent whisperings beyond the curtains of his bed. The soft closure of the door was followed by a strange silence and, finally, a discreet cough. He sat up, sensing something at once out of sorts. It did not seem quite light enough for the normal morning routine whereby his servants would respectfully wake him, then offer his furred robe and slippers that he might either move towards his little oratory for immediate prayer, or towards the close stool for physical easement. He waited for a few more seconds, expecting the curtain to twitch and the familiar face of his body servant. Then the dry, discreet cough again.

Puzzled, Henry drew back his own curtain and found his confessor, Father Gregory, kneeling at his bedside. The monk kept his head bowed. "Good morning, Your Grace. I trust you slept well." Henry realised that there was no-one else in the chamber. His mind was sliding over possibilities: if there was news from Europe, or Scotland, it would be delivered by one of his privy council. The presence of a cleric, and a private one at that, could presage only one thing.

"Tell me, and tell me quickly. My mother?"

Your Grace, as far as I know your lady mother is well." The friar hesitated then took a deep breath. "*Si bona de manu Dei suscipimus, mala autem quare non sustineamus?*" Henry stared, processing a rapid translation. "What evil thing must I face this morning, Father? What evil thing has God sent to me? What is so bad that they have sent you to tell me?"

Father Gregory was nothing if not courageous. "Sir, it is news from Ludlow. Our beloved Prince of Wales has departed this life to seek eternal glory in Heaven, where I am sure his soul is already with the angels."

It was the disbelief on his king's face that upset him so much. He watched as Henry Tudor drew back slightly; as his eyes narrowed then widened. Then he heard an animal-like sound of agony coming from somewhere in his king's throat, a tearing, sobbing sound. Henry was stumbling from the bed, his legs thin and white beneath his night-gown, which rode up and exposed his thighs. Friar Gregory tried to look away but Henry Tudor was clutching him, clawing at his coarse grey habit. "You have it wrong! You are mistaken!"

The door opened a little way and Father Gregory looked over the head of the weeping man.

"Send for Her Grace the Queen."

When Bessy came, she found king and confessor kneeling together before Henry's prie-dieu. The fire in the hearth had gone out, for no-one had dared to enter. Bessy wondered, momentarily, if this really was the worst moment of her life and decided it was. Her father's death; Richard's defeat at Bosworth; her mother's death; young Ned before the executioner's block; Perkin Warbeck swinging from the gallows at Tyburn; two children lost in infancy … and now this. Images flashed before her mind of Arthur at different ages: the swaddled baby at Winchester who had grown into the kindest of little boys; the youth who had smiled at her with his grandfather's eyes and the promise of becoming the king she could believe had been worth every sacrifice …

"Wife?" Henry sounded utterly broken.

"I am here."

"Arthur is dead. My son is dead."

She determined that he should never know the depth of her own misery. It was hers, and hers alone. If he had said "our son" she might have found it easier to weep with him. *How many times have I had to hide my true feelings before this man? I can do it again.*

"You still have a prince. And two fair princesses. You still have me, Your Grace, and we are young enough to make another prince." She astonished herself with the level tone she managed to produce. *Forgive me, Arthur. No-one will ever replace you. I have to say what he needs to hear. My mother lost all her princes; my Uncle Richard lost his only prince. And my husband killed my Uncle George's prince.*

Her apparently calm demeanour and rational comments seemed to help him. He focused upon her and saw that she, too, was in her night-shift albeit with a thick, sleeveless overgown thrown on hastily. He registered her bare forearms, slightly freckled, and her bare neck, and the hint of flesh where her full breasts separated. Her hair lay in a thick braid down her back. *She is thirty six and her mother had children well into her forties.* He swept his own lank, greying hair out of his eyes and back over his head – the gesture of a man trying to make quick sense of a crazy situation.

"You bring me to my senses, wife. God's will be done."

"Your Lady Mother had but one son, and yet God has preserved you," said Bessy. *Though why, and how, I cannot tell.*

Father Gregory patted his arm encouragingly, thankful for the Queen's common sense. "We will have Masses said later today, Your Graces."

Henry looked at Bessy bleakly. "What else should we do – now?"

She bit her lip and willed her mind away to somewhere where Arthur yet lived. "Your privy council will wish to send your instructions to Ludlow."

"My instructions?" He looked genuinely nonplussed.

Again, Father Gregory dared to lay a gentle hand upon the sleeve of the king's night-gown.

"As to where you might wish His Grace the Prince of Wales to be laid to rest."

Another awful sob escaped from Henry's throat and he laid his head in despair upon the velvet padded bar of his prie-dieu.

"Your Grace, why not return to your rooms for a while? His Grace the King needs time."

Dry-eyed, Bessy nodded acquiescence. She could do no more.

As she walked back to her own apartments the early morning mist was just lifting off the river and the lawns. She paused by an open window and leaned on the casement. Behind her, Kateryn Huntley also stopped respectfully. Bessy could feel her heart pounding in her chest; could almost feel the blood throbbing in her veins. Far away in Ludlow, Arthur's body was probably lying in the round chapel in the castle courtyard. She imagined her cousin Meg kneeling by the black catafalque with Catalina, his five-month widow. She could smell the incense. She could see the finely-drawn features of her first-born son: the dark shadow above his lip; the tender mouth; the blue Plantagenet eyes beneath the pale eyelids. *Could God be so cruel? Why?*

"Your Grace. Once you comforted me. Let me now comfort you." Kateryn Huntley, who might or might not be her sister-in-law, was holding out her arms and Bessy stumbled towards them.

Katherine: *The rain in Shropshire and Worcestershire that April was so bad that Arthur's body could not be brought to London for burial. Instead, he found his final resting place in the cathedral at Worcester, where our ancestor King John also lay. They told us that the roads were such quagmires that oxen had to be used to pull the hearse because the horses nearly perished in the mud. Together, Bessy and I read Meg's letter, which told of Arthur's sudden, catastrophic descent into fever and death. He had been coughing, on and off, since Christmas but Meg had thought him slightly improved. The ink was splashed with tears and many words indecipherable. Clearly, she blamed herself: unable to save her only brother from Henry Tudor's axe, and unable to save her nephew from some virulent form of sickness.*

333

12

"Upon Friday following … Sir James Tyrrell was brought out of the Tower to the scaffold upon the Tower Hill, and there hanged, beheaded and quartered. And the residue remained in prison at the king's grace." Great Chronicle of London

The Tower of London 30th April 1502

William Courtenay had spent two months adjusting to his new circumstances. Pessimism was not normally part of his character but the sheer unexpectedness of his arrest, and the appalling possibilities that lay before him caused some heart-stopping moments. Quite frankly, William did not much care who sat upon the throne of England as long as he ruled well and wisely, though he knew such sentiments were best kept close to his heart. His father's loyalties lay firmly with the House of Lancaster, in the new shape of the Tudors. William felt less certain, judging that seventeen years did not necessarily make a dynasty. Edmund de la Pole's arguments about the Plantagenet claims had sometimes made for intriguing listening. He could have kicked himself, though, for too much hob-nobbing with the Earl of Suffolk. In hindsight, he could see that he might well have been after some Courtenay promise about support in the West Country – not that his father would ever have agreed to anything so ludicrous.

There were worse corners of the Tower than this one. William had heard the rumours of subterranean chambers where the King's enemies were encouraged to confess what they knew, courtesy of the Duke of Exeter's daughter (a charming maiden, made of wood and rope, whose main aim was to stretch a man into submission). So far, though, his royal brother-in-law seemed happy enough to leave him in the Beauchamp Tower, unlike other men arrested at the same time.

The most frustrating thing was the lack of physical freedom. For an energetic man like William, used to riding, jousting, tennis and hunting, sitting still was something reserved for the end of the day. The long hours spent in attendance upon the king had invariably contained some form of exercise and it was the lack of it that William felt would drive him mad. The Tower's Lord Lieutenant had taken one look at him pacing up and down, likely to wear away the stone floor, and suggested he could go outside on to the rampart walkway. He also offered his private garden so William imposed upon himself the discipline of at least two hours walking up and down, up and down, every afternoon.

He wrote to Katherine; to his parents; to his children – unsealed letters read by the Lord Lieutenant. When the first parcel of clothing came from the Queen, his gaolers' attitude changed to a sort of apologetic deference. *Thank God for Her Grace!* Deliveries were regular: good wine, decent food, warm bedding and firewood. But no word of release. Fortunately the days were lengthening but the temperature inside the stone and brick building were always cool. The Beauchamp tower was part of the inner defences, so there was no view over the river, just an outlook on to a further stone perimeter wall.

At night, when the whole complex grew quiet, William lay in bed, missing the warmth of Katherine's body, and marvelling that he could be held prisoner in a place he had come to as the Queen's brother-in-law on countless occasions over the past seven years. He had feasted and jousted here; overseen some of the military armaments; prayed in the two chapels; visited the lions in the menagerie and seen the King's coins at the royal mint. *Really, you had to laugh at the irony of it all.* Sometimes he thought of Katherine's two lost brothers, and wondered again about the young man who had tried to take the city of Exeter and met his end, battered beyond recognition, on the end of the hangman's rope.

One morning the key grated in the lock and a warder he had not seen before stood in the doorway. A burly man, in his forties; a seasoned soldier, by the look of him. William waved at his empty plate. "It was good bread. Makes all the difference."

The man smiled faintly. "My wife baked it, my lord." There was a hint of West Country in the way his r rolled in the last word and in his lingering vowels.

"Really? Please convey my thanks."

"My wife prepares most of your meals, my lord."

William's hand paused in mid-air. He was in the middle of writing to Katherine and his quill dripped a little ink on to the paper. It occurred to him that although he knew that the Queen paid for him to be decently fed he had not given any thought as to who might actually be producing the food. He had presumed the Lord Lieutenant was sending up dishes from his kitchen.

"That's … that's extremely kind of her. And she would be Mistress …?"

"Mistress Darch, my lord. I am Christopher Darch."

"Darch? That's a Devon name!"

"It is indeed, my lord. My father was Robert Darch, from Tiverton."

William was dumbfounded. "You are from my family's estates?"

"Not as such, my lord. My father was a blacksmith in the town but looking for a bit of adventure in my youth I followed your father the Earl to Redemore Plain, and after the battle just never made it home to Devon again. Met my wife, so to speak. Ended up here."

William stood up and held out his hand. The soldier looked wary but then took it, clasping it firmly. His ruddy complexion deepened; he had never shaken hands with a lord before.

"I am just writing to *my* wife …" William looked at Christopher Darch keenly. Could he ask him to take a letter out, without the Lord Lieutenant's knowledge?

The captain rocked slightly on his heels. "I came to tell you, my lord, that your wife will be in the Tower this very night."

William went as pale as yesterday's milk. "Jesu! She is not arrested, too? He has not stooped to taking women!" He thumped the table and the ink pot wobbled precariously.

The captain realised his error. "Sweet Virgin! No, sir! Your lady comes with her sister the Queen. To the royal apartments in the White Tower."

William closed his eyes and breathed again. The world righted itself. "And the King?"

"The King does not come, sir. Just the Queen." Darch collected up the empty plate and tankard. "And the Lord Lieutenant is away at present." He made for the door.

A slow, incredulous smile began to creep across William's face. "Are you, by any chance, trying to tell me something, Captain Darch, late of Tiverton?"

"Just that your lady wife is one of the most persistent women I have ever come across, my lord. This will be the second time I have been persuaded to give her access to one of my prisoners."

When Katherine fell into his arms William was not ashamed to weep too. The world was reduced to a microcosm in which they hungrily kissed each other's lips and breathed in the familiar scent of each other's skin. He was thinner, she noticed, but his linen was clean and his face freshly shaven. He saw the fine bone structure of her face; the skin stretched taut over her cheekbones; the dark shadows under her peat-brown eyes. Tenderly, he removed her headdress, pulled the ivory pins from her hair and lost himself in the rosemary-scented fragrance. The knife he had used to cut his meat had not yet been removed and he reached for it, wiped away the grease, and used it to sever a tress.

"I must have something of you, beloved, to hold at nights."

"And me, you." She waited while he cut a length of his own curling, chestnut hair. "Bessy knows I have come to you. She is our saviour, William."

He drew her down on to his narrow bed and held her close again. "How long have we got?"

"A couple of hours. But William, I must not be with child again. I dare not. If he knew … if he finds out that Bessy … what she risks for me…" His mouth was on hers, his hands already on the satin skin of her thighs, and she felt his hardness. How many times had they enjoyed each other's bodies since their marriage? There had been a time when she had tried to count but had given up. It was an utterly natural and fulfilling part of their relationship, every time an affirmation of the quality of their love. Katherine's most secret triumph in life was that although Henry Tudor had chosen her husband, thinking to force her into obscurity he had unwittingly provided her with a man who adored the very ground whereon she walked.

"You will not be with child, beloved." His whisper was warm in her ear.

"Is that not a sin?"

"A waste, but not a sin."

She sighed, and gave herself up to his lovemaking.

When they had finished, Katherine sat quietly between his legs, while he ran his fingers through her hair, combing it back into some kind of order.

"How does your sister the Queen?"

"Grieving. She was very ill for days after we heard about Arthur. The apothecary has prescribed tinctures for her but in truth she does not seem much improved. She does not sleep at night, I am often her bedfellow."

"She must be glad to have you close again. Is the little Spanish princess back in London yet?"

"Bessy has sent a litter for her. She has been ill herself."

"Really? Does she carry Arthur's child?"

337

"We shall not know for several weeks. Oh William, how can everything have gone so horribly wrong? Arthur dead, and you, in here." She wound her fingers together. "The others who were arrested ... some are to stand trial at the Guildhall. Everyone says ... everyone says they will be executed. Oh, Jesu, William – what will happen to you?"

His lifted the heavy skeins of her hair and kissed the vulnerable nape of her neck. "I don't believe he will be able to find any evidence to prove that I supported Suffolk. Mainly because there isn't any, beyond a few dinners and drinking expeditions. I told you, I wrote to him – about horses. Where's the treason in that? He wanted to breed from Seaton and we discussed terms. How is he, by the way? Missing me?"

"I have sent him down to Devon with a couple of the grooms. Your father will look after him – until you are set free."

"And the children?"

"You ask about your horse before your children. Typical!"

"No!" he protested. "I would have asked first but for your distress."

"They are well. Edward loves your letters. He thinks you are abroad on the King's business and Joanna does not tell him otherwise. The people at Dagenham are loyal to Bessy. Please God you will see them before the summer is out."

William sat back, locking his hands behind his head. "We have to face facts. I think it most unlikely Tudor will set me free as long as Suffolk parades freely around Antwerp, or wherever he has fetched up. He will hold me as some sort of political hostage – as a warning to others. A sign that he trusts no-one. If the Queen's brother-in-law can be suspected, then so can anyone else, no matter how high born. Do you know, when I think back to Arthur's wedding I believe he was watching then – watching, and waiting to pounce. Suffolk had named me as one of his jousting team – remember he was supposed to have been there? But he saw his opportunity and slipped away. Doubtless, Tudor's spies have told him that anyone on Suffolk's team must have had his confidence. No, my beloved girl, I fear we are in this for the long-run." He pulled her back down again and held her fiercely. "I wish you were out of London, Katherine. I wish you would take the children and go down to my parents in Devon. It would give me peace of mind to think of you there, far away ... from *this.*" He gestured helplessly around the room, the stone walls and narrow lancet windows.

She looked up into his handsome face, and ran her fingers either side of his eyes, across his strong, straight nose and firm lips, around his jawline and then sweeping back up again to his forehead – like a blind woman committing his features to the innermost recesses of her mind. "Not just yet. Bessy needs me, and she promises the children will be educated with Harry and Mary. That has to be a better prospect for them."

The precious time was passing. Around them the Tower began to settle for the night, like some mythical, heraldic beast taking up its *couchant* pose. The daily workers flowed out through the main gate leaving the vast complex to its guests and permanent inhabitants. The very stones seemed to exhale in relief, and possibly pity for those who did not choose to be there.

"I am surprised Her Grace wanted to come here on her own. You've always said she only just tolerates it when the king orders it."

"No, it's not on Bessy's list of favourite palaces, but there's a reason." Katherine stared up at the vaulted ceiling, noting the cobwebs and dark patches of mildew. "James Tyrrell is held here."

William breathed out in a long whistle. Tyrrell had been loyal to King Richard but quickly pledged allegiance to the Tudors. A capable administrator, he had risen in Henry's favour, as lieutenant of the castle at Guisnes, near Calais. "He took a huge risk harbouring Suffolk, then ensuring his safe passage on to Antwerp. He will die for it."

Katherine nodded. "But he has asked to see Bessy – privately. We think he may know something about our brothers. Maybe, finally, we will have some truth. This has been such a terrible month but if Tyrrell is prepared to shed some light upon what happened it may help my sister."

"It's nigh on twenty years, Katherine. Don't expect too much. And don't believe in fairy tales."

There was a knock on the door, a moment of respectful waiting, then Christopher Darch's broad face appeared.

"I'm sorry. You must leave now, my lady."

Stricken, Katherine clutched at her husband. "Jesu, I cannot bear to leave you."

"You must. Stay strong, Katherine, and all will be well. I have Captain Darch here to look after me, and the wonderful Mistress Darch, too. As long as Her Grace the Queen can send me necessities I can survive quite happily. Well, maybe not *happily* but I can survive. I am in good health and good spirits."

Katherine turned beseechingly to Darch. "And you will admit me, when I come here with my sister the Queen?"

"As long as there is no specific order to the contrary, then yes, my lady. We have many prisoners here who see their families."

She gave him a wry smile. "Who would have thought our paths would cross again, Captain Darch?" She hesitated. "But will you take some money this time, in return for your kindness?"

"Unlike many in this place, I am not to be bribed, my lady."

"No! No, not a bribe … I did not mean … I meant to thank you for your trouble. And your wife."

"A few years ago, I told you, my lady that I believe God sees what is right and what is wrong."

The White Tower held many secrets. Dark stone staircases led down into a Hades world of cells and chambers where thick walls and locked doors muffled the cries of Henry Tudor's enemies. This was where the Feigned Lad had been battered and disfigured. This was where James Tyrrell had found himself facing the King's interrogators and telling all he knew of how Edmund de la Pole, the Earl of Suffolk, had made his escape from England and passed through Guisnes on his way to the Emperor Maximilian's court.

To be honest, it had been a relief to tell. And they knew it all anyway. Why suffer on the rack in some foolish attempt to maintain personal integrity? James Tyrrell was not that sort of man. Once, in his youth, he had followed his dreams, and fought for York at Tewkesbury, and been knighted by the Sun in Splendour himself, King Edward. Golden days, when it had seemed the house of York would shine forever. How wrong could you be? James Tyrrell had sacrificed idealism for pragmatism long ago.

An approaching candle glimmered in the darkness. A key clunked in the lock and the door to his cell swung open. The guard was accompanied by a serious-faced young man, clad in the dark robes of a lawyer, who gestured that he should follow him. They climbed an endless, spiral stone staircase ending in another door which opened out into a broad passage lit by sconces. Tyrrell judged they were now on the first or second floor of the Tower; he puffed from the exertion, and his legs ached.

"Her Grace the Queen waits for you in here." The young man knocked, then opened a door. Tyrrell followed him into a small room where two women sat side by side in the candlelight. He was suddenly conscious of how bad he smelt.

"Thank you, Master More. The Archbishop was not wrong when he told me you are a young man to be trusted. Please be good enough to wait outside. I will speak privately with Sir James, as he has requested." The lawyer bowed and retreated.

When Tyrrell looked at the Queen he could see the resemblance to her father in her broad, high brow and the shape of her mouth. Like her father, she was putting on weight in her middle years, and her blue eyes were full of sadness. Tyrrell remembered that the Prince of Wales was dead. She introduced her companion.

"My sister, Lady Courtenay, whose husband is also held here at present."

Tyrrell bowed, as best his could. His very bones seemed to throb with pain from the cramped and damp conditions of the cell where they had held him for weeks. "My apologies, Your Grace, but I have had no clean linen for days now."

"You sent word that you wished to meet with me. That you had something to tell me. You may speak before my sister. We have no secrets."

Tyrrell stared at his feet. His boots had once been supple and shining; now the soles were cracked and the leather stained. What a sight he must look. Unshaven. Dishevelled. Fingernails black with grime. He cleared his throat but at first no words would come. *It must be nigh on midnight.* There was a full moon which shone in through the casement and gave the chamber an eerie pale glow.

"I know I am to die. In a day or so I must stand before God. I have a confession to make."

He looked up at the two women. The younger one, Lady Courtenay, was wide-eyed, like a startled young doe. The Queen's expression did not change, except that she lowered her chin slightly and pursed her lips.

"It concerns Your Grace's brothers."

"Edward, and Richard."

Tyrrell started. Hearing their Christian names moved him. He swallowed hard and began the story he knew he must tell these Plantagenet princesses.

"My father was a Lancastrian and died for it, but I supported your own house of York. I loved your kingly father. And I was your uncle's body knight. When your father died, I found it easy to follow your uncle – he was a good man. He only wanted what was best for this country and when the news broke that your father had been pre-contracted to Shrewsbury's daughter he believed that only a legitimate, adult king could take the helm. And, forgive me, but he could not stomach your mother's Wydville family; he feared they would seize control, and rule through the boy."

Bessy and Katherine were silent; he told them nothing new.

"For a while he could see no alternative to ..." Tyrell gathered himself. "No alternative to … removing them. Indeed, he sent orders that it should be done, and thought it *had* been done but…" He had thought that a confession would be easy – to put the blame for it all on King Richard but now it came to it he realised the only way his soul would be eased was if he told the entire truth. The Queen was staring at him intently and the younger sister clasped her hands in her lap.

"He gave orders that the Constable at the time, Robert Brackenbury, should hand over the keys for a night, and I came here … but when I saw the boys I knew that King Richard's decision was a rash one – something he would regret. So I had them removed ... but to my own home in Gipping, in Suffolk. I decided to keep them safe there, until such times as your uncle was secure upon the throne, with his own heirs, and then I thought maybe the boys could be accepted again – as your other bastard brother is accepted. No-one has ever thought Master Arthur Plantagenet a threat."

"You are telling us that my royal brothers did *not* die here in the Tower?" Bessy's breast rose and fell; her voice rose to an incredulous whisper. "Did my Uncle Richard know this?" Her mind was racing over the past. Sometimes she wondered if she remembered it differently to others.

"Your Grace, your uncle died believing that he had been responsible for their deaths. Events happened so swiftly – his son dying, his wife dying, then your husband coming from Brittany. I never dreamed that King Richard would be defeated. I was in France then, at Guisnes, and when the news came of Henry Tudor's victory I did not know what to do. The boys were still sequestered in Suffolk. I panicked. I was afraid for my family. So I sent word to my Lady the King's Mother."

The silence that followed was profound. Neither woman stirred. Tyrrell knew there was nothing but to press on; he had no idea whether the Queen was fully grasping the implications of his story. The only certainty was the executioner's axe that awaited him. He had to ease his own soul, not hers. He opened his mouth to continue but the Queen's soft voice forestalled him.

"So you told Lady Stanley that the princes lived. And she told her son. And he gave orders that they should not live. Because if they lived they he was not truly the king, even if he had defeated my uncle at Redemore Plain."

"Aye. But that it not quite the end, Your Grace. The new Tudor king said that if I killed them both my family and my fortune would stay intact. The oldest boy was ill already – a terrible malady of the jaw; he was fading fast even then, but the younger one…"

"Dickon," breathed Katherine, "my playmate."

"He had won the hearts of all at Gipping and I could not let him die. We took him to the coast and smuggled him out to Flanders. To his aunt. When your husband's men came to Gipping they did indeed find two dead boys but one was a village lad who had died the day before of the sweating sickness."

"Finish your story, Sir James," said Bessy quietly.

"Madam, I confess that I killed your brother Edward. I had him smothered in his bed. God forgive me. But your brother Richard I saw safely on to a boat for Bruges." He gave a hollow laugh. "Your husband rewarded me for my loyalty. He issued a pardon for my former support of the house of York, and even restored me to my position at Guisnes. I took good care over the years to be seen to serve him well…"

"Whilst all the time keeping an eye on Dickon as he grew to manhood in Flanders!" exclaimed Katherine. "Oh, Holy Mother of God, Bessy! Oh, Jesu!" She found her eyes welling with tears. "And when you heard of *his* death you gave your support instead to our cousin, Edmund?"

"Sir James, what exactly are you expecting me to do with this revelation that my husband and his mother gave orders for my brothers' murder?" To discover that she had lived under an extraordinary delusion for seventeen years was, strangely, no real surprise.

Tyrrell found he could not look at either of them. "I don't know, Your Grace. All I know is that I felt you were owed the truth. To do with as you wish."

"And what can I do with it?" An edge of hysteria threatened. "Can I accuse my husband? Or my esteemed mother-in-law? No, Sir James, I must do what I have always done – stay silent and pray that those I love stay safe."

"Have you made your *confession* to anyone else? A priest? The men who questioned you?" Katherine asked sharply.

"No, my Lady. I said that I would speak only to the Queen."

"But the King is *bound* to know."

Tyrrell hesitated. "That young lawyer who bought me up – you say he is to be trusted?"

"He is spoken of as a young man of integrity beyond his years," replied Bessy. "It was he who brokered this meeting."

"Then let him go back to your husband and tell him that Sir James Tyrrell has confessed to killing the York princes on King Richard's orders. That way he gets want he wants; you are protected and my family also. I can go to my grave knowing that I at least told the truth to those who deserve to know."

Katherine turned an urgent face towards her sister. "He's right, Bessy. We can do nothing for our brothers now. You once told me we should look only to the future. Harry is the future and he will need so much of your attention and guidance. We can still have a boy with our York blood who can learn how to be a good king."

"I can do nothing to save you, Sir James. You will go to the block shortly for your open support of my cousin. But I will speak for your son."

"May God bless you, Your Grace."

Bessy rose to summon More back into the room. His open, intelligent face betrayed a curiosity. Both women seemed in total command of themselves and Tyrrell simply stood staring ahead.

"Master More, Sir James has just told us a tale the King will wish to be informed of at the earliest opportunity. It concerns the deaths of my young brothers, here in the Tower, many years ago, on the orders of my uncle King Richard. Sir James is willing to repeat it now to you." If More was astonished he gave no sign but merely inclined his head. He began to usher the prisoner back into the corridor but Katherine darted in front of them both.

"Where were … the boys buried?"

Tyrrell was transported back nineteen years. He had been a handsome fellow then, the girls had whispered coyly; strong enough to wield the sharp spade necessary to dig down through the sub soil; strong enough to carry the heavy stones needed to disguise the grave. He could smell the metallic tang of the dank earth and the stench emanating from the decaying bodies, pitifully slender in their winding sheets. It had taken several days to bring them on a cart from Suffolk. He had refused to bury them like that and someone had brought an old wooden chest used for storing clothes. When they lifted the lid the sharp aroma of wormwood, valerian and cedar leaves wafted up. It had been difficult to manouevre the already stiff corpses inside. A King's son and a brewer's son, shoved like offal into a dark runnel. No prayers; no candles to light their way to heaven. And then, a couple of years later, dug up again when Henry Tudor and his mother's consciences pricked them. Tyrrell hoped that maybe they had finally been laid to rest somewhere like the royal chapel at Windsor or the Plantagenet castle at Fotheringhay.

"I am sorry, my lady. Truly, I do not know." His wrists chafed where the manacles bit into new flesh. Strange, he thought, that this time next week I, too, shall lie in a grave. He knew his family would beg for burial at Austin Friars, where his cousin Alice knew the Augustinian brothers. Sometimes it was useful to have an Abbess in the family. More was already in the passage, waiting for him but Tyrrell twisted his head back to look at the two women. "Your Grace," he mouthed, "I have a sister, Mary, who lives in the Minories, not far from here, and two cousins, Alice and Joyce. They will remember the boys who came to stay at Gipping."

Then he was gone, swallowed into darkness, the chains between his hands clinking softly then fading to nothing. In the distance a door slammed shut.

Katherine: *When I think back, it is hard to know what grieved my sister most in those days: the loss of her dearest boy Arthur? The shocking truth of our brother Edward's demise? The knowledge that her husband and his mother had ordered both our brothers' deaths? The realisation that the young man who had died on the gallows at Tyburn had, indeed, been sweet Dickon? And yet, through it all, her concern was also for me. Every morning, her first prayers were for me, my husband and children. Truly, she was my rock.*

13

Richmond Palace May 1502

Henry Tudor had certainly scored a triumph in his remodelling of Richmond, which seemed to rise directly from the Thames, its stupendous reflection glittering in the bright water of a May morning. It was truly a palace of miracles: clear water spouted from taps; sunlight caught on the glass windows and warmed the bricks to a rich terracotta; onion-shaped domes searched for the sky and red roses adorned everything, from the extraordinary cistern in the courtyard to the timbers in the Great Hall. Bessy and Katherine walked together through gardens where the topiaries of mythical beasts seemed as real as the gorgeous illustrations in their books of hours.

Katherine felt she was living some surreal existence. Less than ten miles away William was incarcerated in two rooms and yet here she was, with the freedom to explore what was surely the most exquisite dwelling in England. In the Great Hall stood statues of all the kings in English history. Her brother-in-law had been careful to place his own on a slightly higher plinth. Really, she could have laughed if other things were not so dreadful. Each night, at supper, Henry Tudor bowed to her politely, for all the world as if he had no idea her husband was imprisoned at his command.

She marvelled at Bessy's composure. Her sister welcomed the little Spanish widow, and seemed to find comfort in caring for her. They sat for hours, talking about Arthur. Catalina related the poignant story of their few months together; her English was much improved and she tried hard to make her mother-in-law smile with tales of how she and Arthur had passed the cold winter, playing chess, and wrapping up in furs to ride out into the surrounding villages. She had never seen snow before, and had been enchanted by the sleigh Arthur had ordered, and the bells on the horses, and the thick fustian boots over their hooves. Until he had started coughing so badly.

They waited a few weeks to see if Catalina showed any signs of pregnancy but finally Bessy sighed sadly. "She tells me that much as she loved him, there will be no child."

It was a warm afternoon. Bees buzzed and hummed amongst the blossom. Tonight there would be a pageant upon the river; picnics and music, masques and dancing on the lawns. The window was open in Bessy's presence chamber as she sat at her writing table, a pile of documents in front of her. She was working her way through them, methodically checking and adding her signature.

"I am sending more clothes to William. Holland cloth for shirts, fox fur to line a gown of russet … oh, and a night bonnet. Is there anything more he needs at present?"

Katherine looked up gratefully from her lute. She strummed a minor chord softly. "You are so kind. He writes that he is well provided for. And these summer months should not be so bad, he says."

"And the children?"

"Are well. Though I miss them."

"What do they need?"

"Joanna requests hose, shoes, laces, soap. If that is possible."

"Only think how they will have grown when you see them next!" There seemed to be a forced brightness to Bessy's voice. She continued checking and writing while Katherine picked out the melody to a new tune she was composing. In her mind it spoke of love and loss; the fingers on her left hand moved deftly up and down the fretboard whilst those on the right plucked gently. Bessy's voice broke again through her reverie.

"What do you say to a new saddle? Something rather lovely in black velvet, with some sable trappings for your pretty mare?"

"I do not really need one, but if you have plans to travel, and you wish for my company?"

"Exactly so. I feel restless."

"You wish to go on pilgrimage somewhere?"

"Not specifically. But I should like to go on my own progress this summer."

Katherine looked at her with astonishment. To her knowledge, Bessy had never gone away anywhere by herself, other than short trips to local shrines to pray and make offerings. And why would she choose to be away from Harry,

Margaret and Mary at a time when they needed her? And why away from her husband? It was only eight weeks since Arthur's death; the royal family still wore the dark blue of mourning.

"Is there something you wish to share with me, Bessy?" she ventured. Normally she would never dream of probing at the intimacies of her sister's life and thoughts; she always waited for her to confide. To her consternation, Bessy suddenly buried her head in her hands. She took several deep breaths, as if trying to calm herself and then whispered desperately, "I *have* to get away! He forces himself upon me, night after night. It's my own fault – I said we were still young enough to have another child but he's like a man possessed. And he will not listen when I speak of poor William – and he will not listen when I speak of Cecily –"

Katherine put down her lute and rushed to take her sister in her arms. "Hush! Oh hush! I had no idea! And whatever has Cecily done that causes you to plead for her?"

Bessy laid her hands helplessly on the table. "Married again. Married a man called Thomas Kyme. A *squire,* if you please, from Lincolnshire. And Henry is furious."

Serious though the matter was, Katherine could not help the twitches that threatened at the corners of her mouth. That Cecily should throw caution to the winds and marry some obscure man without the King's permission! It was typical of her impetuosity. There was simply no-one else who would dare. She knew exactly how Cecily's mind would have worked: one husband never mentioned; one husband dead; two children dead – why should she care for the Tudor's wrath? A chance of happiness had presented itself and Cecily had seized it. Katherine found herself wanting to applaud her wayward elder sister. A giggle worked its way up and out.

"Well, I hope he's handsome!"

And then they were both laughing; a crazy, splintered laughter that acknowledged both Cecily's bravado and foolishness.

"But you'll never guess who *is* on her side!"

"Not My Lady the King's Mother?" Katherine was round-eyed.

"I know – just when you want to hate her more than life itself, she does something so you can't. She's always liked Cecily, and Cecily's always played up to her. Now it seems it's been worth it, for Lady Margaret declares the happy couple can live at her house in Northamptonshire while it all blows over. She has her reasons; Cecily has a lifelong interest in the Welles lands in Lincolnshire and

I'm sure Lady Margaret will broker some sort of deal that sees money falling into her own coffers, and Henry's. Cecily is banished from court, though," she added regretfully. "Heaven knows when we will see her again."

A large vase of early summer flowers stood in the centre of the table: irises and cornflowers as blue as Cecily's eyes, with early white lilies. On the wall opposite the window hung an exquisite tapestry from Bruges depicting the Annunciation, the gold threads in the Madonna's halo glowing in the sunlight. Everything in the room was freshly carved, or freshly painted – designed to give pleasure and speak of wealth. To live in such an environment was something the Plantagenet sisters had been born to, and come to value again.

"Cecily would have known that," said Katherine, "I doubt she cares if she ever sees London again."

"But *us,* Katherine?"

"We don't see Bridget. We don't see Anne. It does not mean they do not love us; it does not mean we do not think of them, and pray for them."

"But I shall miss her so much. She was by my side for so many years, and then always here for important events. If Henry never allows her back ... if we never travel into the Midlands again..." Bessy's voice trailed off. Katherine bit her lips. She had begun to think of perhaps spending part of the year with William's parents in Devon but saw now that if she, too, left court Bessy would be bereft.

"Well, then *we'll* have to do the travelling!" She pulled a face." It will keep us from dwelling too much on other matters. Where do you propose going this summer?"

"I want to go to Raglan, in Wales. Lord Herbert's wife is our cousin and they both knew our Uncle Richard's daughter, Katherine, who married the Earl of Huntingdon."

"Ah! The *other* Katherine Plantagenet."

"Richard spoke of her and his boy so fondly. I have a fancy to meet with her family and ask if..."

"If they knew anything of our brothers?"

"Yes. Since Tyrrell confessed I feel sure there must be more people who knew the truth at the time."

"It's a long way to Raglan, Your Grace."

"Well, I mean to go by pretty routes – Woodstock, and Gloucester, and Monmouth."

"Then I will definitely need that new saddle!"

Katherine: *If my royal brother-in-law was surprised by Bessy's desire to separate from him that summer he hid it well. Later I was to learn that he already knew that Bessy was pregnant, so maybe he just wished to humour her. We left Windsor together early one morning in mid-July, and crossed the Thames at leafy Datchett. As they ferried us across I sent a silent farewell downstream to William in his prison in the Tower. By nightfall we had reached the Abbey at Notley where the Abbot made us welcome in his own house. It was there that dreadful tidings reached us ...*

The Abbot's hall was spacious and cool. On a hot July morning the great fireplace was filled with scented flowers and herbs from the gardens and the casement window at the far end was open, admitting a welcome breeze. It should have been an idyllic resting place for the sisters at the beginning of their journey. From the abbey came the clamour of bells calling the monks to prayer at Sext, the midday office, but they moved with heavy hearts for news was spreading that the messenger who had arrived two hours earlier had brought sad news for the Queen's sister, Lady Courtenay. As they all knelt on the stone flags Father Simon invoked them to pray for the lately departed soul of Lord Edward Courtenay, aged six years.

Katherine's grief was profound and silent. All she could think of was Edward's last brave little wave and smile as he had turned in the saddle before kicking his pony on towards Havering. To think that she would never see him again was unbearable. Never hold his warm, firm little body and bestow a kiss upon his springy hair. Never hear him say his prayers before watching him take a flying leap into bed. Never hear his delighted shouts of laughter as his father swung him upwards and on to Seaton's broad back. She could not speak. She felt utterly crushed by sorrow. The messenger was Joanna's nephew, who delivered the formal news in a letter from Lady Margaret Cotton, the governess appointed by Bessy, but he also brought personal tidings from Joanna.

"Your Grace, my sister says he was gone in a day – a sudden fever and a rash, and he complained that his neck hurt. There was no time to send for a doctor. My aunt did what she could but he died in her arms. The other children are well, says my aunt, and no sign of sickness amongst any other members of the household."

Katherine nodded dumbly and gripped Bessy's hand even tighter. What had they done that God had seen fit to take both their sons this year?

"Katherine, he was a king's grandson. A Plantagenet prince as much as my own boys. He will not lack for a royal burial. I will write today to the Abbot at Westminster. You will want to go to Havering to be with Hal and Margaret."

"But I cannot leave you, alone..."

"And I cannot not ask you to come with me. Not now. It's five months since you saw your children. Go to them" Bessy's voice was low and insistent. "And anyway, I will hardly be alone – with four other ladies-in-waiting."

The next day Katherine departed back along the route they had only just covered – back to Windsor and then down river to the city, and finally along the eastern road through the forest and villages to Havering. When she arrived at the old manor it was to find a household in mourning. Edward's little coffin lay in the chapel, awaiting removal to Westminster. Katherine knelt alongside and rested her forehead against the wood. Inside this box lay her firstborn.

"At least I will know where you lie, my sweeting," she whispered. "Which is more than my own mother did, with *her* Edward." She raised her eyes towards the crucifix on the altar and the statue of the Virgin close by. "Now I know what it feels like, Holy Mother of God."

A patter of steps and four-year-old Hal was by her side, his hand firmly held by Joanna and behind them her daughter Philippa carrying baby Meggie who had turned into a plump toddler with a burgeoning vocabulary. Hal looked at her curiously.

"Are you my lady mother?" He was not fearful of her, just anxious to sort things in his mind.

Joanna looked mortified. "Forgive me, Your Grace, we have talked of you, and my Lord William every day since we have been here. My little Lord Hal, you *know* this is your mother!"

He gave her a dazzling smile. "I did *really*! I was just pretending! This is Meggie; she is my little sister, and I have to look after her now that God has taken my brother, and while my father is away. " He looked askance at the little girl whose unmistakable Wydville silver gilt hair was escaping from her holland cap. "I s'pose I'll have to find her a husband one day."

Common sense told her that, rich or poor, children died every day; she was lucky to have had all three survive thus far. The passage from childhood to adulthood was fraught with illness, disease, accidents, and worse. It was the will of God – hard to comprehend and even harder to accept but His will nevertheless.

Joanna placed a gentle hand on her shoulder. "He is surely with the angels in Heaven, my lady."

"Where he will not lack for company," she whispered, thinking of York children gone before her own son: her royal brothers; her Uncle Richard's legitimate heir, Edward, and his bastard boy, John, dead by Henry Tudor's command; Bessy's tiny Elizabeth and young Edmund, and now Arthur; Cecily's two girls and Anne's babies. She sighed deeply. You had to live for the living. You had to bury the pain and hurt deep in your heart and make plans for those who survived. It did not mean forgetting.

Supper in the hall at Havering was a muted affair. Katherine sat with Lady Margaret Cotton, a motherly, sensible woman who spoke with warmth of little Edward's progress and behaviour since she had taken over the Courtenay children's governance. She produced little books of his writing – the script wobbly but bold. "Keep them, my lady. In my experience it helps to have little things to look at. But Lord Hal has the makings of a scholar too!"

Katherine smiled, despite her sadness. The idea of her four-year-old ever writing anything decipherable was almost incredible. Lady Margaret patted her hand. "It's true. He has learnt how to hold the quill and make a mark!" She chatted on, sensitive to Katherine's sorrow concerning her dead son and imprisoned husband, but focusing on Hal and Meggie, their sweet ways and endearing mischief.

"Will you stay awhile, my lady? Or are you needed at court?"

"No, nothing calls me back to court. Her Grace the Queen is on progress this summer into Wales and bids me be with my children. There is nothing I can do In London, and I would rather be here than anywhere else in the world."

Katherine: *And so I stayed in that lovely place, amongst the ancient woodlands and ripening cornfields of Essex, taking time to mourn one child and reacquaint myself with the other two. It was good to be outdoors in that humid late summer, even if it meant dodging the showers and sometimes the sudden thunderstorms. It had been so hard to write to William about our firstborn but I forced myself to send cheerful news of the children's progress: how Hal was now able to ride alone on his pony, and how little Meggie's conversation had begun to include choice phrases overheard in the kitchen. Letters also came from Bessy.*

She reached Raglan Castle by mid-August and stayed for two weeks then began a long, slow journey back through Chepstow, Berkeley and the Cotswolds. It became clear from her letters that she was with child, and not feeling as well as in previous pregnancies. She stopped at many shrines to make offerings and wrote of her dependence upon her apothecary, for it seemed the early sickness still plagued her. Wherever she stayed, my sister bestowed gifts and rewards I knew she could ill afford. New clothes came for my children: Hal was resplendent in a gown of expensive black damask, another of tawny and a little waterproof coat for riding. For Meggie there were kirtles embroidered with daisies, and new shoes. She paid also for Joanna's brother to travel up to London with our messages for William. Every day I blessed my sister for her generosity and wondered what on earth my life would be without her.

14

"Queen Elizabeth, lying at the Tower of London was brought to bed on Candlemas Day and delivered of a fair daughter who was there christened and named Katherine, and on 11th February the most virtuous princess and gracious queen there died …." Richard Grafton, citizen of London

February 1503 The Tower of London

Bessy had always planned to give birth to this final child at Richmond. In mid-January she summoned Katherine from Havering, writing that she felt she simply could not be without her. The last month of her pregnancy was presenting new problems. She was enormous, still nauseous, her hands and feet swollen, exhausted and impatient for it all to be over. But by the time Katherine reached Richmond new instructions diverted her to the Tower, where it seemed Henry Tudor was determined to spend the feast of Candlemas and wanted Bessy's company. Katherine felt a mixture of emotions: elation at the opportunity it might offer for her to see William, and outrage for her sister whom she knew simply wished to be comfortable in the quiet and beauty of her favourite riverside palace, not trapped in the place she associated with so much suffering and misfortune.

As her barge drew up at the Tower wharf Katherine's gaze flickered over the yeoman warders lined up to carry her boxes. Sure enough, she spotted the broad shoulders of Christopher Darch. Poker-faced, he handed her ashore but she felt her hand squeezed. She passed under the court gate of the Byward Tower and into the main complex.

Bessy was in the newly-constructed Queen's Lodgings, a pleasing timber-framed set of apartments. Lady Margaret Beaufort ushered Katherine in, her usually stern expression overlaid with anxiety. Katherine was shocked at her sister's appearance. Bessy had been through six pregnancies and, whilst bothered by passing discomforts, had never before looked ill.

She looked up wearily from her bed and held out a hand.

"Bless you for coming, Katherine. Lady Margaret and all my ladies are kind and cannot do enough or me, but to have someone of my own flesh and blood …"

"There is no chance Cecily might be allowed to be with us?"

Bessy looked at Lady Margaret, who shook her head. "None at all. My son the King is still furious with her for *dragging the royal name down into the mud of Lincolnshire.*"

"There was a time when Cecily would have agreed with him," said Katherine wryly.

Bessy shifted position, grimacing at the effort involved. Beneath her loose gown her belly was taut. She had put aside her headdress and her thick hair was pulled off her face into a braid. Her complexion was very pale and she sank back again listlessly against her cushions.

Katherine thought of the choppy waters she had just encountered. Despite the skill of the rowers it had not been a pleasant experience on a windy day when the Thames was in full winter flow. "Do you think you will cope with the trip downriver back to Richmond?"

"Maybe not. Kateryn Huntley has sent for Alice Massey, the midwife who attended me with Mary and Edmund. To tell the truth, I shall not complain if this babe puts in an early appearance. It lies so heavy and I can barely sleep."

"Pray God it is a son," said Lady Margaret. "We need another boy. In fact, I shall return to my devotions now that Lady Courtenay is come." She bestowed the nearest she could come to a smile upon them and closed the door behind her.

"Goodness," said Katherine, "is she mellowing these days?"

"She found Arthur's death as hard as anyone," replied Bessy generously, "and I think she appreciates me being pregnant again. And Henry does needs another boy. He says he cannot feel safe while we have just Harry. A new Tudor prince will help in so many ways. Why, it might even mean the release of your William." She gave a wan but affectionate smile. "The other day a woman came with two fine capons for my table, and I sent one to him, and some oranges and pomegranates that Patch the Fool brought from the fruit merchants."

"Bessy, I don't know where to begin to –"

"You have no need to thank me. I love you, and I love William, and your children. *He* cannot forbid me to stop loving my family." She paused. "Will you go to your husband? I thought maybe if I stayed here it would give you chance to slip away."

There was a quiet knock at the door and Lady Kateryn Huntley entered. *Still she wears black. Two years later and she mourns him as if it were yesterday.* She bobbed a curtsy but then came quickly to Bessy's side, more like a sister than a servant, a steaming cup in one hand and a small basket in the other.

"Warmed cider, infused with oranges, Your Grace; they say it helps the swelling in your hands and feet. And cabbage leaves. To wrap around them. We use them in Scotland." She was brisk and competent, leaning in to plump up Bessy's pillows and smooth the fur coverlet. Bessy sipped cautiously but pronounced the drink to be palatable. Pulling a comical face she stuck out her feet to allow Kateryn to swathe them with the huge leaves which she secured with thin cord. The effect was hilarious.

Kateryn looked up. "How does your husband fare, Lady Courtenay?"

"I thank you. He is well."

"I am glad. I was so sorry to hear about your son."

"As we were once sorry to hear about yours."

Bessy said quietly, "I have told her Tyrrell's story."

Kateryn sank by Bessy's bed in a billow of dark velvet, her auburn hair a vivid band at the edge of her hood. "We were together for nearly two years, and he told me everything he could remember about his childhood. Your lady mother, and the time you all spent in sanctuary. About how Tyrrell came here to the Tower, and took him and his brother in a boat down the Thames and east to Suffolk. About how they had to be two distant cousins, whose parents had died. They had to call each other by new names, Peter and Matthew – Dickon was Peter. They could never mention their past life, or think about the future. Then Dickon's brother sickened; he could not eat … and they feared for his life. One morning Dickon was told he had died, and the next thing he knew he was travelling across the sea to his aunt in Antwerp. She wept when she saw him, and told him that her brother Richard was dead in battle, and that England had a false king…" Her hand stole out to grasp Bessy's. "When he came to Scotland as a man, my cousin the King believed in him, and offered me as his bride."

"Did he speak of us, his sisters?"

"All the time. He remembered Bessy and Cecily very clearly, and described them so well that I would have known them even in a market place. Anne, you and Bridget were less distinct in his mind – names he loved, little moments of memory. He told me how Bridget was so quiet, and you so lively. He recalled how a sister ran out from sanctuary with him when they came to steal him from his mother."

"How can you bear it … now he is gone? And your child gone, too?"

"A first I could not. I wanted to die too. I thought of throwing myself in the river, or jumping from a high window, but when I confessed my thoughts the priest reminded me it was a sin, and I should never go to heaven." She was silent for a moment. "I must bear it as best I can."

Katherine saw a look pass between Bessy and Kateryn that she could not interpret. On Kateryn's side it seemed to indicate a sort of helpless guilt and sorrow, and from Bessy pity and forgiveness. She was aware, though, that all three were now caught in a complex web of secrets that must remain forever hidden from all others.

Bessy finished her drink like an obedient child and contemplated her feet. "I hope your strange Scots remedy works, Kateryn, for the King requests my presence at the Candlemas service tomorrow. Tell my sister your old Scots rhyme."

A slow smile spread across Kateryn's pretty face. "'Tis one my mother taught me when I was a bairn.

If Candlemass day be dry and fair, Then half o' winter to come and mair. If Candlemass day be wet and foul. Then half o' winter gane at Yule."

"So," said Bessy, "I don't mind at all if it's a horrible day tomorrow, for if it is Lady Kateryn promises that winter will soon be over."

* * *

In the Beauchamp Tower, Lord William Courtenay dozed by a good fire after a fine meal of roast capon. In a week or so it would be a whole year since his arrest and imprisonment and nigh on ten months since he had seen his wife. And now he knew he would never see his son Edward again. The terrible news from Havering had thrown him into despair. For days he had simply stared at the walls of his room, hearing a far-away echo of the boy's piping voice and feeling the little hand that used to slip so trustingly into his own. In the drowsy hinterland of sleep he saw his face. The weeks and months had a worrying habit of merging into something he just called "time"; he found he liked to sleep more because it was an escape from sorrow and the drab boredom of reality. He had no cause for complaint – there had been no interrogation, or maltreatment. His meals were delivered daily, his chamber kept swept and clean linen provided regularly. The Constable of the Tower, John de Vere, Earl of Oxford was rarely present and the day to day running was left to his Lieutenant Sir John Digby, who lived close by. Supper with the Digby family was one of the highlights of William's life these days, along with the loyal service of Christopher Darch and his wife. Digby spoke optimistically of William soon being allowed "the Liberty of the Tower" – the privilege of not being locked up other than within the Tower precincts. It would mean he could wander around, take better exercise, and speak to others more freely. Yet no-one, it seemed, could guess at when the King's displeasure with him might subside. Katherine's letters spoke of endless pleading and endless silence. He knew she was back in residence with her royal sister, for John Digby saw no reason to keep it secret. The Lieutenant had shared an orange with William and spoken of how much the Queen was looking forward to Katherine's arrival. A visit from Lady Courtenay to her husband need not be a secret, he said affably. The King had not forbidden it, but it must be conducted in daylight hours with a third party present. At present Lady Courtenay was attending the Queen. William was content. He had waited for months; he could wait a day or so longer. He knew she would come as soon as humanly possible.

* * *

On the first floor of the White Tower, the Chapel of St John the Evangelist received the King and Queen for the Candlemas service. Wan February light filtered through the stained glass windows, casting watery colours on solid, Romanesque pillars of pale Caen stone. The very simplicity of the place attracted Katherine as she knelt to pray where her Angevin and Plantagenet ancestors had knelt for four hundred years. She guessed it looked no different today, its austere beauty set ablaze by all the candles for the Mass to celebrate the presentation of the Christ child at the Temple, and rejoicing in the light brought into the world by the new born baby. It was forty days since Christmas; at Havering-atte-Bower the first snowdrops would be poking through the grass. Spring was perhaps not too far away.

As the priest intoned the familiar Latin words, Katherine contemplated the story of Mary and Joseph taking their boy to the temple in Jerusalem and encountering the blind Simeon:

"Nunc dimittis servum tuum, Domine, secundum verbum tuum in pace:
Quia viderunt oculi mei salutare tuum
Quod parasti ante faciem omnium populorum:
Lumen ad revelationem gentium, et gloriam plebis tuae Israel."

How beautiful, to feel so peaceful and content – to be so sure of salvation and the future of all people. Her eyes stole to the kneeling figure of Henry Tudor, his head resting on the rail of his prie-dieu, who longed so much for the birth of another son to help light the Tudor path into the future. His tall, thin frame seemed weighed down by his black furred gown. Kneeling by his side, with the support of Kateryn Huntley, Bessy appeared almost double his width, the train of her gown spread out behind her.

The Mass was long. The royal couple made their offerings at the altar and Katherine could sense Bessy's restlessness. At one point she was sure she heard her sister catch her breath and saw how she leaned heavily against Kateryn. Suddenly there was consternation in front of the altar – Bessy was crying out with pain and fear and a pool of liquid was trickling out from beneath her skirts across the cold stone slabs.

Jesu, she has started her travail! Katherine darted from her place to join the women clustering around the Queen. Bessy was white as a linen sheet; her legs had given way and she was clutching Henry Tudor as the nearest thing to prevent her falling prostrate upon the floor. His leather shoes were dark from where he was paddling in his wife's waters. Katherine locked eyes with her sister. "Stay calm, Your Grace, we will get you to your bed. The midwife will be summoned." She tried to smile brightly, "You said you hoped the babe would not tarry!"

Bessy's labour was savage. Throughout the afternoon and into the evening she thrashed and screamed upon the pallet bed they had brought hastily from some other part of the Tower. She was beyond any help that had seen her through previous births: there was no prayer, nor holy relic that reached her. A shocked Lady Margaret Beaufort retreated to the chapel to pray on her daughter-in-law's behalf. When the daylight faded they had to bring in scores of candles so the midwife could see what she was doing. Mistress Massey wore an expression of concern and disbelief. "Her Grace is like a frightened first time girl, out of her mind, I have never seen her like this. With the two babes I attended she was calm and endured it as a queen should." She greased her hands and motioned to Katherine and Kateryn to hold Bessy firmly whilst she investigated inside the Queen's body. Bessy was lost, far away in an ocean of agony. The midwife waited until yet another contraction seemed to subside, then slipped her long fingers in. A deep gasp escaped from Bessy's lips.

"The babe is likely stuck for some reason. She'll never deliver it like this. We must get her on to the birthing stool."

With Bessy slumped between them they rocked her on the stool – forward into Katherine's arms, backwards into Kateryn's, whilst Alice Massey hovered underneath, greasing and probing, massaging and stretching. Bessy alternated between sobbing, screaming and groaning. When the violent contractions came they seized her body and soul, and Katherine wondered whether any prisoner in the Tower could ever have suffered worse torture. Outside, the whole inner ward seemed to shudder with her shrieks. The wives of the yeomen warders clutched their rosaries. Their husbands looked up at the window where Henry Tudor kept vigil in his own apartments; the doors were firmly shut and only a faint light could just be distinguished behind the shutters. What was happening in the Queen's rooms was women's work.

It was nearly midnight before the child was born. Bessy lost consciousness a couple of times and the midwife was forced to burn pungent herbs under her nose, and once to slap her into wakefulness. When a live child was finally expelled from her body, it was a miracle. Katherine knelt before the little portable altar that had once belonged to Elizabeth Wydville and still travelled with Bessy from residence to residence. "Blessed Lord, why did she have to suffer so?" The candle flames danced, and the faces of the saints leered at her. Kateryn Huntley had called for more attendants and they were now lifting Bessy from where she was slumped virtually insensible on the birthing stool and carrying her to the pallet bed

The midwife looked at her sharply. "You know as well as I, my lady, that it is the fault of Eve. Her Grace has come through it. The child is alive too. We should rejoice."

Katherine bit her lip, knowing that any midwife feared being held responsible for a dead mother or a dead child. In their world of herbs and folk lore, an accusations of witchcraft was the flip side of admiration. She held the new scrap of Tudor humanity in her arms – no replacement prince but a tiny girl with a screwed-up face, who had struggled to draw her first few breaths. She was not large and it seemed extraordinary that her mother should have suffered so badly. Even more female servants were in the room now, cleaning up with hushed expressions of shock. The birthing stool was carried away to be sluiced. A young nursemaid held out her arms to receive the baby for swaddling. Bessy took no interest in the new baby but simply lay back upon the bed, eyes closed, refusing the birthing ale and turning her face away from the cradle. She was whispering something, over and over again. Katherine leaned close.

"Never! I will never lie with him again. I will never endure this again ... I have finished with him."

The baby was baptised in the Tower's other chapel, the little church of St Peter ad Vincula which had once stood outside its confines and was now the place of worship for all who worked there. Henry Tudor declared that she should be another Katherine, named for his maternal grandmother, the Valois princess of France who had married the sixth Henry and afterwards Owen Tudor. It was a short ceremony, with nothing of the pomp that had attended the christenings of the other Tudor children. The baby hardly stirred as she was undressed and presented at the font by her grandmother. As soon as possible she was wrapped up again and returned to her warm cradle in the corner of Bessy's chamber.

Katherine, like her own mother, had always recovered quickly from childbed and whilst glad of a few days' rest had then become rather bored in the weeks following confinement. On all three occasions, by the time she was churched, her young body was well on its way to its customary slimness. Those who could remember Elizabeth Wydville remarked on the similarity. With Bessy, though, each successive child had brought a slightly longer period of recovery and a thickening of her waist and hips. Now she lay in her own bed and gave no signs of wanting to move. She complained of headaches and feeling her heart pounding in her breast. At times she groaned, and asked when the baby would be born.

"Is it the childbed fever?" Kateryn Huntley had not moved from Bessy's side and was cooling her forehead and neck with endless basins of cold water.

Katherine gave a helpless shrug. "Who knows? We can only wait. She's so pale still."

"I will go to the King and his mother, and tell him she needs a physician. He will listen to me."

Katherine heard the determination in her voice, and the tinge of something else – a sort of resigned acceptance. Kateryn handed Katherine the basin, veiled her eyes and left the room. On the bed Bessy stirred a little and the shifting of the covers caused an unpleasant smell to waft out. In the far corner the bay was being rocked gently by the wet nurse, who exclaimed at the foetid air.

"Oh, my Lady! That's the same smell as my sister had, when she died of her last babe! The midwife said as how it was something rotting inside, something that should have come away but didn't!"

It was fortunate that Bessy seemed totally unaware of her deteriorating condition. Ever fastidious, she would have been deeply distressed by the betrayal of her own body. For a week, days merged into nights until both Katherine and Kateryn were exhausted. They took it in turns to snatch a few hours of sleep, refusing to allow any other of Bessy's ladies to take over. Lady Margaret returned and took it upon herself to pray continuously. *She thinks of her own experience of childbirth when she was only a child herself, nearly torn in two by this son she now worships.* The King visited, throwing protocol to the winds. However, he did not enter the room but stood on the threshold, holding a gloved hand over his mouth and nose. What Katherine could see of his face seemed emaciated: sharpened cheekbones and dark eye sockets where terror lurked. It was just ten months since Arthur had died and now his carefully constructed world threatened to crack again. He had sent for Bessy's best physician; even now Dr Aylesworth was travelling on the incoming tide from Gravesend, and should be here by daybreak. Framed in the doorway, Henry Tudor appealed to his sister-in-law, whose husband he held prisoner in a tower they could all see from the window. "What more can I do?"

Katherine stared at him. "Join your mother, and pray for her," she said shortly.

The end, when it came, in the early hours of the morning, was sudden and shocking. Bessy surfaced to ask for drink and Kateryn was supporting her whilst Katherine held a cup of weak small ale to her lips. When they laid her back upon her pillows she gave a faint cry and whispered, "Oh, I am wet…" Kateryn lifted the bedcovers and cried out in horror. A flood of blood was soaking the bleached linen sheets below Bessy's body. On her thirty seventh birthday, the Queen's life bled away in a haemorrhage that could not be staunched.

Men go into battle and women endure childbirth. Which is worse? An hour later, Katherine surveyed a scene that would have rivalled a butcher's shop in the shambles. Blood was smeared in scarlet streams across the wooden floor and piles of blood-soaked linen lay abandoned in the corners of the room. The robe of the priest who had rushed to adminster the last rites was spattered with dark flecks. A metallic tang hung in the air. Henry Tudor sat by the bed clutching Bessy's lifeless hand, dry-eyed but speechless. Appalled, he and his mother gazed upon the dead body of the woman whose lineage had given credence to the Tudors' place upon the throne. Without her, what would happen? Outside, some yeoman warder was shouting that the doctor's boat had just arrived at the wharf.

Katherine: *How to describe the loss of my beloved sister? I cannot. It was beyond words. We did what had to be done: we washed her poor body clean with rosewater, and I combed through that thick, strawberry- blonde, York hair one last time and helped to dress her in her finest gown of scarlet and ermine. When her children came from Eltham to say goodbye they found her lying as if asleep. My niece, the Queen of Scots wept bitterly, while little Mary stood with her thumb in her mouth, and trembled as I held her other hand. Prince Harry was dumbstruck, his face as red as his hair. He set his obstinate little mouth and refused to utter a word, either to bid his mother farewell or even pray for her soul. I understood his grief for I was tongue-tied too. Finally he came to my other hand and held it so fiercely I thought he might crush my fingers. The King had left us – gone alone to Richmond with orders that none might follow him. To her credit, Lady Margaret Beaufort took control of the situation, spoke firmly to the children about Bessy's assured place in Heaven, and busied herself decreeing what mourning they all should wear. I waited outside whilst the sergeant of the chandlery and the King's plumber came to embalm my sister's body and encase her in lead. The hot, sweet scents of wax and spices seeped under the door and I heard the dull thuds as they finally nailed down the lid of the holly wood coffin. Then they carried her to the chapel of St John where a thousand candles burned, day and night, for the windows had been draped with black and no chink of daylight entered. Kateryn and I kept vigil, seated before the coffin at the altar. We had no mourning gowns, for who would have thought that Bessy would die? Instead, we chose the simplest kirtles in our travelling boxes and tied threadbare kerchiefs under our chins. As if our sadness was not enough, my tiny namesake was also taken; she died quietly one night in her cradle. I wished we could have laid her in her mother's arms.*

"... and was with all funeral pomp carried through the City of London to Westminster, and there buried ..." Richard Gratfton

February 22nd 1503

All of London mourned the York princess who had become their queen and taught them to tolerate the Tudor invader, and then to love her Tudor children. Bravely, the noontime sun chased away the rain clouds and shone upon the wet streets as Bessy was taken on her last journey to the abbey at Westminster.

Whiterose shifted restlessly, her hooves muffled by the deep sawdust in the Tower courtyard. Katherine stroked her neck gently and saw how her black velvet glove left a faint indentation in the mare's thick coat and then how, gradually, the hairs sprang back into place. The yeoman warders formed a guard of honour as the coffin was brought out of the White Tower, borne carefully down the exterior staircase. At the foot, a small group of noble prisoners had been allowed to gather. Amongst them she could discern William's tall figure and curly chestnut hair. Her heart ached – there had been no time to visit and now at all costs she must maintain her composure. Resolutely, she turned her head away. He would understand, she knew.

But Katherine was not alone. Her three sisters were lined up behind her, the first time they had all been together in eleven years. Strangely, they had Margaret Beaufort to thank for this, for with her son gone to ground at Richmond she judged the mood of the moment and gave London what it wanted. Unmistakably sisters, they sat easily upon their horses with the grace and dignity of their Plantagenet birthright. That it had taken such a tragedy to allow their reunion! Katherine turned in her saddle to look at them, so identical in their mourning gowns and long trains. Why, we might be taken for that phenomenon of four girls born to the same parents on the same day! Cecily, inheritor of the eternal Wydville youthfulness, her thirty four years sitting lightly upon her; Bridget, in her nun's wimple, serene and mature at twenty three and Anne, so joyful at being summoned from Norfolk.

The chariot bearing Bessy's coffin was draped in black velvet, as were the six horses who drew it. At each corner, white banners stirred slightly in the fresh air, the metallic threads in their beautifully embroidered images of the Virgin catching the light. Katherine could not bear to look at the wooden effigy lying on the top. As they passed through the city streets it seemed the whole of London had emerged to pay their last respects. They moved slowly, every little church wishing its solemn peal to be heard; every individual district determined to present its thirty seven virgins with their hair unbound, carrying lighted candles to pay homage to Bessy's age and passing in childbed. As they passed by the Chère Reine Eleanor cross, the sisters rode four abreast behind the chariot. The crowds stood in silence, scores deep and it seemed the procession had gathered thousands – besides the nobles of the court there was every last civic dignitary and craftsmen from the guilds, merchants, bishops, abbots, priests and choirs. The rich wash of sung anthems drenched the narrow streets as they drew near the abbey.

Bridget flashed a rare and beautiful smile. For a moment she looked so extraordinarily unlike a nun that someone yelled, "Bless you, Princess Bridget!" Her brows arched like finely drawn bows.

"They are still our people!" said Anne in wonder, under her breath. "They have never forgotten us!"

"They will never forget Bessy!" muttered Cecily fiercely, "they know she was their true queen! They remember our name, and our father, and our brothers!"

As the great door opened Katherine could not help but recall the last time the four of them had followed Bessy into the abbey, at her coronation. Now they took the same steps up the same aisle, not towards the coronation chair but instead the huge black catafalque constructed before the altar, where their sister's body would lie overnight. When the coffin was placed there, Katherine finally allowed herself to look upon the effigy. It was distressingly lifelike, with a fall of wavy red-gold hair and dressed in the same robes of estate that she had worn when the children had paid their last respects. Katherine was no fool; she knew that someone must have fashioned the features directly from Bessy's dear, dead face. Bridget stared, and gasped. With a stab of pity. Katherine realised this was the first time her little sister had looked upon Bessy's face since she was a child. The cloying smell of incense clouded the air as the priests waved their silver-gilt censors. The funeral began.

There were nearly twenty four hours, and two services, to be endured. After the first one Katherine and her sisters were escorted back to the Westminster Hall for refreshments and a night of wakeful sleep in the rooms where they had grown up. The next morning, even before daylight, they were back in the vast dimness of candle-lit abbey for the final ceremonies. Tradition demanded that the women closest to the Queen should offer palls of jewel-like cloth of gold, one for each year of her life. One by one they stepped up to kiss them and lay them beside the coffin in glowing folds. Kateryn Huntley joined them, her dark eyes brimming with tears as she placed hers on the top. Then the four sisters, and Kateryn knelt in a row and held each other's hands through the final Requiem Mass, and as the officiating bishop preached his sermon. How bereft they all were, he declared loftily, to lose their virtuous queen and her princely son in so short a space of time.

Katherine was glad that women were not required to witness the actual burial. The idea of having to watch as Bessy was laid below the cold, stone slabs, in a damp, silent vault made her almost physically sick. Her heart thudded in her chest and her head swam. Somewhere near here her own little Edward mouldered in an honourable but unmarked grave. It was too much to contemplate. She knew that their souls were free but still the thought of what must happen to their physical remains disturbed her. Yet it was mid-morning before they left Bessy to the reverend ministrations of the clergy, her gentleman ushers and the other men. They made their last obeisances and turned away. Once outside, despite the welcome fresh air, the world seemed empty and pointless. A covered chariot was waiting to take them all back to the Tower, from where they would disperse.

The vehicle creaked and rattled its way back past the Eleanor Cross, back through Cheapside and Fenchurch, through Temple Bar and Mark Lane and under the portcullis of the Tower itself. In Bessy's rooms, Kateryn supervised the serving women who were quietly packing up the dead queen's bed, tapestries and linen, and the sisters said their farewells, not knowing when they might meet again. They shared out little mementoes of their beloved sister – not her jewels for they would have to be returned to the Wardrobe, but Cecily claimed her book of hours, Anne her favourite hood with its red and gold partlets, and Katherine her ivory comb and collection of music. Bridget, who had made her vow of poverty, could take nothing but her sisters' kisses. She was the first to leave, for the abbess at Dartford had requested her prompt return. They all gathered on the Tower wharf, by the great watergate, where a couple of winter seagulls were perched, bickering and squawking. The wind, which blew across from the marshes on the opposite bank, was cold upon their cheeks and hands. Bridget stepped into the plain barge they had sent for her then looked back up at them all, her face sweet and loving but already distant.

"You are forever in my prayers," she said gravely, as the vessel bobbed up and down on the rising tide, and added, "Be at peace. Our brother-in-law the King has paid for Masses, and for alms to be distributed in Bessy's name to the blind, the lepers and countless unfortunates here in the city. Her soul will not stay long in Purgatory. All the sisters at the priory will pray for her." Katherine stared at her, remembering the quiet little playmate of her childhood, now a pious young nun, certain of her role as the family's intercessor. It was clear that she was keen to return to her religious life.

"God go with you, Bridget, and thank your Mother Abbess for letting you come." Cecily put an arm around Katherine and Anne's waists and the three of them waved until Bridget's boat was a just a distant speck upon the grey-green water. Anne gave a sudden sob. "I cannot bear it! I don't want to go back to Thetford! I would much rather stay here with you both!"

"Don't be a fool, Anne. No-one is staying anywhere," replied Cecily. "I am commanded by the King to retrace my steps back to my lowborn husband, and never trouble him further. Which, quite frankly, is what I had in mind anyway. If I never clap eyes on him again it will be too soon for me. But I shall persuade my Thomas that we should take a trip into Norfolk, and come and vist you, Anne, if your highborn husband-duke will admit us. I think he will, as he likes to keep in with my Lady the King's Mother." Her blue eyes danced with the spirit Katherine had sorely missed but softened immediately into genuine compassion as she turned to her younger sister. "And you, Katherine? What are you to do now?"

Katherine tried to smile but somehow her lips refused and set themselves instead into a rueful grimace. "I will do as my husband bids me, and seek refuge with his family in Devon, for as long as his Grace the King sees fit to hold William here."

"It won't be for long," said Cecily, "for they say he ails from the quinsy, and a cough, and fevers and grows weaker by the day. Lady Margaret writes that he cannot swallow. God willing, he'll never come out of his room in Richmond where he's hiding away, pretending to mourn our sister so grievously!"

"Cecily! Guard your tongue! It is treason to –"

"And when did our family ever pay heed to that?" Cecily tossed her head like a wilful pony. "I tell you, our fortunes could yet change. The Tudor rose is not so well established that it may not wither. You both heard them in the streets yesterday – there are still men enough in England who would rejoice in the chance to bring our family back."

"Sometimes, I think you are quite mad. Do you not think William, and all the other men arrested, are in enough danger without your foolish imaginings?" As on so many occasions Katherine found the love she felt for Cecily competing with exasperation. "Oh, go back to Lincolnshire, or Northamptonshire, or wherever it is that is far enough away so I do not have to listen to your dangerous words! I'll wager you keep them quiet from Lady Margaret, your benefactress!"

"Please don't quarrel!" Anne was clutching at both their sleeves. "Bessy would not wish it. We only have each other in this world."

Moodily, Cecily pulled away and strode back into the Tower precincts. Anne looked stricken but Katherine gave a short laugh. "You know Cecily, she hates to be told when she's in the wrong. She'll come round and before you know it you'll be having her to stay, as she's planning."

"Will you be able to travel into Norfolk? I am sure my husband's family would make you welcome."

Katherine hugged her quiet, uncomplaining sister, whose sad eyes gave away the secrets of her difficult relationship with her ambitious Howard relatives. "Maybe next year. I do need to face my own in-laws, and arrange what I can for the children's futures."

"When will you have the chance to speak to William?"

"Tomorrow, after you and Cecily have gone. It's not forbidden."

"You are very brave, sister."

Katherine shrugged. "So are you. So is Cecily, in her own way. So is Kateryn Huntley, especially as she has to stay here. So was Bessy. It's how we have all survived – up until now."

* * *

William Courtenay held his young wife in his arms as if he would never let her go and they wept quiet tears together over their lost boy. He listened in silence to her honest account of the horror of Bessy's death, and the funeral. They were both acutely aware that the Queen's passing left them unprotected and impecunious. William tried to disguise his fears.

"I'm young and I'm healthy. I have yet a wife who loves me, and two beautiful, living children. What more can a man ask for? It's much better here now than when they first arrested me – why, you have seen with your own eyes how I am free to come and go, within reason. Captain Darch is a decent man; I'm really lucky that he is my warder. This time next year it will all be different – you'll see. The King will have tired of his ridiculous game, and I'll be back

368

with you and my parents in Devon. We can build a new life there, Katherine. Forget about Henry Tudor."

She reached up and smoothed his cheek where the day's stubble was just beginning to emerge, and loved him for his optimism. "But without Bessy's gifts ..."

"I have clothes enough to last a season, and I may have to swop meat for pottage, but the Darches won't see me starve. The Lieutenant is a decent man too; he knows the ways of the wheel of fortune. There could yet come a time when our star could rise. Look to the future, Katherine. Look to better times, for they will surely come. Just promise me ..." he tilted her chin so he could look deeply into her eyes. "Just promise, right wellbeloved, to be faithful, and not ..."

"Do not doubt me, "she responded fiercely.

The Traitor's Faithful Spouse

1503 -1509

1

Katherine: *Without Bessy, and as the wife of a prisoner, I was no-one. My children arrived from Havering with nothing but the clothes they stood up in, apart from the faithful Joanna and her daughter Philippa. We had to rely on William's parents sending a chariot, horses and servants from Devon to escort us into the West Country. In the meantime we lived on the charity of old friends, moving between the homes of courtiers who had loved my sister, or discreet friends of the Courtenay family – eating their food, sleeping in their beds, accepting their little gifts of money and goods. I was not proud; I thanked them all for whatever we were given. Finally, in the late spring, when the roads had improved, we set out for our new home. Leaving London was both a blessing and a curse. I longed to put distance between my children and Henry Tudor, yet every mile took me further from William, planting an ache in my heart the like of which I had ever known before.*

> **"Alack, alack, what shall I do?**
> **For care is cast unto my heart,**
> **And true love locked thereto."** poem by King Henry VIII

Colcombe Castle, East Devon Summer 1504

It was strange, thought Katherine, how quickly you could adapt to new surroundings. Even more extraordinary how a landscape could unexpectedly work its way into your heart to give you ease and comfort. Devon's vivid summer colours surprised her every morning: the rich red soil; the emerald grass and the azure sky which melted into the sea on a distant horizon. She had lived in palaces

370

and castles and in the grandeur of Warwick Lane yet this manor house of Colcombe pleased her beyond all measure. Built of mellow, pale grey stone it had an air of importance on a human scale. It lay almost hidden, like a secret jewel, in the folds of the rolling fields between the coast and the little market town of Honiton. To call it a castle was faintly ridiculous but its crenellations, moat and gatehouse allowed it. The rooms were wide and airy, with impressive fireplaces and beautiful plasterwork. Deep mullioned windows admitted sunshine from the south west, drenching the rooms in warmth and light, even on a winter's day. The whole house hummed with the activity associated with a busy estate. The kitchens, brew-house, pantries and dairy murmured with the comfortable burr of Devon voices as rich as cream.

She had wondered what reception would await her from William's parents. Would they see her Plantagenet family as the source of all their troubles – would they regret ever having married their beloved son and heir into a maelstrom of intrigue and rebellion?

The Earl himself was phlegmatic. "We do not blame you, my dear; it is the times we live in." Lady Elizabeth Courtenay was harder work. William was her only surviing child and she made it clear that she believed he would not be in the Tower were it not for his wife's treasonous relations. Her former awe of Katherine's royal connections was gone; she treated her daughter-in-law with chilly civility.

When news arrived that the Courtenay estates in Devon were under royal attainder Katherine felt entirely to blame. Henry Tudor would allow the Earl to live off the estates for his natural life, but upon his death William would not inherit. Everything would be forfeit to the crown; the revenues from the manors all over the West Country would roll into the Tudor coffers and leave Katherine's son Hal with nothing. Her little boy might be a king's grandson but he would have no lands, or castles, or income. It was meant as a lesson to anyone with a drop of Plantagenet blood.

However, Sir Edward spotted a lifeline. His side of the Courtenay family came from Boconnoc in Cornwall, and the inheritance of those estates was not mentioned in the attainder. "I believe I can make provision for Hal and Meggie from this. The Boconnoc land should yield a hundred marks a year for them. And we might squeeze out some sort of a dowry in due course, eh Meggie?" He looked down fondly to where his granddaughter sat on the floor playing with her cloth poppets.

The family sat patiently whilst Sir Edward perused the rest of the document. His face was drawn into a myriad of wrinkles and crinkles as he concentrated on the wording no doubt devised by the cleverest of Henry Tudor's new breed of administrator. "Well, there's not much we can do, except to ensure you look after me well, wife – in the hopes that I may live a long life," and added sardonically, "at least he remembers my loyalty to him at Bosworth and Exeter and does not take away our Devon lands immediately. Ah, don't look so miserable, Katherine my dear. The fortunes of this family have ever ebbed and flowed upon the whim of a king. Who knows what the future might bring?" He reached out for his grandson and made room for him on his knee. "We may yet see a bright future, eh young Hal? We just have to live through the shadows."

Lady Elizabeth's sniff conveyed her displeasure. "That's all very well, my lord, but poor William may die in that dreadful place!" She buried her face in her hands and sobbed noisily. Sir Edward looked across at Katherine with an expression of comical dismay.

"Would it not be better, wife, to attend to the next package you are sending up to London for our son, and ensure its safe despatch? What is it he has he asked for, Katherine?"

"Paper, sir, that he might write to us, and money to pay the Darches for decent food."

"The Darches! Good, honourable people! Salt of the earth! How incredible that Christopher Darch holds that position in the Tower! We must indeed be thankful that God has bestowed such good fortune upon us. We can all sleep at night knowing that Captain Darch watches over William." His heartiness was forced, she knew, but it bolstered her hopes.

Every couple of months the Courtenays sent a trusted man up to London with what they could afford; each time a travel-stained letter came home together with whatever news the man could glean. Nothing changed. No specific charge was laid against William. They heard that more men had been arrested for conspiracy and some executed whilst others went free. No doubt because money found its way into Tudor hands. Suffolk himself had been captured and was held at Namur – a thorn in Henry Tudor's side by all accounts but Philip of Burgundy was in no hurry to yield up his interesting captive.

At night Katherine lay awake in her chamber overlooking the pretty gardens, trying to remember what it had been like to sleep in her husband's arms in their own bed. She had grown used to being alone; it was as if the sensual part of her nature had simply been set aside. But sometimes she watched the covert glances between the young male and female servants or caught their sighs, and felt a melancholy steal over her. She was not a widow, but she had no husband, and knew not if she would ever have one again. When she looked up at the full moon riding in the night sky she wondered if William was seeing it too, and when the sun rose each morning she crept to her prie-dieu and sent the first of her daily prayers winging its way up the Great West Road.

Her thoughts ran upon others too. How was young Margaret faring in distant Scotland? And young Catalina, alone at Durham House on the Strand, caught between her father-in-in law's elusive parsimony and her own father's ambition? Did it ever occur to Margaret Beaufort to help young Harry cope with his angry grief? Letters came occasionally from Anne and Cecily, and she wrote back with what news she had.

The summer of 1504 was the hottest in living memory. England sweltered, week after week under a relentless blaze of heat. Streams disappeared and rivers exposed expanses of flat, muddy beds, leaving only channels of slow-moving water. At Colcombe the moat surrounding the little castle dropped daily. The north facing dairy, with its slate slabs became the most popular room in the whole castle but even so milk lasted barely a day and flies buzzed upon any meat left lying out in the kitchens. Even after dark the castle walls glowed with retained heat. Katherine wished she could cast off her garments but propriety forbade it; however, she allowed little Meggie to go barefoot in her shift like a village child. One of her pleasures was to ride out to the cool of the woods with her young son. At eight, Hal was now of an age to sit confidently upon a pony without need of a servant to lead him. He was a well-grown little boy, with his father's unruly nut-brown hair and kind hazel eyes, and his affinity and skill with horses. His ambition was to ride William's courser, Seaton, who lived in the stables and fields at Colcombe in honourable retirement from jousting duties but still much in demand as a sire for the young horses Sir Edward could sell on to buyers all over the West Country.

On a baking afternoon, mother and son trotted through the handsome little village of Colyton where curious householders bowed respectfully, thinking Katherine a very striking young woman and smiling to see the young lord waving back enthusiastically. They crossed the barely moving River Axe at the bridge and meandered for three miles through the wetlands, past Axmouth and on towards the coast at Seaton. It was breezier here, and they rode along the strand of the pebbly beach where the fishermen were hauling small boats ashore and emptying the day's catch into willow baskets. Katherine reined in Whiterose and paused to watch. The bay was vast and blue, shimmering in the heat haze, with white cliffs on one side and red on the other, just as William had once described. Small waves broke with a sigh on the shingle. Hal jumped down and dashed across to see the men, as brown as walnuts. A few shy girls, with kirtles hitched up to their knees, carried the baskets back up the beach; their feet were wrapped in thick fustian and crunched on the shingle. There was just sea, and sky, and sunshine – and air that tasted pure and wholesome. A faint tang as the women passed her, but more from the seaweed and their clothes than the glistening creatures in their creels.

They took the long route home, pausing in the shady woods where the silence of midsummer was, in itself, cooling. Light filtered down through the thick foliage. The only sound was of the horses' tails swishing and the soft movement of ferns as they pushed through along the track.

"Lady Mother?" Hal was riding directly behind her, his pony's nose virtually touching Whiterose's hindquarters. "Will my father die in the Tower?"

Katherine pulled up sharply, and the black pony bumped alongside. Hal's face was covered in a pearly sheen but whether from the heat or anxiety it was hard to tell. His bottom lip was trembling slightly. "I keep thinking of him in this heat, Mama. I heard the messenger saying about *the sweat*," he added.

It was true. They were falling like scythed hay in London. Alive at breakfast and dead by supper, the messenger had told the whole household. And the King's court stayed on the Thames, avoiding Westminster and the city at all costs, seeking out the cleaner air of Greenwich and Richmond.

She took a deep breath. They had long stopped the pretence of William being abroad. She did not want to lie to him but neither did she want to raise false hope. "Your father's fate is in God's hands, Hal. There is nothing you, or I or even your grandfather can do about it. Except pray, of course. But I know you do that."

The little boy nodded dumbly. Both horses had taken advantage of the halt to crop the grass at the side of the track. Hal stared down his pony's neck and wound his fingers into the thick, coarse mane. "But he's in the King's hands too, isn't he, Mama? He is the King's prisoner so the King can decide what to do with him?"

How much to tell a small boy? "Your father is not in a cell, Hal. He is not mistreated or accused of anything. He is just … held."

374

"Mama, I cannot remember what he looks like."

"Oh, Hal!" She reached down and laid her own hand over his. "I sometimes thought that too, about my father, for I was a tiny child when he died."

"Your father was a king, wasn't he, Mama?" She realised that he was beginning to piece together the complicated mosaic of his heritage. No doubt he listened in kitchens and stables, as she had once done.

"He was, indeed. A much loved and handsome king."

"And did *he* keep men prisoner in the Tower, and have them killed?"

She hesitated. Long ago she had always known when the adults lied to her. "That is what kings sometimes have to do, Hal, if they believe someone is their enemy. If they think someone threatens their right to the throne."

He looked puzzled. "But surely my father does not threaten the King? Grandfather is always telling us about how he fought for him, for the House of Lancaster. Why does King Henry think we are traitors? Why has he said my father cannot be the Earl of Devon, or me after him? Why is he going to take all our money and homes away from us? It's not fair!"

It was time to tell him. Here in this lovely place, in high summer while they were quite alone. "It's because of me, Hal. The King does not trust my family, and so anyone who is related to me must come under the same suspicion. Your father is held because the King uses him as an example. He's what is called a political prisoner. The King will keep him as long as it's useful to do so."

Hal hauled his pony's head up from the grass and kicked him on. Katherine understood that her son needed time to make sense of the information she had provided. She let him keep just ahead for a few minutes until they emerged from the copse on to the broader track that led back to Colcombe, then she caught up with him again. The heat of the day had dried his tears but left tell-tale little salty deposits on his cheeks. His hurt was one she understood so well – the pain of a child whose world is destroyed by the power of adults he can neither comprehend nor fight. However, he lifted his chin bravely. "Mama, we *will* be earls of Devon, my father and me. The King won't stop us. I'll find a way!"

2

December 1505

"My lady, we are approaching Richmond." Katherine pulled back the leather curtains which kept the worst of the biting cold out of the chariot and craned her neck to see the palace come into view. Huddled in a corner was young Philippa, who was to serve as Katherine's maid, and a bleary-eyed Hal. Although it was nearly noon, frost still lay like sugar on the lower lawns which stretched down to the river banks, and upon the heads and backs of the fantastic topiary creatures sculpted from the yew hedges. Swathed in furs, and with the hot stones they had given her at the last inn only just now cooling, she smiled encouragingly across at Hal.

"There's nothing to be frightened of. I am sure your royal cousins will welcome you kindly."

It would be the fourth Christmas season without William. They had expected to pass it quietly at home at Colcombe until the letter came summoning Lady Courtenay and her son to attend the court during the festivities. A short letter, written in a scribe's neat hand but signed with a flourish by Prince Harry who said how much he had missed his favourite aunt and how much he would like to see her. And she should bring his namesake cousin.

"He is now always at the King's side," Sir Edward Courtenay told her. "Henry Tudor dare not let him out of his sight. Just one boy who stands between the Tudors and God know what chaos, so they are training him to be a great chivalric king in waiting. My lord prince is adored. Henry cannot say no to him, which is why you are invited to visit. Best go, my dear. You never know; it might do some good."

This had been Bessy's special place and every corridor, every staircase seemed bereft without its queen. Henry's new court had no particular place for women, other than the few who attended upon his mother. There was no quiet chatter against a background of lute music; no little cluster of ladies with their tapestries and embroidery. Without a queen there was no need for ladies-in-waiting, maids of honour and female servants. The male members of her household had either been absorbed into the King's, or simply returned home to their estates and families. Behind closed doors the queen's former rooms were swept clean, and waiting. Whether Henry intended to marry again was anyone's guess. Rumours that he might take Arthur's widow Catalina for himself had been short-lived and the girl herself hovered in an uncertain state of on-off betrothal to Prince Harry.

Katherine and her son were conducted past Bessy's old apartments to the wing used by Margaret Beaufort when in residence. Yeoman of the guard stood smartly to attention outside the double oak doors. Hal was wide-eyed with apprehension and passed his hand yet again over his dampened wavy hair.

"The Lady Courtenay and Lord Henry Courtenay."

Well, at least we are still allowed to use our titles. The room was fairly full. Katherine felt herself raked by scores of pairs of eyes, saw palms raised to hide remarks, and noted that not one person offered even the smallest bow. Rather, they watched the Courtenays with fascinated interest, as if regarding a doomed species. Three female figures sat separately in the deep oriel window embrasure at the far end of the room; another was seated, reading, in a large armchair before the fire. Katherine scanned them, poised to respond accordingly. Lady Margaret glanced up from her book of devotions, no vestige of emotion visible on the small shield-like face framed by a snow-white wimple and draped with a black velvet hood. Her eyes flickered between mother and son. She had the air of one indisputably in charge of her own domain. And so she must be now, more than ever – the first female at court. Margaret R indeed. Katherine's obeisance was faultless. By her side Hal dropped to one knee and remained there, head bowed, the result of endless practising before his grandmother in the Great Hall at Colcombe.

"Lady Courtenay. And your son. My grandson Prince Harry bids me greet you in his name. You are in good health." It was not a courteous enquiry, more an observation. Katherine murmured her own conventional phrases. Clearly her arrival was of little interest to My Lady the King's Mother, who returned to her book. Those in the chamber were also turning back to their cards and conversation, but stepping quickly towards her from the window end was a tall woman in her mid-thirties, dressed in dark blue mourning. She had an oval face and a long, patrician nose. Her eyes were full of love. Next to her stood a short, doll-like, auburn-haired girl in her late teens, in an oddly shabby gown. And behind her, a confident girl of about ten or eleven, incredibly pretty and aware of it. Katherine recognised her cousin, Margaret Pole; the Spanish princess Catalina and Mary, her youngest niece.

"Katherine! Come and tell us your news!" She was being enfolded in her cousin's arms.

She had not seen Meg Pole since Arthur and Catalina's wedding but had of course heard that her husband had died last summer, leaving her a widow with five children. Worry lines etched the fine skin around her eyes and mouth, and across her high forehead. The Spanish princess looked equally anxious. Only young Mary seemed at ease in this room.

"Would my cousin like to see my monkey? May I take him, Grandmama?" Clearly, she was the spoiled darling of the family for even Lady Margaret's austere expression softened as her granddaughter treated them all to a disarming, dimpled, coy smile. Hal looked half-alarmed and half-enchanted at the prosepct of being swept off by this charming cousin of his own age. Lady Margaret nodded assent and they were gone, Mary seizing his arm and bundling him away. Across the palace courtyards the bells for Sext began to sound. The King's mother raised her head in the manner of an alert bird, and a small group of ladies began to gather around her, falling into line like obedient children. She attended every call to prayer, eight times in every twenty four hours. Fortunately, though, she did not seem to expect everyone to follow. As she swept out, the three younger women curtsied again and Katherine heard her cousin whisper, "Just keep your voice low."

She found herself steered into the relative privacy of the window seat where they sat on tasselled velvet cushions embroidered with the Tudor rose. She remembered how well these two knew each other from those few months at Ludlow. To be with someone from her own family was suddenly immensely comforting, especially someone who understood the agony of trying to live an everyday life when the person you loved most in the world was hidden away behind the impenetrable walls of the Tower.

"I did not know you would be here, cousin. Well, to be truthful I did not know who to expect. How are you?"

Meg Pole gave a sad smile. "Surviving. Like you, I imagine. It's not easy though, now, for His Grace has the wardship of my sons and our estates have reverted to the crown. It will be a tough few years before my eldest comes into his majority." She shrugged elegant shoulders. "So to be invited here for Christmas … well, we can at least eat and lodge for free. I don't know how much longer I can carry on at home. God knows what the future holds."

"Lady Pole es muy valiente." Catalina reached over affectionately to pat Meg's knee. "and es muy maravilloso to see her again." The blend of Spanish and English was endearing. Her voice was low-pitched and slightly rasping. How lonely she must be here in England without anyone to love her and so uncertain of her future. Catalina's hand lingered on the rich damask fabric of Katherine's best dark green gown. "Es muy linda! Very pretty!" She gestured to her own clothing apologetically. "I have no good dress. No money of my own. Until His Grace is telling me to come to live in his household I have no firewood some days. My ladies must go to bed if they are cold. And myself also."

Meg Pole frowned. "It's shocking to treat you so, Princess. He's only summoned you here to save money. What does your father say?"

"I am at His Grace's mercy. Since my mother died my father does not take much notice of my letters. But I do not want to return home to Spain. I want ..." a sudden ferocity lanced her words: "I want to be a queen here, as I was brought up to be!" The sudden raw edge of Catalina's emotions was disconcerting. Katherine covered the trembling hand that lay upon her lap and stroked it. This girl, only a few years younger than herself, promised so much and now given so little.

Their hushed conversation was attracting interest. "Look at them," said Meg softly but bitterly. "They don't know which of us is the more deserving of their curiosity – two dead husbands, one in the Tower; one executed brother for me; two lost brothers for you, Katherine. Our children's inheritance snatched away and all three of us wondering what on earth happens next. Any minute now they'll remember the name you and I were born with, Katherine."

Seated between them, Catalina held both their hands. "One day, it is different. I promise you. When Prince Harry make me his wife." Katherine couldn't help but reflect that such an occurrence was the least likely thing she could imagine, and from the tiniest, sideways, grimacing movement of Meg's mouth she guessed her Plantagenet cousin thought the same.

* * * *

Prince Harry towered above the other teenage boys who served as his companions in the schoolroom and in the tiltyard. Before long he would begin to fill out his tall, lithe, athletic frame and his boyish face would harden into masculine lines. His hair had darkened to deep copper and a shadow was visible above his upper lip. When Katherine studied him she could discern fleeting reminders of the Feigned Lad in his easy, long stride and guessed that much of his physical prowess was inherited from his Plantagenet grandfather. She searched, too, for Bessy in his features and demeanour but struggled to find more than the odd gesture of the hand or the sensual little mouth. Maybe he was a throwback to his Beaufort ancestors, the handsome sons of John of Gaunt, or the obscure Tudors from North Wales. Standing next to his father's throne in the presence chamber at Richmond, receiving Christmas gifts from courtiers, the boy dwarfed the man. Henry Tudor seemed a shrunken, pale and shifty-looking satyr alongside a young Adonis. Lady Margaret Beaufort sat to one side, with the Princess Mary. They also made a strange couple: very much the same height but one reminiscent of an old lemon and the other a velvety peach.

Katherine realised she no longer recognised many of those who surrounded the King. New faces abounded: men who had risen in the royal household by merit of their ambition; men who were even now muscling their way into favour with gifts of money. Meg had explained to her how, these days, Henry Tudor controlled loyalty through fines and bonds, the old nobility held to ransom for their good behaviour. All over the country, Henry sniffed out every opportunity to chase up every last penny he could claim due to him as King.

She had no money to give these Tudors who controlled her destiny, only the gift of two embroidered shirts. The King's glance flickered over them; if he recognised the pattern as the same Bessy had once used he gave no sign. If he had any thought at all of her husband in the Tower he gave nothing away. But her nephew Harry seemed touched, stepping forward and holding out a large hand to raise her from her knees.

"Lady Courtenay. Aunt Kaff'ryn!" He chuckled at his own joke, kissed her on the cheek and threw a friendly look over her shoulder to where Hal was bowing. "And my young cousin. It is good to have family here at Christmas, is it not, Mary?" There were few people Harry Tudor could claim as close relatives – no-one on his father's side apart from his grandmother, and out of all his mother's sisters only Katherine had living children who were his first cousins. With his brother dead, his mother dead, and his sister Margaret gone into Scotland his family was sadly reduced. He seemed eager to include his Courtenay relatives in his immediate circle.

Katherine looked into his face and wondered if she would like this young man. What must it feel like to have the weight of the Tudor dynasty riding on your shoulders, however young and broad? Nothing was certain – that much England had learned over the last seventy years. Families swept away in civil war; survivors making unholy alliances with past enemies; families desperately trying to establish new order and new histories. Henry Tudor and his mother were investing everything in these two living, golden children, Harry and Mary. Both were marked with the self-possession born of knowing just how important they were. Harry deferred still to his father but had the confidence to say his piece too. The young Princess Mary reminded Katherine of Cecily – a pretty, wilful girl who would seek to find her own subtle way of triumphing over the men who ruled her life. Even now she was looking under her lashes, assessing every male present. Katherine noted the wink offered to her by Charles Brandon, one of Harry's slightly older companions. Mary stifled a giggle.

Mercifully, the audience was short. It seemed the prince had a short attention span and was soon diverted by introductions of other invited guests and more presents. Katherine melted back into the crowd, pulling Hal with her. It was quite enough to have been recognised. She would be happy to spend the next few days simply observing and learning the protocol of this new court without a queen. The room was hot, the air heavy with the scent of musk rising from furs and velvets.

"Mama? What do we do next?"

"We wait, my son, upon the King's pleasure."

And so followed days of waiting, which fell into weeks. The Christmas and New Year celebrations were drawn out, with days of hunting, hawking, gaming and music, followed by evenings of feasting and dancing, singing and masques. Sometimes Katherine was invited; sometimes she wasn't. It was a most peculiar existence, simply waiting; eating well when the meals were public and going hungry when they were not. Philippa helped her and Meg to dress, and minded the youngest Pole children whilst they alerted each other to opportunities of food, or a chance for the older children to spend time with their royal cousins. Hal was soon under the charismatic spell of the prince, serving him like a young squire, running in and out of his rooms with a shining face and showing his mother cast-off gifts carelessly slung to him: a velvet cap the prince had never worn; a pair of finely tooled leather boots the prince found too tight and thought his young cousin might "grow into one day". Katherine said nothing. If Harry liked Hal some good might come of it.

One morning Hal attended Harry before he went out hunting. Katherine looked down from a window into the courtyard to see her son holding the bridle of the prince's horse, confident in his ability. The creature was quite beautiful, coal black with a much-brushed, sweeping mane and tail. She recognised Hal's handiwork there. When the prince and his entourage came out, laughing and joshing, she saw Harry's appraisal of his mount and how he clapped Hal on the shoulder, drawing his friends' attention to the proud boy. A few minutes later Hal came running into her room, his face pink with excitement.

"The prince says we may visit my father!"

Katherine caught his arm and pulled him close. "No, no, Hal. It is only the King who can give us that permission."

"Yes! The prince asked for us, and the King agreed. We can go today!"

She supposed it was not impossible. In this topsy-turvy world of power games, Henry Tudor might well keep her husband a prisoner yet allow their meeting.

"Tell me more," she demanded.

"I have been telling my cousin how much I missed my father. That I had not seen him for so long and feared he might forget me, and he said he understood, because he missed his mother, and that he would ask as a special favour. He told the King that his mother would surely wish it."

Oh Bessy, still your goodness flows from beyond your grave! Hal was tugging at her. "We can go now, Mama. But we must be back tomorrow."

On the river it was cold and squally. Mother and son were chilled to the bone by the time the hired boat drew up alongside the Tower wharf. Hal proudly clutched the document with the royal seal which would allow them access. He had no real memory of his father but Joanna's stories, his grandparents' discussions and his mother's careful descriptions had created a meaningful emotional bond. He longed to see him. The Lieutenant raised a quizzical eyebrow but then smiled at the eager boy. "Go on, then. Darch! Take them to your prisoner!"

Katherine wanted to cry as she saw Captain Christopher Darch emerge from the line of warders to take her son's hand. He bowed to her gravely. "All is well, my lady. But you'll find him changed." They were following the path that swept around the White Tower towards the Beauchamp.

"But he has his freedom? Within this place? He is not locked in?"

Darch's broad face was troubled. "His status has not changed, but he does not always take advantage of it. I do my best, my lady. But I'm sure seeing you, and the lad, will cheer him. Mind, he's had no warning. It will come as a shock to him."

Katherine grabbed Hal. "Then go and tell him. Allow him to compose himself."

They waited, in the shadow of the massive stone walls. Katherine could feel her stomach clenching in anxiety and Hal's euphoria seemed to have evaporated too. The sky was grey and the buildings were just a darker shade of the same colour. Her legs felt suddenly quite weak and she leaned against the wall for support. When had the family in Devon last managed to send money? She thought William would have come down the staircase to them, two at a time, in the old way, to snatch up his son and hold her to his heart. Instead, she heard the creak of the small window two floors overhead and Darch's voice.

"You can come up now, my lady."

She was glad there was nothing to frighten her son. A decent fire burned in a small brazier; the room was clean, and even had a couple of threadbare tapestries hung on the walls. The bed in the corner was piled with thick covers. A middle-aged woman was just clearing the table of a pewter plate and tankard. She bobbed a curtsey amd sidled out. Darch cleared his throat. "In these instructions," he waved the document, "it says I must remain."

It was hard to say what, exactly had changed in William Courtenay. He sat in the only chair, his hands on his knees, rocking very slightly. Katherine felt Hal's hand creep into hers and sensed his uncertainty. William was looking at them but his eyes were dull and tired. She saw strands of grey by his temples, where a small vein throbbed visibly. Two years had gone by but he seemed ten years older.

"Husband?" She kept her voice deliberately soft, as you might speak to a wary animal. "I am sorry, we did not have time to send a message. But I have brought your son. Here is Hal, so grown, William! Bow to your father, Hal." If she gave him time it might be all right. She would not approach him yet; she would talk of anything. "We have come from Richmond, where His Grace has kept Christmas. It took us four days to travel up from Devon. Your parents are well. Our daughter thrives, too. There has been little sickness on the estates this past year. And the harvest is not so bad, either, considering the heat of the summer." She searched her mind for something that might reach him. "And Seaton is in fine fettle, is he not, Hal? Tell your father."

For all her son's lack of years he had the Plantagenet emotional intelligence. He gazed at the stranger who was his father with an intuitive compassion. "Seaton misses you, my lord Father, but I tell him that you will be home one day. I go to his stable and help to brush him, and clean his feet. Grandpapa says he is doing well for such an old horse." Hal fished inside his doublet and produced a small package wrapped in linen. He held it out, and when William didn't take it simply placed it on his father's lap and unwrapped it himself. "See, Papa, I knew what you would like. I brought you a little bit of Seaton. He didn't mind. I told him it was for you."

A thick clump of black horsetail hair trailed over William's knees. He touched the strands wonderingly, then his fingers closed around them. His eyes filled with tears. Some days it was such memories that kept him going: clinging to a hope that he was not yet thirty and might still live to thunder again down the lists; the weight of the lance finely balanced; the plumed helmet of the opposition visible in the slit of his own visor; the roar of the crowds who appreciated great horsemanship and jousting skills. On other days, like today, he found his thoughts sluggish and dark. He had woken to a cold, grey winter dawn and an encroaching despair. When Darch had whispered to him of his wife and son he had thought it must be a dream. So often he dreamed of them before waking. But here was a very real little boy, looking at him with patient solemnity.

Hal had never actually seen a grown man cry before but he hid his surprise well. Looking at his father he recognised a younger version of his grandfather, whom he had grown to love. When *he* cried, his grandfather Courtenay tended to distract him with stories. Hal decided to try the same tactic. "I like the story of when you and Grandfather fought in Exeter; Grandfather shows me the scar on his arm where the arrow went in. When we went to Exeter he showed me the gate that burned, and we went to the cathedral to find the monk who had saved his life. Then we prayed and left offerings." He laid a hand upon his father's sleeve.

"Grandfather said how brave you were. And he said it's a shame the King can't seem to remember things like that."

Christopher Darch cleared his throat noisily. "For your own sake, my lady, and my lord's, the lad would do well to guard his tongue."

"Of course," said Katherine hastily. "Hal, we do not speak ill of His Grace. Ever. You know that. We are all His Grace's loyal subjects."

William suddenly laughed. A strange, wild, bitter, bark of cynical laughter. He reached out and clamped a hand around Hal's wrist. "You hear that, my boy? Your mother speaks true. We Courtenays are ever loyal and this is how we are rewarded – with imprisonment and attainder. There will be nothing for you, Hal – you know that, do you? No land, no money, no title, no home to call your own. My God, what sort of father am I that I have brought this upon my children? Who will want Meggie for a wife? What will become of my own wife when my father dies?"

Katherine flung herself in front of him on her knees. "Do not speak like that, husband. You have done nothing. If you want to blame anyone, blame me. Hal understands now who I am and why you are here. We can all bear it – until better days come. And they will. I do not know how or when but they will."

"Sometimes I think I will end my life in this place." William still held Hal to him with one hand but used the other to make a gesture of futility. He buried his face in his son's hair.

"No, Papa, you won't," said Hal earnestly. "Prince Harry likes me. And he loves Mama. He says she is his favourite aunt. And he says that when he is king he will set you free."

Katherine looked at Christopher Darch in dismay. However loyal the man was to the Courtenay family; however much of their money made its way into his pockets or however decent a human being he was, there were some things he might be duty bound to report. And mention of Henry Tudor's demise, however obliquely, was certainly bound to be one of them. What her nine-year-old son had said could be construed as treason. Darch looked distinctly uncomfortable, as if he would rather be anywhere else in London than in a small room on the second floor of the Beauchamp Tower with the political prisoner Lord William Courtenay and his family.

"Captain Darch – he's just a small boy," she pleaded. "He merely repeats what he has heard others say. He does not understand the significance of it."

"Then you had best teach him, my lady, before anyone else hears his prattle." Then he saw her consternation. "Ah, no, Jesu, my lady, you are safe enough with me! Never think that I would say anything! But what the lad has said here he might repeat. Or others could make him say it. I do not know how long I am to remain here; there's talk of new postings soon, and there's other warders who will not care a fig for your husband's family."

William looked up. "If you go, Darch, what will become of me?" he asked bleakly.

"I'll do my best, my lord, to have you assigned to a fair guard. It's good that you have money that comes in regularly. But I don't think there's anyone else you could fully trust. I know of no-one here with links to the West Country. It will take more money ... to ensure your welfare."

"Father, you are hurting me," said Hal in a small voice. William relinquished his vice-like grip and Katherine caught hold of his hands. The hands that had been placed over hers at their betrothal ceremony and again at their marriage. The hands that knew every inch of her body. Her own hands were so small in comparison but steady and warm whilst his trembled and were cold. He tried to withdraw from her grasp but she would have none of it.

"My lord husband, as you once told me, this is but the wheel of fortune. I will speak in front of Captain Darch here for I believe now he would never willingly do anything to harm us. We can endure this. Soon Hal and I will go home to Devon but I must have your promise that you will not allow yourself to be defeated by this situation. I made you a promise, remember? You have to make your vow to me too, and to Hal, and Meggie – and God knows, even to your old warhorse of a father and your shrew of a mother, and –" she smiled, "apparently Hal has promised even Seaton. Make a promise before God, William, that you will not give up."

William seemed to draw a long breath. It was almost as if he was trying to inhale the fierce courage and love emanating from his wife's kneeling form. Katherine closed her eyes and pressed her lips against his hands. But he did not seem able to speak.

It was hard to leave him. Katherine had no idea when she might be able to visit again. The next day, at first light, they were back on the river for the long journey back to Richmond. Already a keen, icy wind was whipping across the water and the boatmen were not eager; they'd been hoping for a short run upstream to Westminster perhaps, not a long row in open water. By the time they reached the palace, well after noon, it was clear that they would be unable to return to the city, for a storm was brewing.

What followed was a night of horrendous tempest. The south coast of England was assaulted by the worst rain and gales in living memory. Inside the stone-built palace Katherine, Meg Pole and their children huddled in one bed as Nature wreaked havoc on the black world outside. The rain lashed viciously at Henry Tudor's expensive glass windows and the wind gusted and screamed through every nook and cranny – down chimneys, under doors and over the domed towers. Katherine actually found herself thankful that William was in the Tower, where at least the walls had fended off the weather for the last few hundred years. There was no sleeping; rather, a tense fourteen hours of darkness until eventually the late dawn revealed the extent of the devastation. The parkland surrounding the palace was virtually a lake where the corpses of sheep floated like huge sacks.

It was two days before the wind fully died down and then a series of messengers began to arrive, all demanding audience with the King. The news was astonishing: the Archduke Philip and his wife Juana had been shipwrecked off the coast of Dorset and a quick-thinking West Country lord had ushered the exhausted Burgundian royals inland. Henry Tudor could hardly believe his luck, for Philip was the man who stood between him and the rebel Duke of Suffolk. For months the pair of them had played a cat and mouse game – Philip half-promising to hand over the Yorkist heir to whom he had given a safe haven, and Henry Tudor proferring vast sums of money to support the Hapsburg claim to the throne of Castile. The latest mud-spattered messenger to turn up at Richmond was none other than Philip's own private secretary, sent by his master to agree terms whereby the Burgundians could resume their voyage to Spain.

Henry Tudor listened whilst the Flemish secretary tangled himself in diplomatic knots. He had long learned the power of silence and wished to demonstrate this to his son. Give your enemies half a yard and they might well hang themselves and save you the trouble. He laid his lips lightly upon the tips of his folded fingers and stared down his thin, bony nose. By his side Prince Harry was experimenting with what he felt to be a manly way of standing – feet splayed well apart and his right hand held lightly upon his hip. He rather liked the effect.

"So my royal master requests that his reception in your delightful country be as brief and simple as possible. There is no need for any pomp. The Archduke would welcome the opportunity to be on his way as soon as his fleet is in order to sail again." The secretary dared a hopeful expression. Everyone knew that Philip was now effectively Henry's prisoner and would have to agree specific terms if he was ever to see Castile.

The King pursed his lips as if giving great consideration to the proposal. Philip was trapped but there was no reason why a fellow monarch should lose face; it should be easy to extract maximum benefit from the whole situation. "Please convey our greetings to the Archduke, and our every assurance that shipwrights in the south west will receive direct orders to repair his fleet." He looked into the distance, thoughtfully. "In the meantime, we will send our son of Wales to welcome him at Winchester, and we shall make preparations to receive the Archduke, and his wife, the Queen of Castile at Windsor."

The secretary's discomfiture was plain for all to see. What Henry Tudor meant was this: *the Flemish archduke will come here, where I can keep an eye on him, until such times as he agrees to hand over the Earl of Suffolk, and do anything else of use that occurs to me.* Prince Harry could barely contain his excitement – he was being sent (on his own!) to receive the man who was his chivalric hero and husband to Catalina's sister, Juana! Defeated, the secretary made his bows and retreated from his audience with the English king.

Harry looked at his father cautiously. "Winchester, sir?"

"It's the old capital of England, my son. The seat of King Arthur, for whom your brother was named. I can rely upon it to impress even an arrogant dog like Philip. You can show him the great table there, and maybe he'll get the idea that the Hapsburgs do not have the monopoly on chivalry, style and glamour. Especially not those who need a favour."

"And I am to escort him to Windsor?"

"Yes. Where we will lay on such pleasures and distractions that he will hardly notice signing the odd treaty or two. Carpe Diem, Harry. Besides which, I have a fancy to see his wife. They say she's mad. When your mother and I visited Calais he kept her well out of the way. I'm curious."

"And will you allow the Spanish princess to meet with her sister, sir?" Harry was never entirely sure what his father intended to do with Catalina. He'd been betrothed to his brother's widow but her father Ferdinand never stumped up the hundred thousand scudos dowry payments he'd promised, and Henry Tudor was fasting losing patience. Only last July he had forced Harry into a declaration that his betrothal to Catalina was at an end – something that remained a convenient secret. Yet Harry had a soft spot for his attractive sister-in-law, with her dark blue eyes and long auburn hair. He had a soft spot for most girls, as he was fast discovering. His older friends were not above bringing the odd serving wench into his rooms, late at night. So far he'd not actually done anything, only watched.

"She could be useful," admitted Henry. "She and your sister Mary can devise some form of entertainment at Windsor. It'll need a woman's touch to lighten the proceedings. I cannot ask your grandmother. She doesn't go in for merriment."

Harry hesitated. He thought about Mary's boldness and Catalina's reticence. The two did not always get on, either. Catalina had assumed an elder sister role and often felt the need to restrain Mary, resulting in slammed doors and tears of outrage. "My lord father, would you consider asking my Aunt Katherine to help?"

Henry frowned. "Lady Courtenay? Is she still here?" He did not like to be reminded of her. Harry had already pushed him to the limits in inviting her for Christmas and then asking if she and the boy could visit Courtenay in the Tower. However, the young woman had kept a low profile at court. Somewhere, too, in the back of his mind was Bessy's voice pleading for mercy for her sister and children. He thought rapidly. In the absence of a queen his court would certainly struggle to present an air of elegance; Mary was young and inexperienced and Catalina might simply assume she was in charge. He would not allow that. An older woman, like Katherine Courtenay, with wide knowledge of etiquette, music and dancing would actually be a blessing. And he quite liked the irony that it was all in aid of securing the capture of her Plantagenet cousin. And if, subsequently, Suffolk talked, it might mean the convenient end of her irritating husband in the Tower.

Katherine had hoped to be back at Colcombe by Candlemas to light a candle for Bessy beneath the beautiful new west window in St Andrew's Church in Colyton. In her mind it was also to have been a symbol of hope for William. She had imagined going there one quiet morning, with just Joanna and the two children, and kneeling in front of the altar, commending the soul of her sister to God and praying for Him to watch over her husband. Instead, she found herself unpacking her cedar travelling chest in a room in Windsor Castle. Meg Pole and her children had set off that morning back to the Midlands. The two cousins had clung tearfully to one another and Meg had whispered treason in her ear.

"Pray for his death, Katherine. It's the only way for you and me and our children. A new rose grafted on the stem of the old."

The King commanded her to assist the royal princesses in welcoming the Archduke Philip. It was such a bizarre order. But looking about her she realised that there was, indeed, no-one else with an inkling of what to do. No great duchesses at court to step into the breach. She sent word to the Courtenays in Devon of her delayed return and once again Sir Edward reminded her that it might do some good. Hal, of course, was delighted; it meant more time in the aura of his princely cousin.

She sat down with Catalina and her niece Mary, to discuss ideas. Both were in a state of high excitement, for different reasons. Catalina yearned to see her sister again; it was ten years since Juana had left her family in Spain to marry Philip. Mary was clearly delighted at the prospect of showing off before her first international audience. Catalina was lost in her memories of childhood. "Juana es muy bella! So beautiful! I cried so much when she left us."

Eleven-year-old Mary regarded her sister-in-law sceptically. "I have heard she is *muy loca!* So mad."

"No es loca, mi hermana!" Catalina slipped quickly back into Spanish when emotional. She appealed to Katherine. "Mary must not say such things! It is cruel... and untrue!"

Katherine realised she had her work cut out. Catalina believed that her nine years' seniority and learning gave her a natural precedence over Mary. Mary, however, revelled in her status as beloved daughter of the King and England's true born princess. Seeing the two side by side it was actually hard to take in the age difference: Mary was tall, confident and poised, with a well-developed young figure. Away from her grandmother's eagle eye she took every opportunity to be noticed. Catalina was tiny, anxious and often ill; her thinness betrayed the way she battled with food. The pair of them together took careful handling. Katherine decided to play to both their strengths.

"Highness, Catalina; could you make a list of dances we could perform? Perhaps something Spanish too? If your sister is well enough to travel I am sure she would be cheered by seeing something that reminds her of home. Your Grace, Mary; what lute pieces does your father enjoy best? What have you been learning on the clavichord that would impress the Burgundians? And what shall we all wear? His Grace the King says we may send to the Wardrobe for whatever we need." Her heart felt a little stab; the idea of dressing up in finery while her husband probably still made do with the clothes Bessy had sent to him three years ago felt like a betrayal.

Peace reigned for a few minutes whilst the two girls made their lists. Katherine rose and went to the window. The room faced south, out over the great forest. She liked Windsor; it lacked the modern finesse of Richmond and the charm of Eltham but it had its own comfortable solidity. The royal apartments were relatively new and Henry Tudor had given orders that they should be decorated to impress the shipwrecked Burgundians. No doubt even now the servants were frantically polishing the gold and silver gilt plate, and pinning up the best tapestries. She had seen great beds being positioned in every main room and noted the costly drapery. Clearly, no expense was being spared. The King was out to dazzle his foreign guests with every length of cloth of gold he could lay his hands on. It was a relief to let her eyes rest awhile on the muted browns, greys and occasional green of the forest.

"Aunt, is it true that you have met the Archduke?" Mary's voice broke her reverie.

"Yes. I went with your parents to Calais. It was very interesting."

"He is as handsome as my sister is beautiful, Lady Huntley says," said Catalina. "There is no couple to match them in the whole of Europe."

Katherine felt a sudden surge of joy. "Kateryn Huntley? You know her, Highness?"

"She is one of my ladies-in-waiting. *Por que?* Do you know her? Arthur told me she was some kind of Scottish princess. A widow, like me. She does not speak about her husband. When *La Reina* died she joined my household. I like her very much. She is quiet and thoughtful."

"I ... knew her, Highness. I wondered what had become of her. She was with me in Calais, when we met your brother-in-law."

Mary gave a sly giggle. "My father likes her too! He plays cards with her! Now that Catalina's household has to live with us he sees her quite often. Is she really a princess, aunt? He might marry her if she is. Though I think he wants to marry the Archduke's sister now." She gave a sudden irrepressible shout of laughter. "But she was once marrried to your brother, Catalina! And I'm supposed to marry the Archduke's son! So your sister will be my mother-in-law. Ugh! I hope she is not as mad as they say. Does it run in your family, Catalina?"

The Spanish princess turned pale with fury. With a savage turn of strength from one so slight she seized the edge of the table and upturned it into Mary's lap. Ink spilled out of the pot into the English princess's lap. Shocked, Mary stared at her. A torrent of fast, incomprehensible Spanish tumbled from Catalina, accompanied by dangerous jabbings of her forefingers. Mary stood up and picked up the tipped-over pot – then aimed it and threw the rest of the ink at Catalina.

"Stop it! Stop it, both of you! What a way to behave!"

"She is jealous of me, "said Mary calmly, "because I will be an empress and she will probably soon be sent back to Spain and married off to some second or third son in Portugal, or somewhere equally dreary. She's also jealous because I am younger and prettier."

Katherine played the only card at her disposal. "That's as maybe, Mary. But in the meantime your father will not be pleased if I tell him what has passed between the two of you. Neither will My Lady the King's Mother." To her satisfaction she saw how both girls reacted – exchanging apprehensive glances. She realised how important it would be to foster some form of solidarity between them.

"Mary, no royal girl knows what her destiny is, until it's thrust upon her. Look at your mother and me, and all my sisters. At your age your mother thought to be queen of France. I was meant to be queen of Spain – in my cradle I was promised to Catalina's brother. It all came to nothing. Do not be envious of each other, I beg of you. There may come a day when you need each other. God alone knows what the future will hold for both of you. Neither of you has a mother to advise you, and you may think me rather young to try and step into that role, but I have already experienced great reversals of fortune – and I have learned enough to know that women should support each other, not dwell on pointless jealousies."

Mary looked abashed at her aunt's rebuke and Catalina lowered her eyes. The Spanish princess understood the truth of Katherine's words. She had been raised to be queen of England yet Arthur's death had dashed that reality away; she now laid all her tenuous hopes upon a boy not yet fifteen. As for her sister, Juana – she had left Spain thinking she would be beloved by the most handsome prince in Europe and instead she was trapped in a loveless union with a vain philanderer, and the intensity of her emotional suffering caused her husband to call her mad. What Mary had said touched a raw nerve, for Catalina knew that she, too, felt slights deeply and passionately. Was that madness?

* * *

When Philip le Bel arrived at Windsor Castle he was all too aware of the delicacy of his position. The English king was making a fine charade of friendship but behind all the ostentatious welcomes, invitations and acknowledgements was a powerful political agenda. Philip managed to maintain his equilibrium as Henry Tudor conducted him through a series of magnificent chambers, and plied him with fine wines and food but he was damned if the English were going to make a performing ape out of him. Deliberately, he had dressed in black, and deliberately he had left his wife Juana far behind on the coast. Nevertheless, the English court pressed ahead with their ridiculous entertainments. Philip found himself led by his host into a private chamber where the floor was cleared for dancing. Worse still, he was formally greeted by his wife's sister, Catalina, who looked disturbingly like Juana with her fair complexion, blue eyes and auburn hair.

Philip scowled at her. Catalina looked at him wonderingly, completely thrown by such grumpy demeanour. He refused to sit. He sighed with obvious disdain and boredom.

"Will my brother-in-law, the King of Castile, dance?" Catalina was fast losing confidence. She had expected to see her sister but no-one would explain her absence; she had expected a courtly prince but this rude man seemed utterly disinterested in their relationship. Katherine Courtenay came to her rescue. She curtsied low before the Burgundian archduke.

"There are, of course, other entertainments prepared for Your Highness. Please say what would please you."

Philip looked at her, a flicker of interest crossed his face. Who was this? Ah, he remembered, the late queen's sister – the one whose husband the English king suspected of liaising with Suffolk. And yet she was here – part of the court! The ways of the English never ceased to astonish him. However, he could not recall her name, only the way she had put him in his place six years ago at Calais. Well, he could return the compliment now.

"Ah, the traitor's faithful spouse," he said as he bowed over her hand.

"Better to be a faithful spouse than an unfaithful one," breathed Katherine in rapid French, treating him to her widest smile. He could not be sure he had heard her aright. Already she was presenting the English king's daughter, the girl loosely betrothed to his infant son, Don Carlos. Philip sighed. He could not afford to offend Henry Tudor or he might never reach his goal of Castile. With bad grace he allowed himself to be seated whilst Mary played her lute. Grudgingly, he noted that child was a gifted musician and beautiful too. It was easy to see the woman she would become in a few short years. Ever the connoisseur, Philip found himself thawing a little. He would not be made to dance but he would listen to the music.

Catalina was mortified. First red with embarrassment and then pale with humiliation, she stared at the floor while Mary played. "Princess, there are worse things," whispered Katherine at her elbow. "The man is despicable. I pity your poor sister. Hold your head up and smile. It is what we women have to do. Hold fast to your dignity and never let them see your fear."

3

Katherine: *At the time I was unaware of how Henry Tudor was fast engineering further misery for my family. He detained the Archduke in England until my cousin Edmund de la Pole, Duke of Suffolk, was arrested. When Philip was finally permitted to sail from Cornwall for his wife's kingdom of Castile, my cousin was already in the Tower. I have no doubt he was tortured there. I had no love for Edmund but my heart bled for his wife and daughter. By then Hal and I had returned to Devon and our lives continued quietly at Colcombe. My parents-in-law often left me to my own devices, for Sir Edward was required to spend time at Tiverton, the hub of the Courtenay estates. Wryly, he reasoned that even if all was to go to the Crown upon his death, it could go in good order. I heard little from court – an occasional letter from Catalina or Mary, usually complaining about each other. But both expressed their shock that the Archduke Philip had died suddenly only months after his visit to Windsor – Mary told me with great glee that Catalina's mad sister touted her husband's corpse around Europe. William's letters became less frequent and I fretted terribly, especially in the heat of the summer months and the cold of the winter. Part of me sympathised with the love-crazed young Queen of Castile.*

"Cecily, not so fortunate as fair…" Edward Hall, Chronicler

September 1507: Colcombe Castle, Devon

There were times when Katherine felt that having an imprisoned husband must be one of the worst quirks of fate that life could bestow. Two extremes existed: moments when she could think of nothing else but him, obsessed with imagining the tedium and loneliness of his existence – and moments when, absorbed in some activity, he drifted from her consciousness. Both caused her equal agony.

To forget him, even for a few minutes, was surely a terrible betrayal, yet she needed those snatched minutes of refreshment to sustain her. When she walked in the garden, shading her eyes against the strong sunshine and reading yet again the precious pages of his last letter she found herself praying that he, too, was outside on this lovely morning, able to see the blue sky. Perhaps even now he was on the ramparts, glimpsing the fast-flowing Thames, or in the Lieutenant Governor's garden, breathing in the fragrance of late roses. It was three months since she had heard from him. *At least I have things to tell him,* she thought; *he must struggle to know what to put on the page.* This particular letter was stilted but at least included a few lines for Hal and some words for Meggie.

She had just settled her children at their morning lessons in the schoolroom. A tutor from Axminster had been engaged to instruct them. He was somewhat surprised at Katherine's insistence that Meggie should be taught alongside her brother but at six years old she was bright and eager, in full command of the letters on her hornbook. Lady Elizabeth Courtenay was dubious; what need would her granddaughter have of Latin and French? The best the child could hope for now was marriage into some respectable Devon family of close connection, who might overlook her lack of fortune. Katherine remained firm. Meggie, she pointed out, was also the grandchild of a king. Reference to the Plantagenet name caused the Countess to wrinkle her nose in distaste. To appease her, Katherine acknowledged the importance of learning how to manage a household herself; at Colcombe the staff expected their lady to understand and direct all the daily tasks that in Henry Tudor's palaces she had taken for granted. So she had set herself to learning about the Colcombe estate.

Her natural, pleasant authority meant everyone looked to her for supervision. The steward came to her with his account books, and the cook with her recipes. When anyone was ill they expected her to know what herbs should be prepared and administered. They sought her advice on everything, from the raising of poultry to the buying of wine from the merchants at Topsham. It was very different to life at Warwick Lane, where Katherine had had little cause to involve herself in the running of the household. There had been riches; here were economies to be made. She began to see that Lady Elizabeth had a point. If she had been born into anything but the royal family she too would have been taught how to manage a household. She vaguely remembered her mother Elizabeth Wydville speaking of how she had been raised to handle the everyday maintenance of an estate for her first husband.

There was no society to be had at Colcombe, just a daily, weekly, monthly and seasonal routine, dictated by the Church and the land. The holy days and festivals came and went. She began to take an interest in the tenant farmers and listened attentively whilst they spoke of growing crops and the husbandry of farm animals. She learned about what price their surplus corn and barley might make at market in Honiton. Above all she kept her eye on the household expenditure and felt gratified that adding figures came as easily to her as reading the pricklines in music. Always, in the back of her mind, was the hope that by some miracle the attainder on the estates would be reversed.

Regularly, she had the great leather bound volumes brought before her and calculated the recent expenditure. Noting and approving the amounts, she set her initials in the broad margin. The harvest promised to be good; the crops would sustain the household comfortably throughout the winter ahead. An abundant hay crop would feed the cattle. There would be enough beeswax for all their fine candles, and in any case they could easily use rush lights. Katherine tried hard not to be lulled into a false sense of security for all hung upon the slender thread of Sir Edward Courtenay's life. Thankfully, though, it was a far cry from her cousin Meg Pole's situation: she had been forced off her estates and reduced to pleading with distant relations and the Church to put a roof over hers and her children's heads. Katherine had heard she was now living at Syon Abbey with her youngest children whilst Henry Tudor pocketed all the revenues from her eldest son's wardship. Her mind ran upon what could be sent up to London to supplement William's existence: good woollen clothes and money for everyday necessities.

A quiet cough sounded behind her. She turned to see the Colcombe steward, Robert Anning, a man about five years older than herself. William thought highly of Rob; despite their differences in birth they had shared many a childhood escapade together and Rob had fought at Exeter. Katherine liked his kindly wife, Christian, who helped in the house, and his ten-year-old twins provided company for Hal and Meggie.

"My lady, there is a man arrived in the last hour. He's ridden hard, he says, from Hatfield, and would speak with you. He says his name is Thomas Kyme."

"Jesu! My sister Cecily's husband! Where is he, Rob?" She was already folding the letter and smoothing down her skirts.

"Waiting in the summer parlour, my lady."

The little castle was cool and still inside. Katherine made her way quickly to her favourite room, where the September sunshine still spilled through the diamond-paned windows and made little lozenges of light dance on the floor. Somewhere in the distance a dog was barking. A thickset man in his forties was leaning against the fine stone surround of the fireplace, resting his head against his forearm. His hair was still wet from the water he must have splashed upon his face to sluice off the worst of the dust of the road. Several days' stubble darkened his jawline.

"Sir? I am Katherine Courtenay. Be welcome."

He raised his head and regarded her with soulful eyes, rather like a faithful dog, she thought, who has been whipped unfairly. He wore black, from head to toe and his garments were splashed with mud. In an instant she understood what he had to tell her.

"Oh! When?" she whispered.

"A month ago, my lady. In childbed." He caught his breath. "We had not thought to be so blessed. Ah, Cecily!" His face suddenly collapsed in an agony of emotion. Katherine stood quietly, fighting back tears. It did not take much to recognise devotion.

"Come, sir; sit down and tell me everything." So this was the man her sister had married for love, defying Henry Tudor's authority. He could easily have been taken for a servant, his dress was so plain.

He sat gratefully, heavily, elbows on his knees and his head in his hands. For a few moments there was silence, then he cleared his throat noisily. "I beg your pardon, my lady. Bringing you such sad news." His voice had a northern twang which gave him a sort of solidity and homeliness.

"Sir, you are not a mere messenger. You were her *husband!* It is I who should be comforting and thanking you! God bless you for coming in person at such a time!"

"She gave up everything for me," he said quietly. "God knows, I never thought to marry with a princess. I did not even know she *was* a princess at first."

"Forgive me, sir, I know little of your story. The last time I saw Cecily was when my sister the Queen died, and there was hardly any time to talk ... and I was so caught up in my own problems ..."

"I know about that, my lady; I am sorry for your troubles."

"My husband lives, sir. We are never without hope. But tell me of you and Cecily."

A tired smile broke across his sad features. "We met in Lincolnshire, where her husband's family had manors, and after his death my uncle, William Kyme, was helping her to sort out details of the estate. I fell in love with her. It was as simple as that. My first wife had died, and Cecily came into my life like a rainbow. We did not care about anybody or anything. I knew she was high-born, but they had to tell me who *exactly* she was. By then it was too late. It was hard on her, loving me. She had to fight to keep anything. But she said it was worth it. And we were happy, my lady. Marriage is not often about happiness, is it?"

"Indeed, no," said Katherine softly, "we have been lucky, you and I, sir."

"She longed for another babe, but thought her child-bearing days were over. She was so well, no sickness, or other signs – and she kept meaning to write to you, my lady."

"I kept meaning to write to her."

"Her labour came upon her suddenly. The babe was small but she lost too much blood."

Katherine nodded mutely, vivid pictures of Bessy's last hours flooding into her brain. So many risks that women ran when confined. Bleeding. Fever. Babes too big to bear. Babes too small to live. Death for one, or the other, or both.

"But before she slipped away she pleaded with me to come to you, and give you a message." Despite his bulk and years, Thomas Kyme looked like a small boy searching his mind to remember an important lesson. "Aye. I am to tell you that *white roses will always bloom in men's hearts.* And that she loved you."

Despite her sorrow, Katherine could appreciate the humour. So Cecily, as her elder sister, had been determined to have the last word on the subject which had ever caused sharp words between them. Rebellious Cecily! If she had been born a man she would surely have raised her own army to fight against Henry Tudor and reclaim her family's birthright. A thought struck her. "The baby?"

He shook his head. "There was just time to baptise the little mite. The King's mother paid for the funeral; we laid them to rest with the friars at the priory at King's Langley. They tell me there's an old royal palace hard by, so maybe my Cecily can sleep easy there."

The idea of Cecily being dead was hard to grasp. To think of Cecily was to conjure up images of everything that was vital and passionate, like a stream in full spate. To have to light candles for her soul would be hard indeed. "I pray her passage to heaven is swift, sir, for my sister Bessy surely waits there to greet her, and my parents, and my sister Mary whom I never knew. And her own girls. And my sweet, murdered brothers. As you see, sir, she will not be alone with such a family."

Thomas Kyme regarded her solemnly. "That's what gave her comfort, though I would have given my own life to keep her. I have sent messages to your other sisters. Lady Margaret paid for that too."

This was the one part of Cecily's story that Katherine still found somewhat inexplicable. Margaret Beaufort was her son's champion, and the idea of her taking Cecily's side in the face of the King's displeasure was mystifying. Kyme registered her disbelief. "You're right, my lady, she's an old harridan in many ways, a plotter and a schemer."

"No worse a charge than my sisters laid upon our own mother!"

"But she had no daughter of her own, and Cecily was her god-daughter, and I think she just *liked her.* There was always a room for us in her houses – she charged us our bed and board, mind but we were never turned away. She made money out of Cecily's dower lands, but she helped her to keep an income too. But everything will revert to the Welles family now."

"And what will you do?"

"Return to my family in Lincolnshire. Oh, I own nothing myself but I have cousins who will not see me starve." He gave her a long, level look. "Like you, I will await better times, my lady."

Katherine was always glad that she had met Thomas Kyme. To know that proud Cecily had found happiness with an esquire from the Fenlands, and in doing so gained the support of England's most powerful woman, was a strange but welcome thread in the tapestry of her life.

4

Autumn 1508 The Tower of London

Christopher Darch pushed his tankard of small ale away with a heavy heart. Without comment, his wife, Avis, cleared away his untouched plate of oatcakes and covered it with a cloth. She sat down opposite him and laid her hand over his. Five years now, her husband had had the wardship of Lord William Courtenay; for five years she had laundered his lordship's linen, emptied his slops, baked him pies and sometimes taken him a bunch of gillyflowers to brighten his room. She would greet the messengers from Devon at the main gatehouse, take whatever gifts they had bought and pass on any money to her husband. Christopher she knew to be a moral man – rare among the yeoman warders in the King's service. Occasionally a few extra Courtenay silver shillings came their way but mostly Christopher simply took what he considered to be a fair wage. He would not make money out of a man's misfortune, he said, for who knew when he himself might need aid.

"You knew it would end somehow," she said quietly.

His eyebrows drew together in a fierce frown. "I did not think they would send him to moulder away in some French prison. I imagined that given time they would release him, like some of the others."

"It's better than the scaffold, surely?"

"Is it? I'm not sure I would want to be in some damp cell for the next five years, knowing I'd probably never see England again."

"It has to be. He still has a chance."

Darch snorted with derision. "To sit amongst the rats, hoping the King dies first? His little lad spoke true. But the odds are against him."

"I have grown fond of him." It was true. He might be the son of an earl but he always addressed her politely as Mistress Darch. Of course at first he'd been like an outraged boy confined by his elders but then he'd quietened and become more accepting. Sadly, of late he'd seemed deeply melancholy. His family were far away and visits had dwindled. She could see the sense of that, though – better to send money to him than waste it on travelling. Christopher tried to explain to her the background of the case – something about Lord Courtenay plotting with the Earl of Suffolk against the King but it all seemed a bit far-fetched. Suffolk was held in some other corner of the Tower; Christopher said he'd been racked to try and make him name names but Courtenay's was not one of them.

"So does he know?"

"No. I must go to him now." The great bunch of keys at his waist clunked heavily against the table as he stood up. "Say a prayer for him, wife. Give me half an hour, then follow me with needle and thread. After he had gone Avis latched the door carefully and took out her rosary.

Darch strode across the inner ward to the Beauchamp Tower and ascended the narrow staircase as he had done thousands of times. He found Lord Courtenay as he often did, reading letters. "Ha! Darch! Come in! Listen, my wife writes that she has mastered the art of brewing – or at least she can recognise decent barley now when she sees it!"

Rereading the letters had lifted his spirits; William liked to think of Katherine busy at Colcombe. He could lie for hours picturing every nook and cranny of the little castle; in his imagination he walked through its rooms, wandered across the courtyard to the stables, mounted Seaton and rode for miles. Sometimes he was a boy again, in the company of his friend the steward's son, Rob Anning, climbing trees and swimming in the broad River Axe.

"You look glum, Darch. Has the good Mistress Darch been scolding you?"

"My lord, I'm afraid I have bad news."

"Jesu, my wife? My children?"

"No, sir, but brace yourself. This day you are to be taken from here under escort to Dover, and thence to Calais."

William was bewildered. "Calais? Why should I go to Calais?"

"To the castle, my lord. Where you will be imprisoned, together with Sir Thomas Grey."

It was best, thought Darch, to give it to him straight. If he had learned anything about this gentleman it was his appreciation of honesty. "I regret, sir, that this is the end of our acquaintance."

There was silence as William took it in. A great weight seemed to press upon his chest; a band tightened around his head as if someone was trying to force too small a helmet upon him. His mouth worked as he fought to keep his emotions under control. Thomas Grey – surely he was the son of Katherine's half brother? Yes, and another drinking friend of Edmund de la Pole – one of the group who had regularly dined and roistered with Suffolk. God, but Henry Tudor was wily! Waiting and waiting to round up every one of Suffolk's known associates. To Calais, to the cells in the great castle there – a conveniently far-flung outpost of Henry Tudor's domains where embarrassing prisoners could be forgotten and, presumably, die without fuss. You had to hand it to him. A master-stroke of expediency. So, no public execution – just spirited away across the Channel. Rather like being dropped down an "oubliette".

"It will be ... different to here?"

Darch's expression was grave and pained. "I fear so, my lord."

"The cells are underground there. I've seen them. They will chain me. I will be a proper prisoner. Oh, Jesu, my poor family." He began to scrabble furiously for clean paper and ink. "I must write to her... tell her." Then he realised he was weeping, like a child. When had he last wept? When his tutor had beaten him with a birch for failing to recite his lesson? No, when he had held his first-born son in his arms. No, when the boy had died. No, when Katherine had come and they had shed tears together.

Darch was moving round the room, gathering up William's thickest cloak and the strong box that held his money. The key was on a chain round his neck, under his shirt. "My wife will sew your money into your cloak, sir. If you have some silver things will go better for you." Wordlessly, William fished around his neck and handed over the key just as Avis Darch slipped around the door. Her homely face was creased with pity.

William pulled himself together. "As always, Mistress Darch, you have my welfare at heart." She took a few steps towards him, halted as if uncertain then held out her arms.

"My poor young lord. Forgive us, we are unable to do more."

William allowed himself to be drawn into her warm, motherly embrace. Birth and rank were forgotten and he drew comfort from the scent of lavender that clung to her plain gown. He had been fortunate beyond measure to encounter these two good souls in so unhappy a place. Formally, he bowed and kissed her hand as if she were a great lady. She blushed but then laid the same hand on his

403

head in a mother's traditional blessing. "God go with you, sir. He will guard you, of that I am certain."

* * *

My second crossing to Calais, thought William wryly, hunkering down against the bulwark of the galley. The swell underneath was causing an alarming lurching of his empty stomach. Tom Grey leaned against him, groaning. They were shackled together, had been so since leaving London and would be so until they reached the castle at Guisnes. It was late October, cold and wet. As they came into port the flat, featureless character of the marshy landscape made William feel sad; it was a far cry from the red cliffs, rolling hills and valleys of East Devon.

They were loaded into a cart and conveyed across the town, over the moat and under the portcullis of the brooding fortress that guarded the last frontier of English rule in France. Much as William had suspected, they were to be held in the prison cells now – no more mention of being "political prisoners"; no more named guards – and certainly no liberty to stroll in the castle bailey. Tom Grey shivered and looked up at the dismal sky whose colour matched his name. They spoke in low voices as the cart creaked to a halt.

"It's a cruel thing, to send us here, Will. We'll be forgotten, like something swept under the rushes."

"That's what he hopes. He's sent us here to die conveniently far from home."

"You think he'll have us poisoned, or executed?"

"If we persist in living, yes. But he'll hope that gaol fever will carry us off first, no doubt, to save him the trouble."

"Can your family send anyone here?"

"Can yours?"

"My Lord Courtenay! My Lord of Dorset!" A tall, dark haired man in his mid-thirties stood to attention as they clambered awkwardly from the cart, the chain between their legs clanking. "I am Richard Carew, His Grace's governor in Calais. I'm sorry you have to come here in such circumstances." William thought he detected a glimmer of sympathy in his direct gaze but it was quickly hidden. "Take these men down." Two soldiers came forward to seize them but William straightened up.

"There's no need for that. Lord Dorset and I are honourable men. If you would be so good as to release us from this…" he gestured to their legs" we …will go where we must."

Carew gave a quick nod and the irons were removed. William resisted the temptation to rub his sore ankle. "Carew? Of Devon? "

"Of Beddington, Surrey. But I have cousins in the West Country."

"I fought with Sir Edmund Carew at Exeter."

Richard Carew's eyebrows raised slightly. "Indeed? A connection then, but remote, I fear."

"It was worth pointing it out," responded William dryly. The cloak wrapped firmly around his body betrayed a satisfying heaviness in the hem where his silver lay secretly. It was a wonder nobody had thought to check it, or take it from him. Thankful for small mercies he took in a last deep breath of clean air before they were herded down a stone staircase into the foetid bowels of the castle.

Colcombe February 1509
"Whereto should I express
My inward heaviness
No mirth can make me fain
Till that we meet again." poem by King Henry VIII

Meggie Courtenay was nearly eight years old and a fair copy of her mother, with the same unusual combination of dark eyes and blonde hair. She knew she was clever because she had almost caught up with Hal's lessons, and Hal was nearly three years older. It wasn't that he lacked intelligence, just that he hated to be in the schoolroom with their kindly old tutor when he could be riding, or swimming, or fishing with Adam Anning, the steward's son. And they made it quite clear to Meggie that her company was not required. Not that Joanna or Phillipa would have let her, anyway, for they were forever reminding her that she was a lady and should behave like one. Often though, even when it was cold outside, she wished she could follow the boys down to the river to escape the terrible sadness that lay upon Colcombe.

Everything had changed of late. Servants moved on tiptoe, placing pewter plates on the table with delicate care. The usual singing in the kitchens was hushed and even the horses in the stables seemed to know something was wrong.

Ever since her lord grandfather Edward's visit two months ago, Mama had cried so much. She kept trying to stop but the tears would burst out afresh. At dinner she did her best to maintain her composure but sometimes in vain. Hal cried too – great noisy sobs, of which he was ashamed yet unable to quell. He'd rushed off to the stables to bawl into old Seaton's mane, pushing her out of the way as he fled from the Great Hall.

It was all about her father, she'd gathered that much. Meggie was deeply jealous that Hal had visited him once, for she had no recollection of him at all. He was just a name: *your lord father* – a ghost father who was not dead. Mama showed her letters with bits addressed to *my beloved daughter Margaret* – sentences exhorting her to be dutiful, and pious, and obedient. She was jealous too, of Adam's twin sister, Damaris Anning, who had a father who lifted her up and swung her round, and planted kisses on her head. Meggie sighed. Ever since she had been aware of anything she had known that her father was a prisoner in London; it still did not make much sense because everyone said he had done nothing. Damaris had whispered a bit more, for she was twelve years old and heard her parents talking. Apparently it was the King who kept Meggie's father in the Tower, and nobody could release him except the King. Meggie had never seen the King but he sounded horrible. And now he had sent her father far away to France, to a prison in a town that belonged to England, but was definitely on the other side of the sea that formed the edge of Devon. That water stretched as far as the eye could see, and Meggie was fearful of where her lord father might be now.

"Will we ever be happy again?" she asked Philippa, as they sat in the winter parlour, sewing. At least, Mistress Anning and Philippa were hemming bed sheets, Damaris reluctantly learning and Meggie kept occupied with simple embroidery. The needle was large and tricky for small fingers to push through the cloth.

"I know it's hard, and with your lady grandmother having passed away, too..." Philippa was twenty, good-natured and patient, trained by her mother Joanna to be a trustworthy and discreet servant in the Courtenay family.

"Hal says Grandfather wants us to go and live with him at Tiverton, now. Is that true?"

"It would make sense, my sweet, for he and your lady mother could be of much support to each other."

"Do you think my father will ever come home?" It was said in a small, frightened voice. Philippa looked at the child sympathetically. "It will be as God decides, Lady Meggie."

Every evening the whole household came together for prayers and after the Latin the chaplain included the English words Meggie had come to know by heart: prayers for the health and welfare of Lord William Courtenay, followed by prayers for their dread and sovereign lord, King Henry VII. Hal and Meggie noticed how their mother set her chin at the latter and they were not always sure that she said "Amen" even if her lips formed the words, but to be honest the enthusiasm of the whole Colcombe household seemed lacking at that point.

News from London was much sought-after. And it appeared that Rob Anning was particularly good at keeping his ears open, whether in the inns of Honiton, or upon the quaysides of Beer, Axmouth or Topsham, Honiton stood fair and square upon the Great West Road, and travellers to and from London often broke their journey there, or at the abbey at Dunkeswell. And on the coast the men from fishing fleets and the merchants gossiped as eagerly as washerwomen.

"Father says that the King is very ill, doesn't he, Mother?" remarked Damaris conversationally, her tongue protruding as she concentrated on trying to keep her stitches even.

Christian Anning pinned her needle into the linen and gave her daughter a severe look.

"Don't repeat rumours," she reprimanded.

"But I heard you both talking, last night," Damaris remonstrated, "and Father said it was true."

Philippa raised her eyebrows questioningly. Everyone at Colcombe was acutely aware of the situation: if the old king died then the new one might well show clemency to the Courtenays. But could poor Lord William survive a winter in that awful prison in Calais?

"Very well," said Christian. "Yes, they say the King is much afflicted, as he is in every cold season, by a troublesome cough and the quinsy."

"And the merchant Father knows said that no-one has seen him for weeks. And that his mother is in charge of the palace. He could have been dead for weeks!"

Christian reached over and slapped Damaris's hand. The needle between her fingers slipped and stabbed her thumb. She gazed at her usually gentle mother in wide-eyed shock, and then sucked furiously to stop the oozing blood dripping on to the pale linen. At that moment the door opened and Katherine bustled in.

Philippa and Christian rose and curtsied. Their lady might well like to sit and gossip but she was still Lady Courtenay. Damaris was in awe of her and sank to her knees. Meggie threw down her sewing and rushed to her mother's side. "Lady Mother, is it true that the king is a-dying?"

The first person that Rob Anning told of the London news had been Katherine herself. Coming hard on the heels of the knowledge of William's removal to Calais, it was the tiniest glimmer of hope. To want somebody dead was wicked; to want the King dead was treason but Katherine found herself happy to be a traitor. She imagined Henry Tudor lying in his sumptuous bed, gasping for breath behind the thick, crewelled curtains. She hoped every breath was an agony for him; hoped that his inflamed throat would close and his lungs heave with foul sputum. Who now cared, beyond his faithful mother? Rob said it was known all over that the King would not survive the winter.

Now she drew Meggie close and motioned that the women, and Damaris, should rise.

"I see then, that those cousins Gossip and Rumour have made themselves at home in the cosiest room in my house!" Christian Anning's face was full of apology but Katherine forced herself to smile. "Your husband brought us welcome news, Mistress Anning. And I am sure it is over half of southern England by now. We will not be the only ones contemplating how our lives may change."

"He well knew how to maintain his royal majesty and all which appertains to kingship at every time and in every place ... but all these virtues were obscured latterly by avarice, from which he suffered." Obituary on Henry VII from the Anglica Historia

Richmond Palace April 23rd 1509

She had devoted her life to her son, believing implicitly that he had been born to greatness, and now he was dead. Margaret Beaufort was on her knees in the chapel, gazing up at the *Pieta* – the poignant representation of the Holy Virgin cradling the dead Christ in her arms. Henry had commissioned it from the workshops of the Italian sculptor Pietro Torrigiani in Rome. In the expression of the Virgin she saw her own pain: to have your son die before you; to have to watch his suffering, being utterly powerless to change the course of events. Beneath her knees the stone floor was cold and unforgiving. Her joints ached with rheumatic stiffness but her eyes were dry and her mouth set with determination. Harry would need her now.

However, an uneasiness set in as she thought about her grandson. Of course he was unfailingly deferential, obedient even, but now he veiled his eyes when she lectured him about his imminent responsibilities. She feared she would not have the strength to control him once he was king. At Mass he glanced too often across at that Spanish chit, Catalina, whose father had never delivered the promised dowry money.

The doors to Henry's private rooms remained resolutely shut. Richmond was a tense palace in waiting. Only his doctors, and closest spiritual and political advisors knew about the cold, stiff body. She understood why it had to be so: no-one must know until the succession was absolutely secured. It was imperative that there should be no challenge to the claim of young Harry. The inner circle of the Council need time to plan a strategy that would ensure the survival of the Tudor dynasty. The king might change but kingship would not.

Lady Margaret squeezed her eyes shut and tried to focus on prayers rather than thoughts. It was not easy, though, for images from the past insisted on crowding into her mind: herself aged just fourteen, almost torn apart as she gave birth to her Tudor son, then just four years later watching forlornly from the battlements of Pembroke Castle as he was taken from her to be raised by Yorkists. She did not see him again for years – just a brief reunion when her cousin King Henry VI momentarily regained his crown, but then King Edward IV was victorious again and fourteen-year-old Henry spirited away into exile in Brittany. He was a man of twenty eight before she beheld him again, after Bosworth Field. Yet never, for a single day, had he ever been out of her thoughts. She had dedicated her life to finding a way to bring him to the throne, and keeping him there. He was fifty two; she was nearly sixty six. The fight against the Yorkists was not yet over, she knew that, for the eldest de la Pole (she refused to accord him his title) was still alive in the Tower, whilst his brother flitted across Europe. There was young Buckingham too (she recalled his father, to whom she had written secret letters) arrogant and ambitious, basking in his own royal blood and only kept at bay by a subtle blend of rewards and warnings. And another boy too, the young son of Katherine Plantagenet and William Courtnenay who might one day seek to shout about his ancestry.

Yes, she understood that in order for Harry to be accepted as king the people must be convinced that the new regime would be different from the old. Henry Tudor had become feared, hated even, for the financial penalties he had inflicted upon anyone who opposed him. A clever ploy, though. Opposition to him was futile for none had the means to fund it. She knew that all across England people would rejoice at her son's death but what was essential was that they should look only to the new young golden Tudor prince, not cast covert glances for any Yorkist replacement.

The general pardons were a sensible idea. They gave a feeling of a fresh start and would reassure people that the new king would listen and justice applied. She wondered where her place would be in this new world. Seventeen- year-old Harry would not be looking to his grandmother for guidance. Maybe she should simply accept this and retire gracefully. Let him marry whom he would. Let him count his father's gold and spend it as he would. But it would hurt to stand aside and watch. She, who had been by the King's elbow for a quarter of a century. Yet perhaps Harry would honour her, and turn to her?

She realised that her legs were numb and her hands cold. It was a feeling she was used to for she often prayed for hours at a time. Unfortunately, with age, it was getting harder. She was obliged to use the altar rail as a support to lever her way back on to her feet.

"Lady Grandmother?" It was Mary, since December married by proxy to the Emperor's grandson, Charles. Her glee in her newfound status caused her to move around Richmond like a ship in full sail, dressed always in gorgeous clothes. The imposed quiet of the past few weeks had irritated her intensely. Lady Margaret composed her face before she turned round to her granddaughter; the girl did not yet know her father was dead. "I am come to bid you join us for dinner," said Mary. "My brother waits for us. Are you not glad, Grandmother, that we can have a pleasant day to celebrate St George? After all these weeks of His Grace my father being ill?"

Lady Margaret allowed Mary to lead the way back towards the great presence chamber adjoining the King's private rooms. It was packed with nobles come to court for the traditional Order of the Garter celebrations. They stood aside for her, bowing and smiling. She took her place at the table, next to young Harry, who shot her a beaming smile. Did he know? Had they told him? She could not tell. The door from Henry Tudor's rooms opened and a group of councillors emerged, chatting. A few of the assembled throng looked up expectantly but there was no announcement and soon the chamber was full again with a hubbub of appreciative dining, pleasant conversation and polite laughter. She watched Mary, making eyes at Charles Brandon, despite the gold ring on her heart finger, and Harry casting his glance down the table to where the Spanish princess sat quietly, toying with her food. *Next door, my son's body lies cold; probably as yet unwashed.*

Later, they all processed back to the chapel for evensong. Lady Margaret knew that Harry would be steered upstairs into the privacy of the holyday closet where the king traditionally heard Mass before joining everyone else for the rest of the service. Sure enough, a small group of councillors herded him like a sheep and shut the door firmly. *They are telling him now. Telling him that he is King Henry, eighth of that name.* All around her nobles in their resplendent Garter vestments and badges were taking their places ready for the service. Their gold collars glinted in the candlelight. In past years Lady Margaret had sat alongside other Ladies of the Garter, Queen Elizabeth and her sister Cecily. She never missed Bessy but she missed Cecily. The sweet voices of the choirboys soared into the first psalm and she bowed her head.

They came to her at the end of the service – two of the council, Archbishop Wareham and Thomas Howard, Earl of Surrey, husband of Anne Plantagenet. They bowed and ushered her quickly along deserted galleries into a small room where her grandson stood with a mixture of incredulity and eager anticipation on his handsome face. Painfully, she sank into an obeisance, her black robes settling like a dark cloud.

"Your Grace, please be seated at the head of the table." They guided Harry to the most important seat and he flushed with excitement. There was no trace of sorrow in his countenance, just a relief that his time had come. He grasped the Archbishops's flowing sleeve. "Will it be you who crowns me?"

"Assuredly sir, but first …"

"When?"

"First, Harry, your lord father must be decently buried!" She could not help it that her retort was sharp. He had the decency to look somewhat abashed as she settled herself in the seat next to him where she had always sat when Henry required her advice.

"Sir, we advise that first you go to the Tower, with chosen members of your household. We will gauge the feeling in the city, and arrange for your honoured father's funeral as soon as may be, *then* we shall be free to plan for your coronation." Thomas Howard was managing him well, with a subtle mix of deference and instruction. "It should be no longer than, say, two or three weeks. The safety of your royal person is our first concern."

The young king seemed to grasp that for the moment he was out-manoeuvred. He must obey them, and bide his time. His grandmother was fixing him with the gimlet stare that used to frighten him as a child but suddenly he saw her for what she was – simply an old woman. He would humour her.

"Will you be coming with me, Lady Grandmother?"

"My Lady the King's Mother –" the Archbishop corrected himself hastily. "My Lady the King's *Grandmother* will stay here to implement the terms of your late father's will. If that pleases you, my lady?"

Her thin lips curved into an unexpected smile. "Of course." It would be her last service to her precious son. She knew what was in it in any case.

"Well, whilst I wait they can construct a tiltyard for me at the Tower," said Harry. "Then afterwards, I shall go to Greenwich."

Already his mind was on the joyful prospect of the summer ahead. A summer by the river, in the palace of his birth; long, sunlit days of jousting, and swimming, and archery – and long, warm nights of dancing, and music … and love.

6

"The Rose both white and red
In one rose now doth grow …
England now gladder flowers
Exclude now all douleurs." John Skelton, poet and tutor to King Henry VIII

Katherine: *The news of my nephew's accession reached us within days as heralds sent out from London reached the towns and villages of the south. I remember how Rob Anning came galloping home from Axminster, across our little drawbridge, his horse's hooves drumming on the wood. I rushed out into the inner courtyard as he threw himself out of the saddle and ran to kiss my hand, his face wreathed in smiles. For we all knew what it meant: King Harry VIII would keep his word to us, and William would be freed. Yet my father-in-law did not live to see his son again. On May 28ᵗʰ he died at Tiverton.*

We waited. It was not hard to wait a few more months – not after seven years. Meanwhile more news poured out of London and down the Great West Road: how young King Harry had married the Princess Catalina and made her his Queen Catherine. They had gone simply, hand in hand, to a private closet at Greenwich and married without fuss. Not two weeks later they took their coronation oaths in the abbey at Westminster. And only days later his grandmother Lady Margaret Beaufort died – they said she had eaten too much roasted cygnet at the banquet but in my view she simply knew that Harry would never be controlled, and she decided not even to try.

"The Lord William was delivered and set at liberty by the noble and famous prince King Henry VIII" Edward Hall, Chronicler

The litter carrying William Courtenay home swayed along the track that wound its way from Exeter up the secretive Exe valley. Labourers and artisans came out to stare at the little cavalcade passing through their villages and hamlets, and cheered and waved when they recognised the Courtenay standard held aloft by the servant riding in front. They saw a thin, pale man who stared back and tried to wave but his hand often fell and tears coursed down his cheeks. The litter creaked as it dipped in the troughs of the rutted trackway running along the floor of the steep and thickly wooded river valley. Oak leaves, just turning tawny, fluttered down, landing on the roof of the litter and the hind-quarters of the horses.

William had parted company with Thomas Grey in London. They were not sorry to see the back of each other; two years sharing a cell with any man was enough to try the patience of a saint. The horrors of sickness, anger, melancholy, despair – each had touched his own nadir in Calais. When they stumbled into the daylight, pardoned by the new king, they had wept on each other's shoulders, not out of regard but sheer relief.

Rob Anning had been waiting at Dover, with the astonishing luxury of clean clothing. William was riddled with lice, dirt ingrained into the very pores of his skin. Rob had half carried him to the nearest bath-house and deposited him in a barrel of steaming, herb-scented water. A girl had oiled his body and scraped off layers of filth. Another had cropped his hair close to his head; for a few weeks at least the shock of white amongst the brown would be disguised. Katherine had sent new shirts, embroidered by her own hand; he pulled one over his head and stared in amazement at its extraordinary whiteness and smelled the unbelievable heaven of lavender.

They trundled through Silverton and finally into Tiverton, past the handsome sandstone church of St Peter's and arrived at the castle itself – the solid-looking gatehouse and, to the left, the round tower. William drew a deep breath to steady himself but winced at the sharp pain stabbing his lungs. Someone was opening the door of the litter and placing a box for him to step on. For a moment he thought his legs would not obey him. A tremor seemed to be coursing through his whole body.

"My lord husband." She was there, in front of him, holding the hand of a young girl who gazed at him with huge, watchful eyes, and next to her a boy with long limbs and a freckled face, holding the reins of …

"Seaton! Dear God, it's Seaton!"

The old warhorse had been brushed and burnished within an inch of his life. Thin with age, but polished like a chestnut, in full Courtenay caparison – the three red *torteaux* against a golden background. The boy commanded him in a high but confident voice "Bow down!" and the horse extended his front legs and lowered his head, before tossing it up again and exhibiting ancient yellow teeth in a loud whinney. Laughter and cheering bounced off the castle walls.

Then Rob Anning was helping him from the litter, discreetly allowing his lord to lean on his shoulder, and he was in Katherine's arms while the whole household clapped wildly. He closed his eyes and pressed his lips against her forehead. "Right well-beloved wife," he whispered, "it is good to be home."

Katherine masked her shock well. The man whom she held was almost unrecognisable – it was like clutching a bag of bones, and when he removed his velvet bonnet it was to reveal a head as smooth and white as an egg. She searched his face for signs of the young man she had loved.

"I am sorry, Katherine, I know I am changed."

"Do not be *sorry!* You have *survived!* That is all that matters!" Fiercely, she raised his arm aloft that he might be seen to acknowledge his homecoming.

At supper she ensured that he took his rightful place upon the dais to absorb the waves of love and respect swelling up to greet him: the smiling servants from the buttery; the grooms from the stable crowded round trestles at the far end of the hall; musicians in the gallery playing long-forgotten favourite tunes and outside a crowd of people come up from the town to wish their lord well on his return.

Katherine sat close by his side, her hand often resting on his, attentive to his mood and needs. His son and daughter sat a little way down the table, trying to resist the urge to stare and stare at this stranger. The celebration was kept within the bounds of what William could tolerate. It was clear that he could stomach little more than a few mouthfuls of food, and he took only sips of small ale.

Katherine sensed his fatigue. "Let us retire to our private chamber."

They sat together in the firelight. He seemed disinclined to talk so she filled the gaps with quiet telling of essential news: the latest information from London; the running of the estates and of course the deaths of his parents.

"I have arranged for work to begin on the tombs in St Peter's. Rob Anning has found a craftsman in Exeter who is equal to the job. I hope that pleases you, my love. We have not settled yet on designs because I knew you would wish to choose for yourself."

William blinked away tears again. He had never been overly emotional but now everything threatened to unman him. In contrast, his wife seemed the epitome of resilience; her hand pouring the wine from pitcher to cup was steady and her voice did not falter. He marvelled at her beauty – the oval face and clear complexion; the determined chin; the peep of thick, wheat-coloured hair under her cap and those dark eyes. The thick fabric of her gown could not hide the fact that her body was still as slim as a girl's.

She seemed to read his thoughts, blushing a little. "I have had my thirtieth birthday, William. I am indeed ageing!"

"It's been nearly eight years, Katherine. My children do not know me. My parents are dead. Look at the state of me – I am a wreck. God knows what the future holds for us. What's he like, this kingly nephew of yours? What can we expect?"

She settled herself on a large cushion at his feet, leaning against his legs and resting her chin on his knees. She loosened the ties on her cap, pulled out the pins from her hair and released the thick plait. Before long, she knew, his hand would stray to stroke the top of her head in the old way. Deliberately, she kept her tone low and even. "Of course your children know you, my lord. They have grown up speaking of you every single day. Hal cannot wait for you to visit the stables with him, and teach him how to carry a lance. You are his hero. As for Meggie, she longs for a father to tell her stories and admire her music, and her reading and writing. In any other circumstances they might have been sent away to learn in other families, and we would *both* feel unfamiliar with them. As for your honoured parents, be thankful that they lived long and useful lives, that they died in their beds. They were good to me, William – and I am thankful for their care while you were … away. Of course I am sorry that they did not live to see you restored to us but your father would be more concerned that the lands and title might pass on to you, and to Hal. He never gave up hope, you know. He never lost faith that our fortunes could turn. "

Sure enough, she felt his palm on the crown of her head. "And you think Harry will set things aright for us?"

"There will be conditions. He wants to be seen as the generous king, the very opposite of *his* father but he's bound to set his own terms. He's extraordinary, William, only eighteen but like a young god. But he's sentimental too, and likes

417

the idea of family. If we play the part of affectionate aunt, respectful uncle and adoring young cousins he will let us into his world. He's already granted me an annuity of two hundred marks. There may be more to come. If we can open up negotiations with him about the Courtenay lands... "

"Jesu, Katherine. I had never thought you so cynical."

"All I want is for us to be safe. Bessy taught me long ago that surviving is the only thing that matters. And you will *get better!* With good food, and good air, and exercise –"

He gave a sudden guffaw, the first sound resembling the old William. "Now you make me sound like Seaton."

She laughed. "Well, has he not survived too? I'll wager you did not expect to see him again."

"I did not. There were times though when I made myself dream of him – tried to remember what it was like to be on his back, galloping down the lists. God knows I did not have much in common with your cousin Tom Grey but we could at least share some stories of our jousting days. I think we relived every tournament, every opponent, every hoofbeat."

"William, it's over. The Tower. Calais. The Tudor Dragon. I tell myself it's Bessy's boy, my father's grandson who rules us now and we can surely find a future in this new England. Why would he not want his *faithful* family close by? My cousin Margaret Pole is back at court, beloved of the new queen. Catalina will soon fill the nurseries at Eltham with a new generation of princes and princesses and we will be welcome."

"Do you want to go back, to that old life of serving a queen?"

"Not entirely," she admitted. "I could live happily enough here in Devon forever, but we have our children to think of. A match for Meggie. A place for Hal."

She felt him caressing the nape of her neck and then the laces of her gown being loosened. A shiver ran down her back. For years she had pushed all carnal thoughts to the very edges of her mind. She had lived like a nun, trying not to see the beauty in a man's form and ignoring the monthly rhythms of her body. Once she had touched herself where her husband had touched her but the exquisite, sudden flood of pleasure had frightened her. What had *he* done, all this time? Had the Courtenay money paid for whores in the Tower? He was a man, after all.

Now he had pulled her to her feet and was sliding her gown down past her shoulders, past her waist, and then his hands pulling at her kirtle, then fumbling at the ribbons on her shift. Neither of them spoke. She found herself helping him out of his hose and shirt and eventually they stood naked in front of each other. His thinness troubled her; she could see his ribs and the muscles of his thighs and calves were wasted.

"Katherine, I am not sure I can be much of a husband to you."

"Shh." Gently she led him to the bed and he lay down, the bed ropes creaking slightly. She drew the bed-curtains and they were cocooned in the darkness. She felt his hands upon her hips, her back, pulling her down on top of him.

"I seem to remember, wife, that we did not always heed the Church's instructions about how to take our pleasure." His voice was a mischievous disembodiment.

"We did not, husband," she whispered.

"Can you recall what we did?"

"I can."

As she lowered herself on to him she heard a great sigh that seemed to signify the release of seven years of longing but whether it was him or her she could not tell. Neither, a little later, could she distinguish between their cries of joy or between his tears and hers.

7

Eltham Palace August 1510

She lay with her eyes closed in the sunshine, listening to the distant, inaudible murmur of conversation. The Queen's ladies had come out for a breath of fresh air on this hot afternoon and were arranged like bright little birds on the edge of the lake. Catalina herself sat upright in a velvet chair, under a canopy, and some of her ladies kept her company in similar dignified state, with their books, or embroidery, or cards, but others reclined on cushions or even, like Katherine, upon the green grass itself. The water of the lake shimmered in the afternoon heat and tiny waves lapped at the reedy banks where insects hummed and buzzed amid the vegetation. Eltham was always idyllic. A perfect place for a woman to while away the long months of pregnancy in the company of good friends; a perfect place for children to be nurtured. *I was born here, thirty one years ago today. When my father was a glorious king. When my mother was the most beautiful queen England had ever seen.*

"Lady Courtenay? Are you awake?" A lilting Scots voice from many years ago. Katherine opened her eyes, squinting against the sharp rays of sunlight as a dark silhouette gradually resolved itself into a recognisable form.

"Kateryn? Is it really you?" She scrambled to her knees, brushing bits of dry grass from her skirts and looked in wonderment upon the much-loved face she had not seen since Bessie's funeral. Her secret sister-in-law. Kateryn Huntley was smiling broadly, all the fears and apprehension of past years wiped away.

"They told me you had come to court. I have been looking out for you."

"But did not expect to find me lying in the water reeds!"

"A cool retreat on such an afternoon," allowed Kateryn, "I will join you, until the queen calls for me." She lowered herself carefully and arranged her skirts neatly. Katherine saw a slim gold band on the heart finger of her right hand.

"Jesu! *Married,* Kateryn?"

"Aye, to one James Strangeways, gentleman usher to His Grace the King."

"A love match?"

Kateryn gave a reproving little smile. "Hardly. I am thirty six. Past the age of romance. But he is a good man with a fine manor in Berkshire. I am glad to have some independence at last, a house of my own to go to when not at court. Your royal nephew allowed it, though he has imposed some odd terms. I am not to go within a hundred miles of Scotland. So I can never go home."

"He would not be Harry without his terms." Katherine twisted up a handful of grass and threw it into the water. "We have been promised that my husband will be restored to his earldom, and our estates secured, but he still watches us. We do our best to live a quiet life, though he likes to have us at court, where he can see us. William hates it. He would much rather stay in Devon."

"It will be different when Harry has a son. He won't think so much about the past. It will all be about the glorious Tudor future."

They both looked across the greensward to where Catalina was sewing in the shade. Katherine masked her lips with her hand. "It is true what they say? That there was no baby the first time?"

"Oh, there was a baby, but she miscarried last January, then the foolish doctor told her she had another left in her womb. She believed it. Harry believed it. But spring came and nothing happened. Her womb has swelled up and down like a pig's bladder."

"And now? Is she pregnant again?"

"We believe so. Her courses have ceased again. Her breasts are tender. Since May she has often vomited."

"Then we must hope that next January or February proves more kind to Her Grace."

"Indeed we must."

They sat companionably by the water's edge, watching brilliant sapphire dragonflies darting close to the surface. Two were coupled together, creating a heart-like shape, their iridescent wings flashing as they flexed and twisted. Kateryn turned her head away. "Och, this sun is so bright! It makes my eyes water."

"You think of him often," said Katherine softly. "It is only natural. And you have no-one with whom you may speak of him, which makes it worse."

"Or better. It means I can keep it all locked away."

"I was always glad when I had Bessy, and my other sisters to talk to. To share memories with. You must have so much you have been forced to bury so deep. Dickon. Your child – "

"You think my child did not survive?"

Time stopped. Even the wisps of cloud high in the sky seemed to halt. The distant music and laughter of the queen, her ladies and musicians was far, far away. Katherine rested her head on her knees and the light silk of her veil fluttered against her cheeks. Kateryn was staring straight ahead across the lake towards the dark green woods beyond. Neither spoke for several minutes. A long legged egret suddenly rose from the reeds, flapping and screeching before flying in a slow circle over their heads then away towards the trees.

"We were told that your babe had died. Before you were brought up from Cornwall …"

"Aye, well, that was the best story to tell. I made sure I was dressed in mourning when I was taken before Henry Tudor."

"Holy Mother of God! Tell me what happened."

Still gazing into the distance she dropped her voice to such a whisper that Katherine had to strain to be sure of each word. "We had sailed from Ireland, and I was near my time. He had to leave me with the monks at St Michael's Mount. They brought a woman across the causeway to help me birth the child – then we heard that he had been captured and I knew it was all over. The woman offered to take my son to safety, to her sister in Wales. I agreed; I wanted him to live."

"Did … did *he* know?"

"Not at first. I let him believe the child had died. But in the end I could not bear it. We found ourselves alone, for a moment, and I told him – but then he tried to escape and they took him to the Tower. Sometimes I think if I had not told him he would have settled for some sort of life at Henry Tudor's court."

"No," said Katherine softly, "sooner or later Henry Tudor would have killed him. Where is your son now?"

"I am not sure. Alive, somewhere in Wales. Called Richard Perkin. I pray he grows to manhood and that nobody ever tells him who he is. I would not wish him to know how his father died."

"I wonder you can bear it. Do you not long to see him?"

"I have longed for many things in my life but they have rarely come my way. It is enough for me to know he survives."

A thought like an arrow. "Did my sister the Queen know?"

Kateryn turned her head sideways, slowly. "Yes. And your sister Cecily. I had to confide in someone. At first I thought it was a secret too dangerous to tell but when Bessy lost Arthur, and Cecily's girls both died they both turned to me for comfort, believing I knew how they felt. But I did not and I felt a fraud when I tried to pretend. I could not lie to your sisters; they were too kind to me."

"May God go with you in your life, Kateryn."

A call from Catalina's little pavilion disturbed their quiet conversation. All her ladies were summoned into the shade for refreshment. Katherine and Kateryn made their way dutifully across the grass to the clipped lawn and under the awning. Pages were pouring frothy small ale and handing round sweetmeats. All the ladies looked uncomfortably warm in their gowns, full sleeves and headdresses. Catalina wafted a large, Spanish-style fan and surveyed them critically.

"In my country, we dressed differently in the summer," she observed. "When I was a girl we lived at the Alhambra in Granada… "She lingered nostalgically over the Spanish names. "My mother, Queen Isabella, dressed us in cool linens and silks, and we sat in courtyards with pools and fountains. Our chambers were tiled, and sometimes we went barefoot …"

Katherine laughed. "Your Grace, do not make us envious! Maybe if we had summers like this every year we too would learn to live differently, but you can be sure it will always rain within a few days and then we are thankful for our wool and velvets, even in August!"

"Lady Courtenay. We are pleased to see you. How is your husband?" Catalina's solicitous manner was genuine. She never forgot that this lady was from the old ruling family – Lady Pole too, and she knew that it was the deaths of their close relations which had brought the Tudors to the throne. She was glad to be able to offer them friendship, to compensate them in some small way for the manner in which Fortune had changed their lives. Catalina knew about Fortune – less than two years ago she herself had been at the very bottom of the wheel, ignored by her father-in-law and politically manipulated by her own father. Sometimes she felt like the damsel in distress from old tales, rescued by the handsome prince from the brink of despair. She had come to realise how powerless women were when at the mercy of some men. It was not something

423

for which her mother had prepared her; on the contrary, Isabella of Castile had led her to believe that women could be just as strong as men. Now, after thirteen years in England she knew it was not true. She had acquired a wariness. Even the golden prince who had rescued her was proving to be not quite what she had imagined. The honeyed early months of their marriage had already been soured by her miscarriage and the rumour that Harry had looked elsewhere for his satisfaction. She prayed that this baby in her womb was a son, the first of many, for only then would she be truly valued.

"I thank Your Grace for asking. William is much better, but often afflicted by a cough."

Catalina cocked her head with concern. "What remedies do you give him?"

"Steeped thyme, and honey."

"I will send you ginger, and liquorice, which are imported from Spain. The King is most interested in medicines and likes to mix his own."

"Your Grace is most kind."

Catalina nodded. "Such things are important to me. Tell me of your children, Lady Courtenay."

"Well, Your Grace, Hal is now twelve, and thinks himself a man. And Margaret, Meggie, is ten."

"You have had no other children … since your husband's return?"

Katherine felt herself colouring slightly. "No … God has not seen fit to bless us again."

A small frown creased Catalina's otherwise smooth little face. "I hope He will bless me, in a few months." The trauma of her first disastrous pregnancy was still raw.

It was important to tread delicately. Tension stretched in the hot, late summer air. Katherine cast around for something to say which might give some confidence to this little Spanish queen. "My own mother, His Grace's maternal grandmother, had ten children. Many women do not have the least trouble in childbirth, and their babies thrive, and I am sure that God will bless you, likewise."

"You are kind, and sensible, Lady Courtenay. I should very much like it if you were to attend me when my time is near. You, and my dear friend, your cousin, Lady Margaret Pole, and Lady Kateryn. My husband speaks of you with great affection – his *favourite aunt,* he always says."

Sweet Virgin, am I never to escape these Tudors? She fastened her brightest smile on her lips and curtsied. "It would be an honour, Your Grace."

Catalina seemed satisfied and fell to talking in Spanish with Maria de Salinas, her devoted chief lady-in-waiting. Katherine realised she had been dismissed and found her way to the edge of the awning where Kateryn stood next to Margaret Pole. The two cousins greeted each other eagerly, their loving embrace an unspoken acknowledgement of their improved circumstances. As the afternoon lengthened so did the shadow cast by the canopy and the women were happy to stay outside. Such days were rare, and to be enjoyed.

In bed that night, Katherine found it hard to sleep, pondering upon Kateryn's revelation. She considered telling Margaret but decided the secret was not hers to share. Yet the thought that somewhere out there, in the depths of Wales, lived a Plantagenet boy the same age as her own beloved Edward, was at once intriguing and desperately sad. But Kateryn was right – no good could ever come of finding him and telling him of his parentage. For such a boy there could be no restoration to a title, or wealth. No, best to leave him in ignorance and safety. Harry still held his cousin Suffolk in the Tower, and the only other de la Pole brother circled the courts of Europe, hiding and surfacing in a game of endless blind man's bluff. She slipped out of bed and found her rosary, then knelt in the sultry darkness praying that a boy called Richard Perkins would be granted health and happiness.

Then she prayed for her husband. William's health gave cause for concern – he succumbed to every cough and cold and in this hot weather she lived in fear of the sweating sickness. She had insisted he stay at home while she came to court and luckily young King Harry did not seem too put out. His Uncle William was perhaps too old, he'd said airily, to join him on his progress with his other young male friends. He had surrounded himself with a coterie of young nobles: Compton, Brandon, Buckingham and others, all perfectly prepared to devote themselves again to the hard task of distracting their monarch whilst his wife coped with the early months of pregnancy. The rumours were everywhere: how the Lady Anne, Buckingham's sister, had suddenly been sent home by her furious husband – for it seemed she had also been distracting the King, with her low-cut gowns and flashes of ankle as she danced. No wonder Catalina seemed so downcast. Katherine wondered if Harry had inherited her own father's easy virtue – would Catalina have to look the other way, as Elizabeth Wydville had done? The rosary beads slid through her fingers; she chided herself as she found it hard to concentrate on her prayers whilst other thoughts pushed themselves to the fore. She hoped Harry's escapades would not bear the sort of fruit that would sadden Catalina – at least not so early in their marriage. It was easier for a queen to turn a blind eye to her husband's indiscretions as long as she had a nursery full of her own children. *God knows how many other half siblings I have out there; they say my father lay with every merchant's wife in London ... are there Courtenay bastards out there too?* She could not bring herself to ask William about his years in the Tower. They had lain together many times now since his return but as she had admitted to Catalina there had been no sign of another child for them. Sometimes she yearned for a new baby, not to replace Edward but to make their little family bigger. Margaret Pole had a whole brood of sons and daughters. Bessy had had six. But then poor Anne had none. Her fist tightened over the coral beads. Why did God favour some women and not others?

8

Richmond January 1511

There was a new Prince of Wales; the capital and the country went wild with joy. The Spanish queen had done her duty and presented her eighteen-year-old husband with his first son. Bonfires burned on every hillside, and in every inn and family home the queen was the toast of the land. The carpenters, busy carving Catalina's pomegranate badge in churches and halls, paused to survey their handiwork with satisfaction: the fruit of Spain had indeed ripened in England's hot summer. With a grin from ear to ear Harry mounted his horse and set off immediately to the shrine at Walsingham to give thanks for his heir (and maybe seek other pleasures en route) while Catalina sank back against her pillows in triumph.

"The first of many, I am sure, Your Grace," said Meg Pole kindly, "and worth waiting for. "

William, summoned from Devon, stood alongside Katherine at the font to witness the baptism of their godson, the newest Henry Tudor.

Six weeks later the dark days of winter were just beginning to lengthen. The baby prince was left behind at Richmond, where snowdrops clustered hopefully on banks and under trees, and birds were calling out to prospective mates. Catalina, sorrowful to leave her baby but basking in her glory, was reunited with the King at Westminster. Harry was busy organising jousts. There was to be no expense spared, he declared, in honouring the mother of his son.

Katherine regarded William anxiously as he returned from yet another day of whirlwind planning in the King's rooms. He was grey with exhaustion. "Let the others do it, William, *please*. Or at least do not stay so late."

"I can hardly leave until he dismisses me. And in any case, I'm enjoying it. It's like old times again." He joined her at the table where a late supper awaited them. Their rooms overlooked the main courtyard and they could hear the great gates being closed for the night and in the distance the sonorous abbey bell calling out the hour of Compline.

Katherine served him wine and a plate of cold meats and bread. "So what is his latest scheme?"

He ate hungrily. "Those who compete are all to wear costumes embroidered with their names. Harry is to be *Coeur Loyal*, Tom Knyvet is to be *Bon Espoir*. I am Sir Good Will – *Bon Vouloir*. Edward Neville is *Joyeux Penser*. All in French. He thinks it sound better. And there's to be enough gold to outshine King Midas. Hearts, flowers … Knyvet says he will drape his codpiece with gold."

Katherine grimaced, " Are we meant to be impressed?"

"They are young, beloved. Let them have their day."

She tried hard to suppress the worry in her voice. "What if you are injured?"

He grinned at her, for a fleeting moment the boy who had spoken to her at Kenilworth.

"Don't be cross, Katherine. It doesn't suit you."

"But you are not well enough, I know how you -"

"I shall be *fine.*" A shade of irritation in his voice at her fussing." I know more about jousting than Harry, Knyvet, Nevillle, Brandon and Compton all put together." He caught her hand. "And wait till you see the golden castle and the dancing horses."

The fresh smell of sawdust and paint pervaded the whole tiltyard where the carpenters had worked all night to finish the gallery seating Catalina and her ladies. It rose at a giddy angle, overlooking the lists. Every post, every rail was bright with fresh colour. It was cold and dry, crisp and sunny. Catalina leaned forward in her seat, *"Oh! Mirar el castillo!"*

Gasps of delight and wonderment; exclamations of admiration and incredulity. An enormous platform was being wheeled in front of them, lumbering and creaking over the sanded yard, apparently drawn by a silver antelope and a golden lion. At each corner and along the side men dressed as foresters, in suits of green velvet. In the centre a magnificent golden castle, with crenellations and turrets, and at its portcullis a man making a huge garland of golden roses. He bowed, stepped down and presented it to Catalina, who rose and accepted it with great dignity. She held it aloft and the crowd roared their approval. Nothing was too good or too beautiful for the mother of their prince!

Suddenly, the sides of the castle opened up, creating ramps for four knights to ride down on their horses. Katherine held her breath, scanning the names on their trappings. Harry, though, was unmistakable: the plumes on his helmet were the tallest; his armour the finest; his horse the most beautiful, resplendent in blue velvet, picking his way carefully down the walkway and then prancing proudly towards them all. Harry handled him expertly, using just his hands and heels to bring him to a halt. And behind him *Bon Vouloir,* William, with his visor up and a twinkle in his eye, mounted on one of Seaton's most handsome grandsons, Musbury. Katherine felt a rush of love and pride for this kindest of husbands who was, truly, a chivalrous knight from the stories of old. Maybe Fortune would be kind too, now, and they could go forward in life free of suspicion, hatred and revenge – all the terrible things which had blighted their lives. Maybe William would regain his full health as well as his titles, and maybe there would be another child to set the seal on their joy. Maybe their godson, half Spanish, half Tudor; partly York, partly Lancaster, partly English, partly Welsh, would be the one to unite them all in this new dawn of a century.

The whole day was extraordinary. Knight after knight pounded down the lists. Katherine was relieved to see William pace himself, whilst Harry seemed to go mad, flying past at least twenty times, lance poised and knocking down opponents like ninepins. The whole performance was rounded off by a display of horsemanship unmistakably the work of William Courtenay. The four knights, and their mounts, put on an exhibition of pirouetting, rearing and leaping, with Harry's stallion finally beating its hooves boastfully against the wooden partition that ran the length of the tiltyard whilst the other four sank down in courtly obeisance to Catalina and her ladies. The silence of astonishment gave way to cheers and delighted laughter, then all four knights jumped down from their horses and ran across to the Queen's gallery, leaping over the balustrade to present their shields to the ladies. The Princess Mary screamed with delighted fear as Charles Brandon vaulted and landed practically in her lap.

"Well, I admit I did not exactly *leap,"* admitted William that evening in the White Hall at Westminster. "I think I would describe it as more of a cautious scramble."

"As befits your age and status, cousin," said Meg Pole gravely, before the effort of maintaining a serious expression became too much for her. She felt the relief as much as anybody; a secure Tudor dynasty spelled safety for her own children. Much loved by Catalina, and respected by Harry she felt she could face the future with confidence.

Katherine giggled. "At least you reached me, husband, even if you were the last knight to do so. And I quite glad that you did not carry me off to your pavilion."

Under the table William ran his hand along her thigh, "There was a time, beloved, before you weighed as much as you do now -"

"For shame, I am no different from the day you married me, and well you know it!"

"Look at your nephew, Harry; he is the epitome of the loving husband."

Katherine followed her husband's sightline over the musicians and dancers to where the young king knelt like a devoted pilgrim at Catalina's feet. He was still revelling in his role as Sir Loyal Heart, clasping her hand while she beamed down at him – all rumours of his romantic straying with Anne Stafford clearly forgiven. Now he stood up, and seemed to be inviting the initiation of some foolish game whereby foreign ambassadors should try to seize the golden letters of his costume.

At the far end of the hall the crowd of ordinary Londoners invited for the occasion craned their necks for a glimpse of the proceedings. Their excitement was evident as they jostled and shoved for a better view, their cheers turning into raucous shouts. Katherine touched William's sleeve uneasily. "Jesu! Surely they mean some mischief!"

As she spoke, the rail holding them back gave way and suddenly the hall was overrun with scores of men in drab fustian charging forward towards where the ladies and gentlemen of the court were dancing. There was absolute chaos. The Londoners had one thing on their mind – to seize anything of value and make off with it! Harry's game escalated into a complete free-for-all as men ripped what they could off the gowns and doublets of alarmed nobles. Safe behind a table, Katherine looked on in mesmerised fascination as they chased Thomas Knyvet on to the royal dais and tore the infamous golden codpiece from his nether regions. But then the fun was gone. A few of the ringleaders turned their attention to where Catalina sat, next to the Princess Mary. Out of the corner of her eye Katherine saw that the King's guard had their wits about them and were racing to put themselves between the royal ladies and the mob. William was there too, directly in front of Catalina, shielding her.

Above the din of shouting, screaming and the clash of halberds, the young King was yelling. "Forbear! Forbear! Good people! You shall not go home empty-handed!"

Gradually, the cacophony subsided, leaving just the sobs of a few terrified ladies-in-waiting and men panting from their exertions. Silver gilt platters were strewn over the floor, pastries and sweetmeats trodden underfoot. Harry lifted one foot shod in blue velvet and peeled something flat and sticky from the sole. He burst out laughing.

"Thank you! Thank you all for coming to share in our joy! Now take what you have, and for God's sake go home!" His command of the situation was a relief, his bonhomie unexpected but infectious. Men, whether commoner or noble, pulled each other to their feet; ladies smiled nervously and the citizens retreated, clutching an assortment of the golden letters and symbols. Katherine stood stock still as one man passed close by, cock-a-hoop with delight, a handful of gleaming yellow "H"s dangling from his hand. He grinned at her, revealing a mouth of black stumps.

When they were all gone, the guards shut the huge doors firmly and the musicians were instructed to strike up again. Catalina, however, was pale. Although it had lasted less than a quarter of an hour the intrusion had been frightening. She looked appealingly at Meg Pole and Maria de Salinas to join her. Harry, though, seemed hell-bent upon resuming the celebrations and was leading his sister Mary out on to the dance floor. Within minutes the Tudor siblings were behaving as if nothing untoward had occurred.

William returned to Katherine's side. "Never a dull moment at King Henry VIII's side, eh?"

Richmond 22nd February 1511

Elizabeth Poinz was a cut above the usual wet nurse, her father-in-law being vice-chamberlain of the Queen's household. It was said that the King would have none but a gentlewoman suckle his baby son. She woke early in the chamber adjoining the royal nursery, relieved that in a few minutes she would be able to hold the young prince to her breast and ease the fullness there. The thought of his eager little gums on her nipple caused a sudden wetness against her shift. Her own baby was six months old now and with his own wet nurse, an apple-cheeked country girl on the family estates in Gloucestershire; she would not see him again until this royal baby was weaned and her duties over.

All was peaceful in the nursery. One of the rockers hummed quietly as she gently pushed the cradle every few seconds. The baby had just begun to sleep through a few more hours at night-time. *I will wake him, though,* thought Mistress Poinz, *my breasts ache too much. I need him to suck.*

She settled herself in the comfortable, cushioned chair and unlaced the front of her gown, lifting out a heavy, white breast with its prominent indigo veins and dark, huge nipple. She smiled at the rocker and motioned that she should lift the baby out of his slumber. Obediently, the girl leaned over the vast, painted cradle to gather up the tiny prince. She loved him very much, with his downy thatch of gold-red hair and his little rose-bud mouth. There was no mistaking his parentage; when he screwed up his face to cry he looked exactly like the King. Usually, when disturbed from his slumbers he mewed like a little kitten, and arched himself in resentment.

But he was silent. The girl's scream was a like a vixen's cry, her eyes as wide as her mouth. Mistress Poinz seized him, frantically unwrapping his swaddling bands, then holding him upside down by his ankles, slapping his fragile back and yelling for the doctor who slept nearby.

They laid him on the table to try and breathe life back into him but his lips were blue, his limbs floppy and the puny chest unresponsive. Terrified, Mistress Poinz looked down upon the corpse of Henry, Prince of Wales, not yet nine weeks old. "Jesu, who will tell them?" She felt the hotness of milk from her breasts and tears from her eyes, and an appalling sense of guilt that she was glad it was not her own baby naked and dead with the sunrise.

Katherine: *It was me who told them. No-one else dared. I took Catalina in my arms and held her as she sobbed her lamentations, then left her with my cousin Meg Pole while I sought out my nephew the King. He looked for all the world like a small, angry boy who has had his favourite toy snatched away. When the French ambassador tried to present Louis XII's condolences I warned the Council against it, for there was no predicting my nephew's temper. With Catalina, though, he did his best to hide his feelings and consoled her with the thought that they were both young, and God had shown her to be fertile. Their Tudor children would arrive soon enough. But that year the tragedy of the prince's short life was eclipsed by my own sorrow.*

9

April 1511

The King summoned his aunt and uncle Courtenay to attend him at Westminster. They walked through the sprawling complex of old stone and timber buildings to the royal apartments. Katherine found she knew her way instinctively along the passages and alley ways, staircases and corridors. Inside it was damp and chilly, draughts kept at bay by thick Burgundian tapestries on the walls and even hanging in doorways. They passed by countless Old Testament scenes in fading reds, blues, yellows and greens.

Harry was in his library, engaged in signing documents. A couple of dark-robed attendants were busying themselves either handing him the papers or rolling up those already bearing his name. He threw down his quill with delight as they were announced. Clearly, any excuse to quit the business of day to day government was well-received. Katherine curtsied deeply, taking care to remain with her eyes downcast. William made a similar, respectfully deep bow. Harry liked to be treated with initial deference but then enjoyed the power of dispensing with it. He liked to be exalted but approachable. They were to remain standing whilst he addressed them.

"This business of reversing my father's attainder." He eyed them keenly. "I am minded to do it. Upon certain conditions."

Katherine focused upon the rushes under her feet, and the tiny visible flecks of saffron. She did not dare catch William's eye.

"Your Grace is most merciful," said William politely.

"Always," said Harry gravely, "to those who serve me with loyalty and love."

Katherine remembered the petulant little boy who pushed his sister into rose-beds and hated to share. "What conditions does Your Grace have in mind?"

"Aunt Kaff'ryn, I have been made aware of your claims upon the March lands and fortune."

William raised a quizzical eyebrow. Harry burst out laughing. "Uncle William, has my aunt not acquainted you with this aspect of her ancestry?"

She explained: "My sister the Queen inherited the lands of the earls of March through our Mortimer great grandmother."

"My great-great grandmother," pointed out Harry, "and these lands passed from my mother to my father, and should therefore pass to me – as my lawyers have advised me," He gesticulated in an offhand way in the direction of the two men in plain robes.

A lawyer might argue that as Bessy's sister, and of the blood line of the Mortimers, I have a far stronger claim upon the lands than anyone else living. But it was crystal clear what Harry wanted. And why fight him? She would trade her own birthright for William's restoration to his title and estates. It was not a hard decision.

"Of course, Your Grace. I am sure it is what my sister, your beloved mother, would have wished."

It was a clever move. Harry revered Bessy's memory and from that stemmed his willingness to help his mother's sister.

"So you will agree to renounce *all* claims upon the March lands, and any others purchased by your father, King Edward the fourth?"

It would be so much safer for Hal if his only inheritance was of the house of Courtenay. Any sniff or shadow of the old Plantagenet legacies would fester in Harry's mind and might cause untold trouble in future years. The King was fond of his young Courtenay cousin; she had a duty to ensure the health of that relationship.

"Of course, Your Grace."

Harry looked suspicious for a moment, as if he had missed comprehending why the game had been so easily won, but then beamed at them. After all, winning was what mattered. He rose, and clapped William on the shoulder, and kissed his aunt enthusiastically. Katherine smelled the musky perfume he favoured and felt the softness of his clean-shaven cheek upon hers. It was hard to believe he was only eighteen – he had the physique of a man in his mid-twenties. Today he had adorned himself in a heavy collar of worked gold with large Hs between the links. A huge diamond glittered on his forefinger.

"Well then, Uncle, we shall look to see you made ninth Earl of Devon, as soon as possible! Shall you like to be a Countess, Aunt?" He seemed immensely pleased with his own generosity. Katherine studied him: the broad face, with eyes that seemed a little too small; the mouth and ears surprisingly neat and small on a young man of his build. A rich, dark green velvet cap perched on top of his auburn hair. He caught her staring.

"Do you think I look like your father, Aunt? There are many who say so."

"Your Grace, I have no memories of my father. I was a tiny child when he died. But yes, he was tall like you … and handsome." He was satisfied with her answer, but already his mind was elsewhere; he had achieved his purpose and was tiring of their company.

"But shortly after, when he (Lord William Courtenay) **began to exercise himself in martial feats and warlike study, he sickened of a disease called pleurisy, of which malady, because it was so strange and rare to the physicians, he at the king's manor of Greenwich died, leaving one son behind him to continue his family."** Edward Hall, Chronicler

Greenwich London June 1511

Although the prospect of taking possession again of the house in Warwick Lane was a particular delight, Katherine also looked forward to returning to Devon for the summer months. It would be a chance to spend time with Hal and Meggie, and to ride with William through the countryside visiting many of the manors on the Courtenay estates.

Before going home, though, there was time to enjoy all the rituals of May Day, when William accompanied the King at dawn to fetch in the may blossom and boughs of pale greenery to decorate the Great Hall at Greenwich, followed by four days of merry-making involving wrestling, jousting, dancing, and picnics of cake and cream in the water meadows. Following the ceremony to bestow the earldom of Devon upon William, the Courtenays were high in the King's favour – who else could discuss the finer points of horse-breeding like his Uncle William? Who else could lend beauty and grace to the maypole dancing like his dear Aunt Kaff'ryn? Every day, for a fortnight, Harry dragged William to the stables, tennis courts, bowling alleys and archery butts, amidst a mob of younger courtiers all intent upon proving their physical prowess. It was with relief that they finally waved Harry and Catalina off on their progress though the Midlands; there would be three or four months breathing space before being summoned to court again. Katherine turned to supervising the packing of their own clothes and essentials.

But William caught a summer cold, which escalated into a dry, barking cough. All the exertions in the chill spring air, on top of the two years in Calais gaol had left his lungs weakened and he was soon laid low. After only a week he was complaining of sharp pains every time he tried to draw breath. Within hours each shallow intake was an agony.

The physician gave him poppy syrup to soothe the pain. Katherine looked on helplessly as he slipped in and out of consciousness, his chest still convulsing and his handsome features distorting with discomfort. Her eyes brimmed with tears as she stroked his hair back off the hot forehead; it had grown again, just as springy as in the past, like a bed of camomile, but with the tell-tale streak of white that told of past suffering.

Outside their set of rooms the servants had already begun the ritual cleansing of the palace; she could hear the banging and swishing of the brooms as they swept out the dirty rushes, and the slopping of water in pails as they began to wash down the panelling. She longed for William to recover so they, too, could be on their way down the Great West Road.

But the man who lay exhausted with coughing, as pale as the linen bolsters supporting his head, did not improve. When he managed to speak it was to gasp out complaints of daggers in his chest and a fire in his head.

The physician attending him turned sombre eyes upon Katherine. "My Lady, I think you should send for a priest."

It was as though some strange pageant was being enacted before her. A priest came to give extreme unction, anointing his lips, ears, eyes, nostrils, lips, hands and feet and intoning the prayers while Katherine knelt, a thousand memories dancing before her closed eyes: the boy on the horse; the young man who had held her so close after their betrothal; the ardent young husband gazing in wonderment upon her body; the proud young father holding his firstborn so tenderly; the knight galloping downs the lists, his armour blinding her in the bright sunlight … she could not believe that this could be the end.

Afternoon slid into evening, and evening became the short summer night which eased again towards dawn. William was far away, his eyes closed, and his breathing changed to deep rasps that reverberated around the chamber. She could feel his hands cooling in hers. Occasionally he tried to yawn, as if searching for air. She moistened his dry lips and looked up at the physician in mute appeal, but he shook his head sadly.

"God's will be done, my lady."

The priest began murmuring afresh and she was only vaguely aware of others filling the room, amongst them a shocked Rob Anning who had recently arrived to escort them home, and Philippa. She thought back to the stories of her father's death. That, too, had been shocking and unexpected – a man taken from his wife and family in his prime. Now she understood what her mother must have felt. William was thirty six. It was too soon! He had only just been returned to her. She gave a sudden, hoarse sob. God was unfair!

His soul departed quickly, like an insignificant wave retreating from the shingly shore at Seaton. Suddenly, she was aware the breaths had ceased and as his face relaxed into an expression of peace she knew that his pain was over. The bells of the city were beginning to ring out the hour of Prime. Around her, everyone knelt and prayed. Rob Anning was crying. She kissed her husband's lips softly. "Oh, William, right well-beloved, thank you. I have been blessed amongst women. Godspeed to heaven, and greet our son."

They told her that the idea of taking his body home to Devon was an impossibility in this summer heat but the King, miles away in the midland counties, hearing of her distress, would issue a royal warrant to grant his respected uncle-by-marriage, the newly restored Earl of Devon, a resting place in the priory at Blackfriars.

"He means it as an honour," said Meg Pole, an arm around her cousin's waist as they walked together in the royal privy garden, where golden lions and unicorns perched on colourful striped poles, and June roses hung heavy in the hot sunshine. It was strange to have the palace to themselves. Everyone had gone, either with the court on progress, or home to their own estates. "See how he rewards our loyalty, Katherine. We have nothing to fear now. He wants us, his family, all close by, and wants to please us."

"It was good of you to come; I feel so alone. The children are distraught. They had come to know him again, Meg, and love him."

"He was a rare man, Katherine. You have been fortunate, despite the difficult years. To have a husband who truly loves you … well, they write of such love, and sing of it, but for most of us it remains the stuff of legends. I counted myself lucky in the end that mine was kind and respectful."

"How have your children coped without their father?"

"My eldest, Henry, has done his best to take Richard's place. Geoffrey's a bit of a hot-head and could do with a man's discipline. Arthur is a sweet boy, and Ursula a treasure – they are both too young to know any different."

"And your son Reginald?"

Meg paused. "He does not forgive me for placing him with the brothers at Sheen. I was desperate when Richard died; Henry Tudor took everything and as you know I was forced to take my youngest and live with the nuns at Syon Abbey. Reginald is resentful. He's a difficult boy. Jealous of his brothers and sister, I fear."

"Meg, do you ever worry about your boys? In the future?"

"You mean their bloodline?"

"Yes. Sometimes I wonder whether one day Harry will look at our sons and see them as a threat."

"Then you and I must teach them *not* to be a threat. They must be His Grace's beloved cousins – his most devoted followers. And then, what a future awaits them!"

"Do you know how our cousin Suffolk fares?"

Meg Pole wrinkled her long, elegant nose. "Listen, Katherine, you know as well as I do that Suffolk brought his misfortune upon himself through arrogance and foolish, romantic ambition. He languishes in the Tower still, as my poor brother did, but *he* deserves it, whereas Ned…"

"Forgive me, Meg, I did not mean to open old wounds."

They had criss-crossed the network of paths through the knot garden, where the shrubs and plants were planted in clever patterns – like the devices on a shield, thought Katherine. Now and again the beds of herbs released their aromatic wafts. Katherine breathed in deeply, allowing lavender to soothe her thoughts. "I have been considering, Meg, that I should take a vow of celibacy."

Margaret stopped dead, her shoes scrunching in the gravel. "*What?* You mean to take the *veil? Like Bridget?* Oh, Katherine, *no,* my dear! I am sure you were not made for such a life!"

"No, not to shut myself away in a nunnery but to become a vowess, like our grandmother, Cecily Neville."

Meg scrutinised her younger cousin. "Our grandmother was a very pious woman. To be honest, she had much in common with My Lady the King's Mother, except that one was a Yorkist and the other a Lancastrian! In all good faith,

Katherine, I cannot quite see you draped in black for the rest of your life and on your knees in the chapel for hours on end."

They had reached the far corner of the walled garden, where a low wooden door was almost hidden by rambling roses. Katherine tried the latch and it opened. It was a private route out of the palace, leading firstly into an orchard and then onto the open grassland of the deer park. Here the air was fresher, for a light breeze blew off the river. The panorama was impressive, with the broad Thames on both sides of the headland. Far away to the west were the spires of the city and north-eastwards the dark green of the woods and forests of Essex. The ground was dry, and the grass short where the deer had cropped it. A fallen tree provided a convenient seat.

"I am trying to fathom a way into the future that will protect me, and my children. I'm only thirty one, Meg, and the King could force me into marriage with someone of his choosing, or some man might see me as his way to challenge the Tudor rule. If I take a public vow of chastity I avoid that. I can go back to Devon, and care for the Courtenay estates until Hal is of an age to shoulder the responsibility. I am used to living without a husband – I know I can do it. I want the freedom to do as I wish."

She pulled off her headdress and removed the linen coif covering her hair. The pinned braids caught the sunlight, glinting with shades of creamy gold. Meg sat primly, even disapprovingly, her skirts tucked around her feet. "I think you are over-reacting, cousin. Poor William's death is a tragedy, of course, and I understand your grief, but I am sure there is a safe future for both of us, and all our children. There's no need to go making some grand gesture."

"If William had died without his inheritance I would agree with you, but the attainder has been reversed and it is my duty to be the custodian. And in any case, I never want another husband – or the dangers of childbirth. I want to live, and have control of my own life."

Meg looked dubious. "What woman can ever say that, cousin?"

Katherine looked down to the river, where the freshening wind was catching at the sails of the craft headed downstream to who knows where – Burgundy, France, and all the duchies and states along the North Sea coast; even onwards to Denmark and into the Baltic. Maybe even towards the New World they heard tell of.

"I don't know. But I intend to try."

Katherine: *My husband was interred in the church at Blackfriars. Good Dr Standish preached the funeral sermon and declared that William had never been involved in any plot against Henry Tudor. I admired his courage, as he stood there in the pulpit, warning all princes and lords not to give hasty credence to words without sure ground. Of course, Harry was not there to hear him, but as I left the church I felt William's name had finally been washed clean of all doubt. I pressed forward with my resolve to secure my independence, and only a month after William's death stood in front of the Bishop of London to make my vow of chastity. There was nobody to gainsay me. A letter came from Bridget, with loving words of support: "Sister, you do well to guard yourself from those who would seek to use you."*

My nephew the King and I traded like hard-nosed merchants to achieve a deal of benefit to us both. I relinquished all claims to any ancestral lands, and in return, to my astonishment, received the estates and earldom of Devon in my own right, for my lifetime. It was more than I could have ever hoped for. Even Meg Pole had to agree that my gamble had paid off. My son Hal would be called "Earl" and receive all his inheritance in due course. The fact that no man could now force me into marriage for the sake of my Plantagenet blood seemed to please Harry – who either failed to, or chose not to, see that my resolution prevented him from persuading or coercing me into a second marriage.

I took care to dress modestly, in darker colours and without too many jewels. My widowhood and vow of celibacy became my shield and armour.

The Countess Katherine
1511 -1527

1

Tiverton Castle Spring 1513

Any hope she might have had of dissuading her son from soldiering was clearly pointless. Hal was excited beyond measure at the thought of joining the King's war in France, and could supply an answer to every single one of her protests. Seventeen, he declared, was exactly the same age his father had been when *he* joined King Henry VII's expedition against Maximilian of Austria. And she could not argue that he was not sufficiently grown – like his royal cousin he had the height and build that made him look more like a man of twenty five. She knew he could sit on a war horse as well as any of the experienced officers in Harry's army and months of feverish practising had honed his young body into battle-fitness. He dismissed her concerns about injury, or worse, with a confidence born from youthful arrogance. "And anyway, I am the King's trusted companion and cousin. I am commanded to go with him."

She could hear the pride in his voice. He loved all the Courtenay estates in Devon but his yearning for the world of men, travel, chivalry and adventure was written all over his eager young face. With his mother in charge of all the Courtenay lands there was no need for him to be tied to the West Country. And it was a glorious time to be alive! His cousin the King talked of nothing but going to France and winning back all the lands once held by the fifth King Henry. "And he was a Plantagenet too, Lady Mother!"

"He was not of our mother's family. He was a Lancastrian," said Meggie waspishly. She could always be relied upon to put her brother in his place. They had been playing at cards after supper, and she had won, twice. Quick-witted and clever, she was always one step ahead of him.

In the privacy of the cosy family solar they could speak freely. "There was no such thing as Lancastrians and Yorkist in those days, Meggie. It all came afterwards." Their mother rarely spoke of her bloodline. Her children exchanged swift, meaningful looks.

"Tell us then, Mother," coaxed Meggie.

Katherine hesitated but, in a moment of amused exasperation with them both, gave in.

"I was taught that the troubles began with the death of King Edward III, for it was his grandson who became King Richard II, and he ruled unwisely. So much so that his cousin, Harry of Lancaster –"

"Why was he of Lancaster?" Hal asked.

"Because he married a Lancaster heiress, stupid!" retorted Meggie. "Everyone knows that."

"So why was *your* family of *York,* Mother?"

Meggie sighed. "Because our great- great-great grandfather was created the Duke of York!"

Hal's brows knitted together in an expression of confusion. He was more interested in the here and now, and the future. Meggie seized a quill and sheet of paper, and drew a broad, vertical line, punctuated by horizontal dashes. "Look, Hal – here is our mother, Princess Katherine of York, and her father, King Edward, and his father, the Duke of York. *His* father was called the Duke of Cambridge, and second son of the Duke of York, who was son to King Edward!" She underscored her penmanship with a triumphant flourish.

Katherine took the quill from her daughter and dipped it into the ink-pot. Carefully, she filled in a few more names. "Your Aunt Cecily showed me how to do this when I was a girl. She was fascinated by it all. And so proud of who we were. Look, Hal, here is the fourth Henry, of Lancaster, and *his* son the fifth Henry, and *his* son, the sixth Henry."

Hal frowned. "The mad one? The one who lost all our lands in France and died in the Tower?"

Katherine sighed, "I don't think he was suited to being a king, Hal. He preferred to pray, so my sisters used to tell me." Suddenly, the smell of the ink and scratching of the goose-quill brought back memories of listening to Bessy and Cecily discussing the finer points of their family history.

"Did he not fall asleep, Mother, for months at a time?" Meggie's dark eyes were bright with interest.

"So they say, poor man. It's surely hard to be a king when you are asleep. And my grandfather, Richard of York believed he could be a better king, and challenged him."

She had both children's attention now. Hal stared at the paper, running his eye down the page, watching as she added more names.

She realised that they knew only a world where the Tudors ruled. And even Meggie's superior understanding of her royal connections was limited to a line of names. There was no-one who would have told them of the thirty years of struggle and bloodshed between the two houses. Names of battles and men long-forgotten. *Somewhere, there must still be ancient men who recall the blood-soaked snow at Towton; the terrifying mists of Barnet; the slaughter at Tewkesbury.* All fought before her birth, but haunting the imagination of her childhood. And the legacy of the strife between Lancaster and York, reaching into her life like the cold steel of a sword, twisting and turning …

"What exactly happened to the sixth Henry?" Hal asked.

Katherine paused, the thick goose-quill against her cheek. "He died in the Tower, shortly after my father had won the great victory at Tewkesbury. It was before I was born. Some say that my father and Uncle Richard had him killed. Some say they killed him themselves. I think it quite likely, for I have learned that in this world it is often a case of kill, or be killed."

"Where does the Duke of Suffolk fit in, Mother?"

"I thought you knew that, Hal."

"I have never seen the relationships made so clear before." He followed her finger as she explained, then looked at her with troubled eyes. "The King says he will have him executed – before we go to France."

Katherine swallowed hard. "I am surprised he has lived this long. He was the cause of your father's imprisonment and suffering. Never forget that, Hal. I would not wish death upon anyone, but save your pity. And for goodness sake don't draw any attention to our kinship with him when you are with the King."

"Well, I suppose that means the King will be rewarding someone else with my Lord Suffolk's title and lands," remarked Meggie. "I wonder who that will be? He'll be incredibly wealthy, won't he, Mother?" Sometimes it was hard to believe she was only twelve, such was her insightfulness. She cocked her head like an inquisitive robin. "Who will I marry, Mother?"

Katherine was genuinely startled. Somewhere, certainly, in the back of her mind, was the determination to broker safe, secure and advantageous alliances for her children.

"Who would marry *you*, sister?" asked Hal in acid, brotherly tones. "You would be forever correcting him, and saying you wanted to read books rather than take care of his household. It's a good job our lord grandfather Courtenay settled money on you from his own estates – no man would take you otherwise."

Meggie went scarlet with mortification but fought back. "And what girl will want you, Hal, when you stink of horses and … and … and forget to clean your teeth?"

Hal stretched out his long legs and put his feet up on the table just to annoy her.

"Plenty, sister, because *I* am the Earl of Devon," he replied loftily, "and will probably be a war hero as well."

Katherine had had enough of their bickering. She pushed her son's feet away, and rolled up the paper charting their maternal descent. "Let us pray that you survive to tell the tale, Hal." She knew his youth was no guarantee of safety; soldiers expected to be led, and that was the job of men of high birth, even if they were little more than boys. Hal would want to be noticed, and win the approval of his royal cousin. She fretted that there would be no older close relative to keep a watchful eye on him – no father, or uncle, or brother.

Meggie yawned. "Who will rule the country while Hal and the King are away playing soldiers?"

"Our cousin says he will leave his wife as Regent."

Meggie sat up in surprise. "Really? He will leave a woman in charge?" She shuffled the pack of cards expertly and laid the king and queen of hearts upon the table. She drew the queen towards her. "Queen Catherine will like that, won't she Mother?"

Katherine smiled. "Catalina has always been certain that women are perfectly capable of ruling. Her own mother was Queen of Castile, and led her troops into battle." She remembered Catalina telling stories of her childhood to the two Tudor princesses, Margaret and Mary, and revelling in their expressions of disbelief as she recounted tales of her mother conquering the infidel Muslims in Granada.

Hal came over and tried to pull the cards from his sister's hand. "I'd like to see *you* living in a tent in a field, Meggie; you're too fond of your comforts these days."

She batted him away. "I'm not saying I would want to go to war – you are welcome to your awful beds, and disgusting food, and festering wounds but it will be interesting to see how a woman rules in the King's absence." She frowned. "If we were not always called upon to have children, I am sure we could play a much larger part in government. Don't you think so, Mother?"

Hal shouted with laughter. "Listen to yourself, Meggie! Now I am certain no man will ever marry you, unless Mother sends you to the altar with a gag in your mouth!"

For a moment Katherine felt immense sympathy for her feisty young daughter. It would, indeed, take a young man of rare foresight to cope with Meggie's cravings for education and freedom. She patted Meggie's hand. "Women can influence things in many ways, my sweeting. And have enough power to keep themselves content. Look at me, do I not make all my own decisions now?"

"Now you are a widow, "Meggie responded dolefully, "and now you have made your vow never to marry again."

King Harry's campaign took him away from England for the entire summer and autumn. It seemed that nearly every young nobleman in England went with him. At first, the country was left with a strange feeling of emptiness and of marking time until news came from across the Channel that the English army had put the French to flight at the town of Therouanne. They heard how the enemy turned and fled, thousands of pairs of spurs flashing in the sun as Harry's army pursued them for miles across the flat land of Artois. Hal sent a mud-stained letter recounting the glee with which he and others had chased the French and helped to capture scores of terrified prisoners. He told them that whilst a handful of English lords had perished he was safe, under the command of Charles Somerset, Lord Herbert, and now at Lille, where warfare had given way to jousting. The best bit, he said, was a tournament held indoors, where the horses' feet were covered in felt shoes. Katherine had to smile; Hal was his father's son after all. How William would have loved to ride Seaton on such an occasion! The old warhorse was dead now, of course – but Hal rode one of his descendants in France.

Yet Katherine and Meggie were even more captivated by what Catalina achieved in her husband's absence. Deep in the Devon countryside they felt far removed from the capital but even so news filtered through of astonishing events. The Scottish king had taken advantage of his brother-in-law's preoccupations abroad to launch an invasion across the border. On Catalina's orders, the Earl of Surrey and his army rode into Northumberland and slaughtered over ten thousand Scots outside the village of Branxston. Their king had died fighting alongside his men, cut down by an English arrow and skewered by an English billhook.

"They say her Grace has sent the Scots king's bloodstained coat to her husband in France," said Rob Anning, "and she wanted to send the body as well."

An expression of fascinated horror crossed Meggie's face as they listened to Rob recounting what he had heard in Honiton. "What stopped her?"

"I think she was eventually persuaded that we English are more civilised than that, my lady. But apparently she said it is what her mother would have done."

Battles and bloodshed seemed a world away in the pleasant warmth of an early October. Summer still lingered in Devon; the roads were dry and a group of travelling players had stopped for a few days to entertain the local gentry. Katherine liked to offer hospitality to neighbouring families at the Courtenay castle in Tiverton. The hall was alive tonight with conversation and music but she could see her guests hushing one another as the news spread. Faces were upturned expectantly – it was exciting to have their countess so closely related to kings and queens.

Katherine's heart ached for young Queen Margaret, whom she had last seen as a girl of thirteen, weeping at Bessy's funeral. That summer Henry Tudor had taken her north to her future with a man twice her age. She had heard that King James had proved a loving husband but Margaret had had to share him with several mistresses and numerous illegitimate children; her own efforts to produce a living heir for Scotland had been tinged with tragedy. The new king of Scotland was a mere seventeen months old.

"Mother, what will happen now to my cousin the Queen of Scotland?"

"I suppose she might become Regent, but I cannot see the Scots parliament wanting the sister of their enemy."

"No-one ever really wants a woman in a position of power."

"Hush, Meggie! Now is not the time or the place for your thoughts."

Katherine stood up, knowing that her guests were eager to hear confirmation of the rumours. "We hear that the army sent by the Queen has won a great victory over the Scots at a battle called Flodden Field. My cousin the King will be delighted."

Roars of approval rose up to the, rafters. It was good to be English! Good to have a young belligerent king, unafraid of attacking the perfidious French after all these years, and good to have a brave young queen keeping the country safe from that other slippery customer in the *auld alliance* between the Scots and the French.

"*God save King Henry! God save Queen Catherine!*" Someone raised an enthusiastic toast, taken up by scores of others in Tiverton Castle. So Harry and Catalina had come of age, dignified by their actions into Henry and Catherine. Her friends and neighbours hammered their fists on the trestle boards. At her side, Rob Anning diplomatically filled Katherine's wine-glass. "Always best to be on the winning side," he murmured. She lifted it and acknowledged the cheers.

2

"A nymph from Heaven, a Paradise" Venetian State Papers record the beauty of Princess Mary Tudor

"She consented to his request, and for the peace of Christendom, to marry Louis of France, though he was very aged and sickly, on condition that if she survived him, she should marry whom she liked." Letters from the reign of King Henry VIII

The Princess Mary Tudor's rooms hummed with activity as the women of the court prepared for her imminent departure to France. In the middle of it all, Catalina of Aragon directed operations as effectively as she had organised a battle against the Scots. They were knee-deep in great coffers overflowing with clothes and jewels offered by the King to pacify his demanding little sister.

Only three months ago the princess thought she would be departing to Burgundy, to marry her long-time betrothed, Prince Charles of Castile, but during early summer everything had changed. Emperor Maximilian and Catalina's father, Ferdinand, had made a peace treaty with the French, and Harry Tudor had found himself outflanked. His dreams of another summer of glorious warfare were replaced by a need to make the French his allies even more firmly than Spain and Burgundy. If the English were astonished at the turnabout of events, their eighteen-year-old princess was incandescent with rage. She had expected to marry Catalina's nephew, a teenage boy she thought to twist round her little finger; instead she was told by her brother she must be the wife of an old man in his fifties. The palace of Greenwich echoed with her screams and sobs until the King could bear it no more, and sent to Devon for his Aunt Kaff'ryn to talk some sense into her niece.

Katherine asked to see Mary alone. She knew there was no gainsaying Harry Tudor. He would use his sister as a political pawn, as she herself might have been used in some other life. All she could do was try to help Mary to see another perspective. It would be no easy task, though; Mary was the spoiled darling of the Tudor court, petted and indulged since childhood, used to getting her own way with just a flutter of her eyelashes and pout of her lips. Her brother's command to marry his former enemy had stunned her.

She found her face-down on her bed, weeping noisily. Sometimes, the prettiness of childhood is not fulfilled in later years, but Mary Tudor was astoundingly attractive, even with puffed eyes. That she had worked herself up, yet again, into a state of near-hysteria was obvious. Katherine sat quietly on the coverlet and placed a sympathetic hand upon the princess's heaving back.

"Your Grace. Mary. Will you talk to me?"

"Not if he's sent you to make me agree!" Her voice was half-muffled by the bedclothes but then she raised herself on her elbows and looked at her aunt with an expression of utter tragedy. "How can he *do* it, Aunt Kaff'ryn? To *me?"*

Katherine hesitated. "Mary, you have always known -"

"Yes, *yes* – that I would marry abroad, but to the boy who would one day be Emperor, not to some *stinking old man!"*

"You don't know that he –"

"*All* old men stink! Every single one! They stink like goats! They have no teeth! Their breath smells vile! Why, I hazard he is impotent, too!" She fell into a fresh burst of sobbing. "Does no-one have any pity for me? Ah, Jesu, if my mother were still alive she would not allow this!"

It was probably true, but mention of Bessy hardened Katherine's resolve. "Your mother was also forced to marry someone who repulsed her."

Mary was shocked enough to stop crying. "What do you mean? My father loved my mother. When she died he grieved for her so much ..."

Katherine pulled her niece to her. She was as slender as a young sapling, her red-gold Tudor hair loose over her shoulders and back like molten copper. "Your mother married your father because she had no choice. She did it for the sake of peace in this land, and to help us, her sisters. Lord help us, Mary, *she* thought to be Queen of France as a child. Look, Louis may be old but he will be entranced by you. He will give you whatever you want. More clothes and jewels than you could ever imagine. I think he will be easier to manage than some boy who thinks *you* are too old."

"Charles said that? That I am too old?" Mary was affronted.

449

"He is yet a boy, and you are a woman. Mary, the die is cast, as I think you know, but what you can do is plan how to play a clever game. Make Louis adore you."

She was sure she had caught her niece's attention, for the heaving breaths subsided and she clasped her hands together in her lap, knitting her fingers together to control the trembling. "But I will still have to let him have me …"

"Yes, and I am sorry that you will not have a young husband, but just because he is older does not mean he will not be tender. In fact, if you play your cards right you can turn everything to your advantage. Go to your brother, and beg his pardon; you know there's nothing he likes more than feeling he is right – but ask if you may pick the household who will travel with you, and –" Katherine drew a deep breath, "ask him to promise that when Louis dies you can come home and marry someone of your own choice." She had learned that Harry quite enjoyed bargaining. And all Tudors liked gambling.

Mary was silent, but unknotted her fingers and placed them quietly on her knees. "Someone of my own choice?" Her whisper held a sort of incredulous wonderment. Katherine knew then that the rumours about the flirtation between Mary and Harry's friend Charles Brandon were more than likely true, despite his colourful marital past history and being betrothed to his ward, Elizabeth Grey, an eight year old heiress.

"Mary, you have no choice at the moment but Louis is not in good health. And England needs peace. Would you have more young men die needlessly? That is what your mother thought about when she married your father. A princess can be a powerful force for good."

"*You* were not forced to marry, Aunt Kaff'ryn." She was not going down without a fight.

"Oh yes I was, but I was incredibly lucky. Your father told me I must *marry a Courtenay* – I had no idea who. Luck may yet come your way too, Mary. In the future. If you can be patient."

"And you think Harry will agree to me choosing my own husband – next time?" Her almond-shaped eyes slewed round in thinly-veiled anticipation.

"If I know my nephew he will be so relieved you have stopped screaming he will agree to give you the moon. Just make sure he's on his own, with no advisors around."

Mary stared at the rings on her long, musician's fingers. "And so, if you were my mother, this would be your advice to me?"

Katherine felt a pang, for she now knew that she would never insist upon Meggie marrying anyone who was not acceptable to her. But Meggie was not a princess of England, thank God. "If I were your mother, and a queen, I would know that the King's word was final, whether father, uncle or brother. I would tell you to hold your head high, do your duty, for the moment. You can survive this, Mary"

Within the week a pacified Mary managed to play her part to perfection in the proxy marriage to King Louis. His envoy was his cousin, the Duc de Longueville, who laid a naked leg next to Mary's own shapely limb in a bed hung with gold and purple. Archbishop Wareham solemnly declared the union symbolically consummated. The bride seemed happy, and in the following weeks revelled in the attention of the dressmakers and jewellers. Her husband sent a magnificent diamond, as large as a man's finger, set in a huge pear-shaped pendant pearl, which Mary wore constantly and held to the sunlight, gazing at its flashing fire and smiling secretly.

Now, in her apartments, the final packing was taking place. Catalina poured over lists of tapestries and finest linen, checking and rechecking against the inventories, whilst Mary sat unconcerned in a corner with her lute, surrounded by a group of young nobles, among them Charles Brandon. Katherine was wondering if she was the only one to notice the heightened colour in Mary's cheeks, when she caught the eye of another lady-in-waiting.

Lady Elizabeth Boleyn decided that she liked the King's aunt. They were much the same age, as were their children, and her brother Thomas Howard had been married to Countess Katherine's sister, Anne, until the poor lady had died of consumption three years since. She would never say it aloud, but the Howards thought it no great loss; Anne's children had all died and Lord Howard had already remarried. Lady Boleyn's own family was enormous: she was one of ten siblings, and her father had already embarked upon a second family with her stepmother. The Howard star was rising under the Tudors; her own marriage to Sir Thomas Boleyn was definitely helping to enhance his status.

"Her Grace seems content now," she observed sagely, as she helped Katherine fold yet another length of gorgeous damask into a linen travelling bag before they laid it in a trunk. She held open the neck, as Katherine sprinkled in liberal amounts of aromatic herbs that would ward off damp and moths whilst travelling. "Does your own daughter go with Her Grace to France?"

Katherine shook her head; Mary had offered, but Meggie said she had absolutely no desire to become a lady-in-waiting to her overindulged cousin. What time would there be for reading if she had to scuttle round after Mary Tudor from morning till night? Lady Elizabeth looked surprised. "My eldest is to go. Thank goodness. Her younger sister, Anne, is already abroad and my Mary is desperate – as the eldest she says she should have gone first, but Anne is so clever – her father found her a place with the French Duchess Marguerite in Antwerp last year. They will be together in Paris."

Katherine could hear the pride in Lady Elizabeth's voice. "A great honour and opportunity for them," she said politely. She was wary of the ambitious Howards.

"Well, I hope they can come back in two or three years with some polish. And then their father will have to find husbands for them. We are looking into our Irish connections. Do you have anyone in mind for your daughter?"

Fortunately, Lady Boleyn's desire to gossip was halted by Catalina approaching them, dusting off her hands with satisfaction. "It is like sending an army abroad! It makes me remember when I set out from Spain when I was a girl. Mary, *mi querida,* we are finally ready!" Despite her fluency in English she had never made much attempt to mask her Spanish accent with her "r"s rolled, a certain harsh edge to her pronunciation, and sentences delivered at speed.

Surrounded by her little group of admirers, Mary was barely listening. Charles Brandon leaned over her, ostensibly to turn the page of her music but also casting glances down at her full bosom, hardly concealed by the thin cambric of her chemise. She was now choosing to wear the type of hood thought fashionable in France, which showed much more of her hair than the gabled headdress Catalina liked her ladies to wear. Katherine saw how Catalina's lips pursed with distaste, but whether for Brandon or the French hood was unclear. Katherine rather liked the French hood herself; she wished she could have worn something so becoming as a young woman, and sighed to think that her vow now precluded it. Of Brandon she was less certain. The man was certainly handsome, but an opportunist – too fond of his own importance, his only claim to fame that his father had died for Henry Tudor at Bosworth. Now Harry had given him the dukedom of Suffolk, and all its estates, following the execution of her cousin. He swaggered around court, certain of his good looks, and the Princess Mary's favour.

A commotion at the door, and Harry swept into the room, in the company of even more young men, among them Hal Courtenay. All the ladies sank into billows of respectful curtsies. Beaming, Harry offered a huge hand to his wife, and kissed her cheek solicitously. "I hope you are not tiring yourself, my dear." His eyes flicked to the burgeoning curve of her belly. Catalina's latest pregnancy made him hungry with new hope.

"Not at all, Your Grace. I am simply anxious to ensure that the new Queen of France should have all things prepared for her journey tomorrow."

"And is all now in order?"

Mary threw her brother a brilliant smile. "It is, *now*, sir," she said sweetly. For a moment Harry looked slightly nonplussed but hating to appear anything but in full control of every situation he simply ignored his sister and flung an arm around Hal Courtenay instead. "So, we shall all set out for Dover tomorrow, will we not? The whole family. Cousin Courtenay here, and Aunt Kaff'ryn. We shall give you a fine send off, sister, then I shall trust you to God, and the fortunes of the sea, and the government of the French king, your husband!" He roared with laughter at his joke.

For a moment Mary looked panicked but Charles Brandon, who was gathering up her music and handing it to Lady Boleyn, said quietly, "Indeed, Your Grace, have no fear, for God will surely watch over you."

Katherine: *And so we did, indeed, wave Mary off to France, where she proceeded to dance her exhausted husband into an early grave, after just eighty two days of marriage! After an enforced seclusion of another forty days, to ensure she was not pregnant, my nephew sent his friend Charles Brandon to bring her home but Mary, being Mary, dragged Brandon off to the altar in the chapel at the Palais de Cluny and gave him an ultimatum: marry me now, or never. It was her greatest gamble ever. Harry was furious, mostly with Brandon, for betraying him, but Harry, being Harry, eventually saw a way to save face: his sister and her new husband could come home if Mary turned over all her jewels and plate from France, and promised to repay the £24,000 spent on her marriage to Louis. The new Suffolk family were forgiven but uncertain of where their next penny might come from.*

In a fit of pique, Harry also sold off Brandon's wardship of young Elizabeth Grey. I bought it, with an eye to Hal's future. She was a cousin; her grandfather had been the brother of my mother's first husband, Sir John Grey of Groby. Lisbet was a sweet child, orphaned as I had been. And in the meantime Catalina gave birth to a tiny, premature, stillborn boy who did not even receive a name. I was relieved to go home to Devon, and give my attention to my own family.

3

"There was a lover and his lass, with a heigh and a ho, and a heigh nonny no!" Tradtional 16th century lyric

Tiverton Castle 1515

Sometimes Katherine wondered if her own married life had been a dream. Just seven fleeting years (so hard to recall now) before William's arrest and imprisonment, then just eighteen months together before his death. Those she had loved and lost came to her so clearly in her dreams. Their faces flashed into her mind as if caught in the polished surface of a silvered mirror. The Feigned Lad was there too, arm in arm with Ned of Warwick. They were always sauntering away, though, and just looking back over their shoulders. She thanked God that all of them appeared as they had lived, not as they had died. That would have been unbearable. She had no portrait of William – just an imprint on her memory, an echo of his light, loving voice yet in her dreams she saw him clearly. When she woke at dawn in her great bed at Tiverton, she sometimes thought he was still there with her – could swear for a moment that she could hear his even breathing, and feel his familiar warmth next to her, but then her eyes opened to her loneliness. She had the maids take away the extra pillows. That he was in Heaven she had no doubt; in due time she would join him, but for now there was a life to be lived. She had children to provide for.

Hal seemed perfectly content to marry little Lisbet Grey when she should be old enough. The child often came to stay, hungry for love and affection, adoring Katherine and Meggie, and in awe of the young man they told her would one day be her husband. Katherine felt William would have approved of her plan. There was the worrisome question, though, of a suitable husband for Meggie. They had a heart-stopping moment when Harry suggested her as a bride for the debauched young Earl of Oxford, John de Vere – a wastrel fond of frequenting the stews of Southwark, despite his tender years. It took all of Katherine's tact to steer her nephew's match-making prerogative in other directions. Meggie took to her room and refused to eat for nearly a week. *Why should my cousin the King choose who I marry, Mama? I will die rather than marry that vile boy!* When news came that de Vere had refused her daughter, Katherine did not know whether to laugh or cry. Meggie emerged, thinner but defiant and triumphant. It was a wake-up call that made them both eager to find someone suitable before King Harry thought of another prospective bridegroom.

In the event, all was solved quite miraculously. In France, Hal had made firm friends with Henry Somerset, son of his commander, Lord Herbert, now the Earl of Worcester. His maternal grandmother was Mary Wydville, Katherine's aunt. The names rang bells in Katherine's mind; she suddenly remembered Bessy travelling to stay with her Herbert relations in Wales, the summer before she died. Even more intriguing was the fact that Henry Somerset's grandfather had taken as his second wife that Katherine Plantagenet, the love-child of King Richard. The family had been staunch Yorkists. Somerset's mother, Elizabeth Herbert, had been a heiress in her own right, her title going to her husband.

Meggie was fascinated by the family connections. "So, this Somerset, Mother, is of your Yorkist blood?"

"Oh, Meggie, don't get carried away by romantic notions. His father is a Beaufort, of Lancaster. I have told you, everyone is a cousin sooner or later!"

"But our grandmothers were sisters," insisted Meggie.

"Yes, but at that point they were Lancastrian ladies too! Remember, my mother only became Yorkist when she married King Edward."

Meggie stared at her family ancestry chart – she was forever adding new pages and filling in new names. "It's all fascinating."

"It's all complicated. Why not keep a record of your Courtenay lineage instead?"

"With respect to my father, that's not half so interesting! Courtenays of Boconnoc, and Powderham?"

Katherine smiled. "Your grandmother Courtenay was always keen to impress upon me the fact that there were Courtenays in England almost as long as there had been Plantagenets. She told me once I was not the first princess to marry into their family – but she had no idea who! I asked my sister Bessy, who told me a grand-daughter of the first King Edward had married a Courtenay. So you see,

Meggie, you can be proud of both sides! And we shall get to meet our distant cousin, Lord Somerset. Hal is bringing him to stay. He is anxious to see the Courtenay horses. Hal hopes he will buy a couple. Apparently they call him Somer, because there are so many Henrys now at court."

The two young men arrived in a whirl of energy and enthusiasm. Henry Somerset was eager to claim kinship with his friend's family and bowed low over Katherine's hand. He sat next to Meggie at dinner, affably playing the part of supper companion, helping her to dishes and cutting up her meat with his own knife.

"I do this for my own sister, at home at Raglan," he said.

"And is Raglan a large castle? Bigger than Tiverton?" asked Meggie, accepting his offer of the choicest chicken.

Somerset hesitated, knife mid-air, which he hastily put down. He was a well brought-up young man and did not wish to offend. "A little bigger, yes, but this is … charming."

Katherine hid a smile. Bessy had waxed lyrical about how the Herberts lived in Monmouthshire, in their majestic, luxurious castle, with its parklands, and gardens. Here at Tiverton they lived most comfortably but the castle itself was more like a grand manor house, not the towering edifice that was Raglan.

Meggie was stealing sideways glances at him. He was certainly worth looking at: tall, with hair so dark as to be almost blue-black, and sea-blue eyes framed by strong, dark brows. His mouth was set in a permanently pleasant upward turn, and his ears stuck out rather endearingly. Like Hal, life at the Tudor court gave him opportunities for doing all the things beloved of athletic young men; his wrists were strong from swordplay, and his shoulders broad from carrying a shield and lance. But there was more to him than just physical attributes. After dinner, Hal sprawled in his chair. "Play us one of your songs, Somer. My mother and Meggie are fond of music."

Obligingly, the young man took the lute offered to him, checked the tuning, then balanced it carefully upon his right knee, his left stretched out – muscular in its tight-fitting hose. "This is a song my mother taught me. It's Welsh."

His tuneful voice flowed like honey over the plaintive, plucked chords of the lute. He was utterly at ease with his talent, modestly glad to bring pleasure to his audience. After listening for a couple of verses Katherine was able to harmonise a little and he smiled at her appreciatively. In that moment she knew that she wanted him for Meggie. Her daughter was uncharacteristically quiet for the rest of the evening but in the morning went with the young men to look at the foals and yearlings in the paddocks. She returned bubbling with admiration.

"Mama, he is so *nice!*" adding mischievously, "I cannot believe that he is my brother's friend! "

"Meggie! You never look for the best in Hal!"

She giggled. "Mother, Hal is all horses and swords; Somer is more than that – he writes poetry, and composes music, and likes to read … he knows *The Morte d'Arthur!*"

"Good heavens," observed her mother.

"And he thinks that girls should read too, and write. He says he would willingly educate his own daughters. He says his mother was clever; he says –"

"Clearly, he has said a great deal to impress you."

"Yes," said Meggie simply. "He is the only young man I have ever met who can talk of anything sensible." Her dark eyes shone with honesty. "Mother, I could marry such a man. He is kind."

She was just fourteen. She had lived nearly all her life quietly in Devon. It was unlikely she had ever talked with any man of her own status except her brother. Katherine touched her cheek. "Oh Meggie, my love, his family may have other plans."

"Hal says not." She picked at the lace cuff of her gown.

"You have only just met him. You are still quite young, Meggie. I would not let you become a full wife to any man yet. You understand my meaning?"

She blushed. "Yes. And I would not wish to, yet." Then she turned imploring eyes upon her mother, like a cornered doe. "But neither could I bear it if my cousin the King says I have to marry someone like De Vere." An obstinate little twist curled at the corner of her mouth. "I would rather follow Aunt Bridget to the nunnery at Dartford."

"Let me talk with Somer, and write to his father. If we could persuade the King, between us …" She put her arm around her daughter's waist. "You are a prize for any man, my sweeting; you are the grand-daughter of a King, and the cousin of a King, but for all that that you have no royal title. The Herberts may indeed have a bigger castle but we are their equals in land."

Loud footsteps and laughter heralded the arrival of the two young men, pink-cheeked with fresh air, arms around each other's shoulders.

"Somer is going to have two of the colts, Mother. The black and the bay."

Katherine inclined her head. "A sound choice; they are both from the bloodline of my late husband's favourite courser, Seaton, who carried him in both battles and jousts."

"That is what interests me, my Lady. I want a couple of youngsters I can train up for the tiltyard. Hal tells me your stallions are always named for towns on the Courtenay manors. I like that. Lady Meggie, would you do me the honour of choosing names for my two new horses?" His grin was open, boyish and eager.

Katherine: *Fortunately, the Herbert family were not only interested in the bloodline of the Courtenay horses! Somer must have gone straight home to Raglan, for before the month was out, and whilst I was composing in my head how best to open a dialogue with the Herberts, a letter arrived from the Earl of Worcester, asking if I might consider an alliance with his family. Hal took credit for it all of course, claiming he had identified his friend Somer as the only man who could put up with a girl like Meggie: "They can write poetry together, Mother, and then she can wipe the ink off his fingers." I held firm against an over-early consummation. As yet, Meggie was far more girl than woman. Sixteen had been young enough for me, and sixteen it should be for my beloved daughter. The Herberts were content enough; a marriage suited us both but Somer would have to wait a little while for Meggie to become his full wife. In the meantime she would go to Raglan to learn the ways of her new family. It was hard to let her go but I knew her future was assured.*

Eltham Summer 1515

Harry Tudor decided it had been his idea all along that his young cousin Lady Margaret Courtenay should marry into the Herbert family. The way De Vere had refused her was preposterous, and he had been fined for it. Harry was discovering that fining people was a most satisfactory mode of revenge. Lord Worcester had offered fine military support in France; there was no reason why his son should not be rewarded with a bride from the fringes of the royal family. That was the way loyalty to the Tudors was secured.

He shifted his weight in his wife's bed. Last night he had come to her chamber with all the dignity and pomp suitable to the occasion. He did not always stay until morning but had slept heavily after doing his duty. Once, Catalina's body had delighted him in its pretty daintiness but he had to admit that, these days, gazing at her nakedness by candlelight was no longer guaranteed to arouse him. He found he had to think instead of young Bessie Blount, one of Catalina's ladies, and close his eyes. The image of blonde Bessie, stepping lightly in the dance, and the memory of her lissom waist, usually did the trick.

It was hard to imagine that only five years ago he was chasing Catalina around the bedchamber until they fell, giggling and panting, upon the bed. Then, their coupling was natural and joyful but after each tragic pregnancy Catalina had become more and more detached, until their lovemaking could only be described as a conscientious effort to create a prince. Catalina presented her body to him like an offering at Mass. She lay still and silent until he had finished, then stroked his hair like a mother.

Harry could feel the warmth of her breath now, near his shoulder. He opened his eyes slightly and through his lashes saw how she lay upon her pillow, one arm flung above her head and the other curled against her cheek. *She is nearly thirty. How much longer do we have? Six years and still no son.* Lying so close to her he noted the lines beginning to crease her forehead, and running out from the corners of her eyes and mouth. Bessie Blount's skin was entirely smooth but then she was only seventeen. *Aunt Kaff'ryn is older than my wife but looks younger. She looks more like Hal Courtenay's elder sister than his mother.*

His thoughts wandered on towards what the day might bring: hunting this morning, with his friends William Compton and Charles Brandon. Yes, Charles was his friend again – and he'd reduced his fine, and those young dogs Courtenay and Somerset. Afterwards, some tennis perhaps, or some practising for the next set of jousts, and tonight the Italian ambassador and his followers would dine with him. The actual business of government Harry was more than content to leave to Thomas Wolsey. He could not do without Wolsey. Invaluable as an almoner in the French campaign, and now he was Chancellor he could be even more useful. For Harry was determined only to have advisors who agreed with him. Inheriting his father's advisors had driven him mad – all they wanted him to do was be careful – at least most of them were gone now.

At his side, Catalina stirred. When she realised he was still with her, her eyes flew open in pleasure and she sat up quickly. "Harry! My lord! What can I get for you?"

Only a year ago he would have pushed her back again amongst the rumpled bedding but now he swung his long, muscular legs out of bed and reached for the nightshirt discarded several hours ago. He kissed her hand lightly. "I will leave you to your ladies, my dear."

His rejection, however courteous, hurt her. She grasped his hand and held it tightly against her cheek. "Harry, I will pray that I have conceived a son." Her eyes were filling with tears. She cried very easily these days.

"Of course. As will I." He broke free and called for his page.

"We could go together, to hear Mass, as soon as I have dressed?"

"No, no, my dear. I have urgent business to attend to. You take your time. I will look forward to your company this evening." His page was offering his furred robe, that he might return to his own apartments. The King swept through the open door and the page closed it quietly behind him. Catalina bit her lip and pulled on her shift to cover her nakedness, then waited for the arrival of her ladies, who would wash and dress her for the day ahead.

Harry Tudor strode back to his own side of the palace, whistling good-humouredly. He was fond of Catalina and would continue to accord her every honour as his wife, bedfellow and queen. But he did not want to spend too long with her. So far, he reasoned, his behaviour as a husband had surely been exemplary. Yes, there had been that bothersome business with pretty Anne Stafford during Catalina's first pregnancy, but he'd learned from it – never to let Compton act as his go-between ever again! He was not a king to go whoring. Up until now Catalina had fulfilled his needs but if he had got her with child again then there would be a few months when to pester her would not be chivalric …

In his rooms, a small group of his gentlemen were already gathering. Even if the King had not slept in his own bed, the daily routine rarely varied: he washed and changed his linen with the assistance of his gentlemen, then seated himself to be shaved. The scent of cloves rose from the steaming basin of water. Harry closed his eyes and leaned back as his barber applied hot cloths to his face. He felt the scrape of the knife on his cheek.

"Should I grow a beard, Courtenay? They say the new French king, Francis, has a beard."

"It certainly saves shaving, sir!"

Harry opened one eye to see his young cousin standing close by, ready with a doublet of green velvet lined with cloth of gold. He smiled. "My brother-in-law Brandon has a beard, and my sister says it tickles her every time he kisses her."

A ripple of slightly nervous laughter ran round the room. No-one was entirely sure whether the new Suffolks were forgiven or not.

"And my sister the Scottish queen says her new husband also has a beard, which she mislikes. Maybe *that is* why she has left him and come to England."

More tentative chuckles, but then a guffaw broke from Hal Courtenay. His judgement of his royal cousin's mood often hit the mark. "Then let us regard our lack of beards as a sign of our civilisation, sir!" The Scottish Queen Margaret was also his cousin.

Harry sat while the barber scraped the other side of his face. "Our grandfather Edward IV was clean-shaven, was he not, Courtenay?"

"So they say, sir. So it would appear from his portrait in Your Grace's collection."

"They say we are both like him, Courtenay – what do you say to that?"

This was always dangerous ground. To claim too close an affinity with the King might remind him of possible dangers; to deny it might upset the notion of "family" that he sometimes clung to. The mercurial nature of Harry Tudor's mind was not always open to interpretation. Hal trod carefully. "I do think it must be where we both get our height from, sir. And Your Grace's colouring. But we both owe a great deal to our own fathers' families too." He held out the doublet for Harry to put his arms in. "My grandfather Courtenay was honoured to serve your father at home and abroad." He pulled on the side-laces; the King's torso was long and firm – an athlete's body.

Harry punched him affectionately on the shoulder, like an older brother, "Ha, Hal! You'll make an excellent diplomat for me one of these days! Where shall we send you to – Rome? Paris? Madrid?"

"Wherever Your Grace pleases, but –" he pulled a comical face, "don't expect me to converse in anything other than English. I do not have Your Grace's gift with languages!"

Harry loved to be complimented. He was proud of his scholarship, at ease in French, Italian, Latin and Greek.

"Well, my young cousin, there we *do* differ, indeed." Harry stood while his gentlemen made final adjustments to his clothing. "So, you won't be much use this evening whilst I am entertaining the Italians. Best send your mother instead!" He was pleased with his joke, and already striding out into the ante-chamber thronged with courtiers and petitioners eager to catch his attention for a moment. But Harry was having not of it. This morning his mind was on hunting and he swept past the bowing crowd, through the ante-chambers, down the staircase and out into the courtyard where the horses were waiting.

Hal Courtenay scurried along behind – he was also eager to be out in the fresh air, galloping through the deer park while the greyhounds ran at the horses' heels. It was the best thing about being at court in attendance upon the King – along with all the other forms of exercise that Harry relished. His friend Henry Somerset was already in the saddle, holding the reins of Hal's horse while he vaulted on board.

In the early morning the countryside lay still and silver, the dawn mists clearing. The best hunting would be had a few miles from the palace. Like all the royal hunting grounds the land was flat and lightly forested, with open areas ideal for the chase.

"Better than Devon?" Somer teased.

"Better than Raglan?" Hal could give as good as he got.

Somer acquiesced. "Actually, there's no land as good as your own, I find."

They trotted easily, side by side, their horses occasionally snorting with pleasurable anticipation. "I'm glad you are to be my brother, Somer. Thank God the King has accepted the match. Mama and Meggie were in such a state over De Vere. My mother's incredibly strong but that's one thing she would have been powerless to fight. It would have broken her heart to see my sister traded in marriage to such a man."

"I admire your mother hugely, Hal. The way she runs all your family's estates. My mother was an heiress but she could never have done that on her own."

"Mama is exceptional," agreed Hal.

"And your sister is, too."

"Meggie is …" Hal searched for words to describe his sister, "… unlike other girls."

"You mean because she loves reading and writing? It sets her apart, I agree, but I admire her for it. She will make an excellent wife and mother, I am sure of it." They pulled up on the edge of the wood where distant bluebells shimmered in the shade and their horses' hooves left imprints in the damp grass as they shifted restlessly. The king's hounds and huntsmen had already entered the thickets, and away to the right Harry himself sat poised on his horse, alert for the sound of the horn and ready to take flight in pursuit of the startled deer that would soon emerge.

"Have you met Thomas More, the lawyer?" asked Somer. "He's an interesting fellow – thinks girls can learn exactly like boys, and is educating his daughters to prove it."

"My mother has spoken of him. How do you know him?"

"My father is close to the King since France; Wolsey is close to the King since France; Wolsey speaks highly of More – he's an under sheriff in the city and has recently been sent to Bruges to do the King's business. He's a rising star, my father says."

"My cousin likes to surround himself with capable men. These days it does not matter so much whether you belong to old families, like yours and mine."

"Well, let's face it, most of the old families have been wiped out. We're a dying breed, Hal! The world is changing!"

The high, thin, nasal sound of the hunting horn pierced the air. Their horses shivered with excitement. A large buck broke cover and made a desperate bid for freedom across the open acres. The two young men exchanged delighted glances and pressed their heels against their horses' sides but the creatures needed little urging. Within seconds they had joined the mêleé of galloping riders.

4

"The Queen and I are both young, and if it is a girl this time, by God's grace boys will follow." King Henry VIII

Summer 1516

The baby had been born alive and still survived. England had a princess. She lived beyond the first six weeks of her ill-fated brother and her parents dared to hope that she would thrive. Of course, a boy would have been better, but Harry Tudor shrugged off any criticism. "We are both young. If it was a daughter this time, by God's grace sons will follow." At the christening, when Katherine held little Mary at the font, she was only too well aware of how so many had discreetly averted their gaze from her obvious naked femininity.

Katherine carried the tiny scrap of humanity back to her mother and father. Catalina's chamber was thronged with well-wishers admiring the christening presents, the air thick with the cloying smell of perfumed bodies sweating in their best clothes. A great smile was fixed upon Harry's lips and he declared that the baby girl was *his pearl of the world* but his eyes were hard and empty. Catalina seemed oblivious, chatting in animated Spanish with her favourite lady-in-waiting, Maria de Salinas and her doctor, Vittoria, whom she credited with helping her to a successful birth.

The King gazed down into the gilded cradle with its precious occupant. The baby was now swaddled tightly, her dark blue eyes the only moving part of her. "She does not cry, Aunt."

"Indeed, no, sir. Why would she?"

"And soon she will have brothers."

"I do not doubt it, Your Grace."

He seemed soothed and, when numbers thinned, took her elbow, guiding her to a quieter spot by the window where he seated himself and indicated that she might do likewise.

"Remind me, how many girls did your father have before he had a boy?"

Katherine fought against taking a sudden intake of breath. Harry did not often allude to his Plantagenet family. "There were three girls, sir, before my father gained an heir."

"But both your father and your mother had already proved that they could have sons, with others." His anguish was almost palpable and Katherine felt a rising pity for him. She would always distrust him, and be wary of his company and motives but at that moment he had laid his innermost feeling bare to her. She reached over and laid a small hand upon the huge bejewelled sleeve.

"Your Grace ... Harry." She dared to use his Christian name. "You are young. Your boys will come, in God's good time."

"With her?" His voice was so low that at first she was not sure she had heard correctly.

"Aunt Kaff'ryn, sometimes I almost wish she might ..." he tailed away, his face flushed, then said abruptly, "I do not understand it, after seven years of marriage, why I have no son."

She felt helpless in the face of his bafflement. "We know it is God's will, Harry. He took my son, Edward –"

"But left you with two other children. My sister Mary has a son now, with Brandon. My sister Margaret has a living son –"

"She has lost other children, sir, like you."

He fiddled with the huge round-cut diamond that hung from his collar of gold. It was the size of a walnut. His powerful fingers were also glittering with gold and jewels, and his doublet was encrusted with sapphires. On his velvet cap was an enamelled badge of Saint George and the dragon. Everything about him shouted wealth and power. But he had no son. The most humble cottager was richer than his King, if he had a son.

The baby's godfather, Wolsey, was gliding across towards them like a ship in scarlet rigging. The butcher's son from Ipswich had become a priest, then a canon, then a bishop, then an Archbishop of York and now a cardinal. *Really, it defies comprehension; the man is positively a wonder of the Tudor age.* In his early forties, with a thickset build, his face was fleshy and jowly, his features fixed in the expression of an unctuous sneer. Katherine had heard that once a

466

London merchant had asked Wolsey to bury his dead child and the priest had demanded the child's christening robe as payment. Outraged, the grieving father refused, and later found himself arrested. He had been found dead in his cell.

Wolsey inclined his large head politely in Katherine's direction but then faced the King directly.

"Your Grace. " His voice was gravelly, as if he might benefit from clearing his throat. He had done his best to eradicate all evidence of a Suffolk rural accent but remnants clung to his ponderous speech. Katherine guessed that he still had to think hard about every sentence that left his lips.

"Wolsey! Have you come to tear me away from my own child's christening day to sign papers?"

"Far from it, Your Grace. There is nothing for Your Grace to be concerned about. I merely come to ask for Your Grace's permission to take my leave and return to my work."

That Wolsey was relieving the young king from every tedious aspect of routine state business was common knowledge. They said he rose at dawn and sat at his desk till dusk, while his sovereign amused himself at the archery butts, or in the tennis courts, or in the lists. Hal had told Katherine that the King was utterly bored by the minutae of everyday government but unwilling to relinquish power. Wolsey was the ideal stop-gap: he provided Harry with crisp summaries of issues, selected only the most important documents for him to read, and even drafted responses for him to sign. *He's invaluable, Mama. The King loves him. Everything goes through Wolsey. And you should see how he lives!*

Harry was diverted from his tense mood. "Aunt Kaff'ryn, have you heard of what my lord Archbishop is doing at Hampton?"

She had. Hampton had once been one of Bessy's favourite retreats, situated fifteen miles upstream from Westminster. She had loved to stay there, courtesy of its tenant Giles Daubigny, one of Henry Tudor's councillors. Wolsey had razed the old building to the ground and was busy constructing a palace to rival anything owned by the King. She was surprised that he wanted Harry to see what he was up to. *It comes to something when an upstart like Thomas Wolsey can afford a home equal to his royal master.* Harry had a passion for building new homes and so, it seemed, did his servant.

"It is a goodly spot, sir. The air is clean and wholesome."

Wolsey scrutinised her. "It is, indeed."

"We should all come and see it," announced Harry, eager for distraction.

467

"*All,* Your Grace?" Wolsey looked slightly bewildered.

"When my sister the Queen of Scots arrives. When the weather improves. We shall have a family outing to Hampton – my sisters, my aunt and her son Courtenay. You can give us a picnic, Wolsey. And show us where the best hawking is to be had." Harry was immensely pleased with his plan.

If Wolsey was alarmed at the thought of entertaining the King and half his court at a building site he hid it well. *Serve him right; he's rich enough.*

Hampton Summer 1516

A fine, dry summer's morning. A flotilla of barges cut through the clear waters of the upstream Thames and arrived at the old wharf built by the Knights Hospitaller when Hampton had been little more than a grange to store the grain grown on their estates. The King persisted in calling it a family visit, despite an entourage of at least fifty courtiers in tow. In the water meadows of riverside settlements of Molesy and Ditton, people looked up from their work in astonishment as the gorgeous vessels glided by, bearing the royal standards of England, Scotland and France, for Harry had indeed brought his two sisters with him.

Margaret Tudor, now Stuart, had been in England for several weeks now. Katherine had no difficulty in recognising her niece after twelve years: the same flame-red hair, and in adulthood her features showed a close resemblance to Bessy at a similar age. Her relief in being home again was evident. The last two years had taken their toll on her, mentally and physically. After the death of her husband at Flodden she had tried to hold on to the regency but had fallen in love, and secretly married Archibald Douglas, Earl of Angus. The Scots Council were having none of it. They told her that in remarrying she forfeited her right to her two small boys, and threatened to replace her entirely. Their choice of Regent, Albany (next heir after Margaret's boys) got wind of her plans to appeal to Harry for help, and forcibly removed her sons. The youngest had died soon after. In despair, and pregnant, she had fled across the border, leaving her husband to guard her interests, Privately, Katherine wondered if the Earl of Angus was guarding his self-interests.

Since her arrival, Harry had showered his elder sister with gifts. Her entire wardrobe was refurbished, and a residence prepared her for at Scotland Yard, the ancient guest house of Scottish royalty. Immediately, her baby, *little Marget,* was placed in the royal baby Mary's household. It appeared that Harry could not do enough to make up for his elder sister's trials and tribulations. His younger sister, now Mary Brandon, had her nose put firmly out of joint. Katherine watched with amusement as Harry was besieged by both his siblings, each determined to prove herself the most important; the most beloved. And vying with them both for his attentions was Catalina.

As they all disembarked at Hampton, Catalina and Margaret laid claim to Harry's arms; Mary Brandon had to be content with her husband, a few steps behind. As dowager queen of France she felt herself equally important as her sister and sister-in-law but unfortunately her brother did not possess a third arm. But no matter – she was younger and prettier, and in possession of her baby son. Catalina had no son. Margaret's had been taken from her.

Katherine walked with Hal, and Meggie (for once having agreed to come to court) with her new husband, Somer. Meggie was self-conscious as her position as the King's cousin – she hardly knew him, and overawed to find herself in the company of three queens. Behind them trailed a tail of gentlemen and ladies of the court.

Wolsey's builders had been busy a year now. Already a great courtyard was taking shape, with forty residences for his guests. Workmen were everywhere, swarming over the rose-brick walls. Where once there had been a small manor house, a palatial residence was rising. Inside, carpenters were sawing and hammering, and the scent of clean oak was heady. Where the ceilings were already complete, men lay on their backs on scaffolding, painting bright colours to the bosses. Sunlight flooded in through mullioned windows of the finest glass. Wolsey led them from one area to the next, pointing out where apartments would be built for Harry, Catalina and their daughter, when they might wish to stay.

Katherine lingered, gazing in wonderment. There was something so extraordinarily precise about the design of the whole place – so many squares! It was utterly unlike the rambling palaces of her childhood. At Westminster, and Eltham and Sheen the passages twisted and turned, and staircases ended in unexpected rooms. Here, all was ordered and neat. Where upper floors had been finished, slender brick chimneys spiralled skywards, each like a finger wrapped in patterned material.

"It's beautiful!" breathed Meggie, craning her neck to the rooflines. "The loveliest thing I have ever seen! Who would have thought that an ugly old man like Wolsey could have such ideas!"

"It's a wonder the King is not jealous," observed Hal. "My lord Cardinal seems to have collected up all the best workmen in England."

Somer stood still, then turned slowly in a full circle, taking in every detail. "It's like something the Romans might have built … I bet his new friends in Italy have been telling him how to set about it. It's nothing like a castle, is it? Not like Tiverton, or Raglan, or Windsor. Jesu, he must be rich! Let's go and look at his stables, Hal!"

Far from being jealous, the King just wanted to know more and more about Wolsey's plans, suppliers and workforce. He managed to shake off his womenfolk and strode forward with his Chancellor, deep in conversation. Brandon tagged along, eager for tips for his own intended projects. Katherine and Meggie caught up with the three royal ladies. Catalina smiled, always pleased to see her husband's aunt.

"Lady Courtenay, Wolsey has promised us refreshments in the old gardens. Let us make our way there."

The ancient pleasuances of the old manor house were also undergoing total redesign but Wolsey's staff had erected a number of trestle tables under awnings on the greensward by the river. He had spared no expense in producing an outdoor feast fit for his sovereign. Catalina, Margaret and Mary were led to chairs under individual cloths of estate: the golden lions of England, the red rampant lion of Scotland; the lilies of France. *Oh, very clever! All three queens flattered and appeased!* Catalina's seat was in the middle, slightly raised. *Wait till I write to Meg Pole about this!* With all the niceties of protocol observed, they were served with cool small ale, then Wolsey's servants retired discreetly until their master and the King should arrive. While they waited, the women fell into relaxed conversation. They directed kind questions to Meggie, encouraging her to tell them of her new home at Raglan, and then, like all women, exchanged anecdotes of their own experiences as new brides.

"When I arrived in Scotland, the feasting went on for days, then my husband took me on a tour of my new realm." Katherine stole a glance at Catalina – who had declared war upon Margaret's husband and rejoiced at his death. It seemed extraordinary that they could now sit side by side watching the swans gliding along the peaceful Thames.

"When *I* arrived in Paris, Louis could not take his eyes off me. Every night a banquet! Every night dancing till dawn! Thousands of people in the streets of Paris to see me! My every wish granted!" Mary looked a little wistful for a

470

moment, no doubt contemplating the financial drawbacks of replacing her ancient royal husband with a younger, impecunious version.

"When *I* arrived," said Catalina, "King Henry burst into my chamber and demanded that I should lift my veil. To inspect me, you understand. My *duenna* was horrified. We had much to learn about the ways of you English. And the language."

"But you were happy with my brother, Arthur," said Margaret. "I remember the letters he wrote from Ludlow. My mother could not be parted from them. He wrote of such joy in your company. You were lucky to have a husband so close to yourself in age."

Catalina was suddenly flustered. "He was a sweet boy but we did not spend much time together. It is hard to remember those days now."

Mary looked around quickly, and then leaned in towards Catalina. Her eyes bright with mischief. "*Is* it true – that you were a virgin when you married Harry?" Catalina went white, then red, then looked as if she would like to slap her pampered sister-in-law. "Only Louis couldn't *wait* to get his hands on me. It was horrible. What about you, Margaret? James had lots of mistresses, didn't he? "

Margaret lowered her eyelids. "I did my duty, sister."

"But you prefer your *new* husband? As I prefer mine?" persisted Mary. She went off into peals of laughter. "Jesu, we've *all* had *two* husbands! Do you prefer Harry, Catalina?" She did not wait for an answer but turned her attention to her aunt. "And what about you, Aunt Kaff'ryn? Does your vow of celibacy hold good down there in Devon? Are there no handsome men to tempt you to a second marriage? You do not look your age at all. Brandon says you could easily be taken for another royal sister!"

Catalina was distressed by Mary's audacity. Her first marriage remained a delicate topic, and certainly not one for airy discussion. Her Spanish temper flared suddenly. "*Mi hermana* – you must learn to guard your tongue if you and your husband wish to be welcome here at court. Your brother forgives you much but do not misjudge his tolerance. And your comments to your aunt are thoughtless."

Mary was not easily abashed. She met Catalina's glare with a cool, Tudor stare. "I meant no offence. We are sisters alone here, surely? And I am sure Aunt Kaff'ryn is flattered that the court still thinks her beautiful." She turned a dazzling smile upon Katherine.

"Mary," said Margaret, "you are still the youngest. Have a care."

"Tell us of your new husband," returned Mary pertly. "I am sure you want to. You must miss him."

She had touched a raw nerve, and knew it. Margaret had no idea when she might see Archibald Douglas again. He had seen his new-born daughter briefly before she had fled to her brother's protection. Douglas had stayed put – made his peace with the new Regent. His decision not to follow Margaret and the baby to England had caused Harry to comment scathingly, "done *like a Scot*".

Tight-lipped, Margaret ignored her sister and instead looked out, over her head, to the Thames, where a family of swans was drifting by slowly. The dark grey cygnets paddled in their parents' slipstream. Meggie cast an anxious look at Katherine; this barbed bickering between her royal cousins was disconcerting. She was inexperienced at court and found it hard to read the characters of the three queens but Mary's comment on her mother's vow struck her as insensitive, if not rude. Thank God Mary had not asked telling questions about her own intimate experiences as a bride! She and Somer were six months married but her sixteenth birthday was still a year away. Mama had been adamant, and Somer respectful. No doubt he turned to other women whilst waiting for her to grow up but he did so discreetly. Hal was in the same position, with Lisbet being even younger.

Mary's mischief was halted by the emergence of Harry and Wolsey, and the men of their households. Hampton Court had been thoroughly inspected, from its kitchen to its stables; its public rooms to its private apartments. Harry had secured promises that Wolsey would send his craftsmen on to the houses *he* was improving. Katherine hid a smile; it was Harry aged ten, all over again. He simply could not bear that anyone should have anything better than himself.

5

"Suddenly there came a plague of sickness. This malady was so cruel that it killed within three hours, some within two hours, some merry at dinner and dead at supper." Edward Hall, Chronicler

Summer 1517 Devon

The sweating sickness was no respecter of rank, age or gender. Some whispered darkly that it was God's judgement upon the Tudors, for hadn't it first struck after Bosworth, and then again twenty three years later, just before the old king died? Its horror lay in the speed of its onslaught: you might feel well on rising but by noon your head and stomach would be splitting in two from pain, you would fall to the ground, panting for breath and lie there – cold at first but then as hot as a furnace, sweat pouring from your skin. By sunset you were in your shroud. The lucky ones slipped into sleep before death; the less fortunate lay speechless, as pain stabbed their hearts and lungs.

In Oxford and Cambridge the students fell down at their desks; in London the merchants and tradesmen keeled over in the streets. Harry Tudor was terrified, and fled from Westminster – first to Greenwich, then Windsor, and finally to remote houses in the depths of the countryside. His court was broken up, for at times none knew where the King and Queen might be found. For Katherine, what had begun as a quiet period overseeing her estates in Devon quickly turned into a nightmare.

First to succumb at the castle was Joanna, who had been her own nursemaid as a girl, and then to the Courtenay children. Poor Joanna – to be denied a quiet, dignified deathbed in old age. For Katherine it was like losing a mother all over again, and she held Philippa in her arms like a sister rather than a servant.

Normal life in the busy little town of Tiverton came to a shocking halt. Families were decimated. From the cottages where fullers, tuckers and weavers lived and worked, sad little trails of surviving relatives made their way to the churchyard to bury their dead. Rob Anning suffered most, though. On two consecutive days he lost his quiet, capable wife, Christian and his daughter Damaris.

Katherine was visited by John Greenway, Tiverton's most respected inhabitant – a wool merchant who employed almost threequarters of the town's working men. Wealthy from his enterprises, he was currently embellishing St Peter's Church with an impressive new chantry chapel and a splendid south porch. A serious man in his late fifties, he stood anxiously before her, twisting his plumed cap in his broad hands.

"I have come to ask you, my lady, if you would be so good as to consider giving alms to the most needy. We have children orphaned; families left without their menfolk; fathers left with young children and no mother. It is the duty of the parish to do what we can for poor folk, but never before have we been so stretched. I fear my own resources are simply not enough."

His distress was sincere. Katherine crossed herself. "God rest all their souls, Master Greenway. I will pay for Masses to be said for them, and will instruct my steward to pay monies into your fund. I will send food, too; please assure the townsfolk that none shall starve here in Tiverton."

"God bless you, my lady, for your charity."

"Well, we are well-supplied here. Gifts of food arrive daily from my tenants. And I have heard of your own good works, sir. Are you not already building almshouses in the town?"

He smiled sadly. "Men who work hard for me all their lives deserve to be looked after when they become infirm."

"Et prout vultis ut faciant vobis homines et vos facite illis similiter," said Katherine gravely but realised he did not understand. "Do unto others as you would have them do unto you," she translated quickly. "My husband Lord William would have approved. He set great store by the loyalty of our own servants and the debt we owe them. Your charity does you great credit, Master Greenway."

He was about to go but turned in the doorway. "My lady, you should leave for one of your other houses while this sickness rages. This place may well be moated and walled and embattled, but it cannot keep the bad humours out. I have sent my own wife out of the town and I shall leave myself tomorrow."

"Wait, sir. What do *you* think causes it? "

"Who knows! Some say it is the moist air of this land. Others speak of the impure spirit of the people."

"Joanna Colson and Christian Anning were not *impure,* " said Katherine bitterly. "They were excellent women. Both devoted to my family."

"Well, there was certainly nothing like it in my childhood, and I never heard my parents or grandparents speak of it either," said Greenway cautiously, "and the Great Plague that struck England in *their* grandsires' time was something altogether different. And it's not just the poor that are dying. "

"So, do you … do you believe it came with the Tudors?"

He hesitated. What was she implying? Peace under the Tudors had brought him prosperity. He had risen from weaver to merchant, exporting his cloth across Europe and winning valuable trading contracts for the old king. Surely it was God's will that had brought him wealth? His fleet of merchant ships were always at the Tudors' disposal; indeed, young Harry Tudor had requisitioned some for his recent war in France. How strange that the young King's aunt should be uneasy about it all! Then he remembered who she was – born a Plantagenet. Gracious heavens, after all these years did she look for a sign that her family had been wrongfully usurped?

"Disease can follow hard on the heels of an army, my lady. I know not why. When His Grace King Henry landed in Wales he brought with him men from all over Europe to fight against King Richard. Mayhap they brought the pestilence with them."

He saw that the Countess had a faraway look in her eyes. "Aye, there were not that many Englishmen who would have chosen to fight against Richard."

Greenway was silent. He had been a young man of twenty five at the time, absorbed in transporting wool from Ireland to the mills in Tiverton. He'd owed no allegiance to old Sir Edward Courtenay who'd fought on the side of the Tudor. If anything, he'd quite admired King Richard's plans to preserve his brother's good governance.

"Your father was much loved, my lady. He brought peace to England, and I am sure your uncle meant likewise. And your blessed sister, Queen Elizabeth. Peace brings us a chance to survive and thrive … I cannot believe that then God sends sickness upon us as punishment. Although it is God's will, surely." He was aware of the confusion of his answer and looked abashed. He was no man of letters. Theological debate was beyond his world of sheep fleeces, cloth and boats.

Shouting echoed outside in the courtyard. A few moments later Philippa appeared, her face tight with her recent grief and new concern. "My lady, it is a messenger ridden in from London."

Katherine's thoughts flew in all directions: *not Raglan, so not Meggie; not Surrey, so not Hal; not Bisham in Hampshire, so not Meg Pole. Who? Who?*

John Greenway saw her apprehension and a sort of paternal care for her swept over him. She might think him presumptuous but he was reluctant to let her face bad news alone.

"Shall I stay with you, my lady?"

The mud-stained messenger knelt and held out a letter bearing an unfamiliar seal. He proferred it first to Greenway, impressed by his expensive clothes and thinking he must be a gentleman of the Courtenay family. Philippa sniffed her disapproval.

Embarrassed, Greenway waved it away. "No, no, lad, that is for Her Grace the Countess."

But Katherine's hands were trembling like the leaves of a birch tree. "Open it, if you will, Master Greenway, and tell me the content."

He broke the dark red wax seal, looked first for the name at the end then scanned the text. Reading did not come easily to him and he moved his lips as he had been taught, to follow the neat, square writing. He dismissed the messenger and snapped his fingers at Philippa. "Fetch wine for your lady." Affronted, she stalked from the room.

Katherine stared at him. "Who?"

"I'm so sorry, my lady. It is from the Abbess at Dartford. She writes that they lost six nuns last week, from the Sweat, among them your sister, the Lady Bridget. God rest her soul." Katherine looked stricken. He kept his voice steady. "So there we have our proof, my lady, that God does not send this sickness to those who are impure."

He let her cry quietly a while, until the maid returned. Although she poured carefully for her mistress, he could have sworn she deliberately splashed his hose with the dark liquid. Then he sat next to the countess while she sipped, his big hands splayed upon his knees. His travels had once taken him into Worcestershire where he had stayed a few nights at the Priory at Malvern where the monks had shown him their precious new treasure: a stained glass window depicting King Edward and his family. Even now, years later, he recalled the vivid blue of the girls' dresses and their tall headdresses. Each face had looked identical.

"She was your youngest sister, my lady?"

"Yes. My playmate." She was in control of herself again. "Bridget always said her job was to pray for the rest of us. It is nigh on fourteen years since I last saw her, but to know that her prayers have been with me every day – has always been a great comfort… through all my difficulties. " She glanced at the letter. "Poor Bridget, to die in such a way."

"Mercifully quickly, my lady," interjected Philippa. "And sure of God's grace. 'Tis us left behind who find it hard."

Greenway wondered at the way the young woman dared to speak in such a forthright manner to the countess but then saw how her eyes were brimful with tears too. He kept his counsel.

They sat in the quiet of the morning. Sparrows chirruped on the window ledge outside; cattle lowed in the distance and the bell of St Peter's began yet another melancholy knell. *I am the last of my family.* "Two of my sisters died in childbirth, and one of the consumption. And my broth –" she stopped herself quickly. It would be too easy to confide her sorrows to this kind, honest man.

John Greenway was thoughtful. For all that this lady was a princess, and a countess, she was first and foremost a lonely woman coping with yet another blow to her fortunes. It did not matter how rich you were if God saw fit to take those you loved. He had no children to inherit his wealth; it would all go to the almshouses and the chapel. He coughed.

"When I finish the porch on the church, my lady, might I carve the Courtenay coat of arms too? To honour your husband and you? I have found the most wonderful craftsman in Exeter – he can carve anything! I thought he might show some of my ships, and where they sail to, and details of my trade."

He wished he could just put his arms around her, like a father or a husband, to comfort her. His wife always welcomed his embraces when she felt upset. The maid was eyeing him fiercely, as if she suspected his thoughts. Katherine patted his hand in appreciation. "You are a good man, Master Greenway, and I should indeed be honoured by your suggestion."

"And you will follow my advice to seek cleaner air?"

"I will."

She had a choice: her manor at Columbjohn, just a few miles away at Broadclyst, or the little castle at Colcombe. Colombjohn was pretty and peaceful but low-lying in land that often flooded. She thought of Master Greenways's comments about how the sickness might linger in wetlands. By contrast, Colcombe was situated on a ridge above the floodplain of the Axe, and breezes blew in from the sea only two miles away.

Trotting through Colyton, over the bridge spanning the River Coly, she felt a sense of relief. A heron rose from the shallows and a white egret sat waiting for the fish he left behind. The meadows were rich with emerald summer grasses, dotted with the sheep that kept this area busy with trade. They were glad to be rid of their thick fleeces in this warm weather – already the wool was being carded, spun and woven on broadlooms into the kersey that would be shipped out to Europe on Greenway's boats. Colyton was full of merchants who had travelled as far as Bruges and Antwerp, where they had seen their wool dyed into brilliant colours and woven into the tapestries that graced the King's palaces. The cavalcade rode up the hill and turned left. The castle was visible now through the trees. How could sickness be present in a place like this? The very air was fragrant with summer.

Shocked by her mother's death, Philippa found solace in organising the household. Carts were unloaded; beds, bedding and plate carried in. Coffers containing Katherine's clothes were shouldered to her private chamber, which had been hastily swept and strewn with fresh herbs. She washed off the dust of a day's riding and then threw open the shutters. In the distance the evening sunlight caught the glass in the new octagonal lantern tower of St Andrew's in Colyton, atop its sturdy, square tower. Nearby, the little bell of the Colcombe chantry chapel began ringing the hour of Vespers. She should go down and join the household.

She found them waiting for her. Rob Anning, hollow-eyed with recent grief, already on his knees, oblivious to everything except the loss of his wife and daughter. There had been no point in him staying on in Tiverton; Christian and Damaris were already in their graves. The Colcombe priest led them in their psalms and evening prayers. He was an elderly man, old enough to have buried people in both the other outbreaks of the Sweat. With his voice quavering with compassion, he added prayers for the repose of the soul of the Princess Bridget Plantagenet; for Joanna Colson, Christian and Damaris Anning, and all those taken on Courtenay lands in the West Country.

In the morning, Rob came to her in the Great Hall. "Give me some occupation, my lady. It's the only thing that will help." As her steward at Tiverton, he had a group of mid and east Devon manors in his care but, as the sickness had taken hold, travelling, visiting and administration were reduced to the bare essentials.

Katherine hesitated. She did not wish to add to his troubles. "Rob, no-one expects it of you at the moment. Let someone else …"

"By your leave, no. There's enough chaos as it is. We left several behind at Tiverton, too weak still to travel. Someone needs to keep an eye on your accounts, and see to your needs. We have to order in fresh provisons."

"We shall keep a very quiet household here this summer. No entertaining while the sickness is still abroad. Neither Lady Meggie nor Lord Hal will visit, and I shall remain here. There'll be no going to court, Rob, for there's no court to go to. But –"

"My lady?"

"The anniversary of Lord William's death, Rob – and I have sent no wax for candles at his tomb, or payment to the good friars for their services these last few months. And I would wish to send money to the nuns at Dartford too."

"It will be put right today, my lady." She could see that he was pleased to have something to do, and her heart went out to him, this loyal servant who had been William's childhood companion.

"Rob, you may send payment to St Peter's too; for Christian and Damaris. I have told Philippa there will be Masses sung for those we have lost as often as for Lord William and all my sisters. And Master Greenway has a stone mason who shall make a memorial for them. They will not be forgotten. How does your son, Adam, fare?"

"He has found employment with John Greenway. He's away in Bruges at present, my lady. May God bless you, for your kindness to us."

"That's good, Rob. He's away from this pestilence and safe. Greenway is a fine man. This sickness, Rob, it reminds us all of our mortality, does it not? It matters not *who* we are; what matters is how we do right by each other."

It was a long summer. And strange how the beauty of the season was so much at odds with the suffering of the people. But with Rob Anning's industry, the Courtenay manors survived the worst of it. Most of the harvests were brought in, a fair proportion of rents collected and most pressing creditors paid. It was more than could be said for other estates. Meg Pole wrote of how the King and Queen still flitted round the countryside – now in Surrey, now in Hampshire. In Suffolk, Mary Brandon gave birth to a daughter, Frances, and Margaret, the Scots queen-dowager arrived back at the borders of her little son's kingdom, to discover that her new husband had been living openly with his mistress, Janet Stewart.

Katherine felt far, far removed from the doings of her royal family. She found she cared much more about whether the land up to Axminster was yielding good grain rather than whether Harry Tudor had been sighted within twenty miles of London. When Hal wrote that his royal cousin had turned up in West Horsley it was almost comical:

"He arrived with the Queen and his physician, Dr Linacre, and with Compton and Carew. He insists that we all partake of his own remedy against the Sweat: sage, elder leaves and rue which tastes most foul, and as the sickness has passed us by here we are loath to take it… Her Grace the Queen is exhausted with all their travelling but sending you greetings and prayers, as do I …"

Philippa listened while Katherine read out parts of the letter. "Poor lady. I wonder if there will be any sign of a child next year – she is spending so much time with the King, after all. I hope the little Princess Mary keeps well, bless her sweet head." She looked up from her sewing, a frown creasing her forehead. "My lady, what will happen if there is no prince?"

"Of course there will be a prince; we just have to wait."

"But if there is not. What then?"

"Philippa! The King is only twenty six! He will have many sons."

"Do you think so, my lady? There are many who doubt it."

"You would do well, Philippa, not to listen to such gossip." It was not often that Katherine reprimanded her maid. Philippa was much more than that – at Colcombe now she was her only female confidante.

Philippa went red and bit her lip, ashamed for a moment but then her courage held. "My lady, it's not gossip. People are worried for the Queen. All women are beginning to wonder what the King will do with her if there is no son. She is older than him, and people fear he might put her aside and marry a younger woman to give him sons." The last words tumbled out in a terrified rush.

Katherine looked at her, aghast. Harry Tudor's words on his daughter's christening day, buried somewhere in the back of her mind, came back. She also recognised the fear that she always fought to quell: for if there was no male Tudor heir, where would Harry turn? Would his thoughts go towards his male nephews? The tiny Scots king, or the Brandon boy? And would there be those who would see a chance to stoke the embers of a dying Plantagenet fire? The Duke of Buckingham, son of he who had risen against Richard? The last de la Pole cousin, out in Italy? Meg Pole's sons, with their proud Clarence and Neville ancestry? Or, dear God forbid, her own son, Hal?

Her stomach churned and she felt a bitter taste in her mouth. "Philippa, *promise* me you will not speak of this again. Not with me, not with *anyone.* It's too dangerous. You would not wish to bring trouble upon this family, would you?"

Philippa was shocked into tears. "No! *No,* my dearest lady! Never!" She threw down her sewing and flung herself at Katherine's feet. "You are everything to me, my lady. My mother would have died for you, and so would I."

"I know you would. For goodness sake, get up!" She lowered her voice. I did not mean to frighten you. But no-one must ever hear the slightest whisper against the Tudors in this house. Last time, my husband ended up in the Tower. When others gossip you must keep your counsel, and not be drawn in." Philippa was nodding mutely. "Ah, bless you, Philippa, what would I do without you?"

Her maid dried her eyes with the edge of her apron. "It's Rob Anning who comes back from Honiton with all these tales."

Katherine was alarmed. Surely Rob knew better than to carry tittle-tattle back from the ale houses? He had seen what gossip and rumour had done to his lord.

"Losing Christian and Damaris – it's changed him, my lady. He seems reckless – doesn't care what happens to him. They say he drinks himself into a stupor, and drink always loosens a man's tongue."

"Have him sent to me."

Rob came, shame-faced, fully aware of his indiscretions. Katherine listened silently to his apology. Like Philippa, he was mortified to think that his loyalty was being called into question. Four generations of his family had served the Courtenays.

"My household has to be beyond reproach, Rob. There must never be a breath of criticism of the King. That is treason."

"I know, my lady."

Katherine softened. "If you hear aught in the alehouses or the markets, come and tell *me!* Or better still, keep *out* of the alehouses. Drinking yourself stupid will not bring them back you know. Neither will it help you in your work. Try to look to the future, Rob. It was my sister's advice to me, always."

He looked at her unhappily. "I try, my lady. And it's been better when I'm out and about round the manors, but coming home I hear their voices round every corner; every time a shadow falls in the doorway, I thinks it's Christian, and every time I hear a young woman's voice singing I think it's Damaris. She was to have been married you know, but the lad died too."

"It will feel better with time, Rob. You learn to live on without them. If it had been you who died, what would you have wanted for Christian?"

He was startled. "Why, to find a new husband to care for her."

"Then think on, Rob. There are women who would count it a blessing to care for *you*. Life is not over."

There were few who would have dared to offer him such advice, and even fewer he would have taken it from, such was his grief, but he acknowledged Katherine's right to counsel him.

Katherine: *I saw little of Harry and Catalina for many more months. They continued to keep their distance from any city or town, staying anywhere that was not London, until well into 1518. We heard of little Princess Mary's betrothal to the Dauphin, and of Catalina giving birth to another daughter who did not live long enough to be baptised. Philippa raised her eyebrows to me but said nothing as I read out my son Hal's letter. Sweet Lisbet Grey, the child I had selected for him as a future bride, had also died in the Sweat; now Hal wrote of a girl he admired – Gertrude, the daughter of Sir William Blount. The court was due to reconvene at last, wrote Hal; he was summoned to attend upon the King who would be eager to see again his sweet Aunt Kaff'ryn and his cousin the Lady Margaret Somerset. So would I please tear myself away from Devon, pleaded Hal, and speak to Gertrude's father?*

6

Summer 1519 Greenwich

The King had a son. A son that lived. A bouncing baby boy with unmistakably red Tudor hair. The court was agog with the news that had leaked out from Essex, where Wolsey had judiciously hidden young Bessie Blount and her rounded belly for the past six months. What would happen? Would the King acknowledge the child? Who would tell the Queen?

Clearly, someone had summoned up the courage to do so, for when Katherine arrived at court it was to find Catalina in a state of composure in public but distraction in private. That a chit of a girl from Shropshire could have done what she, an infanta of Spain could not! Her eyes were red and swollen from weeping, her complexion grey with fatigue. She slammed the door of her private chamber in the face of her anxious young lady-in-waiting. Desperately, Katherine tried to think of words that might comfort her.

"Bessie will not return to court, Your Grace. I hear she is to be married. You will never have to see her again."

"And the child? You know that Harry has boasted to everyone he is the father? *Jesu Maria,* he has named him Henry Fitzroy, and has even made Wolsey his *godfather!* How could he *do* this to me?"

"Your Grace, kings have mistresses. My own father had many – and probably many bastard children too. It was no slur upon my mother, as queen, or –"

"But your father had *legitimate* sons! The bastards were of no consequence!"

"And I am sure, in time …"

Catalina's blue eyes flashed with savage bitterness. "In *time?* I have been married for ten years! God does not listen to my prayers. Instead he gives a son to a *whore*." She spat out the last word with the sort of Spanish venom that her mother, Isabella, had directed at the Moors in Granada before she crushed them utterly.

Katherine maintained a diplomatic silence. She was not sure that sixteen-year-old Bessie had been given much choice about warming Harry's bed. *Whore* seemed an unkind word to level at a gentle, musical, pretty virgin seduced by Harry's power and persuasion.

But then a steely defiance replaced Catalina's anger. "Maybe He is telling me I have no need of sons. My mother was queen of her own country, Castile, and my daughter Mary can be queen of this England!"

Katherine judged it best not to mention that little Mary's recent betrothal to the Dauphin might, in that case, mean England slipping under French rule one day. However, it was as if Catalina had read her thoughts.

"And her consort will be my sister Juana's son, the King of Castile! They will reign as joint monarchs, as my parents did! *Pah!* I will not see her married to that *French* boy!"

"How is the princess?" Katherine steered the conversation into safer waters. Immediately, Catalina's face was transformed, lit up by mother-love.

"Ah, very beautiful, and very clever. Now she is three years old we have engaged a musician to teach her how to play the virginals, and already she dances like an angel!"

Katherine thought back to Meggie at the same age, eager to learn the letters on Hal's hornbook. It was not beyond reason that the little princess should be forward in her abilities.

"And Harry adores her," added Catalina firmly.

At the same age, I was once the adored daughter of the King. And my sister Bessy betrothed to another Dauphin. Another time. Another life. These plans can crumble like dust.

Catalina was much calmer now, enquiring politely about the welfare of Hal and Meggie.

"Is there no sign of a child?" Meggie and Somer had been living as husband and wife for two years now.

Katherine shook her head. "No yet. But she is young."

"*Ha!* That is what they told *me* ... but they do not say it any more. And Lord Courtenay?"

"Well." *There is no time like the present.* "He is interested in one of your young ladies-in-waiting."

"Which one?"

"Gertrude Blount."

For a moment the tarnished surname caused Catalina to purse her lips but her mouth worked itself out into a smile. "Gertrude! A dear girl. She cannot help the distant cousin who causes me pain. You know that she is half Spanish? Her mother, Inez de Vegas, came with me as a girl. She would be a good choice for your son. Would you like me to speak to her father on your behalf? I am sure he would be honoured to think his child could make such a match. I am very fond of Lord Mountjoy, as is the King."

"How did she come by such a strange name?"

"I have asked her that. She tells me her father was travelling in the Low Countries when he visited Erasmus, and he liked the names he heard there. She tells me it means *spear of strength*. But a Spanish name would have been prettier."

"It sits oddly upon the tongue," mused Katherine, "but at least she is not another Elizabeth, Margaret or Katherine!"

The Queen's composure was restored by now. She reached for her needlework – she was forever embroidering shirts for her husband, and resumed her neat, diamond-patterned stitching around the neckline. "What you say is true, Katherine, I know. My father, too, had other women, and my mother looked away. It did not mean that he did not love her. He loved her as a queen. Harry will always love me, as his queen, because I am a princess of Spain. It is a different sort of love – between kings and queens. He shows me every respect; he sends away those women who tempt him. And the child will probably die." She wore the expression of a smug cat, sure once again of her importance and status.

Jericho Priory, Blackmore, Essex

Harry Tudor was enchanted by his baby son whom he visited privately whilst staying at his new palace of Beaulieu in Essex. Bessie Blount presented him, blushing with pride. Harry held him briefly, touching the tuft of reddish hair on the baby's crown with his large, bejewelled fingers. The contrast between the golden giant of a man and the three-month-old infant suddenly struck Bessie as hilarious. She giggled – the adorable, infectious giggle that had been part of her appeal over the last eighteen months. Harry laughed too, and handed the child back to his nurse, then sat down and beckoned Bessie to come and sit upon his knee.

She draped her skirts modestly, expecting his hands to rove as they used to. Her body had bounced back to its girlish shape almost immediately after the birth; she could easily have been the baby's older sister rather than his mother. But Harry simply placed his arm lightly around her waist, and with his other hand stroked her cheek as he might a favourite spaniel.

"Sweet Bessie, thank you for my son."

She blushed again, remembering the ease with which he had slipped from her body. The midwives had warned her that first babes often took many hours, and that she would have to be very brave to bear the pain that Eve had brought upon all women, but actually it had hurt very little. She would be happy to give the King more children if that was what he desired. Bessie liked to make everybody happy.

"I must give you to a husband now, my sweet."

She stared at him, wide-eyed. It was what Wolsey had told her but she had not believed it.

"Why, sir? May I not just live here, with little Henry, and you visit us?"

The temptation to establish a second little family with Bessie was almost irresistible. For a moment Harry pictured himself arriving at regular intervals, met by a glowing young mistress and an ever-increasing brood of rosy little Fitzroys. He liked one woman at a time, and was inclined to lose his heart quite romantically; it had happened with Catalina, and then with Anne Stafford, and then with Bessie. But truthfully, he lost interest quickly too. Bessie the virgin, with her long, slender legs and full breasts, had been delightful beyond measure, but Bessie the mother was far too much like the serene portraits of the Madonna and Child, which unnerved him. And Wolsey said he must give her up now. He could not afford to father a whole string of bastards; he must select married girls in future, so that the paternity of any by-blows could be explained away.

"Have I displeased you, sir?" the girl asked timidly, watching the frown growing on his face.

"Displeased me? Never, sweetheart. Wolsey has explained how you will be rewarded?"

For a moment she looked mulish. "With a big dowry, sir, and marriage to one of his wards." She gazed at him, the father of her child, her lover. Sometimes, in bed, she had clean forgotten that he was the King of England – he had just been handsome Harry, and she had fantasised that he was an ordinary young man. Once he had made her pretend to be a milkmaid and said he was a shepherd boy.

Looking back, that was probably the night baby Henry had been conceived. "I would rather have you, sir."

He tipped her off his knee. "Well, I cannot marry you and we need to make an honest woman of you."

"Is it because the Queen is cross?" she whispered. Actually, Bessie really loved Catalina, who had never shown anything but kindness to her young, homesick maid of honour from Shropshire. "Does she know?" Suddenly she realised that she would never be allowed back to court now, and she understood why. There could be no more blithe dancing in the great halls of Harry's palaces; no more happy hours playing her lute while Harry sang; no more nights in his great bed. "Who must I marry? Where must I go?"

"Wolsey thought young Gilbert Tailboys. His father is a lunatic." Bessie gasped. "But the son is of sound mind. His lands are held in trust at present but we will release some estates in Lincolnshire upon his marriage to you." Bessie had no idea where Lincolnshire was but it sounded a long way from anywhere. In that instant she knew she had lost Harry's love.

"What about my son, sir? Will you … will you take him?"

Harry Tudor had fully intended to move the baby into the royal nurseries but the directness of Bessy's question was disconcerting. The loss of his own mother was still sometimes an arrow in his heart. "No, my dear. You shall have him until he is breeched. I will give him everything I can, and you will be honoured as his mother."

"And must I go to Lincolnshire soon?"

He considered the question. The novelty of seeing the healthy baby boy was still too enticing. "No, young Tailboys can come to court and you can stay here for a year or so – where I can visit. Tailboys won't mind. We'll pay him well enough for it. And you'll soon have his child."

Bessy bowed her head. It was impossible to do anything but accept Harry's terms. What woman could ever disobey a man? All her young life she had obeyed her father and now she would have to obey a husband. And they were all bound to obey the King. Being one of Catalina's maids of honour had been lovely but she would never now be promoted to lady-in-waiting. A price had to be paid. She saw that.

Hampton Court Palace May 1520

Thomas Wolsey was well pleased with his new home. His private chamber looked out on to the gardens, whose immaculate lawns ran down to the river. It was far cry from the shambles of Ipswich where his father had traded in cattle and butchered them in front of the house, their blood running down the runnel in the middle of the street. Wolsey saw the irony of his scarlet cardinal's robes but hoped that no-one else did. Sometimes he could still smell the meat hanging from the hooks outside the house, and hear the buzzing of flies on warm summer days or the creaking of the wooden sign in the still, frosty nights. But the shop had made money – enough to send him to school, and then on to Oxford. Ordination; chaplain at Canterbury; trusted emissary of old Henry Tudor; trusted administrator to the new young king; made Lord Chancellor; made an archbishop; made a cardinal. Wolsey had to admit to a feeling of smug satisfaction, knowing that no subject of any monarch had ever held so many important offices, or lived in such luxury.

When he looked about the room he knew that all his possessions were equal to the King's. And in some things he actually outshone Harry Tudor: his servants' livery was newer, brighter; the alms he dispensed on saints' days more lavish; the amount he spent on gifts more generous. Wolsey chuckled; until recently he'd outdone the King on the matter of sons too – his own boy was now a healthy, thriving eight-year-old, living with his foster family in Willesden. It did not do to flaunt Joan Larke, his mistress, too openly. Really, the only thing that galled him was the necessity of travelling on the narrow back of a humble mule instead of spreading his weight across a comfortable horse.

He yawned widely. He'd been hard at it since dawn, putting the finishing touches to Harry Tudor's forthcoming visit to France. Last time, he'd been in charge of all the administration to facilitate the King's invasion and warfare; this time it was to ensure the smooth running of the meeting between Harry and the new French king, Francois. It was no joke, trying to organise how nearly five thousand English should cross the Channel and then be fed, housed and entertained but Wolsey revelled in the challenge. On his desk lay countless lists: provisions, furniture, horses, armour and of course the fabulous designs for the royal lodgings. For three months now the best and brightest of England's talent had been out there in the Golden Vale, near Calais, constructing a temporary palace of illusions. No expense was to be spared in impressing the French king.

England would be empty! Harry and Catalina were taking all their favourite courtiers, churchmen, heralds and servants. The country would be left to the guardianship of the elderly Duke of Norfolk. In the old days, thought Wolsey, no king would ever have dared leave his lands for fear of rebellion but Harry was taking everyone and anyone with him; there would be no-one left behind to lead any insurrection. Wolsey checked his figures one last time – his estimate of £15,000 would not be far out, he thought.

The Field of the Cloth of Gold, June 1520

Hal Courtenay thought that camping in one of the gorgeous blue and gold tents would have been quite an adventure but his status as Harry Tudor's cousin meant that Wolsey had given him and his wife Gertrude rooms in Guisnes Castle itself. His mother was with the Queen, in the extraordinary faux palace, acting as lady-in-waiting but his sister Meggie and her husband Lord Somerset were also in the castle.

Gertrude was dressing. Everyone in the royal entourage had been ordered to attend in their finest clothes, according to their estate. Hal watched as her maid laced her into a peacock-blue satin gown, and attached long, hanging sleeves of darker blue velvet. They had been married for eight months and Hal had a dawning awareness that Gertrude was not quite the girl he had thought. Her father's position as Queen Catalina's chamberlain gave her an instinctive understanding of court life and she had also been trained well in the running of a noble household, taking her new wifely duties very seriously; the house at West Horsley was already becoming a real home under her guidance. What surprised him was her piety. She spent hours on her knees and heard Mass five times a day. When he woke in the morning she was already in the chapel. At first he thought she was praying for a child but soon realised her devotions ran far deeper. She usually dressed sombrely and confided that had he not asked for hand in marriage she would have been content with life as a bride of Christ. Like Meggie she was well-educated but the only texts she cared to read were lives of the saints. She wanted him to purchase relics for the chapel at their Surrey home, and he had a suspicion that she possessed a hair shirt – sometimes her white skin seemed red and irritated, though she maintained she was merely sensitive to the prickling of her woollen bodices through her linen shift. Sometimes Hal felt a little unnerved by her. He put it down to her Spanish heritage. His own brand of religion was more work-a-day.

Now she looked down at her gown, as if slightly astonished at herself. The maid held out at tray of jewellery. Gertrude chose a long string of pearls with a golden crucifix and looped it carefully around her neck, settling the cross in the hollow of her throat.

A knock on the door, and there was Meggie resplendent in honey-coloured damask and Somer looking sheepish in his finery.

"Thank God the tournaments begin tomorrow, Hal! I shall feel much more at home in my armour than trussed up like this! "

"And then we can thrash the French!" Hal spat into the rushes. "That's all they're good for."

Meggie looked alarmed. "You're not supposed to say that, brother. We are here in the spirit of friendship, surely?"

"You may be," retorted Hal. "I am here to bring down as many Frenchmen as I can in the lists. For all this embracing and lovemaking with 'em we can't stand 'em, and they can't stand us."

"It's a cordial hatred!" grinned Somer. "We all know it."

"Exactly."

"I fear we shall roast, slowly, in these garments," said Gertrude ruefully. "They say it is as hot as Spain or Italy out there. I do love this dress but I am not myself in it."

"Appearance is everything, my love," said Hal acidly, " and we must outdo the French in everything, especially you ladies in your sleeves and stomachers."

Meggie laid a hand upon her brother's arm. "You know this is where our father was held prisoner?"

"Aye, I've thought of little else since we arrived. Here *we* are, in the best accommodation, and there *he* was, in the cells below. The wheel of fortune, eh?"

"Has your lady mother said anything?" asked Gertrude, her eyes troubled with anxiety. She was in awe of Katherine but liked her; a girl could do far worse for a mother-in-law.

"She was very quiet as we sailed into Calais, and said she was glad she was not required to stay here at the castle."

"I will pray for your father's soul – later, when we return," she added hastily, seeing Hal's eyebrows shoot up.

"Well, let's go and see the fun," said Somer.

Katherine: *When I remember those two weeks in the hot sunshine of northern France, I often think it was the most ludicrous display of wealth I have ever seen. Some called it the eighth wonder of the world. Never had I seen so much gold or silver; so many gems, or such colour as was in the garments, the paintings on the pretend palace walls or the huge emblems of England and France that hung from the tiltyard walls. Everywhere you looked there were fleur de lys, or English leopards; from every corner trumpets blasted their fanfares; from every fountain wine flowed freely and by the end of each evening hundreds of the local population lay prostrate and inebriated. The hot wind blew the sand from tiltyard into our faces and when we undressed at night-time we each left a little pool of coarse, gritty dust on the smooth, painted floor of the faux palace.*

Katherine watched from Catalina's viewing gallery as her son trotted out to face his French opponent. The heat was intense, for the gallery was glazed, and packed with scores of women sweating into their linen beneath their rich velvets and satins. Katherine wiped the perspiration from her brow and smiled encouragingly at her daughter-in-law who seemed to find watching the jousting distasteful.

"The lances are blunted, Gertrude; Hal is unlikely to come to harm."

"Unless he falls."

"Unless he falls, that is true. I always feared for William in that way."

Next to her, Meggie was gazing intently at the French knight who approached the French queen's gallery on the opposite side of the enormous yard, and took off his helmet. Even at a distance his long nose and dark beard were unmistakable. She saw how Claude, the queen, offered him her favour to tie on to his lance.

"Heaven save us, Mama, it is Francois! Hal is to run a course against the French king!"

491

A tremendous gust of wind caused the whole gallery to sway for a moment and the women screamed and clung to each other. Beyond the tiltyard a few of the canvas tents gave up the battle and took to the air like crazy blue sails.

Katherine found herself gripping the hands of both younger women as Hal's Devon-bred courser, some great grandson of the inimitable Seaton, swivelled on his hocks and prepared for the lists. He reared up, his hooves pawing the air like cymbals, then crashed down, and Englishman and horse launched themelves forward. They were playing at battle, of course; all was arranged to show off talent and skill – but still there could be no doubting the underlying hatred that had existed for centuries between the two nations. Francois thundered down the French side, utterly determined to unseat the young English Lord Courtenay who had pursued the French army into ignominious defeat seven years earlier.

A heavy *thud* echoed off the tiltyard walls and the ranks of three thousand French spectators roared their approval as the English knight swayed precariously in his saddle. But Hal was not William Courtenay's son for nothing. His stallion detected the faltering grip of his rider's knees and slackened his pace sufficiently for Hal to regain his balance. Both riders turned at their respective ends, and squared up for a second joust. When they clashed again it was with equal ferocity. Sparks flew from their armour and this time it was the French king who had to fight to gain control of his mount.

"They will do best of three!" breathed Meggie.

Gertrude thought she might actually be sick, then and there, in the Queen's gallery. With her free hand she clutched the ivory rosary that always hung from her waist.

Katherine felt a sudden surge of pride for her son, who had once been her youngest boy. She prayed that his father and brother looked down from Heaven and would keep him safe. In his veins ran the Plantagenet blood that, a hundred years ago, had defeated the French at Agincourt. She watched as Hal levelled his lance upon his stallion's neck, then hefted the heavy pole into position. She tried to imagine what he might see out of the narrow slit in his visor – how on earth he could adjust the angle of the lance as he galloped. Then something happened – a crisis of confidence in the French horse, or an incorrect stride. Francois was forced to use his legs to steady the creature and in that split second Hal landed a superb blow upon the French king's helmet. If the lance had been sharp it would have pierced through the visor to the eye. A sigh of dismay exhaled through the crowd, followed by shouts of triumph from English trumpets. Both men brought their horses to a halt.

Katherine was aware of Catalina on her feet, applauding wildly. "One in the eye for the French, as they say, Lady Courtenay!" The queen flashed a mischievous, Spanish grin of satisfaction. *She really does not want her daughter to marry the Dauphin!*

Francois was waving away the anxious attendants who had rushed out towards him. He pulled off his battered helm and inclined his head courteously to Hal. *"Bien monte, Mon Seigneur."* His long nose seemed to pinch with pain but he kept his composure. His right eye socket was already darkening with a livid bruise.

Hal discarded his own helmet and threw it to his squire. He jumped off his horse, armour clanging, and bowed deeply to Francois. "You were a fine opponent, *Sire."* And with a snap of his fingers his stallion, flecked with foamy sweat, was also making an obeisance to the French king. *Oh, William! If you could but see!*

Laughter and cheers began to ring out from both sides of the lists. Queen Claude was clapping with delight and King Henry himself striding out from his pavilion, well-satisfied with his cousin's diplomatic modesty. Gertrude thought that maybe she would not disgrace herself by vomiting, after all.

"He came into Harry's bedchamber, and said he wished to serve him as his valet! Imagine, the King of France holding the shaving water for the King of England!" Catalina was helpless with laughter as she recounted the story. "Francois threw him at wrestling, then Harry beat him at the butts; they have even tried to outdo each other with their gifts."

Katherine thought she was beginning to get the measure of Catalina's attitude to the whole visit: in public she was the model wife, sensitive to precedence and totally supportive of Harry Tudor's desire to appear as the equal of the French king, but in private she was dismissive of the need to impress the French. They had just returned from the final ceremony, an open air Mass conducted in the great tiltyard, where Wolsey had laid the foundation stone of a wonderful chapel to be built upon the site.

"Have you enjoyed it, Lady Courtenay? *Nuestro viaje pequeno a Francia?* I certainly enjoyed seeing the French king receive a black eye, courtesy of your son!"

"Your Grace, I think you would not be saying that, were we not alone!" Katherine found herself bubbling up with laughter too. There had been an entertaining moment during the Mass, when each queen had been invited to kiss the Pax held before them by Wolsey. Claude and Catalina clearly wished to preserve the delicate balance of power achieved by their husbands, and ended up kissing each other instead, leaving Wolsey looking nonplussed.

"Ah, I shall be glad to get home, and to see Mary again. I have had enough of this peacemaking in France. Suddenly her face took on the same sly expression Katherine had seen when Hal had bettered Francois in the lists. "But you should know we return by way of Gravelines, where we are to meet with my nephew the King of Castile, and his aunt, Margareta; she was once my sister-in-law, you know, married to my brother Juan."

Katherine could not resist it. "Once, *I* was to have married your brother, Juan."

For a moment, incredulity registered on Catalina's face as she sifted through her knowledge of her own family's past history, and tried to tie it in with her appreciation of who Katherine had been as a girl. "Yes," she said slowly, "I had forgotten. Forgive me. You were once a princess. Of course, of course." She held out a hand in genuine friendship. "How strange our lives have been, Lady Courtenay. How strange. To think, you might have been Juan's wife, and Queen of Spain, and I might have been –" she stopped herself abruptly.

Yes, who would they have married you to, if my Tudor brother-law- had died at Bosworth? There would have been no Arthur, no Harry. If Richard's son Ned had lived, would they have married you to him? Is that how you might have become queen of England?

"The world is full of "what might have beens", "said Katherine lightly.

Catalina's eyes suddenly brimmed with tears. "What might have been if I could have had a son," she said quietly. "There will be no more babies, I know that now. I have only Mary, and I will *not* see her married into France. That is why we go home via Gravelines. I will see her married into my own family. Into Spain." She paused. "I tell you this, Lady Courtenay because I know you are discreet, and because I know you understand my husband like no other. I have humoured him, coming here to France, but I will get what I want."

8

Tiverton April 1521

Spring again. A soft one, with catkins dangling over the River Exe and hedge-sparrows nesting in the castle's nooks and crannies. The incessant bleating of lambs and their mothers in the meadows that stretched out for miles towards Exeter. A feeling of contentment that yet again winter was past, the days were lengthening and soon the milk and butter would taste of fresh grass. In St Peter's churchyard handsome headstones now marked the grave of Joanna Colson, Christian Anning and her daughter Damaris and Masses were offered for their souls in Master Greenway's new chapel.

Life moved on. Philippa had come blushing to Katherine one morning, saying that Rob Anning wished to marry her and, with the Countess's permission, she was minded to accept him. "If only to shut him up, my lady; he never stops pestering me about it."

Katherine smiled. Her household servants in Devon were dear to her. No matter how many weeks or months she spent away there was always something good about returning to the familiar security of her Courtenay estates. She was glad to hear that time had healed the worst of Rob's grief and that he could contemplate a new future. Philippa was still young enough to bear him children.

"Of course you have my permission! And my blessing. I will pay for your ring and your wedding gown – you shall have a marriage portion to take to him, and some marriage money for yourself of course." She realised she sounded more enthusiastic than Philippa herself, who was pink already but rapidly turning the colour of a russet apple.

"I've told him I shall not leave you, my lady."

"Well, there is no need, surely? Rob is my steward, and as his wife you will continue to have your home here."

"But if ..." By this time she was the colour of a cardinal's robes "... if there should be ... babes?"

"Then we shall have a nursemaid for them, and you shall remain at my side whenever I am in Devon," replied Katherine cheerfully. "It will be wonderful to have children in the castle again. And if you wish to attend me at court then Rob will just have to put up with it!"

She saw the relief come into her maid's eyes. It was one thing to acquire a husband; it was quite another to have to submit to his will, as God and the law demanded. Philippa had enjoyed status and freedom as Katherine's maid; she had travelled widely and seen life. Why should she abandon such liberty?

"Philippa, Rob was a loving husband to Christian and there is no reason why he should not be the same to you."

"I know it, my lady."

"Well then, there is nothing more to be said, other than the banns in church!"

Philippa and Rob's wedding was a simple affair. Just a trothplighting ceremony in St Peter's and a wedding feast in the castle's Great Hall. Cider from the orchards; a roasted ox; a great bridal cake made with raisins; sugar candies, comfits and almond tarts – the Courtenay household and a few invited guests enjoyed the Countess's generosity. Katherine stayed for a while, to raise a toast, but slipped away before the real roistering began. However, she had played her part in preparing the wedding bed, gathering rose petals from the garden and insisting that Philippa should have a fine lawn shift for the occasion, in addition to her new velvet dress and kirtle. As the warm, May darkness finally fell, she could hear the shouts of laughter and music as the couple were carried to their bedchamber by their friends. Doors slammed; men whistled; women giggled – and then they returned to the hall where their merrymaking continued into the early hours.

In the morning the little castle was strangely silent. An apologetic, dark-haired young maid came in late to open Katherine's shutters, bringing her fresh water for washing and offering to help her dress. She grinned ruefully, showing good teeth, and executed a neat curtsey.

"They're all mostly still asleep, my lady. Some just where they laid their heads! 'Twill take a good deal of tidying down there. Philippa ... that's Mistress Anning that is now ... sends word that she will be with you bye and bye, my lady."

"Tell her there is no need. She must take a few days as her honeymoon."

"Oh! I'll run and tell her, my lady! They do say as how the first month of a marriage is the sweetest! I can serve you well; I d'know how I must brush out your lovely hair, and how to fold your lovely clothes in the chest. Philippa … that's Mistress Anning, has learned me well."

Katherine rinsed her face and hands in the water, noting how little lavender sprigs bobbed in it. The girl had clearly made an effort. Now she held out a fresh shift, a small garnet and pearl ring glinting on her right hand. Not the sort of ring you might expect to see a maid from Tiverton wearing. Katherine started, splashing water on to the floor.

"That's a goodly ring. Who gave it to you?"

"Oh, 'twas my grandmother's. She did leave it to me in her will when she died. I do wear it all the time, in memory of her."

"Remind me of your second name, child." Katherine had seen her about the castle in the last couple of months but knew her only as Isabel.

"Oh, 'tis Darch, a good Devon name, though I have lived up in London till but recently. I have come home to be married myself this summer, to Master Anning's son, Adam, as works for Master Greenway. So as I shall be *young* Mistress Anning!"

"Are you related to Christopher Darch, who was a warder at the Tower?"

Isabel looked astounded that someone so high born as the Countess should know of her family. "Why, *yes,* indeed! Grandfather Christopher was at the Tower, as a younger man of course."

A sudden, sharp memory of a boy on a narrow pallet, his eyes misted with misery, and the flash of a steel axe on a rain-soaked morning when Plantagenet blood splashed into the sodden straw on Tower Hill. Meg Pole's poor little brother, murdered for his name.

"Your grandfather did my family great service, Isabel. Over many years. Did you know my late husband was once a prisoner in the Tower?"

"I've heard it said," Isabel replied cautiously. "My father did speak of it." She was rapidly feeling out of her depth. Philippa had given her strict instructions about holding her tongue and not rattling on in my lady's presence. On the other hand, she reasoned, if the Countess asked a question she was bound to reply. In her childhood Isabel had often been taken to visit her grandparents in their accommodation at the Tower: she had seen the strange creatures in the menagerie, and remembered the huge bunch of keys her grandfather carried on his belt. Her own father was a sea captain who lived at St Katherine's Wharf near the Tower.

He worked for John Greenway, whose ships sometimes set out of London as well as Topsham. That was how she had met Adam Anning, who'd come up from Devon and lodged awhile with her family. The Annings knew the Darches. The Darches knew the Annings. Both sides were happy with the match. Adam's home was in Tiverton and he wanted her to come back to Devon with him. His mother and sister were dead of the Sweat, he said; his father due to remarry and he, Adam, would take on his own cottage in the town. When she'd arrived, Adam's new stepmother-to-be, Philippa had suggested she could help out with fine sewing and give a hand with the wedding preparations. *But don't go expecting anything like this yourself, my girl. I am the Countess's personal maid and she is doing this for me.*

The Countess had sat down and was unbinding her hair, which was still thick and the colour of ripe wheat. *How old must she be? Surely forty, but she does not look it. Her skin is not yet wrinkled – her arms are smooth and her neck is, too. She could pass for thirty any day of the week.* Isabel took the ivory comb and admired the pretty carving.

"It is a mermaid, my lady! I can see her fishy tail and all the little shells!"

"It's my favourite. It was my sister's. My sister that was queen."

Isabel gulped. She wished she'd paid more heed to Philippa's long-winded explanations. Isabel did not pay much attention to the past and had but a tenuous grasp of who might have been king before the present glorious King Harry.

"However did *my* family help yours, my lady?" She began to pull the comb through the Countess's hair. "I can scarcely imagine such a thing."

"It was your grandfather. He once allowed me to visit a relative held prisoner, and then when my own husband was confined in the Tower he took it upon himself to ensure that my Lord Courtenay was well-looked after. My husband never forgot your grandfather's kindness – and your grandmother too. He tried to find them again when he was released but they had gone from the Tower."

"Grandfather died, and Grandmother came to live with us. She died two years since, but a wonderful age, my lady – nigh on sixty!" Isabel twisted the ring off her finger. "She always wore this – said it was in memory of a young man who had died."

Katherine stared at the little ring, remembering how she had pressed it back into Christopher Darch's hand. "The young man who died was my cousin. I wish your grandparents were alive, that I might thank them for all their goodness. I hope they knew that my lord husband was released, and restored to his family.

"Just before he died, Grandfather went to the funeral of a great lord. Grandmother said they had known him once, and he had kissed her. I always thought it was a story ... how could *my* family know great lords?" Isabel looked suddenly troubled. "Is this *your* ring, my lady?"

"No, child. It is yours. By all that is good and right, it is yours."

9

West Horsley, Surrey May 1521

Hal Courtenay reined in his horse on the summit of Leith Hill. The creature was glad to stop after such a climb; his neck was flecked with foam and he blew heavily. The view was spectacular. Looking south, the county of Surrey stretched into Sussex – a vast, densely wooded plain that reached over twenty five miles to the sea. Hal squinted; he was sure he could see a faint blue smudge on the horizon. Then twisting in the saddle he gazed northwards to London, imagining the crowded and stinking streets of the city. Somewhere, in that direction, lay the Tower and the hill just beyond its gates, where three days ago his cousin the Duke of Buckingham had been executed in front of hundreds of shocked citizens.

Despite the warmth of the early summer afternoon, Hal shivered. The last week had been a lesson for life. A week ago he'd been sitting in Westminster Hall, on a bench with his fellow English peers, looking across at Edward Stafford, third Duke of Buckingham, on trial for high treason.

He's another of my mother's myriad cousins. We're both descendants of Plantagenet kings and their blood courses through our veins. The difference is that I never allude to it, whilst he never lets anyone forget it. That's why he's on trial for his life and I am amongst those who must condemn him.

Buckingham had been foolish beyond words. Predicting that Harry would have no sons and just smiling lazily at the tongue-waggers who said well if that's so then who shall be the next king? Mustering his troops in Wales – saying it was just to protect himself when everyone knew he was flexing his muscles against the King. Trying to bribe the King's own guards, for heaven's sake! And kneeling before the King with a dagger concealed about his person, so that when he rose he could have easily stabbed him! It beggared belief. And yet …

Hal watched Cardinal Wolsey's inscrutable face whilst the charges were read out. It was obvious he wanted Buckingham dead. The accused stood in his usual arrogant pose, flanked by yeomen of the guard, staring back at the men with whom he had, till recently, soldiered, hunted, played tennis, drunk and laughed. He was as finely dressed as a king, and examined his fingernails whilst the charges against him were read out:

"That you did listen to prophecies of the King's death. That you did intend to kill the King."

His own father died for treason against King Richard. Why can the man not be content with his wealth, his title and his estates, as I am? Why could he not see that to move against Harry, and Wolsey, was bound to end badly?

Hal listened to the damning evidence provided by Buckingham's own servants and realised his own hands were trembling. How much of Wolsey's money had bought these men? Or did they already bear grievances against their lord? Could it ever be that anyone in the Courtenay household would turn against him, or his mother?

When it was his turn, Hal pronounced his "Guilty" as firmly as he could, though a bitter gorge was rising in his throat. There could be no other verdict. Harry Tudor would not stomach this subject who thought himself suited to take his place. Buckingham would die for his Plantagenet blood, his presumption and his stupidity. So be it. Harry would seize his lands and his houses. That was the way of kings. The extraordinary noise was the Duke of Norfolk weeping as he passed sentence upon his peer.

Now, Hal dismounted and found a spot out of the wind, where he lay on the rough grass, closed his eyes and allowed his horse to crop steadily beside him. He missed Devon but liked Surrey, with its quiet villages and easy road up to London. His home at West Horsley was comfortable – a house built by a Courtenay bishop of Exeter and equipped with all the luxuries that made life pleasant. Hal made a mental note not to emulate Buckingham and try to make his homes better than the King's. No doubt even now, whilst Buckingham's body was just freshly buried, Harry Tudor would be thinking about which of his estates he coveted the most – beautiful Penshurst in Kent, no doubt. The sun's rays danced a red glow on his eyelids. From up here he was only ten miles away from his own acres, just beyond the little town of Dorking.

The trick is to always convince the King that I am his most loyal cousin. Mama is right; well, she is always right – Harry Tudor is the vainest man alive

501

and those of us who wish to survive must serve that vanity. That way my sons and grandsons, and their grandsons will follow good fortune.

He thought suddenly of Lady Margaret Pole, his mother's Plantagenet cousin, who had married her daughter to Buckingham's heir. *Jesu, how will Harry treat her now? And will his suspicions fall upon others who happen to be descended from the old royal family? Suffolk dead. Buckingham dead. That leaves the Poles and the Courtenays.*

Hal could hear Katherine's voice in his head, warning him when he first went to court and fought for Harry in France: *"He loves us but he hates us, Hal. He loves me for being his mother's sister but he hates me for having been born a Plantagenet. He freed your father, but only because his own father had imprisoned him, and he wanted to be different. Never trust him, and always be wary of how quickly his moods can change."*

*S*ound advice. Hal wondered what his mother might be doing, down in Devon, and whether news of Buckingham's death had reached there yet. He had written immediately after the trial, and the roads were good, so it was very likely. He's been careful what he put in the letter – just a factual account of events. He knew his mother's astuteness – that she would understand how the King would suspect a plot (the Tudors always suspected plots) and she would welcome the opportunity to prepare herself. *Thank God we have always kept our distance from the Buckingham family, but Mama loves Lady Pole and the Poles are now too close to the flame.*

London March 1522

Katherine felt no pity for Buckingham – a man her own age who should have known better. Long ago, Bessy and Cecily had identified the Stafford family's fatal flaw: a belief that their own pedigree outrivalled any Lancastrian or Yorkist king. It did not surprise her, then, that the third duke had gone the same way as the second. The most distressing aspect of the whole business was the effect upon her cousin Meg Pole, no longer safe behind her married name. Dismissed from her position as little Princess Mary's governess; one of her sons thrown in the Tower to cool his heels, another sent from court and another staying out of harm's way in Italy. Time for the Poles to lie low, until such time as Harry Tudor might forget their closeness to the Stafford family.

For the Courtenays, thank God, it was different. If Harry rejected some relatives he cleaved to others. Hal was even elected Knight of the Garter in Buckingham's place. In the lovely chapel at Windsor Katherine watched from Catalina's loft as her son's helm, crest and sword were attached to the stall. Her gaze strayed across to the fine gates guarding her father's tomb, to the coat of gilt mail and banner that still hung there proudly, nearly forty years on. Nearby was Lord Hasting's chantry – her father's friend, killed on her Uncle Richard's instructions. Ironically, the sixth King Henry lay close by too. What on earth would her father have made of lying for all eternity a few feet away from the cousin he had fought so long to replace? Pilgrims still visited saintly Henry's tomb, leaving their offering in the stout iron box alongside his grave.

She was visiting Hal and Gertrude at West Horsley, and found her daughter-in-law debilitated by sickness with her first pregnancy. Gertrude was invited to participate in a pageant at Wolsey's London home but could not even lift her head off the pillow. Katherine took one look at her wan face and offered to go in her stead. Two years' absence from court made her curious.

In the Queen's rooms at Westminster, the two Boleyn girls now appeared to be permanent fixtures. They were like contrasting figures on a chess board – Mary, now Mary Carey, fair of complexion and hair, with eyes as blue as periwinkles, favouring light colours and Anne, olive-skinned with eyes like sloes, her dark brown hair purposefully visible under her fashionable French hood, swishing about the Queen's apartments in sophisticated black. Jane Parker, the betrothed of the Boleyn son, George, was also a new lady-in-waiting. Katherine found it hard to warm to any of them: Mary wore a permanently smug expression; Anne clearly regarded a woman of forty three as unspeakably old, and Jane simply scowled at everyone.

It was with some misgiving then, that she realised they would be her companions at the pageant to entertain the Spanish ambassadors at York Place. Catalina, delighted by Katherine's presence, was gleeful.

"I told you, did I not, that my Mary would not marry the Dauphin! Harry has changed his mind, and now favours my beloved Spain. He has agreed that our daughter shall be the wife of my nephew, Charles!"

Katherine felt it better not point out that Charles would have to wait ten years or so for six-year-old Princess Mary to be his wife. Quite frankly, there was no believing in these alliances until they actually happened. But Catalina seemed thrilled; all her talk was of Spain, and what a fine consort the young emperor would make for Mary. It was obvious she truly believed that Mary could one day be queen in her own right. As she chattered, Katherine saw the Boleyn sisters exchange veiled smiles she found hard to interpret. Were they laughing at Catalina, thinking her naïve? She was suddenly irritated by them and sought to change the subject.

"So, what is this revel we must appear in?"

"*Vraiment*, Lady Courtenay, we are *invited*, not commanded," said Anne Boleyn lightly. "Truly, an honour for my sister and me – and Jane, of course," she added as an afterthought. Jane Parker scowled again. *There is no love lost there.* "An honour to dance with the French queen, and with the King's dear aunt." Her accent was unusual, tinged with French pronunciation, though whether natural or affected Katherine could not judge. *The French queen? Oh, she's talking of Mary Brandon, and she manages to make me sound like some ancient old crone.*

Mary Carey looked up from her embroidery. "Eight of us are to play the parts of ladies defending a castle. We are to have names that describe our good qualities. I am to be Kindness." She giggled. "And Anne is to be Perseverance."

"I *can* persevere, to get what I want," agreed Anne.

"What is it, that you want, Mistress Boleyn?" asked Catalina, trying to make a connection with these two bright young women, trying to join in their banter.

Anne lowered dark lashes. *She's playing at modesty.* "*Ma foi*! Let me think. Perhaps, one day, a husband as wonderful as yours, Your Grace?"

Catalina seemed to think this a witty response. "And do you have anyone in mind, Mistress Anne?"

"Oh! Let me see. An earl? A duke?"

"She's just determined to do better than me, Your Grace," said Mary with sisterly acerbity.

"If possible," Anne's reply was both sweet and barbed. "My father would have me matched with my cousin the Earl of Ormond."

"Lady Carey, your husband, William, is much liked by the King," said Catalina soothingly. "I am sure he has a fine future ahead of him. Has not the King already shown him favour? I believe I heard that he is to be granted some manors in Hertfordshire? No doubt a reward for his good services. My husband enjoys the company of young men who share his interests …"

Yet again, that smug, cat-has-got-the-cream look on Mary Carey's face. Katherine had a moment of absolute revelation. *Jesu! She has found her way into*

Harry Tudor's bed! And he rewards her husband! And Mistress Anne knows! Pity welled up in her heart for Catalina. *Yet, he is no worse than my own father, who whored with any lady-in-waiting willing to have him. But my father had sons. No mistress ever threatened my mother's position. But at least Mary Carey's married. She cannot threaten Catalina.*

Not content with Hampton Court, Wolsey also laid claim to a London home to rival anything possessed by the King. York Place was sumptuous. Wolsey had acquired it, extended it, developed it and filled it with the best tapestries, furniture and silver plate possible. Yet again, Katherine found herself marvelling that a butcher's son from Essex could have risen so fast, so high, and that Harry Tudor just seemed to view such a meteoric career as a reflection of his *own* power.

The pageant was extraordinary, and in the end Katherine gave in to enjoying herself as much as the younger women. Thank God she still had the energy and fleetness of foot to keep pace with the Boleyn girls who were half her age. Twenty-six-year old Mary Brandon, Duchess of Suffolk, once Queen of France for eleven weeks, was radiant as Beauty, and led them all. Katherine was gratified to be Honour, and strange Jane Parker was Constancy. *Certainly constant in looking cross.* No expense was spared, and Katherine had to admit she loved her costume. Years of dressing fairly discreetly and covering her hair, were put aside tonight. Their gowns were low cut. She ran her hand over the white satin and lace from Milan, and tilted her head under the golden bonnet encrusted with jewels. Her hair was loose, and flowed down her back as thickly as Mary Carey's. Her form was still as slender as Anne Boleyn's. Behind her mask she could easily be mistaken for a girl.

The designer of the entertainment had created a huge green castle with three towers, glittering in the torchlight. At the drawbridge choirboys played the parts of the Seven Vices. From the battlements Beauty, Kindness, Perseverance, Bounty, Mercy, Pity and Honour watched as eight lords, led by Ardent Desire, demanded their release. The Vices refused. A chivalric siege commenced: at the signal of gunfire, Katherine joined in with gusto, pelting the men with comfits, and showering them with rosewater. They dodged the dates and oranges which flew back through the air.

Wolsey's great chamber was alive with colour, laughter and music, heady perfumes and sharp citrus. The painted floorcloth in front of the castle was tacky with sticky rosewater, causing the lords to lift their feet like paddling ducks. The audience of courtiers and Spanish ambassadors shouted encouragement as the lords assaulted the castle and triumphantly led out the ladies. Katherine found her hand grasped by Devotion, who led her on to the dance floor.

It was years since she had danced with such abandon. Ever mindful of her vow of celibacy she had carefully avoided drawing too much attention to herself. Yet with her identity concealed and the steps of the galliard imprinted on her memory, she allowed her partner to swing her joyfully through the patterns. He was tall and well built but light on his feet, his eyes smiling at her through his mask. *One of Harry's gentlemen – and he thinks he has caught some young lady-in-waiting!* The rhythm of the drums sent her heart racing and she found herself openly smiling back at him. As the final chord hovered and the last percussion beat crashed they were both out of breath and laughing.

The couples were unmasking. To shouts of delight from the audience the King was revealed to have been Loyalty, and he had rescued Kindness from the castle. Seated with the Spanish ambassadors, Catalina was engaged in animated conversation in her mother tongue and did not see how tightly Mary Carey's fingers were entwined with Harry Tudor's, or how his eyes lingered on her pale flesh. Then he had released her, and was paying court to all the other ladies who had danced. Anne Boleyn curtsied low but she had no bosom to rival her sister and Harry merely grazed her hand disinterestedly with his lips. Then he was in front of Katherine, beaming down at her.

"My favourite aunt! Why, when they said the Countess of Devon I expected your daughter- in-law!"

"Your Grace. Gertrude is expecting a child and is not well. I was happy to take her place."

"Ha! So my cousin Courtenay is to be a father!" She saw his eyes cloud over for a moment. If Hal had a son there would be yet another male with Plantagenet blood, whatever his surname. Then, "*My* boy thrives, you know, down in Essex. A handsome and healthy child." His declaration boomed around the hall. *So it's true – he acknowledges Bessy Blount's child. But he's picked his next mistress more carefully, so that future bastards can be passed off as her husband's. Catalina must have heard but she gives no sign. Her dignity is remarkable in the face of his effrontery.*

"So, who is your partner, Aunt Kaff'ryn? Why, it's Sir Benet Haute! I can leave you in safe hands then, Aunt, for he is a sad and sombre widower, like yourself." And he swept on.

506

Without his mask Devotion was revealed to be a man of her own generation. Silvering dark hair lay damply on his brow. He was regarding her with frank admiration through crinkled hazel eyes. Katherine was suddenly on her guard; no man had looked at her like that for years. They had not dared: she had been Lord Courtenay's faithful wife, then his grieving widow, then an avowed celibate. Just as she had intended, that public statement kept the male nobility of England at a safe distance and in Devon gentlemen amongst her neighbours treated her with deference due to her rank. She gathered her thoughts, aware that the hilarity of the pageant and the dancing had released something she had quelled for years.

"I am sorry, sir. I am not familiar with your name."

"Benedict … Benet they call me. Haute. Of Kent." He hesitated. "If I may presume, I can claim some small degree of kinship, my lady, for I believe our mothers were cousins. At some point a Wydville married an Haute. I'm just a younger son, somewhere along the line, but heigh-ho, His Grace seems to like me …" He opened his palms in a self-deprecating gesture.

If William had lived he would have been about the same age as this man at her side.

"Because you are a good jouster, and can play tennis, and can carry the tenor line."

"Bass, actually. I have a gravelly old voice."

"You are … older than most of His Grace's new friends."

"And wiser. He'll pension me off though, one of these days. As you say, his new friends are the young set: Boleyn, Norris, Weston, Bryan. I can't always keep up with 'em."

"You did tonight."

"It must have been the example set by my partner. Will you take refreshment?" He was steering her towards a space on the table below where Catalina still conversed with the Spaniards. He summoned a servant who filled their glasses and brought them fruit and nuts. From the minstrels' gallery a consort of lute players struck up quiet tunes that allowed conversation to flow freely. *Nobody is watching me. All eyes are the other side of the hall where the King now sits with his young bucks, the Boleyn sisters and all the other youthful beauties.*

It was easy to talk with him. He asked about Devon and was knowledgeable about the challenges of running an estate. He asked about her family – was acquainted with Hal and Somer and said he, too, had fought in France. He told her of his own family – two daughters both recently married but no son. "This particular branch of the Hautes ends with me, it would seem." His wife had died of the Sweat five years ago. No, he had not sought to remarry. He had been invited to court after the King had visited Kent for the hunting at Knole. He'd been one of the local gentlemen invited to show His Grace the best places to follow the chase. Yes, the life of a courtier suited him – kept him busy and kept him fit, too.

He raised an enquiring eyebrow. "You prefer to stay in the country?"

"There are many things that call for my attention there. It's not hard to live in so beautiful a county as Devon."

"Forgive me – I am aware that you have taken vows."

"They do not preclude me from *life,* Sir Benet. I am not a nun."

Amusement flashed across his face. "Indeed not."

She examined her hands in her lap. "You know who I am, Sir Benet. You might say I became a vowess for practical reasons, not through piety."

"Then I would say you made a clever choice. However did you persuade the King?"

"The usual way. By allowing him to think he had thought of it himself."

Benet chuckled. "He's no different to when he was a small boy, is he? I remember coming here as a page, in the old king's time, and seeing him when he was the Duke of York, ordering us all around."

"His Grace has always known what he wants," agreed Katherine carefully.

"What he seems to want now is a worry to us all," said Benet more quietly, "and especially Her Grace."

Another couple arrived, and Benet was forced to shift position to make more room on their bench. Their upper arms, hips and thighs were pressed together for a moment. Katherine's glass threatened to spill as the trestle wobbled, and he reached out a hand to steady it, as hers made exactly the same movement. His fingers closed around her own for a brief moment, warm and strong.

Katherine: *I had expected to stay just a week or so with Hal but Catalina was glad of my company in the new, brittle Tudor court where her husband wooed young Mary Carey. You could hardly condemn Mistress Carey – everyone knew that her mother's family, the Howards, were ambitious, and more than delighted that Mary had caught Harry Tudor's fancy. Catalina's dignity was astounding. Every morning the girl knelt before her as her lady-in-waiting, and every morning the queen smiled at her whilst the rest of us shifted uneasily. When* *the King arrived he was always accompanied by his retinue. Often my son Hal was amongst them, and Sir Benet Haute, who made a point of casually joining me wherever I sat – or inviting me to join the hunt, or politely offering to escort me into supper. So six weeks passed. No-one was interested in me and my doings – the King's love life was far too fascinating. In his wife's rooms, his eyes flickered over us, searching out Mary Carey's bowed blonde head. They said that her young husband had been told to relinquish her – and was rewarded with money and lands.*

10

Tiverton

Back home in Devon, Katherine threw herself into a busy schedule of visiting her estates and meeting her tenants. Rob Anning was taken aback. There was no need, he told her; all the rents were up to date and in any case problems could be dealt with by her central surveyor.

"He thinks you must have lost faith in him," observed Philippa, one morning, as Katherine prepared to ride out to Columbjohn. "I told him, likely as not you just want to see things for yourself," and added pointedly, "to see how *well* he stewards your lands." She offered Katherine her gloves.

Katherine pulled on the fine leather, slowly smoothing out the wrinkles over the back of her hands. She implicitly trusted Philippa's loyalty and discretion but she had not confided in her about Benet Haute. What was there to tell, anyway? Simply that a man of her own age had paid her attention, offered a compliment or two – and made her heart race like girl of eighteen. She had thought about him all summer – shocking in a woman of her age. The only way to stop thinking about him was to fill her head with other thoughts: the repairs needed at Colcombe; the alms to be given to the poor; the offerings to be made at Mass; how four horses should be taken to Meggie and Somer; the preparations to be made for Christmas …

The land around Columbjohn was low lying, on the flood plain of the River Culm, the grass always lush even in late autumn. Katherine liked the mansion house, which sat solidly on a slight incline above the water meadows. It was a peaceful place. Doves fluttered from the dovecote as she rode through the gatehouse arch with Rob. In the large parlour a fire burnt brightly in the hearth; at least twenty tenant farmers steamed gently in the heat. An attorney from Exeter rose hastily to greet her. She smiled at them all.

"I am here merely to ensure you are all content with your manors." There was much shuffling of feet and clearing of throats. A farmer voted their spokesman bowed low.

"Indeed we are, Your Grace. As ever we were upon Courtenay land. We hopes as how our gifts are pleasing to Your Grace? "

Katherine looked questioningly at Rob. "Oxen and lambs, my lady – and pheasants, eels, partridges – salmon from the river ..."

"Of course. Be assured your gifts are much appreciated by all my household at Tiverton. My steward, Mr Anning you all know, and I am in his debt for the way he devotes himself to the business of my lands. If you have any concerns you know you may approach him." Assorted noises of acknowledgement. "And my attorney, Mr Luscombe, will deal with any formalities."

"God bless you, my Lady of Devonshire, and the young Earl too, and his lady."

She left them to their discussions, Rob looking much happier now, and walked out in to garden. A few late roses still bloomed – white roses, the symbol of her house. Over a quarter of a century had passed since she had been the Princess Katherine Plantagenet – a lifetime since she had willingly given herself to William Courtenay. If she closed her eyes his dear face would swim slowly into focus. He was always smiling, always reaching out his hands to her. Every June she gave offerings in his memory; every year Master Lyne the chandler was paid for the annual supply of beeswax candles to light his tomb; every year the Black Friars sang services for him in their priory. He was in Heaven, surely, and looking down upon her. Could he see her now, at Columbjohn, attending to Courtenay business? Had he seen her at York Place, dancing with Benet Haute? She found herself stripping a rose head of its petals; they dropped silently onto the grass. Life, and death. Life, as she had learned, was so precious and fragile. Inevitably her thoughts turned to her siblings, those she had loved and those she had hardly known – all gone now. But reunited in Heaven! Was Elizabeth Wydville, even now, gathering her young princes to her heart? Was Heaven a place where Dickon's death upon the gallows, and Edward's demise at the hands of James Tyrrell's servants, could finally be forgotten? Richard Plantagenet had given orders for their deaths, yet they had died at others' behests – was he then spared from Hell? And where had Henry Tudor gone, upon whose instructions they had both died? She had seen the glorious, half-finished chantry in the Abbey, where his body lay alongside Bessy's. But where was his soul?

Despite her thick riding cloak, she shivered. She remembered kneeling before the Bishop of London after William's death, making her vow: *"for to be chaste in my body and truly and devoutly shall keep me chaste from this time forward as long as my life lasteth"* It had been no hardship – until now. Benet's warm smiles, and the brush of his lips on the back of her hand had kindled emotions not felt for over ten years. Jesu, she was forty three! What business did she have to allow her thoughts to turn to love? It was an age for grandchildren, and sitting by the fire! Yet her own mother had given birth to her at forty two! And she had inherited Elizabeth Wydville's youthful looks – her face was unlined; no need to rinse her hair in urine yet to preserve its blondeness, and her limbs still felt as supple as when she was a girl. With Meggie and Hal gone she was lonely. She styled herself *"the excellent Princess Katherine, Countess of Devon, daughter, sister and aunt of kings"* in her official documents and on her seal – a grand nomenclature that made people keep their distance. Yet Benet Haute had broken through her reserve, and she longed to see him again.

She had hoped that her children might keep Christmas with her at Tiverton, but Hal wrote that the King set great store by his company. Gertrude's first pregnancy had ended in an early miscarriage, but she was with child again, sick again and not up to travelling. Meggie and Somer would come if the roads permitted. In mid-December the first snow fell, a dusting at first but then a two-day blizzard that turned Tiverton into a silent, white world. Drifts piled against the gatehouse and temperatures plummeted. Layers of ice prevented the shutters from opening and a two-inch crust of ice sat on top of the snow; trying to walk on it was like crunching through marchpane. The wind sculpted the snow into fantastical shapes in hedgerows, doorways and ditches with patterns like beautiful seashells and peaks like whipped cream. A magical, transformed, pristine continent. The snow stopped but most routes in and out of the town were obliterated. Katherine resigned herself to a festive season without her family but in the company of her household. At least the castle's butteries and kitchens were piled high with provisions and the meat kept well in such cold. After the fasting of Advent all looked forward to twelve days of merrymaking.

The men waded out into the woodlands and dragged home a huge Yule log and the Great Hall was transformed into a green bower of holly and ivy. A rich, fresh scent of evergreen vegetation hung in the air, competing with spices. There would be players from Exeter if they could make it through the snow, and choirboys from St Peter's. By Christmas Eve the castle was packed with local

512

minstrels and tumblers. Her fool was busy devising tricks and jokes to keep everyone entertained. She ate a quiet supper in her chamber – the cooks were frantically preparing for the great feast tomorrow.

A perfunctory knock, and Philippa's head popped around the door. "My lady, you will barely credit it, but there is a gentleman arrived through the snow from Exeter with his servant. He says he is acquainted with you."

Katherine was puzzled. The men she knew from Exeter were either from the cathedral, or the priories, or else gentlemen who would surely be at home with their own families. Given the weather, the few civic dignitaries invited had politely declined. "Does he give his name?"

"Sir Benedict Haute. A most pleasant gentleman. I have settled him and his boy in the hall with some refreshments and told him to wait."

Surely Philippa could hear the pounding of her heart and see the colour rising in her cheeks?

"Well, we cannot refuse any traveller hospitality at Christmas, and in such weather. I will come down."

He did not hear her enter in her soft-soled, furred winter house boots but when the girl serving him suddenly dipped into a curtsey he turned around. The hall was in shadows, with just the light from a couple of thick candles that had been lit for him, and the slow flicker of flames from the hearth. The tankard beside him was steaming with hot spiced ale. A lad of no more than twelve was fast asleep on the floor. Benet swept her deep, courtly bow.

"My Lady of Devonshire. I sincerely hope you remember me and can afford us somewhere to lay our heads for a night or two. Indeed, it would seem my lad has already made himself more than comfortable in your lovely home."

She knew that their exchange was for the benefit of satisfying Philippa's curiosity.

"Of course I remember you, sir. You serve my nephew the King, and we were introduced by him at York Place. Be welcome. My steward's wife will find you a bed, and there's bound to be a truckle for the lad."

What in Jesu's name are you doing in Tiverton and how did you get here in this weather?

He was obviously reading her thoughts.

"His Grace had Christmas gifts for the Bishop in Exeter, and appointed me to deliver them." *Did he really?* "And when my young friend Hal Courtenay heard I would be but twelve miles from his lady mother, he asked me bring his greetings as he cannot be here in person."

"It cannot have been an easy journey from Exeter!" exclaimed Philippa. "There's nothing been heard of the players yet! However did *you* find your way?"

Benet twinkled at her disarmingly. "Do you know, Mistress, I am not entirely sure. I put it down to your fine church towers here in Devon, and the goodwill of all we met during the day. And the full moon helped too."

Philippa's disapproval was obvious in her sniff. "Foolhardy, I call it, sir. You might have disappeared underneath a snowdrift and never been seen again."

Katherine suppressed the urge to giggle wildly. In the half-light he looked more like some mischievous boy rather than a man past his middle years. She fought hard to maintain a serious, aloof tone.

"Your boy is evidently exhausted, Sir Benet, and no doubt you are too. A few hours' sleep will benefit you both. Please join me in the morning for Mass." She could have sworn that he winked at her. Outside, the bells of Tiverton began to proclaim midnight and Christ's nativity.

As her unexpected, honoured guest from London, he knelt by her side in St Peter's Church, similarly swathed in furs against the cold. Normally she heard Mass in her private chapel but Christmas was a time when Tiverton expected to see its princess. Packed with her household, and townsfolk who had braved the icy cobbles, the building glowed with lighted tapers in the darkness of the winter dawn as the choristers sang the genealogy of Christ. Their breaths, the strange names and familiar names, hovered in the cold air: *Perez and Zereh, Amminnadab and Nahshon ... then Manasseh and Amon, Josiah and Jeconiah ... and finally Jacob, Joseph and the blessed Virgin Mary.* Thus it had been for five hundred Christmas mornings in Tiverton. The prayers, the echoing chants, the swinging censor and its clouds of incense – everything known by heart since her childhood and repeated every day all over the land. The special day of Christ's nativity was always a favourite because it put an end to the hungry days of Advent and heralded the earthly pleasures yet to come.

As the Latin washed over her, understood by only a handful of the educated, but as familiar and comforting to all as mothers' milk, Katherine found herself looking up into the still eyes of the statue of Mary. *Sweet Virgin, show me the way forward for the rest of my life. Protect my family. Grant eternal rest to those already with you in Heaven.*

Benet insisted she tuck her hand into the crook of his elbow as they made their way back to the castle. Once or twice she nearly lost her footing on the icy paving and clutched at his arm, laughing. Tiverton was a clamour of bells ringing out the Christmas morning as the sun edged up over the horizon to seize the few, precious hours of the December day. There would be feasting in the evening but the short day was theirs to do as they wished.

It was too cold for outdoor activities so they played at cards, and dice, and chess in the cosy winter parlour, facing each other across the table, laughing and exclaiming at first his luck, then hers. For years she had not known such easy domesticity in a man's company.

"Now, tell me the truth. Like Philippa, I refuse to believe you rode from Exeter yesterday."

"You doubt my horsemanship?"

"No, I doubt that you could have found a single pathway, in all that snow. The players talk of needing guides from village to village."

"Then I will come clean. I *was* at Exeter with Bishop Veysey until a few days ago. When the King wanted someone to convey his gift I jumped at the chance to come down into Devon. But I left before the snow threatened, and the lad and I have been at an inn these past few days. I've been summoning up my courage." He looked at her levelly over the chessboard, where his vanquished pieces lay on her side. "You have my heart, Katherine. You surely know that. What you do with it is up to you."

It was what she wanted to hear, of course, but …

"I am a vowess, Benet." Her voice was tight in her throat.

"But not from piety – that's what you said. You do not wear the wimple."

"I made vows nevertheless. Before the Bishop of London."

"Such vows have been undone before."

"With a dispensation from His Holiness in Rome."

"We could seek one."

She stared at him. He sighed. "Forgive me if I have misjudged. I thought there was something between us those weeks in the spring. When I saw your face last night I believed I was not mistaken. What is the point of not being honest with you?"

"Benet, we are *old!*"

"What I feel is not old. What I feel is new, and quite wonderful. I could believe I am twenty again, although" he added wryly "if I knelt now at your feet my knees would probably tell me I am not."

"I am the Countess of Devon – my position …"

"Ah, I should not dare look so high, you mean? I am presumptuous, indeed." He spoke lightly but she could tell he was hurt.

She felt her eyes brim with tears. "No, *no* – I did not mean *that.*"

"Then tell me what you *do* mean. I would be your husband, my lady, if you'll have me."

She leaned over the table to grasp his hand. He'd spoken of honesty.

"You have not misjudged. But I was born a Plantagenet, Benet. What you don't know is all that entails. What it still means to Harry Tudor. If I went back on my word to remain unmarried, I would be putting my children, and any grandchildren I might have in danger. "

"How so? You and I would not have children now, more's the pity, so how could he be threatened?"

"Because like his father he fears factions. Fears rebellion. As a widow and a vowess I am just his dear Aunt Kaff'ryn, who lives in faraway Devon and comes to court occasionally. As someone else's wife I could add … credence to a cause."

"Katherine! My family are Hautes! We're just knights from Kent, not descendants of Edward III determined to flaunt the few drops of royal blood in our veins!"

"A man, *any* man, married to me, could find himself drawn into opposition against the Tudors. There are still those out there whom he suspects – my cousin Richard de la Pole for one."

Benet gave a hoot of scoffing laughter. "*The Wanderer of Europe?* There's nobody interested in him. Least of all me! I'm a loyal Tudor man, through and through. No, I understand – I have looked too high. You are offended." He extricated his hand from hers and stood up. "The gulf between us is too much, I see that now. I beg your pardon. " He made for the door.

Katherine scrambled to her feet, bumping against the little table and sending the chess pieces skittering over the floor. She pushed past him and leaned against the door, blocking his way. He looked bemused, and ran his hands through his hair.

"What do you want from me?"

"I don't know … I need time to think. I am just … so aware of consequences. The queen is past child-bearing now; there's no prince, and Harry's grip on the throne is seen as weak. I think turbulent times are coming again. There are new families pushing their way forward – and you might be seen to be doing just that, in marrying me. For I am Hal Courtenay's mother. And Hal is the grandson of a Plantagenet king." Her last two statements came out as desperate excuses against the desires of her heart.

The cosy little room held them together, suspended in time; a middle-aged man and woman, with the chance of love and companionship to brighten the autumn of their lives. Benet held out his arms. "Does that mean we can have nothing together?" It was too much. She stumbled forward into his embrace. Her head fitted neatly under his chin and he held her tightly so that her cheek was pressed hard against the buttons of his leather jerkin. She felt his lips on her hairline and then his hands loosening their hold and sliding down her arms, over the fabric of her sleeves until her caught at her bare hands. They stood there, body crushed to body, fingers interlocked, like a pair of young lovers.

He released her hands and instead cupped her face, and leaned down. His kiss began as something gentle, not entirely certain – an experiment in love, but within seconds became intensely fierce and passionate, and possessive.

The next few days passed in a haze of feasting, dancing and laughter, with the lines between status blurred in the castle as the Lord of Misrule took up his post. This year it was Katherine's fool, Mug, with bells on his ankles and wrists, who directed them all in merrymaking. The players from Exeter performed interludes, and led them all in caroling. They had a new book, with splendid new songs about boars' heads, and hunting, as well as those that told the story of Christ's birth. Katherine's household listened with pleasure as their lady was persuaded to accompany on her harp and lute, and the personable knight from London added his strong voice to the players'. It was good, they told each other, that Sir Benet had sought refuge in the snow, for his presence had much improved what had otherwise threatened to be a dull Christmas in the castle.

As December turned to January a thaw set in. Gradually the familiar landscape emerged. Just a few forlorn ribbons of snow lay on the north-facing field slopes and Tiverton town saw again its tracks and crossroads. The Exe roared with melted water flowing down from the Somerset hills. With regret, the townsfolk spoke of returning to work – to their ploughs, and spinning wheels.

"And I must go soon," said Benet quietly. He lay in Katherine's bed, holding her tenderly after lovemaking. "Your servants will be up and about soon, and it would do your reputation no good at all for Philippa to find me tangled up in your sheets. To be truthful, I think I fear her more than the King!"

Katherine stretched sleepily. Benet's secret visits to her chamber were the joy of her life. He came after midnight, when the household slept, padding barefoot, learning which timbers creaked in the passageway. At Tiverton the only guard was in the gatehouse below. Since her marriage Philippa slept away from the castle, returning early each morning to attend upon the countess – an arrangement that Katherine now blessed.

"What would our children say, if they knew?" She stroked his bare arm with its forest of fine dark hairs.

Benet propped himself up on one elbow and grinned at her. "They would be appalled of course, because we are old enough to know better. That is the one ace we have, Katherine – we're so old no-one will ever suspect us! They all think love is the property of the young."

She closed her eyes. "Did you love your wife?"

"I learned to love her. She was a good woman. Did you love your husband?"

"Against all the odds, I did. When the old king said I was to marry a Courtenay I knew I had no choice – but I was blessed."

He kissed her forehead. "We could be blessed again. You could come to London, in the spring, and we could speak to the King. While he's besotted with Mary Carey he might look favourably upon other lovers."

Such temptation! Laid before her like the sugared plums she had coveted as a child. But at the back of her mind, always, the ring of steel sword upon steel helmet; the flash of the executioner's axe and a young man's broken body dangling from a gallows on Tower Hill.

Instinctively, she pushed him away. "I cannot marry you, Benet. I have told you why. We can have *this,* when I come to court, and you can find excuses again to come here … but beyond that …"

But already he was swinging himself off her bed and pulling on his shirt and hose. The room was still dark, lit only by the night-candle that had burnt low. The little brazier that had glowed for hours was now black and cold. Without Benet's body-warmth beside her Katherine shivered. She was close to tears. *Why could he not understand? Even if Harry Tudor gave them permission to marry, in a fit of love-driven generosity, his good will could change like a weather-vane.*

If Gertrude had a son, and Lord Courtenay's mother married again, the King might be reminded of how fragile was the Tudor hold upon the crown.

Benet was the door, with his shoes in his hand, looking back at her through the shadows.

"I don't want just a lover, Katherine. I could satisfy my desires, foolish man that I am, with any girl from the stews in Southwark. I want a wife. To live with me and share these last years."

The night candle finally guttered. His face was lost in the inky darkness.

"Then you had best go and find one," she whispered.

11
The Red Rose, Suffolk Lane, London

June 1525

Like his cousin the King, Hal Courtenay had no living son as yet. Gertrude's three pregnancies had all ended sadly, in little bundles of flesh wrapped swiftly and buried in the corner of the graveyard at West Horsley. She suffered each time, puking for weeks, and emerging from the late miscarriages as thin and white as a birch sapling. Catalina sent private messages of sympathy to her devout lady-in-waiting. Of all people, she understood the sorrow and shame of a woman's body expelling a half-formed child. The King seemed more fond than ever of his cousin, inviting him to serve in his privy council, confirming him in the traditional hereditary offices of the Courtenays in the west of England, and appointing him to other positions of favour. Hal's wealth and status grew. The Courtenay name was as powerful in the south west as it had ever been in centuries past.

Katherine did not feel comfortable in her son's new townhouse. Formerly, it had been home to her disgraced Suffolk cousins. It was not far from her old home in Warwick Lane but that was lost to her now, seized by the Tudors after William's arrest and sold away to some wealthy merchant. However, it was now easier for Hal to attend upon the King and come home at night, much as William had once done. To have Hal riding high in the King's favour, was worth her own personal sacrifice.

She had not seen Benedict Haute for over two years – but casual questioning had revealed that he was married again now, to a wealthy Kentish girl half his age, who had given him a son. There had been no letter, no message on either part. Did he sometimes think of those magical twelve days of Christmas in the snow at Tiverton? Katherine had put them away carefully in her mind, not with the painful memories, but with the joyous recollections of those she had loved. The whole thing had been such a fleeting episode, though, that sometimes she wondered at its authenticity.

Visits to London were rare these days, but the ceremony to honour her son, and Meggie's message that she could attend too, had brought her together with her children.

"Marquess of Exeter, Hal? *And* Constable of Windsor Castle? *And* High Steward of the Duchy of Cornwall?" Meggie regarded her brother with mock awe. "Are we not in exalted company, Lucy?" The baby girl on her lap rewarded her mother with a gummy grin, and shoved a fistful of bonnet strings into her mouth. Meggie extracted them carefully and handed the child back to her hovering nursemaid. "Take her, but don't let her choke; it's her favourite new trick." Motherhood was something she tolerated. Her firstborn had been a long time coming, and if Somer was disappointed not to have a boy he hid it well but Meggie knew the family at Raglan Castle would expect a male heir next time. The prospect of all that pain again was not something she relished.

The woman curtseyed, took the child and presented her to Katherine for a grandmother's blessing. She laid her hand on the little head, warm in its soft linen. A pair of dark eyes regarded her seriously. She tucked away a few escaping blonde curls. *So the years roll on: little Lady Lucy Somerset, great-grand-daughter of Edward Plantagenet and Queen Elizabeth Wydville. What will become of you, I wonder?* The baby looked back in interest over her nursemaid's shoulder as they left the room. The door closed softly behind them.

It was like old times, just herself and her two children, secure in each other's absolute discretion. Meggie's intelligent eyes sparkled with the delight of being in London again.

Yesterday's ceremony, that had seen Hal made Marquess of Exeter had really been all about Harry Tudor's illegitimate son, raised to the peerage as Duke of Richmond, Duke of Somerset and Earl of Nottingham. "Well! How extraordinary that the child outranks everyone now, except his father," observed Meggie. "And is it true what they say – that the King will now send him to live with his own household at Sheriff Hutton?"

Katherine gasped. Sheriff Hutton was part of the Neville and Plantagenet inheritance – one of the castles from where her uncle Richard had governed the North of England in her father's name. Richard's little boy Edward, a fleeting

521

Prince of Wales, lay in the church there. It was where Bessy had been taken to keep her safe from Henry Tudor's invasion.

"He calls the boy *my wordly jewel,*" said Hal. "And some are already calling him a prince. There is no other acknowledged son. There can be no other legitimate son – from Catalina. Stranger things have happened."

"But the Princess Mary!" interrupted Meggie. "How can she be denied her birthright?"

"He gives her equal honour – at the moment. She is to go into Shropshire, to Ludlow, with our mother's cousin Lady Pole, as her governess."

"I am glad Harry allows the princess to have Meg Pole with her," said Katherine quietly "It means he trusts her again."

"She is a very bright girl, isn't she?" said Meggie. "Maybe the King will come to his senses and see that a woman *could* rule."

"My guess is that he'll continue heaping titles and estates upon the boy until it seems the most obvious thing in the world to make him his heir," said Hal.

"Who would sanction that?"

"Who would oppose it? Why? Who wants civil war again?" he returned.

Meggie looked long and hard at her brother. "You would stand by, while the by-blow of a man whose father had no real claim to *our* grandfather's throne is placed above *you?"*

"Meggie!" whispered Hal fiercely. "I am His Grace's loyal servant! You will not speak treason in my house!"

"Loyal enough to accept Bessie Blount's bastard as your next sovereign? Our Plantagenet grandfather would turn in his grave, brother." Her tone was acidic.

Jesu, if Meggie had been born a boy she would probably be an exile in Europe like her last Suffolk cousin, thought Katherine. *She is the one who studies her lineage with such interest and feels her heritage most keenly. Hal is content to ignore my blood in his veins, and settle for a safe existence. Meggie is Cecily all over again.* Katherine felt a terrible weariness. *Was England destined to return to the same crazy game of thrones that had blighted it in the last century? Did Harry not realise the impact and consequences of trying to foist an illegitimate heir upon the land?*

Hal's discomfiture was only too apparent. He turned appealingly to his mother. "Tell her to curb her tongue, Mama. She'll have us all in the Tower. Thank God these walls are thick and there is none to hear you, you foolish girl. You're not in distant Wales now."

"Don't call me foolish, Hal. I have never been foolish. *You're* the foolish one, if you think that supporting Bessie Blount's boy above our rightful princess is the way to behave."

"Well, maybe our cousin the King has a plan for *both* his children," snapped Hal.

His sister and mother looked at him, aghast … An expression of disgust spread across Meggie's face. "He would not. Surely he would not. It's monstrous. It would be against the laws of God, and Nature."

"Hal, His Holiness in Rome would never allow -"

Hal held up both hands as if to ward off their disapproval.

"It will never come to pass." Katherine found herself saying the words as a talisman, rather than through belief. "Catalina would never agree to such a terrible idea, not in a million years."

Hal sighed. His mother did not see what he saw at court. Every day the queen's influence counted less and less. Her private letters to her nephew the Emperor Charles V intercepted; three of her Spanish ladies expelled and women in Wolsey's pay now serving in her rooms. Some strange air of foreboding hung over the queen's apartments but nobody could quite put their finger upon what, or why. Gertrude came home and whispered of the queen weeping in her private closet where she knelt to pray. What was becoming clear was that Catalina no longer had much, if any, influence upon how her husband chose to deal with Europe. It was Cardinal Wolsey he listened to now, not his wife.

The Queen's Apartments, Greenwich August 1525

Katherine tried hard to hide her shock when she was admitted to Catalina's rooms. The queen was one of those women towards whom age was unfairly cruel. The few strands of hair visible around the edge of her gable headdress were grey and coarse; the backs of her hands mottled with brown spots and her complexion washed out. Here was the wealthiest woman in England but she could not buy back her youth. Her gown and sleeves of red damask were beautiful, as were the rubies round her neck but somehow they served to draw attention to the increasing stoutness of her little body and thickness of her throat. At forty, Catalina looked like the grandmother she should have been. By contrast, six years older, Katherine looked astoundingly youthful.

The queen and her ladies were just emerging from chapel. When Katherine curtsied, Catalina held out a plump hand with the genuine affection she had always shown.

"Lady Courtenay! A ray of sunshine on this gloomy day!"

For outside, it was hard to believe it could be high summer. A chill wind whipped up the Thames estuary and the sun hid behind darkening storm clouds.

"Have you seen the King?" Catalina's enquiry seemed nonchalant but her face was tight with tension.

"No, Your Grace. I believe His Grace's household are moving into the countryside to escape the pestilence in the city." *Has she not been informed?* "My son travels with him – that's the only reason I know."

"Ah, yes. Gertrude!" She called over shoulder. "Our husbands seek pure air together. Good. Good."

Katherine saw her daughter-in-law, pale and thin, her rosary still wound around her fingers. She liked Gertrude but found her piety rather wearing. She rather suspected that Hal would enjoy his weeks away with the King, pestilence or no pestilence. Still, time for Gertrude to recover the roses in her cheeks.

"Has Your Grace heard yet from the Princess Mary?"

Immediately, Catalina's face brightened a little. "Yes! Lady Salisbury writes from Tickenhill that she is safely arrived."

"You know that my cousin will be as a mother to her," said Katherine gently. "She is devoted to her."

"As she was to me when *I* was just a girl in Ludlow, even though her brother … Do you remember, Lady Courtenay, I could speak no English then! Now I barely speak any Spanish. But of course Gertrude here has a little of my own language, from her mother, who came with me from Spain." Since the unkind dismissal of her last Spanish ladies, Catalina valued young Lady Exeter even more.

"I hope my daughter Gertrude continues to give you comfort and company, Your Grace," said Katherine formally.

They passed a happy hour and the visit seemed to bring Catalina pleasure. Katherine was urged to come again but she explained that soon she would be returning to Devon, and Meggie to Raglan. Catalina nodded. "That is wise, with so much disease again this summer. We should all be thankful that we are not compelled to stay in the city. My doctors say the numbers of dead are increasing weekly. But at least none of us have cause to go abroad in the streets."

Katherine looked around at the rest of Catalina's ladies. Several were unknown to her. The two Boleyn sisters were missing, though their brother's wife, Jane, sat quietly in a corner. Catalina smiled ruefully.

"You see how we are quieter than we were. Mistress Anne has gone home to Hever, after an unfortunate entanglement with the Duke of Northumberland's son, and her sister Lady Carey is soon to bear her husband a second child."

Gertrude's anxious eyes implored her mother-in-law to make no comment on this state of affairs. Jane Boleyn simply folded up her embroidery and set her mouth in a straight line. Katherine understood instantly – Mary Carey was to have another child with Harry Tudor. My word, Harry was collecting a whole alternative family with his mistresses. Happily for Catalina, Mary Carey's offspring would be acknowledged by her husband as his own, even if they were unmistakably the King's. The bane of Catalina's life was the existence of the copper-haired six-year-old Henry Fitzroy – the little double duke now living like royalty up in Yorkshire. Katherine wondered if the queen had any idea of the horrible rumours linking his future to the Princess Mary.

As if reading her thoughts, Catalina touched her sleeve. "Would you walk with me before you go, Lady Courtenay? I usually take some air at this hour. We will accompany you back to the jetty."

For Katherine, Greenwich would always take her thoughts back to William's death. The beauty of the gardens had provided a haven in those days of dark despair. She understood why Catalina was eager to be out in the fresh air, even if the gravel paths were darkened by a recent shower, and the topiary rather sinister under the ominous skies. For all her short stature Catalina strode along briskly, until they were out of hearing from the other women.

"They spy on me," she said abruptly. "I know they are Wolsey's creatures. Gertrude does her best but she cannot always field them. Wherever I go there is always some young lady who listens and reports." She looked sideways at Katherine. "Do you think, when your sister was queen, that she ever had to endure such disrespect? No, because she was the mother of princes. And your grandmother also. That is what queens must do, be the mother of boys. It is what I can never do – now." She dashed tears from her face. "I love my husband, Lady Courtenay. He has always grieved with me, never blamed me when … But he has changed and I do not understand why. You have known him … since he was a little boy. He is fond of you, his Aunt Kaff'ryn. He treats your son like a brother. What should I do? I feel so alone."

Katherine felt rather helpless in the face of the queen's distress. Men ruled women's lives. That was God's law and thus the nature of being alive. It had ever been thus. Rapidly, she thought back through what she had been taught about her country's history. Had there ever before been a king left with just a daughter, and his wife too old to bear more children?

"My husband must accept God's will. Mary will make an excellent queen. It's just you English – afraid that a woman cannot rule. But she can! *Jesu Maria*, Mary is ten times more intelligent than the Fitzroy bastard!"

Her words tumbled out at speed as they paced along. "My nephew Charles has broken his betrothal to Mary – he says he cannot wait for her to grow up- and so now the King thinks again of a French marriage for her. Can you imagine, Katherine, my child offered to *that* man whose wife has died from *le mal francais!* A child to be given to an ogre! How can he consider this for our princess? How can he *think* of giving England to France? *France,* who has always been our *enemy!"* Catalina sounded as though she was about to erupt in some Castilian fury.

"Maybe not to Francois himself, Your Grace; he has sons."

"One Frenchman is as bad as another!" spat Catalina. She stopped suddenly and seized Katherine's hands. "I am sorry. It's just that I have so few I can speak to – since Lady Pole has gone with Mary, and my Spanish ladies have been sent away."

The barge that would take her back to the city was bobbing on the water. Katherine kissed the hands, with the puffy flesh bulging around the rings. "I will come again, Your Grace, at Christmas, and I would be honoured to have your letters." When she looked up she saw how Catalina was blanched with anxiety.

"Sometimes I fear he wants rid of me. He sees how his sister Margaret has rid herself of her second husband, and he remembers how his friend Charles Brandon was divorced before marrying his sister Mary. This is what I fear."

"*No*, Catalina! It is not God's law that women are put aside by their husbands simply because they have no sons!"

"Oh, you are right. I am being foolish. There! I am sure I shall be Queen of England till the day I die!"

As the barge pulled away upstream Katherine's eyes watched until the outline of the queen, motionless like a little chess-piece, disappeared behind the bend in the river.

It was late evening before she reached the Red Rose. The city streets were chilly, especially where the overhanging eaves of the houses prevented the sun from warming the narrow streets below. The sour smells of hundreds of people crammed into such cheek-by-jowl existence hung on the air: a day's worth of sweat, cooking, horse dung and human urine. She longed for the sweet scents of August in Devon.

As her litter bumped to a halt outside her son's gatehouse she heard raised, anxious voices. She pulled back the leather covering to find the stricken face of young Isabel Anning, whom she had brought from Devon as her personal maid. A different smell assaulted her nostrils – the vile stench of death.

In the two days of her absence, the plague had rolled through these few streets, claiming rich and poor alike. *Merry at breakfast; dead by supper.* At the Red Rose a kitchen maid and a man-at-arms had fallen sick within minutes of each other and the Lady Meggie, young Lady Somerset, had woken with an unexpected fever, keeled over with dizziness by her baby's cradle before noon and now lay dead in her bed in the fading light of the dismal summer evening. Fat, beeswax candles burned intensely at her head and feet.

"I have washed her," whispered Isabel. "No-one would help me, but I was not afraid. Poor young lady. I made the boy run for a priest and he came in time. She was not alone, my lady. I held her hand."

Her daughter lay like an alabaster effigy, beautiful and cold. It was beyond belief. Only two nights ago they had sat together, laughing because they had the run of the house, Hal being with the King and Gertrude with the queen. They had played duets on their lutes, and Hal's household had applauded, glad to have such sweetness in their midst.

"How many in the household?"

"Four, my lady, including the nursemaid from Wales."

Down the corridor, a baby was crying.

Katherine was dry-eyed, numb with grief, staring at Meggie, whose chin was bound with linen, and whose dark, York eyes were closed forever – whose soul must even now be in purgatory. Her young husband was hundreds of miles away at Raglan. They would not be able to send her body there for burial, or home to Devon. Must she be interred in some local parish grave with all the others who had died this day? Could there even be a decent funeral?

It was as though Isabel read her thoughts. "Blackfriars will take her, my lady, if we send her early in the morning. The brothers say they will lay her near her father, and sing Masses for her. I said you would send money." Her lips flattened in apology. "I have cousins everywhere in this city."

Katherine, the countess, groped for the hand of Isabel the maid, whose little gold, garnet and pearl ring gleamed in the candlelight. Isabel's hand was warm and alive. Meggie's had cooled in this girl's courageous clasp.

"Thank you," mouthed Katherine. "Oh, Jesu, Isabel – the babe! You say the nurse is dead too?"

Isabel looked down compassionately at the still form beneath the coverlet. "Little Lucy is well – listen to her!"

Katherine gathered her wits. By rights they should place a bunch of straw outside the gatehouse, to warn others they were a house of pestilence. They should not go out except for necessities, and none should be allowed in. If she took the babe and set out for Devon she risked taking the contagion with her.

"Who is still here, Isabel?"

"I'm not rightly sure, my lady. It was terrible yesterday – when they all died. Some of my lord's servants fled. The cook is gone, and the steward, and those who have families here in London."

"What can we do?"

"I think we must stay put, my lady. It must surely be God's will whether we survive or not. It's a big house – there's food in the stores, and we can send out for fresh food to be left at the gatehouse for us."

"How can we feed the child now her wet nurse is dead?"

"We must make pap, my lady – soften bread in small ale. She will take that. And if someone will bring us fresh, early morning milk we may give that to her."

"You are a marvel, Isabel."

Together, they found fresh linen sheets in Gerturude's linen press. Katherine's tears came then. She sobbed as she sewed her clever, beloved daughter into her makeshift shroud. At the last moment she paused and cast around the room. A small, velvet covered Book of Hours lay on the table. She opened it and read the inscription: *Cecily Princess of York, her boke.* Tenderly she laid it on her daughter's heart. A thicker volume lay open by the bedside. Meggie's favourite *Morte d'Arthur.* Would it be so wrong to place it in her hands for her final journey? She slipped it inside, under the clasped hands that lay folded on her breast.

The sky lightened by six o'clock and two men from the abbey at Blackfriars came to collect the body. It was like some awful nightmare – they had bought a hastily constructed box, hardly a coffin, and Meggie was laid inside with no ceremony. Katherine was beyond emotion, silently handing them the money required to take away a plague-ridden corpse. She must put her trust in the monks to give her daughter a decent burial. She prayed they would keep their promise to lift the slab in their church and put Meggie with her father. When they were gone, she had Isabel tie thick bunches of straw on to the great iron knocker on the gatehouse. It was fashioned like a rose, the white rose of York, ordered from the blacksmith by the old, royal Suffolk family when the house was first built, and then declared to be a red rose in honour of the Tudors' Lancastrian heritage. Hal had shrugged when she pointed it out. "It's just a rose, Mama. They grow in all our gardens."

Life is for the living. The depleted, appalled Courtenay household gathered in the Great Hall before the Marquess's mother and heard her explain that they must obey the city's rules and stay within the confines of Red Rose for forty days. They saw how she was hollow-eyed with sorrow and exhaustion, and bowed their heads in obedience.

It was early November before Katherine set out along the Great West Road, taking her baby granddaughter, whose father gave orders she should be returned to his family's care. At Salisbury she handed the infant over to a new Welsh nursemaid to begin another journey of her own through Cirencester and Gloucester, over the Severn to Monmouth, and finally to the mighty castle at Raglan.

They called the Yuletide of 1525 the "still Christmas". Harry the King stayed at Eltham, mixing his own potions against the plague. Only Cardinal Wolsey was permitted to visit, confident that his diet of fresh oranges had been successful in keeping infection at bay. Neither the King nor Hal Courtenay saw their wives again until after the New Year of 1526.

12

Tiverton Castle, October 1526

Katherine sat in the solar with two letters on her lap – one from Hal and the other from Catalina. Frequently, her son used a scribe, sensitive in the past to his sister's teasing of his own lopsided script but this time he had managed a whole page: *We have named him Edward for your kingly father, and my sweet brother. Pray God he lives and thrives.* The words slid alarmingly to the right. Katherine allowed herself a quiet smile. How Meggie would have berated her brother for his appalling hand! Finally a Courtenay heir – poor Gertrude had survived the months of sickness and carried a child to full term. The baby was fair and blue-eyed.

Devon, it seemed, was awash with rosy-cheeked, healthy children. They waved at her obediently from their mothers' arms as she toured her estates; they crawled and clambered in cottages and farmhouses, mischievously pulling cats' tails and bawling lustily when a paw swiped back. At church on Sundays she saw how the wool merchants stood proudly with their families, nudging their younger sons into self-conscious bows as she passed. How could it be God's will that ordinary men and women – farmers, millers, tanners, weavers – could be blessed with endless numbers of sons and yet Harry Tudor have none, except the bastard Fitzroy, and the unacknowledged, auburn-haired son of Mary Carey? And how would the King react to the news that his cousin Exeter had a boy?

With surprising good humour, wrote Hal, "for *His Grace appears much distracted by a young lady of the court, the Lady Anne Boleyn. We are all gone French, Lady Mother, for the lady prefers to read and speak and dance and dress in that style, and the King swears he is struck with the dart of love*" ...

Katherine switched to Catalina's letter, also written in her own hand – neat, upright and even: "Mayhap *I was mistaken in my fears. His Grace shows me every courtesy and together we visited our beloved Princess Mary at Hunsdon this summer. You will be welcome at court this Christmas, for we missed you much last year."* No indication that Catalina had the least concern about Harry Tudor's latest dalliance.

The solar was tranquil. Morning sunbeams fell through the wooden slats. A jug of freshly brewed small ale sat on the court cupboard, its pleasant, yeasty smell blending with the honeyed scent of polished wood. On the walls hung her favourite tapestries showing the story of Adam and Eve. Here, everything spoke of security and permanence. In Tiverton most only knew their King as a profile on a coin; a man of legend to be prayed for in church on a Sunday. Philippa, Rob and now Isabel found themselves much in demand, to tell stories of what they had seen in the King's palaces in London. To travel so far was regarded as remarkable. *I have lost count of the times I have trailed up and down the road to London; the inns and monasteries I have stayed in along the way; the long hours spent on horseback, or in a litter.*

So, nearly two hundred miles away in Surrey a new little grandson lay in his cradle whilst his cousin the King pursued a woman as if she were a hind. Katherine pressed the edge of the thick paper of Catalina's letter against her lips, thinking. When Harry had chased other women before there had been no threat to his wife; all kings had mistresses, sooner or later. Why would a queen worry, when she was assured of her husband's love and respect for her as mother of his children? But now Catalina's situation was utterly changed. If he had found someone to replace the queen – oh, no doubt Wolsey and Harry's latest advisor, Thomas Cromwell, would advocate a foreign princess – but if Harry was anything like his maternal grandfather, her own Plantagenet father, he would marry whom he chose. Her mother Elizabeth Wydville had been a commoner, an English girl like Anne Boleyn. Yet surely this could never be? Catalina would never agree to a something so awful as a divorce, and on what grounds, anyway, could Harry procure such a thing? His wife's faithfulness was beyond reproach; he'd married her of his own free will, *chosen* to marry her above all others. She was an anointed queen. He could not just put her aside, like a dish no longer quite to his taste. Could he? For not producing a son? Then no decent woman in England would be safe, whether duke or farmer's wife.

She read on in Hal's letter. He, too, urged her to come to London again for the Christmas season. She would be able to see little Edward, and the King was promising a wonderful Yuletide this year at Greenwich, with days of feasting, merrymaking and tournaments (if the weather held). She would be able to see the Lady Anne Boleyn, too, added Hal. Carefully, she laid both letters in her private coffer and locked it. The morning was bright and dry; she would ride out.

The Courtenay horses were still much sought after. Hal had taken some mares and a stallion up to West Horsley to continue breeding for tournaments but the stables and fields at Tiverton still boasted some of the finest riding horses in the West Country. They brought in a steady income from the county's noble families – from Powderham to Hartland; from Okehampton to Axminster. Katherine loved them all, with their satiny coats and huge eyes, their soft muzzles and swishing tails. Her preferred mount these days was an ebony mare with a gentle nature and a soft mouth. She found her in the stall once inhabited by Whiterose, her name plate *Demirose* now replacing that of her old favourite. The other horses stamped and whickered, hearing her footsteps. All of them could trace a bloodline back to Seaton and beyond, back to the horses bred by William's father in the early days after Bosworth Field.

The groom who rode with her knew to give her plenty of space and lagged behind dutifully as she cantered across the river meadows. Beneath her the mare moved smoothly, enjoying the fresh air as much as her rider. The great oaks were still mainly green, though other trees looked as if some painter had thrown his red and yellow colours through their branches. The year was turning, yet again. It seemed only yesterday that Meggie and Hal had been children riding their ponies here by the banks of the Exe. Most noble siblings were unfamiliar with each other because of the custom of sending young men to be raised in other families but Hal had been spared that – no-one particularly wanted the young son of the disgraced earl of Devon. Instead, he and Meggie had enjoyed most of their childhood together, moving with her from Colcombe to Tiverton to Colcombe again. Theirs had been a strong, loving bond, characterised by teasing. Hal wrote of how much he missed his sister. The shock of her death, in his own house, cast a shadow on his life. Somer was still at Raglan, grieving not only for Meggie but now for his own father: Somer had become the second Earl of Worcester. It was unlikely they would see little Lady Lucy for many a year. Somer would have to remarry, she knew, and Lucy would be absorbed into a new family.

She pulled up. Above her, patches of blue showed through the scudding grey and white clouds. To stay here, in the county she had learned to call home, was tempting beyond words. Yet Hal knew her too well – knew that holding the new baby would be some consolation for the loss of Maggie and Lucy; knew that her

532

curiosity to see the Lady Anne would get the better of any resolution to remain in Devon.

Greenwich Christmas 1526
"And graven in diamonds in letters plain
There is written, her fair neck about:
Noli me tangere, for Caesar's I am ..." Thomas Wyatt on Anne Boleyn

"No more to you at present, mine own darling, for lack of time, but that I would I were in your arms again, or I in yours, for I think it long since I kissed you." Letter from King Henry VIII to Lady Anne Boleyn

The December day was mild and dry. Bored with the fasting required by the season of Advent, the King had swept them all outside into the gardens for fresh air and a game of bowls. Today, his sense of family was buoyant again: Lord Exeter was his "dearest coz"; Katherine his "beloved aunt". Surrounded by young, laughing courtiers he was in high humour. In contrast, Catalina seemed quiet and withdrawn and Harry made little effort to include her. She retreated to a sheltered seat to watch them play, her face pinched, not with cold, but with loneliness. She missed her daughter. Just past her tenth birthday, Mary was instructed by her father to hold a Christmas court on her own at Tewkesbury, where vast numbers were expected to visit her.

Katherine searched her mind for something positive to say. "She will be able to practise being queen. Imagine her being in charge of her own little world, with all the local nobles coming to honour her!"

Catalina managed some semblance of a smile. "She will know what to do. I have taught her well."

The game of bowls was underway: the soft *clunk* of the wooden balls; calls of encouragement or commiseration, and polite rounds of applause. Catalina's ladies clustered around her protectively and she waved a languid hand. "Go and join the King, Lady Courtenay. He enjoys your company."

Underfoot, the grass was soft but not wet. Katherine made her way across the lawns to the closely clipped green where the game was in full flow. By the time she reached the players some sort of dispute seemed to be going on. A tall, handsome young man with a strikingly silky, chestnut beard was engaged in animated conversation with the King.

"I tell you, Wyatt, I have it!" declared Harry. Katherine saw how his flushed, fair face was beginning to broaden out now he was in his thirties. His body-shape was changing too: the lithe, athletic lines of his younger self were beginning to soften, though his height disguised it. Would he eventually run to fat as they said her own father had done?

"Sir, I am closest."

A sudden hush fell upon those watching. The winter morning prickled with tension. Katherine was puzzled. Why had the mood changed so suddenly? Who was the fellow challenging the King? There was very little in it – less than an inch, surely. Didn't he know it was always safest to let Harry believe he'd won? The man was no different to the child who had been allowed to win far too often for his own good. A pity no-one else had dared spank him, as Cecily had once done. No-one had dared reprove him since his formidable grandmother had died. She felt a sharp pang of grief for Bessy, who would have taught her boy a better way to be a man.

Harry was pointing towards his own ball, his hand raised for all to see. He tilted it deliberately so that all had sight of the ring glinting on his little finger, which he waggled provocatively. "It is *mine.*" A note of warning

The man called Wyatt had a charming smile, which he now used to good effect as he reached into his shirt and drew out a silver chain. Lifting it calmly over his head he made towards the two balls and the jack as if to ascertain the distance between each. "If it may like Your Majesty to give me leave to measure it, I hope it will be mine." His voice was attractive, cultured, reasoned and resonant. Everyone heard what he said. Katherine saw a locket was attached to the chain. Harry saw too, and his face mottled with fury. It was also clear to all that Wyatt had, indeed, won the game. He rose up, a pleasant smile on his lips. The eyes of the courtiers swivelled to and fro, as if they were all sitting in the gallery in the tennis court.

"It may be so, but then I am deceived." Abruptly, Harry turned on his heel and strode away. Wyatt carefully tucked the chain and locket back inside his shirt, fastened the points on his doublet and walked away too, in the opposite direction.

For a moment there was a stunned silence, then the King's close companions ran after him in consternation. Then the scrunch of Catalina's footsteps, and those of her ladies, as they also quit the gardens. The remaining courtiers broke up into small groups, huddling together, their conversation suddenly rising like restless sparrows arguing in a hedge. Katherine felt conspicuous – the King's aunt left high and dry with no female company. Then her elbow was touched gently and someone was ushering her across the green towards the nearest gravel pathway. It wasn't until they reached the alley, with its trellises of bare winter branches, that she dared to look sideways.

"Benet!" His name came easily, happily, to her lips.

"My Lady Courtenay. I trust you are well. I saw you looking … as if you had no idea what to do next."

"No more did I. Thank you." He looked no different to when he had left her bed on that dark January morning. Maybe a few more streaks of silver in his dark curls and a few more laughter lines around his mouth and eyes. She did not trust herself to speak. He stood very close, still cradling her elbow in his hand. His warmth seemed to burn through the fabric of her sleeve. She felt her skin tingling.

"Let me escort you to dinner. It's been a long morning. No meat, of course, but I believe there is good fish. Are you hungry?"

She allowed him to propel her along passageways and corridors until they came out on to the main staircase leading into the Great Hall. Scores of people milled about – some cast curious glances at the King's aunt and a few bowed. Benet paused. "You are not expected in Her Grace's rooms? To attend upon her?"

"No, no. I am here as a visitor." She felt a hot blush rise from her breast and suffuse her face.

He found her a place near to the top table, as befitted her status. A servant brought a bowl of scented water and spread the long napkin across her lap. She knew she could invite him to sit with her, as her companion. "Do you wish to keep me company?"

"If *you* wish it, I will do so gladly, my lady."

She must say it. "And your wife, Sir Benet. She is also most welcome. Will you go and find her?"

"You have been awhile from court, my lady," he said gravely. "My wife died." He shrugged. "Childbirth is a perilous thing."

"But I heard –" She stopped herself.

"The boy lived. He is in Kent with my daughter's family."

There was nothing more to be said, though Katherine's mind ached with questions. Had he loved the girl who had died? Did he miss his son? Was he happy here at court living the life of a single man yet again?

"But you have had your own sorrows, my lady. The loss of your daughter. I was sorry to hear of it." He slipped into the space next to her.

Around them the hubbub of conversation ceased as the Latin grace was said. The food was suitable for the fasting season, but plentiful – salmon in wine sauce, and cold spiced vegetables, followed by apples and gingerbread. Benet was a thoughtful mess mate, helping her to dishes and refilling her cup. Apart from the everyday rituals of serving, the atmosphere was light and informal. Katherine looked for her son but could not see him. Benet saw her scanning the tables.

"The King dines alone with his favourites. Or possibly *entirely* on his own today, given this morning's events. "

Katherine was careful to keep her voice low. "Benet, what was going on out there? Why did His Grace lose his temper over a game of bowls?"

Benet shielded his mouth with his hand and she had to lean close to catch his words.

"It was all about the Lady Anne. Tom Wyatt had her locket and the King saw it. He had her ring, and Wyatt saw that. Wyatt tries to lay claim to her still, and it makes the King burn with jealousy."

"She plays a foolish game. If she wants to be his mistress she had best send her other lovers packing,"

"Oh, I don't think she wants to be his *mistress.* " His voice was a whisper and almost drowned out in the chatter surrounding them.

Katherine threw caution to the winds." Do you care to ride out for an hour or so this afternoon, Sir Benet? The weather is still so favourable. My son Hal has horses we may borrow."

They drew breath on rising ground in the parkland behind the palace, from where they could see the great bend in the river and, on the horizon away to the west, the spires and towers of London churches. Katherine was warm from galloping in the winter sunshine and loosened the ties of her furred riding cloak.

"I am truly sorry about your wife, Benet. It is a terrible thing to lose those you love."

He was silent for a moment then sighed. "I would be lying if I said I had loved her. Thomasine was a rich and pretty girl, and I grew fond of her but she was too young for me. Apart from … well, we had little to say to each other."

Katherine was shocked at his detachment. "But she died in childbed, giving you a son!"

"I know; I blame myself for that."

"And your little son – does he thrive?"

"So they tell me. My daughter mothers him for she has none of her own. It's a good arrangement and will suffice for several years yet. The land and money he will inherit is from Thomasine anyway. Her father is glad to have a grandson of his blood."

"Oh, Benet, you should show more interest in him. He is your son. He will think about you as he grows."

"Maybe." He spoke abruptly, making it clear that that he did not wish her to delve more.

She sighed. "Why did you approach me in the garden, Benet? I had not noticed you. You could have just left with the King. I would have been none the wiser."

"Maybe I am just a moth to a flame." He gave a short laugh. "Old fool that I am."

"I think neither of us has learned to avoid singeing our wings!"

"You still think of me, too?"

"I have never stopped thinking of you, Benet, since the day I met you. I will grow old thinking of you. I will die thinking of you."

"Ah, Katherine! Do not speak yet of dying!"

"If I recall, you once said that the greatest cover we had to our feelings for each other was the fact that our children would be horrified! And now we are even older!"

He reached over and caught her horse's reins so that she bumped sideways against his leg. "But you still maintain that you could not become my wife, even in old age?" He nodded back towards the palace of Greenwich, "You do realise that Harry Tudor will move heaven and earth to get himself a legitimate son? What will he care for the Courtenays, or the Poles, or any other cousins when he has his own boy? God knows he's waited long enough."

A few miles upriver was the Tower, that strange combination of palace and prison. "I will not put my son, or his family into any sort of danger," she said resolutely. "You have my love but I cannot give you more. But Benet, what will become of the queen? He cannot divorce her."

He looked troubled. "She must put the country before her own desires. England needs an heir and the king must remarry. He's not yet forty. Look at me, a son at fifty! You should have seen the envy in the King's eyes when someone told him that. Now he's found the Lady Anne he can see another future for himself. God's teeth! She has him panting like a dog after her!"

"But how can he marry *her?* How can he marry anyone, while Catalina is his lawful wife? How could he ever put her aside?"

Benet raised an eyebrow. "By proving that the marriage was never valid in the first place."

"What!"

"I pity the poor lady. I really do. But I pity the country more, if we are to slide back into chaos and war. It's a huge secret but the King has told Wolsey he wants a reason to break with her, and it's Wolsey's job to find it. Meanwhile Mistress Anne refuses him her favours because she says she will not be like her sister, Lady Carey, with a king's bastard, or like Bessie Blount, discarded and married off to the son of a madman."

Katherine studied the pattern on the backs of her gloves. "What manner of woman is she? Have you met her?"

"Frequently. She comes to take supper in his privy chamber; she accompanies him everywhere ... out hunting, at the archery butts, at the card table. Sings with him; plays the lute with him; clings to his arm like a burr ..."

"But what is she *like?"*

"Clever. Witty. Ambitious. I think she's realised that denying the man who has always been given everything is, in fact, the route to a crown on her head."

How much she had missed him – this candid and insightful man.

Katherine returned to the queen's rooms that evening with a private feeling of quiet contentment but she stepped into a hornets' nest. Rumour swept through the palace that Sir Thomas Wyatt had suddenly left court, bound for some diplomatic mission to Venice. His bags had been packed for him and he was on the next boat out of Dover. There was much whisperings in corners and shadows. Catalina wished to play cards and called for companions to join her. Gertrude and Katherine sat down willingly and the queen looked around for a fourth player. "Lady Anne. Won't you join us?" It was obvious that the younger Boleyn sister had been trying to slide surreptitiously from the room but she managed to turn with a brilliant smile in one fluid movement and seat herself gracefully at the table.

"Of course, Your Grace. Would you like me to cut and shuffle, and deal first?"

Her fingers were long, slender and elegant. The cards purred under her deft touch. The game was *Pope Joan,* with its staking board and compartments of Ace, King, Jack, Queen, Game, Pope, Matrimony and Intrigue. They played several rounds, with the luck ebbing and flowing between all four of them. If

Anne felt any awkwardness she did not show it. Rather, she revelled in gathering chips and successfully running down her cards. Katherine noted that Gertrude struggled to contain her dislike. Catalina, though, simply stared at her young lady-in-waiting when she won the final hand.

"Lady Anne, you have the good fortune to always stop at a king. But you are not like the others, you will have all, or none."

The queen's comment silenced the room, her Spanish accent pronounced and harsh as often happened when her emotions threatened her composure. Anne Boleyn met Catalina's gaze with equanimity – some might have said with a hint of insolence in her dark eyes. She smiled slowly. "When I was a girl, at the Burgundian court, the Duchess Margaret taught me that I should always play to win."

"But that involves *always* having luck on your side," said Gertrude tartly.

"Oh, yes," replied Anne. "But I also learned that, once established, a winning streak is to be pursued, not abandoned. Another game, Your Grace?"

"I think not. You may consider your duties finished for the evening."

Anne rose and curtsied stylishly. No-one could fault the respect of her obeisance to the queen. She backed away carefully, then whisked through the doorway and was gone, her light heels tap-tapping down the corridor. Catalina sat upright, and rested her lips upon the tips of her fingers as she held her hands together in a prayer-like pose, whilst Gertrude gathered the counters and cards, and placed them back in their box. Finally, she smiled ruefully at Katherine.

"My father, and yours too, Lady Courtenay, had numerous *amours*. Do you know, I think it might be better to ignore it all. At least with Lady Anne here under my nose I know what is going on! He will tire of her, eventually." Katherine felt pity welling in her heart for this Spanish princess who took so seriously the job of being an English queen. She had failed in the one thing asked of queens, and was now fast losing the respect she so deserved from her husband and his advisor, Wolsey. The English people loved her but was this enough to keep her safe? She spoke quietly to Gertrude in Spanish, and Katherine's daughter-in-law replied in the same language. Other women in the room looked suddenly nonplussed and Katherine saw veiled glances of irritation passing among them. Wolsey's creatures – placed in the queen's rooms to eavesdrop and report.

Catalina was indicating that she would retire for the night when the door opened and one of Harry's own guards, in his scarlet uniform, stood there. For a second Catalina's face lit up with hope and a ripple of surprise spread through the room. This was how the King often summoned his wife to his bed.

"His Grace requests that Lady Courtenay attend upon him at her pleasure."

At her pleasure! That meant immediately. *Jesu,* when had she last spoken to him in private? Years ago, when she bargained for the independence she valued so highly. Wearily, Catalina waved her away – she was neither wanted nor thought of.

Katherine followed the yeoman guard through half-lit passageways and staircases to the other side of the palace, where Harry had his own suite of rooms. As they approached, waves of music and laughter rolled out into the night air. A figure came hurrying down the staircase towards her – Hal!

"Lady Mother!" Hal's expression was a comical mix of concern and delight. Then he whispered urgently in her ear. "*She* is with him. Take care."

Harry Tudor had thrown off his furred gown and sat informally in his loosened shirt and doublet, picking out a tune on his lute. Few ever saw him like this. A small group of people clustered around him, their backs to her, holding sheets of music in their hands. Four men. One woman. Hal ushered her in and the King looked up. Without ceasing his strumming, he motioned that she should stand next to the other woman.

"Mother," explained Hal, "we are singing two to a part, but as you can see … the Lady Anne thought of you!"

Gracious heavens, she had been summoned to sing! For a moment she did not know whether to be outraged, or flattered. Hal passed her a sheaf of manuscript music, the notes waving like robust little flags on the staves.

"It is His Grace's own famous composition." Anne Boleyn slid her a sideways look. " He says you are familiar with it."

They sang the first verse together, their voices blending perfectly through the lilting rhythm:

Pastime with good company
I love and shall unto I die
Grudge who list but none deny
So God be pleased thus live will I.

> *For my pastance*
> *Hunt, song, and dance*
> *My heart is set:*
> *All goodly sport for my comfort*

Who shall me let?

Katherine loved to sing. The sound of the inter-linking harmonies was immensely satisfying as the male singers joined in the second and third verses. The King needed no music and simply gazed at Anne as she sang, his strong fingers moving deftly up and down the fretboard. *He is totally lovestruck, like a boy of sixteen.* Her gown was low cut and although her figure was not full her close-fitting bodice caused her bosom to swell as she took in enough breath to sing through the phrases. Her neck was slender, like the stem of a fragile plant, and her head like an attractive, dark flower with her French hood pushed back and her long dark brown hair waving down her back. The veil she had worn an hour ago in Catalina's presence was gone.

> *Youth must have some dalliance,*
> *Of good or ill some pastance;*
> *Company methinks the best*
> *All thoughts and fancies to dejest:*
> > *For idleness is chief mistress*
> > *Of vices all*
> > *Then who can say*
> > *But mirth and play*
> > *Is best of all?*

Harry Tudor was a genuinely talented composer; the notation was innovative and interesting, weaving patterns of texture and colour. Here, in his private rooms all was relaxed and informal – the King of England could enjoy an hour of absolute pleasure with his closest companions. That Anne Boleyn came here often was all too apparent: she seemed entirely at ease. Whatever anger Harry had felt earlier in the day had been assuaged, his jealousy soothed, his ego restored. Now Anne was leaning over Harry to suggest a couple of corrections in the harmony which he eagerly amended. What a contrast to the strained, chilled atmosphere in Catalina's apartments! They sang the whole song again, and Katherine observed Anne's satisfaction with the changes.

Harry seemed pleased with Katherine's contribution. "You have not lost your touch, Aunt Kaff'ryn, for all that you are a grandmother!"

She inclined her head, deciding to hear the compliment rather than the reference to her age. "It is easy to sing such beautiful music, sir." As always, flattery worked its magic upon her nephew.

"All our family are musical," he acknowledged, "and I was well instructed by my mother when I was a boy."

"You have a lovely voice, Lady Anne." Katherine deliberately continued with her blandishments. "Another of your accomplishments from your time in France, I am sure."

Hal looked alarmed; he knew his mother too well to miss the tiniest hint of disapproval but the King was oblivious and only a flicker of Anne's long eyelashes gave any indication that she might infer criticism from the comment. She turned away – rudely some might have said, and whispered something in Harry's ear.

"Would *you* play, Aunt, while I sing?" He thrust the lute into Katherine's hands, stood up and straightened his doublet. "*Green Groweth the Holly,* I am sure you know it – but Hal, pass your lady mother my music book."

Her son balanced it on the King's carved music stand and she seated herself on his vacated stool. It was a song she had played many times, attractive in its simplicity, and easy to extemporise upon. Harry's pleasant tenor filled the room:

As the holly groweth green
And never changeth hue,
So I am, ever hath been,
Unto my lady true.

Now unto my lady
Promise to her I make,
From all other only
To her I me betake

Adieu, mine own lady,
Adieu, my special
Who hath my heart truly
Be sure, and ever shall.

Katherine: *In that moment I knew that Catalina's cause was lost. I knew that he would find some pretext to set her aside and marry this Circe. Not this year. Maybe not even next. But he would do it. Part of me understood – why should he be denied what countless men could have so easily? And part of me agreed with Benet that the country needed certainty, and peace. Yet the rejection of an anointed queen and the destruction of a marriage hallowed by God seemed two of the most heinous crimes against His laws.*

Christmastide was happy enough. The King was determined upon pleasure and spared no expense with tournaments, masques and banquets. Catalina presided over events with dignified serenity. If anything, she treated Anne Boleyn with remarkable kindness. *That's because she believes her nephew the Emperor will never see her humiliated. She thinks she has just to sit it out. Or she's worked out that if her husband thinks she is passive it gives her time to muster her defences.* Katherine could not help but think of Griselda, the obedient and long-suffering wife from *The Canterbury Tales*, one of the stories she had enjoyed throughout her life. Thank God *she* had never been subjected to the will of a controlling husband. Obeying Willian had been easy because he had never demanded anything of her that she disagreed with. Her loyalty was freely given in return for the respect and love he had accorded her. Of course, she had always been acutely aware that this was not the normal lot of wives.

When a man was full of vanity, as was Harry Tudor, and had never been denied anything in his entire life, then the wife who could no longer satisfy him would face his displeasure and repudiation. Yet what was going on was the strangest mix of behaviours. Some nights the King sat beside his queen, apparently chatting with her wearing a broad smile; Katherine even saw him serve her food in the manner of a devoted husband. *That's because he thinks she knows nothing and he believes he can rid himself of her without fuss. Who is the more clever disguiser? And why?*

Catalina invited her into her box to watch the jousts. Hal acquitted himself well – running against the King always held a modicum of worry for any contestant for it was only a couple of years since Charles Brandon's lance had broken in splinters on the King's brow when he'd failed to pull down his visor in time. But Harry craved opponents who could match him in skill. Such willingness kept Lord Exeter high in his favour.

Gertrude sat close by the Queen, who held her lady-in-waiting's hand as their husbands opposed one another in the lists. *She is much-loved by Catalina, and Hal by the King.* Such a state of affairs must surely be a wonderful thing for the new generation of Courtenays but a nagging doubt lurked in Katherine's mind. What would happen if, somehow, Catalina *was* set aside? She simply could not imagine Gertrude willingly serving a new queen, especially if it turned out to be the Lady Anne. Hal would have to order her to. Momentarily, a sort of dimly-perceived danger occurred to Katherine. She must speak to Hal about Gertrude's passionate loyalty to the queen and make sure he gave her some guidance.

And where would she, Katherine, stand on the matter? How on earth would it be possible to carry on loving courageous Catalina, as she had always done, yet also ensure her family continued to prosper under the Tudors? Maybe at her age it would be possible to curtail her visits to court and sink into some sort of obscurity in the West Country – but Hal and Gertrude played more prominent parts. Who in their right mind would see any political future in supporting an abandoned queen? If there was one thing she had learned in life it was that most men would choose pragmatism over idealism. If ever it came to it, anyone choosing Catalina's camp would be a fool. She sighed heavily, and so audibly that many looked in her direction.

"You are very pensive, Lady Courtenay." It was Benet, assigned to the Queen's box. From the yard below came a surge of cheers, for the King had won his first tilt against Lord Exeter. All eyes were on Harry, in his superb armour made here in the workshops at Greenwich, cantering triumphantly past.

"I just want to go home. I am tired of court."

"Lady Courtenay is unwell," announced Benet to the women in the box, "but do not disturb yourselves, I will see her safely back to her rooms." It was a well-judged moment; no lady-in-waiting or maid of honour really wanted to miss the spectacle. A few, murmured platitudes followed her as Benet handed her down the steps and into the fresh air.

The main rooms of the palace were deserted, except for a few servants preparing for the evening's banquet. The guest wing was quiet too but when Benet opened the door to her chamber they found Isabel brushing out Katherine's clothes. She looked up, startled. The countess was pale and possibly a little tearful; the man accompanying her had his arm about her waist in an affectionate and supportive way, but Isabel could not place him. She remained respectfully silent. It was not for her to pass comment.

"Isabel, this is my … cousin … Sir Benedict Haute. Do you remember he once came to Tiverton in the snow?"

Ah, now she knew him! She cast her eyes downwards, hid a smile and bobbed a curtsey. Best not to let on that she recognised the short, dark and silvery hairs on his head as those that she'd found on the countess's pillows a few years back … or the strange incident of the man's shirt found by Philippa under those pillows when she had stripped the bed-linen for washing. A shirt laundered and then given to her husband Adam Anning.

"God give you good day, sir." She battled to keep her lips in a straight line. He might be old enough to be her father but he was still a fine-looking man. He was looking at the countess with concern and tenderness. Bowing low he kissed her hand.

"I will leave you with your woman, then, my lady, and return to my duties. No doubt I shall be travelling through Devonshire on His Grace's business sometime this summer. I hope I may call upon you then – cousin?"

When he had gone Katherine turned to her maid. "Try to close your mouth, Isabel; it's not becoming. How soon can we be packed and ready to travel? I think I have had enough of Greenwich. I'd like to spend some time with my grandson in Surrey before we head for home."

Litte Edward Courtenay was teething and could go from smiles to sorrow in the twinkling of an eye. Katherine held him firmly on her lap and gave him his coral ring to mouth. At only six months it was too early yet to say how his little features might settle but his eyes were promising to be brown, like hers. Or maybe he just favoured Gertrude's Spanish mother. The baby burbled and crowed happily now, his chubby little hands clasping the ring as though his life depended on it.

"*You* are a future marquess and earl, young man," Katherine informed him solemnly, "and how proud your grandfathers would have been of you." She thought wistfully of her other grandchild, growing up in far-off Raglan with a new stepmother. Lucy was totally absorbed into the Somerset family.

It was peaceful in Hal's country home. The baby's parents stayed on at court. That was the way in noble households, when both parents served their sovereigns. Maybe Gertrude would spend more time in Surrey as her family grew – it could be just the excuse needed to put safe water between the Courtenays and Catalina. Katherine had had no opportunity to speak privately to Hal – it would have to wait.

But oh, the relief of escaping from court! Harry Tudor had barely noted her leaving but Catalina had held her close, sad to see her go. Katherine felt helpless. The fragility of the Queen's position had been made abundantly clear. What Harry Tudor would give to hold a boy like this upon *his* lap – a legitimate male heir, handsome and healthy? Yet who could foresee the future? So Elizabeth Wydville must have dandled her precious, ill-fated princes; so had Queen Anne Neville gazed proudly upon her little boy; so had she seen Bessy bounce Arthur upon her knee. *Dear God, so even Marguerite of Anjou must have held her son who perished in the battle at Tewkesbury all those years ago.*

Katherine shivered violently, and the baby gave her a look of surprise. She hugged him fiercely. "*You* must live, Edward Courtenay!" she whispered into his soft little crown, "for living, and surviving, is all in this world."

The journey home took longer than expected. A troublesome winter cough seemed to have crept upon her without the usual precursor of a cold; it exhausted her and for once she stayed in her litter the whole way, for the early spring air was cruelly cold and stabbed at her chest. At every stopping point Isabel fussed to provide more hot stones for her comfort, and swathed her in furs but still she could never quite get warm enough, even though she could feel a sheen of sweat on her forehead. The undulating, treeless downlands of Salisbury Plain seemed endless and she found herself yearning for the flatter terrain of Somerset where the wheels would roll more swiftly towards Devon.

"All very well, my lady," remarked Isabel, "but there's still the Blackdown Hills to be got through! Up and down there we shall be, like bells in the belfry!"

At Shaftesbury they stopped at the magnificent abbey, where the Benedictine nuns welcomed her. Isabel gazed around in awe at the obvious wealth – the silken bed-hangings, the silver-gilt plate and the quality of the food on the table. "It's better fare than at Greenwich!"

Despite her weariness, Katherine laughed. "If the Abbess here were to marry with the Abbot of Glastonbury I dare say their heir would hold more land than the Tudors!"

With great excitement, they brought before her an elderly priest who claimed he could remember her father. Katherine received him with genuine curiosity – so few people ever seemed to want to refer back to those years of the cousins' wars. The Abbess ushered him in with the same air of importance with which she had shown Katherine her abbey's famous psalter. Clearly, King Edward IV's visit was a proud moment in Shaftesbury's six hundred year history. Katherine was prepared to be entertained. The Abbess offered some of her best Bordeaux wine for the occasion.

"He was the tallest man I ever saw," began the priest, his rheumy old eyes peering at her through lashless lids. "Tall, and golden of hair. A giant of a man! Like a king should be. I can see him know, kneeling before our shrine – still then as tall as them *not* kneeling!"

"He came here, to worship?"

The Abbess nodded. "We have had many royal visitors over the years. Our shrine is that of King Edward the Martyr. I expect your lord father came to pray with his namesake. Father Peter here was a young man then."

"Aye!" said the old fellow eagerly. "He had need of a scribe and in those days I made a fair hand."

"To whom did you write?" asked Katherine, fascinated.

"He wanted to send word to his brother in Yorkshire. Richard, who was king after him. He heard here that the queen was delivered of a child, and wished to tell his dearest brother the glad news. Three pages I wrote, of his greetings, news of the birth and much of his other doings. It was a proper brotherly letter, for the king said he loved Richard like his own soul – his "eyes in the north" he called him."

Katherine felt a catch in her heart. That her father had so loved the brother who would order his sons to be put to death! "When was this?"

The old man searched his memory, looking at the Abbess for help.

"You have always said you were a young fellow of twenty," she prompted.

"That's it! I do recall the king said it might be his last child, for the queen was older … and he asked me if being celibate I would not miss having children, for he said they were a great blessing. And then he laughed. "

"I think he must have been telling of my sister Bridget."

"That's the name! He knelt here at our shrine and said he would dedicate this youngest to God for he had daughters aplenty to marry to kings and princes!" He was into his stride now, and the wine loosened his tongue. "But we didn't care for the queen. Scheming minx, my lord abbot said, when the king died. No, we wanted nothing of her Wydville family! Snared the poor king by enchantment and –"

Consternation spread across the Abbess's refined features and she tugged frantically at his sleeve. Her vision of entertaining her honoured guest with one of her abbey's prized stories was going horribly wrong. He was launching into a part she had never heard before.

"Forgive him, Countess! He is very old!"

But there was no stopping Father Peter, whose recollections came thick and fast. "We gave our allegiance here to Richard, knowing how the old king had loved him so, and wanted him to be Lord Protector to the boy. No, there was no-one here in favour of the Wydvilles. And we wanted a man, not a boy to rule us. *Woe to thee, O land, when thy king is a child and thy princes eat in the morning!*"

If the ground had opened up, the Abbess would willingly have thrown herself in it, and probably have poured the Bordeaux wine in too.

"For that's what the Wydvilles were, jumped-up men who had none of King Richard's understanding of what this land needed! I was at Bosworth, too, lady, and we wept when we lost him to the Tudor!"

He delivered the last few words with passion, then shook uncontrollably. A silence fell, during which a couple of attendant nuns confiscated his cup, tried to take his elbows and steer him away.

"Wait!" Katherine rose and placed herself in front of him. "I take no offence, Mother Abbess. The good father simply speaks the truth as he saw it. It must have been hard to live through those years, trying to gauge men's motivations and ambitions. I am glad you thought well of my kingly father, and my uncle too. Can I ask you, sir, what did they say then of my brothers, the princes?"

The old man shook off the flapping nuns and looked straight into Katherine's eyes. For all his age there was nothing amiss with his mind.

"Men said many things. When they disappeared it was almost a relief, for no good could have come of a boy again as king. You see, we remembered the second Richard and the sixth Henry who both brought this country low. Aye, lady, we were glad to have a king who knew how to govern." He gave a short laugh. "And now you will have my head off for treason."

"No treason, sir. I am sure I have heard nothing but praise for my father. It is a fine story, and I am glad to have met you. For what it's worth, my sister Bessy once called my mother a schemer too. We survived, Father Peter. We survived those terrible times, did we not?"

"We did. But whether we shall survive the times to come is another question."

"What do you mean, sir?"

"The rumours, my lady, about King Harry wanting to take a new wife, and not caring what he does to make it happen. Have you not heard the whisperings about this up in London?"

She realised that all over England her nephew's private life was fast becoming public concern.

The Abbess and the nuns were all looking at her like startled rabbits, their wimpled faces stretched with astonishment. Katherine felt suddenly very tired again. A chill settled upon her and the cough threatened in her chest. Concern crossed the old priest's face. He had heard similar coughs and seen other men and women look fatigued and thin, like the Countess in front of him. It could only have one ending.

"Forgive an old man's ramblings, princess. I just wanted to tell you about the time I met your royal father. You have an air of him. May God bless you."

13

Late summer 1527: Tiverton

"The King is so bent upon this divorce that he has secretly assembled certain bishops and lawyers that they may sign a declaration to the effect that his marriage with the queen is null and void, on account of her being his brother's wife." Mendoza, the Spanish ambassador, in a letter to the Emperor Charles V.

In the late afternoon heat, Sir Benet Haute trotted through the streets of the little Devonshire town with a light heart. It still struck him as ridiculously fortuitous that the King seemed to regard him as the ideal private courier to come into the West Country with messages for the Bishop of Exeter! He had enjoyed four comfortable days in the compact little city, lodging at St Nicholas's Priory and drinking at the inn in St Martin's Lane, the little cobbled throroughfare hard by the cathedral – time made even more pleasurable by the knowledge that he could extend his sojourn in Tiverton.

The news he had brought to the bishop was of progress concerning the King's "great and secret matter": its greatness was beyond doubt; its secrecy less certain. Harry Tudor was keen that all major churchmen should be brought on board with his view that his marriage to the queen must end – that they had been living in mortal sin these past eighteen years, offending God. For the sake of both their souls they must separate. Benet knew the throw upon which the King was staking his future: the revelation that Queen Catherine of Aragon had carnally known his brother Arthur, contrary to the teachings of Leviticus, Chapter 20. Harry Tudor believed that those few words could be his passe-port to annulling his marriage.

Benet was not so certain. For a start off, many clerics were citing another verse in the Bible, advocating a man's duty to marry his widowed sister-in law! Well, Benet had never actually read the Bible for himself – his Latin was not up to it, yet at court a rumour circulated whispering of the Lady Anne Boleyn's support for the new ideas from Europe that people should be able to read the Bible in their own language. Actually, thought Benet, that's not necessarily a bad idea … Even more astonishing, word was that Rome had fallen to the angry, unpaid army of the Emperor Charles, and the Pope humiliated and besieged in his own castle. By anyone's reckoning His Holiness was unlikely to listen to Harry Tudor's plea for an annulment from the woman whose nephew now had him by the short and curlies! No, the King of England would be forced to devise some new stratagem, or at least Wolsey would be forced to think of a new approach to the whole matter. Gradually, the shroud of secrecy was being ripped away from the King's "great matter": the Emperor Charles had declared he would not see his good aunt deserted in her troubles, and his other aunt, Margareta of Austria was also determined to winkle out what was going on.

As the church of St Peter came into view, Benet found himself glad to put official business out of his head. A trip to Devon meant a chance to see Katherine. She would be waiting for him; he had sent word from Exeter. What a handsome church! As he drew closer, Benet admired how the tower soared up into the cloudless summer sky and the tall windows glittered. Exquisite carvings surrounded the entrance porch. He squinted to look more closely at the detail of ships and other symbols of the sea. True to his word, John Greenway had also included the arms of the Courtenay family. The whole effect was as if Devon lacework had been created from stone. A mason working within the porch paused for a moment, hearing hoofbeats, and seeing the quality of Benet's horse and clothing, doffed his headgear.

Round to the right and suddenly he was in front of Katherine's little castle with its round tower and sturdy gatehouse. The last time he'd been here was in those deep snowdrifts five years ago – that magic month of Katherine's love and warmth … until he'd spoiled it all, of course, by trying to push her into the one thing she would not give him. He understood better now; did not agree with her, but understood. Their reunion at Greenwich had taught him to take what she was prepared to offer: the deepest of friendships. And that still came with the warmth of her lips and the invitation of her arms. Truly, the woman was a witch! His oldest Haute aunt, whose own mother had been a Wydville, said Katherine Courtenay was the living image of her mother, Elizabeth Wydville, and if that was so Benet quite understood why King Edward IV had made her his queen.

Surprisingly, the studded oak door was firmly shut. The little castle seemed to drowse in the August heat. A snoozing tabby cat, waiting to be let in, barely

551

stirred as a solitary bumblebee flew by. Benet looked up. Many of the shutters were open, no doubt to allow any breath of air to circulate. He resorted to rapping loudly with the hilt of his sword. With a creak, half of the door was opened and a tousle-haired young guard, still pulling on his leather jerkin, peered at him. The cat shot past his legs into the cool beyond.

"Ah, be you the gentleman come from Exeter?"

"The very same." Benet smiled affably. "Asleep in the sunshine, lad? Good job we're a country at peace with itself!"

"Aye, sir. Well no, sir, not asleep exactly. We're just keeping quiet while Her Grace the Countess rests. Old Mistress Anning's orders."

Was Katherine really one to put her feet up on a summer afternoon? Was she waiting for him in the garden, dreaming amongst the roses? He dismounted and threw the reins into the fellow's hands. "Direct me to where the redoubtable Old Mistress Anning is guarding her mistress."

The lad looked troubled for a moment, then relieved as a young woman came quickly across the courtyard towards the gatehouse. "Here's *young* Mistress Anning, sir."

Benet recognised the maid who had come to Greenwich with Katherine. "Isabel? Your mistress is expecting me. I made good time from Exeter through the valley."

An anxious glance passed between the two Courtenay servants. Here in Devon he knew that the small household was tightly bound with loyalty. "Is something wrong?

"Come away in, sir. You'll be wanting to refresh yourself after your journey." It was true, he had sweated heavily in the heat, probably stank of horse, and had no wish to greet Katherine until he had changed his linen and splashed the dust from his face and hands. He followed her from the shadow of the gatehouse, through the bright sunshine of the courtyard and then into the cool of the main building. Up a short flight of stone stairs and she ushered him into a room he remembered well. Already a clean shirt lay draped over a joint stool, and a bowl of hot water steamed gently.

"Thank you, Isabel. Will you take word to Lady Courtenay that I am arrived? I should be presentable in two shakes of a lamb's tail."

She stared studiously at the rush matting. "I'll tell my stepmother, sir. She will come to you. Wait here."

He pulled off his stained shirt and dabbed at his torso and underarms with a linen cloth. The warm water, scented with lavender, felt good against his face and he closed his eyes, letting it trickle down his chin, then scooped up a handful, splashed it through his hair and shook his head vigorously like a dog. Droplets flew through the air, catching in the sunlight.

The fresh shirt felt soft and cool against his skin. Restored to some sort of respectability, he crossed to the window and leaned out of the casement. His room overlooked the rear of the castle, where the land sloped gently down the River Exe. The grass, the leaves on the trees and all the other vegetation was tinged with that dark green of late summer, the air heavy with late afternoon heat.

A discreet knock, and then Philippa Anning was standing in the doorway. That she knew exactly what he and Katherine meant to each other was clear in the honest expression of her face, framed by her gable headdress; her skin was wrinkled like a Devonshire cider apple. Yet she stood silently, her mouth twitching with emotion, and apprehension stirred in Benet's heart.

"Sir Benet, be welcome." She was fighting to offer him a formal greeting but her voice wobbled precariously and Benet found himself across the room in two strides, taking her worn hands in his. Philippa abandoned all attempts at propriety. "She is not well, sir. This past week or so. These past two months or so ..." Now she was weeping freely. "My mother had care of her since she was a girl, saw her through her childbeds and everything. She's *never* been ill, sir ... and now *this!*"

"Holy Mother of God, tell me, Philippa. Now *what?*"

She freed her hands from his and used them in an arching gesture of helplessness and anger. "What killed her sweet sister Anne – the wasting sickness. She is thin, sir, and coughs, and has fevers."

Benet was thunderstruck. "But I saw her at Christmas. She was entirely well."

"She seemed tired, sir, when she came home. I thought it was the journey – all those nights in priory beds; all those days rattling in her litter – I thought she would soon blossom again in our good Devon air, like she has always done, sir. But she had a cough that would not go away and has sweats at night ..."

His mind raced. "You have a good physician here? You must summon someone from London. The King would send someone if he knew!"

Philippa stiffened slightly. "Master Greenway has supplied the best man he knows, sir. She has been bled, and there are days when she feels much better.

And of course the Marquess has been informed. We expect him and his wife any day, with a doctor from court."

Benet looked at her levelly. "Has she coughed blood yet?"

Philippa's face crumpled. She whispered, "Sweet Jesu. A little. "

"Does she know how ill she is?

"My lady is no fool, sir."

"Can I see her?"

Philippa hesitated. "Sir, the doctor says the disease may be spread from one to another. I do not believe it myself, but I do not care anyway. I have lived my life and would gladly give mine for hers."

"As would I. Lady Courtenay's condition holds no fears for me." It was true. He had seen enough people die – of the Sweat, the pox, the bloody flux and buried two wives. He'd watched men die in agony on the battlefield in France, and the corpses of children pulled out of rivers. When he considered his own age, and Katherine's, it was a miracle that they lived so long. If sickness was in the air and God meant him to die then so he would but until then …

He found her in the room where they had played chess together, and where they had first kissed. Her evident joy in seeing him made him swallow hard. Her cheek bones were razor sharp in her face but her dark eyes danced. Philippa stationed herself close by – clearly taking her role as chaperone seriously. The chamber was redolent with pungent herbs rising from the cup at her side, the floor and the hearth.

"How do you do today, my lady? Philippa tells me you have not been well."

"I am well enough. Sit down, Benet, and tell me all the news from court. "

So he told her – of the gossip trickling out from Westminster into the streets, like blood from the shambles; of how the Spanish ambassador Mendoza had declared that the King's affair was as notorious as if it had been proclaimed by the town crier. "Their Graces have gone off together into Essex this summer but the Lady Anne has gone too. You can guess the rest. It's building and building, Katherine."

She sighed. "If there was no child at all, then I think Catalina might step aside but she will fight for the Princess Mary's birthright until the day she dies. You know, she's completely convinced that Mary could rule England." She felt the tell-tale tightening again in her chest. It did not do to speak too much.

Philippa snorted derisively. "But who would let her try, my lady? By all rights your sweet sister the queen should have been given this land for her own after your brothers. Well, all I'm saying is that there will always be some man to take what is not rightfully his." She glared at Benet as though he were responsible for the transgressions of all men.

Benet sat on the edge of his chair and took Katherine's hand, noting the prominence of the blue veins and how her wedding ring hung loosely on her heart finger. "Well, we have no law against it, as the French have. And I sometimes think if a woman can run an estate as widespread as say … the Courtenay lands, then why should she not take on the whole of England?"

Mollified by his compliment to her mistress, Philippa softened. "Indeed, sir. All she would need is good advisors."

"And maybe a husband, though, to ensure her heirs?" He twinkled at her.

Suddenly Katherine coughed, tried to repress it, but her frame shook with the effort and gave way to a short paroxysm. Philippa's anxious eyes were on the square of linen she held up to her mouth. It came away faintly spotted with pink. The three of them stared at it.

The harbinger of mortality. Wordlessly, Philippa helped her to sip from the cup and the herbal tisane was soothing.

"I am not afraid of dying." She spoke softly. "Just sad to say goodbye to those I love."

The week he then spent with her Benet later counted amongst the most precious in his whole life. Her son was due before the end of the month and Benet knew it would not be possible to linger once the Marquess of Exeter came home to Tiverton. Who was *he,* but a passing courtier, a distant cousin on the distaff side, kindly offered bed and board by the thoughtful Countess when travelling through Devon on the King's business?

He carried Katherine out into the garden, and laid her down in the shade of an old oak tree. Philippa would brook no immodesty, so either she or Isabel Anning always trod behind. This afternoon it was Isabel, tactfully bending over some absorbing piece of household mending.

Grimacing, for his right knee was not entirely reliable, he lowered himself next to her on the cushions and put one on his lap so she could lay her head there. Thus they were both utterly content to pass the hours. On the other side of the wall the River Exe burbled happily. They did not speak any further of her illness, or of his going. Instead, they talked of memories, matching and balancing their individual lives, comparing and contrasting the years. Isabel tried hard not listen but could not help catching snatches of their conversation and when the Countess spoke of the years her husband had been in the Tower she found her heart swelling with pride at the loyalty of her grandfather Darch. *They are old enough to be my parents, yet he holds her like a young lover.*

For a whole week the weather held. Each afternoon he thought of something different: her fools acted out an hilarious interlude; the boys from the church choir came to sing; Master Greenway visited and talked of his ships and on his last day she played her lute while he sang, in the way that men sing who have lovely voices but do not know it. She could not join in – it made her cough too much. Her cook made the most delicious food to tempt her – little honeyed pastries shaped like flowers and birds which she nibbled politely but barely swallowed. Philippa clucked like a mother hen: *Is my lady warm enough? Is my lady tired yet? w*hile Rob brought the household accounts and assured his mistress that all was well with her lands and tenants.

On his last day she asked him to help her check through her will, lying in the sunshine, with a friendly spaniel curled up by her side. Together they scrutinised the wording. All of her servants were to be provided with black mourning gowns and supported for a year after her death, unless taken into the Marquess's service.

"I have decided to lie in John Greenway's beautiful new chapel," she announced, "and I will have three honest priests to pray for the souls of my father, my mother, my son Edward, my husband William, my daughter Margaret and all Christian souls. And," she added, "Master Greenway must select three poor men from the town who will pray for all those departed, especially any of our Courtenay servants. They will be paid well for their time."

She spoke as though she were making practical arrangements before going on a journey. "Hal will be my executor. I can trust him now to do things properly. Who would have thought it, though, when he was a boy?"

In the broad margin of the parchment lay her clear signature; she traced the quill strokes with her finger. "The excellent Princess Katherine, daughter, sister and aunt of kings. Will I be remembered, do you think, Benet? So many kings; so many princesses."

"How could Devon ever forget its very own princess?" he said tenderly. "My name will be dust, but yours will live on, my love."

"Mmmm. We are all scattered … the other princesses, my sisters. But we will meet in Heaven. It will be like old times. Bessy will want to look after us all; Cecily will be stamping her foot at something; Anne will be trying to smooth over our quarrels, and sweet Bridget will say nothing but a prayer for us all, and my brothers …"

Benet breathed in suddenly. He had never heard her speak of her lost brothers before. Her eyes were closed and she lay back on her cushions. "My brothers will know me, of that I am sure." A smile touched her lips. "And of course there will be Meggie, and my little son, and William."

Later, he carried her back to her chamber and laid her tenderly on the bed he had once shared with her. The bedhead was carved with her elaborate coat of arms: the three red spots of the Courtenays, symbolising Christ's blood brought back from the Holy Land by William's crusading ancestors, quartered with the lion rampant of the Devon Redvers; and her own proud ancestry – the royal families of England, France, Ulster and Mortimer, all crowned with the Yorkist crest of a demi-rose and the rays of the sun. Under its grandeur she looked entirely at home. Philippa brought another of her tisanes – this one containing poppy syrup that made her drowsy.

"I am so tired. Why am I so tired?"

He knelt by the bed and kissed her hand. He wanted to remember her like this: Katherine the princess lying at the very centre of her world where she was loved, respected and honoured. He waited until her eyes closed. Her breathing was uneven but she was in no distress. She slipped away from consciousness.

"It's best I go now," he said quietly to Philippa. "While she sleeps. Her son and his family will be here tomorrow."

He felt Philippa's hand on his back. "You love her, sir, as do we. And the Marquess too. She will not be alone. Go in peace."

557

Greenwich, London December 1527

Harry Tudor, King of England, read his cousin Exeter's letter again. He had never been to Tiverton but from Hal Courtenay's words he could imagine the scene. His aunt's coffin covered with a pall of cloth of gold and accompanied by mourners in black gowns; banners depicting the saints and no doubt a procession of local dignitaries. A trio of Abbots and some gleaming silver. An open vault in the pavement of the church and a Requiem Mass sung by the choristers from the cathedral in Exeter.

He nodded his satisfaction as he read. A suitably dignified funeral ceremony for his mother's sister. Harry rarely allowed himself to think about his mother. She was a soft, sorrowful memory in the far reaches of his mind. It did not do to think of the Yorkist past in England – he would only look ahead to the Tudor future. Surely it could not be long now until he and Anne could be allowed to make a boy together? Anne! He felt the familiar hardening beneath his cod piece. He frowned – if the Pope was too frightened to say that his marriage to Catalina could not be annulled, then he, Harry, would be forced to do something … God rot Wolsey if he failed to come up with a solution … he could not wait forever!

Epilogue
1558

"Considering that diverse of you be of the ancient nobility ... my meaning is to require of you nothing more than faithful hearts ..." Queen Elizabeth I's first speech, Hatfield, 20th November 1558

Ightam, Kent 20th November 1558

For several days now, the bells had rung joyously through the cities and counties of England. It was Sunday morning, and yet again a steady peal floated out from the tower of St Peter's in the little village of Ightam. From his bed in his son's house, Sir Benedict Haute could hear them, celebrating the accession of the new young queen, Elizabeth Tudor.

Downstairs, the family was preparing to stroll the hundred yards down the village street to the service where the priest would once more read the Bible in English. He could no longer join them; it was too far to walk for an ancient old man who had just passed his eightieth birthday. On that day his youngest granddaughter, Katherine, had gazed at him with eyes as grey and huge as the pewter plates on the oak board chest. *Eighty years old! And she, Katherine, but eight!*

The door creaked open and the little girl's face peeked around. "We are just going, Grandfather, but Isabel will listen out for you." She regarded him seriously. "Will you still be alive when we get back?" She worried that every day might be his last, for who else could boast a grandfather of such antiquity? She pattered across to the bed, climbed on to the step and bestowed a swift kiss on his cheek. His skin was pale and papery, with thin red veins close to the surface but he smelled nicely of good soap and lavender water. When his eyes opened they twinkled at her, as usual, and she heaved a sigh of relief.

"We are all going to pray for Queen Elizabeth," she announced, and as an afterthought added, "I expect the more of us who pray, the longer she will live."

"Most probably, sweeting," said Benet gravely.

"Father says people will pray all over England, so that must mean she will live for a very long time. I will pray for you too, Grandfather," she added.

"In that case I will surely still be here when you return, and we can finish our game of chess."

She beamed at him, smoothed his coverlet as she had seen Isabel do, climbed down, bobbed a little curtsey and whisked away, clattering down the staircase.

He heard the main door close and the voices of his family fade as they made their way to church. Soon the bells stopped too, for all were safely inside and the service about to begin. Benet pictured them: his son, another Benedict, now over forty himself, and his wife Margery, and his six grandchildren. Five boys and Katherine.

Katherine, Father? For whom do we name her? It's not a name much used in our family. We had thought to call her Joan, or maybe Thomasine, for my mother. But they had humoured him.

Thirty one years ago today she had died. Thank God for that, for at least she had never lived to see the day just eleven years later when her son Hal had his head struck off with a sword on Tower Hill, for treason. Foolish Courtenay, probably not guilty but still daft enough to engage in communication with those other fanatical Plantagenet offshoots, the Pole family. Yes, thank God Katherine had not lived, for surely Harry Tudor would have wreaked his Tudor revenge upon her as he did her cousin, Margaret Pole, whose inept executioner had repeatedly hacked at her as if she were an old tree to be felled for firewood. At least her grandson, *the last sprig of the White Rose* had been spared but only to live out a precarious existence – in and out of the Tower; favoured by Queen Mary; then used by others in plots against her and finally, repudiated by both Mary and Elizabeth Tudor, packed off to exile in Brussels. Benet heard he'd died in Padua two years ago, some said of the French pox; some said of poison; some said because he he'd refused to change his wet clothes after hunting.

He wondered what on earth Hal and Edward Courtenay said for themselves when they met Katherine in Heaven. Did they creep towards her, shame-faced, after all she had sacrificed to keep her bloodline safe? Did she point out that all the Courtenay estates she had fought so hard to maintain had ended up divided, loyal servants forced to seek new employment. At least he had been able to offer a home to Isabel Anning; Katherine would have hated to see her faithful household made destitute.

Daughter, sister and aunt of kings – that's how Katherine had described herself. Sometimes proudly, sometimes sadly, sometimes ruefully. Strange, though, that she'd never included "niece" in her list … he had never heard her pass comment on the third Richard. But what changes England had seen through those years – his own lifetime too … Civil war, conspiracies, rebellions! Five kings! What times they had all gone through.

Benet was old enough to remember when religion was simply the quiet backdrop to everyday life. A time when every household worshipped peacefully; when the gentle click of the rosary and the familiar Latin prayers had washed over them all like the continual sigh of waves upon the shore. When saints' days and church festivals marked the passage of the seasons. Then the earthquake of Harry Tudor's desire for Anne Boleyn, which had ended up creating the chasm of faith into which the monasteries, nunneries, priories and abbeys had fallen. The world Katherine had left on that November Sunday in 1527 seemed so far away now. Strange to think she had known nothing of Princess Elizabeth, or Prince Edward, or how her nephew Harry Tudor would launch himself so desperately into four more marriages. So much hope pinned upon Jane Seymour's boy, but he was dead at sixteen, like young Arthur. Then all that chaos with poor young Jane Grey, herself the great-great granddaughter of Elizabeth Wydville, and great granddaughter of Queen Bessy of York – what would Katherine have made of that?

And Mary had brought such horrors upon them all in trying to turn the tide of the new faith, burning people she called *heretics* in the fires of Smithfield. Once, they had spoken of whether England could be ruled by a woman. The last five years had made Benet very dubious. Catalina's daughter had turned her face to Spain and clung like a burr to her mother's religion in an England that had been dragged kicking and screaming away from its monasteries, superstitions and Latin but actually found a new peace and purity in such reformation.

For a moment Benet wished he could see into the future. For all that this red-headed young queen was Anne Boleyn's daughter, and a proud Tudor, she was also Queen Bessy's granddaughter and Katherine's great niece – a precious drop of Yorkist blood in her veins. A royal girl of English parents, as Katherine had once been. Could anyone dare to hope that she might be their salvation? Where would she take England, this new queen?

561

Such thoughts exhausted him. He would close his eyes and sleep for another hour till Katherine came home.

Historical Notes for the Curious

Catalina of Aragon was indeed set aside by her husband. She was forcibly separated from her daughter Mary, divorced against her will and sent to live in a variety of lonely, dank houses. She died in January 1536.

Anne Boleyn married Harry Tudor but she too failed to give him a son. Cromwell engineered a case for adultery and witchcraft against her and she was executed in May 1536. Harry died believing the Tudor succession was secured by the birth of his son Edward VI. He could never have imagined what would ensue when Edward died of TB at just sixteen in 1554.

Mary Tudor became queen regnant, as Catalina had so fiercely desired but her reign was short and unhappy. Like her mother, she turned to Spain for her support, marrying her cousin King Philip, much to the dissatisfaction of most people in England. Her desperate desire to turn England back towards the Catholic faith was ill-judged. With no heir, she died in 1558.

Cardinal Wolsey failed in his efforts to persuade the Pope to grant a divorce. He died shortly after his arrest.

Mary Brandon (formerly Princess Mary Tudor, Katherine's niece) kept her distance from Anne Boleyn and retreated to her country estates in Suffolk where she died in 1533.

Henry Courtenay (Hal, Katherine's son) came to hate the effects of the Reformation upon his Devon estates and tenants. He drifted into an association with the Catholic Pole family, encouraged by his wife Gertrude. The Courtenay family were arrested in November 1538. Hal was executed shortly afterwards.

Gertrude Courtenay (Katherine's daughter-in-law) remained fiercely loyal to Catalina and her Roman Catholic faith. She was forced to carry the christening robe of the baby Elizabeth Tudor in 1533. She wrote regularly to Catalina and acted as a go-between with the Spanish Ambassador Chapuys. Arrested for treason with her husband, Gertrude spent two years in the Tower. The accession of Mary saw her restored to favour and appointed lady-in- waiting, with some of her lands restored but she lost the Queen's favour when she pushed too hard for her son Edward to be a potential suitor. Her son's exile hit her hard; she wrote loving letters but never saw him again. She died in 1558, just two months before Mary.

Lord Henry Somerset (Baron Herbert) "Somer" (Katherine's son-in-law) Married again and had a large family. His descendants became the Dukes of Beaufort.

Lady Lucy Somerset (Katherine's granddaughter) married John Neville, Baron Latimer and served as lady-in-waiting to his stepmother, Queen Catherine Parr. She had four daughters. The eldest, Katherine, married Henry Percy, the 8th Earl of Northumberland.

Edward Courtenay (Katherine's grandson) was arrested with his parents in 1538. He was kept prisoner in the Tower until 1553. Mary Tudor showed him favour, restoring him to his estates, and creating him Earl of Devon, but rejected him as a suitor. He was later implicated in the Wyatt rebellion of 1554, which aimed to put Elizabeth on the throne. Both he and Elizabeth were imprisoned as a result. It is said that Elizabeth then refused to have anything to do with him because she held him partly responsible for her imprisonment and she also mocked his lack of education and culture. Edward was forced into European exile and died unmarried and childless in Padua in 1556

Mary Carey survived her sister Anne Boleyn's downfall. She made a secret marriage to William Stafford and retreated to Rochford in Essex, where she died in 1543. She lived to see her children begin to rise in the Tudors' favour: her daughter Catherine became a much-loved lady-in-waiting to Elizabeth I and her son Henry became Lord Hunsdon, Elizabeth's Lord Chamberlain.

I like to think that **Sir Benedict Haute** died in his bed, at the incredible age of 85.

Princess Bridget Plantagenet: When I first began to write *Bright Shadow* it was widely accepted that Bridget's death had occurred in either 1513 or 1517. The latter fitted will into my narrative. However, recent research by Margaret M. Condon at the University of Bristol (published in The Ricardian Vol XXX 2020) now pin-points the date as 1507, the same year as Cecily. Evidence comes from the one of Henry VII's books of cash payments which records *"item for a Marbulstone bought to ley vpon my lady Brygett within the quere of Dartford."* This means that by the age of twenty eight, Katherine had lost all of her beloved sisters.